Valley of Silence

NORA ROBERTS

JOVE
New York

A JOVE BOOK
Published by Berkley
An imprint of Penguin Random House LLC
penguinrandomhouse.com

Copyright © 2006 by Nora Roberts
Excerpt from *Naked in Death* by J. D. Robb copyright © 1995 by Nora Roberts
Penguin Random House supports copyright. Copyright fuels creativity, encourages
diverse voices, promotes free speech, and creates a vibrant culture. Thank you for buying
an authorized edition of this book and for complying with copyright laws by not
reproducing, scanning, or distributing any part of it in any form without permission.
You are supporting writers and allowing Penguin Random House to continue to
publish books for every reader.

A JOVE BOOK, BERKLEY, and the BERKLEY & B colophon are
registered trademarks of Penguin Random House LLC.

ISBN: 9780515141672

First Edition: November 2006

Printed in the United States of America
13   15   17   19   21   22   20   18   16   14

Cover design by Rita Frangie
Text design by Kristin del Rosario

Number-one *New York Times* bestselling author Nora Roberts presents the electrifying conclusion to her powerful Circle Trilogy. Worlds have collided and centuries have elapsed as six people have brought their unique powers, their courage and their hearts to a battle that could drown humanity in darkness. . . .

Her face, so pale when she'd removed her cloak, had bloomed when her hand had taken the sword. Her eyes, so heavy, so somber, had gone as brilliant as the blade. And had simply sliced through him, keen as a sword, when they'd met his. . . .

In the kingdom of Geall, the scholarly Moira has taken up the sword of her people. Now, as queen, she must prepare her subjects for the greatest battle they will ever fight—against an enemy more vicious than any they have seen. For Lilith, the most powerful vampire in the world, has followed the circle of six through time to Geall.

Moira also has a personal score to settle. Vampires killed her mother—and now, she is ready to exact her revenge. But there is one vampire to whom she would trust her soul. . . .

Cian was changed by Lilith centuries ago. But now, he stands with the circle. Without hesitation, he will kill others of his kind—and has earned the respect of sorcerer, witch, warrior and shape-shifter. But he wants more than respect from Moira—even though his desire for her makes him vulnerable. For how can a man with an eternity to live love a woman whose life is sure to end—if not by Lilith's hand, then by the curse of time?

Don't miss the other books in the Circle Trilogy

Morrigan's Cross
Dance of the Gods

Turn the page for a complete list of titles by
Nora Roberts and J. D. Robb from Berkley. . . .

Nora Roberts

Ebooks by Nora Roberts

Cordina's Royal Family
AFFAIRE ROYALE
COMMAND PERFORMANCE
THE PLAYBOY PRINCE
CORDINA'S CROWN JEWEL

The Donovan Legacy
CAPTIVATED
ENTRANCED
CHARMED
ENCHANTED

The O'Hurleys
THE LAST HONEST WOMAN
DANCE TO THE PIPER
SKIN DEEP
WITHOUT A TRACE

Night Tales
NIGHT SHIFT
NIGHT SHADOW
NIGHTSHADE
NIGHT SMOKE
NIGHT SHIELD

The MacGregors
PLAYING THE ODDS
TEMPTING FATE
ALL THE POSSIBILITIES
ONE MAN'S ART
FOR NOW, FOREVER
REBELLION/IN FROM THE COLD
THE MACGREGOR BRIDES
THE WINNING HAND
THE MACGREGOR GROOMS
THE PERFECT NEIGHBOR

The Calhouns
COURTING CATHERINE
A MAN FOR AMANDA
FOR THE LOVE OF LILAH
SUZANNA'S SURRENDER
MEGAN'S MATE

Irish Legacy
IRISH THOROUGHBRED
IRISH ROSE
IRISH REBEL

LOVING JACK
BEST LAID PLANS
LAWLESS

BLITHE IMAGES
SONG OF THE WEST
SEARCH FOR LOVE
ISLAND OF FLOWERS
THE HEART'S VICTORY
FROM THIS DAY
HER MOTHER'S KEEPER
ONCE MORE WITH FEELING
REFLECTIONS
DANCE OF DREAMS
UNTAMED
THIS MAGIC MOMENT
ENDINGS AND BEGINNINGS
STORM WARNING
SULLIVAN'S WOMAN
FIRST IMPRESSIONS
A MATTER OF CHOICE

LESS OF A STRANGER
THE LAW IS A LADY
RULES OF THE GAME
OPPOSITES ATTRACT
THE RIGHT PATH
PARTNERS
BOUNDARY LINES
DUAL IMAGE
TEMPTATION
LOCAL HERO
THE NAME OF THE GAME
GABRIEL'S ANGEL
THE WELCOMING
TIME WAS
TIMES CHANGE
SUMMER LOVE
HOLIDAY WISHES

Nora Roberts & J. D. Robb

REMEMBER WHEN

J. D. Robb

Anthologies

FROM THE HEART
A LITTLE MAGIC
A LITTLE FATE

MOON SHADOWS
(with Jill Gregory, Ruth Ryan Langan, and Marianne Willman)

The Once Upon Series
(with Jill Gregory, Ruth Ryan Langan, and Marianne Willman)

ONCE UPON A CASTLE	ONCE UPON A ROSE
ONCE UPON A STAR	ONCE UPON A KISS
ONCE UPON A DREAM	ONCE UPON A MIDNIGHT

SILENT NIGHT
(with Susan Plunkett, Dee Holmes, and Claire Cross)

OUT OF THIS WORLD
(with Laurell K. Hamilton, Susan Krinard, and Maggie Shayne)

BUMP IN THE NIGHT
(with Mary Blayney, Ruth Ryan Langan, and Mary Kay McComas)

DEAD OF NIGHT
(with Mary Blayney, Ruth Ryan Langan, and Mary Kay McComas)

THREE IN DEATH

SUITE 606
(with Mary Blayney, Ruth Ryan Langan, and Mary Kay McComas)

IN DEATH

THE LOST
(with Patricia Gaffney, Mary Blayney, and Ruth Ryan Langan)

THE OTHER SIDE
(with Mary Blayney, Patricia Gaffney, Ruth Ryan Langan, and Mary Kay McComas)

TIME OF DEATH

THE UNQUIET
(with Mary Blayney, Patricia Gaffney, Ruth Ryan Langan, and Mary Kay McComas)

MIRROR, MIRROR
(with Mary Blayney, Elaine Fox, Mary Kay McComas, and R. C. Ryan)

DOWN THE RABBIT HOLE
(with Mary Blayney, Elaine Fox, Mary Kay McComas, and R. C. Ryan)

Also available . . .

THE OFFICIAL NORA ROBERTS COMPANION
(edited by Denise Little and Laura Hayden)

To my own circle,
friends and family.

Good and evil, we know, in the field of this world
grow up together almost inseparably.
—JOHN MILTON

Presume not that I am the thing I was.
—SHAKESPEARE

Prologue

There were pictures in the fire. Dragons and demons and warriors. The children would see them, as he did. The old man knew the very young and the very old often saw what others could not. Or would not.

He had told them much already. His tale had begun with the sorcerer who was called by the goddess Morrigan. Hoyt of the Mac Cionaoith was charged by the gods to travel to other worlds, to other times, and gather an army to stand strong against the vampire queen. The great battle between human and demon would take place on the sabbot of Samhain, in the Valley of Silence, in the land of Geall.

He had told them of Hoyt the sorcerer's brother, killed and changed by the wily Lilith, who had existed near a thousand years as a vampire before making Cian one of her kind. Nearly another thousand years would pass for Cian before he would join Hoyt and the witch Glenna to make those first links in the circle of six. The next links were forged by two Geallians—the shifter of shapes and the scholar who traveled between worlds to gather in those first days. And the last of the circle was joined by the warrior, a demon hunter of the Mac Cionaoith blood.

The tales he had told them were of battles and courage, of death and friendship. And of love. The love that had bloomed between sorcerer and witch, and between the shifter and the warrior, had strengthened the circle as true magic must.

But there was more to tell. Triumphs and loss, fear and valor, love and sacrifice—and all that came with the dark and the light.

As the children waited for more, he wondered how best to begin the end of the tale.

"There were six," he said, still watching the fire while the children's whispers silenced and their squirming stilled in anticipation. "And each had the choice to accept or refuse. For even when worlds are held in your hands, you must choose to face what would destroy them, or to turn away. And with this choice," he continued, "there are many other choices to be made."

"They were brave and true," one of the children called out. "They chose to fight!"

The old man smiled a little. "And so they did. But still, every day, every night of the time they were given, that choice remained, and had to be made anew. One among them, you remember, was no longer human, but vampire. Every day, every night of the time they were given, he was reminded he was no longer human. He was but a shadow in the worlds he had chosen to protect.

"And so," the old man said, "the vampire dreamed."

Chapter 1

He dreamed. And dreaming, he was still a man. Young, perhaps foolish, undoubtedly rash. But then, what he believed was a woman had such beauty, such allure.

She wore a fine gown in a deep shade of red, more elegant than the country pub deserved, with its long, sweeping sleeves. Like a good claret it poured over her form to set her pure white skin glowing. Her hair was gold, the curls of it glinting against her headdress.

The gown, her bearing, the jewels that were sparkling at her throat, on her fingers, told him she was a lady of some means and fashion.

He thought, in the dim light of the public house, she was like a flame that burned at shadows.

Two servants had arranged for a private room for her to sup before she swept in, and simply by being had silenced the talk and the music. But her eyes, blue as a summer sky, had met his. Only his.

When one of the servants had come out again, walked to him and announced that the lady requested he dine with her, he hadn't hesitated.

Why would he?

He might have grinned at the good-natured comments of the men he was drinking with, but he left them without a thought.

She stood in firelight and candlelight, already pouring wine into cups.

"I'm so glad," she said, "you would agree to join me. I hate to dine alone, don't you?" She came toward him, her movements so graceful she almost seemed to float. "I'm called Lilith." And she handed him wine.

In her speech there was something exotic, some cadence of speech that hinted of hot sand and riotous blooming vines. So he was already half seduced, and completely enchanted.

They shared the simple meal, though he had no appetite for food. It was her words he devoured. She spoke of the lands to which she had traveled, those which he'd only read of. She had walked among the pyramids, she told him, in the moonlight, had ridden the hills of Rome and stood in the ruined temples of Greece.

He had never traveled beyond Ireland, and her words, the images they invoked, were nearly as exciting as she herself.

He thought she was young to have done so much, but when he said as much she only smiled over the rim of her cup.

"What good are worlds," she asked, "if you don't make use of them? I'll make use of much more. Wine to be drunk, food to be tasted, lands to be explored. You're young," she said with a slow and knowing smile, "to settle for so little. Have you no wish to see beyond what you've seen?"

"I thought perhaps to take a year when I'm able, to see more of the world."

"A year?" With a light laugh, she snapped her fingers. "That is a year. Nothing, a blink of time. What would you do if you had an eternity of time?" Her eyes seemed like depthless blue seas as she leaned toward him. "What would you do with it?"

Without waiting for his answer, she rose, leaving the trail of her scent behind as she walked to the small window. "Ah, the night, it's so soft. Like silk against the skin." She turned back with a gleam in those bold blue eyes. "I am a night creature. And so, I think, are you. We, such as we, are at our best in the dark."

He had risen when she did, and now as she came back to him, her scent and the wine swam through his senses. And something more, something thick and smoky that hazed over his mind like a drug.

She tipped her head up, and back, then laid her mouth over his. "And why, when we're best in the dark, would we spend the dark hours alone?"

And in the dream, it was like a dream, misty and muddled. He was in her carriage, with her full white breasts in his hands, her mouth hot and avid on his. She laughed when he fumbled with her kirtle, and spread her legs in seductive invitation.

"Strong hands," she murmured. "A pleasing face. It's what I need, and need, and take. Will you do my bidding?" With another light laugh, she nipped at his ear. "Will you? Will you, young, handsome Cian with the strong hands?"

"Aye, of course. Aye." He could think of nothing but burying himself in her. When he did, with the carriage swaying madly, her head fell back in abandon.

"Yes, yes, yes! So hard, so hot. Give me more, and more! And I'll take you beyond all that you know."

As he plunged, his breath coming short as he neared climax, her head reared up again.

Her eyes were no longer blue and bold but red and feral. The shock that rushed into him had him trying to pull back, but her arms suddenly wrapped around him, implacable as iron chains. Her legs hooked around his waist, keeping him inside her, trapped. While he struggled against her impossible strength, she smiled with fangs gleaming in the dark.

"What are you?" There were no prayers in his head; fear left no room for them. "What are you?"

Her hips continued to rise and fall, riding him, so he

was helplessly driven closer to peak. She fisted a hand in his hair, yanking back his head to expose his throat. "Magnificent," she said. "I am magnificent, and so will you be."

She struck, the fangs piercing his flesh. He heard his own scream, somewhere in the madness and pain he heard it. The burn was unspeakable, searing through skin, into blood, beyond the bone. And mixed with it, sliding through it was a terrible, terrible pleasure.

He came, in the whirling, singing dark, betrayed by his body even as it dipped toward death. He struggled still, some part of him clawing for the light, for survival. But the pain, the pleasure dragged him deeper into the abyss.

"You and I, my handsome boy. You and I." She dipped back, cradling him in her arms now. With her own fingernail, she sliced a shallow slice across her breast so that blood dripped from it as it did, horribly, from her lips. "Now drink. Drink me, and you are forever."

No. His lips wouldn't form the word, but it screamed through his mind. Feeling his life slipping away, he struggled weakly for that last hold on it. Even when she pulled his head to her breast he fought her with what was left of him.

Then he tasted it, the rich and heady flavor that flowed from her. The bulging life of it. And like a babe at its mother's breast, he drank his own death.

The vampire woke in absolute dark, in absolute silence. Such was the way for him since the change so long ago, that he roused each sunset with not even the sound of his own heartbeat to stir the air.

Though he had dreamed the dream countless times over countless years, it disturbed him to fall from that edge yet again. To see himself as he'd been, to see his own face—one he'd not seen while awake since that night—made him edgy and annoyed.

He didn't brood over his fate. That was a useless occupation. He accepted and used what he was, and had through his personal eternity accumulated wealth, women, comfort, freedom. What else could a man want?

Having no heartbeat was a small price to pay, in the larger scheme of things. A heart that beat aged and weakened, and eventually stopped like a broken clock in any case.

How many bodies had he seen decay and die over his nine hundred years? He couldn't count them. And while he couldn't see the reflection of his own face, he knew it was the same as the night Lilith had taken him. The bones were still strong, the skin over them firm, supple and unlined. His eyes were sharp of sight and unfaded. There was not, and would never be, any gray in his hair, any sagging in his jowls.

Perhaps there were times, in the dark, in private, when he used his fingers to see his own face. There the high, prominent cheekbones, the shallow cleft in the chin, the deep-set eyes he knew were a strong blue. The blade of his nose, the firm curve of his lips.

The same. Always the same. But still, a small indulgence to spend a moment reminding himself.

He rose in the dark, his leanly muscled body naked, shook back the black hair that framed his face. He'd been born Cian Mac Cionaoith, and had gone by many names since. He was back to Cian—his brother's doing. Hoyt would call him nothing else, and since this war he'd agreed to fight might end him, Cian decided it was only right he should wear the name of his birth.

He'd prefer not to be ended. In his opinion, only the mad or the very young considered dying an adventure. But if that was his fate, at this time and place, at least he'd go out with style. And if there were any justice in any world, he would take Lilith with him to dust.

His eyes were as keen as his other senses, so he moved easily in the dark, going to a chest for one of the packets of blood that had been transported from Ireland. Apparently, the gods had deemed to allow the blood, as well as the vampire who required it, to travel through worlds from their circle of stones.

Then again, it was pigs' blood. Cian hadn't fed on humans in centuries. A personal choice, he mused as he broke open the packet, poured its contents into a cup. A matter of will, he thought, and well, manners, come to that. He lived among them, did business with them, slept with them when he was in the mood. It seemed rude to feed off them.

In any case, he'd found it simpler to live as he liked, to stay off the radar, if he didn't kill some hapless soul on a nightly basis. Live feeding added both thrill and flavor nothing else matched, but it was, by nature, a messy business.

He'd grown accustomed to the more banal flavor of pigs' blood, and the simple convenience of having it at his fingertips rather than having to go out and hunt something up every time hunger stirred in him.

He drank the blood as a man might his morning coffee—out of habit and the need for a kick on waking. It cleared his mind, jump-started his system.

He troubled neither with candles nor fire as he washed. He couldn't say he was overly pleased with the accommodations of Geall. Castle or not, he imagined he was as out of place in this medieval atmosphere as both Glenna and Blair.

He'd lived through this sort of era once, and once was enough for anyone. He preferred—much preferred—the daily conveniences of indoor plumbing, electricity, Chinese bloody takeout, come to that.

He missed his car, his bed, the damn microwave. He missed the life and sounds of city life and all it offered. Fate would have given him a solid kick in the ass if it ended him here, in the era, if not the world, of his beginnings.

Dressed, he left his room to make his way to the stables, and his horse.

There were people about—servants, guards, courtiers— those who lived and worked within the Castle Geall. Most avoided him, averting their eyes, quickening their pace.

Some made the sign against evil behind their backs. It didn't trouble him.

They knew what he was—and had seen what creatures like him were capable of since Moira, the scholarly gladiator, had battled one in the playing field.

It had been good strategy, he thought now, for Moira to ask him along with Blair and Larkin to hunt down the two vampires who'd killed her mother, the queen. Moira had understood the importance, the value of having vampires brought back alive so the people could see them for what they were. And see Moira herself fight and end one, proving herself a warrior.

She would, in a matter of weeks, lead her people to war. When a land had been at peace as long as Geall was reputed to have been, it would take a strong leader, a forceful one, to whip farmers and merchants, ladies-in-waiting and creaky advisors into soldiers.

He wasn't sure she was up to the task. Brave enough, he mused as he slipped out of the castle, crossed a courtyard toward the stables. More than bright enough. And it was true she'd honed considerable fighting skills over the past two months. No doubt she'd been trained since birth in matters of state and protocol, and her mind was clever and open.

In peace, he imagined she'd rule her pretty little world quite well. But in wartime, a ruler was general as well as figurehead.

If it had been up to him, he would have left Riddock, her uncle, in charge. But little of this business was up to him.

He heard her before he saw her, and scented her before that. Cian very nearly turned around to go back the way he'd come. It was just another annoyance to come across the woman when he'd been thinking of her.

The problem was, he thought of her entirely too often.

Avoiding her wasn't an option as they were inexorably bound together in this war. Slipping away now unseen was easily done. And cowardly. Pride, as always, refused to let him take the easy way.

They'd housed his stallion at the far end of the stables, two stalls away from any of the other horses. He understood and tolerated the fact that the grooms and farriers were wary of tending to the horse of a demon. Just as he was aware either Larkin or Hoyt groomed and fed his temperamental Vlad in the mornings.

Now it seemed Moira had taken it upon herself to spoil the animal. She had carrots, Cian saw, and was balancing one on her shoulder, cajoling Vlad to nip it off.

"You know you want it," she murmured. "It's so tasty. All you have to do is take it."

He'd thought the same about the woman, Cian mused.

She was gowned, her dress draped over a plain linen kirtle, so he assumed whatever training she'd done that day was complete. Still, she dressed simply for a princess, in quiet blue with only a hint of lace at the bodice. She wore the silver cross, one of nine Hoyt and Glenna had conjured. Her hair was loose, all that glossy brown falling down her back to her waist, and crowned with the thin circlet of her office.

She wasn't beautiful. He reminded himself of that often, nearly as often as he thought of her. She was, at best, a pretty thing. Slender and small-framed, small of feature as well. But for the eyes. They were long and dominant in that face of hers. Dove gray when she was quiet, pensive, listening. Hell smoke when she was roused.

He'd had his choice of great beauties in his time—as a man with any sense and skill would given a few centuries. She wasn't beautiful, but he couldn't, for all the effort, lock her out of his mind.

He knew he could have her if he put any of that effort into a seduction. She was young and innocent and curious, and therefore, very susceptible. Which was why, above all else, he knew he'd be better off seducing one of her ladies if he wanted the entertainment, the companionship, the release.

He'd had his fill of innocence long ago, just as he'd had his fill of human blood.

His horse, however, appeared to have less willpower. It took only moments before Vlad dipped his head and nipped the carrot from Moira's shoulder.

She laughed, stroked the stallion's ears as he chomped. "There now, that wasn't so hard, was it? We're friends, you and I. And I know you get lonely from time to time. Don't we all?"

She was lifting another carrot when Cian stepped out of the shadows. "You'll make a puppy out of him, then what sort of war horse will he be come Samhain?"

Her body jerked, then stiffened. But when she turned toward Cian, her face was composed. "Sure you don't really mind, do you? He so enjoys a bit of a treat now and then."

"Don't we all," he murmured.

Only the faintest flush of heat along her cheekbones betrayed any embarrassment at being overheard. "The training went well today. People are coming in from all over Geall. So many willing to fight we've decided we'll be setting up a second training area on my uncle's land. We'll have Tynan and Niall working there."

"Lodging?"

"Aye, that's becoming a bit of a thing. We'll house as many here as we can manage, and at my uncle's as well. There's the inn, and many of the farmers and crofters nearby are sheltering family and friends already. No one will be turned off. We'll find a way."

She fiddled with her cross as she spoke. Not, Cian thought, out of fear of him, but out of nervous habit. "There's food as well to think of. So many had to leave their crops and cattle behind to come here. But we'll manage. Have you eaten?"

She flushed a little deeper as soon as the words were out. "What I meant is there'd be supper in the parlor if—"

"I know what you meant. No. I thought to see to the horse first, but he appears well groomed and fed." On the heels of the words, Vlad bumped his head against Moira's shoulder. "And spoiled," Cian added.

Her brows drew together as they did, he knew, when she

was annoyed or thoughtful. "It's only carrots, and they're good for him."

"Speaking of food, I'll need blood in another week. You might make certain the next pigs that are slaughtered, their blood isn't wasted."

"Of course."

"Aren't you the cool one."

Now the faintest sign of irritation crossed her face. "You take what you need from the pig. I'm not after turning my nose up at a slab of bacon, am I?" She shoved the last carrot into Cian's hand and started to sweep out.

She stopped herself, "I don't know why you fire me up so easily. If you mean to or not. And no." She held up a hand. "I don't think I want to know the answer to that. But I would like to speak to you for a moment or two about another matter."

No, avoiding her wasn't possible, he reminded himself. "I have a moment or two."

She glanced around the stables. It wasn't only horses that had ears in such places. "I wonder if you could take that moment or two to walk with me. I'd be private on this."

He shrugged, and giving Vlad the last carrot joined Moira to walk out of the stables. "State secrets, Your Highness?"

"Why must you mock me?"

"Actually, I wasn't. Irritable tonight, are you?"

"It might be I am." She shoved back the hair that spilled over her shoulder. "What with war and end of days, and the practical matters of washing linens and providing food for an army meanwhile, it might be I am a bit irritable."

"Delegate."

"I am. I do. But it still takes time and thought to push chores into other hands—finding the right ones, explaining how it must be done. And this isn't what I wanted to speak to you about."

"Sit."

"What?"

"Sit." He took her arm, ignoring the way the muscles tensed against his hand, and pulled her down onto a bench.

"Sit, give your feet a rest if you won't turn off that busy brain of yours for five minutes."

"I can't remember the last time I had an hour, all to myself and a book. Well, I can, actually. Back in Ireland, in your house. I miss it—the books, the quiet of them."

"You need to take it, that hour now and again. You'll burn out otherwise, and won't be any good to yourself or anyone else."

"My hands feel so full, they make my arms ache." She looked down at them where they lay in her lap, and sighed. "And there, I'm off again. What is it Blair says? Bitch, bitch, bitch."

She surprised a laugh out of him, and turned her head to smile into his face.

"I suspect Geall has never had a queen such as you."

And her smile faded away. "No, you've the right of that. And we'll soon see. We go tomorrow, at first light, to the stone."

"I see."

"If I lift the sword from it, as my mother did in her time, and her father in his, and back to the first, Geall will have a queen such as me." She looked off, over the shrubberies toward the gates. "Geall will have no choice in it. Nor will I."

"Do you wish it otherwise?"

"I don't know what I wish, so I don't wish at all—except that it was done and over. Then I could do, well, whatever needs to be done next. I wanted to tell you." She shifted her gaze from whatever she saw in her mind, and met his eyes again. "I'd hoped we'd find a way to do this thing at night."

Soft eyes, he thought, and so serious. "It's too dangerous to have any sort of ceremony outside after sunset beyond the castle walls."

"I know it. All who wish to witness this rite may attend. You can't, I know. I'm sorry for it. It feels wrong. I feel the six of us, our circle, should be together at such a time."

Her hand reached up for her cross again. "Geall isn't yours, I know that as well, but the moment of this, it's important for what comes after. More than I knew before. More than I could have known."

She took a shaky breath. "They killed my father."

"What are you saying?"

"I have to walk again. I can't sit." She got up quickly, rubbing her arms to warm them from the sudden chill in the air, and in her blood. She moved through the courtyard into one of the gardens.

"I haven't told anyone—I didn't mean to tell you. What purpose does it serve? And I've no proof, just a knowing."

"What do you know?"

Easier than she'd believed it would be to talk to him, to tell him, she realized, because he was also so to the point. "One of the two that killed my mother, that you brought here. The one I fought." She held a hand up, and he watched her draw in her composure again. "Before I killed it, he said something of my father, and how he died."

"Likely trying to get a rise out of you, break your concentration."

"It did that well enough, but was more, you see. I know it, inside me." Looking at him, she pressed a hand to her heart. "I knew it when I looked at the one I killed. Not just my mother, but my father as well. I think Lilith sent them here this time because she'd had success with it before. When I was a child."

She continued to walk, her head bowed with the weight of her thoughts, her circlet glinting in the light of the torches. "They thought it was a bear gone mad. He was in the mountains, hunting. He was killed, he and my mother's young brother. My uncle Riddock didn't go as my aunt was close to her time with child. I . . ."

She broke off again as footsteps echoed, keeping her silence until the sound of them drifted away. "They thought, those who found them and brought them home, they thought it was animals. And so it was," she continued with steel in her tone now. "But these walk like a man. She sent them to kill him, so there would be no child but me."

She turned to him then, the torchlight washing red over

her pale face. "Perhaps, at that time, she knew only the ruler of Geall would be one of the circle. Or perhaps it was easier to kill him than me at that time, as I was hardly more than a baby and kept close watch on. Plenty of time for her to send assassins back for me. But instead they killed my mother."

"Those that did are dead."

"Is that comfort?" she wondered, and thought—from him—it likely was an offer of it. "I don't know what to feel. But I know she took my parents from me. She took them to stop what can't be stopped. We'll meet her on the battlefield come Samhain, because it's meant. Whether I fight as queen or not, I fight. She killed them for nothing."

"And nothing you could have done would have stopped it."

Yes, comfort, she thought again. Oddly, his pithy statement gave her just that. "I pray that's true. But I know because of what was done, what was not done, what had to be, what comes tomorrow is more important than rite and ritual. Whoever holds that sword tomorrow leads this war, and wields it with the blood of my murdered parents. She couldn't stop it. She cannot stop it."

She stepped back, gestured up. "Do you see the flags? The dragon and the claddaugh. The symbols of Geall since its beginning. Before this is done, I will ask that one more be hoisted."

He thought of all she might choose—a sword, a stake, an arrow. Then he knew. Not a weapon, not an instrument of war and death, but a symbol of hope and endurance. "A sun. To shed its light on the world."

Surprise, with pleasure running just behind it, lit her face. "Aye. You understand my thinking, and the need. A gold sun on the white flag to stand for the light, the tomorrows we fight for. This sun, gold as glory, will be the third symbol of Geall, one I bring to it. And damned to her. Damned to her and what she brought here."

Flushed now, Moira drew a deep breath. "You listen well—and I talk too much. You must come inside. The others will be gathering for supper."

He touched a hand to her arm to stop her. "Earlier I thought you'd make a poor wartime queen. I believe it might have been one of the rare times I was wrong."

"If the sword is mine," she said, "you will be wrong."

It occurred to him as they started inside, that they'd just shared their longest conversation in the two months they had known each other.

"You need to tell the others. You need to tell them what you believe about your father. If this is a circle, there should be no secrets to weaken it."

"You're right. Aye, you've the right of it."

Her head was lifted now, her eyes clear as she led the way.

Chapter 2

S he didn't sleep. How could a woman sleep on what
  was, in Moira's mind, essentially the last night of her
life? If in the morning it was her destiny to free the sword
from its stone scabbard, she would be queen of Geall. As
queen she would rule and govern and reign, and those
were duties she'd been trained for since birth. But as queen
on this coming dawn and the ones to follow, she would
lead her people to war. If it wasn't her destiny to raise the
sword, she would follow another, willingly, into battle.

Could weeks of training prepare anyone for such an action, such a weight of responsibility? So this night was the
last she could be the woman she'd believed she would be,
even the queen she'd hoped she might be.

Whatever dawn brought her, she knew nothing would
ever be quite the same again.

Before her mother's death, she'd believed this coming
dawn was years away. She'd assumed she would have years
of her mother's company and comfort and counsel, years of
peace and study so that when her time came she'd be not
only ready for the crown, but worthy of it.

A part of her had assumed her mother would reign for decades longer, and she herself would marry. In the dim and distant future, one of the children she bore would take the crown in her stead.

All of that had changed on the night of her mother's death. No, Moira corrected, it had changed before, years before when her father had been murdered.

Perhaps it had not changed at all, but was simply unfolding as the pages of the book of fate were written.

Now she could only wish for her mother's wisdom, and look inside herself for the courage to bear both crown and sword.

She stood now on the high reaches of the castle under a thumbnail moon. When it waxed full again, she would be far from here, on the cold ground of a battlefield.

She'd come to the battlement because she could see the torches lighting the playing field. Here the sights and sounds of night training could reach her. Cian, she thought, used hours of his night to teach men and women how to fight something stronger and faster than humans. He would push them, she knew, until they were ready to drop. As he had pushed her, and the others of the circle, night after night during their weeks in Ireland.

Not all of them trusted him, she knew that as well. Some actively feared him, but that might be to the good. She understood he wasn't after making friends here, but warriors.

In truth, he'd had a strong part of making one of her.

She thought she understood why he fought with them— or at least had a glimmer of understanding why he would risk so much for humankind. Part of it was pride of which she knew he had abundance. He would not bow to Lilith. Part, whether he admitted it or not, was loyalty to his brother. And the rest, well, it dealt with courage and his own conflicted emotions.

For he had emotions, she knew. She couldn't imagine how they struggled and whirled inside him after a thousand years of existence. Her own were so conflicted and torn after only two months of blood and death she hardly recognized herself.

What must it be like for him, after all he'd seen and done, all he'd gained and lost? He knew more than any of them of the world, of its pleasures, its pains, its potentials. No, she couldn't imagine what it was like to know all he knew and still risk his own survival.

That he did risk it, that he was even now lending his time and skill to train troops, earned her respect. While the mystery of him, the hows and whys of him, continued to fascinate.

She couldn't be sure what he thought of her. Even when he'd kissed her—that single hot and desperate moment— she couldn't be sure. And getting to the inside of matters had always been irresistible to her.

She heard footsteps, and turning, saw Larkin coming toward her.

"You should be in your bed," he said.

"I'd only stare at the ceiling. The view's better here." She reached for his hand—her cousin, her friend—and was instantly comforted. "And why aren't you in yours?"

"I saw you. Blair and I went out to help Cian for a bit." Like hers, his gaze scanned the field below. "I saw you standing up here alone."

"I'm poor company, even for myself tonight. I only wish it were done, then there would be what happens next. So I came up here to brood over it." She tipped her head toward his shoulder. "It passes the time."

"We could go down to the family parlor. I'll let you beat me at chess."

"Let me? Oh, will you listen to him." She looked up at him. His eyes were golden brown, long-lidded like her own. The smile in them didn't quite mask his concern. "And I suppose you've *let* me win the hundreds of matches we've had over the years."

"I thought it good for your sense of confidence."

She laughed even as she poked him. "It's confident I am I can beat you at chess nine times out of every ten."

"We'll just put that to the test then."

"We will not." Now she kissed him, brushing his tawny hair away from his face. "You'll go to your bed and to your lady, and not spend these hours distracting me from my sorry mood. Come, we'll go in. It may be the limited view of my ceiling will bore me to sleep after all."

"You've only to tap on the door if you're wanting company."

"I know it."

Just as she knew she would keep her own counsel until the first light of dawn.

But she did not sleep.

In the way of tradition she would be dressed and tended to by her ladies in the last hour before dawn. Though it was urged on her, she refused the red gown. Moira knew well enough it wasn't a color that flattered her, however royal it might be. In its stead she wore the hues of the forest, a deep green over a paler green kirtle.

She agreed to jewels—they had been her mother's after all. So she allowed the heavy stones of citrine to be fastened around her neck. But she would not remove the silver cross.

She would wear her hair down and uncovered, and sat letting the female chatter chirp around her as Dervil brushed it tirelessly.

"Will you not eat just a little, Highness?"

Ceara, one of her women, once again urged a plate of honey cakes on her. "After," Moira told her. "I'll feel more settled after."

Moira got to her feet, her relief profound when Glenna stepped into the room. "How wonderful you look!" Moira held out her hands. She'd chosen the gowns herself for both Glenna and Blair, and saw now she'd chosen well. Then again, she thought, Glenna was so striking there was nothing that wouldn't flatter her.

Still, the choice of deep blue velvet highlighted her creamy skin and the fire of her hair.

"I feel a bit like a princess myself," Glenna told her. "Thank you so much. And you, Moira, look every inch the queen."

"Do I?" She turned to her glass, but saw only herself. But she smiled when she saw Blair come in. She'd chosen russet for Blair, with a kirtle of dull gold. "I've never seen you in a dress."

"Hell of a dress." Blair studied her friends, then herself. "We've got that whole fairy tale thing going." She threaded her fingers through her short, dark hair to settle it into place.

"You don't mind then? Tradition requires the more formal attire."

"I like being a girl. I don't mind dressing like one, even one who's not in my own fashion era." Blair spotted the honey cakes, and helped herself to one. "Nervous?"

"Well beyond it. I'd like a moment with the ladies Glenna and Blair," Moira told her women. When they scurried out, Moira dropped into the chair in front of the fire. "They've been fussing around me for an hour. It's tiring."

"You look beat." Blair sat on the arm of the chair. "You didn't sleep."

"My mind wouldn't rest."

"You didn't take the potion I gave you." Glenna let out a sigh. "You should be rested for this, Moira."

"I needed to think. It's not the usual way of it, but I want both of you, and Hoyt and Larkin to walk with me to the stone."

"Wasn't that the plan?" Blair asked with her mouth full.

"You would be part of the procession, yes. But in the usual way, I would walk ahead, alone. This must be, as it always has been. But behind me, would be only my family. My uncle, and my aunt, Larkin, my other cousins. After them, according to rank and position would walk others. I want you to walk with my family, as you are my family. I do this for myself, but also for the people of Geall. I want them to see what you are. Cian isn't able to be part of this, as I wish he could."

"It can't be done at night, Moira." Blair touched a hand to Moira's shoulder. "It's too much of a risk."

"I know. But while the circle won't be complete at the place of the stone, he'll be in my thoughts." She rose now to go to the window. "Dawn's coming," she murmured. "And the day follows."

She turned back as the last stars died. "I'm ready for what comes with it."

Her family and her women were already gathered below. She accepted the cloak from Dervil, and fastened the dragon brooch herself.

When she looked up from the task, she saw Cian. She assumed he might have stopped for a moment on his way to retire, until she saw he carried the cloak Glenna and Hoyt had charmed to block the killing rays of the sun.

She stepped away from her uncle's side, and up to Cian. "You would do this?" she said quietly.

"I rarely have the opportunity for a morning walk."

However light his words, she heard what was under them. "I'm grateful you've chosen this morning to take one."

"Dawn's broke," Riddock said. "The people wait."

She only nodded, then drew up her hood as was the custom before stepping out into the early light.

The air was cool and misty with barely a breeze to stir the fingers of vapor. Through the rising curtain of it, Moira crossed the courtyard to the gates alone, while her party fell in behind her. In the muffled quiet, she heard the morning birds singing, and the faint whisper of the damp air.

She thought of her mother, who had once walked this way on a cool, misty morning. And all the others who'd walked before her out of the castle gates, across the brown road, over the green grass so thick with dew it was like wading through a river. She knew others trailed behind her, merchants and craftsmen, harpers and bards. Mothers and daughters, soldiers and sons.

The sky was streaked with pink in the east, and the ground fog sparkled silver.

She smelled the river and the earth, and continued up, over the gentle rise with the dew dampening the hem of her gown.

The place of the stone stood on a faerie hill where a little glade of trees offered shelter. Gorse and moss grew, pale yellow, quiet green, over the rocks near the holy well.

In the spring there would be the cheery orange of lilies, dancing heads of columbine, and later the sweet spires of foxglove, all growing where they would.

But for now, the flowers slept and the leaves of the trees had taken on that first blush of color that portended their death.

The sword stone itself was wide and white, altarlike on an ancient dolmen of flat gray.

Through the leaves and the mists, beams of sun lanced, crossing that white stone and glinting on the silver hilt of the sword buried in it.

Her hands felt cold, so very cold.

All of her life she had known the story. How the gods had forged the sword from lightning, from the sea, and the earth and the wind. How Morrigan had brought it and the altar stone herself to this place. And there she had buried it to the hilt, carved the words on the stone with her fiery finger.

SHEATHED BY THE HAND OF GODS
FREED BY THE HAND OF A MORTAL
AND SO WITH THIS SWORD
SHALL THAT HAND RULE GEALL

Moira paused at the base of the stones to read the words again. If the gods deemed it, that hand would be hers.

With her cloak sweeping over the dew-drenched grass, she walked through sun and mist to the top of the faerie hill. And took her place behind the stone.

For the first time she looked, and she saw. Hundreds of people, her people, with their eyes on hers spread over the field, down toward that brown ribbon of road. Every one of them, if the sword came to her, would be her responsibility. Her cold hands wanted to shake.

She calmed herself as she scanned the faces and waited for the trio of holy men to take their places behind her.

Some were still coming over that last rise, hurrying lest they miss the moment. She wanted her breath steady when she spoke, so waited a little longer and let herself meet the eyes of those she loved best.

"My lady," one of the holy men murmured.

"Yes. A moment."

Slowly, she unpinned the brooch, passed her cloak behind her. The wide sweep of her sleeves flowed back as she lifted her arms, but she didn't feel the chill against her skin. She felt heat.

"I am a servant of Geall," she called out. "I am a child of the gods. I come here to this place to bow to the will of both. By my blood, by my heart, by my spirit."

She took the last step toward the stone.

There was no sound now. It seemed even the air held its breath. Moira reached out, curled her fingers around the silver hilt.

And oh, she thought as she felt the heat of it, as she heard somewhere in her mind the murmur of its music. Of course, aye, of course. It's mine, and always was.

With a whisper of steel against rock, she drew it free and raised its point to the sky.

She knew they cheered, and some of them wept. She knew that to a man they lowered to one knee. But her eyes were on that point and the flash of light that streaked from the sky to strike it.

She felt it inside her, that light, a burst of heat and color and strength. There was a sudden burn on her arm, and as if the gods etched it, the symbol of the claddaugh formed there to brand her queen of Geall. Rocked by it, thrilled and humbled, she looked down at her people. And her eyes met Cian's.

All else seemed to melt away in that moment, for a

moment. There was only him, his face shadowed by the hood of his cloak, and his eyes so brilliant and blue.

How could it be, she wondered, that she should hold her destiny in her hand, and see only him? How, meeting his eyes like this, could it be like looking deeper, deeper yet, into her own destiny?

"I am a servant of Geall," she said, unable to look away from him. "I am a child of the gods. This sword, and all it protects is mine. I am Moira, warrior queen of Geall. Rise, and know I love you."

She stood as she was, the sword still pointing skyward as the hands of the holy man placed the crown on her head.

He was no stranger to magic, the black or the white, but Cian thought he'd never seen anything more powerful. Her face, so pale when she'd removed her cloak, had bloomed when her hand had taken the sword. Her eyes, so heavy, so somber, had gone as brilliant as the blade.

And had simply sliced through him, keen as a sword, when they'd met his.

There she stood, he thought, slender and slight, and as magnificent as any Amazon. Suddenly regal, suddenly fierce, suddenly beautiful.

What moved inside him had no place there.

He stepped back, turned to go. Hoyt laid a hand on his arm.

"You must wait for her, for the queen."

Cian lifted a brow. "You forget, I have no queen. And I've been under this bloody cloak long enough."

He moved quickly. He wanted to get away from the light, from the smell of humanity. Away from the power of those gray eyes. He needed the cool and the dark, and the silence.

He was barely a league away when Larkin trotted up to him. "Moira asked me to see if you wanted a ride back."

"I'm fine, but thanks."

"It was amazing, wasn't it? And she was . . . well, brilliant as the sun. I always knew she'd be the one, but seeing it happen is a different matter. She was queen the moment she touched the sword. You could see it."

"If she wants to stay queen, have anyone to rule, she better make use of that sword."

"So she will. Come now, Cian, this isn't the day for gloom and doom. We're entitled to a few hours of joy and celebration. And feasting." With another grin, Larkin gave Cian an elbow poke. "She might be queen, but I can promise the rest of us will eat like kings this day."

"Well, an army travels on its belly."

"Do they?"

"So it was said by . . . someone or another. Have your feasting and celebration. Tomorrow queens, kings and peasants alike best be preparing for war."

"Feels like we've been doing nothing else. Not complaining, mind," he continued before Cian could speak. "I guess the matter is I'm tired of preparing for it, and want to get to it."

"Haven't had enough fighting the last little while?"

"I've payment to make for what was nearly done to Blair. She's still tender along the ribs, and wears down quicker than she'd admit." His face was hard and grim as he remembered it. "Healing fast, as she does, but I won't forget how they hurt her."

"It's dangerous to go into battle with a personal agenda."

"Ah, bollocks. We've all of us something personal to settle, or what's the point? And you won't tell me that a part of you won't be going into it with what that bitch did to King in your mind and in your heart."

Because Cian couldn't deny it, he left it alone. "Are you . . . escorting me back, Larkin?"

"As it happens. There was some mention of me throwing myself bodily over you to shield you from the sunlight should the magic in that cloak fade out."

"That would be fine. We'd both go up like torches." Cian said it casually, but he had to admit he felt easier when he stepped into the shadow cast by Castle Geall.

"I'm also asked to request you come to the family parlor if you're not too weary. We're to have a private breakfast there. Moira would be grateful if you could spare a few minutes at least."

She would have liked a few minutes herself, alone. But Moira was surrounded. The walk back to the castle was a blur of movement and voices wrapped in mists. She felt the weight of the sword in her hand, the crown on her head even as she was swept along by her family and friends. Cheers echoed over the hills and fields, a celebration of Geall's new queen.

"You'll need to show yourself," Riddock told her. "From the royal terrace. It's expected."

"Aye. But not alone. I know it's the way it's been done," she continued before her uncle could object. "But these are different times. My circle will stand with me." She looked at Glenna now, then Hoyt and Blair. "The people won't just see their queen, but those who have been chosen to lead this war."

"It's for you to say, you to do," Riddick said with a slight bow. "But on such a day, Geall should be free of the shadow of war."

"Until Samhain has passed, Geall remains always in the shadow of war. Every Geallian must know that until that day, I rule with a sword. And that I'm part of six the gods have chosen."

She laid a hand on his as they passed through the gates. "We will have feasting and celebration. I value your advice, as always, and I will show myself, and I will speak. But on this day, the gods have chosen both queen and warrior in me. And this is what I will be. This is what I'll give to Geall, to my last breath. I won't shame you."

He took her hand from his arm, brought it to his lips. "My sweet girl. You have and always will bring me nothing but pride. And from this day, to my last breath, I am the queen's man."

The servants were gathered, and knelt when the royal party entered the castle. She knew their names, their faces. Some of them had served her mother before Moira herself was born.

But it was no longer the same. She wasn't the daughter of the house now, but its mistress. And theirs.

"Rise," she said, "and know I am grateful for your loyalty and service. Know, too, that you and all of Geall have my loyalty and service as long as I am queen."

Later, she told herself as she started up the stairs, she would speak with each of them individually. It was important to do so. But for now, there were other duties.

In the family parlor the fire roared. Flowers cut fresh from garden and hothouse spilled from vases and bowls. The table was set with the finest silver and crystal, with wine waiting for Moira's inner circle to toast the new queen.

She took a breath, then two, trying to find the words she would say, her first, to those she loved best.

Then Glenna simply wrapped arms around her. "You were magnificent." She kissed both Moira's cheeks. "Luminous."

The tension she'd held tight in her shoulders eased. "I feel the same, but not. Do you know?"

"I can only imagine."

"Nice job." Blair stepped up, gave her a quick hug. "Can I see it?"

Warrior to warrior, Moira thought and offered Blair the sword.

"Excellent," Blair said softly. "Good weight for you. You expect it to be crusted with jewels or whatever. It's good that it's not. It's good and right that it's a fighting sword, not just a symbol."

"It felt as though the hilt was made for my hand. As soon as I touched it, it felt . . . mine."

"It is." Blair handed it back. "It's yours."

For the moment, Moira set the sword on the table to accept Hoyt's embrace. "The power in you is warm and steady," he said close to her ear. "Geall is fortunate in its queen."

"Thank you." Then she let out a laugh as Larkin swept her off her feet and in three dizzying circles.

"Look at you. Majesty."

"You mock my dignity."

"Always. But never you, *a stór.*"

When Larkin set her back on her feet, she turned to Cian. "Thank you for coming. It meant a great deal to me."

He neither embraced nor touched her, but only inclined his head. "It was a moment not to be missed."

"A moment more important to me that you would come. All of you," she continued and started to turn when her young cousin tugged on her skirts. "Aideen." She lifted the child, accepted the damp kiss. "And don't you look pretty today."

"Pretty," Aideen repeated, reaching up to touch Moira's jeweled crown. Then she turned her head with a smile both shy and sly for Cian. "Pretty," she said again.

"An astute female," Cian observed. He saw the little girl's gaze drop to the pendant he wore, and in an absent gesture lifted it so that she could touch.

Even as Aideen reached out, her mother all but flew across the room. "Aideen, don't!"

Sinann pulled the girl from Moira, gripped her tight against her belly, burgeoning with her third child.

In the shocked silence, Moira could do no more than breathe her cousin's name.

"I never had a taste for children," Cian said coolly. "You'll excuse me."

"Cian." With one damning look toward Sinann, Moira hurried after him. "Please, a moment."

"I've had enough moments for the morning. I want my bed."

"I would apologize." She took his arm, holding firm until he stopped and turned. His eyes were hard; blue stone. "My cousin Sinann, she's a simple woman. I'll speak with her."

"Don't trouble on my account."

"Sir." Pale as wax, Sinann walked toward them. "I beg your pardon, most sincerely. I have insulted you, and my queen, her honored guests. I ask your forgiveness for a mother's foolishness."

She regretted the insult, Cian thought, but not the act. The child was on the far side of the room now, in her father's arms. "Accepted." He dismissed her with barely a glance. "Now if you'll release my arm. Majesty."

"A favor," Moira began.

"You're racking them up."

"And I'm in your debt," she said evenly. "I need to go out, onto the terrace. The people need to see their queen, and, I feel, those who are her circle. If you'd give me a few minutes more of your time I'd be grateful."

"In the buggering sun."

She managed a smile, and relaxed as she recognized the frustration in his tone meant he'd do as she asked. "A few moments. Then you can go find some solitude with the satisfaction of knowing I'll be envying you for it."

"Then make it quick. I'd enjoy some solitude and satisfaction."

Moira arranged it deliberately, with Larkin on one side of her—a figure Geall loved and respected—and Cian on the other. The stranger some of them feared. Having them flank her would, she hoped, show her people she considered them equals, and that both had her trust.

The crowd cheered and called her name, with the cheers rising to a roar when she lifted the sword. It was also a deliberate gesture for her to pass that sword to Blair to hold for her while she spoke. The people should see that the woman Larkin was betrothed to was worthy to hold it.

"People of Geall!" She shouted it, but the cheering continued. It came in waves that didn't ebb until she stepped closer to the stone rail and raised her hands.

"People of Geall, I come to you as queen, as citizen, as protector. I stand before you as did my mother, as did her sire, and as did all those back to the first days. And I stand as part of a circle chosen by the gods. Not just a circle of Geallian rulers, but a circle of warriors."

Now she spread her arms to encompass the five who stood with her. "With these who stand with me, that circle is formed. These are my most trusted and beloved. As a citizen, I ask you give them your loyalty, your trust, your respect as you do me. As your queen, I command it."

She had to pause every few moments until the shouts and cheers abated again. "Today, the sun shines on Geall. But it will not always be so. What is coming seeks the dark, and we will meet it. We will defeat it. Today, we celebrate, we feast, we give thanks. Come the morrow, we continue our preparations for war. Every Geallian who can bear arms will do so. And we will march to *Ciunas*. We will march to the Valley of Silence. We will flood that ground with our strength and our will, and we will drown those who would destroy us in the light."

She held her hand out for the sword, then held it high again. "This sword will not, as it has since the first days, hang cool and quiet during my reign. It will flame and sing in my hand as I fight for you, for Geall, and for all humankind."

The roars of approval rose like a torrent.

Then there were screams as an arrow streaked the air.

Before she could react, Cian shoved her down. Under the shouting and chaos, she heard his low, steady cursing. And felt his blood warm on her hand.

"Oh God, my God, you're shot."

"Missed the heart." He spoke through gritted teeth. She saw the pain on his face as he pushed away from her to sit.

When he reached up to grip the arrow out of his side, Glenna dropped to a crouch, pushed his hand aside. "Let me see."

"Missed the heart," he repeated, and once again gripped the arrow. He yanked it out. "Bugger it. Bloody fucking hell."

"Inside," Glenna began briskly. "Get him inside."

"Wait." Though her hand trembled a little, Moira gripped Cian's shoulder. "Can you stand?"

"Of course I can bloody stand. What do you take me for?"

"Please, let them see you." Her free hand fluttered over his cheek for just an instant, like a brush of wings. "Let them see us. Please."

When she linked her fingers with his she thought she saw something stir in his eyes, and felt its twin shift inside her heart.

Then it was gone, and his voice was rough with impatience. "Give me some damn room then."

She got to her feet again. Below was chaos. The man she assumed was the assassin was being kicked and pummeled by every hand or foot that could reach him.

"Hold!" She shouted it with all her strength. "I command you, hold! Guards, bring that man to the great hall. People of Geall! You see that even on this day, even when the sun shines on us, this darkness seeks to destroy us. And it fails." She gripped Cian's hand, lifted it high with her own. "It fails because there are champions in this world who would risk their lives for another."

She laid a hand on Cian's side, felt his wince. Then held up her bloody hand. "He bleeds for us. And by this blood he shed for me, for all of you, I raise him to be Sir Cian, Lord of Oiche."

"Oh, for Christ's sake," Cian muttered.

"Be quiet." Moira said it softly, with steel, and her eyes on the crowd.

Chapter 3

Half-vamp," Blair announced as she strode back into the parlor. "Multiple bite scars. Crowd did a number on him," she added. "A regular human would be toast after the beating he took. And he's not feeling so well himself."

"He can be treated after I've spoken to him. Cian requires care first."

Blair looked over Moira's shoulder to where Glenna was bandaging Cian's side. "How's he doing?"

"He's angry and uncooperative, so I would say he's doing well enough."

"We can all be grateful for his reflexes. You handled it," Blair added, looking back at Moira. "Kept your cool, kept control. Tough first day on the job, nearly getting assassinated and all that, but you did good."

"Not good enough to have anticipated a daylight attack. To remember that not all Lilith's dogs require an invitation to come within these walls." She thought of how Cian's blood had run against her hand—warm and red. "I won't make that mistake again."

"None of us will. What we need is to get information out of this asshole Lilith sent. But there's a problem. He either can't or won't speak English. Or Gaelic."

"He's mute?"

"No, no. He talks, it's just none of us can understand him. Sounds Eastern European. Maybe Czech."

"I see." Moira glanced back at Cian. He was stripped to the waist, with only the bandage against his skin. Annoyance more than pain darkened his face as he sipped from a goblet she assumed held blood. Though he didn't look to be in the best of moods, she knew she was about to ask another favor.

"Give me a moment," she murmured to Blair. She approached Cian, ordering herself not to shrink under his hot blue stare. "Is there something more that can be done for you, to make you more comfortable?"

"Peace, quiet, privacy."

Though each of his words had the lash of a whip, she kept her own calm and pleasant. "I'm sorry, but those items are in short supply right at the moment. I'll order them up for you as soon as I can."

"Smart-ass," he mumbled.

"Indeed. The man whose arrow you intercepted speaks in a foreign tongue. Your brother told me once that you knew many languages."

He took a long, deep drink, with his eyes deliberately on hers. "It's not enough that I *intercepted* the arrow? Now you want me to interrogate your assassin?"

"I would be grateful if you would try, or at least interpret. If indeed, his tongue is one you know. There are likely a few things in the world you don't know, so you may be of no use to me at all."

Amusement flickered briefly in his eyes. "Now you're being nasty."

"Tit for tat."

"All right, all right. Glenna, my beauty, stop hovering."

"You lost considerable blood," she began, but he only lifted the goblet.

"Replacing, even as we speak." With a slight grimace, he got to his feet. "I need a goddamn shirt."

"Blair," Moira said in even tones, "would you fetch Cian a goddamn shirt?"

"On that."

"You've made a habit of saving my life," Moira said to Cian.

"Apparently. I'm thinking of giving that up."

"I could hardly blame you."

"Here you go, champ." Blair offered Cian a fresh white shirt. "I think the guy's Czech, or possibly Bulgarian. Can you handle either of those?"

"As it happens."

They went into the great hall where the assassin sat, bruised, bleeding and chained, under heavy guard. That guard included both Larkin and Hoyt. When Cian entered, Hoyt stepped away from his post.

"Well enough?" he asked Cian.

"I'll do. And it cheers me considerably that he looks a hell of a lot worse than I do. Pull your guards back," he said to Moira. "He won't be going anywhere."

"Stand down. Sir Cian will be in charge here."

"Sir Cian, my ass." But he only muttered it as he approached the prisoner.

Cian circled him, gauging ground. The man was slight of build and dressed in what would be the rough clothes of a farmer or shepherd. One eye was swollen shut, the other going black and blue. He'd lost a couple of teeth.

Cian snapped out a command in Czech. The man jolted, his single working eye rolling up in surprise.

But he didn't speak.

"You understood that," Cian continued in the same language. "I asked if there are others with you. I won't ask again."

When he was met with silence, Cian struck out with enough force to have the prisoner slamming back against the wall, along with the chair he was chained to.

"For every thirty seconds of silence, I'll give you pain."

"I'm not afraid of pain."

"Oh, you will be." Cian jerked the chair and the man upright, kept his face close. "Do you know what I am?"

"I know what you are." The man used his bloodied mouth to sneer. "Traitor."

"That's one viewpoint. But the important thing to remember is that I can give you pain beyond what even such as you can stand. I can keep you alive for days, weeks, come to that. And in constant agony." He lowered his voice to a hiss. "I'd enjoy it. So let's begin again."

He didn't bother to ask the question, as he'd warned he wouldn't repeat it.

"Could use a spoon," he said conversationally. "That left eye looks painful. If I had a spoon handy, I could scoop it right out of its socket for you. Of course, I could use my fingers," he continued when that eye wheeled wildly. "But then I'd have a mess on my hands, wouldn't I?"

"Do your worst," the man spat out—but he'd begun to tremble a little. "I'll never betray my queen."

"Bollocks." The shudders and sweat told him this one would be easily and quickly broken. "You'll not only betray her before I'm done with you, you'll do it dancing the hornpipe if I tell you to. But let's just be quick and direct as we've all better things to do."

The man's head jerked back as Cian moved. But instead of going for the face as his quarry anticipated, Cian reached down, gripped the man's cock. And squeezed until there was nothing but screams.

"There's no one else! I'm alone, I'm alone!"

"Be sure." Cian only increased the pressure. "If you lie, I'll find out. And then I'll begin to cut this piece of you off, one inch at a time."

"She sent only me." He was weeping now, tears and snot running down his face. "Only me."

Cian eased the pressure a few fractions. "Why?"

The only answer was raw, rough gasps, and Cian tightened the vise of his fingers again. "Why?"

"One could slip through easily, unnoticed. Un . . . unremarked."

"The logic of that has spared you, at least for the moment, from becoming a eunuch." Cian strolled over, got himself a chair. After placing it in front of the prisoner, he straddled it. And spoke in conversational tones even as the man whimpered. "Now, this is better, isn't it? Civilized. When we're done here, we'll see to those injuries."

"I want water."

"I'm sure you do. We'll get you some—after. So for now, let's talk a bit about Lilith."

It took thirty minutes—and two more sessions of pain— before he was satisfied he knew all the man could tell him. Cian got to his feet again.

The would-be assassin was weeping uncontrollably now. Perhaps from the pain, Cian thought. Perhaps from the belief it was ended.

"What were you before she took you?"

"A teacher."

"Did you have a wife, a family?"

"They were no use but food. I was poor and weak, but the queen saw more in me. She gave me strength and purpose. And when she slaughters you, and these . . . ants who crawl with you, I'll be rewarded. I'll have a fine house, and women of my choosing, wealth and power."

"Promised you all that, did she?"

"That and more. You said I could have water."

"Yes, I did. Let me explain something to you about Lilith." He moved behind the man, whose name he'd never asked, and spoke quietly in his ear. "She lies. And so do I."

He clamped his hands on the man's head and in one fast move, broke his neck.

"What have you done?" Shocked to the pit of her belly, Moira rushed forward. "What have you done?"

"What needed doing. She sent only one—this time. If it upsets your sensibilities, you might want to have your guards take that out of here before I brief you."

"You had no right. No right." Her belly wanted to revolt as it had constantly since he'd begun the torturous interrogation. "You murdered him. What makes you any different from him that you would kill him without trial, without sentence?"

"The difference?" Coolly, Cian lifted his brows. "He was still mostly human."

"Is it so little to you? Life? Is it so little?"

"On the contrary."

"Moira. He's right." Blair moved between them. "He did what had to be done."

"How can you say that?"

"Because I'd have done the same. He was Lilith's dog, and if he'd escaped, he'd have tried again. If he couldn't get to you, he'd kill whoever he could."

"A prisoner of war—" Moira began.

"There are no prisoners in this," Blair interrupted. "On either side. If you'd locked him up, you'd take men out of training, off patrol, to guard him. He was an assassin, a spy sent behind lines during wartime. And mostly human is generous," she added with a glance at Cian. "He'd never be human again. If it had been a vampire in that chair, you'd have staked him without thought or hesitation. This isn't any different."

A vampire didn't leave its body broken on the floor, Moira thought, still chained to a chair.

Moira turned to one of the guards. "Tynan, remove the prisoner's body. See that it's buried."

"Majesty."

She saw Tynan's quick glance at Cian—and recognized the steely approval in the look.

"We'll go back to the parlor," she continued. "No one has eaten. You can . . . brief us while we do."

Lone gunman," Cian said, and wished almost wistfully for coffee.

"Makes sense." Blair helped herself to eggs and a thick slice of fried ham.

"Why?" Moira addressed the question to Blair.

"Okay, they've got some half-vamps trained for combat." She nodded at Larkin. "Like the ones Larkin and I dealt with that day at the caves, but it takes time and effort. And it takes a lot of work and will to keep one in thrall."

"And if the thrall is broken?"

"Insanity," Blair said briefly. "Total breakdown. I've heard stories of half-vamps gnawing off their own hand to get free and back to their maker."

"He was doomed before he came here," Moira murmured.

"From the minute Lilith got her hands on him, yeah. My take on this was it was supposed to be a quick hit, suicide mission. Why waste more than one? Things go right, you only need one."

"Yes, one man, one arrow." Moira considered it. "If he's skilled enough and fortunate enough, the circle is broken, Geall is without a ruler only moments, really, after it regains one. It would have been a good and efficient strike."

"There you go."

"But why did he wait until we were back? Why not try for me at the stone?"

"He didn't get there in time," Cian said simply. "He misjudged the distance he had to travel, and arrived after it was done. You were closed in by people on your way back, and he wasn't able to get a clear shot. So he joined the parade, so to speak, and bided his time."

"Eat something." Hoyt dished food onto Moira's plate himself. "So Lilith knew that Moira would go to the stone today."

"She has her ear to the ground," Cian confirmed. "Whether or not she'd planned to send someone to try to disrupt the ritual, and the result before Blair tangled with Lora is debatable. She was pissed," he said. "Wild, according to our late, unlamented archer. As I've said before, her relationship with Lora is strange and complicated, but very deep, very sincere. She ordered an archer chosen for this while she was still half-crazed. Sent him on horseback for speed—and they have only a limited number of horses."

"And how is the little French pastry?" Blair wondered.

"Scarred and screaming when the man left, and being tended to by Lilith personally."

"More important," Hoyt broke in, "where is Lora, and where are the rest of them?"

"Our informant, while handy with a bow, wasn't particularly observant or astute. The best I could get puts Lilith's main base a few miles from the battlefield. He described what seems to be a small settlement, overlooked by a good-sized farm with several cottages and a large stone manor house, where I'd say the gentry who owned the land lived. She's in the manor house."

"Ballycloon." Larkin looked at Moira, saw her face was very pale, her eyes very dark. "It must be Ballycloon, and the O Neills's land. The family we helped the day Blair and I were checking the traps, the day Lora ambushed her, they were coming from near Drombeg, and that's just a bit west of Ballycloon. We would have gone farther east, to check the last trap, but . . ."

"I was hurt," Blair finished. "We went as far as we could. And lucky for us. If she'd already made her base when we dropped in, we'd have been seriously outnumbered."

"And seriously dead," Cian added. "They moved in the night before your altercation with Lora."

"There would have been people there still, or on the road." It knotted Larkin's stomach to think of it. "And the O Neills themselves. I don't know if they've reached safety. How can we know how many . . ."

"We can't," Blair said flatly.

"You, you and Cian, you thought we should move everyone out, force them out if necessary, from all the villages and farms around the battleground. Burn the houses and cottages behind them so Lilith and her army would have no shelter. I thought it was cold and cruel of her. Heartless. And now . . ."

"It can't be changed. And I couldn't, wouldn't," Moira corrected, "have ordered homes burned. Perhaps it would have been wiser, and stronger, to do just that. But those whose homes we destroyed would have lost the heart they need to fight. So it's done this way."

She had no appetite for the food on her plate, but she picked up her tea to warm her hands. "Blair and Cian know strategy, as Hoyt and Glenna know magic. But you and I, Larkin, we know Geall and its people. We would have broken their hearts and their spirits."

"They'll burn what they don't need or want," Cian told her.

"Aye, but it won't be our hands that light the torch. That will matter. So we believe we know where they are. Do we know how many?"

"He started out with multitudes, but he was lying. He didn't know," Cian said. "However much Lilith may use mortals, she wouldn't count them in her inner circle, or trust any with salient information. They're food, they're servants, they're entertainment."

"We can look." Glenna spoke for the first time. "Hoyt and I, now that we have a general area, can do a locator spell. We should be able to get harder data. Some idea of the numbers. We know from Larkin's trip to the caves and his look at their arsenal they were armed for a thousand or more."

"We'll look." Hoyt laid his hand over Glenna's. "But what I think Cian isn't saying is whatever the numbers they have, whatever we have, in the end they'll have more. Whatever weapons they have will be more. Lilith has had decades, perhaps centuries, to plan this moment. We've had months."

"And still we'll win."

Cian lifted a brow at Moira's statement. "Because you're good and they're evil?"

"No, and there's nothing so simple as that. You yourself are proof of that, for you're neither like her nor like us, but something else altogether. We'll win because we'll be smarter, and we'll be stronger. And because she has no one like the six of us standing with her."

She turned from him to his brother. "Hoyt, you are the first of us. You brought us together."

"Morrigan chose us."

"She, or fate, selected us," Moira agreed. "But it was you who began the work. It's you who believed, who had the power and the strength to forge this circle. So do I believe it. I rule Geall, but I don't rule this company."

"Nor do I."

"No, none of us do. We must be as one, for all our differences. So we look to each other for what we need. I'm far from the strongest warrior here, and my magic is but a shadow. I don't have Larkin's skills, nor the steeliness of mind to kill in cold blood. What I have is knowledge and authority, so I offer those."

"You have more," Glenna told her. "A great deal more."

"I will have more, before it's done. There are things I must do." She got to her feet. "I'll return to work on whatever is necessary as soon as I'm able."

"Pretty royal," Blair commented after Moira left the room.

"Carrying a lot of weight with it." Glenna turned to Hoyt. "Agenda?"

"Best to see what we can of the enemy. Then I'm thinking fire. It's still one of our most formidable weapons, so we should charm more swords."

"Risky enough to put swords in some of the hands we're training," Blair put in. "Much less flaming ones."

"You'd be right." Hoyt considered, nodded. "It will be up to us then, won't it, to decide who'll be—what is it?— issued that sort of weapon. Good men should be placed in positions as close to Lilith's base as we can manage. They'd need shelter that's safe after sunset."

"It's barracks you're meaning. There are cottages and cabins, of course." Larkin narrowed his eyes in thought. "Other shelters can be built in the daylight hours if need be. There's an inn as well, between her base and the next settlement."

"Why don't we go take a look?" Blair shoved her plate aside. "You and Glenna can look your way, and Larkin and I can do a fly-by. You up for the dragon?"

"I am." He smiled at her. "Especially when you're doing the riding."

"Sex, sex, sex. The guy's a machine."

"On that note," Cian said dryly, "I'm going to bed."

With a quick squeeze of Glenna's hand, Hoyt murmured, "A moment," then followed his brother.

"I need a word with you."

Cian flicked him a glance. "I've had my quota of words this morning."

"You'll have to swallow a few more. My rooms are closer, if you would. I'd prefer this private."

"Since you'd just dog me to my room and pester me until I want to rip your tongue out, your rooms will do."

Servants bustled on the route between the parlor and bedchambers. Preparations for the feasting, Cian thought, and wondered if it was Hoyt's talk of fire that put him in mind of Nero and his fiddle.

Hoyt stepped into a chamber, then immediately threw out an arm to block Cian from entering. "The sun," was all he said, then moved quickly to pull the coverings over the windows.

The room plunged into gloom. Without thinking, Hoyt gestured toward a brace of candles. They flared into light.

"Handy bit of business that," Cian commented. "I'm out of practice lighting tinderboxes."

"It's a basic skill, and one you'd have yourself if you'd ever put your mind and time into honing your power."

"Too tedious. Is that whiskey?" Cian moved straight to a decanter, and poured. "Oh, such sobriety and disapproval." He read his brother's expression clearly as he took the first warm sip. "I'll remind you that it's the end of my day—well past it, come to that."

He glanced around, began to wander. "Smells female. Women like Glenna always leave something of themselves behind to remind a man." Then he dropped down into a chair, slouching, stretching out his legs. "Now, what is it you're bound and determined to bore me with?"

"There was a time you enjoyed, even sought my company."

Cian's shoulders moved in something too lazy to be called a shrug. "I suppose that means nine hundred years of absence doesn't make the heart grow fonder."

Regret showed on Hoyt's face before he turned away to add turf to the fire. "Are you and I to be at odds again?"

"You tell me."

"I wanted to speak with you alone about what you did with the prisoner."

"More humanity heard from. Yes, yes, I should have patted his head so he could stand trial, or before the tribunal, whatever goes for the name of justice in this place. I should've invoked the sodding Geneva Convention. Well, bollocks."

"I don't know this convention, but there could be no trial, no tribunal on such a matter at such a time. That's what I'm saying, you great irritating idiot. You executed an assassin, as I would have done—but with more tact and, well, stealth."

"Ah, so you'd have slithered down to whatever cage they put him in and put a knife between his ribs." Cian raised his eyebrows. "That's all right then."

"It's not. None of it's all right. It's a bloody nightmare is what it is, and we're all having it. I'm saying you did the necessary. And that for his trying to kill Moira, whom I love as I did my own sisters, and for putting an arrow in you, I'd have done for him. I've never killed a man, for these things we've ended these past weeks haven't been men, but demon. But I'd have killed this one if you hadn't been there ahead of me."

Hoyt paused, caught his breath if not his composure. "I wanted to say as much to you so you'd know my feelings on it. But it seems I waste both our time as you couldn't give a damn in hell what my feelings are."

Cian didn't move. His only change was to shift his gaze from his brother's furious face down to the whiskey in his hand. "I do, as it happens, give several damns in hell what your feelings are. I wish I didn't. You've stirred things in me I'd calmed too long ago to remember. You've slapped family in my face, Hoyt, when I'd buried it."

Crossing over, Hoyt took the chair that faced his brother's. "You're mine."

Now when Cian lifted his eyes to his brother's they were empty. "I'm no one's."

"Maybe you weren't, from the time you died until the time I found you. But it's no longer true. So if you give those damns, I'm saying to you I'm proud of what you're doing. I'm saying I know it's harder for you to do this thing than any of us."

"Obviously, as demonstrated, killing vampires or humans isn't difficult for me."

"Do you think I don't see how some of the servants melt away when you're near? That I didn't see Sinann rush to take her child, as if you might have snapped its neck as you did the assassin's? These insults to you don't go unnoticed."

"Some aren't insulted to be feared. It doesn't matter. It doesn't," he insisted when Hoyt's face closed up. "This is a fingersnap of time for me. Less. When it's done, unless I get a lucky stake through the heart, I'll go my way."

"I hope your way will bring you, from time to time, to see me and Glenna."

"It may. I like to look at her." Cian's grin spread, slow and easy. "And who knows, she may eventually come to her senses and realize she chose the wrong brother. I've nothing but time."

"She's mad for me." His tone easy again, Hoyt reached over, took Cian's glass of whiskey and had a sip himself.

"Mad is what she'd have to be to put her lot in with you, but women are odd creatures. You're fortunate in her, Hoyt, if I've failed to mention it before."

"She's the magic now." He passed the glass back. "I'd

have none that mattered without her. My world turned when she came into it. I wish you had . . ."

"That isn't written in the book of fate for me. The poet's may say love's eternal, but I can tell you it's a different matter when you've got eternity, and the woman doesn't."

"Have you ever loved a woman?"

Cian studied his whiskey again, and thought of the centuries. "Not in the way you mean. Not in the way you have with Glenna. But I've cared enough to know it's not a choice I can make."

"Love is a choice?"

"Everything is." Cian tossed back the last of the whiskey, then set the empty glass aside. "Now, I choose to go to bed."

"You chose to take that arrow for Moira today," Hoyt said as Cian started for the door.

Cian stopped, and when he turned his eyes were wary. "I did."

"I find that a very human sort of choice."

"Do you?" And the words were a shrug. "I find it merely an impulsive—and painful—one."

He slipped out to make his way to his own room on the northern side of the castle. Impulse, he thought again, and, he could admit to himself, an instant of raw fear. If he'd seen the arrow fly a second later, or moved with a fraction less speed, she'd be dead.

And in that instant of impulse and fear, he'd seen her dead. The arrow still quivering as it pierced her flesh, the blood spilling the life out of her onto her dark green gown and the hard gray stones.

He feared that, feared the end of her, where she would be beyond him. Where she would go to a place he couldn't see or touch. Lilith would have taken one last thing from him with that arrow, one last thing he could never regain.

For he'd lied to his brother. He had loved a woman, despite his best—or worst—intentions, he loved the new-crowned queen of Geall.

Which was ridiculous, and impossible, and in time

something he'd get over. A decade or two and he'd no longer remember the exact shade of those long gray eyes. That quiet scent she carried would no longer tease his senses. He'd forget the sound of her voice, the look of that slow, serious smile.

Such things faded, he reminded himself. You had only to allow it.

He stepped into his own room, closed and bolted the door.

The windows were covered, and no light was lit. Moira, he knew, had given very specific orders on how his housekeeping should be done. Just as she'd specifically chosen that room, a distance from the others, as it faced north.

Less sunlight, he mused. A considerate hostess.

He undressed in the dark, thought fleetingly of the music he liked to play before sleep, or on wakening. Music, he thought, that filled the silence.

But this time and place didn't run to CD players, or cable radio or any damn thing of the sort.

Naked, he stretched out in bed. And in the absolute dark, the absolute silence, willed himself to sleep.

Chapter 4

Moira stole the time. She escaped from her women, from her uncle, from her duties. She was already guilty, already worried she'd be a failure as a queen because she so craved her solitude.

She would have bartered two days' food, or two nights' sleep, for a single hour alone with her books. Selfish, she told herself as she hurried away from the noise, the people, the questions. Selfish to wish for her own comfort when so much was at stake.

But while she wouldn't indulge herself with books in some sunny corner, she would take the time to make this visit.

On this day she was made queen, she wanted, and she needed, her mother. So hiking up her skirts, she went as fast as she was able down the hill, then through the little gap in the stone wall that bordered the graveyard.

Almost instantly she felt quieter of heart.

She went first to the stone she'd ordered carved and set when she'd returned to Geall. She'd set one herself for King in Ireland, in the graveyard of Cian and Hoyt's ancestors. But she'd vowed to have one done here, in honor of a friend.

After laying a handful of flowers on the ground, she stood and read the words she'd ordered carved in the polished stone.

> **King**
> *This brave warrior lies not here*
> *but in a faraway land.*
> *He gave his life for Geall,*
> *and all humankind.*

"I hope you would like it, the stone and the words. It seems so long ago since I saw you. It all seems so long, and still hardly more than a hand clap. I'm sorry to tell you Cian was hurt today, for my sake. But he's doing well enough. Last night we spoke almost as friends, Cian and I. And today, well, not altogether friendly. It's hard to know."

She laid a hand on the stone. "I'm queen now. That's hard to know as well. I hope you don't mind I put this monument here, where my family lies. For to me, that's what you were for the short time we had. You were family. I hope you're resting now."

She stepped away, then hurriedly back again. "Oh, I meant to say, I'm keeping my left up, as you taught me." By his grave she lifted her arms in a boxing stance. "So, for all the times I don't get a fist in my face, thank you."

With the rest of the flowers in the crook of her arm, she picked her way through the long grass, the stones, to the graves of her parents.

She laid flowers at the base of her father's stone. "Sir. I hardly remember you, and I think the memories—most of them—that I have are ones mother passed to me. She loved you so, and would speak of you often. I know you were a good man, for she wouldn't have loved you otherwise. And all who speak of you say you were strong and kind, and quick to laugh. I wish I could remember the sound of that, of your laugh."

She looked over the stones now, to the hills, the distant mountains. "I've learned you didn't die as we always thought, but were murdered. You and your young brother. Murdered by the demons who are even now in Geall, preparing for war. I'm all that's left of you, and I hope it's enough."

She knelt now, between the graves, to lay the rest of the flowers over her mother. "I miss you, every day. I had to go far away, as you know, to come back stronger. *Mathair.*"

She closed her eyes on the word, and on the image it brought to her, clear as life.

"I didn't stop what was done to you, and still I see that night as if behind a mist. Those that killed you have been punished, one by my own hand. It was all I could do for you. All I can do is fight, and lead my people to fight. Some of them to their death. I wear the sword and the crown of Geall. I will not diminish it."

She sat awhile, with just the sound of the breeze through the tall grass and the shifting lights of the sun.

When she rose, turned toward the castle, she saw the goddess Morrigan standing at the stone wall.

The god wore blue today, soft and pale and trimmed in deeper tones. The fire of her hair was unbound to lay flaming over her shoulders.

Her hands empty of flowers, her heart heavy, Moira walked through the grass to meet her.

"My lady."

"Majesty."

Puzzled by Morrigan's bow, Moira clasped her hands together to keep them still. "Do gods acknowledge queens?"

"Of course. We made this place and deemed those of your blood would rule and serve it. We're pleased with you. Daughter." Laying her hands lightly on Moira's shoulders, she kissed both her cheeks. "Our blessings on you."

"I would rather you bless my people, and keep them safe."

"That is for you. The sword is out of its scabbard. Even

when it was forged, it was known that one day it would sing in battle. That, too, is for you."

"She's already spilled Geallian blood."

Morrigan's eyes were as deep and calm as a lake. "My child, the blood Lilith has spilled would make an ocean."

"And my parents are only drops in that sea?"

"Every drop is precious, and every drop serves a purpose. Do you lift the sword only for your own blood?"

"No." Shifting, Moira gestured. "There's another stone here, standing for a friend. I lift the sword for him and his world, and for all the worlds. We're all a part of each other."

"Knowing this is important. Knowledge is a great gift, and the thirst to seek it even greater. Use what you know, and she will never defeat you. Head and heart, Moira. You are not made to give greater weight to one than the other. Your sword will flame, I promise you, and your crown will shine. But what you hold inside your head and your heart is the true power."

"It seems they're full of fear."

"There's no courage without fear. Trust and know. And keep your sword at your side. It's your death she wants most."

"Mine? Why?"

"She doesn't know. Knowledge is your power."

"My lady," Moira began, but the god was gone.

The feast required yet another gown and another hour of being fussed over. With so much on her hands, she'd left the matter of wardrobe to her aunt, and was pleased to find the gown beautiful and the watery blue color flattering. She enjoyed pretty gowns and taking a bit of time to look her best.

But it seemed she was being laced into a new one every time she turned around, and subjected to the chirping and buzzing of her women half the day.

She could admit she missed the freedom of the jeans

and roomy shirts she'd worn in Ireland. Beginning the next day, however it shocked the women, she would dress as best suited a warrior preparing for battle.

But for tonight, she'd wear the velvets and silks and jewels.

"Ceara, how are your children?"

"Well, my lady, and thank you." Standing behind Moira, Ceara continued to work Moira's thick hair into silky braids.

"Your duties and your training keep you from them more than I would wish."

Their eyes met in the mirror. Moira knew Ceara to be a sensible woman, the most centered, in her opinion, of the three that waited on her.

"My mother tends them, and is happy to do so. The time I take now is well spent. I'd rather lose these hours with them than see them harmed."

"Glenna tells me you're very fierce in hand-to-hand."

"I am." Ceara's face tightened with a grim smile. "I'm not skilled with a sword, but there's time yet. Glenna's a good teacher."

"Strict," Dervil piped in. "Not as strict as the lady Blair, but demanding all the same. We run, every day, and fight and tumble and carve stakes. And end each day with weary legs, bruises and splinters."

"Better to be weary and bruised than dead."

At Moira's flat comment, Dervil flushed. "I meant no disrespect, Majesty. I've learned a great deal."

"And are, I'm told, becoming a demon with a sword. I'm proud. And you, Isleen, are said to have a good hand with a bow."

"I do." Isleen, the youngest of the three, flushed with the compliment. "I like it better than the fighting with fists and feet. Ceara always knocks me down."

"When you squeal like a mouse and flutter your hands, anyone could knock you down," Ceara pointed out.

"Ceara's taller, and her arms longer than yours, Isleen. So," Moira said, "you have to learn to be faster, and sneakier.

I'm proud of all of you, for every bruise. Tomorrow, and every day after, for no less than an hour each day, I'll be training with you."

"But, Majesty," Dervil began, "you can't—"

"I can," Moira interrupted. "And I will. I'll expect each of you, and the other women to do their best to knock *me* down. It won't be easy." She stood when Ceara stepped back. "I've learned a great deal as well." She lifted her crown, placed it on her head. "Believe me when I tell you I can knock the three of you, and any else who comes, on your arse."

She turned, resplendent in shimmering blue velvet.

"Any who puts me on mine, or bests me with bare hands or any weapon will be given one of the silver crosses Glenna and Hoyt has charmed. This is my best gift. Tell the others."

It was, Cian thought, like walking into a play. The great hall was the stage, and festooned with banners, enlivened with flowers, blazing with candles and firelight. Knights and lords and ladies were decked in their very best. Doublets and gowns, jewels and gold. He spotted several men and women sporting footwear with the long and pointed upturned toes that he recalled were fashionable when he'd been alive.

So, he thought, even regrettable styles spanned worlds.

Food and drink were so plentiful he imagined the long tables groaned under the platters and pitchers. There was music, bright and lively, from a harper. The talk he overheard ran the gamut. Fashion, politics, sexual gossip, flirtations and finance.

Not so different altogether, he mused, from his own nightclub back in New York. The women wore less there, of course, and the music was louder. But the core of it hadn't changed overmuch through the centuries. People still liked to gather together over food and drink and music.

He thought of his club again, and asked himself if he

missed it. The nightly surge, the sounds, the press of people. And realized he didn't, not in the least.

Very likely, he decided, he'd been growing bored and restless, and would have moved on shortly in any case. It had only taken his brother's sweep through time and space, having Hoyt land—more or less—on his doorstep to up the timetable.

But without Hoyt and his mission from the gods, moving out would have meant a change of name and location, a shifting of funds. Complicated, time-consuming—and interesting. Cian had had more than a hundred names and a hundred homes, and still found the forming of them interesting.

Where might he have gone? he wondered. Sydney perhaps, or Rio. It might have been Rome or Helsinki. It was only a matter, essentially, of sticking a pin in a map. There were few places he hadn't been already, and none he couldn't have made his base if he chose.

In his world, in any case. Geall was a different matter. He'd lived through this sort of fashion and culture once, and had no desire to repeat himself. His family had been gentry, and so he'd attended his share of high-flown feasts.

All in all he'd have preferred a snifter of brandy and a good book.

He didn't intend to stay long, and had come only because he knew someone would come looking for him. While he was confident he could have avoided whoever had come hunting him, he would never avoid the haranguing Hoyt would subject him to the next day.

Easier altogether to put in an appearance, toast the new queen, then slip away.

He had drawn the line at wearing the formal doublet and accessories that had been delivered to his room. He might have been stuck in a medieval timeline, but he'd be damned if he'd dress for it.

So he wore black, pants and sweater. He hadn't packed a suit and tie for this particular journey.

Still he smiled with some warmth at Glenna who drifted

up to him in emerald green, in what he thought had been termed a *robe deguisee* at one time. Very formal, very elegant, and showcasing her very lovely breasts with its low and rounded neckline.

"Now here's a vision I prefer to any goddess."

"I almost feel like one." She spread her arms so the full bell sleeves swayed. "Heavy though. It must be ten pounds of material. I see you went for a less weighty ensemble."

"I believe I'd stake myself before I squeezed into one of those getups again."

She had to laugh. "Can't blame you, but I'm getting a kick out of seeing Hoyt all done up. For me—maybe for you after all this time—it's like a costume ball. Moira chose regal black and gold for the house sorcerer. It suits him, as your more contemporary choice does you. Still, this whole day has been like a very strange dream."

"I was thinking a very strange play."

"Yeah, that works. Whatever, tonight's feasting is a short and colorful respite. We managed to do some scouting today, Hoyt and I magically, Larkin and Blair with the flyover. We'll fill you in when—"

She broke off at the sound of trumpets.

Moira made her entrance, the train of her gown flowing behind her, her crown flaming in the light of a hundred candles.

She glowed, as queens should, as women could.

As his unbeating heart tightened in his chest, Cian thought: Bloody, buggering hell.

He had no choice but to join the others at the high table for the feast. Leaving beforehand would have been an overt insult—not that he minded that overmuch—but it would have drawn attention. So he was stuck again.

Moira sat at the center of the table, flanked by Larkin and her uncle. Cian, at least, had Blair beside him, who was both an informative and entertaining companion.

"Lilith hasn't burned anything yet, which was a surprise," she began. "Probably too busy nursing Fifi. Oh, question. The French bitch has been around about four hundred years, right? And you more than double that. How come both of you still have accents?"

"And why is it Americans believe everyone should speak as they do?"

"Good point. Is this venison? I think it's venison." She took a bite. "It's not too bad."

She wore siren red, which left a portion of her strong shoulders bared. Her short cap of hair was unadorned, but there were ornate gold medallions, nearly big as a baby's fist, dangling from her ears.

"How do you hold your head up with those earrings?"

"Suffering for fashion," she said easily. "So they've got horses," she continued. "A couple of dozen in various paddocks. Might be more stabled. I figure why not have Larkin put down, and we could run the horses off. Just make a nuisance of ourselves. Maybe—if I can talk him into it—light a few fires. Vamps stay inside, they burn. Come out, they burn."

"Good thinking. Unless, of course, she had guards posted inside, with bows."

"Well, yeah, like I didn't think of that. I figure I'll wing a few flaming arrows down, get their attention. I pick my target—cottage nearest the biggest paddock. Gotta be some troops in there, stands to reason. Imagine my surprise and chagrin when the arrows bump off the air, like it was a wall."

His eyes narrowed as he shifted to face her. "Are you talking force field? What is this, bloody *Star Trek*?"

"That's what I said." In tune with him, Blair punched his shoulder. "She's got that wizard of hers, that Midir, working overtime by my guess. And their base camp's in a protective bubble. Larkin flew down, to get a closer look, and we both got a jolt. Like an electric shock. Pisser."

"Yes, it would be."

"Then the man himself comes out—from the big house, the manor house? Creepy-looking guy, let me say. Flying black robes, lots of silver hair. He just stands there, so we're looking down at him, he's looking up at us. Finally, I get it.

Mexican standoff. We can't get anything through, but neither can they. When the shield's up, they're locked down, we're locked out. Good as a freaking fortress. Better."

"She knows how to make the best use of the people she brings in," Cian mused.

"Looks that way. So I was lowered to making rude gestures, just so it wasn't a waste of time. She'd lower the shield at night, wouldn't she?"

"Possibly. Even if they brought enough food with them, the nature of the beast is to hunt. She wouldn't want her troops to get stale, or too edgy."

"So, maybe we can make a night run at it. I don't know. Something to think about. That's haggis, isn't it?" She wrinkled her nose. "I'm skipping that." She leaned a little closer to him, lowered her voice. "Larkin says the word's gone out on how you dealt with the guy who tried to kill Moira. You've got the castle guards and the knights behind you on that one."

"It hardly matters."

"You know better than that. You get what's essentially going to be this army's first line not just accepting you, but respecting you, it matters. Sir Cian."

He winced, visibly. "Just don't."

"Kind of rings for me. This Jell-O sort of thing is a little gritty. Do you know what it is?"

Cian waited, deliberately, until she'd taken a second bite. "Jellied internal organs—likely pig."

When she choked, the laugh just rolled out of him.

It was such a strange sound, Moira thought. To hear him laugh. Strange, a little wicked, and very appealing. She'd made a misstep with the clothes she'd sent for him. He was too much a creature of his own time—or what had come to be his own time—to put on garb from hers.

But he'd come, and she hadn't been sure he would. Not that he'd spoken a word to her. Not a single word.

He'd killed for her, she thought, but didn't speak to her.

So she would put him out of her mind, as he'd so obviously put her out of his.

She only wished the evening would end. She wanted her bed, she wanted sleep. She wanted to peel off the heavy velvet and slide blissfully—for one night—into the dark.

But she had to make a show of eating, despite her lack of appetite. She had to make a pretense, at least, of paying attention to conversations even though her eyes wanted to close.

She'd had too much wine, felt too warm. And there were hours yet before she could lay down her head.

Of course, she had to stop, to smile, and to drink every time one of the knights was moved to toast her. At the rate they were moving, her head would likely spin right off the pillow.

It was with huge relief that she was finally able to announce the dancing could begin.

She had to stand for the first set, as it was expected of her. And found she felt better for moving, for the music.

He didn't dance, of course, but only sat. Like a dyspeptic king, she thought, foolishly irritated because she'd *wanted* to dance with him. His hands on her hands, his eyes on her eyes.

But there he sat, gazing down on the masses and sipping his wine. She spun with Larkin, bowed to her uncle, clasped hands with Hoyt.

And when she looked back again, Cian was gone.

He wanted air, and more, he wanted the night. The night was still his time. What lived inside the mask of a man would always crave it, and always seek it.

He went up, and out, where the dark was thick and the music from the hall only a silvery echo. Clouds had rolled over the moon, and the stars were smothered by them. Rain would come before morning; he could already smell it.

Below, there were torches to light the courtyards, and guards stood at post at the gates, on the walls.

He heard one of them cough and spit, and the quick flap of the flags overhead in a sudden kick of wind. He could hear, if he tuned himself to it, the rustle of mice in their nest tucked in a gap of the stones, or the papery swish of the wings of a bat that circled overhead.

He could hear what others didn't.

He scented human—that salt on the flesh, and the rich run of blood beneath it. There was a part of him—always— that burned a little with the need. To hunt, to kill, to feed.

That burst of blood in the mouth, in the throat. The sheer life of it that could never be tasted in what came in cool packs of plastic. Hot, he remembered, always hot, that first taste. It heated all the places that were cold and dead, and for that moment, life—or its shadow—stirred inside that cold and that dead.

It was good to remember, now and then, the unspeakable pleasure of it. Good to remember what he pit his will against. Vital to remember what it was those they fought craved.

The humans did not, could not. Not even Blair who understood more than most.

Still they would fight, and they would die. More would come behind them to fight, and to die. Some would run, of course—some always did. Some would break with fear and simply stand and be slaughtered, like rabbits caught in a jacklight.

But most wouldn't run, wouldn't hide, wouldn't freeze in terror. In all the years he'd watched humans live and die, he knew when their backs were pressed hardest to the wall, they fought like demons.

If they won, they would end up romanticizing the whole business, songs and stories. Old men would sit by fires years from now and speak of the glory days while they showed their scars.

And others of them would wake in cold sweats from reliving the horror of war in their dreams.

If he lived, what would it be for him? he wondered. Glory days or nightmares? Neither, he thought, for he wasn't human enough to spend his time on what was over and done.

If Lilith managed to end him, well, true death was an experience he'd yet to have. It might be interesting.

And because he heard what others didn't, he caught the footsteps on the stone stairs. Moira's footsteps, as he knew her gait as well as her scent.

He nearly melted back into the shadows, then cursed himself for being a coward. She was only a woman, only a human. She could and would be nothing more to him.

When she stepped out, he heard her sigh once, long and deep as if she'd just shed some enormous weight. She moved to the stone rail, tipped her head back, closed her eyes. And breathed.

Her face was flushed from the heat of the fire, the exertion of the dance, but there were shadows of fatigue haunting her eyes.

Someone had worked slender braids through her long hair, so the weaving of them with their thin ropes of gold rippled through the rain of glossy brown.

He saw the minute she sensed she wasn't alone. The sudden stiffening in her shoulders, and the slide of her hand into the folds of her gown.

"If you've a stake tucked in there," he said, "I'd as soon you didn't point it in my direction."

Though her shoulders didn't relax, her hand dropped to her side as she turned. "I didn't see you. I wanted some air. It's so warm inside, and I've drunk too much."

"More that you didn't eat enough. I'll leave you to your air."

"Oh, stay. I'm only taking a moment, then you can have the damned air to yourself again." She pushed at her hair, then cocked her head.

He got a good look at her face now, her eyes, and thought, yes, indeed, the little queen was on the way to being plowed.

"Do you come out here to think deep thoughts? I can't decide if deep thoughts require space like this, or are better turned over in confines. I imagine you have many thoughts, with all that you've seen."

She stumbled a little, laughed a little when he caught her arm. And immediately released it.

"You're so careful not to touch me," she commented. "Unless you're saving me from death or injury. Or bashing at me in training. I find that interesting. You're a man of interests, how do you find it?"

"I don't."

"Except for that one time," she continued as if he hadn't spoken, and moved a step closer. "That one time you touched me good and proper. You put your hands on me then, and your mouth. I've wondered about that."

He very nearly took a step in retreat, and the realization of it mortified him. "It was meant to teach you a lesson."

"I'm a scholar, and I do love my lessons. Give me another then."

"The wine's made you foolish." He was annoyed with the stiff and pompous sound of his own voice. "You should go in, have your ladies take you to your bed."

"It has made me foolish. I'll be sorry for it tomorrow, but well, that's tomorrow, isn't it? Oh, what a day this has been for me." She did a slow turn that had her skirts swaying over the stones. "Was it only this morning I walked to the stone? How could it be only this morning? I feel I've carried that sword and the stone with it through this day. Now I'm setting them down, until tomorrow, I'm setting them down. I'm the worse for drink, and what of it?"

She stepped closer yet, and pride wouldn't let him back away.

"I'd hoped you'd dance with me tonight. I hoped, and I wondered what it would be like to have you touch me when it wasn't in a fight or out of manners or mistake."

"I wasn't in the mood for dancing."

"Oh, and you're full of moods, you are." She watched his face carefully, studying him, he thought, as she might the pages of a book. "And sure, so am I. I was in an angry mood when you kissed me before. And a little frightened around it. I'm not angry or frightened now. But I think you are."

"Now you're adding ridiculous to foolish."

"Prove it then." She closed that last bit of distance, tipped up her face to his. "Teach me a lesson."

He could hardly be damned for it. He'd been damned long before. He wasn't gentle; he wasn't tender. But yanked her against him and nearly off her feet before his mouth swooped down to plunder hers.

He tasted the wine and the warmth—and a recklessness he hadn't anticipated. That, he knew, was his mistake.

She was ready for him this time. Her hands were in his hair, her mouth open and avid. She didn't melt against him in surrender, or shudder from the onslaught. She strained for more.

Need clawed at him, one more demon sent to torture him.

She wondered the air between them didn't smoke, wondered how it was both of them didn't simply erupt into flame. This was fire, in the blood, in the bone.

How had she lived all of her life without it?

Even when he released her, pushed her back, it stayed inside her like a fever.

"Did you feel that?" Her whisper was full of wonder. "Did you feel that?"

The taste of her was inside him now, and everything in him craved more of her. So he didn't answer, didn't speak at all. He slipped into the dark and was gone before she could take another breath.

Chapter 5

She awoke early and energized. All through the day before she'd dragged such weight with her, as if it had been shackled to her leg. Now that chain was broken. It didn't matter that rain poured out of moody gray skies that smothered even a hint of sun. She had the light inside her again.

She dressed in what she thought of as her Irish clothes—jeans and a sweatshirt. The time for ceremony and decorum was past, and sensibilities be damned until she could spend time soothing them again.

She might be a queen, she thought as she twisted her hair into a long, single braid, but she would be a working one.

She would be a warrior.

She laced on her boots, strapped on her sword. This woman Moira saw in the looking glass, she recognized and approved of. She was a woman with purpose, and power, and knowledge.

Turning, she studied the room. The queen's chamber, she thought. Once her mother's sanctuary, and now hers. The bed was wide and beautifully draped in deep blue velvet and

frothy snow-white lace, for her mother had loved the soft
and the pretty. The posts were thick, polished Geallian oak,
and deeply carved with Geall's symbols. Paintings that
graced the walls were also of Geall, its fields and hills and
forests.

On a table near the bed stood a small portrait in a silver
frame. Moira's father had watched over her mother every
night—now he would watch over his daughter.

She glanced over toward the doors that led to her mother's balcony. The drapes were still pulled tight there, and
she would leave them that way. At least for now. She
wasn't ready to open those doors, to step out on the stones
where her mother had been slaughtered.

Instead, she would remember the happy hours she'd
spent with her mother in this chamber.

She went out, making her way to the door of Hoyt and
Glenna's chamber where she knocked. Because it took
several moments, she remembered the hour. She'd nearly
stepped away again, hoping they hadn't heard her knock
when the door opened.

Hoyt was still pulling on his robes. His long dark hair
was tousled, and his eyes heavy with sleep.

"Oh, I beg your pardon," she began. "I didn't think—"

"Has something happened? Is something wrong?"

"No, no, nothing. I didn't think how early it was. Please,
go back to your bed."

"What is it?" Glenna moved into view behind him.
"Moira? Is there a problem?"

"Only with my manners. I was up and about early, and
wasn't considering others would still be abed, especially
after last night's festivities."

"It's all right." Glenna laid a hand on Hoyt's arm, signaling him to step aside. "What did you need?"

"Only a private word with you. The truth of the matter
is I was going to ask if you'd have breakfast with me in my
mother's—in my sitting room, so I could speak with you
about something."

"Give me ten minutes."

"Are you certain? I don't mind waiting until later in the day."

"Ten minutes," Glenna repeated.

"Thank you. I'll see food's prepared."

"She looks . . . ready for something," Hoyt commented when Glenna went to the bowl and basin to wash.

"Or other." Glenna dipped her fingers into the water, focused. She might not be able to take a shower, but she'd be damned if she'd wash in cold water.

She did the best she could with what she had as Hoyt beefed up the fire. Then, giving into vanity, she did a subtle glamour.

"It might be she just wants to talk about today's training schedule." Glenna fixed on earrings she'd have to remember to take off for training. "I told you she's offered a prize—one of our crosses—to any of the women who takes her down in a match today."

"It was clever of her to offer a prize, but I wonder if it would be the best use of the cross."

"There were nine of them," Glenna reminded him as she dressed. "Five for us, and King's, of course, making six. The two we agreed to give to Larkin's mother and pregnant sister. There's a purpose for the ninth. This may be it."

"We'll see what the day brings." He smiled as she pulled a gray sweater over her head. "How is it, *a ghrá*, that you look lovelier every morning?"

"You've got love in your eyes." She turned into his arms when he moved to her—and looked wistfully at the bed. "Rainy morning. It'd be nice to snuggle in for an hour and have my way with you." She tipped her head up for a kiss. "But it looks like I'm having breakfast with the queen."

Moira was, as was her habit, sitting by the fire with a book when Glenna entered. Moira looked up, smiled sheepishly.

"Shame on me, taking you from your husband and your warm bed at such an hour."

"Queen's privilege."

With a laugh, Moira gestured to a chair. "The food will

be along. One day, if the seeds I brought and potted thrive, I'll be able to have the orange juice in the mornings. I miss the taste of it."

"I'd kill for coffee," Glenna admitted. "Then again, in a way, I am. For coffee, apple pie, TiVo and all things human." She sat and studied Moira. "You look good," she decided. "Rested, and as Hoyt said, ready."

"I am. Yesterday, there was so much inside my head and my heart, so it was all so very heavy. The sword and the crown were my mother's, and only mine now because she's dead."

"And you've had no time to grieve, not really."

"I haven't, no. Still, I know she would want me to do as I have, for Geall, for all, and not close myself off somewhere to mourn for her. And I had fear as well. What manner of queen would I be, and at such a time."

With some satisfaction, Moira looked down at her rough pants and boots. "Well, I know what manner of queen I'll try to be. Strong, even fierce. There's no time to sit on a throne and debate matters. Politics and protocol, they'll have to wait, won't they? We've had our ceremony and our celebration, and they were needed. But now it's time for the dirt and the sweat of it."

She got to her feet when the food was brought in. She spoke to the young boy—still sleepy around the edges—and the serving girl who was with him.

Spoke easily, Glenna noted. Called them both by name as the food and dishes were laid out. And while they both looked puzzled by their queen's choice of dress, Moira ignored it, dismissing them with thanks—and orders she and her guest not be disturbed.

When they sat together, Glenna noticed that Moira, who'd picked at her food for days, ate with an appetite to rival Larkin's.

"It'll be muddy and miserable for training today," Moira began, "and that's good, I'm thinking. Good discipline. I wanted to say that while I'll be participating, and likely every day now, you and Blair are still in charge of the thing. I want everyone to see that I'm training, just like the rest. That I'll get dirty and bruised."

"Sounds like you're looking forward to it."

"By the gods, I am." Moira scooped up eggs she'd coached the cooks to prepare as Glenna often had. Scrambled up with chunks of ham and onion right in them. "Do you remember when Larkin and I first came through the Dance to Ireland? I could plant an arrow anywhere I liked, nine of ten, but any one of you could plant *me* on my arse without half trying."

"You always got up."

"Aye, I always got up. But I'm not so easy to plant these days. That's something I want everyone to see as well."

"You showed them a warrior when you fought and killed the vampire."

"I did. Now I'll show them a soldier who takes her lumps. And there's more I want of you."

"I thought there was." Glenna poured them both more tea. "Spill it."

"I've never explored the magic I have. It isn't much of a thing, as you've seen yourself. A bit of a healing gift, and a kind of power that can be opened and reached by others with more. As you and Hoyt have done. Dreams. I've studied dreams, read books on their meanings. And books on magic itself, of course. But it seemed to me there was no real purpose for what I had other than to offer some ease to someone in pain. Or a way of knowing which direction to take to find a buck when hunting. Little things. Small matters."

"And now?"

"And now," Moira said with a nod. "I think there's a purpose, and there's a need. I think I need all I have, all I am. The more I know what's in me, the better I use it. When I touched the sword, when I put my hand on its hilt, it poured into me. The knowing that it was mine, had always been mine. And a power with it, like a strong wind, just blowing into me. More through me, I think. Do you know?"

"Exactly."

Nodding again, Moira continued to eat. "I've neglected this because it wasn't a particular interest. I wanted to read and to study, to hunt with Larkin, to ride."

"To do the things a young woman enjoys," Glenna interrupted. "Why shouldn't you have done what you liked to do? You didn't know what was coming."

"I didn't, no. I wonder, if I'd looked deeper, if I might have."

"You couldn't have saved your mother, Moira," Glenna said gently.

Moira looked up, her eyes very clear. "You see my thoughts so easily."

"I think because in your place, I'd have the same ones. You couldn't have saved her. More—"

"Weren't meant to," Moira finished. "I'm coming around to that, inside my heart. But if I'd explored what I have, I might have seen something of what was coming. For whatever difference it would have made. Like Blair, I've seen the battleground in dreams. But unlike her, I didn't face it. I turned away. That's done, too. I'm not . . . wait." She searched for the phrase. "Beating myself up? Right?"

"Yeah, that's right."

"I'm not beating myself up over it. I'm after changing it. So I'm asking, if you can make the time to help me hone whatever I might have, the way I've honed my fighting skills."

"I can. I'd love to."

"I'm grateful."

"Don't be grateful yet. It'll be work. Magic's an art, and a craft. And a gift. But comparing it to your physical training isn't far off. It's also, well, like a muscle." Glenna tapped a hand on her biceps. "You have to exercise it, and build it. Like medicine it's said we practice magic, so it's never done."

"Every weapon I take into battle is another strike against the enemy." Brows lifted, Moira flexed her arm. "So I'll build that muscle as I have this one, strong as I can.

I want to crush her, Glenna. More than defeat her, to crush her. For so many reasons. My parents, King. Cian," she added after a pause. "He'd dislike that, wouldn't he, knowing I think of him as a victim?"

"He doesn't see himself that way."

"He doesn't, refuses to. It's why he thrives, in his way. He's made his . . . I can't say peace as he's not a peaceful sort, is he? But he's accepted his lot. I suppose, in some sort of way, he's embraced it."

"I'd say you have his number, as much as any could."

Moira hesitated now, making a business of rearranging the food left on her plate. "He kissed me again."

"Oh. Oh." And after a pause. "Oh."

"I made him."

"Not to belittle your charm or powers, I don't think anyone can make Cian do much of anything he doesn't want to do."

"Could be he wanted to, but he wasn't going to until I pushed him into it. I'd had a bit to drink."

"Hmm."

"I wasn't the worse for it," Moira said with a laugh that had some nerves at the edges. "Not really. Just a little looser in my manners, so to speak, and more determined in my mind. I wanted air and some quiet, so I went up, out on one of the battlements. There he was."

She pictured it again. "He might have gone anywhere, and sure I could have gone somewhere else. But neither of us did, so we both ended up in the same place, at the same time. In the night," she said quietly. "With the music and the lights barely reaching us."

"Romantic."

"I suppose it was. With the rain that would come before dawn just beginning to scent the air, and the thin slice of moon very white against the sky. There's a mystery to him I keep wanting to pick at until I find the pieces of it."

"You wouldn't be human if you didn't find him fascinating," Glenna said. They both knew what she hadn't said. He wasn't. He wasn't human.

"He was being all stiff, the way he can be with me, and it was irritating. And well, I'll admit, challenging. At the same time . . . It comes in me sometimes, when I'm with him. The way knowledge does, or magic. Something rising."

She pressed a hand to her belly, then drew it upward toward her heart. "Just . . . pulling up from the center of me. I never had strong feelings, in this way, for a man. Little flutters of them, you know? Comfortable and interesting, but not strong and hot. There's something about him that compels me. He's so . . ."

"Sexy," Glenna finished. "At the outrageous level."

"I wanted to know if it would be like it had been the other time, the only time, when we'd both been so angry and he'd taken hold of me. I told him to do it again, and wouldn't take no for an answer."

She cocked her head now, as if puzzling it out. "Do you know, I think I made him nervous. Seeing him flustered a bit, and trying not to be, that was as intoxicating to me as the wine had been."

"God yes." On a long breath, Glenna picked up her tea. "It would be."

"And when he kissed me it was like the other time, only more. Because I was waiting for it. For that moment, he was as much caught as I was. I knew it."

"What are you looking for from him, Moira?"

"I don't know. Perhaps just that heat, just that power. That pleasure. Is it wrong?"

"I can't say." But it worried her. "He'd never be able to give you more. You have to understand that. He wouldn't stay here, and even if he did, for a time, you could never have a life with him. You're stepping onto dangerous ground."

"Every day from now till Samhain is dangerous ground. I know what you're saying is good, solid sense, but still in my mind and heart I want. I need to let them both settle a bit before I know what should be done about it next. But I do know that I don't want to go into battle stepping back from this only because I'm afraid of what it could be, or what it couldn't."

After a moment's debate, Glenna sighed. "It may be good solid sense, but I very much doubt I'd take my own advice if I were in your place."

Reaching over, Moira took Glenna's hand. "It helps, being able to talk to another woman. Just to be able to say what's in my mind and heart to another woman."

In another part of Geall, in a house shrouded against even the weak and watery light, two other females sat and talked.

It was the end of their day, not the beginning, but they shared a quiet meal.

Quiet because the man they were draining was beyond protest or struggle.

"You were right." Lora leaned back, delicately dabbing blood from her lips with a linen cloth. The man had been chained to the table between them as Lilith wanted her injured companion to sit, to eat, rather than lie in bed and sip from cups. "Getting up, having a civilized kill was what I needed."

"There, you see." Pleased, Lilith smiled.

Lora's face was still badly burned. The holy water that bitch of a demon hunter had hurled at her had wreaked terrible damage. But Lora was healing, and the good fresh meal would help her get her strength back.

"I wish you'd eat a little more though."

"I will. You've been so good to me, Lilith. And I failed you."

"You didn't. It was a good plan, and nearly worked. It's you who paid such a high price for it. I can't stand to think of the pain you were in."

"I would have died without you."

They had been lovers and friends, competitors and adversaries. They had been everything to each other for four centuries. But Lora's injuries, the near end of her, had brought them closer than they'd ever been.

"Until you were hurt, I didn't know how much I loved

and needed you. Here now, sweetheart, just a little more."

Lora obeyed, taking the man's limp arm, sinking her fangs into the wrist.

Before the burns, she'd been pretty, a youthful blonde with a swaggering style. Now her face was raw and red, riddled with half-healed wounds. But the glassy glaze of pain had faded from her blue eyes, and her voice was coming back strong again.

"It was wonderful, Lilith." She sat back again. "But I just can't drink another drop."

"Then I'll have it taken away, and we'll sit by the fire for a bit before bed."

Lilith rang a little gold bell, signaling one of the servants to clear. The leftovers, she knew, would hardly go to waste.

She rose to help Lora across the room where she'd already had pillows and a throw placed on the sofa.

"More comfortable than the caves," Lilith commented. "But still I'll be glad to be out of this place, and into proper accommodations."

She settled Lora before she sat, regal in her red gown, her hair piled high and gold as she'd wanted to add a touch of glamour to the evening.

Her beauty hadn't diminished in the two thousand years since her death.

"Do you have pain?" she asked Lora.

"No. I feel almost myself. I'm sorry I behaved so childishly yesterday morning, when that bitch flew over on her ridiculous dragon-man. Seeing her again just brought it all flooding back, all the fear, the agony."

"We gave her a surprise though, didn't we?" Soothing, Lilith smoothed the throw, tucking it around Lora. "Imagine her shock when her arrows met Midir's shield. You were right to talk me out of killing him."

"The next time I see her, I won't weep and hide under the covers like a frightened child. The next time I see her, she dies, by my hand. I swear it."

"Do you still have a yearning to change her, for a playmate?"

"I'd never give that whore such a gift." Lora's mouth tightened on a snarl. "She'll get only death from me." Then with a sigh, Lora laid her head on Lilith's shoulder. "She would never have been what you are to me. I thought to have a bit of fun with her. And I thought she'd be entertaining for both of us in bed—all that energy and violence inside her was so appealing. But I could never have loved her as I love you."

She tilted her head up now so their lips met in a long, soft kiss. "I'm yours, Lilith. Eternally."

"My sweet girl." Lilith pressed another kiss to Lora's temple. "Do you know when I first saw you, sitting alone on the dark, damp streets of Paris, weeping, I knew you'd belong to me."

"I thought I loved a man," Lora murmured. "And he loved me. But he used me, spurned me, tossed me aside for another. I thought my heart was broken. Then you were there."

"Do you remember what I said to you?"

"I will never forget. You said, 'My sweet, sad girl, are you all alone?' I told you my life was over, that I would be dead of grief by morning."

Lilith laughed, stroked Lora's hair. "So dramatic. How could I resist you?"

"Or I you. You were so beautiful—like the queen you are. You wore red, as you do tonight, and your hair so bright, all curls. You took me to your house, and fed me bread and wine, and listened to my sad tale and dried my tears."

"So young and charming you were. So sure this man who had cast you aside was all you could ever want."

"I don't remember his name now. Or his face."

"You came so willingly into my arms," Lilith murmured. "I asked if you would wish to stay young and lovely forever, if you would wish to have power over men like the one who hurt you. You said yes, and yes again. Even when I tasted you, you held tight to me and said again, yes and yes."

Hints of red stained the whites of Lora's eyes as she remembered that magnificent moment. "I'd never known such a thrill."

"When you drank from me, I loved you as I had no other."

"And when I lived again, you brought him to me, so I could have the one who scorned me for my first kill. We shared him, as we've shared so much."

"When Samhain comes, we will share all there is."

While the vampires slept, Moira stood on the playing field. She was filthy and drenched. Her hip throbbed from a blow that had slipped past her guard, and her breath was still wheezing out of her lungs from the last bout.

She felt wonderful.

She held out a hand to help Dervil to her feet. "You did very well," Moira told her. "You nearly had me."

Wincing, Dervil rubbed her ample rump. "I think not."

Hands on hips, her head covered with a wide-brimmed and now sodden leather hat, Glenna surveyed both of them. "You stayed on your feet longer this time, and got back on them quicker." She nodded approval at Dervil. "Improvement. From what I'm told there are several men on the other side of this field that you could take."

"There are several men on the other side of the field she *has* taken," Isleen called out, and got a number of bawdy laughs.

"And I know what to do with them when I take them," Dervil retorted.

"Put some of that energy into your next match," Glenna suggested, "and you might win it instead of ending up in the mud. Let's finish up with some archery practice, and call this a day."

Even as the women responded with relief that the session was nearly done, Moira waved a hand. "I haven't yet met Ceara in hand-to-hand. I've been saving what I'm told is the best for last. So I can retire full champion from the field."

"Cocky. I like it." Blair spoke as she moved through the rain and the mud. "Weapon details moving along," she added. "We've kicked production up a notch." She tipped back her head. "Let me tell you, this rain feels great after a couple hours with an anvil and forge. So, what's the score here?"

"Moira's taken all comers with sword and hand-to-hand. She's challenged Ceara here to a bout before we finish up with bows."

"Good enough. I can take a group to the targets while you finish up here."

There was immediate and vocal protest from the women who were eager to watch the last match.

"Bloodthirsty." Blair nodded approval. "I like that, too. All right, ladies, give them room. Who's your money on?" she murmured to Glenna as the two women squared off.

"Moira's hot, and motivated. She's just plowed through the field today. I'd have to put my money on her."

"I'll take Ceara. She's tricky, and she's not afraid to take a hit. See," she added when Ceara went sprawling facedown in the mud, and sprang up again to charge.

She feinted, pivoting at the last minute, then swept up a foot to catch Moira midbody. The queen shot back from the hit, managed to catch her balance and duck the next blow. She came up hard, flipped Ceara over her shoulder. But when she spun around, Ceara wasn't flat on her back, but had pumped off her own hands, and striking out with her feet, kicked Moira into the mud.

Moira was up quickly, and with a light in her eyes. "Well now, your reputation hasn't been exaggerated, I see."

"I'm after the prize." Ceara crouched, circled. "Be warned."

"Come get it then."

"Good fight," Blair commented as fists and feet and bodies flew. "Ceara, keep your elbows up!"

Glenna jabbed Blair with her own. "No coaching from

the peanut gallery." But she was smiling, not just because it was a good, strong fight, but because the rest of the women were shouting and calling out advice.

They'd made themselves a unit.

Moira fell back, scissored out her legs and swept Ceara's from under her. But when she rolled up again to pin her opponent, Ceara thrust up and flipped Moira over her head.

There were several sounds of sympathy as Moira landed with a bone-rattling thud. Before she could shove up again, Ceara was straddling her, an elbow to Moira's throat, and a fist to her heart.

"You're staked."

"Damn me, I am. Get off me, gods' pity, you're crushing my lungs."

She sucked in breath as she struggled to push her still-vibrating body into a sitting position. Ceara simply dropped down to sit in the mud beside her, and the two of them panted and eyed each other.

"You're a great bitch in battle," Moira said at length.

"The same to you, with all respect, my lady. I've bruises on top of my bruises now, and knots on top of those."

Moira swiped some of the mud from her face with her forearm. "I wasn't fresh."

"That's true, but I could take you fresh as well."

"I think you're right. You won the prize, Ceara, and won it fair. I'm proud to have been bested by you."

She offered her hand, and after shaking it, raised it high. "Here's the champion of the hand-to-hand."

There were cheers, and in the way of women, hugs. But when Ceara offered a hand to help Moira to her feet, Moira waved her off. "I'm just going to sit here another minute, catch my breath. Go on, get your bow. And with that you nor any will best me."

"It couldn't be done if we had a thousand years. Your Majesty?"

"Aye? Oh God, I won't sit easy for a week," she added, rubbing her sore hip.

"I've never been prouder of my queen."

Moira smiled to herself, then simply sat quiet, taking stock of her aches and pains. Then her gaze was drawn up to the spot where she'd stood with Cian the night before.

And there he was, standing in the gloom and the rain, looking down at her. She could feel the force of him through the distance, the allure he exuded, she thought, as other men never could.

"So what are you looking at?" she said to herself. "Is it amusing to you to see me on my arse in the mud?"

Probably, she decided, and who could blame him? She imagined she made quite the picture.

"We'll have a match of our own, I'm thinking, sooner or later. Then we'll see who bests who."

She pushed herself to her feet, gritted her teeth against the need to limp. So she could walk away steady, and without a backward glance.

Chapter 6

After scraping off an acre of mud, Moira joined the others for a strategy session. She walked in at that tenuous point between discussion and argument.

"I'm not saying you can't handle yourself." Larkin's tone as he addressed Blair had taken on that last ragged edge of patience. "I'm saying Hoyt and I can manage this."

"And I'm saying three would get it done faster than two."

"What would that be?" Moira asked.

The answer came from several sources, with steadily rising voices.

"I can't make much of that out." She held up a hand for peace as she took her seat at the table. "Am I understanding that we're after sending a party out to set up a base near the battlefield, scouting as they go?"

"With the first troops moving out behind them, in the morning," Hoyt finished. "We have locations marked where shelter can be found. Here," he said, tapping the map spread out on the table. "A day's march east. Then another, a day's march from that."

"But the fact is, with Lilith dug in here." Blair laid her fist on the map. "She's taken the advantage of primo location and facilities. We can crisscross our bases, establish a kind of jagged front line. But we need to start moving troops, and we need to secure bases for them before we send them out. Not only along the route, but at the best points near the valley."

"True enough." Considering, Moira studied the map. She saw how it was meant to work, with daylight jumps from position to position. "Larkin can cover the distance faster than any—we'd agree on that?"

"The way things are. But if we recruited other dragons—"

"Blair, I've said that can't be."

"Dragons?" Moira held up a hand again to silence Larkin's interruption. "What do you mean?"

"When Larkin shape-shifts he can communicate, at least on a rudimentary level, with what he becomes," Blair began.

"Aye. And?"

"So if he calls other dragons when he's in that form, why couldn't he convince some of them to follow him—with riders?"

"They're peaceful, gentle creatures," Larkin interrupted. "They shouldn't be drawn into something like this where they could be harmed."

"Wait, wait." Rolling it over in her mind, Moira sat back. "Could it be done? I've seen some take a baby in as a kind of pet from time to time, but I've never heard of anyone riding a full-grown dragon except in stories. If it could be done, it would allow us to travel swiftly, and even by night. And in battle . . ."

She broke off when she saw Larkin's expression. "I'm sorry, truly. But we can't be sentimental about it. The dragon is a symbol of Geall, and Geall needs its symbols. We ask our people, our women, the young ones, the old ones, to fight and to sacrifice. If such a thing could be done, it should be done."

"I don't know if it can be."

Moira knew when Larkin was being mule-headed. "You'll need to try. We love our horses, too, Larkin," Moira reminded him. "But we'll ride them into this. Now, Hoyt, would you tell me plain, is it best for you and Larkin to go on your own, or for the three of you to do this?"

He looked pained. "Well, you've put me between the wolf and the tiger, haven't you? Larkin's concerned that Blair's not fully recovered from the attack."

"I'm good to go," she insisted, then punched Larkin— not so lightly—in the arm. "Want to go one-on-one with me, cowboy, and find out?"

"Her ribs still pain her by end of day, and the shoulder that was hurt is weak yet."

"I'll show you weak."

"Now, now, children." Glenna managed to sound light and sarcastic. "I'm going to stick my neck into this. Blair's fit for duty. Sorry, honey," she said to Larkin, "but we really can't keep her on the disabled list."

"It would be best if she went." Hoyt sent a look of sympathy toward Larkin. "With three, we shouldn't need to be gone more than a day. The first troops could be sent out at first light, and make their way to the first post."

"That leaves three of us here to continue to work and train and prepare." Moira nodded. "This would be best. Would you think Tynan should lead those first troops, Larkin?"

"Do you ask as a sop to my wounded pride, or because you want my opinion of it?"

"Both."

She charmed a reluctant laugh out of him. "Then, aye, he'd be the one for it."

"We should get started." Blair glanced around the table. "With the time Larkin can make in the air, we'd be able to set up the first base, maybe the first two, before nightfall."

"Take whatever you need," Moira told them. "I'll speak to Tynan, and have him lead the first troops out at dawn."

"She'll be expecting you." Cian spoke for the first time since Moira had entered. "If Lilith hasn't thought of this move, one of her advisors would have. She'll have troops posted to intercept and ambush."

Blair nodded. "Figured that. It's why we're better with three, and coming from the air. They won't take us by surprise, but we might just take them."

"Better chance of that if you come from this direction." He got up to come around to the map and illustrate. "Circle around, come at the first location from the east or the north. More time, of course, but they'd likely be watching for you from this direction."

"Good point," Blair acknowledged, then gave Larkin a considering frown. "Hoyt and I could put down, out of sight, and send our boy here to get the lay. Maybe as a bird, or some animal they wouldn't think twice about seeing in the area. Have to take extra provisions," she added, "the way he burns up the fuel with the changes, but better safe than otherwise."

"Keep it small," Cian warned Larkin. "If you go as a deer or any sort of game, they might shoot you for sport or an extra meal. They'll be bored by this time, I'd imagine. If the weather there's as it's been here today, they'll likely be inside or under shelter. We don't care to be drenched any more than humans do."

"Okay, we'll work it out." Blair got to her feet. "Any magic tricks up your sleeve," she said to Hoyt, "don't forget to pack them."

Be careful." Glenna fussed with Hoyt's cloak as they stood at the gates.

"Don't worry."

"Goes with the territory." She held both hands on his cloak as she looked up into his eyes. "We've stuck pretty tight together since this started, you and I. I wish I were going with you."

"You're needed here." He touched her cross, then his own. "You'll know where I am, and how I am. Two days, at most. I'll come back to you."

"Make damn sure of it." She pulled him to her, kissed him hard and long while her heart trembled. "I love you. Be safe."

"I love you. Be strong. Now go inside, out of the rain."

But she waited while Larkin shimmered into the dragon, then Hoyt and Blair loaded on the packs and weapons. She waited while they vaulted on the dragon's back, and rose up, flying through the gray curtain of rain.

"It's hard," Moira said from behind her, "to be the one who waits."

"Horrible." She reached back, took a strong grip on Moira's hand. "So keep me busy. We'll go in, have our first lesson." They turned, walked away from the gates. "Do you remember when you first knew you had power?"

"No. It wasn't definite, as it was with Larkin. It was more that I sometimes knew things. Where to find something that was lost. Or where someone was hiding if we were playing a game. But it always seemed it could have been as much luck, or just good sense as anything else."

"Was your mother gifted?"

"She was. But softly, if you understand me. A kind of empathy, you could say. A gift for growing things." Idly she tossed her braid behind her shoulder. "You've seen the gardens here, and those were her doing. If she was able to attend a birth or help at a sick bed, she could bring comfort and ease. I thought of what she had, and what I have, as a kind of woman's magic. Empathy, intuition, healing."

They stepped through the archway, moved to the stairs. "But since I began to work with you and Hoyt, I felt more. Like a stirring. It seemed to me it was a kind of echo, or reflection of the stronger power both of you have. Then I took hold of the sword."

"A talisman, or conduit," Glenna speculated. "Or more simply a key that opened a door to what was already in you."

She led the way into the room where she and Hoyt worked. It wasn't so different from the tower room in Ireland. Bigger, Moira thought, and with an arched doorway that led to one of the castle's many balconies.

But the scents were the same, herbs and ash and something that was a mix of floral and metallic. A number of Glenna's crystals were set around on tables and chests. As much Moira supposed for aesthetics as for magical purposes.

There were bowls and vials and books.

And crosses—silver, wood, stone, copper—hung at every opening to the outside.

"Damp and chilly in here," Glenna commented. "Why don't you light the fire?"

"Oh, of course." But when Moira started across to the wide stone hearth, Glenna laughed and grabbed her hand.

"No, not like that. Fire. It's elemental, one of the basic skills. To practice magic, we utilize the elements, nature. We respect them. Light the fire from here, with me."

"I wouldn't know how to begin."

"With yourself. Mind, heart, belly, bone and blood. See the fire, its colors and shapes. Feel the heat of it, smell the smoke and burning turf. Take that from your mind, from inside you, and put it in the hearth."

Moira did as she was told, and though she felt something ripple along her skin, the turf remained quiet and cold.

"I'm sorry."

"No. It takes time, energy and focus. And it takes faith. You don't remember taking your first steps, pulling yourself up with your mother's skirts or on a table, or how many times you fell before you stood. Take your first step, Moira. Hold out your right hand. Imagine the fire lighting inside you, hot, bright. It flows out, up from your belly, through your heart, down your arm to your fingertips. See it, feel it. Send it where you will."

It was almost a trance, Glenna's quiet voice and that building of heat. A stronger ripple now, under her skin, over it. And a weak tongue of flame spurted along a brick of turf.

"Oh! It was a flash inside my head. But you did most of it."

"A little of it," Glenna corrected. "Just a little push."

Moira blew out a long breath. "I feel I've run up a mountain."

"It'll get easier."

Watching the fire catch hold, Moira nodded. "Teach me."

By the end of two hours, Moira felt as though she'd not only climbed a mountain, but had fallen off one— on her head. But she'd learned to call and somewhat control two of the four elements. Glenna had given her a list of simple spells and charms to practice on her own.

Homework, Glenna had called it, and the scholar in Moira was eager to apply herself to it.

But there were other matters to be seen to. She changed to more formal attire, fixed the mitre of her office on her head, and went to meet with her uncle regarding finance.

Wars cost coin.

"Many had to leave their crops unharvested," Riddock told her. "Their flocks and herds untended. Some will surely lose their homes."

"We'll help them rebuild. There will be no tax or levy imposed for two years."

"Moira—"

"The treasury will stand it, Uncle. I can't sit on gold and jewels, no matter what their history, while our people sacrifice. I would melt the royal crown of Geall first. When this is done, I will plant crops. Fifty acres. Another fifty for grazing. What comes from it will be given back to those who fought, the families of any who perished or were injured serving Geall."

He rubbed his own aching head. "And how will you know who has served and who has hidden themselves away?"

"We'll believe. You think I'm naive and softhearted. Perhaps I am. Some of that will be needed from a queen when this is done. I can't be naive and softhearted now, and I must push and prod and ask my people to give and give. I ask a great deal of you. You're here, while strangers turn your home into a barracks."

"It's nothing."

"It's very much, and won't be the last I ask of you. Oran marches tomorrow."

"He's spoken to me." There was pride in Riddock's voice, though his eyes were heavy with sorrow. "My younger son is a man, and must be a man."

"Being yours he could be no less. For now, even as troops begin to march, work has to continue here. Weapons must be forged, people must be fed and housed. Trained. Whatever is required you have leave to spend. But . . ." She smiled now, thinly. "If any merchant or craftsman seeks too heavy a profit, he will have an audience with the queen."

Riddock returned her smile. "Very well. Your mother would be proud of you."

"I hope she would. I think of her every day." She rose, and the gesture brought him to his feet. "I must go to my aunt. She's so good to stand as chatelain these weeks."

"She enjoys it."

"I wonder that she could. The kitchens, the laundry, the sewing, the cleaning. It's beyond my ken with so many to tend. I'd be lost without her."

"She'll be pleased to hear it. But she tells me you come, every day, to speak with her, and to tour those kitchens, the laundry. Just as I'm told you go speak to the smithies, the young ones you have carving stakes. And today you trained with the other women."

"I never thought my office would be an idle one."

"No, but you need rest, Moira. Your eyes are shadowed."

She told herself to ask Glenna to teach her to do a glamour. "There's time enough to rest when this is done."

She spent an hour with her aunt going over household accounts and duties, then another speaking with some of those who performed those duties.

When she started toward the parlor with the idea of a light meal and a vat of tea, she heard Cian's laugh.

It relieved her to know he was keeping Glenna company, but she wondered if she herself had the energy to deal with him after such a long day.

She caught herself turning away, felt a quick flare of anger. Did she need a headful of wine just to sit comfortably in the same room with him? What sort of coward was she?

Straightening her spine, she strode in to see Glenna and Cian sitting by the fire with fruit and tea.

They looked so easy with each other, Moira thought. Did Glenna find it comforting or strange that Cian looked so like his brother? Little differences, of course. That cleft in Cian's chin his brother lacked. And his face was leaner than Hoyt's, his hair shorter.

There was his posture, and his movements. Cian always seemed at his ease, and walked with a near animal fluidity.

She liked watching him move, Moira admitted. He always put her in mind of something exotic—beautiful in its way, and just as lethal.

He knew she was there, she was sure. She'd yet to see anything or anyone come up on him with him unaware. But he continued to slouch in the chair where most men would rise when a woman—much less a queen—entered the room.

It was like his shrug, she thought. A deliberate carelessness. She wished she didn't find that so appealing as well.

"Am I interrupting?" she asked as she crossed the room.

"No." Glenna shifted to smile at her. "I asked for enough for three, hoping you'd have time. Cian's just been entertaining me with stories of Hoyt's exploits as a child."

"I'll leave you ladies to your tea."

"Please don't go." Before he could rise, Glenna took his arm. "You've been working hard to keep me from worrying."

"If you knew it, I wasn't working hard enough."

"You gave me a breather, and it's appreciated. Now, if everything's gone as planned, they should be at the projected base. I need to look." Her hand was steady as she poured tea for Moira. "I think it would be better if we all looked."

"Can you help them if . . ." Moira let it trail off.

"Hoyt's not the only one with magic up his sleeve. But I'll be able to see more clearly, and help if necessary if the two of you work with me. I know you've had a long one, Moira."

"They're my family as well."

With a nod, Glenna rose. "I brought what I thought I'd need." She retrieved her crystal globe, some smaller crystals, some herbs. These she arranged on the table between them. Then she took off her cross, circled the ball with its chain.

"So." She kept her voice light, placed her hands over the ball. "Let's see what they're up to."

It had rained across Geall, making the trip a small misery. They'd circled wide, coming down nearly a quarter mile east of the farm they intended to use for a base. Its location was prime, nearly equidistant from the land Lilith now occupied and the field of battle.

Because it was, Cian's assumption that it would be laid for ambush rang true.

The two riders dismounted from the dragon's back, then off-loaded packs and supplies. There was some cover—the low stone wall separating the fields, and the scatter of trees that ran with it.

Nothing stirred in the rain.

Dragon turned to man, and Larkin scooped both hands through his dripping hair. "Filthy day all in all. You saw the goal right enough?"

"Two-story cottage," Blair answered. "Three outbuildings, two paddocks. Sheep. No smoke or sign of life, no horses. If they're there, they'd have guards posted, a couple in each building, most likely. Taking shifts while the others sleep. They'd need food, so they may have prisoners. Or if they're traveling light, they'd have what they need in canteens—water bags."

"I could risk a look," Hoyt said. "If she sent along any with power though, they could sense it, and us."

"Simpler if I take a run at it." Larkin paused to crunch into an apple. The long trip had hunger gnawing at his belly. "They wouldn't put up the shield, as they have around their main base. Not if they're hoping to snatch some of us if and when we come along."

"Go in small," Blair reminded him. "Cian had a good point about that."

"Aye, well." He stuffed some bread in his mouth. "A mouse is small enough and worked before. It'll take longer than it would as wolf or deer." He slipped off his cross. "You'll need to keep this for me."

"I hate this part." Blair took the cross. "I hate you going in without a weapon or shield."

"Have a little faith." He cupped her chin, kissed her. Then stepping back changed into a small field mouse.

"Can't believe I just kissed that," Blair muttered, then closed her hand tight over his cross as the mouse streaked across the grass. "Now we wait."

"Best if we take precautions. I'll cast a circle."

Larkin was nearly to the first outbuilding when he spotted the wolf. It was large and black, crouched in a thicket of berries. It paid no mind to him while its red eyes scanned the field and the road to the west. Still, he gave it a wide berth before squirming under the doorway.

It was a rough stable, and there were two horses in the stalls. And two vampires seated on the floor having a game of dice. The mouse cocked its head in some surprise. Larkin hadn't considered vampires would game. The wolf, he deduced, was their outlook. A signal from it, and they'd come to action. But for now, they were too involved in the dice to notice a small mouse.

There were swords, and two full quivers with bows. Inspired, he dashed over to where the bows rested against a stall. And busily gnawed at the strings.

One vampire was cursing his fellow's luck when Larkin scrambled out again.

He found similar setups in each building, with the main body of the troop in the cottage. Though he smelled blood, he saw no human. In the cottage, four vampires slept in the loft while five others kept watch.

He did what could be done by a mouse to sabotage, then hurried away again.

He found Hoyt and Blair where he'd left them, sitting now on a damp blanket in a circle that simmered low. "Fifteen by my count," he told them. "And a wolf. We'd need to get past that one for any chance at taking the others by surprise."

"Have to be quiet then." Blair picked up a bow. "And from downwind. Hoyt, if Larkin can give me the exact position, is there a way you can help me see it?"

"I can give you the exact position," Larkin said before Hoyt spoke, "because we'll be going together now. You won the round to come, but you won't go into that nest of demons alone."

"She won't, no. Of the three of us, you've the best hand with a bow, so you'll take the shot," Hoyt told Blair. "But we'll be covering your flank while you're at it. I'll do what I can to help you get a clear shot."

"No point in arguing that one moves faster and quieter than three? Didn't think so," Blair said when she met stony silence. "Let's move out then."

They had to circle widely to keep out of sight, and prevent their scent from carrying. But when they came up behind the wolf, Blair shook her head. "I don't think I can get the heart from here. Moira, maybe, but I'm not that good. Gonna take more than one shot."

She thought it over, saw how it could best be done.

"You take the first one," she whispered to Larkin. "Get as close as you can. If it rears or rolls, shifts around, I can take it. One, two," she added, using her fingers. "Has to be fast, has to be quiet."

He nodded, pulled an arrow from the quiver, notched it in his bow. It was a long shot for him, and the angle poor. But he took aim, breathed out, breathed in. And let the arrow fly.

It took the wolf between the shoulder blades, and its body jerked up. Blair's arrow struck home.

"Nice work," she said as black smoke and ash flew.

Hoyt started to speak, then Glenna's voice sounded in his head as clearly as if she'd been standing beside him.

Behind you!

He spun, pivoted. A second wolf leaped, its body slamming Hoyt aside, knocking him to the ground as it fell on Larkin. Man and wolf grappled, an instant only. Even as Blair drew her sword, and Hoyt his, the wolf was rolled beneath a bear.

The bear's claws swiped, slicing deep across the throat. There was a gush of blood. The bear collapsed on the black ash, and became a man again.

Blair dropped to her knees, running her hands frantically over Larkin. "Are you bit? Are you bit?"

"No. Scratched up here and there. No bites. Ah, the stench of that one." Out of breath, he pushed to his elbows, looked down in disgust at his bloody shirt. "Ruined a good hunting tunic." He looked over at Hoyt. "All right then?"

"I might not have been. Glenna. They must be watching. I heard her in my head." Hoyt held out a hand to help Larkin to his feet. "If you wear that, they'll smell us a half league away. You'll need to . . . wait, wait." And his smile came slow and grim. "I've an idea."

The black wolf crouched over the bloody figure, and from outside the rear of the stables, sent out a low howl. In moments, a vampire armed with a battle-ax opened the door.

"What do we have here?" He glanced over his shoulder. "One of the wolves brought us a present."

Facedown, Hoyt let out a quiet moan.

"It's still alive. Let's get it inside. No need to share it with the others, right? I could use something fresh for a change."

As they stepped out, the second spared the wolf a brief grin. "Yeah, good dog. Let's just have a—"

He exploded into ash as Blair rammed the stake through

his back and into his heart. The second didn't have time to lift his ax before Hoyt sprang off the ground and sliced his sword through its neck.

"Yeah, good dog." Blair mimicked the vampire, and added a quick ruffle of Larkin's fur. "I say we stick with a winner, use the same gambit on the next outbuilding."

They had nearly identical results with the second building, but on the third, only one came out. It was obvious by the way he glanced surreptitiously back at his post that he intended to keep the unexpected meal for himself. When he rolled Hoyt over, the unexpected meal put a stake through his heart.

Using hand signals now, Blair indicated she would go in first, with Hoyt covering her.

Quick and quiet, she thought as she slipped inside. She saw the other guard had made himself a cozy nest with blankets and was taking an afternoon nap in what she thought was a dovecote.

He was actually snoring.

She had to bite back the half a dozen smart remarks that trembled on her tongue, and simply staked him while he slept.

She blew out a long breath. "I don't mean to complain, but this is almost embarrassing, and a little bit boring."

"You're disappointed we're not fighting for our lives?" Hoyt asked.

"Well, yeah. Some."

"Take heart." Larkin stepped in, surveyed the area. "There are nine in the cottage, where we'll be severely outnumbered."

"Ah, thanks, honey. You always know just what to say to perk me up." She hefted the battle-ax she'd taken from the first kill. "Let's go kick some ass."

Bellied down behind a water trough, Blair and Hoyt studied the cottage. The wounded man/wolf gambit wasn't going to work here, and the alternate they'd agreed on was risky.

"He's already gone through a lot of changes," Blair murmured. "It starts taking a toll."

"He ate four honey cakes."

She nodded, hoping it was fuel enough as the dragon landed lightly on the thatched roof. Larkin shimmered free of it, then picked up the scabbard and the sheath for his stake. He signaled down to them before swinging down to peer in one of the second-story windows.

Apparently, Blair thought, he didn't have to change into a monkey to climb like one. Larkin held up four fingers.

"Four up, five down." She moved into a crouch. "Ready?"

Keeping low, they rushed to either side of the doorway. As agreed, she counted to ten. Then kicked in the door.

With the battle-ax, she decapitated the one on her right, then used the staff of it to block the hack of a sword. Out of the corner of her eye she saw a ball of fire flash into Hoyt's hand. Something screamed.

From overhead, Larkin and a vampire flew off the loft to land hard on the floor. She tried to hack her way to him, took a hard kick in her healing ribs. The pain and the force knocked her back into a table that broke beneath her weight.

She used the splintered leg to dust the one that leaped on her. Then she threw the makeshift stake, striking one that rushed Hoyt from behind. She missed the heart, swore and shoved herself breathlessly to her feet.

Hoyt thrust out with a back kick that made her warrior's heart sing. When the vampire fell, Larkin finished it with a sword clean through the throat.

"How many?" Blair shouted. "How many?"

"I took two," Hoyt said.

"Four, by the gods." Even as he grinned, he was grabbing Blair's arm. "How bad?"

"Off my game. Caught my ribs. I only got two. There's another left."

"Gone out the window above. Here, sit, sit. Your arm's bleeding as well."

"Shit." She looked down, saw the gash she hadn't felt. "Shit. Your nose is bleeding, mouth, too. Hoyt?"

"A few nicks." He limped toward them. "I don't think we'd need worry overmuch about the one that escaped. But I'll be doing a spell to revoke any invitation. Let me see what I can do for your arm."

"Spell first." Breathing through her teeth, she looked at Larkin. "Four, huh?"

"It seems two of them were mating, and distracted with it when I came through the window. So I had them both with one blow."

"Maybe we should only count that as one."

"Oh, no, we won't." He finished tying a field dressing on her wounded arm, swiped blood from under his own nose. "Jesus, I'm starving."

It made her laugh, and despite her aching ribs, she wrapped her arms around him to hug.

They're fine." Glenna let out a shuddering breath. "A little battered, a little bloody, but fine. And safe. Sorry, sorry. But watching it like this, not being able to help . . . I'm just going to have a short breakdown."

As promised, she buried her face in her hands and wept.

Chapter 7

◈

Escaping, Cian left Glenna to Moira. In his experience, women dealt best with women's tears. His own
reaction to what they'd seen in the crystal hadn't been fear,
or relief, but sheer and simple frustration.

He'd been delegated to do no more than watch while
others fought. Cozied in the bloody parlor with women and
teacups, like someone's aged grandfather.

While the training sessions were some level of entertainment, he hadn't had a good fight since they'd left Ireland. Hadn't had a woman in longer than that. Two very
satisfying ways of releasing tension and energy had been
denied to him—or he was denying them to himself.

Hardly a wonder, he thought, he was tied up in nasty
knots over a pair of steady gray eyes.

He could seduce a serving girl, but that was fraught
with complications and probably not worth the time or
effort. He could hardly pick a fight with one of the very
handy humans, which was too damn bad.

If he went out on a hunt he could likely scare up at least
one or two of Lilith's troops. But he couldn't rev himself

up to go out into the endless rain on the chance of a lucky kill.

At least back in his own time, his own world, he'd had work to occupy him. Women if he wanted one, of course, but work to pass the time. The endless time.

With none of those options available to him, he closed himself in his room. He fed, and he slept.

And he dreamed as he hadn't dreamed in decades and more of hunting human.

The strong and salty scent of them stung the air, rising as even their puny and smothered instincts warned them they were prey.

It was a seductive and primitive perfume to stir needs in the belly and in the blood.

She was only a whore, working the alleyways of London. Young though, and fair enough despite her trade, which told him it was unlikely she'd been at it very long. As the aroma of sex clung to her, he knew she'd made a few coppers that night.

He could hear tinny music and the raucous, drunken laughter from some gin parlor, and the clopping of a carriage horse moving away. All distant—too distant for her human ears to catch. And too distant for her human legs to run, if she tried.

She hurried through the thick yellow fog, quickening her pace with nervous glances over her shoulder as he deliberately allowed her to hear his footsteps behind her.

The smell of her fear was intoxicating—so fresh, so alive.

It was so easy to catch her, to cover the squeak of her mouth with his hand—to cover the rabbit-rapid jump of her heart with the other.

So amusing to see her eyes take in his face, young and handsome—the expensive clothing—and go sly, go coy, as he eased his hand from her mouth.

"Sir, you frighten a poor girl. I thought you be a brigand."

"Nothing of the sort." The cultured accent he used was

in direct opposition to squawking cockney. "Simply in need of a little comfort, and willing to pay your price."

With a flutter and a giggle, she named one he knew would be double her usual rate. "For that I think you should make me very comfortable."

"I'm sorry to ask for pay from such a fine and handsome gentleman, but I have to earn my keep, I do. I have a room nearby."

"We won't need it."

"Oh!" She laughed when he pulled up her skirts. "Here, is it?"

With his free hand he yanked down her bodice, covered her breast. He needed to feel her heart, beating, beating, beating. He drove into her, pumping hard so that her bare buttocks slapped against the damp stone wall of the alley. And he saw the shock and surprise in her eyes that he could give her pleasure.

That beat beneath his hand quickened, and her breath went short and expelled on gasps and moans.

He let her come—a small gesture—and let her dazed and sleepy eyes meet his before he showed his fangs.

She screamed—just a quick, high sound he cut off when he sank his fangs into her throat. Her body convulsed, bringing him to a very satisfactory orgasm as he fed. As he killed.

That beating under his hand slowed, stilled. Stopped.

Replete and sated, he left her in the alley with the rats, the price she'd named tossed carelessly beside her. And he strolled away to be swallowed by the thick yellow fog.

He woke in the here and now on an oath. The dream memory had awakened appetites and passions long suppressed. He almost, almost, tasted her blood in his throat, almost smelled the richness of it. In the dark, he trembled a little, an addict in withdrawal, so forced himself to get up and drink what he allowed himself as substitute for human.

It will never satisfy you. It will never fill you. Why do you struggle against what you are?

"Lilith." He said it softly. He recognized the voice in his

head, understood now who and what had put that dream into his mind.

Had it even been his memory? It seemed false now that he was steadier, like a stage play he'd stumbled into. But then he'd killed his share of whores in alleys. He'd killed so many, who could remember the details?

Lilith shimmered into the dark. Diamonds glittered at her throat, her ears, her wrists, even in her luxurious hair. She wore a gown of regal blue trimmed in sable, cut low to highlight the generous mounds of her breasts.

She'd gone to some trouble with her dress and appearance, Cian thought, for this illusionary visit.

"There's my handsome boy," she murmured. "But you look tense and tired. Hardly a wonder with what you've been up to." She wagged her finger playfully. "Naughty of you. But I blame myself. I wasn't able to spend those formative years with you, and as the twig is bent."

"You deserted me," he pointed out. Though he didn't need them, he lighted candles. Then poured himself a cup of whiskey. "Killed me, changed me, set me on my brother, then left me broken at the bottom of the cliffs."

"Where you let him toss you. But you were young, and rash. What could I do?" She tugged her bodice lower to show him the scar of the pentagram. "He burned me. Branded me. I was no good to you."

"And after? The days and months and years after." Odd, he thought, odd to realize he had this resentment, even this hurt buried inside him. Like a child tossed aside by its mother. "You made me, Lilith, birthed me, then left me with less sentiment than an alley cat leaves a deformed kitten."

"You're right, you're right. I can't argue." She wandered the room, lazy sweeps that had the skirts of her gown brushing through a table. "I was careless with you, darling boy. And what did I do but take out my temper for your brother on you. Shame on me!"

Those pretty blue eyes twinkled with merriment, and the curve of her lips was charmingly female. "But you did

so well for yourself—initially. Imagine my shock when
Lora told me the rumors I'd heard were true, and you'd
stopped hunting. Oh, she sends her regards, by the way."

"Does she? I imagine she's a pretty sight at the moment."

Lilith's smile faded, and a hint of red showed in her
eyes. "Careful there, or when the time comes it won't just
be that fucking demon hunter I rip to pieces."

"Think you can?" He slouched into a chair with his
whiskey. "I'd wager you on that, but you wouldn't be able
to pay up, being a pile of ash at the end of it."

"I've seen the end of it, in the smoke." She came to him,
leaning over the chair—so real he could almost smell her.
"This world will burn. I'll have no need of it. Every human
on this foolish island will be slaughtered, screaming and
drowning in their own blood. Your brother and his circle
will die most horribly. I have seen it."

"Your wizard would hardly show you otherwise," Cian
said with a shrug. "Were you always so gullible?"

"He shows me *truth*!" She shoved away, her gown
sweeping in a furious arch. "Why do you persist in this
doomed adventure? Why do you oppose the one who gave
you the greatest gift? I came here to offer you a truce—a
private and personal agreement, just between you and me.
Step away from this, my darling, and you have my pardon.
Step away and come to me, and you have not only my pardon but a place at my side come the day. Everything you
hunger for and have denied yourself I'll lay at your feet—
in repentance for abandoning you when you needed me."

"So, I just go back to my time, my world, and all's
forgiven?"

"I give you my word on it. But I'll give you much,
much more if you come to me. To me." She purred it,
molding her breasts with her hands. "Remember what we
shared that night? The spark, the heat of it?"

He watched her run her hands over her body, white
against red. "I remember, very well."

"We can have that again, and more. You'll be a prince in

my court. And a general, leading armies instead of slogging through the muck with humans. You'll have your pick of worlds and all their pleasures. An eternity of desires met."

"I remember you promising something along those lines before. Then I was alone, broken and lost, with the graveyard dirt barely washed off me."

"And so this is my penance. Come now, come. You have no place here, Cian. You belong with your own kind."

"Interesting." He tapped his fingers on the side of his cup. "So, all I need do is take your word that you'll reward me rather than torturing and ending me."

"Why would I destroy my own creation?" she replied in reasonable tones. "And one who's proven himself to be a strong warrior?"

"For spite, of course, and because your word is as much an illusion as your appearance here. But I'll give you mine on one vital matter, Lilith, and my word is as hard and as bright as those diamonds you're wearing. It will be I who comes for you. It will be I who does for you."

He picked up a knife and slashed it over his own palm. "I swear it to you, in blood. Mine will be the last face you see."

Fury tightened her face. "You've damned yourself."

"No," he murmured when her image vanished. "You damned me."

It was deep night, and he was done with sleep.

At least at such an hour he could wander where he liked without bumping into servants or courtiers or guards. He'd had enough of company—human and vampire. Still he needed distraction, movement, something to clear away the bitter dregs of the dream, and the visitation that followed it.

He admired the architecture of the castle—something a few steps up, and over into fantasy than what would have been usual when he was alive. It was storybook, inside and out, he mused, with the shifting lights of torches rising from their dragon sconces, the tapestries of faeries and festivals, the polished, jewel-toned marble.

Of course, it hadn't been built as a fortress, but more as a lavish home. Fit, most certainly, for a queen. Until Lilith, Geall had existed in peace and so could focus its energies and intellects on art and culture.

He could, in the quiet and dark, take time to study and admire the art—the paintings and tapestries, the murals and carvings. He could drift through the dark with the perfume of hothouse flowers sweetening the air or wander to the library to peruse the tall shelves.

Since its creation, Geall had been a land for art and books and music rather than warfare and weaponry. How apt, how cold, that both gods and demons should select such a place for bloody war.

The library, as Moira had indicated when falling in love with his own, was a quiet cathedral of books. He'd passed some of his time with a few of them already, and had been both interested and entertained that the stories he'd found there weren't so different from ones written in his own lifetime.

Would Geall, if it survived, produce its own Shakespeare, Yeats, Austen? Would its art go through revivals and renaissance and offer its version of Monet or Degas?

A fascinating thought.

For now, he was too restless, too edgy to settle himself down with a book, and instead moved on. There were rooms he'd yet to explore, and by night he could go wherever he wanted.

As he walked through shadows, the rain drummed steadily.

He moved through what he supposed had been a kind of formal drawing room and was now serving as an armory. He lifted a sword, testing its weight, its balance, its edge. Geall's craftsmen might have devoted their time, previously, to arts, but they knew how to forge a sword.

Time would tell if it would be enough.

Without aim, he turned and stepped into what he saw was a music room.

A gilded harp stood elegantly in one corner. A smaller

cousin, shaped just as a traditional Irish harp, graced a stand nearby. There was a monochord—an early forefather of the piano—enhanced with lovely carving on its soundbox.

He plucked its string idly, pleased its sound was true and clear.

There was a hurdy-gurdy, and when he turned its shaft, slid the bow over its strings, it sang with the mournful music of bagpipes.

There were lutes and pipes, all beautifully crafted. There was comfortable seating, and a pretty hearth from the local marble. A fine room, he mused, for musicians and those who appreciated the art.

Then he saw the vielle. He lifted it. Its body was longer than the violin that would come from it, and it held five strings. When the instruments had been popular, he'd had no interest in such matters. No, he'd been for killing whores in alleyways.

But when a man has eternity, he needs hobbies and pursuits, and years to study them.

He sat with the vielle over his lap, and began to play.

It came back to him, the notes, the sounds, and calmed him as it was said music could do. With the rain as his accompaniment, he let himself fall into the music, drifted away on the tears of it.

She would never have come upon him without him being aware otherwise.

She'd heard it, the quiet sobbing of music as she'd made her own wanderings. She'd followed it like a child follows a piper, then stood just inside the doorway, stunned and enchanted.

So, Moira thought, this is how he looks when he's peaceful, and not just pretending to be. This is how he might have looked before Lilith had taken him, a little dreamy, a little sad, a little lost.

All that had stirred and risen inside her for him seemed to come together inside her heart as she saw him unmasked. Sitting alone, she thought, seeking the comfort of music. She wished she had Glenna's skill with paints or chalk, for she would have drawn him like this. As few, she was sure, had ever seen him.

His eyes were closed, his expression, she would have said, caught somewhere in the misty place between melancholy and contentment. Whatever his thoughts, his fingers were skilled on the strings, long and lean, seducing the instrument into wistful music.

Then it stopped so abruptly she let out a little cry of protest as she stepped forward with her candle. "Oh please, continue, won't you? Sure it was lovely."

He had preferred she come at him with a knife than that innocent, eager smile. She wore only nightrobes, white and pure, with her hair unbound to fall like the rain over her shoulders. The candlelight shifted over her face, full of mystery and romance.

"The floors are cold for bare feet," was all he said, and rose to set the instrument down.

The dreamy look was gone from his eyes, so they were cool again. Frustrated, she set the candle down. "They're my feet, after all. You never said you played."

"There are a lot of things I never said."

"I have no skill at all, to the despair of my mother and every teacher she hired to school me in music. Any instrument I picked up would end by making a sound like a cat being trod on."

She reached over, ran her hand over the strings. "It seemed like magic in your hands."

"I've had more years to learn what interests me than you've been alive. Many times more years."

She looked up now, met his eyes. "True enough, but the time doesn't diminish the art, does it? You have a gift, so why not accept a compliment on it with some grace?"

"Your Majesty." He bowed deeply from the waist. "You honor my poor efforts."

"Oh bugger that," she snapped and surprised a choked laugh out of him. "I don't know why you look for ways to insult me."

"A man must have a hobby. I'll say good night."

"Why? This is your time, isn't it, and you won't seek your bed. I can't sleep. Something cold." She hugged her elbows, shivered once. "Something cold in the air woke me." Because she was watching him, she caught the slight change in his eyes. "What? What do you know? Has something happened. Larkin—"

"It's nothing to do with that. He and the others are well enough as far as I know."

"What then?"

He debated for a moment. His personal desire to be away from her couldn't outweigh what she should know. "It's too cold in here for nighttime confessions."

"Then I'll light the fire." She walked to the hearth, picked up the tinderbox that rested there. "There was always whiskey in that painted cabinet there. I'd have some."

She didn't have to see to know he'd lifted a brow, a gesture of sarcasm, before he crossed to the cabinet.

"Did your mother always fail to teach you that it would be considered improper for you to be sharing a fire and whiskey alone with a man, much less one who is not a man, in the middle of the night?"

"Propriety isn't an immediate concern of mine." She sat back on her haunches, watching for a moment to be sure the turf caught. Then she rose to go to a chair, and held out her hand for the whiskey. "Thanks for that." She took the first swallow. "Something happened tonight. If it concerns Geall, I need to know."

"It concerns me."

"It was something to do with Lilith. I thought it was just my own fears, creeping in while I slept, but it was more than that. I dreamed of her once, more than a dream. You woke me from it."

And had been kind to her after, she remembered. Reluctant, but kind.

"It was something like that," she continued, "but I didn't dream. I only felt . . ."

She broke off, her eyes widening. "No, not just felt. I heard you. I heard you speaking. I heard your voice in my

head, and it was cold. *It will be I who does for you.* I heard
you say that, so clearly. As I was waking, I thought I would
freeze to death if you spoke so cold to me."

And had felt compelled to get out of bed, she thought.
Had followed his music to him. "Who was it?"

Later, he decided, he might try to puzzle out how she
could hear, or feel, him speak in her dreams. "Lilith."

"Aye." Her eyes on the fire, Moira rubbed a hand up
and down her arms. "I knew. There was something dark
with the cold. It wasn't you."

"You could be sure?"

"You have a different . . . hue," she decided. "Lilith is
black. Thick as pitch. You, well, you're not bright. It's
gray and blue. It's twilight in you."

"What is this, an aura thing?"

The chilly amusement in his tone had a flush creeping
up her neck. "It's how I see sometimes. Glenna told me to
pursue it. She's red and gold, like her hair—if you have an
interest in it. Was it a dream? Lilith?"

"No. Though she sent me one that may have been a
memory. A whore I fucked and killed in the filth of a
London alley." The way he lifted his glass and drank was
a callous punctuation to the words. "If it wasn't that particular one, I fucked and killed others, so it hardly matters."

Her gaze never wavered from his. "You think that
shocks me. You say it, and in that way, to put something
cruel between us."

"There's a great deal of cruelty between us."

"What you did before that night in the clearing in Ireland when you first saved my life isn't between us. It's behind you. Do you think I'm so green I don't know you've
had all manner of women, and killed all manner of them as
well? You only insult me, and your own choices since by
pushing them into the now."

"I don't understand you." What he didn't understand
he usually pursued. Understanding was another kind of
survival.

"Sure it's not my fault, is it? I make myself plain in

most matters. If she sent you the dream, true or not, it was to disturb you."

"Disturb," he repeated and moved away toward the fire. "You are the strangest creature. It excited me. And it unnerved me, for lack of a better term. That was her purpose, and she succeeded very well."

"And having served her purpose, dug into some vulnerability in you, she came to you. The apparition of her. As Lora did with Blair."

He turned back, holding the whiskey loosely in one hand. "I got an apology, centuries overdue, for her abandonment of me when I was only days into the change, and near dead from Hoyt tossing me off a cliff."

"Perhaps tardiness is relative, given the length of your existence."

Now he did laugh, couldn't stop himself. It was quick and rich and full of appreciation. "Aye, the strangest creature, with a sharp wit buried in there. She offered me a deal. Are you interested to hear it?"

"I am, very interested."

"I have only to walk away from this. You and the others, and what comes on Samhain. I do that, and she'll call it quits between her and me. Better, if I walk away from you, and into her camp, I'll be rewarded handsomely. All and anything I can want, and a place at her side. Her bed as well. And any others I care to take to mine."

Moira pursed her lips, then sipped more whiskey. "If you believe that, you're greener than you think me."

"I was never so green as you."

"No? Well, which of the two of us was green enough to sport with a vampire and let her sink fangs into him?"

"Hah. You've got a point. But then you've never been a randy young man."

"And women, of course, have no interest in carnal matters. We much prefer to sit and do our needlework with prayers running through our heads."

His lips twitched before he shook his head. "Another point. In any case, no longer being a randy young man or with any sprig of green left in me, I'm fully aware Lilith would imprison and torture me. She could keep me alive, as it were, for . . . well, ever. And in unspeakable pain."

He considered it now, his thoughts sparked by the brief debate with Moira. "Or, more likely, she'd keep her word—on sex and other rewards—for as long as it suited her. She would know I'd be useful to her, at least until Samhain."

In agreement, Moira nodded. "She would bed you, lavish gifts on you. Give you position and rank. Then, when it was done, she'd imprison and torture you."

"Exactly. But I have no intention of being tortured for eternity, or being of use to her. She killed a good man I had affection for. If for nothing else, I owe her for King."

"She would have been displeased by your refusal."

He sent Moira a bland look. "You're the queen of understatement tonight."

"Then let me also be the mistress of intuition and say you told her you would make it your mission to destroy her."

"I swore it, in my own blood. Dramatic," he said, glancing at the nearly healed wound on his hand. "But I was feeling theatrical."

"You make light of it. I find it telling. You need her death by your own hands more than you'll say. She doesn't understand that, or you. You need it not just for retribution, but to close a door." When he said nothing, she cocked her head. "Do you think it odd I understand you better than she? Know you, better than she could."

"I think your mind is always working," he replied. "I can all but hear the wheels. It's hardly a surprise you're not sleeping well these past days with all the bloody noise that must go on inside that head of yours."

"I'm frightened." His eyes narrowed on her face, but she wouldn't meet them now. "Frightened to die before I've really lived. Frightened to fail my people, my family, you and the others. When I feel that cold and dark as I did tonight, I know what would become of Geall if she wins this.

Like a void, burned out, hulled, empty and black. And the thought of it frightens me beyond sleep."

"Then the answer must be she can't win."

"Aye. That must be the answer." She set the whiskey aside. "You'll need to tell Glenna what you told me. I think it would be harder to get the answer if there are secrets among us."

"If I don't tell her, you will."

"Of course. But it should come from you. You're welcome to play any of the instruments you like whenever you're moved to. Or if you'd rather be private, you could take any you like to your room."

"Thank you."

She smiled a little as she got to her feet. "I think I could sleep for a bit now. Good night."

He stayed as he was as she retrieved her candle and left him. And stayed hours longer in the fire-lit dark.

In the raw, rainy dawn Moira stood with Tynan as he and the handpicked troops prepared to set out.

"It'll be a wet march."

Tynan smiled at her. "Rain's good for the soul."

"Then our souls must be very healthy after these last days. They can move about in the rain, Tynan." She touched her fingers lightly to the cross painted on his breastplate. "I wonder if we should wait until this clears before you start this journey."

With a shake of his head, he looked beyond her to the others. "My lady, the men are ready. Ready to the point that delay would cut into morale and scrape at the nerves. They need action, even if it's only a long day's march in the rain. We've trained to fight," he continued before she could speak again. "If any come to meet us, we'll be ready."

"I trust you will." Had to trust. If not with Tynan, whom she'd known all of her life, where would she begin? "Larkin and the others will be waiting for you. I'll expect their return shortly after sunset, with word that you arrived safe and have taken up the post."

"You can depend on it, and on me. My lady." He took both her hands.

Because they were friends, because he was the first she would send out, she leaned up to kiss him. "I do depend." She squeezed his fingers. "Keep my cousins out of trouble."

"That, my lady, may be beyond my skills." His gaze shifted from her face. "My lord. Lady."

With her hands still caught in Tynan's, Moira turned to Cian and Glenna.

"A wet day for traveling," Cian commented. "They'll likely have a few troops posted along the way to give you some exercise."

"So the men hope." Tynan glanced over to where nearly a hundred men were saying goodbye to their families and sweethearts, then turned back so his eyes met Cian's. "Are we ready?"

"You're adequate."

Before Moira could snap at the insult, Tynan roared out a laugh. "High praise from you," he said and clasped hands with Cian. "Thank you for the hours, and the bruises."

"Make good use of them. *Slán leat.*"

"*Slán agat.*" He shot Glenna a cocky grin as he mounted. "I'll send your man back to you, my lady."

"See that you do. Blessed be, Tynan."

"In your name, Majesty," he said to Moira, then wheeled his mount. "Fall in!"

Moira watched as the scattered men formed lines. And watched in the rain as her cousin Oran and two other officers rode out, leading her foot soldiers to the first league toward war.

"It begins," she murmured. "May the gods watch over them."

"Better," Cian said, "if they watch over themselves."

Still he stood as she did until the first battalion of Geall's army was out of sight.

Chapter 8

Glenna frowned over her tea as, with Moira's prod-
ding, Cian related his interlude with Lilith. The three of
them took the morning meal together, in private.

"Similar to what happened with Blair then, and with me
back in New York. I'd hoped Hoyt and I had blocked that
sort of thing."

"Possibly you have, on humans," he added. "Vampire
to vampire is likely a different matter. Particularly—"

"When the one intruding is the sire," Glenna finished.
"Yes, I see. Still, there should be a way to shut her out."

"It's hardly worth your time and energies. It's not a
problem for me."

"You say that now, but it upset you."

He glanced at Moira. "Upset is a strong word. In any
case, she left in what we'll call a huff."

"Something good came out of it," Glenna continued.
"For her to come to you, try to deal, she can't be as confident as she'd like to be."

"On the contrary, she believes, absolutely, that she'll
win. Her wizard's shown her."

"Midir? You said nothing of this last night."

"It didn't come up," Cian said easily. In truth, he'd thought long and hard before deciding it should be told. "She claims he's shown her victory, and in my opinion, she believes. Any losses we've dealt her thus far are of little importance to her. Momentary annoyances, slaps to the pride. Nothing more."

"We make destiny with every turn, every choice." Moira kept her eyes level with Cian's. "This war isn't won until it's won, by her, by us. Her wizard tells her, shows her, what she wants to hear, wants to see."

"I agree," Glenna said. "How else would he keep his skin intact?"

"I won't say you're wrong, either of you." With a careless shrug, Cian picked up a pear. "But that kind of absolute belief can be a dangerous weapon. Weapons can be turned against the one who holds them. The deeper we prick under her skin, the more reckless she might be."

"Just what do we use for the needle?" Moira demanded.

"I'm working on that."

"I've something that may work." Glenna narrowed her eyes as she stirred her tea. "If her Midir can open the door for her to come into your head, Cian, I can open it, too. I wonder how Lilith would like a visit."

Biting into the pear, Cian sat back. "Well now, aren't you the clever girl?"

"Yes, I am. I'll need you. Both of you. Why don't we finish off breakfast with a nice little spell?"

It wasn't little, and it wasn't nice. It took Glenna more than an hour to prepare her tools and ingredients.

She ground fluorite, turquoise, set them aside. She gathered cornflower and holly, sprigs of thyme. She scribed candles of purple, of yellow. Then set the fire under her cauldron.

"These come from the earth, and now will mix in water." She began to sprinkle her ingredients into the cauldron.

"For dreaming words, for sight, for memory. Moira, would you set the candles in a circle, around the cauldron?"

She continued to work as Moira set the candles. "I've actually been thinking about trying this since what happened with Blair. I've been working it out in my head how it might be done."

"She's hit you hard every time you've used magic to look into her bases," Cian reminded her. "So be sure. I wouldn't enjoy having Hoyt try to toss me off a cliff again because I let something happen to you."

"It won't be me—at least not front line." She brushed her hair back as she looked over at him. "It'll be you."

"Well then, that's perfect."

"It's risky, so you're the one who has to be sure."

"Well, it's the guts and glory business, isn't it?" He moved forward to peer into the cauldron. "And what will I be doing?"

"Observing, initially. If you choose to make contact . . . it'll be up to you, and I'll need your word that you'll break it off if things get dicey. Otherwise, we'll yank you back—and that won't be pleasant. You'll probably have the mother of all headaches, and a raging case of nausea."

"What fun."

"Fun's just beginning." She walked over, unlocked a small box. Then held up a small figure carved in wax.

Cian's brows shot up. "A strong likeness. You are clever."

"Sculpting's not my strongest skill, but I can handle a poppet." Glenna turned the figure of Lilith around so Moira could see. "I don't generally make them—it's intrusive, and dangerous to the party you've captured. But the harm-none rule doesn't apply to undead. Present company excepted."

"Appreciated."

"There's just one little thing I need from you."

"Which is."

"Blood."

Cian did nothing more than look resigned. "Naturally."

"Just a few drops, after I bind the poppet. I have nothing of hers—hair, nail clippings. But you mixed blood, once upon a time. I think it'll do the job." She hesitated, twisting the chain of her pendant around her fingers. "And maybe this is a bad idea."

"It's not." Moira set the last candle. "It's time we push into her mind, as she's pushed into all of ours. It's a good, hot needle under the skin, if you're asking me. And Cian deserves to give her a taste of her own."

She straightened. "Will we be able to watch?"

"Thirsty for some vengeance yourself?" Cian questioned.

Moira's eyes were cold smoke. "Parched. Will we?"

"If all goes as it should." Glenna took a breath. "Ready for some astral projection?" she asked Cian.

"As I'll ever be."

"Step inside the circle of candles, both of you. You'll need to achieve a meditative state, Cian. Moira and I will be your watchers, and the observers. We'll hold your body to this plane while your mind and image travel."

"Is it true," Moira asked her, "that it helps hold a traveling spirit to the safety of its world if it carries something from someone of it?"

Glenna pushed at her hair again. "It's a theory."

"Then take this." She tugged off the band of beads and leather that bound her braid. "In case the theory's true."

After giving it a dubious frown, Cian shoved it in his pocket. "I'm armed with hair trinkets."

Glenna picked up a small bowl of balm. "Focus, open the chakras," she said as she rubbed the balm on his skin. "Relax your body, open your mind."

She looked at Moira. "We'll cast the circle. Imagine light, soft, blue light. This is protection."

While they cast, Cian focused on a white door. It was his habitual symbol when he chose to meditate. When he was ready, the door would open. And he would go through it.

"He has a strong mind," Glenna told Moira. "And a great deal of practice. He told me he studied in Tibet.

Never mind," she said with a wave of her hand. "I'm stalling. I'm a little nervous."

"Her wizard isn't any stronger than you. What he can do, you can do."

"Damn right. Gotta say though, I hope to hell Lilith is sleeping. Should be, really should be." Glenna glanced at the window at the thinning rain. "We're about to find out."

She'd left an opening in the poppet, and prepared to fill it with grains of graveyard dirt, rosemary and sage, ground amethyst and quartz.

"You have to control your emotions for the binding, Moira. Set aside your hatred, your fear. We desire justice and sight. Lilith can be harmed, and we can use magic to do so, but Cian will be a conduit. I wouldn't want any negativity to backwash on him."

"Justice then. It's enough."

Glenna closed the poppet with a plug of wax.

"We call on Maat, goddess of justice and balance to guide our hand. With this image we send magic across air, across land." She placed a white feather against the doll, wrapped it in black ribbon. "Give the creature whose image I hold, dream and memory ancient and old."

She handed the ritual knife to Moira, nodded.

"Sealed by blood she shed, bound now with these drops of red."

Cian showed no reaction when Moira lifted his hand to draw the knife over his palm.

"Mind and image of the life she took joins her now so he may look. And while we watch we hold him safe in hand and heart until he chooses to depart. Through us into her this magic streams. Take our messenger into her dream. Open doors so we may see. As we will, so mote it be."

Glenna held the poppet over the cauldron, and releasing it, left it suspended on will and air.

"Take his hand," she said to Moira. "And hold on."

When Moira's hand clasped his, Cian didn't go through the door. He exploded through it. Flying through a dark even his eyes couldn't conquer, he felt Moira's hand tighten strong on his. In his mind, he heard her voice, cool and calm.

"We're with you. We won't let go."

There was moonlight, sprinkling through the dark to bring blurry smears of shape and shadow. There were scents, flowers and earth, water and woman.

Humans.

There was heat. Temperature meant little to him, but he could feel the shift of it from the damp chill he'd left behind. A baking heat, eased only a little by a breeze off the water.

Sea, he corrected. It was an ocean with waves lapping at the sugar of sand. And there were hills rising up from the beach. Olive trees spread over the terraces of those hills. And on one of the rises—the highest—stood a temple, white as the moonlight with its marble columns overlooking that ocean, the trees, gardens and pools.

Overlooking, too, the man and woman who lay together on a white blanket edged in gold on the sparkling sand near the play of white foam.

He heard the woman's laugh—the husky sound of a roused woman. And knew it was Lilith, knew it was Lilith's memory, or her dream he'd fallen into. So he stood apart, and watched as the man slid the white robe from her shoulders, and bent his head to her breasts.

Sweet, so sweet, his mouth on her. Everything inside her ebbed and flowed, as the tide. How could it be forbidden, the beauty of this? Her body was meant for his. Her spirit, her mind, her soul had been created by the gods as the mate for his.

She arched, offering, with her fingers combing gently through his sun-kissed hair. He smelled of the olive trees, and the sunlight that ripened their fruit.

Her love, her only. She murmured it to him as their lips met again. And again, with a hunger that built beyond bearing.

Her eyes were full of him when at last his body joined with hers. The pleasure of it brought tears glimmering, turned her sighs to helpless gasps.

Love swarmed through her, pounded in her heart, a thousand silken fists. She held him closer, closer, crying out her joy with an abandon that dared even the gods to hear.

"Cirio, Cirio." She cradled his head on her breast. "My heart. My love."

He lifted his head, brushing at her gilded hair. "Even the moon pales against your beauty. Lilia, my queen of the night."

"The nights are ours, but I want the sun with you—the sun that gilds your hair and skin, that touches you when I cannot. I want to walk beside you, proud and free."

He only rolled onto his back. "Look at the stars. They're our torches tonight. We should swim under them. Bathe this heat away in the sea."

Instantly pique hardened the sleepy joy from her face. "Why won't you speak of it?"

"It's too hot a night for talk and trouble." He spoke carelessly as he sifted sand through his fingers. "Come. We'll be dolphins and play."

But when he took her hands to pull her up she drew them away with a sharp, sulky jerk. "But we *must* talk. We must plan."

"My sweet, we have so little time left tonight."

"We could have forever, every night. We have only to leave, to run away together. I could be your wife, give you children."

"Leave? Run away?" He threw back his head with a laugh. "What foolishness is this? Come now, come, I have only an hour left. Let's swim awhile, and I'll ride you on the waves."

"It's not foolishness." This time she slapped his hand away. "We could sail from here, to anywhere we wished. Be together openly, in the sunlight. I want more than a few hours in the dark with you, Cirio. You promised me more."

"Sail away, like thieves? My home is here, my family. My duty."

"Your coffers," she said viciously. "Or your father's."

"And what of it? Do you think I would smear my family name by running away with a temple priestess, living like paupers in some strange land?"

"You said you could live on my love alone."

"Words are easy in the heat. Be sensible." His tone cajoling, he skimmed a finger down her bare breast. "We give each other pleasure. Why does there need to be more?"

"I *want* more. I love you. I broke my vows for you."

"Willingly," he reminded her.

"For love."

"Love doesn't feed the belly, Lilia, or spend in the marketplace. Don't be sad now. I'll buy you a gift. Something gold like your hair."

"I want nothing you can buy. Only freedom. I would be your wife."

"You cannot. If we attempted such madness and were caught, we'd be put to death."

"I would rather die with you than live without you."

"I value my life more, it seems, than you value either of ours." He nearly yawned, so lazy was his voice. "I can give you pleasure, and the freedom of that. But as for a wife, you know one has already been chosen for me."

"You chose me. You said—"

"Enough, enough!" He threw up his hands, but seemed more bored by the conversation than angry. "I chose you for this, as you chose me. You were hungry to be touched. I saw it in your eyes. If you've spun a web of fantasy where we sail off, it's your own doing."

"You pledged yourself to me."

"My body. And you've had good use of it." He belted on his robes as he rose. "I would have kept you as mistress, happily. But I have no time or patience for ridiculous demands from a temple harlot."

"Harlot." The angry flush drained, leaving her face

white as the marble columns on the hillside. "You took my innocence."

"You gave it."

"You can't mean these things." She knelt, clasping her hands like a woman at prayer. "You're angry because I pushed you. We'll speak no more of it tonight. We'll swim, as you said and forget all these hard words."

"It's too late for that. Do you think I can't read what's in your mind now? You'll nag me to death over what can never be. Just as well. We've challenged the gods long enough."

"You can't mean to leave me. I love you. If you leave me, I'll go to your family. I'll tell—"

"Speak of this, and I'll swear you lie. You'll burn for it, Lilia." He bent down, ran a finger over the curve of her shoulder. "And your skin is too soft, too sweet for the fire."

"Don't, don't turn from me. It will all be as you say, as you like. I'll never speak of leaving again. Don't leave me."

"Begging only spoils your beauty."

She called out to him in shock, in terrible grief, but he strode away as if he couldn't hear her.

She threw herself down on the blanket, wildly weeping, pounding her fists. The pain of it was like the fire he'd spoken of, burning through her so that her bones seemed to turn to ash. How could she live with the pain?

Love had betrayed her, and used her and cast her aside. Love had made her a fool. And still her heart was full of it.

She would cast herself into the sea and drown. She would climb to the top of the temple and fling herself off. She would simply die here, from the shame and the pain.

"Kill him first," she choked out as she raged. "I'll kill him first, then myself. Blood, his and mine together. That is the price of love and betrayal."

She heard a movement, just a whisper on the sand, and flung herself up with the joy. He'd come back to her! "My love."

"Yes. I will be."

His hair was black, flowing past his shoulders. He wore long robes the color of the night. His eyes were the same, so black they seemed to shine.

She grabbed up her toga, held it to her breasts. "I am a priestess of this temple. You have no leave to walk here."

"I walk where I will. So young," he murmured as those black eyes traveled over her. "So fresh."

"You will leave here."

"In my time. I've watched you these past three nights, Lilia, you and the boy you waste yourself on."

"How dare you."

"You gave him love, he gave you lies. Both are precious. Tell me, how would you like to repay him for his gift to you?"

She felt something stir in her, the first juices of vengeance. "He deserves nothing from me, neither he nor any man."

"How true. So you'll give to me what no man deserves."

Fear rushed in, and she ran with it. But somehow he was standing in front of her, smiling that cold smile.

"What are you?"

"Ah, insight. I knew I'd chosen well. I am what was before your weak and rutting gods were belched out of the heavens."

She ran again, a scream locked in her throat. But he was there, blocking her way. Her fear had jumped to terror. "It's death to touch a temple priestess."

"And death is such a fascinating beginning. I seek a companion, a lover, a woman, a student. You are she. I have a gift for you, Lilia."

This time when she ran, he laughed. Laughed still when he plucked her off her feet, tossed her sobbing to the ground.

She fought, scratching, biting, begging, but he was too strong. Now it was his mouth on her breast, and she wept with the shame of it even as she raked her nails down his cheek.

"Yes. Yes. It's better when they fight. You'll learn. Their

fear is perfume; their screams music." He caught her face in his hand, forced her to look at him.

"Now, into my eyes. Into them."

He drove himself into her. Her body shuddered, quaked, bucked, from the shock. And the unspeakable thrill.

"Did he take you so high?"

"No. No." The tears began to dry on her cheeks. Instead of clawing, beating, her hands dug into the sand searching for purchase. Trapped in his eyes, her body began to move with his.

"Take more. You want more," he said. "Pain is so . . . arousing."

He plunged harder, so deep she feared she might rend in two. But still her body matched his pace, still her eyes were trapped by his.

When his went red, her heart leaped with fresh fear, and yet that fear was squeezed in a fist of terrible excitement. He was so beautiful. Her human lover pale beside this dark, damning beauty.

"I give you the instrument of your revenge. I give you your beginning. You have only to ask me for it. Ask me for my gift."

"Yes. Give me your gift. Give me revenge. Give me—"

Her body convulsed when his fangs struck. And every pleasure she had known or imagined diminished beside what rushed into her. Here, here was the glory she'd never found in the temple, the burgeoning black power she'd always known stretched just beyond her fingertips.

Here was the forbidden she'd longed for.

It was she, writhing in that pleasure and power, that brought him to climax. And she, without being told, reared up to drink the blood she'd scored from his cheek.

Smiling through bloody lips, she died.

And woke in her bed two thousand years after the dream.

Her body felt bruised, tender, her mind muddled. Where was the sea? Where was the temple?

"Cirio?"

"A romantic? Who would have guessed." Cian stepped out of the shadows. "To call out for the lover who spurned and betrayed you."

"Jarl?" It was the name she'd called her maker. But as dream separated from reality, she saw it was Cian. "So, you've come after all. My offer . . ." But it wasn't quite clear.

"What became of the boy?" As if settling in for a cozy chat, Cian sat on the side of the bed.

"What boy? Davey?"

"No, no, not the whelp you made. Your lover, the one you had in life."

Her lips trembled as she understood. "So you toy with my dreams? What does that matter to me?" But she was shaken, down to the pit of her. "He was called Cirio. What do you think became of him?"

"I think your master arranged for him to be your first kill."

She smiled with one of her sweetest memories. "He pissed himself as Jarl held him out to me, and he sniveled like a child as he begged for his life. I was new, and still had the control to keep him alive for hours—long after he begged for his death. I'll do better with you. I'll give you years of pain."

She swiped out, cursed when her raking nails passed through him.

"Entertaining, isn't it? And Jarl? How long before you did for him."

She sat back, sulking a little. Then shrugged. "Nearly three hundred years. I had a lot to learn from him. He began to fear me because my power grew and grew. I could smell his fear of me. He would have ended me, if I hadn't ended him first."

"You were called Lilia—Lily."

"The pitiful human I was, yes. He named me Lilith when I woke." She twirled a lock of her hair around her finger as she studied Cian. "Do you have some foolish hope that by learning my beginning you'll find my end?"

She tossed the covers aside, rose to walk naked to a silver pitcher.

When she poured the blood into a cup, her hands trembled again.

"Let's speak frankly here," Cian suggested. "It's only you and I—which is odd. You don't sleep with Lora or the boy, or some other choice today?"

"Even I, occasionally, seek solitude."

"All right. So, to be frank. It's strange, isn't it, disorienting, to go back even in dreams to human? To see your own end, own beginning as if it just happened. To feel human again, or as best we can remember it feels to be human."

Almost as an afterthought, she shrugged into a robe. "I would go back to being human."

His brows lifted. "You? Now you surprise me."

"To have that moment of death and rebirth. The wonderful, staggering thrill of it. I'd go back to being weak and blind, just to experience the gift again."

"Of course. You remain predictable." He got to his feet. "Know this. If you and your wizard steer my dreams again, I'll return the favor, threefold. You'll have no rest from me, or from yourself."

He faded away, but he didn't go back. Though he could feel the tugs from Moira's mind, from Glenna's will, he lingered.

He wanted to see what Lilith would do next.

She heaved the cup and what was left of the blood in it against the wall. She smashed a trinket box, pounded holes into the wall with her fists until they bled.

Then she screamed for a guard.

"Bring that worthless wizard to me. Bring him in chains. Bring him— No, wait. Wait." She turned away in an obvious fight for control. "I'll kill him if he crosses paths with me now, then what good will he be to me? Bring me someone to eat."

She whirled back. "A male. Young. Twenty or so. Blond if we have one. Go!"

Alone, she rubbed her temple. "I'll kill him again," she

murmured. "I'll feel better then. I'll call him Cirio, and kill him again."

She snatched her precious mirror from the bureau. And seeing her own face reminded her why she would keep Midir alive. He'd given her this gift.

"There I am," she said softly. "So beautiful. The moon pales, yes, yes, it does. I'm right here. I'll always be here. The rest is ghosts. And here I am."

Picking up a brush, she began to groom her hair, and to sing. With tears in her eyes.

Drink this." Glenna pushed a cup to Cian's lips, and immediately had it pushed aside.

"I'm fine. I'm not after drinking whiskey, or swooning on you without it."

"You're pale."

His lips quirked. "Part of the whole undead package. Well. That was quite a ride."

Since he refused it, Glenna took a sip of the whiskey herself, then passed it off to Moira. "E-ticket. She didn't sense us," she said to Moira. "I'd like to think my blocks and binding were enough, but I think, in large part, she was just too caught up to feel us."

"She was so young." Moira sat now. "So young, and in love with that worthless prick of a man. I don't know what language they were speaking. I could understand her, strangely enough, but I didn't know the tongue."

"Greek. She started out a priestess for some goddess. Virginity's part of the job description." Cian wished for blood, settled for water. "And save your pity. She was ripe for what happened."

"As you were?" Moira shot back. "And don't pretend you felt nothing for her. We were linked. I felt your pity. Her heart was broken, and moments later, she's raped and taken by a demon. I can despise what Lilith is and feel pity for Lilia."

"Lilia was already half mad," he said flatly. "Maybe the change is what kept her relatively sane all this time."

"I agree. I'm sorry," Glenna said to Moira. "And I got no pleasure out of seeing what happened to her. But there was something in her eyes, in her tone—and God, in the way she ultimately responded to Jarl. She wasn't quite right, Moira, even then."

"Then she might have died by her own hand, or been executed for killing the man who used her. But she'd have died clean." She sighed. "And we might not be here, discussing the matter. It all gives you a headache if you think about it hard enough. I have a delicate question, which is more for my own curiosity than anything else."

She cleared her throat before asking Cian. "How she responded, as Glenna said. Is that not usual?"

"Most fight, or freeze with fear. She, on the other hand, participated after the . . . delicacy escapes me," Cian admitted. "After she began to feel pleasure from the rape. It was rape, no mistake, and no sane woman gains pleasure from being brutalized and forced."

"She was already his before the bite," Moira murmured. "He knew she would be, recognized that in her. She knew what to do to change—to drink from him. Everything I've read has claimed the victim must be forced or told. It must be offered. She took. She understood, and she wanted."

"We know more than we did, which is always useful," Cian commented. "And the episode unnerved her, an added benefit. I'll sleep better having accomplished that. Now it's past my bedtime. Ladies."

Moira watched him go. "He feels. Why do you think he goes to such lengths to pretend he doesn't?"

"Feelings cause pain, a great deal of the time. I think when you've seen and done so much, feelings could be like a constant ache." Glenna laid a hand on Moira's shoulder. "Denial is just another form of survival."

"Feelings loosed can be either balm or weapon."

What would his be, she wondered, if fully freed?

Chapter 9

The rain slid into a soggy twilight that curled a
smoky fog low over the ground. As night crept in, no
moon, no stars could break through the gloom.

Moira waded through the river of fog over the courtyard
to stand beside Glenna.

"They're nearly home," Glenna murmured. "Later than
we'd hoped, but nearly home."

"I've had the fires lit in your room and Larkin's, and
baths are being prepared. They'll be cold and wet."

"Thanks. I didn't think of it."

"When we were in Ireland, you thought of all the comfort details. Now it's for me." Like Glenna, Moira watched
the skies. "I've ordered food for the family parlor, unless
you'd rather be private with Hoyt."

"No. No. They'll want to report everything at once.
Then we'll be private." She lifted her hand to grip her
cross and the amulet she wore with it. "I didn't know I'd
be so worried. We've been in the middle of a fight, outnumbered, and I haven't obsessed like this."

"Because you were with him. To love and to wait is worse than a wound."

"One of the lessons I've learned. There have been so many of them. You'd be worried about Larkin, I know. And about Tynan now. He has feelings for you."

Moira understood Glenna didn't mean Larkin. "I know. Our mothers hoped we might make a match of it."

"But?"

"Whatever needs to be there isn't there for me. And he's too much a friend. Maybe having no lover to wait for, no lover to lose, makes it easier for me to bear all of this."

Glenna waited a beat. "But."

"But," Moira said with a half laugh. "I envy you the torture of waiting for yours."

From where she stood Moira saw Cian, the shape of him coming through the gloom. From the stables, she noted. Rather than the cloak the men of Geall would wear against the chill and rain, he wore a coat similar to Blair's. Long and black and leather.

It billowed in the mists as he crossed to them with barely a sound of his boots against the wet stones.

"They won't come any sooner for you standing in the damp," he commented.

"They're nearly home." Glenna stared up at the sky as if she could will it to open and send Hoyt down to her. "He'll know I'm waiting."

"If you were waiting for me, Red, I wouldn't have left in the first place."

With a smile, she tipped her head so it leaned against his shoulder. When he put his arm around Glenna, Moira saw in the gesture the same affection she herself had with Larkin, the kind that came from the heart, through family.

"There," Cian said softly. "Dead east."

"You see them?" Glenna strained forward. "You can see them?"

"Give it a minute, and so will you."

The moment she did, her hand squeezed Moira's. "Thank God. Oh, thank God."

The dragon soared through the thick air, a glimmer of gold with riders on its back. Even as it touched down, Glenna was sprinting over the stones. When he dismounted, Hoyt's arms opened to catch her.

"That's lovely to see." Moira spoke quietly as Hoyt and Glenna embraced. "So many said goodbye today, and will tomorrow. It's lovely to see someone come home to waiting arms."

"Before her, he'd most often prefer coming back to solitude. Women change things."

She glanced up at him. "Only women?"

"People then. But women? They alter universes just by being women."

"For better or worse?"

"Depends on the woman, doesn't it?"

"And the prize, or the man, she's set her sights on." With this, she left his side to rush toward Larkin.

Despite the fact that he was dripping, she hugged him hard. "I have food, drink, hot water, all you could wish. I'm so glad to see you. All of you." But when she would have turned from Larkin to welcome the others, he gripped her hard.

Moira felt her relief spin on its head to fear.

"What? What happened?"

"We should go in." Hoyt's voice was quiet, and tight. "We should go in out of the wet."

"Tell me what happened." Moira drew away from Larkin.

"Tynan's troop was set upon, at the near halfway point."

She felt everything inside her freeze. "Oran. Tynan."

"Alive. Tynan was injured, but not seriously. Six others . . ."

She took Larkin's arm, digging her fingers in. "Dead or captured?"

"Five dead, one taken. Several others wounded, two badly. We did what we could for them."

The cold remained, like ice over her heart. "You have the names? The dead, the wounded, and the other?"

"We have them, yes. Moira, it was young Sean taken. The smithy's son."

Her belly twisted with the knowledge that what the boy faced would be worse than death. "I'll speak to their families. Say nothing to anyone until I've spoken to their families."

"I'll go with you."

"No. No, this is for me. You need to get dry and warm, and fed. It's for me to do, Larkin. It's my place."

"We wrote down the names." Blair took a scrap of paper out of her pocket. "I'm sorry, Moira."

"We knew this would come." She slipped the paper inside her cloak, out of the wet. "I'll come to the parlor as soon as I'm able, so you can tell me the details of it. For now, the families need to hear this from me."

"Lot of weight," Blair declared when Moira walked away.

"She'll bear it." Cian looked after her. "It's what queens do."

She thought it would crush her, but she did bear it. While mothers and wives wept in her arms, she took the weight. She knew nothing of the attack, but told each and every one their son or husband or brother had died bravely, died a hero.

It was what needed to be said.

It was worse with Sean's parents, worse to see the hope in the blacksmith's eyes, the tears of that hope blurring his wife's. She couldn't bring herself to snuff it out, so left them with it, with the prayers that their son would somehow escape and return home.

When it was done, she went to her rooms to put the names into a painted box she would keep now beside her bed. There would be other lists, she knew. This was only the first. And every name of every one who gave his or her life would be written down, and kept in that box.

With it, she put a sprig of rosemary for remembrance, and a coin for tribute.

After closing the box, she buried her need for solitude, for grieving, and went to the parlor to hear how it had been done.

Conversation stopped when she entered, and Larkin rose quickly.

"My father has just left us. I'll go bring him back if you like."

"No, no. Let him be with your mother, your sister." Moira knew her pregnant cousin's husband was to lead tomorrow's troop.

"I'll warm you some food. No, you will eat," Glenna said even as Moira opened her mouth. "Consider it medicine, but you'll eat."

While Glenna put food on a plate, Cian poured a stiff dose of apple brandy into a cup. He took it to her. "Drink this first. You're white as wax."

"With this I'll have color, and a swimming head." But she shrugged, tossed it back like water.

"Have to admire a woman who can take a slug like that." Impressed, he took the empty glass, then went back to sit.

"It was horrible. At least I can admit that here, to all of you. It was horrible." Moira sat down at the table, then pressed her hands to her temples. "To look into their faces and see the change, and know they'll forever be changed because of what you've brought to them. To what's been taken from them."

"You didn't bring it." Anger lashed in Glenna's voice as she slapped a plate down in front of Moira. "You didn't take it."

"I didn't mean the war, or the death. But the news of it. The hardest was the one who was taken prisoner. The smithy's boy, Sean. His parents still have hope. How could I tell them he's worse than dead? I couldn't cut that last thread of hope, and wonder if it would be kinder if I had."

She let out a breath, then straightened. Glenna was right, she would eat. "Tell me what you know."

"They were in the ground," Hoyt began, "as they were when they set upon Blair. Tynan said no more than fifty, but the men were taken by surprise. He told us it seemed they didn't care if they were cut down, but charged and fought like mad animals. Two of our men fell in the first instant, and they gained three horses from us in the confusion of the battle."

"Nearly a third of the horses that went with them."

"Four, maybe five of them took the smithy's son, alive from what those who tried to save him said. They took him off, heading east, while the rest held their line and battled back. They killed more than twenty, and the others scattered and ran as the tide turned."

"It was a victory. You have to look at it that way," Blair insisted. "You have to. Your men took out over twenty vamps on their first engagement. Your casualties were light in comparison. Don't say every death is one too many," she added quickly. "I know that. But this is the reality of it. Their training held up."

"I know you're right, and I've already told myself the same. But it was their victory, too. They wanted a prisoner. No reason else to take one. Their mission must have been to take one alive, whatever the cost of it."

"You're right, no argument. But I don't see that as a victory in their column. It was stupid, and it was a waste. Say five for the prisoner. Those vamps had stayed and fought, they'd have taken more of ours—alive or dead. My take is that Lilith ordered this because she was feeling pissy, or it was impulse. But it was also bad strategy."

Moira ate food she couldn't taste while she considered it. "The way she sent King back to us. It was petty, and vicious. But playful in her way. She thinks these things will undermine us, crush our spirits. How can she know us so little? You've lived half her time," she said to Cian. "You know better."

"I find humans interesting. She finds them . . . tasty at best. You don't have to know the mind of a cow to herd them up for steaks."

"Especially if you've got a whole gang to handle the roping and riding," Blair put in. "Just following your metaphor," she said to Cian. "I hurt her girl, so she needs some payback for that. We took three of her bases—should add we cleared out the second two locations this morning."

"They were empty," Larkin stated. "She hadn't bothered to set traps there, or base any of her troops. Added to that, Glenna told us how you played with her while we were gone."

"Sum of it is, this was tit for tat. But she loses more than we do. Doesn't make it any easier on the families of the dead," Blair added.

"And tomorrow, I send more out. Phelan." Moira reached out for Larkin. "I can't hold him back. I'll speak to Sinann, but—"

"No, that's for me. I expect our father has already talked to her, but I'll see her myself."

She nodded. "And Tynan? His wounds?"

"A gash along the hip. Hoyt treated the wounded. He was doing well when we left them. They're secured for the night."

"Well then. We'll pray for sun in the morning."

She had another duty to see to.

Her women had a sitting room near her own chambers where they could sit and read, or do needlework, or gossip. Moira's mother had made it a cheerful, intensely female space with soft fabrics, many cushions, pots filled with flowering plants.

The fire here was habitually of apple wood for the scent, and there were wall sconces of pretty winged faeries.

When she was crowned, Moira had given her own women leave to make any changes they liked. But the room remained as it had in all her memory.

Her women were there now, waiting for her to retire for the night, or simply dismiss them.

They rose when she entered, and curtseyed.

"We're all women here now. For now, in this place, we're all only women." She opened her arms to Ceara.

"Oh, my lady." Ceara's eyes, already red and swollen from weeping overflowed as she rushed into Moira's embrace. "Dwyn is dead. My brother is dead."

"I'm sorry. I'm so sorry. Here now, here." She led Ceara to a seat, holding her close. And she wept with her as she'd wept with Ceara's mother, and all the others.

"They buried him there, in a field by the road. They couldn't even bring him home. He had no wake."

"We'll have a holy man consecrate the ground. And we'll build a monument to those who fell today."

"He was eager to go, to fight. He turned and waved at me before he marched off."

"You'll have some tea now." Her own eyes red from weeping, Isleen set the pot down. "You'll have some tea, Ceara, and you, my lady."

"Thank you." Ceara mopped at her damp face. "I don't know what I'd have done these past hours without Isleen and Dervil."

"It's good that you have your friends. But you'll have your tea, then you'll go to your family. You'll need your family now. You have my leave for as long as you want it."

"There's something more I want, Your Majesty. Something I ask you to give me, in my brother's name."

Moira waited, but Ceara said nothing more. "Would you ask me to give you my word on something without knowing what I promise?"

"My husband marches tomorrow."

Moira felt her stomach sink. "Ceara." She reached over, smoothed a hand on Ceara's hair. "Sinann's husband marches with the sunrise as well. She carries her third child, and still I can't spare her from his leaving."

"I don't ask you to spare me. I ask you allow me to march with him."

"To—" Stunned, Moira sat back. "Ceara, your children."

"Will be with my mother, and as safe and well as they can be, here, with her. But my man goes to war, and I've trained as he has. Why am I to sit and wait?" Ceara held out her hands. "Peck at needlework, walk in the garden when he goes to fight. You said we would all need to be ready to defend Geall, and worlds beyond it. I've made myself ready. Your Majesty, my lady, I beg your leave to go with my husband on the morrow."

Saying nothing, Moira got to her feet. She moved to the window to look out at the dark. The rain, at last, had stopped, but the mists from it swarmed like clouds.

"Have you spoken with him on this?" Moira asked at length.

"I have, and his first thought was for my safety. But he understands my mind is set, and why."

"Why is it?"

"He's my heart." Ceara stood, laid a hand on her breast. "I wouldn't leave my children unprotected, but trust my mother to do all she can for them. My lady, have we, we women, trained and slogged in the mud all this time only to sit by the fire?"

"No. No, you haven't."

"I'm not the only woman who wants this."

Moira turned now. "You've spoken to others." She looked at Dervil and Isleen. "Both of you want this as well?" She nodded. "I see I was wrong to hold you back. Arrangements will be made then. I'm proud to be a woman of Geall."

For love, Moira thought as she sat to make another list of names. For love as much as duty. The women would go, and fight for Geall. But it was the husbands and lovers, the families inside of Geall that made them reach for the sword.

Who did she fight for? Who was there for her to turn to the night before a battle, to reach for that warmth, for that reason to fight?

The days ticked away, and Samhain loomed like a bloodied ax over her head. And here she sat, alone as she sat alone every night. Would she reach for a book again, or another map, another list? Or would she wander the room again, the gardens and courtyards, wishing for . . .

Him, she thought. Wishing he would put his hands on her again and make her feel so full, so alive, so bright. Wishing he'd share with her what she'd seen in him the night he'd played music and had stirred her heart as truly as he'd stirred her blood.

She'd fought and she'd bled, would fight and bleed again. She would ride into battle as queen, with the sword of gods in her hand. But here she sat in her quiet room, wishing like a blushing maid for the touch and the heat of the only one who'd ever made her pulse quicken.

Surely that was foolish and wasteful. And, it was an insult to women everywhere.

She rose to pace as she considered it. Aye, it was insulting, and small-minded. She sat and wished for the same reasons she'd held back sending the women on the march. Because it was traditional for the man to come to the woman. It was traditional for the man to protect and defend.

Things had changed, hadn't they?

Hadn't she spent weeks in a world and time where women, like Glenna and Blair, held their own—and more—at every turn?

So, if she wanted Cian's hands on her, she'd see that he put them there, and that would be that.

She started to sweep out of the room, remembered her appearance. She could do better. If she was about to embark on seducing a vampire, she'd have to go well armed.

She stripped off her dress. She might have wished for a bath—or oh, the wonderfully hot shower of Ireland—but she made do washing from the basin of scented water.

She creamed her skin, imagined Cian's long fingers skimming over it. Heat was already balling in her belly and throbbing along nerves as she chose her best nightrobe.

Brushing her hair she had a moment to wish she'd asked
Glenna to teach her how to do a simple glamour. Though
it seemed to her that her cheeks were becomingly flushed,
her eyes held a glint. She bit her lips until they hurt, but
thought they'd pinked and plumped nicely.

She stood back from the long glass, studied herself carefully from every angle. She hoped she looked desirable.

Taking a candle she left the room with the sheer determination she wouldn't return to it a virgin.

I n his room, Cian pored over maps. He was the only
one of the circle who'd been denied a look at the battlefield, either in reality or dreams. He was going to correct that.

Time was a problem. Five days' march, well, he could
ride it in two, perhaps less. But that meant he'd need a safe
place to camp during the daylight.

One of the bases the others had secured would do. Once
he'd taken his survey, he could simply relocate in one of
those bases until Samhain.

Get out of the bloody castle, and away from its all-too-
tempting queen.

There'd be objections—that was annoying. But they
could hardly lock him in a dungeon and make him stay put.
They'd be leaving themselves in another week or so. He'd
just ride point.

He could ride out with the troops in the morning, if the
sun stayed back. Or simply wait for sundown.

Sitting back he sipped blood he'd laced with whiskey—
his own version of a sleep-inducing cocktail. He could just
go now, couldn't he? No arguments from his brother or the
others if he just rode off.

He'd have to leave a note, he supposed. Odd to have
people who'd actually be concerned for his welfare, and
somewhat pleasant though it added certain responsibilities.

He'd just pack and go, he decided, pushing the drink
aside. No muss, no fuss. And he wouldn't have to see her
again until they caught up to him.

He picked up the band of beaded leather he'd failed to give back, toyed with it. If he left tonight, he wouldn't have to see her, or smell her, or imagine what it would be like to have her under him in the dark.

He had a bloody good imagination.

He got to his feet to decide what gear would be most useful for the journey, and frowned at the knock on his door.

Likely Hoyt, he decided. Well, he just wouldn't mention his plans, and thereby avoid a long, irritating debate on the matter. He considered not answering at all, but silence and a locked door wouldn't stop his brother the sorcerer.

He knew it was Moira the moment his hand touched the latch. And he cursed. He opened the door, intending to send her on her way quickly so he could be on his.

She wore white, thin, flowing white, with something filmy over it that was nearly the same gray as her eyes. She smelled like spring—young and full of promise.

Need coiled inside him like snakes.

"Do you never sleep?" he demanded.

"Do you?" She swept by him, the move surprising him enough that he didn't block it.

"Well, come right in, make yourself at home."

"Thank you." She said it politely, as if his words hadn't dripped with sarcasm. Then she set down her candle and turned to the fire he hadn't bothered to light.

"Let's see if I can do this. I practiced until my ears all but bled. Don't speak. You'll distract me."

She held out a hand toward the fire. Focused, imagined. Pushed. A single weak flame flickered, so she narrowed her eyes and pushed harder.

"There!" There was absolute delight in her voice when the turf caught.

"Now I'm surrounded by bloody magicians."

Both her hair and her robes fanned out as she turned. "It's a good skill, and I intend to learn more."

"You won't find a tutor in sorcery here."

"No." She brushed back her hair. "But I think in other

things." Walking back to the door, she locked it, then turned to him. "I want you to take me to bed."

He blinked as otherwise he might have goggled. "What?"

"There's not a thing wrong with your hearing, so you heard me well enough. I want to lie with you. I thought I might try being coy or seductive, but then it seemed to me you'd have more respect for plain speaking."

The snakes coiled inside him began to writhe. And bite. "Here's plain speaking. Get out."

"I see I've surprised you." She wandered, running a finger over a stack of books. "That's not easy to do, so as Blair would say, points for me." She turned again, smiled again. "I'm green at this, so tell me, why would a man be angry to have a woman want to lie with him?"

"I'm not a man."

"Ah." She lifted a finger to acknowledge his point. "But still, you have needs, desires. You've desired me."

"A man will put his hand on nearly any female."

"You're not a man," she shot back, then grinned. "More points for me. You're not keeping up."

"If you've been drinking again—"

"I haven't. You know I haven't. But I've been thinking. I'm going to war, into battle. I may not live through it. None of us may. Good men died today, in mud and blood, and left broken hearts behind them."

"And sex reaffirms life. I know the psychology of it."

"That, aye that, true enough. And on a more personal level, I'm damned—I swear it—if I'll die a virgin. I want to *know* what it is. I want to feel it."

"Then order up a subject for stud, Majesty. I'm not interested."

"I don't want anyone else. I never wanted anyone before you, and haven't wanted any but you since I first saw you. It shocked me, that I could have any such feelings for you, knowing what you are. But they're inside me, and they won't leave. I have needs, like anyone. And wiles enough, I think, to overcome your resistance if need be— though you may no longer be a randy young man."

"Found your feet, haven't you?" he muttered.

"Oh, I've always had them. I'm just careful where I step." Watching him, measuring him, she trailed a hand down one of the bedposts. "Tell me, what difference would it make to you? An hour or two. You haven't had a woman in some time, I'm thinking."

He felt like an idiot. Stiff and foolish and needy. "That wouldn't be your concern."

"It might be. I've read that when a man's been denied, we'll say, for a while, it can affect his performance. But you shouldn't worry about that, as I've nothing to compare it to."

"Isn't that lucky for me? Or would be if I wanted you."

Her head cocked, and all he could see on her face was curiosity and confidence.

"You think you can insult me away. I wager—any price you name—that you're hard as stone right now." She moved toward him. "I want so much, Cian, for you to touch me. I'm tired of dreaming of it, and want to feel it."

The ground was crumbling under his feet. Had been, he knew, since the moment she'd walked in. "You don't know what you're asking, what you're risking. The consequences are beyond you."

"A vampire can lie with a human. You won't hurt me." She reached up, drew the cross over her head, set it aside on the table.

"Trusting soul." He tried for sarcasm, but the gesture had moved him.

"Confident. I don't need or want a shield against you. Why do you never say my name?"

"What? Of course, I do."

"No, you don't. You refer to me, but you never look at me and say my name." Her eyes were smoke now, and full of knowledge. "Names have power, taken or given. Are you afraid of what I might take from you?"

"There's nothing for you to take."

"Then say my name."

"Moira."

"Again, please." She took his hand, laid it on her heart. "Don't do this."

"Cian. There's your name from me. Cian. I think if you don't touch me, if you don't take me, a part of me will die before I ever go to battle. Please." She framed his face in her hands, and saw—at last—what she needed to see in his eyes. "Say my name."

"Moira." Lost, he took her wrist, turned his lips into her palm. "Moira. If I wasn't damned already, this would send me to hell."

"I'll try to take you to heaven first, if you teach me."

She rose to her toes, drawing him down. Her sigh trembled out when his lips met hers.

Chapter 10

He'd believed his will would prevent this. A thousand years, he thought, and sank into her, and the male still deluded itself it could control the female.

She was leading him, and had in her way been leading him to this from the first instant. Now he would take what she offered him, what she demanded from him, however selfish the act. But he would use the skill of a dozen lifetimes to give her what she wanted in return.

"You're foolish, reckless to give up your innocence to such as me." He skimmed a fingertip across her collarbone. "But you won't leave now until you have."

"Virginity and innocence aren't always the same. I lost my innocence before I met you." The night her mother had been murdered, she thought. But memories of that weren't for tonight.

Tonight was for knowing him.

"Should I disrobe for you, or is that for you to do?"

He gave a short, almost pained laugh before resting his brow to hers in a gesture she found surprisingly tender. "In such a hurry," he murmured. "Some things, especially the first time they're tasted, are better savored than gulped."

"There, you see. I've learned something already. When you kiss me, things wake up inside my body. Things I didn't know were sleeping there until you. I don't know what you feel."

"More than I'd like." He combed his fingers through her hair as he'd longed to for weeks. "More than could be good for either of us. This . . ." He kissed her, softly. "Is a mistake." And again, deeper.

Like her scent, her taste was of springtime, of sunlight and youth. He craved the flavor of it, filled himself on it and the quick catch of her breath as he skimmed his teeth lightly, very light, over her bottom lip.

He let his hands plunge into her hair, the long, sleek fall of it, then under it to tease and waken the nerves along her spine.

When she trembled, he brought his hands to her shoulders to slide the robes down and bare that soft flesh for his lips. He could feel the yielding in her as well as the tremors, and when his mouth brushed along her throat, that seductive pulsing of blood under the skin.

She didn't jolt when his teeth grazed there, but stiffened when he brushed his hand over her breast.

No one had ever touched her so intimately. The flash of heat his hands brought her was a shock, as was the knowledge only a thin layer of material was between his hand and her flesh.

Then even that was gone, and her nightrobes pooled around her feet. Her hand came up instinctively to cover herself, but he only took it, nipped his teeth lightly at her wrist while his eyes watched hers.

"Are you afraid?"

"A little."

"I won't bite you."

"No, no, not of that." She turned the hand he held so her palm cupped his cheek. "There's so much happening inside of me. So much new. No one's ever touched me like this." Gathering her courage, she took his other hand, brought it to her breast. "Show me more."

He brushed his thumb over her nipple, watched the shock of pleasure flicker over her face. "Turn that busy mind off, Moira."

It was already as if mists clouded it. How could she think when her body was swimming in sensation?

He lifted her off her feet so that her face was suddenly on level with his. Then his mouth took hers into the heat again.

The bed was beneath her? Had he crossed the room? How had . . . but her mind misted over again as his hands, his mouth, slid like flaming velvet over her body.

She was a feast, and he'd fasted far too long. But still he sampled slowly, lingering over tastes and textures. And with each shiver, each sigh or gasp, she fed his own arousal.

When her curious hands came too close to breaking his control, he caught them in his own, trapping them as he slowly, mercilessly ravished her breasts.

She was building beneath him; he could feel the power filling her, harder, fuller. And when he pushed her to peak, she bowed up, riding it with a strangled cry.

She melted down, her hands going limp under his.

"Oh." The word was a long expulsion of breath. "Oh, I see."

"You think you do." His tongue traced over the thick beat of the pulse in her throat. As she sighed, he glided his hand between her legs, and sliding into the wet heat, showed her more.

Everything went bright. It blinded her, the brilliance of it all but seared her eyes, her skin, her heart. She was nothing but feelings now, a mass of pleasures beyond any possibility. She was the arrow from the bow, and he'd shot her high, on an endless flight.

His hands simply ruled her until she was a hostage to this never-ending need. Half-mad she struggled with his shirt.

"I need—I want—"

"I know." He pulled off his shirt so she could touch and taste him in turn. And let himself glide on the pleasure of her eager explorations. Her breath against his skin, warm and quick, her fingers tracing, then digging. When her hands gripped his hips, he let her help him strip the rest of his clothes away.

And wasn't sure whether to be amused or flattered when her eyes went huge.

"I . . . I didn't realize. I've seen a cock before, but—"

Now he laughed. "Oh, have you now?"

"Of course. Men bathe in the river, and well, and being curious . . ."

"You've spied on them. A man's pride isn't at its, ah, fullest after a bath in a cold river. I won't hurt you."

He'd have to, wouldn't he? she thought. She'd read of such things, and certainly she'd heard the women speak of it. But she wasn't afraid of the pain. She feared nothing now.

So she laid back again, braced for him. But he only began to touch her again, rouse her again, undo her again as if she were a knot of string.

He wanted her drenched, drowning, beyond thought and nerves. That tight and slender body she'd stiffened in anticipation went loose again. Warm and soft again, with that erotic flush of blood spreading under the skin.

"Look at me. Moira *mo chroi*. Look at me. Look into me."

This he could do, with will and control. He could ease that moment, that flash of pain and give her only the pleasure. When those heavy gray eyes blurred, he pierced her. He filled her.

Her lips trembled, and the moan they formed was low and deep. He kept her trapped in his eyes as he began to move, long, slow thrusts that had the thrill of it rippling over her face, over her body.

Even when he released her from the thrall, when she began to move with him, her eyes stayed locked on his. Her heart was raging, a wild drum against his chest, so vital it seemed—for a moment—as if it beat inside him.

She came with a cry of wonder and abandonment. At last, at last, he let his own need take him with her.

She curled up against him, a cat who'd lapped up every drop of cream. He would, he was sure, berate himself later for what he'd done. But for now he was content to wallow a bit.

"I didn't know it could be like that," she murmured. "So enormous."

"Being so well-endowed, I've likely ruined you for anyone else."

"I didn't mean the size of your pride, as you called it." Laughing, she looked up at him, and saw from his lazy smile he'd understood her meaning perfectly. "I've read of the act, of course. Medical books, storybooks. But the personal experience of it is much more satisfying."

"I'm happy to have assisted you in your research."

She rolled over so she could splay herself on him. "I'll need to do considerably more research, I'm thinking, before I know all there is to know. I'm greedy for knowledge."

"Damn you, Moira." He said it with a sigh as he played with her hair. "You're perfect."

"Am I?" Her already glowing cheeks went pinker with pleasure. "I won't argue because I feel so perfect right now. Thirsty though. Is there any water about?"

He nudged her aside, then rose to fetch the jug. She sat up as he poured, and her hair spilled over her shoulders and breasts. He thought if he had a heartbeat, the sight of her like this might stop it.

He handed her the cup, then sat across from her on the bed. "This is madness. You know it."

"The world's gone mad," she replied. "Why shouldn't we have a piece of it? I'm not being foolish, or careless," she said quickly, laying a hand over his. "I have to do so many things, Cian, so many things where there's no choice for me. This was my choice. My own."

She drank, handed him the cup so he could share. "Will

you regret something that gave us pleasure and harmed no one?"

"You haven't thought about what others will think of you for sharing a bed with me."

"Listen to you, worrying about my reputation of all things. I'm my own woman, and I don't need to explain to anyone whose bed I share."

"Being queen—"

"Doesn't make me less a woman," she interrupted. "A Geallian woman, and we're known for making up our own minds. I was reminded of that earlier tonight." Now she rose, picking up her outer robe to wrap it around her.

He thought it was like she wrapped herself in mist.

"One of my ladies, Ceara—do you know who I mean?"

"Ah, tall, dark blond hair. She took you down in hand-to-hand."

"That she did. Her brother was killed today, on the march. He was young, not yet eighteen." It pierced her heart, again. "I went to the sitting room where my ladies gather and found her there when I would have given her leave to be with her family."

"She's loyal, and thinks of her duty to you."

"Not just to me. She asked if I would give her one thing, in her brother's name. One thing." Emotion quivered in her voice before she conquered it. "And that was to march in the morning with her husband. To go from here, from her children, from safety and face whatever might be on the road. She's not the only woman who asks to go. We're not weak. We don't sit and wait, or no longer will. I was reminded of that tonight."

"You'll let her go."

"Her, and any who wish it. In the end, some who may not wish it will be sent. I didn't come to you because I'm weak, because I needed comfort or protection. I came because I wanted you. I wanted this."

She cocked her head, and with a little smile, let the robe fall. "Now it seems I'm wanting you again. Do I need to seduce you?"

"Too late for that."

Her smile widened as she moved toward the bed. "I've heard—and I've read—that a man needs a bit of time between rounds."

"You force me to repeat myself. I'm not a man."

He grabbed her hand, flipped her onto the bed—and under him.

She laughed, tugged playfully at his hair. "Isn't that handy, under the circumstances."

Later, for the first time in too long to remember, Cian didn't slip into sleep in silence, but to the quiet rhythm of Moira's heart.

It was that heart that woke him. He heard the sudden and rapid beat of it even before she thrashed in sleep.

He cursed, remembering only then she wasn't wearing her cross, nor had he taken any of Glenna's precautions against Lilith's intrusion.

"Moira." He took her shoulders, lifting her. "Wake up."

He was on the point of shaking her out of it when her eyes flew open. Instead of the fear he'd expected, he saw grief.

"It was a dream," he said carefully. "Only a dream. Lilith can't touch you in dreams."

"It wasn't Lilith. I'm sorry I woke you."

"You're shaking. Here." He pulled up a blanket, tossed it over her shoulders. "I'll get the fire going again."

"No need. Don't trouble," she said even as he got up. "I should go. It must be nearing dawn."

He simply crouched down, placed the turf in the hearth. "You won't trust me with this."

"It's not that. It's not." She should have gotten up quickly, she realized. Left straight on waking. For now she couldn't seem to move. "It wasn't Lilith, it was just a bad dream. Just . . ."

But her breath began to hitch and heave.

Rather than go to her, he lit the turf, then moved around the room to light candles.

"I can't speak of it. I can't."

"Of course you can. Maybe not to me, but to Glenna. I'll go wake her."

"No. No. No." She covered her face with her hands.

"So." Since he was up, and unlikely to sleep again for now, he poured himself a cup of blood. "Geallian women aren't weak."

She dropped her hands, and the eyes she'd hidden with them went hot with insult. "You bloody bastard."

"Exactly so. Run back to your room if you can't handle it. But if you stay, you'll pull out whatever's knotted up your guts. Your choice." He took a chair. "You're big on choices, so make one."

"You want to hear my pain, my grief? Why not to you then, who it would mean so little to? I dreamed, as I do over and over, of my mother's murder. Every time, it's clearer than it was before. At first, it was so muddled and pale—like I saw it through a smear of mud. It was easier then."

"And now?"

"I could see it."

"What did you see?"

"I was sleeping." Her eyes were huge on his face, and full of pain. "We'd had supper, and my uncle, Larkin, the family had come. A little family party. My mother enjoyed having them every few months. We had music after, and dancing. She loved to dance, my mother. It was late when we went to bed, and I fell asleep so quickly. I heard her scream."

"No one else heard?"

Moira shook her head. "No. She didn't scream, you see. Not out loud. I don't think she screamed out loud. In her head, she did, and I heard it in mine. Just once. Only once. I thought I imagined it, must have imagined it. But I got up, and went down to her room. Just to ease my mind."

She could see it even now. She hadn't bothered with a candle because her heart was beating so fast and hard. She'd simply run from her room and down to her mother's door.

"I didn't knock. I was saying to myself, no, you'll wake her. Just ease inside and see for yourself that she's sleeping.

"But when I opened the door, she wasn't in her bed, she wasn't sleeping. I heard such sounds, such horrible sounds. Like animals, like wolves, but worse. Oh, worse."

She paused, tried to swallow through her dry throat. "The doors to her balcony were open, and the curtains moving with the breeze. I called out for her. I wanted to run to the doors, but I couldn't. My legs felt as if they'd turned to lead. I could barely make one step in front of the other. I can't say it."

"You can. You walked to the door, to the balcony door."

"I saw . . . Oh God, oh God, oh God. I saw her, on the stones. And the blood, so much blood. Those things were . . . I'll be sick."

"You won't." He got up now, crossed to her. "You won't be sick."

"They were ripping at her." And the words tore out of her now. "Ripping at her body. Demons, things of nightmares, tearing at my mother. I wanted to scream, but I couldn't scream. I wanted to run out and beat them off. One, one looked at me. His eyes red, my mother's blood all over his face. My mother's blood. He charged at the door, and I stumbled back. Back, away from her when I should have gone to her."

"She was dead, Moira, you knew it. You'd be dead if you'd stepped out that door."

"I should have gone to her. It leaped at me, and then I screamed, and screamed and screamed. Even when it fell back as if it had struck a wall, I screamed. Then it all went to black. I did nothing but scream while my mother lay bleeding."

"You're not stupid," he said flatly. "You know you were in shock. You know that what you saw was the same as being struck a stunning physical blow. Nothing you could have done would have saved your mother."

"How could I leave her there, Cian? Just leave her

there." Tears spilled from her eyes to slide down her cheeks. "I loved her more than anything in this world."

"Because your mind couldn't cope with what you saw, with what was—to you—impossible. She was already dead, before you came into the room. She was dead, Moira, the moment you heard her scream."

"How can you be sure? If—"

"They were assassins. They would have killed her instantly. What came after was indulgence, but death was the goal."

Now he took her cold hands in his to warm them. "She would have had only a moment to feel afraid, to feel the pain. The rest, she was beyond the rest of it."

She went very still, stared hard into his eyes. "Will you swear to me you believe that?"

"It's not a matter of believing, but knowing. I can swear that to you. If they'd wanted to torture her, they'd have taken her somewhere where they could have taken their time. What you saw was a cover-up. Wild animals, it would have been said. The way it was with your father."

She let out a long breath, then another as she saw the horrible logic of it. "I've been sick at the thought that she might have been alive when I got there. Still alive while they tore at her. It's somehow easier to know she wasn't."

She knuckled a tear away. "I'm sorry I called you a bastard."

"I pissed you off."

"With cool deliberation. I haven't spoken of that night to anyone before this. I couldn't pull it out of me and look at it, speak of it."

"Now you have."

"Maybe now that I have I won't see her the way she was that night. Maybe I'll see her as she was when she was alive, and happy. All those paintings I have inside my head of her, instead of that last one. Would you hold on to me for a bit?"

He sat, put his arm around her, stroked her hair when she rested her head on his shoulder. "I feel better that I've told you. It was kind of you to piss me off so I would."

"Anytime."

"I wish I could stay, just stay here in the dark and quiet. Stay with you. But I need to go and dress. I need to see the troops off at first light."

She tipped her head up. "Will you kiss me good morning?"

He met her lips with his, drew the kiss out until it brought a pang to his belly.

She opened sleepy eyes. "I could feel that one right down to the soles of my feet. I hope that means I'll walk lighter today."

Rising, she reached for her robes. "You could miss me a little these next hours," she told him. "Or just lie when I see you again and say you did."

"If I tell you I missed you, it won't be a lie."

Dressed, she caught his face in her hands for one more kiss. "Then I'll settle for whatever happens to be the truth."

She picked up her candle, went to the door. After shooting him a last quick grin over her shoulder, she unlatched it.

And opened it an instant before Larkin could knock.

"Moira?" His smile was quick and baffled. It faded instantly when he saw the rumpled bed and Cian lazily wrapping a blanket around his waist.

It was wild rage now that had him shoving Moira aside and charging.

Cian didn't bother to block the blow, but took it full on the face. The second fist he caught in his hand an inch before it struck. "You're entitled to one. But that's enough."

"He's entitled to nothing of the sort." Moira had the presence of mind to shut and latch the door. "Strike out again, Larkin, I'll kick your arse myself."

"You fucking bastard. You'll answer for this."

"Undoubtedly. But not to you."

"It will be me, I promise you."

"Stop it. I mean it!"

When Larkin's fists bunched again, Moira had to fight the urge to bean him with a candlestick. "Lord Larkin, as your queen I command you to step back."

"Oh, don't start bringing rank into it," Cian said easily. "Let the boy try to defend his cousin's honor."

"I'll beat you bloody unconscious."

Out of patience, Moira shoved between them. "Look at me. Damn your thick skull, Larkin, look at me. What room are we in here?"

"The bloody buggering bastard's."

"And do you think he dragged me in here by the hair, forced himself on me? You're a numbskull is what you are. I walked here, and I knocked on Cian's door. I pushed myself into this room, into this bed, because it's what I wanted."

"You don't know what—"

"If you dare, if you *dare* to say to me that I don't know what I want I'll beat *you* bloody unconscious." She drilled a finger into his chest to emphasize the point. "I've a right to this private matter, and you've no say in it at all."

"But he—you. It's not proper."

"Bollocks to that."

"It's hardly a surprise your cousin objects to you sleeping with a vampire." Cian moved away from them, picked up his cup. Deliberately he dipped a finger in, licked the blood from it. "Nasty habit."

"I won't have you—"

"Wait." Larkin interrupted Moira's furious spate. "A moment. I'd like to speak with Cian in private. Talk only," he said before Moira could object. "My word on it."

She pushed a hand through her hair. "I don't have time for either of you, and this foolishness. Be men then, and discuss what is none of your business or concern as if I'm addle-brained. I have to dress and speak to the troops who march today."

She strode to the door. "I'll trust you not to kill each other over my private relationships."

She went out, slammed the door.

"Make it quick," Cian snapped. "I'm suddenly weary of humans."

The worst of the temper had faded out of Larkin's face.

"You think I hit you, that I'm angry because of what you are. I would have had the same reaction, done the same to any man I'd found her with like this. She's my girl, after all. It wasn't part of what I was thinking, as I wasn't thinking in any case."

He shifted his feet, blew out a hard breath. "And now that I do, well, it adds a complicated layer to it all. But I don't want you thinking I planted one on you because you're a vampire. The fact is, I don't think of you that way unless, well, unless I think about it. You're a friend to me. You're one of the six of us."

Even as he spoke, the flush of temper came back. "And I'm saying clear, me demanding, here and now, what the sodding hell you were thinking of taking advantage of my cousin has nothing to do with whether or not you have a fucking heartbeat."

Cian waited a moment. "Are you done with that part of the speech?"

"I am, until I have an answer."

With a nod, Cian sat, picked up his cup again. "You put me in a position, don't you? Calling me a friend, and one of you. I may be the first, but I'll never be the second."

"Bollocks. That's a kind of way out of things. I trust you as I trust few others. And now you've seduced my cousin."

Cian let out a snorting laugh. "You're not giving her enough credit. Neither did I." Idly, Cian traced a finger over the beaded leather. "She unraveled me like a ball of yarn. It doesn't excuse not making her leave, but she's persuasive and stubborn. I couldn't— I didn't resist her."

He glanced over at the maps he'd neglected since she'd knocked on the door. "It won't be a problem as I'm leaving tonight. Earlier if the weather cooperates. I want a first-hand look at the battlefield. So she's safe from me, and me from her, until this is over."

"You can't. You can't," Larkin repeated when Cian merely lifted a brow. "If you go like this, she'll think it's because of her. It'll hurt her. If I'm responsible for you planning to leave—"

"I'd decided it before she came here last night. Partially because I'd hoped to keep my hands off her."

Obviously frustrated, Larkin dragged his hands through his hair. "As you didn't make it away quick enough for that, it'll just have to wait. I'll take you there myself, by air, in a few days or whenever it can be done. But we six need to be together."

Calmer, Larkin studied Cian's face. "We need to be one circle. This is bigger than lying with or not lying with each other. And that, now that my blood's cooler, I can say is between the two of you. It's not my place to interfere. But damn it," he continued, "I'm going to ask you one thing. I'm going to ask you as a friend, and as her blood kin standing for her father. Have you feelings for her? True feelings?"

"You play the friendship card handily, don't you?"

"You are my friend, I care for you as I would a brother. That's the truth from me."

"Damn it." Cian slammed down the cup, then scowled at the blood that splattered on the maps. "You humans crowd me with these feelings. You push them at me, and into me without a single thought for how I can survive them."

"How can you survive without them?" Larkin wondered.

"Comfortably. What difference does it make to you what I feel? She needed someone."

"Not someone. You."

"Her mistake," Cian said quietly. "My damnation. I love her, or I would have taken her before this for the sport of it. I love her, or I'd have sent her away from me last night. How, I'm not sure, but I love her otherwise I wouldn't feel so goddamn desperate. And you repeat that to anyone, I'll snap your head from your shoulders, friend or not."

"All right." With a nod, Larkin got to his feet, offered his hand. "I hope you'll make each other as happy as you're able, for as long as you're able."

"Hell." Cian accepted the hand. "What the hell are you doing here at this hour anyway?"

"Oh, I forgot completely. I thought you'd not yet be in bed. I wanted to ask if you'd be willing to let us—my family—mate your stallion with one of our mares. She's in season, and your Vlad would be a fine sire."

"You want to use my horse as stud?"

"I would, yes, if it's no problem for you. I'd have her brought to him this morning."

"Go ahead. I'm sure he'll enjoy it."

"Thanks for that. We'll pay you the standard fee."

"No. No fee. We'll consider this a gesture between friends."

"Between friends then. Thanks. I'll just go and find Moira, and let her break her temper over my head as I deserve." Larkin paused at the door. "Oh, the mare I've in mind for your stallion. She's fetching."

The quick grin, the quick wink as Larkin went out had Cian laughing despite the mess of the morning.

Chapter 11

At Moira's orders, the flags flew at half-staff, and pipers played a requiem in the dawn light. She would do more, if the gods were willing, for those who gave their lives in this war. But for now, this was all that could be done to acknowledge the dead.

Standing in the courtyard, she was torn between grief and pride as she watched the men and women—the warriors—prepare for the long march east. She'd already bid her farewells to her women, and to Phelan, her cousin's husband.

"Majesty." Niall, the big guard who was now one of her trusted captains, stepped before her. "Should I order the gates opened?"

"In a moment. You wish you were going today."

"I serve at your pleasure, my lady."

"Your wishes are your own, Niall, and I understand them. But I need you here a bit longer. You'll have your time soon enough." They would all have their time, she thought. "Your brother and his family? How are they?"

"Safe, thanks to Lord Larkin and the lady Blair. Though my brother's leg is healing, he won't be able to fight on his feet."

"There will be more to this than swinging a sword on the battlefield."

"Aye." His hand closed over the hilt of the blade at his side. "But in truth I'm ready to swing mine."

She nodded. "You will." She drew a breath. "Open the gates."

For the second time she watched her people march away from the safety of the castle. It would be a scene repeated, she knew, until she herself rode through the gates, leaving behind the very old, the very young, the ill and infirm.

"It's a clear day," Larkin said from beside her. "They should reach the first base safely."

Saying nothing, Moira looked over to where Sinann stood, a child in her arms, another in her belly, one more at her skirts. "She never wept."

"She wouldn't send Phelan off with tears."

"They must be like a flood inside her, yet even now she won't let her children see them. If courage of heart is a weapon, Larkin, we'll sweep the enemy out of existence."

When she turned to go he fell into step with her. "There wasn't time," he began, "to speak with you before. Or after."

"Before the ceremony." Her voice was cool as the morning now. "After you invaded my private life."

"I didn't invade it. I was just there, at what was an awkward time for everyone involved. Cian and I resolved matters between us."

"Oh, did you?" Her eyebrows winged up as she spared him a glance. "Hardly surprising, as men will resolve matters between them one way or another."

"Don't take that royal tone with me." He took her arm, drew her toward one of the gardens, and more privacy. "How, I'm asking you, would you expect me to react when I've seen you've been with him?"

"I suppose expecting you to be well-mannered enough to excuse yourself is too much to ask."

"That's damn right. When I think a man of damn near eternal experiences seduces you—"

"It was the other way around. Entirely."

He flushed, scratched his head, turned a frustrated circle. "I don't want to know the details of it, if you don't mind. I've apologized to him."

"And to me?"

"What do you want from me, Moira? I love you."

"I expect you to understand I'm a woman grown, and one capable of making her own decisions about taking a lover. Don't wince at the term," she snapped impatiently. "I can rule, I can fight, I can die if need be, but your sensibilities are bruised at the thought I can have a lover?"

He thought it over. "Aye. But they'll get over it. I only want, more than anything, never to see you hurt. Not in battle, not in the heart. Is that enough?"

Her feathers smoothed out, and her heart softened as it always did with him. "It must be, as I want the same for you. Larkin, would you say that I have a good, strong mind?"

"Almost too much of both at times."

"In my mind, I know that I can't have a life with Cian. In my head I understand that what I've done will one day cause me grief and pain and sorrow. But in my heart I need what I can have with him now."

She brushed her fingers over the leaves of a flowering shrub. The leaves would fall, she thought, with the first frost. Many things would fall.

"When I put my head and heart together, I know, in both, that he and I are better for what we gave to each other. How can you love and turn away?"

"I don't know."

She looked back toward the courtyard where people were once again going about their business, their routines. Life went on, she mused, whatever fell. They would see that life went on.

"Your sister watched her man ride away from her, and

knows she might never see him alive again. But she didn't weep in front of him, or in front of their children. When she weeps, she'll weep alone. They're her tears to shed. So will mine be, when this ends."

"Will you do something for me?"

"If I can."

He touched her cheek. "When you have tears, will you remember I have a shoulder for you?"

She smiled now. "I will."

When they parted, she went to the parlor where she found Blair and Glenna already discussing the day's schedule.

"Hoyt?" Moira asked as she poured herself tea.

"Hard at work. We had a slew of new weapons finished yesterday." Glenna rubbed tired eyes. "We'll be charming them twenty-four/seven. I'm going to work with some of those who'll be staying here when the rest of us leave. Basic precautions, defensive, offensive tutorials."

"I'll help you with that. And you, Blair?"

"As soon as Larkin's finished playing pimp, we're—"

"I'm sorry, what?"

"He's got a horny mare, and cleared it with Cian to have Vlad give her a bang. She doesn't even get dinner and drinks first. I thought he told you."

"No, we had other matters, and it must have slipped his mind. So he's having Cian's stallion stand as stud." Her smile came slowly. Yes, life went on. "That's a fine thing. Strong and hopeful—and damn clever, too, as he may be starting a brilliant line there. So, that's what he was about, knocking on Cian's door before sunrise."

"He figured if Cian gave the go-ahead, he could— Wait." Blair held up a hand. "Replay. How do you know he knocked on Cian's door before sunrise?"

"Because I was just leaving the room when Larkin arrived." Moira sipped her tea calmly while Blair slanted a look at Glenna, then puffed out her cheeks.

"Okay."

"Aren't you going to berate and damn Cian for seducing an innocent?"

Blair ran her tongue over her teeth. "You were in his room. I don't think luring you in there to look at his etchings is his style."

Moira slapped a hand to the table with satisfaction. "There! I knew a woman would have more sense—and a bit more respect for my own wiles. And you?" She lifted her eyebrows at Glenna. "Have you nothing to say about it?"

"You're both going to be hurt, and you both know it already. So I'll say I hope you're both able to give and take whatever happiness you can, while you can."

"Thanks."

"Are you all right?" Glenna asked. "The first time is often difficult or a little disappointing."

Now Moira smiled fully. "It was beautiful, and thrilling, and more than I imagined. Nothing I'd played through my mind was near the truth of it."

"A guy isn't good at it after a few hundred years' practice," Blair speculated. "He'd be hopeless. And Larkin walked in when . . . he must've flipped."

"He punched Cian in the face, but they've made it up now. As men do when they pound each other. We've agreed that my choice of bedmate is mine, and moved on."

There was a moment of unified silence as all three women rolled their eyes.

"There's little time left before we leave the safety of this place. And, we can hope, plenty of time after Samhain to debate my choices."

"Then I'll move on, too," Blair told her. "Larkin and I—after considerable browbeating by yours truly—are heading out in a couple of hours to see if we can wrangle ourselves some dragons. He's still not sold on the idea, but he's agreed we'll give it a shot."

"If it's possible, it would be a great advantage for us." Propping her chin on her fist, Moira turned it over in her mind. "I think we could cull out those we feel may not be as strong on the field. If they could ride . . . archers in the air."

"Flaming arrows," Blair said with a nod. "Their aim doesn't have to be on the money."

"As long as they don't shoot the home team," Glenna finished. "There isn't much time left to train, but it's worth the try."

"Fire, aye," Moira agreed. "It's a strong weapon—stronger yet coming from the air. A pity you can't charm the sun onto the tip of an arrow, Glenna, then this would be done."

"I'm going to see if I can move Larkin along." Blair got to her feet, hesitated. "You know, my first time, I was seventeen. The guy, he was in a hurry, and left me thinking at the end: So this is it? BFD. Something to be said for being initiated by someone who knows what he's doing, and has a sense of style."

"There is." Moira's smile was slow and satisfied. "There certainly is." She sensed Blair and Glenna exchange another look over her head, so continued to drink her tea as Blair left the room.

"Do you love him, Moira?"

"I think there's a part of me, inside me, that's waited all my life to feel what I feel for him. What my mother felt for my father in the short time they had. What I know you feel for Hoyt. Do you think I only imagine it's love because of what he is?"

"No, no, I don't. I have strong, genuine feelings for him myself. They have everything to do with who he is. But, Moira, you know you won't be able to have a life with him. That is because of what he is. What neither of you can change any more than the sun can fly on an arrow."

"I listened to everything he and Blair have told us about . . . we'll say his species." And read, Moira thought, countless volumes of fact and lore. "I know he'll never age. He'll be forever as he was in that moment before he was changed. Young and strong and vital. I will change. Grow old, frailer, gray and lined. I'll have sickness, and he never will."

She rose now to walk to a window and the slant of sunlight. "Even if he loved as I love, it's no life for either of us. He can't stand here as I am now and feel the sun warm on

my face. All we'd have is the dark. He can't have children.
So I won't be able to take away from this even that much of
him. I might think, just a year together, or five, or ten. Just
that much. I might think and wish for that," she murmured.
"But however selfish my own needs might be, I have a
duty."

She turned back. "He could never stay here, and I can
never go."

"When I fell in love with Hoyt, and believed that we'd
never be able to be together, it broke my heart every day."

"But still, you loved him."

"But still I loved him."

Moira stood with the sun slanting at her back, glinting
on her crown. "Morrigan said this is the time of knowing. I
know my life would be less if I didn't love him. The more
life, the longer and harder we'll fight to keep it. So, I have
another weapon inside me. And I'll use it."

Moira discovered a long day of teaching children
and the old how to defend themselves and each
other from monsters was more tiring than hours of sweaty
physical training. She hadn't known how hard it would be
to tell a child that monsters were real after all.

Her head ached from the questions, and her heart was
bruised from the fear she'd seen.

She stepped out into the garden for some air, and to
check the sky, again, for Larkin and Blair's return.

"They'll be back before sunset."

She whirled at the sound of Cian's voice. "What are
you doing? It's still day."

"Shade's deep here this time of day." Still, he leaned
back against the stones, well out of direct light. "It's a
pretty spot, a quiet one. And sooner or later, you end up
here for a few minutes."

"So, you've studied my habits."

"It passes the time."

"Glenna and I have been with the children and the old

ones, teaching them how to defend themselves if there's an attack here after we leave. We can't spare many of the able-bodied to hold the castle."

"The gates stay locked. Hoyt and Glenna will add a layer of protection. They'll be safe enough."

"And if we lose?"

"There'll be nothing they can do."

"I think there's always something, if you put choice and a weapon in someone's hands." She walked toward him. "Did you come here to wait for me?"

"Yes."

"Now that I'm here, what do you choose to do?"

He stayed where he was, but she could see the war inside him. Though the air suddenly seemed to lash and swirl with that battle, she stood calmly, her eyes grave and patient.

He took her with both hands, a quick and violent jerk that slammed her body to his. His mouth was ravenous.

"A fine choice," she managed when she could speak again.

Then his lips were assaulting hers again, stealing both breath and will.

"Do you know what you've let loose here?" he demanded. Before she could speak, he turned, gripped her hands to drag her up onto his back.

"Cian, what—"

"You'd better hold on," he ordered, interrupting her baffled laugh.

He leaped up. Her arms tightened around his neck as she gasped. He'd simply soared up, more than ten feet in the air from a stand, and was scaling the walls.

"What are you doing?" She risked a look down, felt her stomach shudder at the drop. "You could have warned me you'd lost your bloody mind."

"I lost it when you walked into my room last night." Now he swung through the window, flicked the drapes shut behind him and plunged them into the dark. "This is the price you pay for it."

"If you'd wanted to come back inside, there are doors—"

She let out a quick cry of alarm when he swooped her up. It felt as though she was flying through the air, blind in the dark. Her next cry was of stunned excitement as she found herself under him on the bed, and his hands tugged aside clothes to take flesh.

"Wait. Wait. I can't think. I can't see."

"Too late for both." His mouth silenced her, and his hands drove her to a hard, violent crest.

Her body strained beneath his, and he knew she was reaching, reaching for the burning tip of that crest. Her breath sobbed against his lips as she reached it, and her body went limp.

He gripped her wrists in his hand, pulling her arms over her head. She was one long line of surrender now, and he sheathed himself in her.

She would have cried out again, but she had no voice. No sight, and with her hands captured, no hold. She could do nothing but feel as he plunged himself into her, battering her body with dark, desperate pleasure until she was writhing, then rising, then recklessly matching him beat for violent beat.

This time the hot tip of the crest shattered her.

She lay, scorched skin over melted bones, unable to move even when he left her to light the fire and candles.

"Choice isn't always an issue," he said, and she thought she heard liquid being poured into a cup. "Nor is it a weapon."

She felt the cup bump against her hand, and managed to open her heavy eyes. She made some sound, took the cup, but wasn't at all sure she could swallow any water.

Then she saw the raw red burn on his hand. She pushed up quickly, nearly sloshing water over the rim. "You've burned yourself. Let me see. I—" And she did see, that the mark was the shape of a cross.

"I would have taken it off." Hurriedly, she pushed the cross and chain under her bodice.

"Small price to pay." He lifted her wrist, noted the faint bruising. "I have less control with you than I'd like."

"I like that you have less. Give me your hand. I have a little skill with healing."

"It's nothing."

"Then give me your hand. It's good practice for me." She held hers out expectantly. After a moment he sat beside her, laid his hand in hers.

"I like that you have less," she said again, drawing his eyes to hers. "I like knowing I can be wanted that much, that there's something in me that pulls something in you enough that something strains, nearly snaps."

"Dangerous enough when you're dealing with a human. When a vampire's control snaps, things die."

"You'd never hurt me. You love me."

His face went carefully blank. "Sex rarely has anything to do with—"

"Being inexperienced doesn't make me stupid, or gullible. Is it better?"

"What?"

She smiled at him. "Your hand. The redness has eased."

"It's fine." He drew it away. In fact there was no longer any burning. "You learn quickly."

"I do. Learning is a passion for me. I'll tell you what I've learned of you, when it comes to me. You love me." Her lips were softly curved as she brushed at his hair. "You might have taken me last night—in fact you would have, with less resistance—if it had been just for sex. If it had been only need, only sex, you wouldn't have taken me with such care, or trusted me enough to sleep awhile with me."

She held up a finger before he could speak. "There's more."

"With you, there tends to be."

She rose, straightening her clothes. "When Larkin came in, you did nothing to stop him from striking you. You love me, so you were guilty about taking what you saw as my innocence. You love me, so you've watched me enough to know one of my favorite places. You waited for me there, then you brought me here because you needed me. I pull at you, Cian, as you pull at me."

She watched him as she sipped water. "You love me, as I love you."

"To your peril."

"And yours," she said with a nod. "We live in perilous times."

"Moira, this can never—"

"Don't tell me never." Passion vibrated in her voice and turned her eyes to hellsmoke. "I know. I know all about never. Tell me today. Between you and me let it be today. I have to fight for tomorrow, and the day after and into always. But with this, with you, it's just today. Every today we can have."

"Don't cry. I'd rather have the burn than the tears."

"I won't." She shut her eyes for a moment, and willed herself to keep her word. "I want you to tell me what you've shown me. I want you to tell me what I see when you look at me."

"I love you." He came to her, gently touched her face with his fingertips. "This face, those eyes, all that's inside them. I love you. In a thousand years I've never loved another."

She took his hand, pressed her lips to it. "Oh! Look. There's no burn now. Love healed you. The strongest magic."

"Moira." He kept her hand in his, then laid hers against his chest. "If it beat, it would beat for you."

Tears stung her eyes again. "Your heart may be still, but it isn't empty. It isn't silent because it speaks to me."

"And that's enough?"

"Nothing will ever be enough, but it will do. Come, we'll—"

She broke off when she heard shouting from outside. Turning, she rushed to the window, drew back one of the drapes. Her hand went to her throat. "Cian, come look. The sun's low enough. Come look."

The sky was full of dragons. Emerald and ruby and

gold, their sleek bodies soared above the castle like flashing jewels in the softening light. And their trumpeting calls were like a song.

"Have you ever seen anything so beautiful?"

When his hand laid on her shoulder, Moira reached up, clasped it. "Listen how the people cheer them. Look at the children running and laughing. It's the sound of hope, Cian. The sound, the sight."

"Getting them here, and getting them to be ridden, and to respond in battle like warhorses, two different matters, Moira. But yes, it's a beautiful sight, and a hopeful sound."

She watched as they began to land. "In all your years, I imagine there's little you haven't done."

"Little," he agreed, then had to smile. "But no, I've never ridden a dragon. And yeah, damn right I want to. Let's go down."

There was still enough sunlight that he needed the bloody cloak in open spaces. But despite it, Cian discovered he could still be enchanted and surprised—when he looked into a young dragon's golden eye.

Their sinuous bodies were covered in large, jewel-toned scales that were smooth as glass to the touch. Their wings were like gossamer, and kept close into the body when they grazed along the ground. But it was the eyes that captivated him. They seemed to be alive with interest and intelligence, even humor.

"Figured the younger ones would be easier to train," Blair said to him as they stood, watching. "Larkin's best at communicating with them, even in his regular form. They trust him."

"Which is making it harder on him to use them in battle."

"Yeah, my guy's a softie, and we went around and around about it. He was hoping to convince everyone we could use them for transportation only. But they could make a hell of a difference on the field. Or above it. Still, I have to admit, I get a little twinge at the idea myself."

"They're beautiful—and unspoiled."

"We're going to change the second part." Blair let out a sigh. "Everything's a weapon," she murmured. "Anyway, want to go up?"

"Bet your ass."

"First flight's with me. Yeah, yeah," she said when she saw the objection on his face. "You pilot your own plane, ride horses, leap tall buildings in a single bound. But you've never ridden a dragon, so you're not going solo yet."

She walked slowly toward one of ruby and silver. She'd ridden it back, and still held out her hand so it would test her scent. "Go ahead, let her get acquainted."

"Her?"

"Yeah, I checked out the plumbing." Blair grinned. "Couldn't help it."

Cian laid his hand on the dragon's side, worked his way slowly to the head. "Well now, aren't you a gorgeous one." He began to murmur to her in Irish. She responded with what could only be termed a flirtatious swish of her tail.

"Hoyt's got the same way with them you do." Blair nodded toward where Hoyt was stroking sapphire scales. "Must be a family trait."

"Hmm. Now why is it that Her Majesty there is mounting one by herself?"

"She's ridden a dragon before. That is, she's ridden Larkin in dragon form, so she knows the ropes. Not all she's riding lately."

"Beg your pardon?"

"Just saying. You two look a lot more relaxed than either of you did yesterday." She gave him a wide, toothy grin, then swung onto the dragon. "Alley-oop."

He mounted the same way he'd scaled the walls. With an easy and fluid leap. "Sturdy," Cian commented. "More comfortable than they look. Not so very different from horseback all in all."

"Yeah, if you're talking Pegasus. Anyway, you don't give them a little kick like a horse or cluck. You just—"

Blair demonstrated by leaning down on the dragon's

neck, gliding a hand over its throat. With a sound like silk billowing, it spread its wings. And it rose up into the sky.

"Live long enough," Cian said behind Blair, "you do every damn thing."

"This has got to be one of the best. There are still logistics. The care and feeding, dragon poop."

"I bet it'll make the roses bloom."

She threw back her head and laughed. "Could be. We've got to train them, and their riders. But these beauties catch on fast. Watch." She leaned to the right, and the dragon swerved gently to follow her direction.

"A bit like riding a motorcycle."

"Some of that principle. Lean into the turns. Look at Larkin. That showoff."

He was riding a huge gold, and doing fancy loops and turns.

"Sun's nearly set," Cian commented. "Give it a few minutes, so I won't fry, and we'll give him a run for his money."

Blair shot a look over her shoulder. "You got it. Going to say something."

"When did you not?"

"She's carrying the weight of the fricking world. If what you two have going lightens that a little, I'm for it. Being with Larkin shifted some of mine, so I hope it's working for the two of you."

"You surprise me, demon hunter."

"I surprise myself, vampire, but there it is. Sun's down. You ready to rock?"

With enormous relief, he shoved back the hood of the cloak. "Let's show your cowboy some real moves."

Chapter 12

Davey had been Lilith's for nearly five years. She'd slaughtered his parents and younger sister one balmy summer night in Jamaica. The off-season vacation package—airfare, hotel and continental breakfast included—had been a surprise thirtieth birthday gift from Davey's father to his wife. Their first night there, giddy with holiday spirit and the complimentary glasses of rum punch, they had conceived a third child.

They were, of course, unaware of this, and had things gone differently the prospect of a new baby would have put the skids on tropical vacations for some time to come.

As it was, it was their last family holiday.

It had been during one of Lilith's brief and passionate estrangements from Lora. She'd chosen Jamaica on a whim, and entertained herself picking off locals and the occasional tourist. But she'd grown tired of the taste of the men who trolled the bars.

She wanted some variety—something a little fresher and sweeter. She found just what she was looking for with the young family.

She'd ended the mother's and little girl's giggling moonlight walk along the beach swiftly and viciously. Still she'd been impressed with the woman's panicked and ineffectual struggle, and her instinctive move to protect the child. As they'd satisfied her hunger, she might have left the man and boy splashing unaware in the surf down the beach. But she'd wanted to see if the father would fight for the son. Or beg, as the mother had begged.

He had—and had screamed at the boy to run. Run, Davey, run! he'd shouted. And his terror for his son enriched his blood to make the kill all the sweeter.

But the boy hadn't run. He'd fought, too, and that had impressed her more. He'd kicked and he'd bitten, and had even tried to leap on her back to save his father. It was the wildness of his attack combined with his angelic face that had decided her on changing him rather than draining him and moving on.

When she had pressed his mouth to her bleeding breast, she had felt something stirring inside her that had never stirred for another. The almost maternal sensation had fascinated and delighted her.

So Davey became her pet, her toy, her son, her lover.

It pleased her how quickly, how naturally he'd taken to the change. When she and Lora had reconciled, as they always did, Lilith had told her Davey was their vampiric Peter Pan. The little boy, eternally six.

Still like any boy of six, he needed to be tended to, entertained, taught. Only more so, in Lilith's opinion, as her Davey was a prince. As such, he had both great privilege, and great duty.

She considered this specific hunt to be both.

He quivered with excitement as she dressed him in the rough clothes of a peasant boy. It made her laugh to see his eyes so bright as she added to the game by smearing some dirt and blood on his face.

"Can I see? Can I look in your magic mirror and see myself? Please, please!"

"Of course." Lilith sent a quick and amused look toward

Lora—adult to adult. Picking up the game, Lora shuddered as she picked up the treasured mirror.

"You look terrifying," Lora told Davey. "So small and weak. And . . . *human*!"

Carefully taking the mirror, Davey stared at his reflection. And bared his fangs. "It's like a costume," he said, and giggled. "I get to kill one all by myself, right, Mama? All by myself."

"We'll see." Lilith took the mirror, and bent down to kiss his filthy cheek. "You have a very important part to play, my darling. The most important part of all."

"I know just what to do." He bounced up and down on his toes. "I practiced and practiced."

"I know. You've worked very hard. You're going to make me so proud."

She put the mirror aside, facedown, forcing herself not to take a peek at herself. Lora's burns were still raw and pink, and her reflection so distressing that Lilith only looked into the charmed mirror when Lora was out of the room.

At the knock at the door, she turned. "That will be Midir. Let him in, Davey, then go out and wait with Lucius."

"We're going soon?"

"Yes. In just a few minutes."

He raced to the door, then stood, shoulders straight while the sorcerer bowed to him. Davey marched out, her little soldier, leaving Midir to shut the door behind him.

"Your Majesty. My lady."

"Rise." Lilith gave a careless wave of the hand. "As you see, the prince is prepared. Are you?"

He stood, his habitual black robes whispering with the movement. His face was hard and handsome, framed by his flowing mane of silver hair. Eyes, rich and black, met Lilith's cool blue.

"He will be protected." Midir glanced toward the large chest at the foot of the bed, and the silver pot that stood opened on it. "You used the potion, as I instructed."

"I did, and it's your life, Midir, if it fails."

"It will not fail. It, and the chant I will use, will shield him from wood and steel for three hours. He will be as safe as he would be in your arms, Majesty."

"If not, I'll kill you myself, as unpleasantly as possible. And to make certain of it, you'll go with us on this hunt."

She saw, for just a moment, both surprise and annoyance on his face. Then he bowed his head, and spoke meekly. "At your command."

"Yes. Report to Lucius. He'll see you mounted." She turned away in dismissal.

"You shouldn't worry." Lora crossed to Lilith, slipped her arms around her. "Midir knows it's his life if any harm comes to our sweet boy. Davey needs this, Lilith. He needs the exercise, the entertainment. And he needs to show off a bit."

"I know, I know. He's restless and bored. I can't blame him. It'll be fine, just fine," she said as much to assure herself. "I'll be right there with him."

"Let me go. Change your mind and let me go with you."

Lilith shook her head, brushed a kiss over Lora's abused cheek. "You're not ready for a hunt. You're still weak, sweetheart, and I won't risk you." She took Lora's arms, gripped tight. "I need you on Samhain—fighting, killing, gorging. On that night, when we've flooded that valley with blood, taken what's ours by right, I want you and Davey at my side."

"I hate the wait almost as much as Davey."

Lilith smiled. "I'll bring you back a present from tonight's little game."

Davey rode pinion with Lilith through the moonstruck night. He'd wanted to ride his own pony, but his mama had explained that it wasn't fast enough. He liked going fast, feeling the wind, flying toward the hunt and the kill. It was the most exciting night he could remember.

It was even better than the present she'd given him on

his third birthday when she'd taken him through the summer night to a Boy Scout camping ground. And that had been such *fun*! The screaming and the running and the crying. The *chomp, chomp, chomp*ing.

It was better than hunting the humans in the caves, or burning a vampire who'd been bad. It was better than anything he could remember.

His memories of his human family were vague. There were times he woke from a dream and for a moment was in a bedroom with pictures of race cars on the walls and blue curtains at the windows. There were monsters in the closet of the bedroom, and he cried until she came.

She had brown hair and brown eyes.

Sometimes he would come in, too, the tall man with the scratchy face. He'd chase the monsters away, and she would sit and stroke his hair until he fell asleep again.

If he tried very hard, he could remember splashing in the water, and the feel of the wet sand going gooshy under his feet and the man laughing as the waves splashed them.

Then he wasn't laughing, he was screaming. And he was shouting: Run! Run, Davey, run!

But he didn't try very hard, very often.

It was more fun to think about hunting and playing. His mother let him have one of the humans for a toy, if he was very, very good. He liked best the way they smelled when they were afraid, and the sounds they made when he started to feed.

He was a prince, and could do anything he wanted. Almost.

He would show his mother tonight that he was a big boy now. Then there would be no more almost.

When they stopped the horses, he was almost sick with the thrill of what was to come. They would go on foot from here—and then it would be his turn. His mother held tight to his hand, and he *wished* she wouldn't. He wanted to march like Lucius and the other soldiers. He wanted to carry a sword instead of the little dagger hidden under his tunic.

Still, it was fun to go so fast, faster than any human, across the fields toward the farm.

They stopped again, and his mother crouched down to him to take his face in her hands. "Do just the way we practiced, my sweet boy. You'll be wonderful. I'll be very close, every minute."

He puffed out his chest. "I'm not afraid of them. They're just food."

Behind him Lucius chuckled. "He may be small, Your Majesty, but he's a warrior to the bone."

She rose, and her hand stayed on Davey's shoulder as she turned to Midir. "Your life," she said quietly. "Begin."

Spreading his arms in the black robes, Midir began his chant.

Lilith gestured so that the men spread out. Then she, Lucius and Davey moved closer to the farm.

One of the windows showed the flickering glow of a fire banked for the night. There was the smell of horses closed inside the stable, and the first hints of human. It stirred hunger and excitement in Davey's belly.

"Be ready," she told Lucius.

"My lady, I would give my life for the prince."

"Yes, I know." She laid a hand briefly on Lucius's arm. "That's why you're here. All right, Davey. Make me proud."

Inside the farmhouse, Tynan and two others stood guard. It was nearly time to wake their relief, and he was more than ready for a few hours' sleep. His hip ached from the wound he'd suffered during the attack on their first day's march. He hoped when he was able to close his gritty eyes he wouldn't see the attack again.

Good men lost, he thought. Slaughtered.

The time was coming when he would avenge those men on the battlefield. He only hoped that if he died there, he fought strong and brave first and destroyed a like number of the enemy.

He shifted his stance, preparing to order the relief watch when a sound brought his hand to the hilt of his sword.

His eyes sharpened; his ears pricked. It might have been a night bird, but it had sounded so human.

"Tynan."

"Yes, I hear it," he said to one of the others on guard.

"It sounds like weeping."

"Stay alert. No one is to . . ." He trailed off as he spotted a movement. "There, near the northmost paddock. Do you see? Ah, in the name of all the gods, it's a child."

A boy, he thought, though he couldn't be sure. The clothes covering him were torn and bloody, and he staggered, weeping, with his thumb plugged into his mouth.

"He must have escaped some raid near here. Wake the relief, and stay alert with them. I'll go get the child."

"We were warned not to step outside after sundown."

"We can't leave a child out there, and hurt by the look of him. Wake the relief," Tynan repeated. "I want an archer by this window. If anything out there moves but me and that child, aim for its heart."

He waited until the men were set, and watched the child fall to the ground. A boy, he was nearly sure now, and the poor thing wailed and whimpered pitifully as it curled into a ball.

"We could keep an eye on him until morning," one of the others on duty suggested.

"Are Geallian men so frightened of the dark they'd huddle inside while a child bleeds and cries?"

He shoved the door open. He wanted to move quickly, get the child inside to safety. But he forced himself to stop his forward rush when the boy's head came up and the round little face froze in fear.

"I won't hurt you. I'm one of the queen's men. I'll take you inside," he said gently. "It's warm, and there's food."

The boy scrambled to his feet and screamed as if Tynan had hacked him with a sword. "Monsters! Monsters!"

He began to run, limping heavily on his left leg. Tynan dashed after him. Better to scare the boy than to let him get away and very likely be a snack for some demon. Tynan caught him just before the boy managed to scramble over the stone wall bordering the near field.

"Easy, easy, you're safe." The boy kicked and slapped and screamed, shooting fresh pain into Tynan's hip. "You need to be inside. No one's going to hurt you now. No one . . ."

He thought he heard something—chanting—and tightened his grip on the child. He turned, ready to sprint back for the house when he heard something else, something that came from what he held in his arms. It was a low, feral growl.

The boy grinned, horribly, and went for his throat.

There was something beyond agony, and it took Tynan to his knees. Not a child, not a child at all, he thought as he fought to free himself. But the thing ripped at him like a wolf.

Dimly he heard shouts, screams, the thud of arrows, the clash of swords. And the last he heard was the hideous sound of his own blood being greedily drunk.

They used fire, tipping arrows with flame, and still, nearly a quarter of their number were killed or wounded before the demons fell back.

"Take that one alive." Lilith delicately wiped blood from her lips. "I promised Lora a gift." She smiled down at Davey who stood over the body of the soldier he'd killed. It swelled pride in her that her boy had continued to feed even when troops had dragged the body, with the prince clinging to it, away from the battle.

Davey's eyes were red and gleaming, and his freckles stood out like gold against the rosy flush the blood had given his cheeks.

She picked him up, held him high over her head. "Behold your prince!"

The troops who hadn't been destroyed in the brief battle knelt.

She lowered him to kiss him long and deep on his mouth.

"I want more," he said.

"Yes, my love, and you'll have more. Very soon. Toss that thing on a horse," she ordered with a careless gesture toward Tynan's body. "I have a use for it."

She mounted, then held out her arms so that Davey could leap into them. With her cheek rubbing against his hair, she looked down at Midir.

"You did well," she said to him. "You can have your choice of the humans, for whatever purposes you like."

The moonlight shone on his silver hair as he bowed. "Thank you."

Moira stood in the brisk wind and watched dragons and riders circle overhead. It was a stunning sight, she thought, and would have sent her heart soaring under any other circumstances. But these were military maneuvers, not spectacle.

Still, she could hear children calling out and clapping, and more than a few of them pretending they were dragon or rider.

She smiled a greeting when her uncle strode over to watch beside her. "You're not tempted to fly?" she asked him.

"I leave it for the young—and the agile. It's a brilliant sight, Moira. And a hopeful one."

"The dragons have lifted the spirits. And in battle, they'll give us an advantage. Do you see Blair? She rides as if she was born on the back of one."

"She's hard to miss," Riddock murmured as Blair drove her mount toward the ground at a dizzying speed, then swept up again.

"Are you pleased she and Larkin will marry?"

"He loves her, and I can think of no other who suits him so well. So aye, his mother and I are pleased. And will miss him every day. He must go with her," Riddock said before Moira could speak. "It's his choice, and I feel—in my heart—it's the right choice for him. But we'll miss him."

Moira leaned her head against her uncle's arm. "Aye, we will."

She would be the only one to remain, she thought as she went inside again. The only one of the first circle who would remain in Geall after Samhain. She wondered how she would be able to bear it.

Already the castle felt empty. So many had already gone ahead, and others were busy with duties she'd assigned. Soon, very soon, she would leave herself. So it was time, she determined, to write down her wishes in the event she didn't return.

She closed herself in her sitting room and sat to sharpen her quill. Then changed her mind and took out one of the treasures she'd brought back with her from Ireland.

She would write this document, Moira determined, with the instrument of another world.

She'd use a pen.

What did she have of value, she wondered, that wouldn't by rights belong to the next who ruled Geall?

Some of her mother's jewelry, certainly. And this she began to disburse in her mind between Blair and Glenna, her aunt and cousin, and lastly, her ladies.

Her father's sword should be Larkin's, she decided, and the dagger he'd once carried would go to Hoyt. The miniature of her father would be her uncle's if she died before him, as her father and uncle had been fast friends.

There were trinkets, of course. Bits of this and that which she gave thought to bequesting.

To Cian she left her bow and quiver, and the arrows she'd made with her own hand. She hoped he'd understand that these were more than weapons to her. They were her pride, and a kind of love.

She wrote it all carefully, sealed it. She would give the document to her aunt for safekeeping.

She felt better having done it. Lighter and clearer in her mind somehow. Setting the paper aside, she rose to face the next task. Moving back into the bedroom, she crossed to the balcony doors. The drapes still hung there, blocking the light, the view. And now she drew them back, let the soft light spill through.

In her mind's eye she saw it again, the dark, the blood, the torn body of her mother and the things that mutilated her. But now she opened the door and made herself walk through them.

The air was cool and moist, and overhead the sky was full of dragons. Streaks and whirls of color riding the pale blue. How her mother would have loved the sight of them, loved the sound of the wings, the laughter of the children in the courtyard below.

Moira walked to the rail, laid her hands on it and felt the sturdy stone. And standing as her mother had often done, she looked out over Geall, and swore to do her best.

She might have been surprised to know that Cian spent a large portion of his restless day doing what she had done. His lists of bequests and instructions were considerably longer than hers and minutely more detailed. But then he'd lived considerably longer and had accumulated a great deal.

He saw no reason for any of it to go to waste.

A dozen times during the writing of it he cursed the quill and wished violently for the ease and convenience of a computer. But he kept at it until he believed he'd spread his holdings out satisfactorily.

He wasn't certain it could all be done as some of it would be up to Hoyt. They'd speak about it, Cian thought. If he could count on anything, he could count on Hoyt doing everything in his considerable power to fulfill the obligation Cian meant to give him.

All in all, he hoped it wouldn't be necessary. A thousand years of existence didn't mean he was ready to give it up. And he damn well didn't intend to go to hell until he'd sent Lilith there before him.

"You were always one for business."

He pushed to his feet, drawing his dagger in one fluid motion as he turned toward the sound of the voice. Then the dagger simply fell out of his limp fingers.

Even after a millennium, there can be shocks beyond imagining.

"Nola." His voice sounded rusty on the name.

She was a child, his sister, just as she'd been when he'd last seen her. Her long dark hair falling straight, her eyes deep and blue. And smiling.

"Nola," he said again. "My God."

"I thought you would say you have no god."

"None that would claim me. How can you be here? Are you here?"

"You can see for yourself." She spread her arms, then did a little turn.

"You lived, and you died. An old woman."

"You didn't know the woman, so I'm as you remember me. I missed you, Cian. I looked for you, even knowing better. For years I looked and I hoped for you and for Hoyt. You never came."

"How could I? You know what I was. Am. You understand that now."

"Would you have hurt me? Or any of us?"

"I don't know. I hope not, but I didn't see any reason to risk it. Why are you here?"

He reached out, but she held up her hand and she shook her head. "I'm not flesh. Only an apparition. Here to remind you that you may not be what you were when you were mine, but you're not what she would have made you."

Because he needed a moment, he bent to pick up the dagger he'd dropped, then sheathed it again. "What does it matter?"

"It does. It will." And apparition or not, her eyes swam as they locked on his. "I had children, Cian."

"I know."

"Strong, skilled, gifted. Your blood, too."

"Were you happy?"

"Oh, aye. I loved a man, and he loved me. We had those children, and lived a good life. And still my brothers left a place in my heart I could never fill. A little ache inside.

I would see you, and Hoyt, sometimes. In the water, or the mist, or the fire."

"There are things I've done I wouldn't have you see."

"I saw you kill, and feed. I saw you hunt humans as you'd once hunted deer. And I saw you stand by my grave in the moonlight and lay flowers on it. I saw you fight beside the brother we both love. I saw my Cian. Do you remember how you'd pull me up on your horse and ride and ride?"

"Nola." He rubbed his fingers over his brow. He hurt too much to think of it. "We're both dead."

"And we both lived. She came to my window one night."

"She? Who?" Inside him, he went cold as winter. "Lilith."

"We're both dead," Nola reminded him. "But your hands go to fists and your eyes go sharp as your dagger. Would you still protect me?"

He walked to the fire, kicked idly at the simmering turf. "What happened?"

"It was more than two years after Hoyt left us. Father had died and Mother was ill. I knew she would never be strong again, that she would die. I was so sad, so afraid. I woke from sleep in the dark, and there was a face at my window. So beautiful. Golden hair and a sweet smile. She whispered to me, called me by name. 'Ask me in,' she said, and promised me a treat."

Nola tossed back her hair, and her face was full of disdain. "She thought since I was only a girl, the youngest of us, I'd be foolish, I'd be easy to trick. I went to the window, and I looked in her eyes. There's power in her eyes."

"Hoyt must have told you not to take such risks. He must have—"

"He wasn't there, and neither were you. There was power in me as well. Have you forgotten?"

"No. But you were a child."

"I was a seer, and the blood of demon hunters was in my veins. I looked in her eyes and I told her it was my blood who would end her. My blood who would rid the worlds of

her. And for her there would be no eternity in hell, or anywhere. Her damnation would be an end of all. She would
be dust, and no spirit would survive."

"She wouldn't have been pleased."

"Her beauty remains even when she shows her true self.
That's another power. I held up Morrigan's cross, that I
wore always around my neck. The light flashed from it,
like a sunbeam. She was screaming when she ran."

"You were always fearless," he murmured.

"She never came back while I lived, and never came
again until you and Hoyt went home together. You're
stronger than you were without him, and he with you. She
fears that, hates that. Envies that."

"Will he live through this?"

"I can't know. But if he falls, it will be as he lived. With
honor."

"Honor's cold comfort when you're in the ground."

"Then why do you hold your own?" she demanded with
a whip of impatience in her voice. "It's honor that brings
you here. Honor that you'll carry into battle along with
your sword. She couldn't drain it out of you, and just the
little she left was enough for you to draw on again. You
made this choice. You've still more to make. Remember
me."

"Don't. Don't leave."

"Remember me," she repeated. "Until we see each
other again."

Alone, he sat, lowering his head into his hands. And
remembered far too much.

Chapter 13

For the most part, Cian avoided the tower room where Hoyt and Glenna worked their magicks. Such things often involved considerable light, flashes, fire and other elements unfavorable to vampires.

But in a way he hadn't—or hadn't admitted to in centuries—he needed his brother.

He noted before he knocked that one or both of his magically inclined relations had taken the precaution of drawing protection symbols on the tower door to keep the curious out. He'd have preferred to stay out himself, but he knocked.

When Glenna answered, there was a dew of sweat on her skin. Her hair was bundled up, and she'd stripped down to a tank and cotton pants. Cian lifted a brow.

"Am I interrupting?"

"Nothing physical, unfortunately. It's just viciously hot in here. We're working on a lot of heat and fire magicks. Sorry."

"I'm not bothered much by temperature extremes."

"Oh. Right." She closed the door behind him. "We've

got the windows blocked off—keeping everything contained—so you won't have to worry about the light."

"It's nearly sundown."

He looked over to where Hoyt stood over an enormous copper trough. Hoyt had his hands spread above it, and there was a sensation, even across the room, of more heat, of power and energy.

"He's fire-charging weapons," Glenna explained. "And I've been working on, well, it's a kind of bomb, really. Something we may be able to drop from the air."

"The NSO would love to have you on staff."

"I could be their version of Q." She swiped at her damp brow with the back of her hand. "You want a tour?"

"Actually . . . I wanted to . . . I'll just speak with Hoyt when he's not so involved."

"Wait." It was the first time Glenna could remember seeing Cian flustered. No, not flustered, she thought. Upset. "He needs a break. So do I. If you can stand the heat, just hang out a few more minutes. He's nearly done. I'm going to go get some air."

Cian caught her hand before she turned to go. "Thank you. For not asking."

"No problem. And if it is a problem, I'll be around."

When she went out, Cian leaned against the door. Hoyt remained just as he'd been, hands spread over the silver smoke that rose from the trough. His eyes were darkened as they were when he held his power strong and steady.

It had always been so, Cian thought, since they were children.

Like Glenna, Hoyt had stripped down for work, and wore a white T-shirt and faded jeans. It was odd, even after the past months, to see his brother in twenty-first-century clothing.

Hoyt had never been one for fashion, Cian recalled. But for dignity and purpose. However much they looked alike, they'd approached life from different poles. Hoyt for solitude and study, and he himself for society and business—and the pleasure both brought him.

Still, they'd been close, had understood each other on a level few others could. Had loved each other, Cian thought now, in a way that was as strong and as steady as Hoyt's power.

Then the world, and everything in it, had changed.

So what was he doing here? Looking for answers, for comfort, when he knew there could be neither? None of it could be taken back, not a single act, a single thought, a single moment. It was a foolish waste of time and energy on all counts.

The man who stood like a statue in the smoke wasn't the man he'd known, any more than he was the same man he'd been. Or a man at all for that matter.

Too much time spent with these people, these feelings, these needs made him forget what could never be altered. He pushed away from the door.

"Wait. A moment more."

Hoyt's voice stopped him—and it irritated him to understand Hoyt had known he wasn't simply shifting position but leaving.

Hoyt lowered his hands, and the smoke whisked away.

"Sure we'll go into this well-armed." Hoyt reached into the trough and lifted a sword by the hilt. Spinning, he pointed it toward the hearth. And shot a beam of fire.

"Will you be using one of these?" Hoyt turned the sword in his hand, eying its edge. "You've skill enough not to burn yourself."

"I'll use whatever comes best to hand—and do my best to stay away from those you arm who are considerably less skilled."

"It's not worry over poor swordsmanship that brings you here."

"No."

Since he was here, he'd do what he'd come to do. But he wandered the room first while Hoyt removed the other weapons from the trough. The room smelled of herbs and smoke, of sweat and effort.

"I've chased your woman away."

"I'll find her again."

"Since she's not here, I'll ask you. Are you afraid you'll lose her in this?"

Hoyt laid the last sword on the worktable. "It's my last thought before sleep, my first on waking. The rest of the time I try not to think of it—or let out the part of myself that wants to lock her away safe until this is over."

"She isn't a woman you could lock away, even with your skill."

"No, but knowing that doesn't stop the fear. Are you afraid for Moira?"

"What?"

"Do you think I don't know you're with her? That your heart is with her?"

"A temporary madness. It'll pass." At his brother's quiet, steady look, Cian shook his head. "I've no choice in it, and neither does she. What I am doesn't run to white picket fences and golden retrievers." He waved it away when Hoyt's look turned puzzled. "To home and hearth, brother. I can't give her a life—if I wanted to—and what passes for mine will go on long after hers is ended. And that's not what I've come to tell you."

"Tell me this first. Do you love her?"

It came into him, the truth of it, swirling through his heart and into his eyes. "She is . . . She is like a light for me when I've lived eternally in the dark. But the dark is mine, Hoyt. I know how to survive there, to be content and productive and entertained there."

"You don't say happy."

Frustration snapped into his voice. "I was happy enough before you came. Before you changed everything again, as surely as Lilith had done to me. What would you have me do? Wish for what you have, and will have with Glenna if you live? What good will it do me? Will it start my heart again? Can your magic do that?"

"No. I've found nothing that can take you back. But—"

"Let it be. I am what I am, and I've done more than well enough. I'm not whining about it. She's an experience.

Love is an experience, and I've always sought them out."
He dragged his hands through his hair. "Christ. Is there
anything to drink in this place?"

"There's whiskey." Hoyt lifted his chin toward a cabinet. "I'll have one as well."

Cian poured whiskey generously into cups, then crossed
to where Hoyt drew two three-legged stools together. So
Cian sat, and they drank for a few moments in silence.

"I've written out a document, a kind of will, should my
luck run out on Samhain."

Hoyt lifted his eyes from his whiskey and met Cian's.
"I see."

"I've accumulated considerable property and holdings,
assets, personal items. I expect you'll see to them, as I've
instructed."

"I will, of course."

"It'll be no small task as they're spread out over the
world. I don't keep a great many eggs in one basket. There
are passports and other identification papers in the New
York apartment, and in safety deposit boxes here and
there. If any are useful to you, you're welcome to them."

"Thanks for that."

Cian swirled the whiskey in his glass, kept his eyes on
it. "There are some things I'd like Moira to have, if you
can get them here."

"I'll get them here."

"I thought to leave the club and the apartment in New
York to Blair—and to Larkin. I think they'd suit them better than you."

"They would. They'll be grateful, I'm sure."

Annoyance rose up at his brother's easy and practical
tone. "Well, don't let sentiment choke you, as it's more
likely I'll be holding a wake for you than you for me."

Hoyt angled his head. "Do you think so?"

"I damn well do. You haven't had three decades and
I've had near a hundred. And you never were as good in a
fight as me when we were both alive, however many tricks
you have up your sleeve."

"But then again, as you said, we aren't what we were, are we?" Hoyt smiled pleasantly. "I'm determined we'll both come through this, but if you fall, well . . . I'll lift a glass to you."

Cian let out a half laugh as Hoyt did just that.

"And would you be wanting pipes and drums as well?"

"Oh, bugger it." Now a wicked gleam came into Cian's eyes. "I'll toss in some fifes for yours, then console your grieving widow."

"At least I won't have to dig a hole for you, seeing as you'll just be dust, but I'll show you the honor of having a stone carved. 'Here doesn't lie Cian, for he's blown off with the wind. He lived and he died, then stayed on like the last annoying guest to leave the ball.' Does that suit you?"

"I'm thinking I'll go back and change some of those bequests, for principle only, seeing as I'll be singing 'Danny Boy' over your grave."

"What's 'Danny Boy'?"

"A cliche." Cian picked up the bottle he'd set on the floor and poured more whiskey into the cups. "I saw Nola."

"What?" Hoyt lowered the cup he'd just lifted. "What did you say?"

"In my room. I saw Nola, spoke with her."

"You dreamed of Nola?"

"Is that what I said?" Cian snapped. "I said I saw her, spoke with her. As awake then as I am now, looking and speaking to you. She was still a child. Jesus, there isn't enough whiskey in the world for this."

"She came to you," Hoyt murmured. "Our Nola. What did she say?"

"She loved me, and you. She missed us. She'd waited for us to come home. Damn it. Goddamn it." He pushed up to pace. "She was a child, exactly as she'd been the last I saw her. It was a lie, of course. She'd grown up, grown old. She'd died and gone to dust."

"And why would she come to you as a grown woman, or an old one?" Hoyt demanded. "She came to you as you remembered her, as you think of her. She gave you a gift. Why are you angry?"

It was fury in him now, fury to wrap tight around the pain. "How can you know what it is to feel this, to have it ripping inside you? She looked the same, and I'm not. She talked of how I'd swing her up on my horse and take her riding. And it was like it was yesterday. I can't have those yesterdays in my head and stay sane."

He turned back. "At the end of this, you'll know you did what you could, what was asked of you—for her, for all of them. If you live, whatever pang you feel at leaving them behind will be balanced out by that knowing, and by the life you make with Glenna. I have to go back where I was. I have to. I can't take this with me and survive it."

Hoyt was quiet a moment. "Was she in pain, afraid, grieving?"

"No."

"And you can't take that with you and survive it?"

"I don't know, that's the plain truth. But I know that one feeling leads to another until you drown in them. I'm half drowned now with what's in me for Moira."

He calmed himself, sat again. "She wore the cross you gave her, Nola did. She said she wore it always, just as you told her. I thought you should know. And I thought you should know she told me Lilith had come back, and tried to lure her into an invitation."

As Cian's had done, Hoyt's hand fisted. "That hell-bitch went for our Nola?"

"She did, and got a boot up the ass for the trouble— metaphorically." He told Hoyt what Nola had said, watched Hoyt's grim face soften a little with pride and satisfaction. "Then she flashed that cross of yours and sent her packing. According to Nola she never came back again, until we did."

"Well now, well. Isn't that interesting. The cross didn't just shield the wearer, it frightened Lilith enough to send her haring off. That, and the prediction we'd end her."

"Which may be why she's so determined to end us."

"Aye. Nola's threat could have added weight to that. Imagine how it must have been for Lilith, being frightened off by a child."

"She wants her own back, no doubt of it. She wants to win this, of course. To set herself up as a kind of god, but under that, it's us. The six of us and the connection between us. She wants us destroyed."

"Hasn't had much luck with that, has she?"

"And what do you think of that? The gods depose, don't they? We've all of us had our close calls, and bled for it. But we're all of us, Lilith included, being driven toward one time and place. The fact of the matter is, I don't care for being led by the nose by gods any more than demons."

Hoyt lifted his brows. "What choice is there?"

"They all talk of choice, but which of us would turn away from this now? It's not just humans who have pride, after all. So, the time clicks away." He rose. "And we'll see what we see on that reckoning day. The sun's well down. I'm going out for air."

He walked to the door, paused to glance back. "She couldn't tell me if you survived it."

Hoyt lifted a shoulder, finished off his whiskey. Then he smiled. " 'Danny Boy,' is it?"

Cian went to see to his horse. Then, though he knew it was risky, saddled Vlad and rode out through the gates. He needed the speed, and the night. Maybe he needed the risk as well.

The moon was past half full now. When that circle was complete, blood—human and demon—would soak the ground.

He hadn't fought in other wars, hadn't seen the point of them. Wars for land, for riches and resources. Wars waged in the name of faith. But this one had come to be his.

No, it wasn't only humans who had pride, or even honor. Or love. So for all of that, this was his. If his luck was in, he'd ride one day again in Ireland—or wherever he chose. And he'd think of Geall with its lovely hills and thick forests. He'd think of the green and the tumbling water, the standing stones, and the fanciful castle on the rise near the river.

He'd think of its queen. Moira, with the long gray eyes and the quiet smile that masked a clever, flexible brain and a deep, rich heart. Who would have believed that after all these lifetimes he would be seduced, bewitched, drowned in such a woman?

He took Vlad leaping over stone walls, galloping over fields where the air was sweet and cool with the night. The moonlight rained down on the stones of her castle, and the windows glowed with candles and lamps. She'd kept her word, he thought, and had hoisted that third flag, so there was claddaugh, dragon, and now the bright gold sun.

He wished, with all that was in him, that she would give Geall, and all the worlds, the sun after the blood spilled.

Maybe he couldn't take all these feelings, these needs and wants with him and survive. But he wanted to take this. When he went back to the dark, he wanted to take this much of her, and have that single glimmer of light through all his nights.

He rode back, and found her waiting, with her bow in her hands and the sword of Geall strapped to her side.

"I saw you ride out."

He dismounted. "Covering my back, were you?"

"We'd agreed none of us would go out alone, particularly after dark."

"I needed it," was all he said, and led the stallion to the stables.

"So it seemed, from the way you were riding. I didn't see any hounds of hell, but it appeared you did. Would you trust one of the stable boys to cool him and settle him for the night? It helps them to have the work, as much as it might help you to have a wild ride."

"There's a scolding under that accommodating tone, Majesty. You do it very well."

"Learned at my mother's knee." She took the reins herself, then passed them with instructions to the boy who came hurrying out from the stables.

When she'd finished, she looked up at Cian. "Are you in a mood?"

"Always."

"I should have said a difficult mood, but the answer might be always to that as well. If you're not, more than usual, I'd hoped you'd have a meal with me. In private. I'd hoped you'd stay with me tonight."

"And if I am in a difficult mood?"

"Then a meal and some wine might sweeten it enough for you to lie with me, and stay with me. Or, we can argue over the food, then go to bed."

"I'd have to have taken a spill from the horse and damaged my brain to turn down that offer."

"Good. I'm hungry."

And furious, he thought with some amusement. "Why don't you get the lecture out of your system. It's liable to give you indigestion."

"I don't have a lecture, and if I did, it's not what would suit me." She walked—regally, he thought—across the courtyard. "What I'd like is to give you a good, strong kick in the ass for taking a chance like that. But . . ."

She drew a long breath, then a second as they entered the castle. "I know what it is to need to get away, to just go for a bit. How it feels you'll rip apart from the pressure inside if you don't. I can go into a book and be quiet in my mind again. You needed the ride, the speed of it. And, I think, there are times you just need the dark."

He said nothing until they'd come to the door of her room. "I don't know how you can understand me that way."

"I've made a study of you." Now she smiled a little, looking up and into his eyes. "I'm a good study. And added to it, you're inside my heart now. You're inside me, so I know."

"I haven't earned you," he said quietly. "That occurs to me now. I haven't earned you."

"I'm not a wage or a prize. I wouldn't care to be earned." She opened the door to her sitting room.

She'd had the fire lit, and the candles. The cold supper and the good wine were already laid out, with flowers from one of the hothouses.

"You've gone to some trouble." He shut the door behind them. "Thank you."

"It was for me, but I'm glad you like it. I wanted a night, just one, where it would be only the two of us. As if none of this was happening. Where we could sit and talk and eat. And where I might drink just a little too much wine."

She laid down her bow and quiver, unhooked her sword. "One night when we don't talk of battles and weapons and strategy. You'd tell me you love me. You wouldn't even have to say it, because I'd see it when you looked at me."

"I do love you. I looked back at the castle, and saw the glow in the windows from these candles. That's how I think of you. A steady glow."

She stepped toward him, took his face in her hands. "And if I think of you as the night, it's the mystery of it, and the thrill. I'll never be afraid of the dark again, because I've seen into it."

He kissed her brow, her temples, then her lips. "Let me pour you the first glass of too much wine."

She sat at the little table and watched him. This was her lover, she thought. This strange and compelling man who carried wars inside him. And she'd have this night with him, the whole of it, and a few hours of peace for them both.

She chose food for his plate, knowing it was a wifely gesture. She'd have that as well, this one night. When he sat across from her, she lifted her glass to his. "*Sláinte.*"

"*Sláinte.*"

"Will you tell me the places you've seen? Where you've traveled? I want to go there in my mind. I studied the maps in your library in Ireland. Your world is so big. Tell me the wonderful things you've seen."

He took her to Italy during the Renaissance, and Japan in the time of samurai, to Alaska during the gold rush, to Amazon jungles and to African plains.

He tried to paint quick snapshots with words, so she could see the variety, the contrasts, the changes. He could all but see her mind opening to take it in. She asked dozens of questions, particularly when something he related expanded or contradicted what she'd read when in his library.

"I've wondered what lies beyond the sea." She propped her chin on her fist as he poured more wine. "Other lands, other cultures. It seems that if we were once a part of Ireland, that there may be parts of Italy and America, Russia, all those wondrous places here, in this world, too. One day . . . I'd like to see an elephant."

"An elephant."

She laughed. "Aye, an elephant. And a zebra and a kangaroo. I'd like to see the paintings from the artists you've seen, and the ones I found in your books. Michelangelo and DaVinci, Van Gogh, Monet, Beethoven."

"Beethoven was a composer. I don't believe he could paint."

"That's right, sure, that's right. The *Moonlight Sonata*, and all those symphonies with numbers. It's the wine muddling it up a bit. I'd like to see a violin, and a piano. And an electric guitar. Do you play any of those?"

"Actually, it's a little known fact that there were six original Beatles. Never mind."

"I know. John, Paul, George and Ringo."

"You've got a memory like that elephant you'd like to see."

"As long as you remember it, it belongs to you. I'll likely never see an elephant, but I'll have orange trees one day. The seeds in the hothouse pots are sprouting." She held her thumb and forefinger up, close together. "That bit of green coming out of the dirt. Glenna tells me the blossoms will be very fragrant."

"Yes, they will be."

"And I took other things."

It amused him to hear the confessional tone in her voice. "So, you've sticky fingers, have you?"

"I thought, if I'm not meant to take them to Geall, they won't go. I took a cutting of your roses. All right, well, three cuttings. I was greedy. And a photograph Glenna took of Larkin and me. And a book. I confess it, I took a book right out of your library. It's a thief I am."

"Which book?"

"It was poems by Yeats. I wanted it particularly because he was Irish it said, and it seemed important I bring something that was written down by an Irishman."

Because you were Irish, she thought. Because the book was yours.

"And the poems were so beautiful and strong," she continued. "I told myself I was going to give it back to you once I'd copied more down, but that's a lie. I'm keeping it."

He laughed, shook his head. "Consider it a gift."

"Thank you, but I'll happily pay you for it." She rose, stepped over to where he sat. "And you may name the price." She sat on his lap, linked her arms around his neck. "He wrote something, your Yeats, that made me think of you, and especially what we have between us tonight. He wrote: 'I spread my dreams at your feet. Tread softly because you tread on my dreams.'"

She combed her fingers through his hair. "You can give me your dreams, Cian. I'll tread softly."

Impossibly moved, he rested his cheek against hers. "You're unlike any other."

"With you, I'm more than I ever was. Will you come out, stand for a while on the balcony with me? I'd like to look at the moon and the stars."

He rose with her, but when he turned, she drew him back. "No, the bedroom balcony."

He thought of her mother, of what she'd seen. "Are you sure?"

"I am. I stood out there today, alone. I want to stand there with you, in the night. I want you to kiss me there so I'll remember it all of my life."

"You'll want a cloak. It's cold."

"Geallian woman are made of sterner stuff."

And when she led the way, when her hand gripped his tight as she opened the balcony doors, he thought, yes, yes, she was.

Chapter 14

He kissed her on the balcony, and she would remember it, all of it. She wouldn't forget the quiet music of the night, the chill in the air, the easy skill of his mouth.

Tonight she wouldn't think of sunrise and the obligations that came with it. The night was his time, and while she was with him, it would be hers.

"You've kissed many women."

He smiled a little, brushed his lips over hers again. "I have."

"Hundreds."

"At least."

Her eyes narrowed. "Thousands."

"Very likely."

"Hmm." She wandered away from him, then turned, leaning back on the stone rail. "I think I'll make a decree, that every man must come and kiss their queen. So I can catch up. At the same time it would be a kind of study, a comparison. I could see how you rate in this particular skill."

"Interesting. I'm afraid you'd find your countrymen sadly lacking."

"Oh? How can you be sure? Have you ever kissed a man of Geall?"

He laughed. "Clever, aren't you?"

"So I'm told." She stayed as she was when he moved to her, when he caged her in by laying his hands on the rail on either side of her. "Does your taste run to clever women?"

"Currently, when their eyes are like night fog, and their hair the color of polished oak."

"Gray and brown. I always thought they were such dull colors, but nothing about me feels dull when I'm with you." She laid a hand on his heart. Though it didn't beat, she saw the pulse of it in his eyes. "I don't feel shy with you, or nervous. I did, until you kissed me."

She pressed her lips to where her hand had laid. "Then I thought, well of course. I should have known. A curtain lifted inside me. I don't think it will ever close again."

"You bring the light inside me, Moira." He didn't say, not to her, not to himself, that when he left her it would go out again.

"The moon's clear tonight, and the stars shine." She laid her hands on his. "We'll leave the drapes open until it's time for sleep."

She went inside with him, into a room shimmering with moonlight and candlelight. She knew what it would be now, the warmth that went to heat, and the heat that went to fire. And all the thrills and sensations that came between.

From somewhere outside an owl called. For its mate, she thought. She knew what it was now to pine for her mate.

She lifted off her circlet, set it aside, then reached up to take off her earrings. When she saw him watching her she realized these small acts, this prelude to disrobing, could arouse.

So she took them off slowly, watching him as he watched her. She took the cross she'd tucked under her bodice, drawing it over her head. This, she knew, was an act of trust.

"I have no ladies. Would you see to my laces?"

She turned her back, lifted her hair.

"I think I'll try to make a zipper. It's a simple thing, really, and makes dressing easier."

"A lot of charm is lost to convenience."

She sent him a smile over her shoulder. "Easy for you to say." But then again, feeling him loosen those laces brought a flutter to her belly. "What invention pleased you the most over your time?"

"Indoor plumbing."

The quickness of his answer made her laugh. "Larkin and I were spoiled, and miss it sorely. I studied the pipes and the tanks. I think I could fashion something like your shower."

"A queen and a plumber." He laid his lips on her shoulder as he eased the material away. "There's no end to your talents."

"I wonder how I'll be as a gentleman's valet." She turned to him. "I like buttons," she said as she began to undo his shirt. "They're sensible, and pretty."

So was she, he thought as she worked her way down efficiently. Then she shoved at her hair.

"I think I should cut this off. Like Blair's. That's sensible, too."

"No. Don't." His belly quivered as her fingers paused on the button of his jeans. His combed down through the length of her hair, from crown to waist. "It's beautiful. The way it falls over your shoulders, spills down your back. It all but glows against your skin."

Charmed, she glanced over toward the long looking glass. And was jolted to see herself standing half dressed. And alone.

She looked away quickly, sent him an easy smile. "Still, it's a great deal of trouble, and—"

"Does it frighten you?"

There was no point pretending she didn't understand

him. "No. It's a bit of a shock is all. Is it hard for you? Not being able to see your reflection?"

"It just is. You adjust. Just another irony. Here, you've got eternal youth, but you won't be able to admire yourself. Still . . ."

He turned her around so they both faced the mirror. Then he lifted her hair, let it fall. When she let out a laugh at watching her hair seem to fly around on its own, he laid his hands on her shoulders.

"There are always ways to amuse yourself," he told her. He lifted her hair again, and this time brushed his lips—and just a hint of teeth—along the nape of her neck.

He heard the quick intake of her breath, saw her eyes widen.

"No, no," he murmured when she started to turn. "Just watch." And trailed his fingers along her skin—bare shoulders, and down to where her loosened bodice clung tenuously to her breasts. "Just feel."

"Cian."

"Did you ever dream of a lover coming to you in the night, in the dark?" He nudged the dress down to her waist then glided his fingertips over her breasts. "Overtaking you. Hands and lips heating your skin."

She lifted her hands to his, needing to feel them. Then flushed and dropped them again as the reflection showed her cupping her own breasts.

Behind her, invisible, he smiled. "You said I didn't take your innocence. You might have been right, but I think I will now. It's . . . succulent, and what I am craves it."

"I'm not innocent," she said, but trembled.

"More than you know." He circled her breasts with his thumbs, moving in slowly until they rubbed stiffened peaks. "Are you afraid?"

"No." And shuddered. "Yes."

"A little fear can add to excitement." He pushed the dress to the floor, leaned close to her ear. "Step out," he whispered. "Now watch. Watch your body."

Fear twisted with arousal so it was impossible for her to

tell them apart. Her body was helpless, her mind transfixed. Hands and lips she couldn't see roamed over her,
erotically intimate, lazily possessive. She could see herself
quivering, and the startled pleasure on her own face.

The clouds of surrender in her own eyes.

Her phantom lover ran his hands down her, fingers toying, tracing, leaving a trail of shivering flesh. This time
when they took her breasts, she covered his hands with
hers, shameless.

She moaned for him, and still her eyes stayed on the
glass. His scholar would never shut her eyes to new experience, to new knowledge. He could feel her trembles,
and the instinctive movement of her hips as pleasure took
her over. Candlelight played over her skin and sensation
warmed it so it bloomed like a rose.

She moaned again as he trailed his fingers over her
belly, and melting into him, hooked her arm back around
his neck.

He only teased, skimming his fingers along her thighs,
over the most sensitive flesh, hinting, only hinting at what
was to come until her breath was sobbing out.

"Take," he murmured. "Take what you want." He gripped
her hand, pressed it to his between her thighs. Trapped it
there.

She felt her body buck against him, against herself as he
stroked her toward a new, towering pleasure. His body was
solid behind hers, and his voice murmured words she no
longer understood, but in the glass there was only her own
form, lost now to its own rising needs.

Release left her breathless, limp and amazed.

He spun her around so quickly she couldn't find her balance, and knew she'd have lost it again in any case when
his mouth took hers with a wild urgency. She could only
cling, could only give while her heart slammed an anvil
beat against his chest.

Of all he'd had and taken and tasted, he'd never known
such hunger. A kind of madness of need that could only
be met with her. For all his skill, all his experience, he was

helpless when she held him against her. As ready and wrecked as she, he pulled her to the floor, and plunged inside her to forge that first desperate link.

He turned her face to the mirror once again as he ravished her, as her body went wild under his strong, thrusting hips. And when she came, quaking, he chained need with will until her heavy eyes opened, met his. Until she saw who had her.

He took her again, building and building until her need paced his own. Then burying his face in her hair, emptied himself into her.

She might have lain there, spent, for the rest of her life, but he lifted her. Simply scooped her up, she realized, and stood with her in his arms all in one effortless motion.

And her heart did a little jig in her chest.

"It's foolish," she said as she nuzzled his neck, "and I'm thinking it's female. But I love it that you're so strong, and that for a moment when we love each other, I make you weak."

"There's a part of me, *mo chroi*, that's always weak when it comes to you."

My heart, he'd called her, and it made her own dance again. "Oh, don't," she said after he'd laid her on the bed and turned to close the drapes. "Not yet. There's so much night left." She rolled off the bed again and grabbed her night robe. "I'm going to get the wine. And the cheese," she decided. "I'm half starving again."

As she ran out he went to the fire, tossed on another brick of turf. He closed his mind to the part of him that asked what he was doing. Every time he was with her, there was another scar to his heart, for the day that would come when he'd never be with her again.

She'd survive it, he reminded himself. And so would he. Survival was something humans and demons had in common. Nothing really died of a broken heart.

She came back, carrying a tray. "We can eat and drink in bed, full of decadence." She set the tray on the bed, and climbed up after it.

"I've certainly given you enough of that."

"Oh?" She brushed back her hair and gave him a slow smile. "And here I was hoping there'd be more to come. But if you've shown me all you know, I suppose we can just begin repeating ourselves."

"I've done things you can't imagine. Things I wouldn't have you imagine."

"Now you're bragging." She made herself say it lightly.

"Moira—"

"Don't be sorry for what's between us, or for what you believe can't be, or shouldn't." Her gaze was clear, direct. "Don't be sorry when you look at me for whatever you might have done in the past. Whatever it was, each time, it was a step to bringing you here. You're needed here. I need you here."

He crossed to the bed. "Do you understand I can't stay?"

"Yes, yes. Yes. I don't want to speak of it, not tonight. Can't we have an illusion for just one night?"

He touched her hair. "I can't be sorry for what's between us."

"That's enough then." Had to be enough, she reminded herself, though with every minute that passed there was something inside her going wild, and wilder still with grief.

She lifted one of the goblets, offered it with a steady hand. When he saw it was blood, he lifted a brow at her.

"I thought you might need it. For energy."

He shook his head and sat on the bed with her. "So, should we talk about plumbing?"

She hadn't been sure what he'd say, but that was the last on any list she might have made. "Plumbing."

"You're not the only one who's made studies. Added to the fact that I was around when that kind of thing was being incorporated into daily life. I have some ideas how you could install some basics."

She smiled and sipped her wine. "Educate me."

They spent considerable time at it, with Moira going off

for paper and ink so they could draw basic diagrams. The fact that he took such an interest in something she imagined people of his time took for granted opened another facet of him for her.

But she realized she shouldn't have been surprised by it, not when she considered the extent of his library in Ireland. And in a house, she remembered, he didn't visit more than once or twice a year.

She understood, too, that he could have been anything he'd wanted. He had a quick, curious mind, clever hands, and from the way he'd played music, the soul of a poet. And a way with business as well, she reminded herself.

In Geall, in her time, he would have been prosperous, she was certain. Respected, even renowned. Other men would have come to him for advice and counsel. Women would have flirted with him at every opportunity.

But she and he would have met, and courted, and loved, she was sure of it. And he would have ruled by her side over a rich and peaceful land.

There would be children, with his beautiful blue eyes. And a boy—at least one boy—with that little cleft in the chin like his father.

And on nights like this, late and quiet, they'd talk of other plans for their family, for their people, for their land.

She blinked herself back when his fingers brushed her cheek.

"You need sleep."

"No." She shook her head, tried to refocus on the diagrams again—to hold off those minutes that drained away her time with him. "My mind was wandering off."

"You'd've been snoring in a minute."

"Well, what a lie. I don't snore." But she didn't argue when he gathered up the papers. She could barely keep her eyes open. "Perhaps we'll rest a little while."

She rose to snuff candles as he moved to close the drapes. But when she moved back toward the bed, he was opening the doors and stepping out.

"For heaven's sake, Cian, you're next to naked." Plucking

up his shirt, she hurried out after him. "At least put this on. You may not mind the cold, but I mind having one of the guards see you standing here in your altogether. It's not proper."

"There's a rider coming."

"What? Where?"

"Due east."

She looked east, but saw nothing. Still, she didn't doubt him. "A single rider?"

"Two, but the second's being led by the first. They're coming at a gallop."

With a nod, she strode back into the bedchamber and began to dress. "The guards are instructed not to pass anyone in. I'll have a look. It may be stragglers. If so, we can't leave them outside the gates and unprotected."

"Invite no one," Cian ordered as he yanked on his jeans. "Even if they're known to you."

"I won't, and neither will any of the guards." With a small pang of regret, she put on her circlet and became queen again. And as queen, she lifted her sword.

"It'll be stragglers," she said. "In need of food and shelter."

"And if not?"

"Then they've ridden a long way to die."

When she stood at the post on top of the wall she could see the riders, or the shape of them. Two as Cian had said, with the first leading the second horse. They wore no cloaks though there was a chill in the air, and a hint of the first frost.

She glanced at Niall who'd been awakened when the guards had spotted the riders. "I'll want a bow."

Niall gestured to one of the men, took a bow and quiver from him. "Seems fruitless for the enemy to ride straight at us. Two of them against us? And unable to pass through the gates unless we welcome them."

"Likely they aren't the enemy. But the gates aren't to be

raised until we know. Two men," she murmured as they rode close enough for her to be sure. "The one being led looks to be injured."

"No," Cian said after a moment. "Dead."

"How can you—" Niall cut himself off.

"You're certain?" Moira murmured.

"He's tied to the horse, and he's dead. So's the lead rider, but he's been changed."

"All right then." Moira let out a sigh. "Niall, tell the men to keep a sharp eye for others. They're to do nothing without a command. We'll see what this one wants. A deserter?" she said to Cian, then dismissed the idea before he answered. "No, a deserter would have gone as far east or north as possible, and kept hidden."

"Could be he thinks he has something to trade," Niall suggested. "Make us think the one he's bringing is still alive, so we'd let them in. Or he's got information he feels we'd value."

"No harm in listening," Moira began, then gripped Cian's hand. "The rider. It's Sean. It's Sean, the smithy's son. Oh God. Are you sure he's—"

"I know my own kind." And with eyes keener than Moira's he recognized the dead. "Lilith sent him—she can afford to lose one so newly changed. She sent him because you'd know him, and feel for him. Don't."

"He was little more than a boy."

"Now he's a demon. The other was spared that. Look at me, Moira." He took her shoulders, turned her to face him. "I'm sorry. It's Tynan."

"No. No. Tynan's at the base. We had word he reached it safely. Injured, but alive, and safe. It can't be Tynan."

She pushed away from Cian, leaning on the wall, straining her eyes. She could hear the murmurs now, then the shouts as the men began to recognize Sean. There was hope in the shouts, and welcome.

"It's no longer Sean." She lifted her voice, cut through the calls of the men. "They killed the one you knew and sent a demon with his face. The gates stay locked, and not

a man here will pass what rides here through them. I command it."

She turned back. Every bone in her body went brittle
as she saw Cian had been right. It was Tynan, or Tynan's
mauled body, tied to the second horse.

She wanted to weep, wanted to burrow herself into Cian
and scream and sob. She wanted to sink to the stones and
cry out her grief and her rage.

She stood straight, no longer feeling the wind that blew
at her cloak, at her hair. She notched the arrow, and she
waited for the vampire to bring its vile gift.

"No one is to speak to it," she said coldly.

What had been Sean lifted its face, raised a hand to
wave to those gathered on the wall.

"Open the gates!" it shouted. "Open the gates! It's
Sean, the blacksmith's son. They may be after me still.
I've Tynan here. He's badly hurt."

"You will not pass," Moira called out. "She killed you
only to send you here to die again."

"Majesty." It managed an awkward bow as it pulled the
horses to a halt. "You know me."

"Aye, I do. How did Tynan die?"

"He's hurt. He's lost blood. I escaped the demons and
made my way to the farm, to the base. But I was weak and
hurt myself, and Tynan, bless him, came out to help me.
They set upon us. We barely escaped with our lives."

"You lie. Did you kill him? Did what she made you turn
you so you'd kill a friend?"

"My lady." It broke off when she lifted the bow and
aimed the arrow at its heart. "I didn't kill him." It held
up its hands to show them empty of weapons. "It was
the prince. The boy." It giggled, then pressed a hand to
its mouth to muffle it in a gesture so like Sean's it ripped
her heart. "The prince lured him outside and had the kill.
I've only brought him back to you, as the true queen commanded. She sends a message."

"And what would it be?"

"If you surrender, and accept her as ruler of this world

and all others, if you place the sword of Geall in her hand, and set the crown on her head, you'll be spared. You may live out your lives here as you like, for Geall is a small world and of little interest to her."

"And if we don't?"

He took out a dagger, and leaning over, cut the ropes securing Tynan to the horse. A careless kick sent the body tumbling to the ground. "Then your fate is as his, as will be the fate of every man, every woman, every child who stands against her. You'll be tortured."

It ripped off its tunic, and the moonlight fell on the burns and gashes yet to heal on its torso. "Any who survive Samhain will be hunted down. We'll rape your women, we'll mutilate your children. When it's done, not a single human heart will beat on Geall. We are forever. You'll never stop the flood of us. Give your answer, and I'll take it to the queen."

"This is the answer of the true queen of Geall. When the sun rises after Samhain, you and all like you will be dust that blows out to sea on the wind. Nothing will be left of you in Geall."

She passed her bow back to Niall. "You have your answer."

"She'll come for you!" it shouted. "And for the traitor to his kind who stands beside you."

It wheeled the horse, kicked it to a gallop.

On the wall, Moira lifted her sword, and flinging it out, shot a stream of fire. The vampire screamed once as the flames struck, then the ball of fire that was left of it fell to the ground, and went to ash.

"He was of Geall," Moira murmured, "and deserved to end with its sword. Tynan—" Her throat simply locked.

"I'll bring him in." Cian touched her shoulder, and looked over her head into Niall's eyes. "He was a good man, and a friend to me."

Without waiting, Cian vaulted over the wall. He seemed almost to float to the ground.

Niall slapped the back of his hand on the arm of the

guard beside him when he saw the man made the sign against evil. "No man stands with me who insults Sir Cian."

Below, Cian picked Tynan up in his arms and, bearing his weight, looked up and met Moira's eyes.

"Open the gates," she ordered. "So Sir Cian can bring Tynan home again."

She tended the body herself, removing the torn and filthy clothes.

"Let me do this, Moira."

She shook her head, and began to wash Tynan's face. "This is for me. We were friends since childhood. I need to do this for him. I don't want Larkin to see him until he's clean."

Her hands trembled as she brushed the cloth gently over the tears and bites, but she never faltered.

"They were playmates, you see. Larkin and Tynan. Was it the truth, do you think, that the child did this to him?"

When Cian said nothing, she looked over.

"He's her child," Cian said at length. "He would be vicious. Let me wake Glenna, at least."

"She was fond of Tynan. Everyone was. No, there's no need for her to come now, so late. They tore my mother like this. Worse, even worse. And I turned away from that. I can't turn away from this."

"Do you want me to go?"

"You think because I see these wounds, these bites and tears, as if an animal had been at him, I could think you're the same as what did this? Do you think me so weak of mind and heart, Cian?"

"No. I think the woman I saw tonight, the woman I heard, has the strongest mind and heart I've ever known. I never ripped at a human that way."

He steadied himself as she turned those ravaged eyes on his again. "I need you to know that, at least. Of all the things I've done, and some were unimaginably cruel, I never did what was done to him."

"You killed more cleanly. More efficiently."

He felt the words slice into him. "Yes."

Moira nodded. "Lilith didn't train you, but abandoned you, so you have little of her in you. Not like this boy must. And, I think, some manner of your upbringing remained. Just as I heard Sean's tone, saw his mannerisms in that thing tonight, so some of yours stayed as they were. I know you're not human, Cian, just as I know you're not a monster. And I know there's some of both in you that has you constantly struggling to keep them balanced."

She washed Tynan's body as gently as she would have washed a child. When she was done she began to dress him in the clothes she'd had sent over from his quarters.

"Let me do that, Moira, for God's sake."

"I know you mean well. I know you're thinking of me. But I need to do this one thing for him. He was the first to kiss me." Her voice wavered a bit before she clamped down and finished. "When I was fourteen, and he two years older. It was very sweet, very gentle. Shy for both of us, as a first kiss in the springtime should be. I loved him. I think in a way like you loved King. She's taken that from us, Cian. Taken them from us, but not the love."

"I swear before any gods you wish, I'll end her for you."

"One of us will." She bent, brushed her lips over Tynan's cold cheek.

Then she stepped back from him.

Now she sank to the floor on a keening wail. When Cian knelt beside her, she curled into him and wept out her shattered heart.

Chapter 15

They buried Tynan on a brilliant morning with cloud shadows dancing over the hills and a lark singing joyfully in a rowan tree. The holy man blessed the ground before they lowered him into it, with a fife and drum sounding the dirge.

All who knew him, and many who didn't, were there so that mourners stretched across the sun-drenched graveyard and up the rise toward the castle. The three flags of Geall flew at half staff.

Moira stood beside Larkin, dry-eyed. Though she heard Tynan's mother weeping, she knew her time for tears had passed. The others of her circle stood behind her, and she could feel them, took some comfort from that.

Now two stones would stand for friends here, along with the markers for her parents. All of them victims of a war that had raged long before she'd known of it. And would end with her, one way or another.

At last, she moved away to give the last moments to the family and their privacy. When Larkin took her hand, she gripped it firmly. She looked at Cian, could just see his eyes under the shadow of his hood. Then she looked at the others.

"We have work to do. Larkin and I need to speak with Tynan's family again, then we'll meet in the parlor."

"We'll head in now." Blair stepped forward, laid her cheek against Larkin's. Moira couldn't hear the words Blair murmured to him, but Larkin released her hand and pulled Blair into a hard embrace.

"We'll be in shortly." Larkin eased back, then took Moira's hand again. She would have sworn she could feel his grief coming through his skin.

Before Moira could move back toward the family, Tynan's mother broke away from her husband and pushed her way to Cian. Her eyes were still spilling tears.

"It's your kind did this. Your kind killed my boy."

Hoyt made a move forward, but Cian shifted to block his path. "Yes."

"You should be in hell instead of my boy being in the ground."

"Yes," Cian repeated.

Moira stepped up to put an arm around her, but the woman shook it off. "You, all of you." She whirled, jabbing out an accusing finger. "You care more about this *thing* than my boy. Now he's dead. He's dead. And you have no right to stand here by his grave." She spat at Cian's feet.

As she wept into her hands, her husband and daughters carried her off.

"I'm sorry," Moira murmured. "I'll speak with her."

"Leave her be. She wasn't wrong." Saying nothing more, Cian walked away from the fresh grave, and the lines of stones that marked the dead.

Niall caught up with him as he reached the gates. "Sir Cian, a word with you."

"You can have as many words as you want once I'm out of this shagging sun."

He didn't know why he'd gone to the graveyard. He'd seen more than enough dead in his time, heard more than enough weeping for them. Tynan's mother wasn't the only one who looked at him with fear and hate, and here he was out in the daylight with the only things between him and the killing sun some rough cloth and a charm.

His blood cooled the moment he was inside, out of the light.

"Say what you need to say." Cian shoved back the detested hood of the cloak.

"So I will." A big man with his usually cheerful face tight and grim, Niall nodded sharply. His wide hand rested on the hilt of his sword as he looked hard into Cian's eyes. "Tynan was a friend, and one of the best men I've known."

"You're saying nothing I haven't heard before."

"Well, you haven't heard me say it, have you? I saw what had become of Sean, what had been a harmless and often foolish lad. I saw him kick Tynan's body from the horse as if it were no more than offal to be tossed in a ditch."

"To him it wasn't any more than that."

Again, Niall nodded, and his fingers tightened on the sword's hilt. "Aye, that's what was made of him. And of you. But I watched you lift Tynan's body off the ground. I watched you carry it in, as a man would carry a fallen friend. I saw none of what was Sean in you. Tynan's mother's grieving. He was her first-born, and she's mad with grief. And she was wrong in what she said to you by his grave. He'd not have wanted you insulted by his blood. So as his friend, I'm telling you that. And I'm telling you any man who fights with me fights with you. That's my word on it."

He lifted his hand from the hilt of his sword and held it out to Cian.

Humans never failed to surprise him. Irritate, annoy, amuse, occasionally educate. But most of all they continued to surprise him with the twists and turns of their minds and hearts.

He supposed that was one reason he'd been able to live among them so long and still be interested.

"I'll thank you for it. But before you take my hand, you need to know that what was in Sean is in me. There's a thin difference."

"Not thin by my measure. And I'm thinking you'll use what's in you to fight. I'll put my back to yours, Sir Cian. And my hand's still out."

Cian shook it. "I'm grateful," he said. But when he went up the stairs, he went alone.

Heartsick, Moira walked back to the castle. There was little time for grieving, she knew, little time for comfort. What Lilith had done to Sean, to Tynan, she'd done to cut at their hearts. And she'd aimed well.

So they would heal them now with action, with movement.

"Can the dragons be used? Are they trained enough to carry men?"

"They're smart, and accommodating," Larkin told her. "Easily ridden by any who have a good seat, and aren't afraid of the height. But so far, it's been like a game for them. I can't say how they'll do in battle."

"For now, it's more a matter of transportation. You'd know the best of them, you and Blair. We'll need—" She broke off as her aunt crossed the courtyard to her. "Deirdre." She kissed her aunt's cheek, held an extra moment. She knew Larkin's and Tynan's mothers were close. "How is she?"

"She's prostrate. Inconsolable." Deirdre's eyes, swollen from her own tears, locked on Larkin's face. "As any mother would be."

He embraced her. "Don't fret for me, or for Oran."

"Now you ask the impossible." Still she smiled a little. But the smile faded as she turned to Moira again. "I know this is a difficult time, and you've much on your mind, on your heart. But I would speak with you. Privately."

"Of course. I'll join you shortly," she said to the others, then laid her arm around Deirdre's shoulders. "We'll go to my sitting room. You'll have tea."

"You needn't trouble."

"It'll do us both good." She caught the eye of a servant as they passed into the hall, and asked that tea be brought up.

"And Sinann?" Moira continued as they climbed the stairs.

"Fatigued, and full of grief for Tynan, of worry for her husband, her brothers. I couldn't allow her to go to the grave today, and made her rest. I worry for her, and the babe she carries, her other children."

"She's strong, and has you to tend her."

"Will it be enough if Phelan falls as Tynan has? If Oran has already . . ."

"It must be. We have no choice in this. None of us."

"No choice, but for war." Deirdre entered the sitting room, took a chair. Her face, framed by her wimple, was older than it had been weeks before.

"If we don't fight they'll slaughter us, as they did Tynan. Or do what they did to poor Sean." Moira went to the hearth to add bricks to the fire. Despite the bright autumn sun, she was cold to the bone.

"And fighting them, how many will die? How many will be slaughtered?"

Moira straightened, and turned. Her aunt wasn't the only one who would question, who would look to their queen for the impossible answer.

"How can I say? What would you have me do? You who were confidant to my mother before she was queen, and all during her reign. What would you have had her do?"

"The gods have charged you. Who am I to say?"

"My blood."

Deirdre sighed, looked down at her hands lying empty in her lap. "I'm weary, to the bottom of my soul. My daughter fears for her husband, as I do for mine. And for my sons. My friend buried her child today. And I know there is no choice in this, Moira. This blight has come to us, and must be cut out."

A servant hurried in with the tea.

"Leave it please," Moira said. "I'll pour. Is food being sent to the parlor?"

The young girl curtseyed. "Aye, Your Majesty. The cook was seeing to it when I left with the tea."

"Thank you. That's all then."

Moira sat, poured out the tea. "There's biscuits as well. It's good to have small pleasures in hard times."

"It's pleasures in hard times I need to speak with you about."

Moira passed the cup. "Is there something I can do to ease your heart? Sinann's and the children's?"

"There is." Deirdre took a small sip of the tea before setting the cup aside. "Moira, your mother was my dearest friend in this world, and so I sit here in her stead, and I speak to you as I would my own daughter."

"I'd have it no other way."

"When you spoke of this war that's upon us, you spoke of no choice. But there are other choices you've made. A woman's choices."

Understanding, Moira sat back. "I have."

"As queen, one who's claimed herself a warrior, one who's proven herself as one, you have the right, even the duty, to use any and all weapons that come to your hand to protect your people."

"I do, and I will."

"This Cian who comes here from another time and place. You believe the gods sent him."

"I know it. He fought by your own son. He saved my life. Would you sit here and look at me, and damn him as Tynan's mother damned him?"

"No." Deirdre took a careful breath. "In this matter of war, he is a weapon. By using him you may save yourself, my sons, all of us."

"You're mistaken," Moira said evenly. "He's not to be used like a sword. What he's done, and what he will do to cut out this blight, he does of his own will."

"A demon's will."

Moira's eyes chilled. "As you like."

"And you've taken this demon to your bed."

"I've taken Cian to my bed."

"How can you do this thing? Moira, Moira." She reached out her hands. "He's not human, yet you gave yourself to him. What good can come of it?"

"Much has already, for me."

Deirdre sat back a moment, pressed her fingers to her eyes. "Do you think the gods sent him to you for this?"

"I can't say. Did you ask yourself that question when you took my uncle?"

"How can you compare?" Deirdre snapped. "Have you no shame, no pride?"

"No shame, and considerable pride. I love him, and he loves me."

"How can a demon love?"

"How can a demon risk his life, time and again, to save humanity?"

"It's not his bravery I question, but your judgment. Do you think I've forgotten what it is to be young, to be stirred, to be foolish? But you're queen, and you have responsibility to your crown, your people."

"I live and breathe that responsibility, every moment, every day."

"And at night you bed a vampire."

Unable to sit any longer, Moira rose, moved to the window. The sun still shone, she thought, bright and gold. It sparkled on the grass, on the river, on the gossamer wings of dragons who flew lazy loops around Castle Geall.

"I don't ask you to understand. I demand your respect."

"Do you speak to me as my niece, or as the queen?"

She turned back, framed by the window and the sunlight. "The gods have deemed me both. You come to me out of concern, and that I accept. But you also come with condemnation, and that I don't. I trust Cian with my life. It's my right, my choice, to trust him with my body."

"And what of your people? What of those who question how their queen could take one of these creatures of darkness as lover?"

"Are all men good, Aunt? Are they all kind and good and strong? Are we as we're made, or how we choose to make ourselves thereafter? I'll say this about my people, about those I'll give my life fighting to defend. They have more important things to worry about, to think about, to talk about than what their queen does in the privacy of her bedchamber."

Deirdre got to her feet. "And when this war is over, will you continue this? Will you put this thing you love on the throne at your side?"

The sun still shone, Moira thought again, even when the heart goes bleak. "When this is over, if we live, he'll go back to his time and his place. I'll never see him again. If we lose, I'll give my life. If we win, I'll forfeit my heart. Don't speak to me of choices, of responsibilities."

"You'll forget him. When this is done, you'll forget him and this momentary madness."

"Look at me," Moira said quietly. "You know I won't."

"No." Deirdre's eyes swam with tears. "You won't. I'd spare you from this."

"I wouldn't. Not a moment of it. I've been more alive with him than I ever was before, or will be again. So no, not a moment of it."

They were all gathered in the parlor around the table and food when Moira came in. Glenna reached over to remove a cover from the plate at the head of the table.

"It should still be warm," she told Moira. "Don't waste it."

"I won't. We need to eat, to stay strong." But she stared at the food on her plate as if it were bitter medicine.

"So." Blair gave her a bright smile. "How's your day been so far?"

The laugh, however quick and humorless, eased some of the knots in Moira's stomach. "Crappy. That would be the word, wouldn't it?"

"Right down to the ground."

"Well." She made herself eat. "She's struck at us, as is her habit, to incite fear and carve away at morale and confidence. Some will believe what she had Sean tell us. That if we surrender, she'll leave us in peace."

"Lies are often more attractive than the truth," Glenna commented. "Time's running out either way."

"Aye. We, we six, will have to make preparation to leave the castle, head toward the battleground."

"Agreed." Hoyt nodded. "Before we do, we'll need to be certain the bases we've set up are still in our hands. If Tynan was killed, they may have taken that stronghold. We've only the word of a demon it was the child who killed him, and him alone."

"It was the child." Cian drank tea that was nearly half whiskey. "The wounds on the body," he explained. "They weren't made by a full-grown vampire. Still, it doesn't answer if the strongholds are still secured."

"Hoyt and I can look," Glenna said.

"I'll want you to, but looking isn't enough." Moira continued to eat. "We need to gather reports from those who survived."

"If they did."

She looked at Larkin and felt what he felt. The constant thrum of fear for Oran.

"If they did," she repeated.

"If she'd wiped out the base," Cian put in, "the messenger she sent would have bragged about it, and likely she'd have sent more bodies."

"Aye, I can see that. But to keep what she accomplished from happening again, we'll want to add reinforcements."

"You want us to go by dragon." Larkin nodded. "That's why you asked if they were ready to be ridden."

"As many as can be used for this. Those who must go on foot or horseback from here will, from today on, be watched over by riders in the air. If you, Larkin, and Blair could go this morning, take a small number with you. On dragon-back, you can travel to all the bases, transport more weapons, more men, see to the reports and what you think must be done when you see for yourself where we stand. You could be back before nightfall, or failing that, stay at one of the bases until the morning."

"You're cutting too many of us out by sending two," Cian interrupted. "And I should be the one to go."

"Hey." Blair wagged a piece of soda bread. "How come you get to have all the fun?"

"Practicalities. First, all but Glenna and I have seen some of the ground of or near the battlefield firsthand. It's time I got the lay of it. Second, with that bloody cloak, I can start the journey during the day, but I can travel more quickly and more safely than any of you at night. And being a vampire myself, I'll recognize signs of them quicker than even our resident demon hunter."

"He makes a good argument for it," Larkin pointed out.

"I've been planning to go, nose around a bit in any case. So this will kill all the birds with one stone. And the last of it, I think we can all agree, the mood here would settle if I wasn't around."

"She was out of line," Blair muttered.

Cian shrugged, knowing she spoke of Tynan's mother. "All a matter of perspective—and where you draw that line. Time's getting short, and one of us should be on the battleground, particularly at night when Lilith might be scouting around herself."

"You don't mean to come back," Moira said slowly.

"There's no point in it." Their eyes met, held, and said a great deal more than words. "One of the men can come back with your reports and so on. And I'd fill in the rest of it when all of you arrive."

"You've already decided this." Moira watched his face carefully. "I see. We're a circle here, equal links. For such a decision, I think we should all have a say. Hoyt?"

"I don't like any of us going off without the others, truth be told. But it needs to be done, and Cian makes the most sense of it. We can watch as we watched when Larkin went to the caves back in Ireland. If need be we can intervene." He looked at his wife. "Glenna?"

"Yes. Agreed. Larkin?"

"The same. With one change in it. I think you're wrong, Cian, to say we'd be cutting it too thin to send two out. I think no one goes on their own. I can get you there in dragon form. And," he continued before there were objections, "I'm more experienced with the dragons than you, should there be any trouble with them, or the enemy. So I'm saying we go together, you and I. Blair?"

"Damn it. Dragon-boy's right. You may move faster alone, Cian, but you're going to need a dragon wrangler to get there, especially if you're leading men."

"Yes, it's smarter." Glenna considered. "All around smarter. It gets my vote."

"And mine as well," Hoyt said. "Moira?"

"Then that's what we'll do." She got to her feet knowing she was sending the two men she loved most away from her. "The rest of us will finish the weapons, secure the castle and follow in two days."

"Big push." Blair considered, nodded. "We can do it."

"Then we will. Larkin, I'll leave it to you to pick the dragons for this, and to you and Cian to pick the men." Moira laid it out in her mind, the overview, the details. "I'll want Niall left back, if you will, to go at the end of it with the rest of us. I'll go now, see to the supplies you'll need."

When she'd done all she could, and hoping she was calm, Moira went to Cian's bedchamber. She knocked, then opened the door without waiting for his response. With the curtains drawn there was barely enough light to see, so she flicked her hand, her power toward a candle. The way the flame spurted warned her she wasn't as calm as she'd hoped.

He continued to pack what he wanted to take in a duffle.

"You said nothing of these plans to me."

"No."

"Were you going to leave in the night, with no word?"

"I don't know." He stopped, looked at her. There were a great many things he couldn't give her, or ask of her, he reflected. At least honesty was a quality they could share.

"Yes, at least initially. Then you came to my door one night, and my plans changed. Or, they were postponed."

"Postponed." She nodded slowly. "And when Samhain's come and gone, will you leave without a word?"

"Words would be useless, wouldn't they?"

"Not to me." There was panic rising up in her at the knowledge they were moving toward the end. How could she not have known that was waiting in her to push its way out and choke her? "Words would be precious to me. You want to leave. I can see it. You want to go."

"I should have gone before. If I'd been quicker, I'd have been out the door and gone before you came to me. You'd be better off for it. This . . . with me. It's no good for you."

"How dare you? How *dare* you speak to me like a child who wants too many sweets? I'm sick to death of being lectured on what I should think, feel, have, do. If you want to go, you'll go, but don't insult me."

"My going has nothing to do with what's between us. It's just something that has to be done. You agreed, and so did the rest."

"If I hadn't, they hadn't, you'd have gone anyway."

He watched her as he strapped on his sword. Pain was already slicing thin wounds in both of them, as he'd known it would from the moment he'd touched her. "Yes, but it's less complicated this way."

"Are you done with me then?"

"And if I am?"

"You'll be fighting on two fronts, you right bastard."

He laughed, couldn't help himself. It wasn't only pain between them, he realized. He'd do well to remember that. "Then it's lucky for me I'm not done with you. Moira, last night you knew you had to be the one to end what had once been a boy you'd known, you'd been fond of. I knew it, so I stopped myself from doing it, from sparing you from that. I know I have to go, and go without you for now. You know that, too."

"It doesn't make it easier. We may never be alone again, never be able to be with each other as we were again. I want more time—there hasn't been enough time, and I need more."

She moved to him, held him hard and tight. "We didn't have our night. It didn't last till morning."

"But the hours mattered, every minute of them."

"I'm greedy. And already fretting that you'll go while I stay."

Not just today, he thought. Both of them knew she didn't speak only of today. "Do women of Geall follow the tradition of sending their men off with a favor?"

"What would you have from me?"

"A lock of your hair." The sentiment of it surprised him, and embarrassed a little. But when she drew back, he could see his request had pleased her.

"You'll keep it with you? That part of me?"

"I would, if you'll spare it."

She touched her hair, then held up a hand. "Wait, wait. I have something. I'll have to get it." She heard the trumpet call of dragons. "Oh, they're ready for you. I'll bring it to you, outside. Don't leave. Promise me you'll wait until I come to say goodbye."

"I'll be there." This time, he thought as she rushed out.

Outside, in the shelter of shade, Cian studied the dragons Larkin had chosen, and the men they'd decided on together.

Then he frowned down at the ball of hardened mud Glenna held out to him. "Thanks, but I had quite enough at breakfast."

"Very funny. It's a bomb."

"Red, it's a ball of mud."

"Yes, a ball of earth—charmed earth, holding a ball of fire inside. If you drop it from the air." She used her hands waving them down as she made a whistling noise—then a puff of breath to simulate an explosion. "In theory," she added.

"In theory."

"I've tested it, but not from a dragon perch. At some point you could try it out for me."

Frowning, he turned it over in his hands. "Just drop it?"

"Right. Somewhere safe."

"And it's not likely to explode in my hands and turn me into a fireball?"

"It needs velocity and force. But it wouldn't hurt to be sure you had good altitude when it's bombs away." She rose on her toes, kissed him on both cheeks. "Be safe. We'll see you in a couple of days."

Still frowning, he secured the ball into one of the pockets of the weapon harness Blair had fashioned for Larkin.

"We'll be watching." Hoyt laid a hand on Cian's shoulder. "Try to stay out of trouble until I'm with you again. And you as well," he said to Larkin.

"I've already told him I'll kick his ass if he gets himself killed." Blair gripped Larkin's hair, pulled his head down for a hard kiss. She turned to Cian.

"We're not doing a group hug."

She grinned. "I'm with you on that. Stay away from pointy wooden objects."

"That's the plan." He looked over her head as Moira ran toward the stables.

"I'd hoped to be quicker," she said breathlessly. "You're ready then. Larkin. Be safe." She hugged him.

"And you." He gave her a last squeeze. "Mount your dragons!" he called out, and with a last flashing grin for Blair, changed.

"I have what you asked me for." Moira held out a silver locket while Blair harnessed Larkin. "My father gave it to my mother when I was born, so she could keep a lock of my hair in it. I left that one, and put in another."

And had added what magic she could.

Rising on her toes, she put the chain over his head. To make a point, to him, to any who watched, she took his face in her hands, and kissed him long and warm and tender.

"I'll have another of those waiting for you," she told him. "So don't do anything foolish."

He put on the cloak, lifting the hood and securing it. He mounted Larkin, looked into Moira's eyes.

"In two days," he said.

He rose up into the sky on the golden dragon. Others soared behind him, trumpeting.

As she watched, as those glints of color grew smaller with distance, Moira was struck with a sudden knowledge, a certainty that the six of them would not come back from the valley to Castle Geall as a circle.

Behind her, Glenna gestured to Hoyt, sending him away. She hooked an arm around Blair's waist, around Moira's. "All right, ladies, let's get busy packing and stacking so we can get you back together with your men."

Chapter 16

✦

He wished for rain. Or at the very least a thick layer of cooling clouds to smother the sun. The damn cloak was hot as the hell he was eventually bound for. He just wasn't used to feeling extremes in temperatures.

Being undead, Cian mused, tended to spoil a man.

Soaring on a dragon was a thrilling experience, no question. For the first thirty minutes or so. And another thirty could be spent admiring the green and pastoral countryside below.

But after an hour in a fucking wool sauna, it was just misery.

If he had Hoyt's patience and dignity, he supposed he would ride steely-eyed and straight-backed until dooms-day. Even with the intolerable heat melting the flesh from his bones. But then he and his twin had had some basic differences even before he'd become a vampire.

He could meditate, he supposed, but it seemed unwise to risk a self-induced trance. He had the sun beating over-head just waiting to fry him like bacon, and a magic bomb strapped on Larkin that for all he knew could burst into flame just for the fun of it.

Why exactly had he thought he had to do this idiotic thing?

Ah yes. Duty, honor, love, pride—all those emotional weights that dragged a man down into the drowning pool, however hard he struggled to keep his head above the surface. Well, there was no going back now. Not on the flight, not on the feelings crowding inside him.

My God, he loved her. Moira the studious, Moira the queen. The shy and the valiant, the canny and the quiet. It was stupid, destructive, hopeless to love her. And it was more real than anything he'd known in a thousand years.

He could feel the locket she'd put around his neck—another weight. She'd called him a bastard one minute, then had given him one of what he was certain was her most valued treasures the next.

Then again, she'd once aimed an arrow at his heart, then apologized with a simple sincerity and flushed mortification. It was probably at that moment when he'd fallen for her. Or at least tripped.

He continued to study the land as his mind wandered. Good farmland, he mused, with rich, loamy soil and gentle rises. Streams and rivers thick with fish running through forests that teemed with game. The mountains in the distance rich with minerals and marbles. Deep bogs for cutting turf for fuel.

She'd brought orange seeds through the Dance. Who would think of such a thing?

She'd need to plant them in the south. Did she know that? Foolish thought, the woman knew everything, or had a way of finding out.

Orange seeds and Yeats. And, because he'd seen it on the writing table in her sitting room, a roller ball pen.

So she'd grow her orange saplings in the hothouse, then plant them in the south of Geall. If they pollinated—and how could they refuse her?—she'd have an orange grove one day.

He'd like to see it, he realized. He'd like to see her orange blossoms bloom from the seeds she'd taken from his kitchen in Ireland.

He'd like to see her lovely eyes light with humor and appreciation as she poured a glass of the orange juice she'd become addicted to.

If Lilith had her day, there'd be no grove, no blossoms, no life here at all.

Already he could see some of the death, some of the destruction. What had been tidy cottages and little cabins were rubble of scorched rock and wood. Cattle and sheep continued to graze in the fields, but there were carcasses rotting in the sun under a black cloud of flies.

Cattle killed by deserters, he decided. Scavenging where and when they could.

They'd have to be hunted down and destroyed, every last one. If even one survived, it would feed and it would breed. The people of Geall and their queen would have to be cautious and vigilant long after Samhain.

He began to put his mind to that particular problem until, at last, Larkin began to circle.

"Thank all your gods," Cian murmured on the descent.

It was a neat and pretty farm, as farms went. Soldiers were spread out, training, posted at points for guards. Women were among them, working alongside the men. And the smoke that rose from the chimney carried a scent that told him there was stew in a pot, likely simmering throughout the day.

On the ground, hands were shading eyes as faces looked up, or were being raised in waves and salutes of welcome.

They were surrounded the minute Larkin landed. Cian dismounted, began to unload the supplies. He'd leave it to Larkin and the other men to answer questions, and ask them. Now, he needed shadow and shade.

We haven't had any trouble at all." Isleen spooned up stew Cian didn't want. But he thought it best to wait to dip into his supply of blood until he had privacy.

Larkin dove into his bowl the instant they were set down. "Thanks," he said with his mouth full. "It's fine stew."

"You're very welcome. I'm doing the cooking by and large, so I'm thinking our troop here is eating better than the others." She dimpled into a smile. "We've been keeping up with our training, every day, and locking up tight before sunset. We haven't seen hide nor hair of anyone since we arrived and sent the other troop on its way."

"It's good to know that." Larkin picked up the tankard she'd set beside his bowl. "Could you do me a favor then, Isleen darling? Would you fetch Eogan—Ceara's Eogan. We've some talking to do."

"Sure I'll do that right away. Oh, and you can bed down here, or upstairs if you'd rather."

"We'll be moving on to the next base after a bit, and leaving three of the men we brought behind here with you."

"Oh. I noticed you brought red-haired Malvin along." She said it casually, with just the hint of a laugh. "I wonder if he'd be one you'd leave behind with us."

Larkin grinned and spooned up more stew. "That wouldn't be a problem, not at all. Fetch Eogan now, won't you, sweetheart?"

"You've had a bit of that, have you?" Cian murmured.

"Had— No." Then his tawny eyes glinted with humor. "Well, a bit, but nothing substantial you could say."

"How do you want to handle this business?"

"Eogan's a sensible man, a solid one. He'd have heard of Tynan by now from those we brought with us. So, I'll answer the questions he'll have on that. I'd like it best if you'd go over the precautions and orders again with him. Then if he's nothing more to report than we've just heard from Isleen, we'll leave Malvin and two others here, and go on to the next. Aren't you hungry then?"

"As a matter of fact, but I'll wait."

"Ah." Larkin nodded his understanding. "You have what you need in that area?"

"I do. The horses and cows are safe."

"I saw the carcasses along the way. Not like an army had fed, but a few scavengers. Deserters, would you say?"

"It's exactly what I'd say."

"An advantage now," Larkin murmured, "with her losing troops here and there. A problem for later."

"It will be, yes."

"We'll think of something." Larkin looked over as the door opened. "Eogan. We've much to talk about, and little time."

There was little more at the next stronghold, but at the third, Lilith had left her mark.

Two of the outbuildings had been burned to rubble, and in the fields the crops had been torched. The men talked of a night of fire and smoke, and the screams of the cattle as they were slaughtered.

With Larkin, Cian stood and studied the scorched earth.

"It's as you said, you and Blair. She would lay waste to the farms and the homes."

"Stone and wood."

Larkin shook his head. "Livestock and crops. Sweat and blood. Hearth and home."

"All of which can be bred and grown, shed and built again. Your men withstood the siege, with no casualties. They fought, and held the ground—and took some of Lilith's forces to hell. Your glass is miraculously half full, Larkin."

"You'd be right, I know it. And I hope if she tries to drink what's left in it, it burns her guts black. We'll move on then."

There were fresh graves at the next base, burned earth and wounded men.

The sick dread in Larkin's belly eased, finally, when he saw his younger brother, Oran, limp out of the farmhouse. He strode to Oran quickly, and in the way of men gave him a hard punch in the arm, then a bear hug.

"Our mother will be pleased you're among the living. How bad are your wounds?"

"Scratches. How is it at home?"

"Busy. I've seen Phelan at one of the other camps, and he's safe and well."

"It's good to hear. Good to hear. But I have hard news, Larkin."

"We know of it." He laid a hand on Oran's shoulder. His brother had been little more than a boy when he'd marched away from home, Larkin thought. Now he was a man, with all the weight that went with it. "How many besides Tynan?"

"Three more. And another I fear won't make the night. Two others taken, dead or alive, I can't say. It was a child, Larkin. A demon child who killed Tynan."

"We'll go inside, and talk of it."

They used the kitchen with Cian sitting back from the window. He understood why Larkin listened to the whole account, though they knew or could imagine most of it. Oran had to speak it all, see it all again.

"I'd had the watch before his, and was still sleeping when I heard the alarm. It was already too late for Tynan, Larkin, already too late. He'd gone out, alone, thinking there was a child hurt and lost and afraid. It lured him, you see, some distance from the house. And though there were men posted, bows ready, when it turned and ripped at him, it was too late."

He wet his throat with ale. "Men rushed out. I think back, I think, I was second in command, and should have ordered them to hold. It was too late to save him, but how could we not try? And because we did, more were lost."

"He would have done the same for you, for anyone."

"They took his body." Oran's young face was alive with grief, and his eyes very old. "We searched. The next morning we searched, for him and the two others, but found only blood. We fear they've been changed."

"Not Tynan." Cian spoke now, waited for Oran's weary gaze to meet his. "We can't say about the other two, but

Tynan wasn't changed. His body was brought back to Castle Geal. He was given a full burial early this morning."

"I'll thank the gods for that, at least. But who brought the body?"

As Larkin gave the account, Oran's face hardened again.

"Young Sean. We couldn't save him in the ambush along the road. They came out of the ground like hellhounds. We lost good men that day, and Sean was lost as well. Is he at peace now?" He looked to Cian. "Now that what took him over is gone, is he at peace?"

"I don't have the answer."

"Well, I'll believe he is, just as Tynan is, and the others we've buried. He can't be held accountable by men or gods for what was done to him."

They double posted guards for the night, and at Cian's instructions small bladders were filled with blessed water. These would be hooked to arrows. With this, even a miss of the heart would cause considerable damage, and possible death.

In addition, more traps had been set. Men who couldn't sleep whiled away the time carving stakes.

"Do you think she'll send out a raiding party tonight?" Larkin asked Cian.

They sat in what had been a small parlor, and was now in use for weapon storage.

"To one of the other points, she may. Here? Little point in it, unless she's bored—or wants to exercise some of her troops. She's done what she had in mind to do at this base." Since they were alone, Cian drank blood from a pottery cup.

"And if you were her?"

"I'd send out small parties to distract and harass. Chipping away at enemy troops and morale at every base. The trouble with that is your men tend to stand firm, while we know some of hers desert. But your individual losses echo with you, where hers mean less than nothing."

He drank again. "But then I'm not her. Being me, I'd find satisfaction in seeking out a raiding party, taking it by surprise before it reached its objective. And killing the hell out of it."

"Isn't that peculiar," Larkin said with a grin. "Not being her, and not being you, the exact same thought had planted itself in my mind."

"Well then. What are we waiting for?"

They left Oran in charge of the base. Though there was considerable argument, discussion, debate, Larkin and Cian set out alone. One dragon and one vampire, Cian had reasoned, could travel swiftly, and undetected.

If they found a party and opted to land for hand-to-hand, Larkin's weapon harness was well-loaded. Cian swung a quiver over his back, loaded extra stakes in his sword belt.

"It'll be interesting to see how the idea of aerial warfare flies—as it were."

"Ready then?" Larkin changed, stood gold and sinuous as Cian strapped on the harness.

They'd agreed to keep it short and simple. They would fly in widening circles, looking for any sign of a party or a camp. If they spotted one, they'd strike—quick and clean.

The flight up toward a moon approaching its third quarter was exhilarating. The freedom of the night swept over Cian. He flew without cloak or coat, reveling in the cool and the dark.

Beneath him, Larkin soared, his dragon's wings barely a whisper on the air, and so thin Cian could see the glimmer of stars through them when they swept the air.

Clouds drifted, thin wisps that slid like gauze over stars, sailed like ghost ships over the waxing moon.

Far below, the first fingers of fog began their crawl over the ground.

If nothing else, the pleasure of the flight balanced out the smothering discomfort of the day's journey. As if he sensed it, Larkin aimed higher, rising in lazy loops. For one indulgent moment, Cian closed his eyes and just enjoyed.

Then he felt it, a stroke along the skin. Cold, seeking fingers that seemed to slide into him and swirl through his blood. And a whisper inside his head, a quiet siren's song that called to what he was beneath the form of a man.

And when he looked down, the savage ground of the battlefield spread below.

Its utter silence was a scream of violence. It burned into him like molten steel, brilliant and dark, deep and primal. The grass was wild sharp blades, the rocks rough death. Then even they would give way to black pits of chasms and caves where nothing dared to crawl.

Guarded by the mountains the damned ground waited for blood.

He had only to lean forward—such a short distance—and sink his teeth in the neck of the dragon to find the blood of a man. Human and rich, that gush of life, and a taste no other living thing could match. A flavor he'd denied himself for centuries. And why? To live among them, to survive wearing the mask of one of them?

They were beneath him, so much less—fleas on a dog. They were nothing but flesh and blood, created for him to hunt. The hunger gnawed in him, and the desire, the feral thrill of it pumped through him like a heartbeat.

The memory of the kill, of that first hot spurt of life gushing into his mouth, riding down his throat, was glorious.

Shaking like an addict in the throes of withdrawal, he fought it. He would not end it this way. He would *not* go back to being a prisoner of his own blood.

He was stronger than that. Had made himself more than that.

His belly cramped with need and nausea as he leaned toward Larkin. "Put down here. Stay in this form. Be ready to fly again, to leave me if you need. You'll know."

It dragged at him, that cursed ground, as they lowered toward it. It murmured and sang and promised. It lied.

The heat was in him like a fever as he leaped down. He would not, he swore, he would not turn himself and kill a friend as he'd once tried to kill his brother.

"It's this place. It's evil."

"I told you not to change forms. Don't touch me!"

"I feel it inside me." Larkin's voice was calm and even. "It must burn in you."

Cian turned, his eyes red, his skin slicked with sweat from his inner war. "Are you stupid?"

"No." But Larkin hadn't, and didn't now draw a weapon. "You're fighting it, and you'll beat it back. Whatever it is this place calls to in you, there's more. There's what Moira loves."

"You don't know the hunger of it." Deep in his throat a groan waited. It hummed in Cian's ears, and with it, he could hear the beat of Larkin's pulse. "I can smell you, the human."

"Do you smell fear?"

Shudders ran through him, hard enough he thought his bones might crack to pieces. His head was screaming, screaming, and still he couldn't block out the sound, the vicious temptation of that beating heart.

"No. But there could be. I could bring it into you. Fear sweetens it. God, God, what sick hand forged this place?"

His legs wouldn't hold him, so he lowered to the ground and struggled to tighten his slippery grip on his will. As he did, he closed his fingers around the locket she'd put around his neck.

The sickness ebbed, just a little, as if a cool hand had stroked a fevered brow. "She brings me light, that's what she brings to me. And I take it, and feel like a man. But I'm not. This is a hard reminder that I'm not."

"I see a man when I look at you."

"Well, you're wrong. But I won't drink tonight, not from you. Not from a human. It won't swallow me tonight. And it won't take me like this again, now that I know."

The red was fading from his eyes as he looked up at Larkin. "You were a fool not to draw a weapon."

In answer, Larkin lifted the cross from its chain.

"It might have been enough," Cian considered. He scrubbed his sweaty palms dry on the knees of his jeans. "Fortunately for us both, we don't have to test it."

"I'll take you back."

Cian looked at the hand Larkin offered. Humans, he thought, trusting and optimistic. He took it, pulled himself to his feet. "No, we'll go on. I need to hunt something."

He'd won the battle, Cian thought as they rose into the air again. But he wouldn't deny he was relieved to be heading away from that ground.

And he was darkly thrilled when he spotted the movements below.

A dozen troops, he noted, on foot and moving with that fluid swiftness of his kind. For all the speed, there was a precision to it, an order in the ranks that told him they were trained and seasoned soldiers.

He felt the shift of the dragon's body when Larkin saw them, and once again Cian leaned down.

"Why don't we try out Glenna's newest weapon? When they cross the next field, fly directly over the center of the squad. They've got archers, so once the shit hits, you'll have to go into evasive maneuvers."

As Larkin flew into position, Cian reached into the harness pocket and took out the ball.

How is a dragon like a plane? he considered, and put his centuries of experience as a pilot to use gauging airspeed, distance, velocity.

"Bomb's away," he murmured, and let the ball drop.

It smashed into the ground, causing the baffled squad to stop, draw weapons. Cian was about to chalk Glenna's experiment up to a loss when there was a towering burst of flame. Those closest to it were simply obliterated, while a few others caught fire.

Watching the panic, hearing the screams, Cian notched an arrow. Ducks in a barrel, he mused, and picked off what was left.

Once again Larkin touched down, and changed. "Well." He kicked carelessly at a pile of ash. "That was quick."

"I feel better for having killed something, but it was detached, impersonal. Human style. Doesn't have the same kick as a true hunt. Same reason we don't use guns or modern weaponry," Cian added. "There's just no thrill in it."

"I'm sorry for that, but the results of it suit me well enough. And Glenna's fireball worked a treat, didn't it now?"

Larkin began to gather the weapons scattered over the ground. As he bent down, an arrow whizzed over his back, and planted itself in Cian's hip.

"Oh well, bugger it! I must have missed one."

"Take the harness." Larkin tossed it at Cian. "And get on."

He flashed to dragon, and since he considered the arrow might slow him down a little on foot, Cian vaulted up. He caught the next arrow in the air before it could strike. Then Larkin was rising and diving and swerving.

"There, I see them. Second party entirely. Likely a hunting party looking for stray humans or whatever comes to hand."

He used the bow again, taking out a few as they scattered and took cover.

"It's just no fun this way," he decided. Drawing his sword, he leaped off Larkin and dropped thirty feet to the ground.

If dragons could curse, Larkin would have turned the air blue.

They came at Cian like the points of a triangle, two male, three female. He sliced the arrow coming at him in two with his sword, then spun the blade back to block the oncoming attack.

The dregs of what he'd felt on the battleground were in him, and he used them. That need for blood, if not to drink, then to shed it. He fought at first to wound, so he could smell it—the rich copper of it, and ride on it as he hacked and sliced.

The dragon's tail whipped down, slapped one of the females back as she lifted her bow again. Then its claws raked at the throat.

To amuse himself, Cian flipped back, shot a vicious kick into the face of an opponent. When it stumbled he took its head even as he yanked the arrow from his hip and plunged it into the heart of the one coming from his left.

He spun around, saw that Larkin had changed and was ramming a spent arrow in the heart of the last one.

"Is that it then?" Larkin said breathlessly. "Is that the last of them?"

"By my count."

"And you counted so well the last time." He rose, brushed himself off. "Bloody dust. Are you feeling more yourself now?"

"Top of the world, Ma." Cian rubbed absently at his wounded hip. Since it was pouring blood, he ripped off the sleeve of his shirt. "Give me a hand, will you? Quick field dressing."

"You want me to bandage your arse?"

"It's not my ass, you git."

"Close enough." But Larkin walked over to see to it. "Drop your drawers then, sweetheart."

Cian spared him a single dark look, but obliged.

"And what do you think Lilith's mood will be when not a one of her raiding or hunting parties comes back?"

"She'll be pissed." Cian craned his head to watch Larkin's work. "Royally."

"Makes a body feel good, doesn't it? You'll have a fine hole in your bum for a bit."

"Hip."

"Looks like your ass to me. And I'm hungry enough to eat a donkey, hide and all. Time we went back, had ourselves a meal and a tankard. There, you'll do. It was a good night's work," he added when Cian pulled his pants up again.

"Turned out that way. It could have gone otherwise back there at the valley, Larkin."

Philosophically, Larkin pulled up some clumps of grass to wipe most of Cian's blood from his hands. "I don't think that's the truth of it. I don't think it could have gone any way but what it did. Now if your ass isn't too sore, you'll help me gather up all these nice weapons to add to our supply."

"Leave my ass out of it."

Together they began to gather swords, bows, arrows. "I'm sure that portion of you will be fine again shortly. If not, Moira'll kiss it well for you when they arrive."

Cian looked over as Larkin whistled a tune and loaded swords in the harness. "You're a funny guy, Larkin. A damn funny guy."

In Geall, Moira walked away from the crystal to stand at the window with her arms folded. "Am I mistaken in it, or were they not told to go check the bases, take no risks?"

"They disobeyed," Blair agreed. "But you've got to admit it was a good fight. And that fire ball was excellent."

"The delay's a little concern." Glenna continued to watch as they flew back toward base. "I'll work on that. I'm a little more worried about the effect the battlefield had on Cian."

"He fought it off," Hoyt replied. "Whatever tried to take hold of him, he fought it off."

"He did, to his credit," Glenna agreed. "But it was hard won, Hoyt. It's something we have to think about. Maybe we can work a charm or spell that will help him block it."

"No." Moira spoke without turning. "He'll do it himself. He'll need to. Isn't it his will that makes him what he is?"

"I suppose you're right." Glenna studied Moira's rigid back. "Just as I suppose the two of them had to go out tonight, and do what they did."

"That may be. Are they back safe yet?"

"Coming in for touchdown," Blair told her. "And all's quiet on the western front. Well, eastern front, but that doesn't have the same literary ring."

"Quiet for the moment." Moira turned back. "I think it's safe to say they'll be tucked up for the night now, and it's unlikely there'll be another raid on the base. We should all get some sleep."

"Good idea." Glenna gathered up the crystal.

They said good night, went their separate ways. But none of them went to bed. Hoyt and Glenna went to the tower to work. Blair headed to the empty ballroom to train.

Moira went to the library and pulled out every book she could find on the lore and legend and history of the Valley of Silence.

She read and studied until the first light of dawn.

When she slept, curled in the window seat as she'd often done as a child, she dreamed of a great war between gods and demons. A battle that had raged for a century, and more. A war that had spilled the blood of both until it ran like an ocean.

And the ocean became a valley, and the valley became Silence.

Chapter 17

"Sinann, you should be in bed still."

With her hand resting on her belly, Sinann shook her head at Moira. "I couldn't let my father leave without seeing him off. Or you." Sinann looked around the court-yard where horses and dragons and men were preparing for the journey. "It will seem so empty now, with so few of us left inside the walls." She managed a smile as she watched her father hoist her son high in the air.

"We'll come back, and the noise will be deafening."

"Bring them back to me, Moira." The strain began to leak through now, through her eyes, her voice. "My hus-band, my father, my brothers, bring them back to me."

She took Sinann's arms. "I'll do everything in my power."

Sinann pressed Moira's hand to her belly. "There's life. Feel it? Tell Phelan you felt his child move."

"I will."

"I'll tend your seedlings, and keep a candle lit until you all come home again. Moira, how will we know? How will we know if you . . ."

"You'll know," Moira promised. "If the gods don't send a sign of our victory, then we will. I promise. Now go kiss your father, and I'll kiss all your other men for you when I see them."

Moira moved to her aunt, touched a hand to Deirdre's arm. "I've spoken with the men I can leave with you. My orders are clear, simple and to be followed exactly. The gate stays locked, and no one leaves the castle—day or night—until word comes that the battle is done. I count on you as the head of my family who remains here, to see these orders are followed. You are my regent until my return. Or in the event of my death—"

"Oh, Moira."

"In the event of my death, you will serve until the next rightful ruler is chosen." She pulled off a ring that had been her mother's, and pushed it into Deirdre's hand. "This is a sign of your authority, in my name."

"I'll honor your wishes, your orders and that name. I swear it to you. Moira." She gripped her niece's hands. "I'm sorry we quarreled."

"So am I."

Though her eyes were wet, Deirdre managed a tremulous smile. "Though we both part here believing we had the right of it."

"We do. I don't love you less because of it."

"My child." Deirdre held her close. "My sweet girl. Every prayer I know goes with you. Come back to us. Tell my sons they have my heart and my pride."

"Sorry." Blair touched Moira's shoulder. "Everything's ready."

"I'll say goodbye to you." Deirdre stepped forward to kiss Blair's cheeks. "And trust you'll keep my eldest out of trouble."

"Do my best."

"You'll need to. He's a handful." She opened her mouth to speak again, then took a steadying breath. "I was going to say be safe, but that's not what warriors want to hear. So I'm saying fight well."

"You can count on it."

Without pomp or pageantry, they mounted horses and dragons. Groups of children were gathered, clucked over by the women who remained behind. The old leaned on walking sticks, or the arms of the younger.

There were tears glimmering. While they might look through the mist of them to loved ones leaving them behind, Moira knew they looked to her as well.

Bring them back to me. How many had that single desperate wish in their hearts and minds? Not all would have that wish granted, but she would—as she'd sworn to Sinann—do her best.

And she wouldn't leave them or lead them with tears.

Moira signalled to Niall, who would lead the ground force. When he called for the gates to be raised, she lifted the sword of Geall high. And leading the last of the troops from Castle Geall, she shot an arc of fire into the pale morning sky.

The dragon riders arrived first to mobilize the troops. They would abandon the first base to begin the next leg of the march to the battlefield. Supplies and weapons were packed, and men were taken up on dragons, or onto horses when they arrived. Those who went on foot were flanked by riders—air and ground.

So they traveled across the land and the skies of Geall.

At the next stop they rested and watered their mounts.

"You'll have tea, my lady." Ceara joined Moira near a stream where dragons drank.

"What? Oh, thanks." Moira took the cup.

"I've never seen such a sight."

"No." Moira continued to watch the dragons, and wondered if any of them would see such a sight again. "You'll ride with your husband, Ceara."

"I will, my lady. We're near ready."

"Where is the cross you won, Ceara? The one you're wearing is copper."

"I . . ." Ceara lifted her hand to the copper cross. "I left it with my mother. Majesty, I wanted my children protected if . . ."

"Of course you did." She wrapped her fingers around Ceara's wrist and squeezed. "Of course." She turned as Blair strode toward them.

"Time to round them up. Mounts are rested and watered. Supplies and weapons are packed, except for what we're leaving behind with the squad that'll hold this base until tomorrow."

"The troops behind us should arrive well before sunset." Moira looked to the skies. "Do they have enough protection if there's a change in the weather. Natural or otherwise?"

"Lilith may have some snipers and scouts scattered this far west, but nothing the troops can't handle. We have to move on, Moira. Leap-frogging this way keeps soldiers from being exposed and vulnerable at night, but it takes time."

"And we've a schedule to keep," Moira agreed. "Give the order then, and we'll move on."

It was well past midday when the first of them arrived at their final destination. Below where she flew, men stopped and cheered. She saw Larkin come out of the house, lift his face. Then change into a dragon to fly up and join them.

And she saw the dark earth of fresh graves.

Larkin circled her with a quick, showy flourish, then paced himself to Blair's mount. Moira lost her breath when Blair stood on her dragon's back, then sprang off into the air. The cheers from below rose up like thunder as Blair landed on Larkin, and rode him down.

Like a festival, Moira thought, as other riders executed showy turns and dives. Perhaps they needed the show and the foolishness for these last few hours of daylight. Night would come soon enough.

She would have seen to her own mount as she had along the way, but Larkin plucked her off her feet, gave her a whirl and a kiss.

"That doesn't sweeten me up," she told him. "I've a bone to pick with you. You were to travel, gather reports and secure. Not go out looking for trouble."

"We do what we must when we must." He kissed her again. "And all's well, isn't it?"

"Is it?"

"It is. He is. Go inside. There are plenty here to see to the mounts. You've had a long journey. No trouble along the way, Blair says."

"No, none." She let him lead her inside.

There was a pot of stew simmering over the fire, and the scent of it, of men and mud filled the air. Maps were spread over a table where she imagined a family had once gathered. Hangings over the windows were homespun and cheerful, and the walls were clean and whitewashed.

Weapons stood at every door and window.

"You've a chamber upstairs if you want a bit of a rest."

"No, I'm fine. But in fact I could use a whiskey if there's any to be had."

"There is."

She could see by his face that Blair had come behind them.

"Mounts are being tended," Blair began. "Supplies and weapons unloaded. Hoyt's on it. What's the setup here?"

"We've troops bunking in the stables, the barn, the dovecote and the smokehouse as well as in here. There's a loft that's roomy enough, and we're using it as a kind of barracks."

He poured a whiskey as he spoke, cocked his head at Blair, but she shook hers.

"Sitting room here is serving as the main arsenal," he continued. "And we've weapons stockpiled in all the buildings. The men take shifts, day and night. Training continues daily. There were raids, as you know, but none since Cian and I arrived."

"Saw to that, didn't you?" Moira asked before she drank.

"We did, and gave Lilith a good boot in the arse. We lost

another man yesterday, one who was wounded in the raid that killed Tynan. He didn't die easy."

Moira looked down into her whiskey. "Are there more wounded?"

"Aye, but walking. There's a kind of parlor open to the kitchen, and we've been using that for tending those who need it."

"Glenna will have a look at that, and arrange it as she sees best. Well." She downed the rest of the whiskey. "We all know there's not enough room inside shelters for all the troops. Nearly a thousand here tonight, and half again that many who'll be here within the next two days."

"Then we'd better get busy making camp," Blair said.

There was some pride in it, Moira discovered, at seeing so many of her people—men and women, old and young—working together. Tents began to spread over the field while wood and turf was gathered for cook fires. Wagons of supplies were unloaded and stacked.

"You have your army," Glenna said from beside her.

"One day I hope crops will be planted here again instead of tents. There are so many. There never seemed so many before. Can you hold so many within a protective circle?"

Glenna's face tightened with sheer determination. "Lilith's pet dog managed to shield their entire base. I hope you're not suggesting Hoyt and I can't measure up."

"Wouldn't think of it."

"Damn big circle to cast," Glenna admitted. "And the sun's getting low, we'll have to get started. We could use you."

"I was hoping you could."

With them, Moira walked the field from end to end and, as Glenna had instructed, gathered blades of grass, small stones, bits of earth as she went. They met again in the center.

As word had passed that magic would be done, the troops fell silent. In the hush, Moira heard the first whispers of power.

They called on the guardians, east and west, north and

south. On Morrigan, their patron. She took up the chant with them as she'd been given it.

"In this place and in this hour, we call upon the ancient powers to hear our needs and grant our plea to shelter all in this company. Upon this grass, this earth, this stone, protection from harm bestow. Only life at its fullest may cross this ring, and none may enter with harm to bring. Within this circle that was cast no enemy nor his weapon may pass. Night or day, day or night shield earth and air within its light. Now our blood will seal this shield and circle it round this field."

As Hoyt and Glenna did, Moira cut her palm with an athame, then fisted it around the dirt, the grass, the stones she'd gathered.

It pumped and plunged through her, the heat—hers and theirs—and the wind they raised blew in widening circles, slapping at the tents, singing through the grass until it whipped around and around the edges of the field in a cyclone of light.

With Hoyt and Glenna, she threw down the blood-soaked earth, felt the shudder under her feet as three small flames bloomed and died. When they clasped hands, her body bowed back from the force of what joined them.

"Rise and circle," she shouted with them, "circle and close and bar this place from all our foes. Blood and fire here mix free, as we will, so mote it be."

Around the field red flames speared up. When the earth was scorched white in a perfect ring, the flames vanished in a thunderclap.

Moira's vision wavered, and the voices that spoke to her seemed to blur as well, as if the world were suddenly underwater.

When she came back to herself she was on her knees. Glenna was gripping her shoulders and saying her name.

"I'm all right. I'm all right. It was just . . . it was so much. Just need my breath back."

"Take your time. It was a powerful spell, only more so because we used blood."

Moira looked down at the slice on her hand. "Everything's a weapon," she stated. "As Blair says. Whatever it takes, as long as it works."

"I'd say it has," Hoyt said quietly.

Following his direction, Moira saw Cian standing outside the circle. Though the cloak protected him from the last rays of the sun, she could see his eyes, and the fury in them.

"Well then. We'll leave the men to finish setting up camp."

"Lean on me," Glenna told her. "You're white as a sheet."

"No, it won't do." Though her knees were still like pudding. "The men can't see me drooping now. I'm just a bit off in the stomach is all."

As she crossed the field, Cian turned on his heel and strode back to the house.

He was waiting inside, and something of his mood must have translated as he was alone.

"Are you trying to lay her out before Lilith gets the chance?" he demanded. "What are you thinking, dragging her into magicks like that, strong enough to brew up your own personal hurricane."

"We needed her," Hoyt said simply. "It isn't an easy matter to throw a net over an area so large that holds so many. And as it stopped you on the edge, the spell holds."

It hadn't just stopped him, but had shot jolts of electricity through him. He was surprised his hair wasn't standing on end. "She's not strong enough to—"

"Don't tell me what I'm not strong enough to do. I've done what was needed. And isn't that the same you'd say to me if I dared question your reckless journey to the valley? Both are done now, and we're able to stand here and argue about it, so I'd say both are well done. I'm told I have a chamber upstairs. Does anyone know where it might be?"

"First door, left," Cian snapped.

When she walked, haughtily, he thought, up the stairs, he cursed. Then followed her.

She sat in the chair by the fire that had yet to be lit, with her head between her knees.

"My head's light, and it doesn't need you bringing a scold down on it. I'll be myself again in a moment."

"You seem yourself to me." He poured water into a cup, held it down so she could see it. "Drink this. You're white as a corpse. I've made corpses with more color than you."

"A lovely thing to say."

"Truth is rarely pretty."

She sat back in the chair, studying him as she drank the water. "You're angry, and that's just fine and good, as I'm angry right with you. You knew I was here, but you didn't come down."

"No, I didn't come down."

"You're a great fool, is what you are. Thinking you'd ease back from me, that I'd let you. We've only days left before we end this thing, so you go ahead and take steps back from me. I'll just take them toward you until your back's in the corner. I've not only learned to fight, I've learned not to fight clean."

She gave a little shiver. "It's cold. I've nothing left after that spell to get the fire lit."

He moved toward the hearth, and before he bent down for the tinderbox, she took his hand. And she pressed it against her cheek.

It broke him, a snap like glass. He lifted her out of the chair, holding her off the floor while his mouth plundered hers. She simply wrapped herself around him, wantonly, arms and legs.

"Aye, that's better," she said breathlessly. "Much warmer now. The hours seemed endless since I watched you go. So little time, so little, for eternity."

"Look at me. Yes, there's that face." He held her close again so her head rested on his shoulder.

"Did you miss it, my face?"

"I did. You don't have to fight dirty when you've already carved yourself inside me."

"Easier to be angry with each other. It hurts less." She squeezed her eyes tight for a moment, then eased back when he set her on her feet. "I brought the vielle. I thought you might like to have it, to play it. We should have music, like we should have light and laughter, and all the things that remind us what we're ready to die for."

She walked to the window. "The sun's setting. Will you go back to the battlefield tonight?" She glanced around when he didn't speak. "We saw you go with Larkin two nights ago, and saw you go alone last night."

"Each time I go, I'm a little stronger. I won't be any good to you or myself if what's soaked into that ground turns me."

"You're right on that, and tonight I'll be going with you. You can waste time arguing, Cian," she said as he began to. "But I'll be going. Geall is mine, after all, and every inch of its ground, whatever is under it. I haven't been on the edges of that place since my childhood, except in my dreams of it. I need to see it, and at night, as it will be on Samhain. So I'll be going with you, or I'll be going alone."

B ut I want to go! I want to. Please, please, please!" Lilith wondered if her head could actually explode from the boy's incessant whining and wheedling. "Davey, I said no. It's too close to Samhain, and much too dangerous for you to leave the house."

"I'm a soldier." His little face went sharp and vicious. "Lucius said so. I have a sword."

He unsheathed the small blade she'd had made for him—to her current regret—after his field kill. "It's just a hunting party," she began.

"I want to hunt. I want to fight!" Davey slashed at the air with his sword. "I want to *kill*."

"Yes, yes, yes." Lilith waved him away. "And you will, to your heart's content. *After* Samhain. Not another word!"

She snapped the order out while a tinge of red smeared the whites of her eyes. "I've had enough from you for one day. You're too young and too small. And that's the end of it. Now go to your room and play with that damned cat you wanted so much."

His eyes gleamed red, and his lips peeled back in a snarl that stripped away even the mask of human innocence. "I'm not too small. I hate the cat. And I hate you." He stormed off, his little legs pumping in his tantrum. He swung his sword wildly as he went, slicing through the torso of a human servant who wasn't quick enough to leap aside.

"Damnation! Look at that mess." Lilith threw up her hands at the blood spatter on the walls. "That boy's driving me mad."

"Needs a good swat, if you ask me."

Face livid now, Lilith rounded on Lora. "Shut your mouth! Don't tell me what he needs. I'm his mother."

"Bien sûr. Don't bite at me because he's being a brat." Sulking, Lora slumped into a chair. Her face was nearly healed now, but the scars that remained burned into her like poison. "Simple to see where he gets his bitchy attitude."

One of Lilith's hands curled, the red-tipped nails like talons. "Maybe you're the one who needs a good swat."

Knowing Lilith could do worse than a swat in her current mood, Lora shrugged. "I wasn't the one who hammered at you the last hour, was I? I backed you up with Davey, and now you're taking it out on me. Maybe we're all on edge, but you and I should stick together."

"You're right, you're right." Lilith dragged her hands through her hair. "He actually gave me a headache. Imagine."

"He's just, how do they say it? Acting out. He's so proud of himself for that kill in the field."

"I can't let him go out."

"No, no." Lora waved a hand. "You did absolutely right. We've lost a hunting party and a raiding party, and it's no place for Davey out there. I still say you should've given him a good slap for talking back to you."

"He may get one yet. Have someone clean that up." She gestured vaguely toward the body of the servant. "Then make sure the hunting party gets on its way. Maybe they'll be luckier tonight and track down the odd human. The troops are tired of sheep's blood.

"Oh, one more thing," she said as Lora started out. "I want a little something to eat—to calm myself down. Do we have any children left?"

"I'll check."

"Something small in any case. I don't have much of an appetite tonight. Have it sent up to my room. I need some quiet."

Alone, she paced the room as if it were a cage. Her nerves were stretched, she could admit that. So much on her mind, so many details, so many responsibilities with it all coming to the end of the circle at last.

The loss of troops was infuriating and worrisome. Deserters had been a problem, but she sent out scavengers nightly to hunt them down and destroy them. It simply wasn't possible two full squads had deserted.

More human traps? she wondered. They were costing her dearly—and would cost the humans a great deal more when she was done.

No one understood the pressure she was under, the weight of her responsibility. She had worlds to decimate. Her destiny was pressing down on her and she was surrounded by fools and incompetents.

Now her own sweet Davey, her own darling boy, was behaving like a snarling, spitting brat. He'd actually sassed her, something she took from no one. She wasn't certain if she should be proud or furious.

Still, she thought, he'd looked so cute and fierce waving that miniature sword. And hadn't he nearly cut that stupid servant in two, then stomped right out, almost swaggered, without a backward glance?

It was annoying, of course, but how could she not be a little proud?

She walked to the door, stepped out so she could feel the night slide over her, into her. He felt trapped in this house, poor Davey. So did she. But soon . . .

Of course, of course, what a terrible mother she was! She'd arrange a hunt right here, on the shielded grounds. Just the two of them. It would perk up her appetite, her spirits. And Davey would be thrilled.

Pleased with the idea, she went back in, and stepping over the bleeding body, went upstairs.

"Davey. Where's my bad little boy? I have a surprise for you."

She opened the door of his room. The smell came first. There was a considerable amount of blood, on the floor, on the walls, on the bed covers she'd had made for him of royal blue silk.

Pieces of the cat were strewn everywhere. It had been, she recalled, a very large cat.

She sighed, then felt a laugh bubbling up. What a temper her little darling had.

"Davey, you naughty boy. Come out from wherever you're hiding, or I might change my mind about the surprise." She rolled her eyes. Being a mother was such work. "I'm not angry, my sweetheart. I've just had so much on my mind, and I forgot you and I need to have some fun."

She searched the room as she spoke, then frowned when she didn't find him. There were little pricks of concern as she stepped again. Lora dragged a woman behind her by a neck shackle.

"We're out of children, but this one's small."

"No, no, not now. I can't find Davey."

"Not in his room." Lora peeked in. "Ah, creative. He's hiding somewhere because you're angry with him."

"I have something . . ." Lilith pressed a hand to her belly. "Something tight inside me. I want him found. Quickly."

They called out a search, scoured the manor house, the

outbuilding, the fields within the protected area. The tightness in Lilith's belly became strangling knots when they discovered his pony missing.

"He's run away. He's run off. Oh, why didn't I make certain he was in his room? I have to find him."

"Wait. Wait," Lora insisted and grabbed Lilith hard. "You can't risk going outside the safety area."

"He's mine. I have to find him."

"We will. We will. We'll send our best trackers. We'll use Midir. I'll go myself."

"No." Struggling for calm, Lilith closed her eyes. "I can't risk you. Lucius. Find Lucius, and have him come to me in Midir's lair. Hurry."

She cooled her blood and her mind. To rule took heat, she knew, but it also took ice. It was ice she needed to hold strong until the prince was safe again.

"I depend on you, Lucius."

"My lady, I'll find him. I give you my word, and my word that I would give my life to see him safely home."

"I know it." She laid her hand on his shoulder. "There's no one I trust more. Bring him back to me, and anything you ask of me is yours."

She whirled on Midir. "Find him! Find the prince in the glass."

"I am searching."

On the wall was a large oval of glass. It reflected the wizard in his dark robes, the room where he worked his dark magicks, and none of the three vampires who watched him.

Smoke slithered over the glass, swirled, and clawed its way to the edges. Through the haze of it, night began to bloom. And in the night came the shadow of a boy on a pony.

"Oh there, there he is." Crying out, Lilith gripped Lora's hand. "Look how well he rides, how straight in the saddle. Where is he? Where in this cursed land is the prince?"

"He's behind the hunting party," Lucius told her as he studied the vision in the glass. "And moving toward the battleground. I know that land, my lady."

"Hurry then, hurry. Willful brat," she muttered. "I'll take your advice this time, Lora. When he's back he'll have a good hiding. Keep him in that glass, Midir. Can you send me to him, the illusion of me?"

"You ask for many magicks at once, Majesty." Robes swirling, he moved to his cauldron and, letting his hands flow through the air over it, brought up a pale green smoke.

"I'll need more blood," he told her.

"Human, I suppose."

His eyes glittered. "It would be best, but I can make do with the blood of a lamb or young goat."

"This is the prince," she said coldly. "We don't make do. Lora, have the one I was going to have brought in. Midir can have it."

In the dark, Davey rode quickly. He felt strong and fierce and fine. He would show them, show them all that he was the greatest warrior ever made. The Prince of Blood, he thought with a glinting smile. He'd make everyone call him that. Even his mother.

She'd said he was small, but he *wasn't*.

He'd thought to trail behind the hunting party, then move in among them and order them to let him take the lead. None would dare question the Prince of Blood. And he would have the first kill.

But something was pulling him away from them, from the scent of his own kind. Something strong and tempting. He didn't need to stay with a hunting party, trail along after them like a baby. They were all less than he was.

He wanted to follow the music that was humming in his blood, and the smell of ancient death.

He rode slowly now, and with excitement bubbling inside him. There was something wonderful out in the dark. Something wonderful and his.

In the moonlight he saw the battlefield, and the beauty of it made him shake as he did when his mother let him put himself into her and ride as if she were a pony.

While it burned through him he saw figures on the high ground. Two humans, he thought, and a dragon.

He would have them all, slaughter them, drain them, and take their heads to drop at his mother's feet.

No one would ever call him small again.

Chapter 18

There was a hard place in the middle of Moira's chest, like a fist poised to strike. Breathing around it was an effort, but she stood as Cian did, at the edge of Silence.

"What do you feel?" she asked him.

"Pulled. You're not to touch me."

"Pulled how?"

"Chains on my feet, around my throat, pulled in opposite directions."

"Pain."

"Yes, but it's mixed with fascination. And thirst. I can smell the blood in the ground. It's thick and it's rich. I can hear your heartbeat, taste your scent."

Yet his eyes were Cian's eyes, she thought. They didn't burn red as they had the night he'd come here with Larkin. "They'll be stronger here than on other ground."

He looked at her then, realizing he should have known she would understand that. "They'll be stronger here. There'll be more of them than there are of you. Driven by what's bred in this place, by Lilith's power over them, death won't mean to them what it does to you. They'll come and they'll come without thought of their own survival."

"You think we'll lose. We'll die here, every one of us."

Truth, he thought, would shield her better than platitudes. "I think the chances of beating this diminish."

"You may be right. I'll tell you what I know of this place. What I've read, and what I think is the truth of it."

She looked out again, across the pitted land called *Ciunas*. "Long, long ago, before the worlds had separated, and were one instead of many, there were only gods and demons. Man had yet to come between to fight either, to tempt either. Both were strong and fierce and greedy, both wanted dominion. But still, the gods, however cruel, didn't hunt and kill their own kind, didn't hunt and kill demons for sport or food."

"So had the margin of good against evil?"

"There has to be a line, even if it's only that. There was war. Eons of it, all leading to this place. This was their last battle. The bloodiest, the most vicious, and most fruitless, I think. There was no victory. Only an ocean of blood that rose here, formed this harsh valley, and in time ebbed away, so that blood soaked into the earth, deep and deep."

"Why here? Why in Geall?"

"I think when the gods made Geall, deemed it would live centuries in peace, in prosperity, this valley was the price. The balance."

"Now payment's due?"

"It's always been coming to this, Cian. Now the gods charge the humans to fight the battle with this demon that began as human. Vampire against what is its source and its prey. It balances here, or it all falls. But Lilith doesn't understand what may happen if she wins this."

"We'll burn out. My kind." He nodded, having come to the same conclusion himself. "In chaos nothing thrives."

Moira said nothing for a moment. "You're calmer now, because you're thinking."

He let out a half laugh. "You're right. Still, it's the last place in this world or any I'd want to spread out for a picnic."

"We'll have a moonlight one, after Samhain. There's a place that's a favorite of mine and Larkin's. It's—"

Though he'd told her not to touch him, he gripped her wrist now. "Ssh. Something . . ."

Saying nothing, Moira reached into the quiver on her back for an arrow.

In the shadows, Davey grinned and drew his treasured sword. Now, he would fight the way a prince was supposed to fight. He'd slice and thrust and bite.

And drink, and drink, and drink.

He leaned low over the saddle, preparing to loose a war cry. And Lilith appeared before him.

"Davey! You turn that pony around this minute and come home."

The fierceness on his face turned into a childish pout. "I'm hunting!"

"You'll hunt when and where I tell you. I don't have time for this nonsense, this worry. I have a war to wage."

Now his face tightened into stubborn lines, and his eyes gleamed against the dark. "I'm going to fight. I'm going to kill the humans, then you won't treat me like a baby."

"I made you, and I can *un*make you. You'll do exactly what I . . . what humans?"

He gestured with his sword. As she turned, and she saw, true fear bloomed in Lilith's belly. Uselessly she grabbed for the bridle, but her hand passed through the pony's neck.

"Listen to me, Davey. Only one of them is human. The male is Cian. He's very powerful, very strong, very old. You have to run. Make this pony run as fast as it can. You're not meant to be here. We're not meant to be here now."

"I'm hungry." His eyes were turning, and his tongue flicked out over fang and lip. "I want to kill the old one. I want to drink the female. They're mine, they're mine. I'm the Prince of Blood!"

"Davey, no!"

But with a violent kick of his heels, he sent the pony racing forward.

It was all so quick, Moira thought. Flashing moments. The silver snick of Cian's sword leaving its scabbard, the shift of his body in front of hers like a shield. The rider flew out of the dark, and her arrow was notched and ready.

Then she saw it was a child, a little boy on a sturdy roan pony. Her heart stumbled; her body jerked. And her arrow went wide of the mark.

The child was screaming, howling, snarling. A wolf cub on the hunt.

Lilith flew behind the pony, an emerald and gold she-demon, streaking through the air, hands curled into claws, fangs gleaming.

Moira's second arrow spiked through her heart and soared into the air.

"She's not real!" Cian shouted. "But he is. Take the dragon and go."

Even as she reached for a third arrow, Cian shoved her aside, leaping over the charging pony.

A little boy, Moira thought. A little boy with eyes burning red and fangs spearing. It waved a shortened sword, as it dragged on the reins. Lilith's screams were like lances of ice through Moira's brain as the boy tumbled off the pony and fell hard on the rocky ground.

It bled, Moira saw, where the rocks struck and scraped. It cried, as a boy would when he had a fall.

Her breath caught in denial as Cian advanced with the illusion of Lilith clawing at him with intangible hands. Sick in heart and mind, Moira lowered her bow.

The second rider came out of the moon-struck dark like fury. Not a boy now, but a man armed for battle, his broadsword already cleaving the air.

Cian pivoted, and met the charge.

Swords clashed and crashed, the deadly music of them ringing over the valley. Cian leaped, dismounting the rider with a vicious kick to the throat.

With no clear shot, Moira tossed down her bow and

drew her sword. Before she could rush to fight with Cian, the boy gained his hands and knees. He lifted his head, stared at her with those gleaming eyes.

It growled.

"Don't." Moira backed up a step as Davey crouched to spring. "I don't want to hurt you."

"I'll rip out your throat." His lips peeled back as he circled her. "And drink and drink. You should run. I like it best when they try to run."

"I won't run. But you should."

"Davey, run! Run now!"

He whipped his head toward Lilith and snarled like a rabid dog. "I want to play! Hide-and-seek. Tag, you're it!"

"I won't play." Moira circled with him, trying to work him back with thrusts of the sword.

He'd lost his sword in the fall, but Moira told herself she would use hers if he sprang at her. He wasn't unarmed; no vampire ever was. And those fangs glinted, sharp and keen.

She spun, kicking out, aiming low to hit him in the belly and drive him back.

Lilith's form crouched over him, hissing. "I'll kill you for that. I'll peel the skin from your bones before I do. Lucius!"

Lucius hacked out at Cian. There was blood on them both, blood in their eyes. They leaped at each other, meeting violently in midair.

"Run, Davey!" Lucius shouted. "Run!"

Davey hesitated, and something came over his face. Moira thought, for an instant, she could see the child the demon had swallowed. The fear, the innocence, the confusion.

He ran as a child runs, limping on his scraped knees. And gaining speed, gaining that eerie grace as he rushed toward the slashing swords.

Dropping her own sword, Moira grabbed up her bow. A moment too late, as Davey leaped onto Cian's back, struck with fang and fist. If she shot now, the arrow could go through the boy, and into Cian.

A fingersnap. More flashes of time. The boy tumbled

through the air, propelled by a savage blow. He knuckled his hands over his burning eyes and cried for his mother.

Again, Lilith called out. "Lucius, the prince! Help the prince."

His loyalty, his years of service cost him. As Lucius turned his head a fraction toward Lilith, Cian took it with one singing strike of his sword.

Davey scrambled to his feet, wild panic on his face now.

"Take him," Cian called out as Davey began to run. "Take the shot."

Now those flashes of time slowed down. Wild screams, wild weeping, echoing through the dragging air. The figure of a child running on bleeding, tired legs. Lilith, her face alive with fear and horror, standing between the child and Moira, her arms spread in defense or plea.

Moira looked into Lilith's eyes as her own blurred. Then with a tear in her heart, she blinked them clear, and sent the arrow flying.

The shriek was horribly human as the arrow passed through Lilith. That shriek went on and on and on as the arrow continued, straight and true into the heart of what had once been a little boy who'd played in the warm surf with his father.

Then Moira was standing alone with Cian on the edge of a valley that hummed with the hunger for more blood.

Cian bent, picked up the swords. "We need to go, now. She'll have already sent others."

"She loved him." Moira's voice sounded strange and thin to her own ears. "She loved the child."

"Love isn't exclusive to humans. We need to go."

Her mind dull, she tried to focus on Cian. "You're hurt."

"And I don't relish leaving any more blood here. Get mounted."

She nodded, taking her own weapons before pulling herself onto the dragon. "She'd killed him," Moira murmured as Cian vaulted on behind her. "But she loved him."

She said nothing more as they flew away from the battlefield.

* * *

Glenna took over the moment they got back, herding them both into the parlor for first aid.

"I'm not hurt," Moira insisted, but sat heavily. "I wasn't touched."

"Just sit." Glenna got to work on Cian's buttons. "Off with your shirt, handsome, so I can see the damage."

"Some cuts, a few punctures." He bit back a wince as he shrugged out of the shirt. "He was good with a sword, quick on his feet."

"I'd say you were better and quicker." Blair handed him a cup of whiskey. "That's a nasty bite on the back of your shoulder, pal. What? This guy fought like a girl?"

"It was the boy," Moira said before Cian could answer. She shook her head at the whiskey Blair offered. "Lilith's boy, the one she called Davey. He came at us, riding a little pony, waving a sword no bigger than a toy."

"He wasn't a boy," Cian said flatly.

"I know what he was." Moira simply closed her eyes.

"A kiddie vamp did all this?" Blair demanded.

"No." With some annoyance, Cian scowled at her. "What do you take me for? The soldier—trained and seasoned—Lilith must have sent after the whelp did this, except for the shagging bite."

"How do I treat it?" Glenna asked him. "A vampire bite on a vampire?"

"Like any other wound. You can sure as hell hold the holy water. It'll heal quick enough, like the others."

"It was a foolish risk going out there," Hoyt said.

"It was necessary," Cian shot back. "For me. And our happy news is whatever holds that place doesn't stop me from dusting another vampire. Moira." Cian waited until she opened her eyes and met his. "It had to be done. There might have been others coming behind the one she called Lucius. If I'd gone after the young one, it would have taken time and left you alone. He was no less your enemy because of his size."

"I know what he was," she said again. "He was what killed Tynan, what tried to kill Larkin. What would have killed us both tonight if it had gone another way. Still, I saw his face—under what it was, I saw his face. It was young and sweet. I saw Lilith's face, and it was the face of a mother, terrified for her child. I put the arrow into it as it ran away, crying for its mother. I know, whatever comes now, nothing I ever do will be worse than that. And I know I can live with it."

She let out a shuddering breath. "I think I'll be having that whiskey now after all. I'll take it up with me if you don't mind. I'm tired."

Cian waited until Moira left the room. "Lilith will try for her. She may not be able to get physically into the house, but in dreams, or illusions."

Hoyt rose. "I'll see to it, make certain the protection we have is strong enough."

"She won't want me now," Larkin murmured. "Or any of us," he added with a quiet look for Cian. "She'll need to curl up with it for a while. And she will live with it, just as she said."

He sat now, across from Cian. "You said the one you fought was called Lucius?"

"That's right."

"That's the one I tangled with, along with the boy, in the caves. I'd say you've just taken out one of Lilith's top men. A kind of general. This would be a very hard night for Lilith, thanks to you and Moira."

"She'll come harder now because of it. We've destroyed or damaged those closest to her, and she'll come at us like bloody vengeance."

"Let her come," Blair said.

She would have come, then and there, so mad was her fury, her rage, her grief. It took six guards, and Midir's magic to hold her down while Lora dosed her with drugged blood.

"I'll kill you all! Every one of you for this. Take your hands off me before I cut them off and feed them to the wolves."

"Hold her!" Lora ordered and forced more blood down Lilith's throat. "You can't go to their base tonight. You can't go with the army and attack. Everything you've worked and planned for would be lost."

"Everything is lost. She put an arrow in him." She whipped her head, flashed fangs and sank them into one of the restraining hands. Her own screams mixed with the howls of the wounded.

"Release her, and I'll take more than your hand," Lora warned. "There's nothing to be done for him, my love, my darling."

"It's a dream. Just a dream." Bloody tears ran down Lilith's face. "He can't be gone."

"There now, there." Signalling the others back, Lora gathered Lilith into her arms. "Leave us. All of you. Get out!"

She sat on the floor, rocking Lilith, cooing to her while their tears mixed together.

"He was my precious," Lilith wept.

"I know. I know, and mine."

"I want that pony found. I want it slaughtered."

"It will be. There now."

"He only wanted to play." Seeking comfort, she nuzzled at Lora's shoulder. "In a few days, I could have given him everything. And now . . . I'll peel the skin from her bones, pour her blood into a silver tub. I'll bathe in it, Lora. I swear it."

"We'll bathe together, while we drink from that turncoat who took Lucius."

"Lucius, Lucius." Tears ran faster. "He gave his eternity trying to save our Davey. We'll build a statue of him, of both of them. We'll grind the bones of humans and build it from their dust."

"They'd be so pleased. Come with me now. You need to rest."

"I feel so weak, so tired." With Lora's help she gained her feet. "Have whatever humans we have left in stock executed and drained. No, no, tortured and drained. Slowly. I want to hear their screams in my sleep."

Moira didn't dream. She simply dropped into a void and floated there. She had Hoyt to thank for the hours of peace, she thought as she began to wake. Hours of peace where she hadn't seen a child's face blurred together with that of a monster.

Now there was work to be done. The months of preparation had whittled down to days that could be counted in hours. While the vampire queen mourned, the queen of Geall would do whatever needed to be done next.

She stirred, sat up. And saw Cian sitting in the chair near the simmering fire.

"It's still shy of dawn," he said. "You could use more sleep."

"I've had enough. How long have you watched over me?"

"I don't count the time." She'd slept like the dead, he thought now. He hadn't counted the time, but he had counted her heartbeats.

"Your wounds?"

"Healing."

"You'd have had fewer of them, but I was weak. I won't be again."

"I told you to go. Didn't you trust me to deal with two of them, especially when one was half my size? Less."

She leaned back. "Clever of you to try to turn this into a matter of my trust in your fighting skills instead of my lack of spine."

"If you'd had less spine and more sense, you'd have gone when I told you to."

"Bollocks. The time for running is well done, and I would never have left you. I love you. I should have taken him with the sword, quickly. Instead, I wavered, and tried to find a way to drive him off so I wouldn't be the one to end him. That moment of weakness could have cost us both. Believe me when I tell you it's burned out of me."

"And the misplaced guilt that goes with it?"

"May take a bit longer, but it won't get in the way. We have only two days left. Two days." She looked toward the window. "It's quiet. This time just before dawn is quiet. She killed a young boy, and came to love what she'd made of it."

"Yes. It doesn't make either of them less of a monster."

"Two days," she said again, almost in a whisper. Something inside her was already dying. "You'll go when this is done, if we win, if we don't, you'll go back through the Dance. I'll never see you again, or touch you, or wake to find you've watched over me in the dark."

"I'll go," was all he said.

"Will you come, hold me now, before the sun comes?"

He rose, went to her. Sitting beside her, he drew her against him so her head lay on his shoulder.

"Tell me you love me."

"As I've loved nothing else." He met her lips when she turned them to his.

"Touch me. Taste me." She shifted so she lay over him, trembling body, seeking lips. "Take from me."

What choice did he have? She was surrounding him, saturating his senses, stoking his needs till they burned. Offering as much as demanding as she pressed his lips to her breast.

"Take more. More and more."

Her mouth was hot and desperate as she pulled away clothes, her teeth nipping at his jaw in sharp, quick bites while her breath shuddered.

She was alive now, burning and alive, with everything inside her rising, aching. How could she step back from this? The love, the heat, the *life*.

If she was destined to die in battle, then she'd accept it. But how could she live—day after day, night after night— without her heart?

She straddled him, taking him in, hips whipping as she fought to feel more, to take more. To know more.

Her eyes gleamed, almost a madness, and stayed locked on his. Then she leaned to him, and her hair fell, curtaining them both, trapping him in its texture and fragrance.

"Love me."

"I do."

His fingers dug into her hips as she drove him toward the jagged edge of peak.

"Touch me, taste me, take me." On a cry, she lowered her throat to his lips, pressed that soft flesh with its pounding blood against him. "Change me."

It was beyond him to stop the flood, it gushed through him, hot, strong, turbulent—and through her, he knew, as her body bucked and quaked. And shuddering, she rubbed that throbbing pulse against his mouth.

"Make me what you are. Give me forever with you."

"Stop." As his body shook, he shoved her away with a force strong enough to nearly send her to the floor. "You'd use what I am against me?"

"Yes." Her chest burned with the tears that streamed through her voice. "Anything, anyone. Why should we find this only to lose it? Two days, only two days left. I want more."

"There's no more to have."

"There could be. Lilith loved what she'd made, I saw it. You love me now, and I love you. We wouldn't stop with the change."

"You know nothing of it."

"I do." She grabbed his hand as he rolled out of bed. "There's nothing I haven't read. How can we just turn away from each other, and go on? Why should I choose death on the field rather than by your hand? It's not true death if you change me."

He pulled his hand free, then seemed to sigh. With a gentleness she couldn't see in his eyes, he framed her face. "Not for all the worlds."

"If you loved me—"

"A poor female trick, that phrase. Not worthy of you. If

I loved you less, I might do exactly what you ask. I have before."

He moved to the window. Dawn was upon them, but there was no need to draw the drapes. Dawn had come with rain.

"I cared for a woman once, long ago. And she loved me, or loved what she believed I was. I changed her because I wanted to keep her." He turned back to where Moira knelt on the bed, silently weeping. "She was beautiful and amusing and bright. We'd make interesting companions, I thought. And we were, for almost a decade until she ran afoul of a well-aimed torch."

"It wouldn't be that way."

"She was twice the killer I was. She liked children best. She was beautiful and amusing and bright—and no less so for the change. Only once she was like me, she put those qualities to use luring toddlers."

"I could never—"

"You could," he said flatly. "And most certainly would. I won't turn the brightest light of my life into a monster. No, I'd never see you like me."

"I don't see a monster when I look at you."

"I would be, again, if I did this. It wouldn't just be you who changed, Moira. Would you damn me all over again?"

She pressed her hands to her eyes. "No. No. Stay then." She dropped her hands. "Stay with me, as we are. Or take me with you. Once Geall is safe, I can leave it in my uncle's hands, or—"

"And what? Live in the shadows with me? I can't give you children. I can't give you any kind of true life. How will you feel in ten years, in twenty, when you age and I don't? When you look in the mirror and see in your nature what you'll never see in mine? We've already stolen these weeks. They'll have to be enough for you."

"Can they be for you?"

"They're more than I ever had, or thought to. I can't be a man, Moira, not even for you. But I can feel hurt, and you're hurting me now."

"I'm sorry, I'm sorry. I feel as if everything in me is being squeezed. My heart, my lungs. I had no right to ask you, I know it. I knew it even when I did. Knew it was selfish and wrong. And weak," she added, "when I'd sworn not to be weak again. I know it can't be. I know it can't. What I don't know is if you can forgive me."

He came to her again, sat beside her. "The woman I changed didn't know what I was until that moment. If she had, she'd have run screaming. You know what I am. You asked because you're human. If I don't need to ask you to forgive me for being what I am, you don't need to ask me to forgive you for being what you are."

Chapter 19

For most of the day, Moira worked with Glenna forming, forging and charming the fireballs. Every hour or so two or three people would come into the tower and haul away what was done to store them in their stockpile outside.

"I never thought I'd say it," Moira began after the fourth straight hour, "but magic can be tedious."

"Hoyt would say what we're doing here is nearly as much science as magic." Glenna swiped at her damp face with her arm. "And yes, both can be boring as ever-living hell. Still, your doing this with me cuts back on the time and increases the payload. Hoyt's bound to be closeted with Cian over maps and strategy all day."

"Which is probably just as tedious."

"Betcha more."

Once again Glenna walked the line of the hardened balls they'd made, hands stretched out, eyes focused as she chanted. From where she stood at the worktable Moira could see the constant use of power was taking its toll.

The shadows under Glenna's green eyes seemed to deepen every hour. And each time the flush the miserable heat brought to her cheeks faded, her skin looked more pale, more drawn.

"You should stop for a bit," Moira told her when Glenna completed the line. "Get some air, have a bite."

"I want to finish this batch, but I will take a minute first. It reeks of sulphur in here." She walked to the window, leaned out to draw in cool, fresh air. "Oh. This is a sight, Moira, come look. Dragons circling over tent city."

Moira wandered over to watch dragons, most of them mounted by riders training them to dive or turn on command. They were quick studies, she mused, and made a bold, bright show against a hazy sky.

"You're wishing you could take a picture of it, or sketch it at least."

"I'll spend the next ten years doing sketches and art-work of what I've seen these past months."

"I'll miss you so much when this is done and you're not here anymore."

Understanding, Glenna draped an arm over Moira's shoulders, then pressed a kiss to her hair. "You know if there's a way to come, we will. We'll visit you. We have the key, we have the portal, and if what we've done here doesn't earn the gods' blessing, nothing could."

"I know. As horrible as these past months have been in so many ways, they've given me so much. You and Hoyt and Blair. And . . ."

"Cian."

Moira kept her eyes on the dragons. "He won't come back to visit, with or without the blessing of the gods."

"I don't know."

"He won't, even if it were possible for him, he won't come back to me." Little deaths, Moira thought, every hour, every day. "I knew it all along. Wanting it different doesn't change what is, or can't be. It's one of the things Morrigan was telling me, about the time of knowing. Us-ing my head and my heart together. Both my head and my heart know we can't be together. If we tried it would tear at us until neither of us could survive it. I tried to deny that, disgracing myself, hurting him."

"How?"

Before Moira could answer, Blair strode in. "What's up? A little girl time? What's the topic? Fashion, food or men? Oh-oh," she added when they turned and she saw their faces, "must be men, and me with no chocolate to pass around. Listen, I'll get out of your way, I just wanted to let you know the last incoming troops have been sighted. They'll be here within the hour."

"That's good news. No, stay a moment, would you?" Moira asked. "You should know what I was about to confess. Both of you have put your heart and blood into all of this. You've been the best friends to me I've ever had, or will have."

"You've got a serious voice on there, Moira. What did you do? Decide to turn to the dark side and hang out with Lilith?"

"It's not so far from that. I asked Cian to change me."

Blair nodded as she walked closer. "I don't see any bites on your neck."

"Why aren't you angry, or even surprised? Either one of you."

"I think," Glenna said slowly, "I might have done the same in your place. I know I'd have wanted to. If we walk away from this, Blair and I walk away with our men. You can't. Do you want us to judge you for trying to find some way to change that?"

"I don't know. It might be easier if you did. I used his feelings for me as weapons. I asked—all but begged him to make me like him when we were at our most intimate."

"Below the belt," Blair stated. "If I were going to do it, that's the method I'd have picked. He turned you down, which tells me there can't be any doubt what you are to him. Back to me again, I'd feel better knowing he was going to be just as miserable and alone as I was when he had to take a walk."

Moira let out a surprised and muffled laugh. "You don't mean that."

"I said it to lighten things up, but down in the gut? I don't know. I might. I'm sorry you're getting the shaft in this. Sincerely."

"Ah well, maybe I'll have a bit of luck and die in battle tomorrow night. That way I won't be miserable and alone after all."

"Positive thinking. That's the ticket." In lieu of chocolate, Blair gave her a hug. And met Glenna's eyes over Moira's shoulder.

It was important, Moira knew, for the last of the troops to be welcomed by their queen, and to show herself to as many as she could in the final hours before the last march. She walked among the tents as twilight came, as did the other members of the royal family. She spoke to all she could. She dressed as a warrior, with her cloak pinned with a simple claddaugh brooch and the sword of Geall at her side.

It was well after dark when she returned to the house, and to what she knew would be the final strategy meeting with her circle.

They were already gathered around the long table with only Larkin standing apart, scowling down at the fire. Something new, she thought with a little quiver in her belly. Something more.

She unpinned her cloak as she studied the faces of those she'd come to know so well.

"What plans are you making that has Larkin so worried?"

"Sit down," Glenna told her. "Hoyt and I have something. If it works," she continued as Moira walked to the table, "it would win this."

As Moira listened, the little quiver became a frozen knot. So many risks, she thought, so many contingencies, and so many ways to fail. For Cian most of all.

But when she looked into his eyes, she understood he'd already made his decision.

"It lays most on you," she said to him. "The timing . . . if it's off by a moment—"

"It lays on all of us. We all knew what we were taking on when we started this."

"No one of us should be risked more than the others," Larkin interrupted. "We may sacrifice one of us without need, without—"

"Do you think I bring this lightly?" Hoyt spoke quietly. "I lost my brother once, then found him again. Found more, I think, than either of us had before. Now doing this, doing what I was charged to do, I may lose him again."

"I'm not getting a sense of confidence in my abilities." There was a tankard on the table, and Cian lifted it to pour ale. "Apparently surviving over nine hundred years isn't considered a strong point on my résumé."

"I'd hire you," Blair said, and held out her cup. "Yeah, it's risky, a lot of steps, a lot of variables, but if it works, it'd be one hell of a thing. I'm figuring you'll make it through." She tapped her cup to Cian's. "So this has my vote."

"I'm not a strategist," Moira began. "And my magic is limited. You can do this?" she asked Hoyt.

"I believe it can be done." He reached for Glenna's hand.

"We got the idea, actually, from something you said back at Castle Geall," Glenna told her. "And we're using Geall's symbols. All of them. It would be strong magic, and—I think—though it takes blood to bind it, pure."

"I believe separately we have more true power than Midir." Hoyt scanned the faces around him. "Together, we'll crush him, and the rest."

Moira turned to Cian. "If you stayed back? A signal to you, to all of us once all the steps have been taken—"

"Lilith's blood on the battleground is essential. She has to be wounded, at least, by one of the six of us. And Lilith's mine," Cian said flatly. "If I get through or don't, she's mine. For King."

For King, Moira thought, and for himself as well. Once he'd been innocent, too. Once he'd been a victim and his life taken from him. She'd shed his blood, fed him hers. Now, what they'd shared might be vital to the survival of mankind.

She rose, carrying the weight of it, and walked to Larkin. "You've already decided." She looked back at the four who sat at the table. "Four of the six, so it would be done as you've planned however Larkin and I vote on this. But it's best if we're together. If the circle agrees, with no breaks, no doubts." She took Larkin's hand now. "It's best."

"All right. All right." Larkin nodded. "We're together then."

"If we could go over it once more." Moira came back to the table. "The details and the movements of it, then we'll pass this on to the squadron leaders."

It would be like a brutal and bloody dance, Moira thought. Sword, sacrifice and magic playing the tune. And the blood, of course. There must always be blood.

"The first preparations in the morning then." She'd risen to pour and pass short cups of whiskey for each. "Then we'll each do our part, and the gods willing, we'll end this. And end it, fittingly I think, with the symbols of Geall. Well, to us then and the hell with them."

When they'd drunk, she walked over to the vielle. "Would you play?" she asked Cian. "There should be music. We'll have music, and send it out to the night. I hope she hears it, and trembles."

"You don't play," Hoyt began.

"I didn't speak Cantonese once upon a time. Things change." Still Cian felt a little odd, sitting down with the vielle, testing the strings for tune.

"What is that thing?" Blair wondered. "Like a violin with gout?"

"Well, it would be a predecessor." He began to play, slowly, feeling his way back from war to music. The oddness faded away with the quiet, haunting notes.

"It's lovely," Glenna said. "A little heartbreaking." Because she couldn't resist, she went for paper and charcoal to sketch him as he played.

From outside, pipes and harps began to play, blending in with Cian's music.

Each note, Moira thought, like a tear.

"You've a hand with that," Larkin told Cian when the notes faded away. "And a heart for music, that's the truth. But would you be after playing something a bit livelier? You know, with a little jump to it?"

Larkin lifted his pipe and blew out quick, cheerful notes, so those echoes of melancholy were swept away in joy. More music poured in from outside, drums and fifes, as Cian matched melody and rhythm. With a quick hoot of approval, Larkin stomped his feet, his knees like loose hinges while Moira clapped the time.

"Come on then." Tossing his pipe to Blair, Larkin grabbed Moira's hands. "Let's show this lot how Geallians dance."

Laughing, Moira swung into step with him in what Cian saw was cousin to an Irish step-dance. Quick feet, still shoulders, all energy. He bent over the vielle, smiling a little at the persistence of the human heart as shadows and firelight played over his face.

"We won't let them get the better of us." Hoyt yanked Glenna to her feet.

"I can't do that."

"Sure you can. It's in the blood."

The floorboards rang with booted feet, and it flowed out into the night, the dance, the tune, the laughter. It was, Cian thought, so human of them, to take the joy, to not only use it, but to squeeze every drop of it.

There, his brother, the sorcerer who prized his dignity as much as his power, whirling around with his sexy red-headed witch who giggled like a girl as she tried to do the steps.

The kick-your-face-and-your-ass demon hunter mixing a little twenty-first-century hip-hop into the folk dance to make her shape-shifting cowboy grin.

And the queen of Geall, loyal, devoted and carrying the

weight of her world, flushed and glowing with the simple pleasure of music.

They might die tomorrow, every one, but by the gods, they danced tonight. Lilith, for all her eons, all her power and ambition would never understand them. And the magic of them, the light of them, might just carry the day.

For the first time, he believed—whether he survived or not—humankind would triumph. It couldn't be snuffed out, not even by itself. Though he'd seen, too often, it try.

There were too many others like these five, who would fight and sweat and bleed. And dance.

He continued to play when Hoyt paused long enough to drink some ale. "Send it to her," Cian murmured.

"Look at my Glenna, dancing as if she'd been born to it." Hoyt blinked, frowned. "What's that you said?"

Cian glanced up, no longer smiling though the music he played was as cheerful as a red balloon. "Send Lilith the music, send it out, just as Moira said. You can do that. Let's rub her fucking face in it."

"Then we will." Hoyt laid a hand on Cian's shoulder. "Damn right we will."

Power rippled, warming Cian's shoulder as he played, and played.

In the dark, Lilith stood watching her troops fight yet another training battle. As far as she could see—and her eyes were keen—vampires, half-vampires, human servants were spread in an army she'd spent hundreds of years building.

Tomorrow, she thought, they would swarm over the humans like a plague until the valley was a lake of blood.

And in it, she would drown that whore who called herself queen for what had been done to Davey.

When Lora joined her, they slid arms around each other's waists. "The scouts are back," Lora told her. "We outnumber the enemy by three to one. Midir is on his way, as you commanded."

"It's a good view from here. Davey would have enjoyed standing here, seeing this."

"By this time tomorrow, or soon after, he'll be avenged."

"Oh, yes. But it won't end there." She felt Midir as he climbed to the rooftop where she and Lora stood. "It begins soon," she said without turning to him. "If you fail me, I'll slit your throat myself."

"I will not fail."

"Tomorrow, when it begins, you'll be in place. I want you standing on the high ridge to the west, where all can see."

"Majesty—"

She turned now, her eyes cold and blue. "Did you think I'd let you stay here, locked and closeted within this shield? You'll do and be where I say, Midir. And you'll stand on that ridge so our troops, and theirs, can see your power. An incentive for them, and for you," she added. "Make your magic strong, or you'll pay the price of it during the battle, or after."

"I've served you for centuries, and still there is no trust."

"No trust between us, Midir. Only ambition. I prefer that you live, of course." She smiled now, thinly. "I have uses for you even after my victory. There are children inside Castle Geall, protected. I want them, all of them, when I've taken the night. From among them I'll choose the next prince. The others will make a fine feast. You'll stand on the ridge," she said as she turned back again. "And you'll cast your dark shadow. There's no cause for concern. After all, you've seen the outcome of this in your smoke. And so you've told me countless times."

"I would be more use to you here, with my—"

"Silence!" She snapped it out, tossed up a hand. "What's that sound? Do you hear it?"

"It sounds like . . ." Lora frowned out into the dark. "Music?"

"Their sorcerer sends it." Midir lifted face and hands

into the air. "I feel him reaching out, pale and petty power in the night."

"Make it stop! I won't be mocked on the eve of this. I won't have it. Music." She spat it out. "Human trash."

Midir lowered his arms, folded his hands. "I can do what you will, my queen, but they make a small and foolish attempt to anger you. See your own troops, training, wielding weapons, preparing for battle. And what does your enemy do with these final hours?" He dismissed them with a flick of his fingers that sizzled out fire. "They play like careless children. Wasting the short time they have left before the slaughter on music and dance. But if you will it—"

"Wait." She held up a hand again. "Let them have their music. Let them dance their way to death. Go back to your cauldron and smoke. And be prepared to take your place tomorrow, and hold it. Or I'll toast my victory with your blood."

"As you wish, Majesty."

"I wonder if he spoke the truth," Lora said when they were alone again. "Of if he hesitated to strike his power against theirs."

"It doesn't matter." Lilith couldn't let it matter, not this close to the fulfillment of all she coveted. "When everything is as I want it, when I crush these humans, drink their children, he'll have outlived his uses."

"*Certainement.* And his power could be turned against you once *he* has what he wants. What do you propose to do about him?"

"I'm going to make a meal of him."

"Share?"

"Only with you."

She continued to stand, watching the training. But the music, the damned music soured her mood.

It was late when Cian lay beside Moira. In these last hours, their circle was in three parts. He'd seen the fire flare and the candle flames flash, and knew Hoyt and Glenna were wrapped in each other.

As he'd been with Moira. As he imagined Larkin was with Blair.

"It was always meant to be this way," Moira said quietly. "The six of us making the circle, with each of us forming a stronger link with another. To gather together, to learn of and from one another. To know love. And this house is bright with love tonight. It's another kind of magic, and as powerful as any other. We have that, whatever comes."

She lifted her head to look down at him. "What I asked you to do was a betrayal."

"There's no need for that."

"No, I want to tell you what I know, as much as I know anything. It was a betrayal of you, of myself, of the others and all we've done. You were stronger, and now so am I. I love you with everything I am. That's a gift for both of us. Nothing can take it or change it."

She lifted the locket he wore. It held more than a lock of her hair, she thought. It held her love. "Don't leave this behind when you go. I want to know you have it, always."

"It goes where I go. My word on that. I love you with everything I am, and all I can't be."

She laid the locket back over his heart, then a hand over the stillness. Tears filled her, but she fought to hold them. "No regrets?"

"None."

"For either of us. Love me again," she murmured. "Love me again, one last time before dawn."

It was tender and slow, a savoring of every touch, every taste. Long, soft kisses were a kind of drug against any pain, silky caresses a balm over wounds that must be endured. She told herself her heart beat hard and strong enough for both of them now, this last time.

Her eyes stayed open and on his, drinking in his face so that at the peak of pleasure she saw him slide away with her.

"Tell me again," she murmured. "Once more."

"I love you. Eternally."

Then they lay together in the quiet. All the words had been said.

In the last hour before dawn they rose, the six, to prepare for the final march to battle.

They went on horse, on dragon, on foot, in wagons and carts. Above, clouds shifted over the sky, but didn't block out the sun. It beamed through them in shimmering fingers and sudden flashes to light the way to Silence.

The first arrived to lay traps in the shadows and in the caves while guards flew or rode over and around the valley with their eyes trained for any attack.

And there found traps laid for them. Under a man's feet, a pool of blood would spread, sucking him down. Ooze, black as pitch, bubbled up to burn through boots and into flesh.

"Midir's work," Hoyt spat as others ran to save who they could.

"Block it," Cian ordered. "We'll have a panic on our hands before we start."

"Half-vamps." Blair shouted the warning from dragonback. "About fifty. First line, let's go." She dived down to lead the charge.

Arrows flew, and swords slashed. In the first hour, the Geallian forces were down fifteen men. But they held ground.

"They just wanted us to have a taste of it." With her face splattered with blood, Blair dismounted. "We gave them a bigger one."

"The dead and wounded have to be tended to." Steeling herself, Moira looked at the fallen, then away. "Hoyt's pushing back Midir's spell. How much is it costing him?"

"He'll have whatever he needs to have. I'm going up again, do a couple of circles. See if she's got any more surprises for us." Blair vaulted back on her dragon. "Hold the line."

"We weren't as prepared as we might have been for the traps, for a daylight attack." Sheathing his stained sword,

Larkin stepped to Moira. "But we did well. We'll do better yet."

He laid a hand on her arm, drawing her away so only she would hear. "Glenna says some are already here, under the ground. Hoyt can't work with her now, but she thinks between herself and Cian they can find at least some, and deal with it."

"Good. Even a handful will be a victory. I need to steady the archers."

The sun moved to midday, then beyond it. Twice she saw the ground open up where Glenna held a willow rod. Then the flash of fire as the thing burrowed in the earth caught the sun and flamed in it.

How many more, she wondered. A hundred? Five hundred?

"He's broken off." Hoyt swiped a hand over his sweaty face when he joined her. "Midir's traps are closed."

"You beat him back."

"I can't say. He may have gone to other work. But for now, he's blocked. This ground, it shakes the soul of a man. It pours up this evil it holds, all but chokes the breath. I'll help Cian and Glenna."

"No, you need to rest a few moments, save your energies. I'll help them."

Knowing he needed to gather himself, Hoyt nodded. But his eyes were grim as he scanned the valley, passed over where Glenna and Cian worked. "They won't be able to find them all. Not in this ground."

"No. But every one is one less."

Still when she reached Glenna, Moira could see the work was taking its toll. Glenna was pale, her skin clammy as Hoyt's had been. "It's time to rest," Moira told her. "Restore yourself. I'll work it awhile."

"It's beyond your power. It's on the edge of mine." Grateful, Glenna took the water bag Moira offered. "We've only unearthed a dozen. A couple more hours—"

"She needs to stop. You need to stop." Cian took Glenna's arm. "You're nearly tapped out, you know it. If you don't have anything left come sundown, what good will you be?"

"I know there are more. A lot more."

"Then we'll be ready when this ground spits them out. Go. Hoyt needs you. He's worn himself thin."

"Good strategy," Cian told Moira when Glenna walked away. "Using Hoyt."

"It is, but it's also true enough. We're draining them both. And you," she added. "I can hear in your voice how tired you are. So I'll say what you said to her. What good are you if you're worn out by sundown?"

"The bloody cloak smothers me. Then again, the alternative's not pleasant. I need to feed," he admitted.

"Then go, up to the high ground and see to it. We've done nearly all we can, all we set out to do by this time."

She saw Blair and Larkin with Hoyt and Glenna now. The six of them, together as the sun sank lower might push their strengths up again. They went across the broken ground, climbed over an island of pocked rock, and began up the hard slope.

Everything in her wanted to shudder when they reached the ridge. Even without Midir's spell, the ground seemed to pull at her feet.

Cian took out a water bag she knew held blood.

"Waiting on you," Blair began. "A lot of your troops have the jitters."

"If you're meaning they won't stand and fight—"

"Don't get all Geallian pride on me." Blair held up a hand for peace. "What they need is to hear from you, to get revved. They need their St. Crispin's Day speech."

"What's this?"

Blair arched her brows at Cian. "Guess you missed *Henry V* when you mowed through Cian's library."

"There were a lot of books, after all."

"It's about stirring them up," Glenna explained. "About getting them ready to fight, even die. Reminding them why they're here, inspiring them."

"I'm to do all of that?"

"No one else would have the same impact." Cian closed the water bag. "You're the queen, and while the rest of us might be generals, in a manner of speaking, you're the one they look to."

"I wouldn't know what to say."

"You'll think of something. While you are, Larkin and I will get your troops together. Add a little *Braveheart* to *Henry*," he said to Blair. "Get her on horseback."

"Excellent." Blair headed off to get Cian's horse.

"What did this Henry say?" Moira wondered.

"What they needed to hear." Glenna gave Moira's hand a squeeze. "So will you."

Chapter 20

I don't have a thing in my head."

"It's not going to come from there. Or not only from there." Glenna handed Moira her circlet. "Head and heart, remember? Listen to both and whatever you say, it'll be the right thing."

"Then I wish you'd say it instead. Foolish to be afraid of speaking to them," Moira said with a weak smile. "And not as afraid to die with them."

"Put this on." Blair held out Moira's cloak. "Good visual, the cloak billowing in the wind. And speak up, kiddo. You have to project to the ones in the peanut gallery."

"I'll ask you what that means later." Moira took one huffing breath, then mounted the stallion. "Here we go then."

She walked the horse forward, then her heart gave a hard thud. There were her people, more than a thousand strong, standing with the valley at their backs. Even as the sun dipped lower in the sky, it glinted off sword and shield and lance. It washed over their faces, those who had come here, ready to give their lives.

And her head understood the words in her heart.

"People of Geall!"

They cheered as she trotted her horse in front of their lines. Even those already wounded called out her name.

"People of Geall, I am Moira, warrior queen. I am your sister; I am your servant. We have come to this time and this place by order of the gods, and so, to serve the gods. I know not all of your faces, all of your names, but you are mine, every man and woman here."

The wind caught at her cloak as she looked into those faces. "Tonight, when the sun sets, I ask you to fight, to stand this bitter ground that has already tasted our blood this day. I ask this of you, but you don't fight for me. You don't fight for the queen of Geall."

"We fight for Moira, the queen!" someone shouted. And again, her name rose up above the wind in cheers and chants.

"No, you don't fight for me! You don't fight for the gods. You don't fight for Geall, not this night. You don't fight for yourselves, or even your children. Not for your husbands, your wives. Your mothers and fathers."

They quieted as she continued to ride the lines, looking into those faces, meeting those eyes, "It's not for them you come here to this bitter valley, knowing your blood may spill on its ground. It's for all humankind you come here. For all humankind you stand here. You are the chosen. You are the blessed. All the worlds and every heart that beats in them is your heart now, your world now. We, the chosen, are one world, one heart, one purpose."

Her cloak snapped in the wind as the stallion pranced, and the dying sun glinted on the gold of her crown, the steel of her sword. "We will not fail this night. We cannot fail this night. For when one of us falls, there will be another to lift the sword, the lance, to fight with stake and fist the pestilence that threatens humanity and all it is. And if that next of us should fall, there will come another and another, and still more for we are the *world* here, and the enemy has never known the like of us."

Her eyes were like hell-smoke in a face illuminated with passion. Her voice soared over the air so the words rang out, strong and clear.

"Here, on this ground, we will drive them down even past hell." She continued to shout over the cheers that rippled and rose from the men and women like a wave. "We will not yield this night, we will not fail this night, but will stand and triumph this night. You are the heart they can never have. You are the breath and the light they will never know again. This night, they will sing of this Samhain, sing of The Battle of Silence, in every generation that comes after. They will sit by their fires and speak of the glory of what we do here. This night. The sun sets."

She drew her sword, pointed west where the sun had begun to bleed red. "Come the dark, we'll raise sword and heart and mind against them. And as the gods witness this, I swear it, we will raise the sun."

She sent fire rippling down the blade of her sword, and shooting into the sky.

"Not too shabby," Blair managed as the troops erupted with shouts and cheers. "Your girl's got a way with words."

"She's . . . brilliant." Cian kept his eyes on her. "How can they stand against that much light?"

"She spoke the truth," Hoyt stated. "They've never seen the likes of us."

The squadron leaders split the troops so they began to move into position. Moira rode back, dismounted.

"It's time," she said and held out her hands.

The six formed a circle to forge that final bond. Then released each other.

"See you on the flip side." Blair flashed a gleaming smile. "Go get 'em, cowboy." She leaped on her dragon, then shot skyward.

Larkin swung onto his own. "Last one to the pub when this is done buys the round." He flew up, and away from Blair.

"Blessed be. And let's kick ass." With Hoyt, Glenna started toward their posts, but she'd seen the look that had passed between the brothers. "What's going on with Cian? Don't lie this close to what might be bloody death."

"He asked for my word. If we're able to bring the spell into play, he asked for my word we not wait for him."

"But we can't—"

"It was the last he asked of me. Pray we won't have to make the choice."

Behind them, Moira stood with Cian. "Fight well," she said to him, "and live another thousand years."

"My fondest hope." He covered the lie by taking her hands a last time, pressing them to his lips. "Fight well, *mo croi*, and live."

Before she could speak again, he'd leaped onto his horse and galloped away.

From the air, Blair called out commands, directing her mount with her legs and scanning the ground for what would come with the dark. The sun fell, plunging the valley into night, and in that night, the ground erupted. They poured out of the ground, from earth, from rock, from crevice, in numbers too great to count.

"Showtime," she whispered to herself, swinging south as arrows from Moira and her archers rained down. "Hold them, hold them." A quick glance to where Niall's foot soldiers' voices rose like chants told her Niall was waiting for the signal.

A little longer, a little more, she thought as vampires swarmed up the valley, as arrows pierced some, missed others.

She flashed the firesword and dove. As men charged, she yanked the rope on her harness, dropping the first bomb.

Fire and flaming shrapnel flew, and there were screams as vampires were engulfed. And still they spewed from the ground pushing their lines toward the Geallians.

Freed of his cloak, Cian sat his horse, his sword raised to hold the men at his back. Bombs exploded fire, scorching the enemy and the ground. But they came, slinking and slithering, clawing and leaping. On a cry of battle, Cian slashed his sword and led his troops into the firestorm.

With flashing hooves and hacking steel, he cleaved a hole in the advancing army's line. It closed again, surrounding him and his forces.

Screams came in a torrent.

On her sloping plateau, Moira gripped her battle-ax. Her heart knocked in her throat as she saw the vampires break through the line to the east. She led the charge even as Hoyt led his so that they took their warriors in a stream of steel and stake to flank the enemy's lines.

Over the screams, the crashes, the fire, came the trumpeting call of dragons. The next wave of Lilith's army was advancing.

"Arrows!" Moira shouted as her quiver emptied, and another, filled, was tossed at her feet.

She notched and loosed, notched and loosed until the air was so full of smoke the bow was useless.

She raised the fiery sword and rushed with her line into the thick of it.

Of all she'd feared, all she'd known, all she'd seen in the visions the gods had given her, what came through the smoke and stink was worse. Men and women already slaughtered, ash of vanquished enemy coating the bitter ground like fetid snow. Blood spurted like a fall of water, painting the yellowed grass red.

Shrieks, human and vampire, echoed in the dark under the pale, three-quarter moon.

She blocked a sword strike, and her body moved with the instinct of hard training to spin, to pivot, to block the next. When she leaped over a low slash, she felt the wind of the sword under her boots, and with a scream of her own slashed for the throat.

Through the haze she saw the dragon that held Blair spiraling to the ground with its side pierced with arrows. The ground was littered with stakes. Grabbing one in her free hand, she rushed forward, then flung it through the back and into the heart of one who charged at Blair.

"Thanks. Duck." Blair shoved Moira aside, and severed the sword arm of another. "Larkin."

"I don't know. They keep coming."

"Remember your own hype." Blair leaped up, striking with her feet, then rammed a stake through the one she'd kicked.

Then she was lost in the waves of smoke, and Moira was once again battling for her life.

As Blair hacked through the line, they closed in around her. She struck, sword, stake, fought to gain ground. And was suddenly soaked. As her attackers screamed from the flood of blessed water that rained down from above, Larkin flew out of the smoke, grabbing her lifted arm to haul her up behind him.

"Nice job," she told him. "Drop me off. There, big, flat rock."

"You drop me. It's my time to have a go down here. You're out of water, but there are two fireballs. She's pushing in hard from the south now."

"I'll give her some heat."

He leaped off, and she soared.

Through the melee, Hoyt searched with his eyes, with his power. He felt the brush of Midir's dark, but there was so much black, so much cold, he wasn't sure of its direction.

Then he saw Glenna, fighting her way back up a ridge. And standing on it like a black crow, was Midir. In horror, he watched a hand snake out of a fold of earth and rock and grab Glenna's leg. In his mind he heard her scream as she kicked, as she clawed to keep from being dragged into the crevice. Even knowing he was too far away, he rushed through swords. Continued to run even when the fire she shot from fingertips coated what dragged at her.

Sensing power, Midir hurled lightning, black as pitch, and had her flying back.

Mad with fear, Hoyt fought like a wild man, ignoring blows and gashes as he worked his way toward her. He could see the blood on her face as she answered Midir's lightning with white fire.

* * *

The stake missed Cian's heart by a hairsbreadth, and the pain buckled his knees. As he went down, he thrust his sword up, all but cleaving his attacker in two before he managed to roll. A lance dug into the stony ground beside him. He gripped it, heaved it up to strike at another heart. Then planting it, he vaulted up, kicking out to send another flying to the wooden stakes the Geallians had hammered into the ground.

He saw Blair through the smoke that billowed from the fireballs and flaming arrows. With a pump of his legs, he leaped up, grabbing her dragon's harness to swing behind her an instant before she released another bomb.

"Didn't see you," she called out.

"Got that. Moira?"

"Don't know. Take over here. I'm going down."

She jumped down to the table of a rock. Cian saw her flip off, shooting stakes from both hands before the haze buried her. He swung his mount, aiming his sword, sending out fire. The ground continued to pull at him; its intoxicating scents of blood and fear driving hunger into him as keenly as a sharpened stake.

Then he saw Glenna, struggling her way up a sheer slope, and outnumbered three-to-one. Her battle-ax flamed, and each time she took an enemy, more crawled their way up toward her.

And when he saw the black figure on the high ridge, he understood why so many would go against a single woman.

The power of the circle battled back the hunger as he swept through the air toward his brother's wife.

He sent three tumbling down against rock, into traps of stakes and pools of holy water with a wild strike from the dragon's tail. His sword took two more even as Glenna's fiery ax turned enemies into flaming dust.

"Give you a lift?" He swooped down, circled her waist with his arm and hauled her up.

"Midir. The bastard."

Understanding, Cian soared up again. But when he struck out with the dragon's tail, it bounced off as if it hit rock.

"He's shielded. The coward." Breath short and choppy, Glenna searched the ground for Hoyt. And felt the lock on her lungs release when she saw him fighting his way up the slope.

"Set me down on the ridge, and go."

"The hell I will."

"This is what's needed, Cian. It's magic against magic for this. This is why I'm here. Find the others, get ready. Because by all the gods and goddesses, we're going to do this."

"Okay, Red. My money's on you."

He flew over the ridge, pausing while she slid down. And left her to face the black sorcerer.

"So, the red witch has come here to die."

"I didn't come for the ambiance."

She raised a hand, and charged with a swing of her ax. The widening of his eyes told her the move had surprised him. The flaming edge of the ax cut through the shield, but the blade missed its mark. She was propelled back, lifted into the air, slammed hard into the ground.

Though she threw out her own power, the scorching heat of his black lightning seared the palms of her hands. She held them out, held her power in them as she pushed painfully to her feet.

"You can't win this," he told her as dark shimmered around him. "I've seen the end, and your death."

"You've seen what whatever devil you sold yourself to wants you to see." She hurled fire, and though he deflected it with a snap of his wrist, she knew he felt her burn even as she'd felt his. "The end's what we make it."

With icy fury on his face, he brought a cutting wind that slashed at her skin like knives.

They were holding, Blair thought. She believed they were holding, but for every foot of ground the Geallians held, more vampires swarmed through the night and over it.

She'd lost track of her kills. A dozen at least with sword

and stake, at least that many with air attacks. And still it wasn't enough. Bodies littered the ugly ground, and even her strength was pushed to its limit.

They needed to pull the rabbit out of the hat, she thought, and screamed in vengeance as she slayed a vampire who'd stopped to feed on one of the fallen.

Whirling, slashing at others, she saw Glenna and Midir on the high ridge, and the firestorm of black against white as they battled.

She grabbed a lance from a dead hand, shot it out like a javelin. The spear tip went through two vampires fighting back to back, and the wood pole pierced hearts.

Something leaped down from above. Her senses caught just the edge of it, and her instincts had her pumping up into a high, wide flip. She slashed her sword as she touched ground, and clashed it against Lora's.

"There you are." Lora slid her blade down until it met Blair's to form a V. "I've been looking for you."

"Been around. You got something on your face there. Oh! Gee, is that a scar? Did I do that? My bad."

"I'll be eating your face shortly."

"You know that's wishful thinking, right? In addition to being disgusting. Enough small talk for you?"

"More than."

The swords sang as they slid apart. Then the music crescendoed as blade struck blade.

In moments, Blair understood she was facing the most formidable enemy of her career. Lora might look like a B movie dominatrix wrapped in snug black leather, but the French bitch could fight.

And take a punch, she thought when she finally got past Lora's guard long enough to slam a fist in the vampire's face. Blair felt the burn shoot a line across her knuckles as fangs sliced her flesh.

Blair flipped up to the jagged teeth of a rock, hacked down. And met air as Lora rose off the ground as if she had wings. Lora's sword whistled past Blair's face, and the tip of it sliced her cheek.

"Oh, will that leave a scar?" Lora landed on the rock with her. "My bad."

"It'll heal. Nothing about you is going to last much longer."

She answered first blood with a lightning parry of her own, gashing Lora's arm, then followed it through with a ripple of fire.

But Lora's sword struck the blade aside, going black against the red flame. The fire spurted and died.

"You think we weren't ready for that?" Lora bared her teeth as they hacked and thrust and swung. "Midir's magic is more than your magicians can ever hope for."

"Then why don't all of your troops have swords like yours? He couldn't pull it off." Blair flew up again, flipping over and striking Lora with her feet. The vampire used the momentum to soar up, driving down with the sword on her descent.

Raising hers to block, Blair didn't see the dagger that flew out of Lora's other hand. She stumbled from the shock, the pain, when it pierced her side.

"Look at all that blood. It's just pouring out of you. Yum." Lora laughed, a tinkling sound of delight, when Blair fell to her knees. And her eyes gleamed red as she raised the sword high for the killing blow.

With a mad, undulating howl, the gold wolf pounced from above. Claws and fangs raked as he leaped over the swinging sword, as he lunged and snapped. When he bunched to spring for the throat, Blair cursed.

"No! She's mine. You gave your word." Her breath whistled as she stayed on her knees, the dagger still lodged in her side. "Back off, wolf-boy. Back the hell off."

The wolf shimmered into a man as Larkin stepped back. "Get it done then," he snapped, his eyes grim. "And stop messing about."

"Pussy-whipped, is he?" Lora circled so that she could keep them both in her line of sight—the bleeding woman, the unarmed man. "But he's right, we really should stop messing about. I've a busy schedule."

She swung the sword down, and Blair thrust hers up to meet it, to block it, to hold it. The muscles in her arms screamed with the strain and her side wept blood and agony.

"I'm no pussy," she panted. "He's not whipped. And you're done."

She yanked the dagger from her side, stabbed it to its bloodied hilt into Lora's belly.

"That hurts, but it's steel."

"So's this." With all her remaining strength, Blair shoved Lora's sword aside, and plunged her own into the vampire's chest.

"Now you're just annoying me." Lora hefted her sword, point down. "Now who's done?"

"You," Blair replied as the blade still in Lora's chest erupted with flame.

Burning, screaming, Lora started to tumble from the rock. Blair yanked the sword free, swung it, hard and true, and cut off the flaming head.

"Fucking well done." Blair stumbled, swayed, would have fallen if Larkin hadn't sprung forward to catch her.

"How bad? How bad?" He pressed his hand to her bleeding side.

"Through and through, I think. No organs hit. Quick patch to stop the bleeding and I'm back in the game."

"We'll see about that. Get on."

When he shimmered into a dragon, Blair crawled onto his back. As they soared she saw Glenna on the ridge clashing with Midir. And she saw her friend fall.

"Oh God, she's hit. She's done. How fast can you get there?"

Inside the dragon Larkin thought: Not fast enough.

Glenna tasted blood in her mouth. There was more seeping out of a dozen shallow slices in her skin. She knew she'd hurt him, knew she'd chipped at his shield, his body, even his power.

But she could feel her own power ebbing out of her along with her blood.

She'd done all she could, and it hadn't been enough.

"Your fire's cooling. Barely an ember left to glow." Midir stepped closer now to where she lay on the scorched and bloody ground. "Still it might be enough to trouble myself to take, along with what's left of your life."

"It'll choke you." She gasped out the words. He'd bled, she thought. She'd made him bleed onto the ground. "I swear it will."

"I'll swallow it whole. It's so small, after all. Can you see below, can you? Where what I helped wrought runs over you like locusts. It's as I foretold. And as you fall, one by one, my power grows. Nothing will hold it now. Nothing will stop it."

"I will." Hoyt swung, bloody and battered, over the lip of the ridge.

"There's my guy," Glenna managed, gritting her teeth against the pain. "I softened him up for you."

"Now here is something more to chew on." Whirling, Midir shot black lightning.

It crashed, sizzled, spewed bloody flames when it struck against Hoyt's blinding white. The force blew them both back, searing the air between them. On the ground, Glenna rolled away from a streaking line of flame, then clawed to her hands and knees.

Whatever she had left, she gathered to send to Hoyt. Closing a trembling hand around the cross at her neck she focused her power into it, and to its twin Hoyt wore.

While she chanted, the sorcerers—black and white— battled on the smoke-hazed ridge, and in the filthy air above it.

The fire that sliced at Hoyt carried the burn of ice. It sought his blood—what was shed, what it aimed to shed, to draw away his power.

It clawed and slashed at him while the air flashed and boomed with magicks, sending smoke billowing high to drown the swimming moon. The ground beneath his feet cracked, splitting fissures under the enormity of pressure.

While his lungs labored and his heart pounded, he ignored those earthly demands on his body, ignored the pains from his wounds and the sweat that ran salt into them.

He was power now. Beyond that moment at the beginning of this journey when he'd wavered for an instant over the black. Now, on this ridge over blood and death, over the courage of man, the sacrifice and the fury, he was the white-hot flame of power.

The cross he wore flashed silver and brilliant as Glenna joined her magic to his. With one hand he reached for hers, gripping it firmly when she linked fingers with him and pulled herself to her feet. With the other he raised a sword, and the fire on it went pure white.

"It is we who take you," Hoyt began and slashed away a thunderbolt with his sword. "We who stand for the purity of magic, for the heart of mankind. It is we who defeat you, who destroy you, who send you forever into the flames."

"Be damned to you!" Midir shouted, and lifting both arms hurled twin thunderbolts. Fear rushed over his face when Glenna waved a hand over the air and turned them to ash.

"No. Be damned to you." Hoyt swung down the sword. The white fire leaped from the blade to strike Midir's heart like steel.

Where he dropped and died, the ground turned black.

High ground, Moira thought. She had to get back to higher ground, regroup the archers. She'd heard the shouts warning that their line had broken again to the north. Flaming arrows would drive that invading force back, give the troops in its path time to forge their lines again. She searched through the melee for a horse or dragon that would take her where she knew she was most needed.

And looking up saw Hoyt and Glenna bathed in brilliant white, facing Midir. A spurt of fresh hope had her racing forward. Even as the ground seemed to catch at her feet, she swung her sword at an advancing enemy. The gash she served it slowed it down, and as she poised to strike again, Riddock took it from behind.

With a fierce grin, he charged with a handful of men toward the broken line. He lived, she thought. Her uncle lived. As she raced to join him, the ground bucked under her feet, sent her sprawling.

As she pushed up she looked down into Isleen's dead and staring eyes.

"No. No. No."

Isleen's throat was torn open, the leather strap where Moira knew she'd worn a wooden cross was snapped and soaked with blood. Grief struck so strong, so deep, she gathered the body up against her.

Still warm, she thought as she rocked. Still warm. If she'd been faster, she might have saved Isleen.

"Isleen. Isleen."

"Isleen. Isleen." The words were a mocking mimic as Lilith flowed out of the smoke.

She'd dressed for battle in red and silver, a mitre like Moira's banding her head. Her sword was bloody to its jeweled hilt. Seeing her crashed waves of fear and fury through Moira that had her surging to her feet.

"Look at you." The grace and deftness with which Lilith spun the sword as she circled warned Moira this vampire queen knew the art of the blade. "Small and insignificant, covered with mud and tears. I'm amazed I wasted so much time planning your death when it's all so simple."

"You won't win here." Queen to queen, Moira thought, and blocked Lilith's first testing thrust. Life against death. "We're beating you back. We'll never stop."

"Oh please." Lilith waved the words away. "Your lines are crumbling like clay, and I've two hundred yet in reserve. But that's neither here nor there. This is you and me."

With barely a blink, Lilith shot out a hand, grabbing the soldier who charged her by the throat. And snapping his neck. She tossed him carelessly to the ground, while slicing down at Moira's swinging fire sword.

"Midir has his uses," Lilith said when the fire died.

"I want to take my time with you, you human bitch. You killed my Davey."

"No, you did. And with what you made of him destroyed, I hope what he was, the innocent he was, is cursing you."

Lilith's hand streaked out, flashing like the fangs of a snake. She raked her nails down Moira's cheek.

"A thousand cuts." She licked the blood from her fingers. "That's what I'll give you. A thousand cuts while my army feeds its belly full on yours."

"You won't touch her again." On his stallion's back, Cian rode slowly forward, as if time had stopped. "You'll never touch her again."

"Come to save your whore?" From her belt, Lilith drew a gold stake. "Gilded oak. I had this made for you, for when I end you as I made you. Tell me, doesn't all this blood stir you? Warm pools of it, bodies not yet cooled waiting to be drained. I know what's in you wants that taste. I put it in you, and I know it as I know myself."

"You never knew me. Go," he said to Moira.

"Yes, run along. I'll find you later."

She flew at Cian, then sprang up a sword's length away to spin over his head. As she sliced down, her sword met air while he threw his body up and back, with the heels of his boots barely missing her face.

They moved so fast, that eerie speed, that Moira saw little more than a blur, heard the clash of swords like silver thunder. This would be his battle, she knew, the one only he could fight. But she wouldn't leave him.

Leaping onto the horse, she drove Vlad up blood-slicked rock until she was positioned over their heads. There she shot fire from her sword to hold off Lilith's men who tried to reach their queen. She vowed that she and the sword of Geall would stand for her lover to the last.

Lilith was skilled, Cian knew. After all, she had centuries to learn the arts of war just as he had. Her strength and speed were as great as his. Perhaps greater. She blocked him, drove him back, slithered away from the force of his attack.

This ground was still hers, he knew. This pocket of black. She fed off it, as he didn't dare. She fed off the screams that echoed through the air and the blood that seemed to spew through it like rain.

He fought her, and the war inside him, the thing that struggled to claw free and revel in what it was. What she'd made him. Taking her advantage, she beat his sword aside, and in that flash of an instant he was open, plunged the stake at his heart.

It struck with a force that sent him staggering back. But as her cry of triumph echoed away, he continued to stand whole and unharmed.

"How?" was all she said as she stared at him.

He felt the imprint of Moira's locket against his heart, and the pain was sweet. "A magic you'll never know." He sliced out, scoring across the scar of the pentagram. The blood that welled from the wound was black and thick as tar.

Pain and fury brought the demon to her eyes, the killing red. Now her screams rang as she came at him with a new and wild strength. He slashed back, spilled more blood, drove as he was driven as the locket seemed to pulse like a heart on his chest.

Her sword ripped down his arm, sending his clattering against the rocks. "Now you! Then your whore!"

When she charged, he gripped the wrist of her sword arm in his bloody hand. She smiled at him. "This way then. It's more poetic."

She bared her fangs to strike at his throat. And he plunged the stake she had made for him into her heart.

"I'd say go to hell, but even hell won't have you."

Her eyes went wide, faded to blue. He felt the wrist he held dissolve in his hand, and still those eyes stared into his another moment.

Then there was nothing but the ash at his feet.

"I've ended you," he declared, "as you ended me so long ago. That's poetic."

The ground under his feet began to quake. So, he thought, it comes.

The black stallion leaped from the rocks, scattering ash. "You've done it." Moira vaulted from the saddle into his arms. "You've beaten her. You've won."

"This saved me." He dragged her locket out, showed her the deep dent in the silver from the force of the stake. "You saved me."

"Cian." As the rock behind her split like an egg, she jumped down, and her face went pale again. "Hurry. Go, hurry. It's begun. Her blood, her end, was the last of it. They've started the spell."

"It's you who beat her, you who won. Remember that." He pulled her into his arms, crushed his mouth to hers. Then he was flying onto the horse, and was gone.

Everything around her was chaos. Screams and shouts through the haze, the moans of wounded, the rush of the enemy in mad retreat.

A gold dragon speared through it, Blair on its back. With the ground rippling in waves under her, Moira lifted her arms so Larkin could cradle her in his claws. She flew over the quivering land toward the high ridge.

On it, Hoyt gripped Moira's hand. "It must be now."

"Cian. We can't be sure—"

"I gave my word to him. It must be now." He raised their joined hands, and together they lifted their faces, their voices to the black sky.

"In this place once damned we hold the power, and we wield it in this final hour. On this ground blood was shed in blackest night, theirs for dark and ours for light. Black magic and demon here are felled by our hand, and now we claim this bloody land. Now call forth all we have done. Now through dark we raise the sun. Its light will strike our enemy. As we will, so mote it be."

The ground trembled, and the wind blew like a fury.

"We call the sun!" Hoyt shouted. "We call the light!"

"We call the dawn!" Glenna's voice rose with his, and the power grew as Moira clasped her free hand. "Burn off the night."

"Rise in the east," Moira chanted, staring through the

smoke that swirled up around them while Larkin and Blair completed the circle. "Spread to the west."

"It's coming," Blair cried. "Look. Look east."

Over the shadow of mountains the sky lightened, and the light spread and speared and grew until it was bright as noon.

Below, fleeing vampires burned to nothing.

On the rocky, broken ground, flowers began to bloom.

"Do you see that?" Larkin's hand tightened on Moira's, and his voice was thick, reverent. "The grass, it's greening."

She saw it, and the sweet charm of the white and yellow flowers that spread over its carpet. She saw the bodies of the fallen on the meadow of a lush and sun-lit valley.

But nowhere did she see Cian.

Chapter 21

Though the battle was won, there was still work. Moira labored with Glenna in what Glenna called triage for the wounded. Blair and Larkin had taken a party out to hunt down any vampires that might have found shelter from the sun while Hoyt helped transport those whose wounds were less severe back to one of the bases.

After rinsing blood from her hands again, Moira stretched her back. And spotting Ceara wandering as if in a daze, rushed to her.

"Here, here, you're hurt." Moira pressed a hand to the wound on Ceara's shoulder. "Come, let me dress this."

"My husband." Her gaze roamed from pallet to pallet even as she leaned heavily against Moira. "Eogan. I can't find my husband. He's—"

"Here. He's here. I'll take you. He's been asking for you."

"Wounded?" Ceara swayed. "He's—"

"Not mortally, I promise you. And seeing you, he'll heal all the quicker. There, over there, you see? He's—"

Moira got no further as Ceara cried out and in a stumbling run rushed to fall to her knees beside where her husband lay.

"It's good to see, good for the heart to see."

She turned, smiled at her uncle. Riddock, his arm and leg bandaged, sat on a supply crate.

"I wish all lovers would be reunited as they are. But . . . we lost so many. More than three hundred dead, and the count still coming."

"And how many live, Moira?" He could see the wounds she bore on her body, and in her eyes the wounds she bore on her heart. "Honor the dead, but rejoice in the living."

"I will. I will." Still she scanned the wounded, those who tended them, and feared for only one. "Are you strong enough to travel home?"

"I'll go with the last. I'll bring our dead home, Moira. Leave that for me."

She nodded, and after embracing him went back to her duties. She was helping a soldier sip water when Ceara found her again.

"His leg, Eogan's leg . . . Glenna said he won't lose it, but—"

"Then he won't. She wouldn't lie to you, or to him."

On a steadying breath, Ceara nodded. "I can help. I want to help." Ceara touched her bandaged shoulder. "Glenna looked after me, and said I'm well enough. I've seen Dervil. She came through very well. Cuts and bruises for the most of it."

"I know."

"I saw your cousin Oran, and he said Sinann's Phelan's already on his way back to Castle Geall. But I haven't found Isleen as yet. Have you seen her?"

Moira lowered the soldier's head, then rose. "She did not come through."

"No, my lady, she must have. You just haven't seen her." Again, Ceara searched the pallets that stretched over the wide field. "There are so many."

"I did see her. She fell in the battle."

"No. Oh no." Ceara covered her face with her hands. "I'll tell Dervil." Tears flowed down her cheeks when she lowered her hands. "She's trying to find Isleen now. I'll tell her, and we'll . . . I can't fathom it, my lady. I can't fathom it."

"Moira!" Glenna called from across the field. "I need you here."

"I'll tell Dervil," Ceara repeated and hurried away.

Moira worked until the sun began to dim again, then exhausted and sick with worry, flew on Larkin to the farm where she would spend one last night.

He would be here, she told herself. Here is where he would be. Safe out of the sunlight, and helping organize the supplies, the wounded, the transportation. Of course, he would be here.

"Near dark," Larkin said when he stood beside her. "And there'll be nothing in Geall that will hunt in it tonight but that which nature has made."

"You found none at all, no enemy survivors."

"Ash, only ash. Even in caves and deep shade there was ash. As if the sun we brought burned through it all, and there was none of them could survive it no matter where they hid."

Her already pale face went gray, and he gripped her arm.

"It's different for him, you know it. He'd have had the cloak. He'd have gotten it in time. You can't believe any magic we'd bring would harm one of our own."

"No, of course. Of course, you're right. I'm just tired, that's all."

"You'll put something in your belly, then lay your head down." He led her into the house.

Hoyt stood with Blair and Glenna. Something on their faces turned Moira's knees to water.

"He's dead."

"No." Hoyt hurried forward to take her hands. "No, he survived it."

Tears she'd held for hours spilled out of her eyes and flooded her cheeks. "You swear it? He's not dead. You've seen him, spoken to him?"

"I swear it."

"Sit, Moira, you're exhausted."

But she shook her head at Glenna's words and kept her eyes on Hoyt's face. "Upstairs? Is he upstairs?" A shudder passed through her as she understood what she read in Hoyt's eyes. "No," she said slowly. "He's not upstairs. Or in the house, or in Geall at all. He's gone. He's gone back."

"He felt . . . Damnation, I'm sorry for this, Moira. He was determined to go, straightaway. I gave him my key, and he was going by dragon-back to the Dance. He said . . ."

Hoyt took a sealed paper from a table. "He asked if I'd give you this."

She stared at it, and finally nodded. "Thank you."

They said nothing as she took the paper and went upstairs alone.

She closed herself in the room she'd shared with him, lit the candles. Then sitting, simply held the letter to her heart until she had the strength to break the seal.

And read.

Moira,

This is best. The sensible part of you understands that. Staying longer would only prolong pain, and there's been enough of it for a dozen lifetimes. Leaving you is an act of love. I hope you understand that, too.

I have so many pictures of you in my head. Of you sitting on the floor in my library surrounded by books, poring through them. Of you laughing with King or Larkin as you so rarely laughed with me in those first weeks. Courageous in battle or lost in thought. You never knew how often I watched you, and wanted you.

I'll see you in the morning mists, drawing a shining sword from a stone, and flying a dragon with arrows singing from your bow.

I'll see you in candlelight, holding out your arms

*to me, taking me into a light I've never known before
or will know again.*

*You've saved your world and mine, and however
many others there might be. I think you were right
that we were meant to find each other, to be together
to forge the strength, the power needed to save those
worlds.*

Now it's time to step away.

*I'm asking you to be happy, to rebuild your world,
your life, and to embrace both. To do less would be a
dishonor to what we had. To what you gave me.*

With you, somehow with you, I was a man again.

*That man loved you beyond measure. What I am
that is not a man loved you, despite everything. In all
the centuries I've loved you. If you loved me, you'll
do what I ask.*

*Live for me, Moira. Even a world apart, I'll know
that you do and be content.*

Cian

She would weep. A human heart needed to shed such
a deep well of tears. Lying on the bed where they'd loved
each other for the last time, she pressed the letter to her
heart, and let it empty.

*New York City
Eight weeks later*

He spent a great deal of time in the dark, and a
great deal of time with whiskey. When a man had eternity, Cian figured he could take a decade or two to brood.
Maybe a century since he'd given up the love of his endless
bloody life.

He'd come around, of course. Of course he would. He'd
get back to business. Travel for a while. Drink a bit longer
first. A year or two of a sodding drunk never hurt the undead.

He knew she was well, helping her people recover, planning the monument she would build in the valley come the next spring. They'd buried their dead, and she herself had read every name—nearly five hundred of them—at the memorial.

He knew because the others were back now as well, and had insisted on giving him details he hadn't asked for.

At least Blair and Larkin were in Chicago now and wouldn't be hammering at him to talk or get together with them. You'd think humans, after spending such an intense amount of time with him, would know he wasn't feeling sociable.

He was going to wallow, goddamn it. The lot of them would be long dead, by his estimation, before he was finished wallowing.

He poured more whiskey. He told himself at least he had enough standards left not to drink it straight from the bottle.

And here were Hoyt and Glenna nagging at him to spend Christmas with them. Christmas, for bleeding Judas's sake. What did he care for Christmas? He wished they would go the hell back to Ireland and the house he'd given them and leave him be.

Did they have Christmas in Geall? he wondered, running his fingers over the dented silver locket he wore night and day. He'd never asked about that particular custom—but why should he have. It would likely be Yule there, with burning logs and music. Whatever, it was nothing to him now.

But she should celebrate, Moira should. Light a thousand candles and set Castle Geall glowing. Hang the holly bushes and strike up the bloody band.

When the hell was this pain going to ebb? How many oceans of whiskey would it take to dull it?

He heard the hum of the elevator and scowled over at it. He'd told the shagging doorman no one was to be let up, hadn't he? He ought to snap the idiot's neck like a used chopstick.

But no matter, he mused, he'd locked the mechanism from inside as second line of defense.

They could come up, but they couldn't get in.

He could barely drum up a curse when the doors slid open, and he saw Glenna step into the dark.

"Oh for pity's sake." Her voice was impatient, and an instant later, the lights flashed on.

They seared his eyes so that this time his curses were loud and heartfelt.

"Look at you." She set aside the large and elegantly wrapped box she'd carried in. "Sitting in the dark like a—"

"Vampire. Go away."

"It reeks of whiskey in here." As if she owned the place, she walked into his kitchen and began making coffee. While it was brewing she came out to find him exactly as he'd been.

"Merry Christmas to you, too." She angled her head. "You need a shave, a haircut—and one day when you're not sulking I'm going to ask how you accomplish that sort of thing. A shave," she repeated, "a haircut, and since whiskey's not the only reek in here, a bath."

His eyes remained hooded, and his lips curved without a whiff of humor. "Going to give me one, Red?"

"If that's what it takes. Why don't you clean yourself up, Cian, come back to the apartment with me? We have plenty of leftover Christmas dinner. It's Christmas Day," she said to his blank look. "Nearly nine o'clock Christmas night, actually, and I've left my husband home alone because he's as stubborn as you and won't come back here without an invitation."

"That's something anyway. I don't want leftovers. Or that coffee you're making in there." He lifted his glass. "I've got what I want."

"Fine. Stay drunk and smelly and miserable. But maybe you'll want this, too."

She marched over to the box, hefted it, then brought it over to drop it in his lap. "Open it."

He studied it without interest. "But I didn't get anything for you."

She crouched at his feet now. "We'll consider your opening it my gift. Please. It's important to me."

"Will you go away if I open it?"

"Soon."

To placate her, he lifted the lid with its silver paper and elaborate bow, brushed aside the top layer of sparkling tissue.

And Moira looked out at him.

"Ah, damn you, damn you, Glenna." Neither whiskey nor will could hold against the image of her. Emotion shook in his voice as he lifted the framed portrait. "It's beautiful. She's beautiful."

Glenna had painted her in that moment Moira had drawn the sword free from the stone. The dreaminess and power of it, with green shadows, silver mists, and the new queen standing with the shining sword pointed toward the heavens.

"I thought, hoped, that having it would remind you what you helped give her. She wouldn't have stood there without you. There'd be no Geall without you. I wouldn't be here without you. None of us would have survived this without each one of us." She laid a hand on his. "We're still a circle, Cian. We always will be."

"I did the right thing for her, leaving. I did the right thing."

"Yes." She squeezed his hand now. "You did the right thing, an enormous and pure act of love. But knowing you did the right thing for all the right reasons doesn't stop the pain."

"Nothing does. Nothing."

"I'd say time will, but I don't know if it's true." Sympathy swam in her voice, in her eyes. "I will say you have friends and family who love you, and will be there for you. You have people who love you, Cian, who hurt for you."

"I don't know how to take what you want to give me, not yet. But this." He traced his finger around the frame. "Thank you for this."

"You're welcome. There are photographs, too. Ones I took in Ireland. I thought you might like to have them."

He started to lift the next layers of tissue, then stopped. "I need a moment."

"Sure. I'll go finish the coffee."

Alone, he uncovered the large manila envelope, and opened it.

There were dozens of them. One of Moira and his books, and with Larkin outside. One of King reigning over the stove in the kitchen, of Blair, eyes intense, sweat sheening her skin as she held a sword in warrior position.

There was one of himself and Hoyt he hadn't known she'd taken.

As he studied each one his feelings swirled and mixed, pleasure and sorrow.

When he looked up at last he saw Glenna leaning against the doorjamb with a mug of coffee in her hand. "I owe you more than a gift."

"No, you don't. Cian, we're going back to Geall for New Year's. All of us."

"I can't."

"No," she said after a moment, and the understanding in her eyes nearly broke him. "I know you can't. But if there's any message—"

"There can't be. There's too much to say, Glenna, and nothing to say. You're sure you can go back?"

"Yes, we have Moira's key, and an assurance of Morrigan herself. You didn't wait around long enough for the thanks of the gods."

She walked over, set the coffee on the table beside him. "If you change your mind, we're not leaving until midday, New Year's Eve. If you don't, after that Hoyt and I will be in Ireland. We hope you'll come see us. Blair and Larkin are taking my apartment here."

"Vampires of New York, beware."

"Damn right." She leaned over, kissed him. "Happy Christmas."

He didn't drink the coffee, but he didn't drink any more whiskey either. Surely that was a step somewhere. Instead he sat and studied Moira's portrait, and the hours passed that way toward midnight.

A swirl of light brought him out of the chair. Since it

was the closest weapon, he grabbed the whiskey bottle by the neck. As he wasn't nearly drunk enough for hallucinations, he decided the goddess standing in his apartment was real.

"Well, this is a red-letter day. I wonder if such as you has ever paid a call on such as me before."

"You are of the six," Morrigan said.

"I was."

"Are. Yet you hold yourself apart from them again. Tell me, vampire, why did you fight? Not for me or mine."

"No, not for the gods. Why?" He shrugged, and now did drink from the bottle in a kind of defiance, of disrespect. "It was something to do."

"It's foolish for such as you to pretend with such as me. You believed it was right, that it was worth fighting for, even ending your own existence for. I've known your kind since they first crawled through the blood. None would have done what you did."

"You sent my brother here to see I fell into line."

The god lifted her brow at his tone, then inclined her head. "I sent your brother to find you. Your will was your own. You have love for this woman." She gestured toward Moira's portrait. "For this human."

"You think we can't love?" Cian's voice shook with rage, with grief. "You think we aren't capable of love?"

"I know that you are, and while that love may run deep in your kind, its selfishness runs as strong. But not yours." Robes flowing, she walked to the portrait. "She asked you to make her one of you, but you refused. You could have kept her had you done as she asked."

"Like a goddamn pet? Kept her? Damned her is what it would have done, killed her, crushed out that light in her."

"Given her eternity."

"Of dark, of a craving for the blood of what she'd been. Condemned her to a life that is no life. She didn't know what she asked me."

"She knew. Such a strong heart and mind she has, and courage, yet she asked and she knew, and would have given you her life. You've done well, haven't you? You have culture and wealth, skills. Fine homes."

"That's right. Made something of my dead self. Why shouldn't I?"

"And enjoy it—when you're not sitting in the dark brooding over what can't be. What you can't have. You enjoy your eternity, your youth, your strength and knowledge."

He sneered now, damning the gods. "Would you rather I beat my breast over my fate? Endlessly mourn my own death? Is that what the gods demand?"

"We demand nothing. We asked, and you gave. Gave more than we believed you would. If it were otherwise, I wouldn't be here."

"Fine. Now you can go away again."

"Nor," she continued in the same easy tone, "would I give you this choice. Continue to live, grow wealthier yet. Century upon century, with no age, no sickness, and the blessings of the gods."

"Got that already, without your blessing."

Her eyes sparkled a little, but he couldn't tell—didn't care—if it was amusement or temper. "But now it's given to you, the only of your kind who has it. You and I know more of death than any human can. And fear it more. There need be no end to you. Or you can have an end."

"What? Staked by the gods?" He snorted out a laugh, took another long pull from the bottle. "Burned in god-fire? A purification of my condemned soul?"

"You can be what you were, and have a life that comes to an end as all do. You can be alive, and so age and sicken and one day know the death as a man knows it."

The bottle slipped out of his fingers, thudded on the floor. "What?"

"This is your choice," Morrigan said, holding out both hands, palms up. "Eternity, with our blessing to enjoy it. Or a handful of human years. What will you, vampire?"

* * *

In Geall, a quiet snow had fallen, a thin blanket over the ground. The morning sunlight glinted off it, and sparkled on the ice that coated the trees.

Moira passed her cousin's infant back to Sinann. "She's prettier every day, and I could spend hours just looking at her. But our company's coming after midday. I haven't finished preparing."

"You brought them home to me." Sinann nuzzled her daughter. "All I love. I wish you could have all you love, Moira."

"I had a lifetime in a few weeks." She gave the baby a last kiss, then glanced around in surprise as Ceara rushed in.

"Majesty. There's someone . . . downstairs, there's someone who wishes to see you."

"Who?"

"I . . . I was only told there's a visitor who's traveled far to speak with you."

Moira's eyebrows shot up when Ceara dashed away again. "Well, whoever it is has her fluttered up. I'll see you again later."

She went out, brushing at her trousers. They'd been cleaning for days in preparation of the new year and her most anticipated guests. To see them again, she thought, to speak with them. To watch Larkin grin over his new niece.

Would they bring any word, any at all, of Cian?

She pressed her lips together, reminded herself not to let her inner grieving show. It was a time of celebration, of holiday. She would not put a pall over Geall after all they'd fought to preserve.

Something trembled along her skin as she started down the stairs. Shivered up her spine and to the base of her neck where her lover had liked to press his lips.

Then it trembled in her heart, and she began to run. That trembling heart began to race. And then to soar.

What she believed never could be was, and he was there, standing there, looking up at her.

"Cian." The joy that had been shut away burst out of her, like music. "You came back." She would have launched herself into his arms, but he was staring at her so intently, so strangely she wasn't sure she'd be welcomed. "You came back."

"I wondered what I'd see on your face. I wondered. Can we speak in private?"

"Of course. Aye, we'll . . ." Flustered, she looked around. "It seems we are. Everyone's gone." What could she do with her hands to stop them from touching him? "How did you come? How—"

"It's New Year's Eve," he said, watching her. "The end of the old, the start of the new. I wanted to see you, on the edge of that change."

"I wanted to see you, no matter when or where. The others come in a few hours. You'll stay. Please say you'll stay for the feasting."

"It depends."

Her throat burned as if she'd swallowed flame. "Cian. I know what you said in your letter was true, but it was hard, so hard, not to see you again. To have our last moment together standing in blood. I wanted . . ." Tears flooded her eyes, and she nearly lost the war to will them back. "I wanted just a moment more. Now I have it."

"Would you take more than a moment, if I could give it?"

"I don't understand." Then she smiled and choked back a sob when he drew the locket she'd given him from under his shirt. "You still wear it."

"Yes, I still wear it. It's one of my most treasured possessions. I left nothing of me behind for you. Now I'm asking, would you take more than that moment, Moira? Would you take this?" He lifted her hand, pressed it to his heart.

"Oh, I was afraid you didn't want to touch me." Her breath shuddered out with relief. "Cian, you know, you must know, that I . . ."

The hand beneath his trembled, and her eyes went wide. "Your heart. Your heart beats."

"Once I told you if it could beat, it would beat for you. It does."

"It beats under my hand," she whispered. "How?"

"A gift from the gods in the last moments of Yule. They gave me back what was taken from me." Now he drew out the silver cross that hung around his neck with her locket. "It's a man who stands before you, Moira."

"Human," she whispered. "You live."

"It's a man who loves you." He pulled her toward the doors, flung them open so the sun poured over them. And because it was still so miraculous, he lifted his face, closed his eyes and let the stream of it bathe his face.

She couldn't stop the tears now, or the sobs that came with them. "You're alive. You came back to me and you're alive."

"It's a man who stands before you," he said again. "It's a man who loves you. It's a man who asks if you'll share the life he's been given, if you'll live it with him. If you'll take me as I am, and make a life with me. Geall will be my world, as you're my world. It will be my heart, as you're my heart. If you'll have me."

"I've been yours from the first moment, and I'll be yours until the last. You came back to me." She laid a hand on his heart, and the other on her own. "And my heart beats again."

She threw her arms around him, and those who'd gathered in the courtyard, and on the stairs cheered as the queen of Geall kissed her beloved in the winter sunlight.

So they lived," the old man said, "and they loved. So the circle grew stronger, and formed circles out from it as ripples spread in a pool. The valley that had once been silent sang with music of summer breezes through green grass, the lowing of cattle. Of pipes and harps and the laughter of children."

The old man stroked the hair of a little one who'd climbed into his lap. "Geall flourished under the rule of Moira, the warrior queen and her knight. For them, even in the dark of night, a light shone.

"And that brings the tale of the sorcerer, the witch, the

warrior, the scholar, the shifter of shapes and the vampire to its own circle."

He patted the rump of the child on his lap. "Off with you now, all of you, while there's still sunlight to enjoy."

There were shouts and whoops, and he smiled as he heard the arguments already starting for who would be the sorcerer, who would be the queen.

Because his senses were still keen in some areas, Cian lifted his hand to the back of the chair, and covered Moira's.

"You tell it well."

"Easy to tell what you've lived."

"Easy to *enhance* what was," she corrected, coming around the chair. "But you stayed very close to the truth."

"Wasn't the truth strange and magical enough?"

Her hair was pure white, and her face as she smiled at him, lined with the years. And more beautiful than any he'd known.

"Walk with me before twilight comes." She helped him to stand, hooked her arm through his. "And are you ready for the invasion?" she asked, tipping her head toward his shoulder.

"When it comes, at least you'll be finished fussing over it."

"I'm so anxious to see them all. Our first circle, and the circles they've made. Once a year for the whole of them is so long to wait, even with the little visits between. And listening to little pieces of the tale brings it all back so clear, doesn't it?"

"It does. No regrets?"

"I've never had a one when it comes to you. What a fine life we've had, Cian. I know we're in the winter of it, but I don't feel the cold."

"Well, I do, when you put your feet on my arse in the night."

She laughed, turned to kiss him with all the warmth, all the love of sixty years of marriage.

"There's our eternity, Moira," he said, gesturing toward

their grandchildren, and great-grandchildren. "There's our forever."

Hands linked, they walked in the softening sunlight. Though their steps were slow and measured from age, they continued through the courtyards and the gardens, and out through the gates while the sound of children playing rang behind them.

High above on the castle peaks, the three symbols of Geall, the claddaugh, the dragon and the sun, flew—gold against the white.

Glossary of Irish Words, Characters and Places

a chroi (ah-REE), Gaelic term of endearment meaning "my heart," "my heart's beloved," "my darling"

a ghrá (ah-GHRA), Gaelic term of endearment meaning "my love," "dear"

a stór (ah-STOR), Gaelic term of endearment meaning "my darling"

Aideen (Ae-DEEN), Moira's young cousin

Alice McKenna, descendant of Cian and Hoyt Mac Cionaoith

An Clar (Ahn-CLAR), modern-day County Clare

Ballycloon (ba-LU-klun)

Blair Nola Bridgitt Murphy, one of the circle of six, the "warrior"; a demon hunter, a descendant of Nola Mac Cionaoith (Cian and Hoyt's younger sister)

Bridget's Well, cemetery in County Clare, named after St. Bridget

Burren, the, a karst limestone region in County Clare, which features caves and underground streams

cara (karu), Gaelic for "friend, relative"

Ceara, one of the village women

Cian (KEY-an) *Mac Cionaoith/McKenna,* Hoyt's twin brother, a vampire, Lord of Oiche, one of the circle of six, "the one who is lost"

Cirio, Lilith's human lover

ciunas (CYOON-as), Gaelic for "silence"; the battle takes place in the Valley of Ciunas—the Valley of Silence

claddaugh, the Celtic symbol of love, friendship, loyalty

Cliffs of Mohr (also Moher), the name given to the ruin of forts in the south of Ireland, on a cliff near Hag's Head, "Moher O'Ruan"

Conn, Larkin's childhood puppy

Dance of the Gods, the Dance, the place in which the circle of six passes through from the real world to the fantasy world of Geall

Davey, Lilith's, the Vampire Queen's, "son," a child vampire

Deirdre (DAIR-dhra) *Riddock,* Larkin's mother

Dervil (DAR-vel), one of the village women

Eire (AIR-reh), Gaelic for Ireland

Eogan (O-en), Ceara's husband

Eoin (OAN), Hoyt's brother-in-law

Eternity, the name of Cian's nightclub, located in New York City

Faerie Falls, imaginary place in Geall

fàilte à Geall (FALL-che ah GY-al), Gaelic for "Welcome to Geall"

Fearghus (FARE-gus), Hoyt's brother-in-law

Gaillimh (GALL-yuv), modern-day Galway, the capital of the west of Ireland

Geall (GY-al), in Gaelic means "promise"; the city from which Moira and Larkin come; the city which Moira will someday rule

Glenna Ward, one of the circle of six, the "witch"; lives in modern-day New York City

Hoyt Mac Cionaoith/McKenna (mac KHEE-nee), one of the circle of six, the "sorcerer"

Isleen (Is-LEEN), a servant at Castle Geall

Jarl (Yarl), Lilith's sire, the vampire who turned her into a vampire

Jeremy Hilton, Blair Murphy's ex-fiance

King, the name of Cian's best friend, whom Cian befriended when King was a child; the manager of Eternity

Larkin Riddock, one of the circle of six, the "shifter of shapes," a cousin of Moira, Queen of Geall

Lilith, the Vampire Queen, aka Queen of the Demons; leader of the war against humankind; Cian's sire, the vampire who turned Cian from human to vampire

Lora, a vampire; Lilith's lover

Lucius, Lora's male vampire lover

Malvin, villager, soldier in Geallian army

Manhattan, city in New York; where both Cian McKenna and Glenna Ward live

mathair (maahir), Gaelic word for mother

Michael Thomas McKenna, descendant of Cian and Hoyt Mac Cionaoith

Mick Murphy, Blair Murphy's younger brother

Midir (mee-DEER), vampire wizard to Lilith, Queen of the Vampires *miurnin* (also sp. miurneach [mornukh]), Gaelic for "sweet-heart," term of endearment

Moira (MWA-ra), one of the circle of six, the "scholar"; a princess, future queen of Geall

Morrigan (Mo-ree-ghan), Goddess of the Battle

Niall (Nile), a warrior in the Geallian army

Nola Mac Cionaoith, Hoyt and Cian's youngest sister

ogham (ä-gem) (also spelled ogam), fifth/sixth century Irish alphabet

oiche (EE-heh), Gaelic for "night"

Oran (O-ren), Riddock's youngest son, Larkin's younger brother

Phelan (FA-len), Larkin's brother-in-law

Prince Riddock, Larkin's father, acting king of Geall, Moira's maternal uncle

Region of Chiarrai (kee-U-ree), modern-day Kerry, situated in the extreme southwest of Ireland, sometimes referred to as "the Kingdom"

Samhain (SAM-en), summer's end (Celtic festival); the battle takes place on the Feast of Samhain, the feast celebrating the end of summer

Sean Murphy (Shawn), Blair Murphy's father, a vampire hunter

Shop Street, cultural center of Galway

Sinann (shih-NAWN), Larkin's sister

sláinte (slawn-che), Gaelic term for "cheers!"

slán agat (shlahn u-gut), Gaelic for "good-bye," which is said to the person staying *slán leat* (shlahn ly-aht), Gaelic for "good-bye," which is said to the person leaving

Tuatha de Danaan (TOO-aha dai DON-nan), Welsh gods

Tynan (Ti-nin), guard at Castle Geall

Vlad, Cian's stallion

Can't get enough of Nora Roberts?

Try the #1 *New York Times* bestselling
In Death series, by Nora Roberts
writing as J. D. Robb.

Turn the page to see where it began . . .

Naked in Death

She woke in the dark. Through the slats on the window shades, the first murky hint of dawn slipped, slanting shadowy bars over the bed. It was like waking in a cell.

For a moment she simply lay there, shuddering, imprisoned, while the dream faded. After ten years on the force, Eve still had dreams.

Six hours before, she'd killed a man, had watched death creep into his eyes. It wasn't the first time she'd exercised maximum force, or dreamed. She'd learned to accept the action and the consequences.

But it was the child that haunted her. The child she hadn't been in time to save. The child whose screams had echoed in the dreams with her own.

All the blood, Eve thought, scrubbing sweat from her face with her hands. Such a small little girl to have had so much blood in her. And she knew it was vital that she push it aside.

Standard departmental procedure meant that she would spend the morning in Testing. Any officer whose discharge of weapon resulted in termination of life was required to undergo emotional and psychiatric clearance before resuming duty. Eve considered the tests a mild pain in the ass.

She would beat them, as she'd beaten them before.

When she rose, the overheads went automatically to low setting, lighting her way into the bath. She winced once at her reflection. Her eyes were swollen from lack of sleep, her skin nearly as pale as the corpses she'd delegated to the ME.

Rather than dwell on it, she stepped into the shower, yawning.

"Give me one oh one degrees, full force," she said and shifted so that the shower spray hit her straight in the face.

She let it steam, lathered listlessly while she played through the events of the night before. She wasn't due in Testing until nine, and would use the next three hours to settle and let the dream fade away completely.

Small doubts and little regrets were often detected and could mean a second and more intense round with the machines and the owl-eyed technicians who ran them.

Eve didn't intend to be off the streets longer than twenty-four hours.

After pulling on a robe, she walked into the kitchen and programmed her AutoChef for coffee, black; toast, light. Through her window she could hear the heavy hum of air traffic carrying early commuters to offices, late ones home. She'd chosen the apartment years before because it was in a heavy ground and air pattern, and she liked the noise and crowds. On another yawn, she glanced out the window, followed the rattling journey of an aging airbus hauling laborers not fortunate enough to work in the city or by home 'links.

She brought the *New York Times* up on her monitor and scanned the headlines while the faux caffeine bolstered her system. The AutoChef had burned her toast again, but she ate it anyway, with a vague thought of springing for a replacement unit.

She was frowning over an article on a mass recall of droid cocker spaniels when her telelink blipped. Eve shifted to communications and watched her commanding officer flash onto the screen.

"Commander."

"Lieutenant." He gave her a brisk nod, noted the still-wet hair and sleepy eyes. "Incident at Twenty-seven West Broadway, eighteenth floor. You're primary."

Eve lifted a brow. "I'm on Testing. Subject terminated at twenty-two thirty-five."

"We have override," he said, without inflection. "Pick up your shield and weapon on the way to the incident. Code Five, Lieutenant."

"Yes, sir." His face flashed off even as she pushed back from the screen. Code Five meant she would report directly to her commander, and there would be no unsealed interdepartmental reports and no cooperation with the press.

In essence, it meant she was on her own.

Broadway was noisy and crowded, a party that rowdy guests never left. Street, pedestrian, and sky traffic were miserable, choking the air with bodies and vehicles. In her old days in uniform she remembered it as a hot spot for wrecks and crushed tourists who were too busy gaping at the show to get out of the way.

Even at this hour steam was rising from the stationary and portable food stands that offered everything from rice noodles to soy dogs for the teeming crowds. She had to swerve to avoid an eager merchant on his smoking Glida-Grill, and took his flipped middle finger as a matter of course.

Eve double-parked and, skirting a man who smelled worse than his bottle of brew, stepped onto the sidewalk. She scanned the building first, fifty floors of gleaming metal that knifed into the sky from a hilt of concrete. She was propositioned twice before she reached the door.

Since this five-block area of West Broadway was affectionately termed Prostitute's Walk, she wasn't surprised.

She flashed her badge for the uniform guarding the entrance.

"Lieutenant Dallas."

"Yes, sir." He skimmed his official CompuSeal over the door to keep out the curious, then led the way to the bank of elevators. "Eighteenth floor," he said when the doors swished shut behind them.

"Fill me in, Officer." Eve switched on her recorder and waited.

"I wasn't first on the scene, Lieutenant. Whatever happened upstairs is being kept upstairs. There's a badge inside waiting for you. We have a homicide, and a Code Five in number eighteen-oh-three."

"Who called it in?"

"I don't have that information."

He stayed where he was when the elevator opened. Eve stepped out and was alone in a narrow hallway. Security cameras tilted down at her, and her feet were almost soundless on the worn nap of the carpet as she approached 1803. Ignoring the hand plate, she announced herself, holding her badge up to eye level for the peep cam until the door opened.

"Dallas."

"Feeney." She smiled, pleased to see a familiar face. Ryan Feeney was an old friend and former partner who'd traded the street for a desk and a top-level position in the Electronics Detection Division. "So, they're sending computer pluckers these days."

"They wanted brass, and the best." His lips curved in his wide, rumpled face, but his eyes remained sober. He was a small, stubby man with small, stubby hands and rust-colored hair. "You look beat."

"Rough night."

"So I heard." He offered her one of the sugared nuts from the bag he habitually carried, studying her, and measuring if she was up to what was waiting in the bedroom beyond.

She was young for her rank, barely thirty, with wide brown eyes that had never had a chance to be naive. Her doe-brown hair was cropped short, for convenience rather than style, but suited her triangular face with its razor-edge cheekbones and slight dent in the chin.

She was tall, rangy, with a tendency to look thin, but Feeney knew there were solid muscles beneath the leather jacket. But Eve had more—there was also a brain, and a heart.

"This one's going to be touchy, Dallas."

"I picked that up already. Who's the victim?"

"Sharon DeBlass, granddaughter of Senator DeBlass."

Neither meant anything to her. "Politics isn't my forte, Feeney."

"The gentleman from Virginia, extreme right, old money. The granddaughter took a sharp left a few years back, moved to New York and became a licensed companion."

"She was a hooker." Dallas glanced around the apartment. It was furnished in obsessive modern—glass and thin chrome, signed holograms on the walls, recessed bar in bold red. The wide mood screen behind the bar bled with mixing and merging shapes and colors in cool pastels.

Neat as a virgin, Eve mused, and cold as a whore. "No surprise, given her choice of real estate."

"Politics makes it delicate. Victim was twenty-four, Caucasian female. She bought it in bed."

Eve only lifted a brow. "Seems poetic, since she'd been bought there. How'd she die?"

"That's the next problem. I want you to see for yourself."

As they crossed the room, each took out a slim container, sprayed their hands front and back to seal in oils and fingerprints. At the doorway, Eve sprayed the bottom of her boots to slicken them so that she would pick up no fibers, stray hairs, or skin.

Eve was already wary. Under normal circumstances there would have been two other investigators on a homicide scene, with recorders for sound and pictures. Forensics would have been waiting with their usual snarly impatience to sweep the scene.

The fact that only Feeney had been assigned with her meant that there were a lot of eggshells to be walked over.

"Security cameras in the lobby, elevator, and hallways," Eve commented.

"I've already tagged the discs." Feeney opened the bedroom door and let her enter first.

It wasn't pretty. Death rarely was a peaceful, religious experience to Eve's mind. It was the nasty end, indifferent to saint and sinner. But this was shocking, like a stage deliberately set to offend.

The bed was huge, slicked with what appeared to be genuine satin sheets the color of ripe peaches. Small, soft-focused spotlights were trained on its center where the naked woman was cupped in the gentle dip of the floating mattress.

The mattress moved with obscenely graceful undulations to the rhythm of programmed music slipping through the headboard.

She was beautiful still, a cameo face with a tumbling waterfall of flaming red hair, emerald eyes that stared glassily at the mirrored ceiling, long, milk-white limbs that called to mind visions of *Swan Lake* as the motion of the bed gently rocked them.

They weren't artistically arranged now, but spread lewdly so that the dead woman formed a final X dead-center of the bed.

There was a hole in her forehead, one in her chest, another horribly gaping between the open thighs. Blood had splattered on the glossy sheets, pooled, dripped, and stained.

There were splashes of it on the lacquered walls, like lethal paintings scrawled by an evil child.

So much blood was a rare thing, and she had seen much too much of it the night before to take the scene as calmly as she would have preferred.

She had to swallow once, hard, and force herself to block out the image of a small child.

"You got the scene on record?"

"Yep."

"Then turn that damn thing off." She let out a breath after Feeney located the controls that silenced the music. The bed flowed to stillness. "The wounds," Eve murmured, stepping closer to examine them. "Too neat for a knife. Too messy for a laser." A flash came to her—old training films, old videos, old viciousness.

"Christ, Feeney, these look like bullet wounds."

Feeney reached into his pocket and drew out a sealed bag. "Whoever did it left a souvenir." He passed the bag to Eve. "An antique like this has to go for eight, ten thousand for a legal collection, twice that on the black market."

Fascinated, Eve turned the sealed revolver over in her hand. "It's heavy," she said half to herself. "Bulky."

"Thirty-eight caliber," he told her. "First one I've seen outside of a museum. This one's a Smith and Wesson, Model Ten, blue steel." He looked at it with some affection. "Real classic piece, used to be standard police issue up until the latter part of the twentieth. They stopped making them in about twenty-two, twenty-three, when the gun ban was passed."

"You're the history buff." Which explained why he was with her. "Looks new." She sniffed through the bag, caught the scent of oil and burning. "Somebody took good care of this. Steel fired into flesh," she mused as she passed the bag back to Feeney. "Ugly way to die, and the first I've seen it in my ten years with the department."

"Second for me. About fifteen years ago, Lower East Side, party got out of hand. Guy shot five people with a twenty-two before he realized it wasn't a toy. Hell of a mess."

"Fun and games," Eve murmured. "We'll scan the collectors, see how many we can locate who own one like this. Somebody might have reported a robbery."

"Might have."

"It's more likely it came through the black market." Eve glanced back at the body. "If she's been in the business for a few years, she'd have discs, records of her clients, her trick books." She frowned. "With Code Five, I'll have to do the door-to-door myself. Not a simple sex crime," she said with a sigh. "Whoever did it set it up. The antique weapon, the wounds themselves, almost ruler-straight down the body, the lights, the pose. Who called it in, Feeney?"

"The killer." He waited until her eyes came back to him. "From right here. Called the station. See how the bed-side unit's aimed at her face? That's what came in. Video, no audio."

"He's into showmanship." Eve let out a breath. "Clever bastard, arrogant, cocky. He had sex with her first. I'd bet my badge on it. Then he gets up and does it." She lifted her arm, aiming, lowering it as she counted off, "One, two, three."

"That's cold," murmured Feeney.

"He's cold. He smooths down the sheets after. See how neat they are? He arranges her, spreads her open so nobody can have any doubts as to how she made her living. He does it carefully, practically measuring, so that she's perfectly aligned. Center of the bed, arms and legs equally apart. Doesn't turn off the bed 'cause it's part of the show. He leaves the gun because he wants us to know right away he's no ordinary man. He's got an ego. He doesn't want to waste time letting the body be discovered eventually. He wants it now. That instant gratification."

"She was licensed for men and women," Feeney pointed out, but Eve shook her head.

"It's not a woman. A woman wouldn't have left her looking both beautiful and obscene. No, I don't think it's a woman. Let's see what we can find. Have you gone into her computer yet?"

"No. It's your case, Dallas. I'm only authorized to assist."

"See if you can access her client files." Eve went to the dresser and began to carefully search drawers.

Expensive taste, Eve reflected. There were several items

of real silk, the kind no simulation could match. The bottle of scent on the dresser was exclusive, and smelled, after a quick sniff, like expensive sex.

The contents of the drawers were meticulously ordered, lingerie folded precisely, sweaters arranged according to color and material. The closet was the same.

Obviously the victim had a love affair with clothes and a taste for the best and took scrupulous care of what she owned.

And she'd died naked.

"Kept good records," Feeney called out. "It's all here. Her client list, appointments—including her required monthly health exam and her weekly trip to the beauty salon. She used the Trident Clinic for the first and Paradise for the second."

"Both top-of-the-line. I've got a friend who saved for a year so she could have one day for the works at Paradise. Takes all kinds."

"My wife's sister went for it for her twenty-fifth anniversary. Cost damn near as much as my kid's wedding. Hello, we've got her personal address book."

"Good. Copy all of it, will you, Feeney?" At his low whistle, she looked over her shoulder, glimpsed the small gold-edged palm computer in his hand. "What?"

"We've got a lot of high-powered names in here. Politics, entertainment, money, money, money. Interesting, our girl has Roarke's private number."

"Roarke who?"

"Just Roarke, as far as I know. Big money there. Kind of guy that touches shit and turns it into gold bricks. You've got to start reading more than the sports page, Dallas."

"Hey, I read the headlines. Did you hear about the cocker spaniel recall?"

"Roarke's always big news," Feeney said patiently. "He's got one of the finest art collections in the world. Arts and antiques," he continued, noting when Eve clicked in and turned to him. "He's a licensed gun collector. Rumor is he knows how to use them."

"I'll pay him a visit."

"You'll be lucky to get within a mile of him."

"I'm feeling lucky." Eve crossed over to the body to slip her hands under the sheets.

"The man's got powerful friends, Dallas. You can't afford to so much as whisper he's linked to this until you've got something solid."

"Feeney, you know it's a mistake to tell me that." But even as she started to smile, her fingers brushed something between cold flesh and bloody sheets. "There's something under her." Carefully, Eve lifted the shoulder, eased her fingers over.

"Paper," she murmured. "Sealed." With her protected thumb, she wiped at a smear of blood until she could read the protected sheet.

ONE OF SIX

"It looks hand printed," she said to Feeney and held it out. "Our boy's more than clever, more than arrogant. And he isn't finished."

Eve spent the rest of the day doing what would normally have been assigned to drones. She interviewed the victim's neighbors personally, recording statements, impressions.

She managed to grab a quick sandwich from the same Glida-Grill she'd nearly smashed before, driving across town. After the night and the morning she'd put in, she could hardly blame the receptionist at Paradise for looking at her as though she'd recently scraped herself off the sidewalk.

Waterfalls played musically among the flora in the reception area of the city's most exclusive salon. Tiny cups of real coffee and slim glasses of fizzling water or champagne were served to those lounging on the cushy chairs and settees. Headphones and discs of fashion magazines were complimentary.

The receptionist was magnificently breasted, a testament to the salon's figure-sculpting techniques. She wore a snug, short outfit in the salon's trademark red, and an incredible coif of ebony hair coiled like snakes.

Eve couldn't have been more delighted.

"I'm sorry," the woman said in a carefully modulated voice as empty of expression as a computer. "We serve by appointment only."

"That's okay." Eve smiled and was almost sorry to puncture the disdain. Almost. "This ought to get me one." She offered her badge. "Who works on Sharon DeBlass?"

The receptionist's horrified eyes darted toward the waiting area. "Our clients' needs are strictly confidential."

"I bet." Enjoying herself, Eve leaned companionably on the U-shaped counter. "I can talk nice and quiet, like this, so we understand each other—Denise?" She flicked her gaze down to the discreet studded badge on the woman's breast. "Or I can talk louder, so everyone understands. If you like the first idea better, you can take me to a nice quiet room where we won't disturb any of your clients, and you can send in Sharon DeBlass's operator. Or whatever term you use."

"Consultant," Denise said faintly. "If you'll follow me."

"My pleasure."

And it was.

Outside of movies or videos, Eve had never seen anything so lush. The carpet was a red cushion your feet could sink blissfully into. Crystal drops hung from the ceiling and spun light. The air smelled of flowers and pampered flesh.

She might not have been able to imagine herself there, spending hours having herself creamed, oiled, pummeled, and sculpted, but if she were going to waste such time on vanity, it would certainly have been interesting to do so under such civilized conditions.

The receptionist showed her into a small room with a hologram of a summer meadow dominating one wall. The quiet sound of birdsong and breezes sweetened the air.

"If you'd just wait here."

"No problem." Eve waited for the door to close then, with an indulgent sigh, she lowered herself into a deeply cushioned chair. The moment she was seated, the monitor beside her blipped on, and a friendly, indulgent face that could only be a droid's beamed smiles.

"Good afternoon. Welcome to Paradise. Your beauty needs and your comfort are our only priorities. Would you like some refreshment while you wait for your personal consultant?"

"Sure. Coffee, black, coffee."

"Of course. What sort would you prefer? Press C on your keyboard for the list of choices."

Smothering a chuckle, Eve followed instructions. She spent the next two minutes pondering over her options, then narrowed it down to French Riviera or Caribbean Cream.

The door opened again before she could decide. Resigned, she rose and faced an elaborately dressed scarecrow.

Over his fuchsia shirt and plum-colored slacks, he wore an open, trailing smock of Paradise red. His hair, flowing back from a painfully thin face, echoed the hue of his slacks. He offered Eve a hand, squeezed gently, and stared at her out of soft doe eyes.

"I'm terribly sorry, Officer. I'm baffled."

"I want information on Sharon DeBlass." Again, Eve took out her badge and offered it for inspection.

"Yes, ah, Lieutenant Dallas. That was my understanding. You must know, of course, our client data is strictly confidential. Paradise has a reputation for discretion as well as excellence."

"And you must know, of course, that I can get a warrant, Mr.—?"

"Oh, Sebastian. Simply Sebastian." He waved a thin hand, sparkling with rings. "I'm not questioning your authority, Lieutenant. But if you could assist me, your motives for the inquiry?"

"I'm inquiring into the motives for the murder of De-Blass." She waited a beat, judged the shock that shot into his eyes and drained his face of color. "Other than that, my data is strictly confidential."

"Murder. My dear God, our lovely Sharon is dead? There must be a mistake." He all but slid into a chair, letting his head fall back and his eyes close. When the monitor offered him refreshment, he waved a hand again. Light shot from his jeweled fingers. "God, yes. I need a brandy, darling. A snifter of Trevalli."

Eve sat beside him, took out her recorder. "Tell me about Sharon."

"A marvelous creature. Physically stunning, of course, but it went deeper." His brandy came into the room on a silent automated cart. Sebastian plucked the snifter and took one deep swallow. "She had flawless taste, a generous heart, rapier wit."

He turned the doe eyes on Eve again. "I saw her only two days ago."

"Professionally?"

"She had a standing weekly appointment, half day. Every other week was a full day." He whipped out a butter yellow scarf and dabbed at his eyes. "Sharon took care of herself, believed strongly in the presentation of self."

"It would be an asset in her line of work."

"Naturally. She only worked to amuse herself. Money wasn't a particular need, with her family background. She enjoyed sex."

"With you?"

His artistic face winced, the rosy lips pursing in what could have been a pout or pain. "I was her consultant, her confidant, and her friend," Sebastian said stiffly and draped the scarf with casual flair over his left shoulder. "It would have been indiscreet and unprofessional for us to become sexual partners."

"So you weren't attracted to her, sexually?"

"It was impossible for anyone not to be attracted to her

sexually. She . . ." He gestured grandly. "Exuded sex as others might exude an expensive perfume. My God." He took another shaky sip of brandy. "It's all past tense. I can't believe it. Dead. Murdered." His gaze shot back to Eve. "You said murdered."

"That's right."

"That neighborhood she lived in," he said grimly. "No one could talk to her about moving to a more acceptable location. She enjoyed living on the edge and flaunting it all under her family's aristocratic noses."

"She and her family were at odds?"

"Oh definitely. She enjoyed shocking them. She was such a free spirit, and they so . . . ordinary." He said it in a tone that indicated ordinary was more mortal a sin than murder itself. "Her grandfather continues to introduce bills that would make prostitution illegal. As if the past century hasn't proven that such matters need to be regulated for health and crime security. He also stands against procreation regulation, gender adjustment, chemical balancing, and the gun ban."

Eve's ears pricked. "The senator opposes the gun ban?"

"It's one of his pets. Sharon told me he owns a number of nasty antiques and spouts off regularly about that outdated right to bear arms business. If he had his way, we'd all be back in the twentieth century, murdering each other right and left."

"Murder still happens," Eve murmured. "Did she ever mention friends or clients who might have been dissatisfied or overly aggressive?"

"Sharon had dozens of friends. She drew people to her, like . . ." He searched for a suitable metaphor, used the corner of the scarf again. "Like an exotic and fragrant flower. And her clients, as far as I know, were all delighted with her. She screened them carefully. All of her sexual partners had to meet certain standards. Appearance, intellect, breeding, and proficiency. As I said, she enjoyed sex, in all of its many forms. She was . . . adventurous."

That fit with the toys Eve had unearthed in the apartment. The velvet handcuffs and whips, the scented oils and hallucinogens. The offerings on the two sets of colinked virtual reality headphones had been a shock even to Eve's jaded system.

"Was she involved with anyone on a personal level?"

"There were men occasionally, but she lost interest quickly. Recently she'd spoken about Roarke. She'd met him at a party and was attracted. In fact, she was seeing him for dinner the very night she came in for her consultation. She'd wanted something exotic because they were dining in Mexico."

"In Mexico. That would have been the night before last."

"Yes. She was just bubbling over about him. We did her hair in a gypsy look, gave her a bit more gold to the skin—full body work. Rascal Red on the nails, and a charming little temp tattoo of a red-winged butterfly on the left buttock. Twenty-four-hour facial cosmetics so that she wouldn't smudge. She looked spectacular," he said, tearing up. "And she kissed me and told me she just might be in love this time. 'Wish me luck, Sebastian.' She said that as she left. It was the last thing she ever said to me."

The Circle Trilogy begins with an epic tale that breaks down the boundaries between reality and the otherworldly, while forging together the passions of the men and women caught in a battle for the fate of humanity.

In the last days of high summer, with lightning striking blue in a black sky, the sorcerer stood on a high cliff overlooking the raging sea. . . .

Belting out his grief into the storm, Hoyt Mac Cionaoith rails against the evil that has torn his twin brother from their family's embrace. Her name is Lilith. Existing for over a thousand years, she has lured countless men to an immortal doom with her soul-stealing kiss. But now, this woman known as vampire will stop at nothing until she rules this world—and those beyond it.

Hoyt is no match for the dark siren. But his powers come from the goddess Morrigan, and it is through her that he will get his chance at vengeance. At Morrigan's charge, he must gather five others to form a ring of power strong enough to overcome Lilith. A circle of six: himself, the witch, the warrior, the scholar, the one of many forms, and the one he's lost. And it is in this circle, hundreds of years in the future, where Hoyt will learn how strong his spirit—and his heart—have become. . . .

Don't miss the other books in the Circle Trilogy

Dance of the Gods
Valley of Silence

Turn the page for a complete list of titles by
Nora Roberts and J. D. Robb from Berkley. . . .

Nora Roberts

Series

Irish Born Trilogy
BORN IN FIRE
BORN IN ICE
BORN IN SHAME

Dream Trilogy
DARING TO DREAM
HOLDING THE DREAM
FINDING THE DREAM

Chesapeake Bay Saga
SEA SWEPT
RISING TIDES
INNER HARBOR
CHESAPEAKE BLUE

Gallaghers of Ardmore Trilogy
JEWELS OF THE SUN
TEARS OF THE MOON
HEART OF THE SEA

Three Sisters Island Trilogy
DANCE UPON THE AIR
HEAVEN AND EARTH
FACE THE FIRE

Key Trilogy
KEY OF LIGHT
KEY OF KNOWLEDGE
KEY OF VALOR

In the Garden Trilogy
BLUE DAHLIA
BLACK ROSE
RED LILY

Circle Trilogy
MORRIGAN'S CROSS
DANCE OF THE GODS
VALLEY OF SILENCE

Sign of Seven Trilogy
BLOOD BROTHERS
THE HOLLOW
THE PAGAN STONE

Bride Quartet
VISION IN WHITE
BED OF ROSES
SAVOR THE MOMENT
HAPPY EVER AFTER

The Inn BoonsBoro Trilogy
THE NEXT ALWAYS
THE LAST BOYFRIEND
THE PERFECT HOPE

The Cousins O'Dwyer Trilogy
DARK WITCH
SHADOW SPELL
BLOOD MAGICK

The Guardians Trilogy
STARS OF FORTUNE
BAY OF SIGHS
ISLAND OF GLASS

Ebooks by Nora Roberts

Cordina's Royal Family
AFFAIRE ROYALE
COMMAND PERFORMANCE
THE PLAYBOY PRINCE
CORDINA'S CROWN JEWEL

The Donovan Legacy
CAPTIVATED
ENTRANCED
CHARMED
ENCHANTED

The O'Hurleys
THE LAST HONEST WOMAN
DANCE TO THE PIPER
SKIN DEEP
WITHOUT A TRACE

Night Tales
NIGHT SHIFT
NIGHT SHADOW
NIGHTSHADE
NIGHT SMOKE
NIGHT SHIELD

The MacGregors
PLAYING THE ODDS
TEMPTING FATE
ALL THE POSSIBILITIES
ONE MAN'S ART
FOR NOW, FOREVER
REBELLION/IN FROM THE COLD
THE MACGREGOR BRIDES
THE WINNING HAND
THE MACGREGOR GROOMS
THE PERFECT NEIGHBOR

The Calhouns
COURTING CATHERINE
A MAN FOR AMANDA
FOR THE LOVE OF LILAH
SUZANNA'S SURRENDER
MEGAN'S MATE

Irish Legacy
IRISH THOROUGHBRED
IRISH ROSE
IRISH REBEL

LOVING JACK
BEST LAID PLANS
LAWLESS

BLITHE IMAGES
SONG OF THE WEST
SEARCH FOR LOVE
ISLAND OF FLOWERS
THE HEART'S VICTORY
FROM THIS DAY
HER MOTHER'S KEEPER
ONCE MORE WITH FEELING
REFLECTIONS
DANCE OF DREAMS
UNTAMED
THIS MAGIC MOMENT
ENDINGS AND BEGINNINGS
STORM WARNING
SULLIVAN'S WOMAN
FIRST IMPRESSIONS
A MATTER OF CHOICE

LESS OF A STRANGER
THE LAW IS A LADY
RULES OF THE GAME
OPPOSITES ATTRACT
THE RIGHT PATH
PARTNERS
BOUNDARY LINES
DUAL IMAGE
TEMPTATION
LOCAL HERO
THE NAME OF THE GAME
GABRIEL'S ANGEL
THE WELCOMING
TIME WAS
TIMES CHANGE
SUMMER LOVE
HOLIDAY WISHES

Morrigan's
Cross

NORA ROBERTS

JOVE
New York

A JOVE BOOK
Published by Berkley
An imprint of Penguin Random House LLC
penguinrandomhouse.com

ISBN: 9780515141658

Jove mass-market edition / September 2006
Jove trade paperback edition / January 2016

Printed in the United States of America
17   19   21   22   20   18   16

Cover image by IgorZh / Shutterstock
Cover design by Rita Frangie
Book design by Kristin del Rosario

For my brothers,
Jim, Buz, Don and Bill

None but the brave deserves the fair.
—DRYDEN

Finish, good lady; the bright day is done,
And we are for the dark.
—SHAKESPEARE

Prologue

It was the rain that made him think of the tale. The lash of it battered the windows, stormed the rooftops and blew its bitter breath under the doors.

The damp ached in his bones even as he settled by the fire. Age sat heavily on him in the long, wet nights of autumn— and would sit heavier still, he knew, in the dark winter to come.

The children were gathered, huddled on the floor, squeezed by twos and threes into chairs. Their faces were turned to his, expectant, for he'd promised them a story to chase boredom from a stormy day.

He hadn't intended to give them this one, not yet, for some were so young. And the tale was far from tender. But the rain whispered to him, hissing the words he'd yet to speak.

Even a storyteller, perhaps especially a storyteller, had to listen.

"I know a tale," he began, and several of the children squirmed in anticipation. "It's one of courage and cowardice, of blood and death, and of life. Of love and of loss."

"Are there monsters?" one of the youngest asked, with her blue eyes wide with gleeful fear.

"There are always monsters," the old man replied. "Just as there are always men who will join them, and men who will fight them."

"And women!" one of the older girls called out, and made him smile.

"And women. Brave and true, devious and deadly. I have known both in my time. Now, this tale I tell you is from long ago. It has many beginnings, but only one end."

As the wind howled, the old man picked up his tea to wet his throat. The fire crackled, shot light across his face in a wash like gilded blood.

"This is one beginning. In the last days of high summer, with lightning striking blue in a black sky, the sorcerer stood on a high cliff overlooking the raging sea."

Chapter 1

Eire, the region of Chiarrai
1128

There was a storm in him, as black and vicious as that which bullied its way across the sea. It whipped inside his blood, outside in the air, battling within and without as he stood on the rain-slickened rock.

The name of his storm was grief.

It was grief that flashed in his eyes, as bold and as blue as those lightning strikes. And the rage from it spit from his fingertips, jagged red that split the air with thunderclaps that echoed like a thousand cannon shots.

He thrust his staff high, shouted out the words of magic. The red bolts of his rage and the bitter blue of the storm clashed overhead in a war that sent those who could see scurrying into cottage and cave, latching door and window, gathering their children close to quake and quail as they prayed to the gods of their choosing.

And in their raths, even the faeries trembled.

Rock rang, and the water of the sea went black as the mouth of hell, and still he raged, and still he grieved. The rain that poured out of the wounded sky fell red as blood—and sizzled, burning on land, on sea, so that the air smelled of its boiling.

It would be called, ever after, The Night of Sorrows, and those who dared speak of it spoke of the sorcerer who stood tall on the high cliff, with the bloody rain soaking his cloak, running down his lean face like death's tears as he dared both heaven and hell.

His name was Hoyt, and his family the *Mac Cionaoith*, who were said to be descended from Morrigan, faerie queen and goddess. His power was great, but still young as he was young. He wielded it now with a passion that gave no room to caution, to duty, to light. It was his sword and his lance.

What he called in that terrible storm was death.

While the wind shrieked, he turned, putting his back to the tumultuous sea. What he had called stood on the high ground. She—for she had been a woman once—smiled. Her beauty was impossible, and cold as winter. Her eyes were tenderly blue, her lips pink as rose petals, her skin milk white. When she spoke, her voice was music, a siren's who had already called countless men to their doom.

"You're rash to seek me out. Are you impatient, Mac Cionaoith, for my kiss?"

"You are what killed my brother?"

"Death is . . ." Heedless of the rain, she pushed back her hood. "Complex. You are too young to understand its glories. What I gave him is a gift. Precious and powerful."

"You damned him."

"Oh." She flicked a hand in the air. "Such a small price for eternity. The world is his now, and he takes whatever he wants. He knows more than you can dream of. He's mine now, more than he was ever yours."

"Demon, his blood is on your hands, and by the goddess, I will destroy you."

She laughed, gaily, like a child promised a particular treat. "On my hands, in my throat. As mine is in his. He is like me now, a child of night and shadow. Will you also seek to destroy your own brother? Your twin?"

The ground fog boiled black, folded away like silk as she waded through it. "I smell your power, and your grief, and your wonder. Now, on this place, I offer this gift to you. I will make you once more his twin, Hoyt of the Mac

Cionaoiths. I will give you the death that is unending life."

He lowered his staff, stared at her through the curtain of rain. "Give me your name."

She glided over the fog now, her red cloak billowing back. He could see the white swell of her breasts rounding ripely over the tightly laced bodice of her gown. He felt a terrible arousal even as he scented the stench of her power.

"I have so many," she countered, and touched his arm—how had she come so close?—with just the tip of her finger. "Do you want to say my name as we join? To taste it on your lips, as I taste you?"

His throat was dry, burning. Her eyes, blue and tender, were drawing him in, drawing him in to drown. "Aye. I want to know what my brother knows."

She laughed again, but this time there was a throatiness to it. A hunger that was an animal's hunger. And those soft blue eyes began to rim with red. "Jealous?"

She brushed her lips to his, and they were cold, bitter cold. And still, so tempting. His heart began to beat hard and fast in his chest. "I want to see what my brother sees."

He laid his hand on that lovely white breast, and felt nothing stir beneath it. "Give me your name."

She smiled, and now the white of her fangs gleamed against the awful night. "It is Lilith who takes you. It is Lilith who makes you. The power of your blood will mix with mine, and we will rule this world, and all the others."

She threw back her head, poised to strike. With all of his grief, with all of his rage, Hoyt struck at her heart with his staff.

The sound that ripped from her pierced the night, screamed up through the storm and joined it. It wasn't human, not even the howl of a beast. Here was the demon who had taken his brother, who hid her evil behind cold beauty. Who bled, he saw as a stream of blood spilled from the wound, without a heartbeat.

She flew back into the air, twisting, shrieking as lightning tore at the sky. The words he needed to say were lost in his horror as she writhed in the air, and the blood that fell steamed into filthy fog.

"You would dare!" Her voice gurgled with outrage, with pain. "You would use your puny, your pitiful magic on me? I have walked this world a *thousand* years." She slicked her hand over the wound, threw out her bloody hand.

And when the drops struck Hoyt's arm, they sliced like a knife.

"Lilith! You are cast out! Lilith, you are vanquished from this place. By my blood." He pulled a dagger from beneath his cloak, scored his palm. "By the blood of the gods that runs through it, by the power of my birth, I cast you back—"

What came at him seemed to fly across the ground, and struck with the feral force of fury. Tangled, they crashed over the cliff to the jagged ledge below. Through waves of pain and fear he saw the face of the thing that so closely mirrored his own. The face that had once been his brother's.

Hoyt could smell the death on him, and the blood, and could see in those red eyes the animal his brother had become. Still, a small flame of hope flickered in Hoyt's heart.

"Cian. Help me stop her. We still have a chance."

"Do you feel how strong I am?" Cian closed his hand around Hoyt's throat and squeezed. "It's only the beginning. I have forever now." He leaned down, licked blood from Hoyt's face, almost playfully. "She wants you for herself, but I'm hungry. So hungry. And the blood in you is mine, after all."

As he bared his fangs, pressed them to his brother's throat, Hoyt thrust the dagger into him.

With a howl, Cian reared back. Shock and pain rushed over his face. Even as he clutched at the wound, he fell. For an instant, Hoyt thought he saw his brother, his true brother. Then there was nothing but the screams of the storm and the slashing rain.

He crawled and clawed his way up the cliff. His hands, slippery with blood and sweat and rain, groped for any hold. Lightning illuminated his face, tight with pain, as he inched his way up rock, tore his fingers in the clawing. His neck, where the fangs had scraped, burned like a brand. Breath whistling, he clutched at the edge.

If she waited, he was dead. His power had waned with

exhaustion, drained with the ravages of his shock and grief. He had nothing but the dagger, still red with his brother's blood.

But when he pulled himself up, when he rolled to his back with the bitter rain washing over his face, he was alone.

Perhaps it had been enough, perhaps he'd sent the demon back to hell. As he had surely sent his own flesh and blood to damnation.

Rolling over, he gained his hands and knees, and was viciously ill. Magic was ashes in his mouth.

He crawled to his staff, used it to help him stand. Breath keening, he staggered away from the cliffs, along a path he'd have known had he been blinded. The power had gone out of the storm as it had gone out of him, and now was merely a soaking rain.

He smelled home—horse and hay, the herbs he'd used for protection, the smoke from the fire he'd left smoldering in the hearth. But there was no joy in it, no triumph.

As he limped toward his cottage, his breath whistled out, hisses of pain that were lost in the rise of the wind. He knew if the thing that had taken his brother came for him now, he was lost. Every shadow, every shape cast by the storm-tossed trees could be his death. Worse than his death. Fear of that slicked along his skin like dirty ice, so that he used what strength he had to murmur incantations that were more like prayers for whoever, or whatever, would listen.

His horse stirred in its shelter, let out a huff as it scented him. But Hoyt continued shakily to the small cottage, dragging himself to the door and through.

Inside was warmth, and the ripple from the spells he'd cast before he'd gone to the cliffs. He barred the door, leaving smears of his and Cian's blood on the wood. Would it keep her out? he wondered. If the lore he'd read was fact, she couldn't enter without an invitation. All he could do was have faith in that, and in the protection spell that surrounded his home.

He let his soaked cloak fall, let it lay in a sodden heap on the floor, and had to fight not to join it there. He would mix potions for healing, for strength. And would sit through the night, tending the fire. Waiting for dawn.

He'd done all he could for his parents, his sisters and their families. He had to believe it was enough.

Cian was dead, and what had come back with his face and form had been destroyed. He would not, could not, harm them now. But the thing that had made him could.

He would find something stronger to protect them. And he would hunt the demon again. His life, he swore it now, would be dedicated to her destruction.

His hands, long of finger, wide of palm, were tremulous as he chose his bottles and pots. His eyes, stormy blue, were glazed with pain—the aches of his body, of his heart. Guilt weighed on him like a shroud of lead. And those demons played inside him.

He hadn't saved his brother. Instead, he had damned and destroyed him, cast him out and away. How had he won that terrible victory? Cian had always been physically superior to him. And what his brother had become was viciously powerful.

So his magic had vanquished what he'd once loved. The half of him that was bright and impulsive where he himself was often dull and staid. More interested in his studies and his skills than society.

Cian had been the one for gaming and taverns, for wenches and sport.

"His love of life," Hoyt murmured as he worked. "His love of life killed him. I only destroyed that which trapped him in a beast."

He had to believe it.

Pain rippled up his ribs as he shucked off his tunic. Bruises were already spreading, creeping black over his skin the way grief and guilt crept black over his heart. It was time for practical matters, he told himself as he applied the balm. He fumbled considerably, cursed violently, in wrapping the bandage over his ribs. Two were broken, he knew, just as he knew the ride back home in the morning would be a study in sheer misery.

He took a potion, then limped to the fire. He added turf so the flames glowed red. Over them he brewed tea. Then wrapped himself in a blanket to sit, to drink, to brood.

He had been born with a gift, and from an early age had soberly, meticulously sought to honor it. He'd studied, often in solitude, practicing his art, learning its scope.

Cian's powers had been less, but, Hoyt remembered, Cian had never practiced so religiously nor studied so earnestly. And Cian had played with magic, after all. Amusing himself and others.

And Cian had sometimes drawn him in, lowered Hoyt's resistance until they'd done something foolish together. Once they'd turned the boy who'd pushed their younger sister in the mud into a braying, long-eared ass.

How Cian had laughed! It had taken Hoyt three days of work, sweat and panic to reverse the spell, but Cian had never worried a whit.

He was born an ass, after all. We've just given him his true form.

From the time they'd been twelve, Cian had been more interested in swords than spells. Just as well, Hoyt thought as he drank the bitter tea. He'd been irresponsible with magic, and a magician with a sword.

But, steel hadn't saved him, nor had magic, in the end.

He sat back, chilled to his bones despite the simmering turf. He could hear what was left of the storm blowing still, splattering on his roof, wailing through the forest that surrounded his cottage.

But he heard nothing else, not beast, not threat. So was left alone with his memories and regrets.

He should've gone with Cian into the village that evening. But he'd been working, and hadn't wanted ale, or the smells and sounds of a tavern, of people.

He hadn't wanted a woman, and Cian had never *not* wanted one.

But if he'd gone, if he'd put aside his work for one bloody night, Cian would be alive. Surely the demon couldn't have overpowered both of them. Surely his gift would have allowed him to sense what the creature was, despite her beauty, her allure.

Cian would never have gone with her had his brother been by his side. And their mother would not be grieving.

The grave would never have been dug, and by the gods, the thing they buried would never have risen.

If his powers could turn back time, he would give them up, abjure them, to have that one night to relive that single moment when he'd chosen work over his brother's company.

"What good do they do me? What good are they now? To have been given magic and not be able to use it to save what matters most? Damn to them all then." He flung his cup across the little room. "Damn to them all, gods and faeries. He was the light of us, and you've cast him into the dark."

All of his life Hoyt had done what he was meant to do, what was expected of him. He had turned away from a hundred small pleasures to devote himself to his art. Now those who had given him this gift, this power, had stood back while his own brother was taken?

Not in battle, not even with the clean blade of magic, but through evil beyond imagination. This was his payment, this was his reward for all he had done?

He waved a hand toward the fire, and in the hearth flames leaped and roared. He threw up his arms, and over-head the storm doubled in power so that the wind screamed like a tortured woman. The cottage trembled under its might, and the skins pulled tight over the windows split. Cold gusts spilled into the room, toppling bottles, flapping the pages of his books. And in it he heard the throaty chuckle of the black.

Not once in all of his life had he turned from his purpose. Not once had he used his gift for ill, or touched upon the black arts.

Perhaps now, he thought, he would find the answers in them. Find his brother again. Fight the beast, evil against evil.

He shoved to his feet, ignoring the scream in his side. He whirled toward his cot and flung out both hands toward the trunk he'd locked by magic. When it flew open, he strode to it, reached in for the book he'd shut away years before.

In it were spells, dark and dangerous magicks. Spells that used human blood, human pain. Spells of vengeance and greed that spoke to a power that ignored all oaths, all vows.

It was hot and heavy in his hands, and he felt the seduction of it, those curling fingers that brushed the soul. Have all, have any. Are we not more than the rest? Living gods who take whatever is desired?

We have the right! We are beyond rules and reasons.

His breath came short for he knew what could be his if he accepted it, if he took in both hands what he'd sworn never to touch. Unnamed wealth, women, unspeakable powers, life eternal. Revenge.

He had only to say the words, to rebuke the white and embrace the black. Clammy snakes of sweat slithered down his back as he heard the whispers of voices from a thousand ages: *Take. Take. Take.*

His vision shimmered, and through it he saw his brother as he'd found him in the muck on the side of the road. Blood pooled from the wounds in his throat, and more smeared his lips. Pale, Hoyt thought dimly. So very pale was his face against that wet, red blood.

Now Cian's eyes—vivid and blue—opened. There was such pain in them, such horror. They pleaded as they met Hoyt's.

"Save me. Only you can save me. It's not death I'm damned to. 'Tis beyond hell, beyond torment. Bring me back. For once don't count the cost. Would you have me burn for all eternity? For the sake of your own blood, Hoyt, help me."

He shook. It wasn't from the cold that blew through the split skins, or the damp that whirled in the air, but from the icy edge on which he stood.

"I would give my life for yours. I swear it on all I am, on all we were. I would take your fate, Cian, if that were the choice before me. But I can't do this. Not even for you."

The vision on the bed erupted in flames, and its screams were past human. On a howl of grief, Hoyt heaved the book back in the trunk. He used the strength left to him to charm the lock before he collapsed on the floor. There he curled up like a child beyond all comfort.

* * *

Perhaps he slept. Perhaps he dreamed. But when he came to, the storm had passed. Light seeped into the room and grew, bold and bright and white, to sear his eyes. He blinked against it, hissing as his ribs protested when he tried to sit up.

There were streams of pink and gold shimmering in the white, warmth radiating from it. He smelled earth, he realized, rich and loamy, and the smoke from the turf fire that was still shimmering in the hearth.

He could see the shape of her, female, and sensed a staggering beauty.

This was no demon come for blood.

Gritting his teeth, he got to his knees. Though there was still grief and anger in his voice, he bowed his head.

"My lady."

"Child."

The light seemed to part for her. Her hair was the fiery red of a warrior, and flowed over her shoulders in silky waves. Her eyes were green as the moss in the forest, and soft now with what might have been pity. She wore white robes trimmed in gold as was her right by rank. Though she was the goddess of battle, she wore no armor, and carried no sword.

She was called Morrigan.

"You have fought well."

"I have lost. I have lost my brother."

"Have you?" She stepped forward, offered him a hand so he would rise. "You stayed true to your oath, though the temptation was great."

"I might have saved him otherwise."

"No." She touched Hoyt's face, and he felt the heat of her. "You would have lost him, and yourself. I promise you. You would give your life for his, but you could not give your soul, or the souls of others. You have a great gift, Hoyt."

"What good is it if I cannot protect my own blood? Do the gods demand such sacrifice, to damn an innocent to such torment?"

"It was not the gods who damned him. Nor was it for you to save him. But there is sacrifice to be made, battles to be fought. Blood, innocent and otherwise, to be spilled. You have been chosen for a great task."

"You could ask anything of me now, Lady?"

"Aye. A great deal will be asked of you, and of others. There is a battle to be fought, the greatest ever waged. Good against evil. You must gather the forces."

"I am not able. I am not willing. I am . . . God, I am tired."

He dropped to the edge of his cot, dropped his head in his hands. "I must go see my mother. I must tell her I failed to save her son."

"You have not failed. Because you resisted the dark, you are charged to bear this standard, to use the gift you've been given to face and to vanquish that which would destroy worlds. Shake off this self-pity!"

His head rose at the sharp tone. "Even the gods must grieve, Lady. I have killed my brother tonight."

"Your brother was killed by the beast, a week ago. What fell from the cliff was not your Cian. You know this. But he . . . continues."

Hoyt got shakily to his feet. "He lives."

"It is not life. It is without breath, without soul, without heart. It has a name that is not spoken yet in this world. It is vampyre. It feeds on blood," she said, moving toward him. "It hunts the human, takes life, or worse, much worse, turns that which it hunts and kills into itself. It breeds, Hoyt, like a pestilence. It has no face, and must hide from the sun. It is this you must fight, this and other demons that are gathering. You must meet this force in battle on the feast of Samhain. And you must be victorious or the world you know, the worlds you have yet to know, will be overcome."

"And how will I find them? How will I fight them? It was Cian who was the warrior."

"You must leave this place and go to another, and another still. Some will come to you, and some you will seek. The witch, the warrior, the scholar, the one of many forms, and the one you've lost."

"Only five more? Six against an army of demons? My lady—"

"A circle of six, as strong and true as the arm of a god. When that circle is formed, others may be formed. But the six will be my army, the six will make the ring. You will teach and you will learn, and you will be greater than the sum of you. A month to gather, and one to learn, and one to know. The battle comes on Samhain.

"You, child, are my first."

"You would ask me to leave the family I have left, when that thing that took my brother may come for them?"

"The thing that took your brother leads this force."

"I wounded her—it. I gave her pain." And the memory of that bubbled up in him like vengeance.

"You did, aye, you did. And this is only another step toward this time and this battle. She bears your mark now, and will, in time, seek you out."

"If I hunt her now, destroy her now."

"You cannot. She is beyond you at this time, and you, my child, are not ready to face her. Between these times and worlds, her thirst will grow insatiable until only the destruction of all humankind will satisfy it. You will have your revenge, Hoyt," she said as he got to his feet. "If you defeat her. You will travel far, and you will suffer. And I will suffer knowing your pain, for you are mine. Do you think your fate, your happiness is nothing to me? You are my child even as you are your mother's."

"And what of my mother, Lady? Of my father, my sisters, their families? Without me to protect them, they may be the first to die if this battle you speak of comes to pass."

"It will come to pass. But they will be beyond it." She spread her hands. "Your love for your blood is part of your power, and I will not ask you to turn from it. You will not think clearly until you have assurance they will be safe."

She tipped back her head, held her arms up, palms cupped. The ground shook lightly under his feet, and when Hoyt looked up, he saw stars shooting through the night sky. Those points of light streamed toward her hands, and there burst into flame.

His heart thumped against his bruised ribs as she spoke, as her fiery hair flew around her illuminated face.

"Forged by the gods, by the light and by the night. Symbol and shield, simple and true. For faith, for loyalty, these gifts for you. Their magic lives through blood shed, yours and mine."

Pain sliced over his palm. He watched the blood well in his, and in hers as the fire burned.

"And so it shall live for all time. Blessed be those who wear Morrigan's Cross."

The fire died, and in the goddess's hands were crosses of gleaming silver.

"These will protect them. They must wear the cross always—day and night—birth to death. You will know they are safe when you leave them."

"If I do this thing, will you spare my brother?"

"You would bargain with the gods?"

"Aye."

She smiled, an amused mother to a child. "You have been chosen, Hoyt, because you would think to do so. You will leave this place and gather those who are needed. You will prepare and you will train. The battle will be fought with sword and lance, with tooth and fang, with wit and treachery. If you are victorious, the worlds will balance and you will have all you wish to have."

"How do I fight a vampyre? I've already failed against her."

"Study and learn," she said. "And learn from one of her kind. One she made. One who was yours before she took him. You must first find your brother."

"Where?"

"Not only where, but when. Look into the fire, and see."

They were, he noted, in his cottage again, and he was standing in front of the hearth. The flames spiked up, became towers. Became a great city. There were voices and sounds such as he'd never heard. Thousands of people rushed along streets that were made of some kind of stone. And machines sped with them.

"What is this place?" He could barely whisper the words. "What world is it?"

"It is called New York, and its time is nearly a thousand

years from where we are. Evil still walks the world, Hoyt, as well as innocence, as well as good. Your brother has walked the world a long time now. Centuries have passed for him. You would do well to remember that."

"Is he a god now?"

"He is vampyre. He must teach you, and he must fight beside you. There can be no victory without him."

Such size, he thought. Buildings of silver and stone taller than any cathedral. "Will the war be in this place, in this New York?"

"You will be told where, you will be told how. And you will know. Now you must go, take what you need. Go to your family and give them their shields. You must leave them quickly, and go to the Dance of the Gods. You will need your skill, and my power, to pass through. Find your brother, Hoyt. It is time for the gathering."

He woke by the fire, the blanket wrapped around him. But he saw it hadn't been a dream. Not with the blood drying on the palm of his hand, and the silver crosses lying across his lap.

It was not yet dawn, but he packed books and potions, oatcakes and honey. And the precious crosses. He saddled his horse, and then, as a precaution, cast another protective circle around his cottage.

He would come back, he promised himself. He would find his brother, and this time, he would save him. Whatever it took.

As the sun cast its first light, he began the long ride to An Clar, and his family home.

Chapter 2

He traveled north on roads gone to mud from the storm. The horrors and the wonders of the night played through his mind as he hunched over his horse, favoring his aching ribs.

He swore, should he live long enough, he would practice healing magic more often, and with more attention.

He passed fields where men worked and cattle grazed in the soft morning sunlight. And lakes that picked up their blue from the late summer sky. He wound through forests where the waterfalls thundered and the shadows and mosses were the realm of the faerie folk.

He was known here, and caps were lifted when Hoyt the Sorcerer passed by. But he didn't stop to take hospitality in one of the cabins or cottages. Nor did he seek comfort in one of the great houses, or in the conversations of monks in their abbeys or round towers.

In this journey he was alone, and above battles and orders from gods, he would seek his family first. He would offer them all he could before he left them to do what he'd been charged to do.

As the miles passed, he struggled to straighten on his horse whenever he came to villages or outposts. His dignity cost him considerable discomfort until he was forced to take his ease by the side of a river where the water gurgled over rock.

Once, he thought, he had enjoyed this ride from his cottage to his family home, through the fields and the hills, or along the sea. In solitude, or in the company of his brother, he had ridden these same roads and paths, felt this same sun on his face. Had stopped to eat and rest his horse at this very same spot.

But now the sun seared his eyes, and the smell of the earth and grass couldn't reach his deadened senses.

Fever sweat slicked his skin, and the angles of his face were keener as he bore down against the unrelenting pain.

Though he had no appetite, he ate part of one of the oat-cakes along with more of the medicine he'd packed. Despite the brew and the rest, his ribs continued to ache like a rotted tooth.

Just what good would he be in battle? he wondered. If he had to lift his sword now to save his life he would die with his hands empty.

Vampyre, he thought. The word fit. It was erotic, exotic, and somehow horrible. When he had both time and energy, he would write down more of what he knew. Though he was far from convinced he was about to save this world or any other from some demonic invasion, it was always best to gather knowledge.

He closed his eyes a moment, resting them against the headache that drummed behind them. A witch, he'd been told. He disliked dealing with witches. They were forever stirring odd bits of this and that in pots and rattling their charms.

Then a scholar. At least he might be useful.

Was the warrior Cian? That was his hope. Cian wielding sword and shield again, fighting alongside him. He could nearly believe he could fulfill the task he'd been given if his brother was with him.

The one with many shapes. Odd. A faerie perhaps, and

the gods knew just how reliable such creatures were. And this was somehow to be the front line in the battle for worlds?

He studied the hand he'd bandaged that morning. "Better for all if it had been dreaming. I'm sick and tired is what I am, and no soldier at the best of it."

Go back. The voice was a hissing whisper. Hoyt came to his feet, reaching for his dagger.

Nothing moved in the forest but the black wings of a raven that perched in shadows on a rock by the water.

Go back to your books and herbs, Hoyt the Sorcerer. Do you think you can defeat the Queen of the Demons? Go back, go back and live your pitiful life, and she will spare you. Go forward, and she will feast on your flesh and drink of your blood.

"Does she fear to tell me so herself then? And so she should, for I will hunt her through this life and the next if need be. I will avenge my brother. And in the battle to come, I will cut out her heart and burn it."

You will die screaming, and she will make you her slave for eternity.

"It's an annoyance you are." Hoyt shifted his grip on the dagger. As the raven took wing he flipped it through the air. It missed, but the flash of fire he shot out with his free hand hit the mark. The raven shrieked, and what dropped to the ground was ashes.

In disgust Hoyt looked at the dagger. He'd been close, and would likely have done the job if he hadn't been wounded. At least Cian had taught him that much.

But now he had to go fetch the bloody thing.

Before he did, he took a handful of salt from his saddlebags, poured it over the ashes of the harbinger. Then retrieving his dagger, he went to his horse and mounted with gritted teeth.

"Slave for all eternity," he muttered. "We'll see about that, won't we?"

He rode on, hemmed in by green fields, the rise of hills chased by cloud shadows in light soft as down. Knowing a gallop would have his ribs shrieking, he kept the horse to a plod. He dozed, and he dreamed that he was back on the cliffs struggling with Cian. But this time it was he who tumbled off, spiraling down into the black to crash against the unforgiving rocks.

He woke with a start, and with the pain. Surely this much pain meant death.

His horse had stopped to crop at the grass by the side of the road. There a man in a peaked cap built a wall from a pile of steely gray rock. His beard was pointed, yellow as the gorse that rambled over the low hill, his wrists thick as tree limbs.

"Good day to you, sir, now that you've waked to it." The man touched his cap in salute, then bent for another stone. "You've traveled far this day."

"I have, yes." Though he wasn't entirely sure where he was. There was a fever working in him; he could feel the sticky heat of it. "I'm to An Clar, and the Mac Cionaoith land. What is this place?"

"It's where you are," the man said cheerfully. "You'll not make your journey's end by nightfall."

"No." Hoyt looked down the road that seemed to stretch to forever. "No, not by nightfall."

"There'd be a cabin with a fire going beyond the field, but you've not time to bide here. Not when you've so far yet to go. And time shortens even as we speak. You're weary," the man said with some sympathy. "But you'll be wearier yet before it's done."

"Who are you?"

"Just a signpost on your way. When you come to the second fork, go west. When you hear the river, follow it. There be a holy well near a rowan tree, Bridget's Well, that some now call saint. There you'll rest your aching bones for the night. Cast your circle there, Hoyt the Sorcerer, for they'll come hunting. They only wait for the sun to die. You must be at the well, in your circle, before it does."

"If they follow me, if they hunt me, I take them straight to my family."

"They're no strangers to yours. You bear Morrigan's Cross. It's that you'll leave behind with your blood. That and your faith." The man's eyes were pale and gray, and for a moment, it seemed worlds lived in them. "If you fail, more than your blood is lost by Samhain. Go now. The sun's in the west already."

What choice did he have? It all seemed a dream now, boiling in his fever. His brother's death, then his destruction. The thing on the cliffs that called herself Lilith. Had he been visited by the goddess, or was he simply trapped in some dream?

Maybe he was dead already, and this was merely a journey to the afterlife.

But he took the west fork, and when he heard the river, turned his horse toward it. Chills shook him now, from the fever and the knowledge that the light was fading.

He fell from his horse more than dismounted, and leaned breathlessly against its neck. The wound on his hand broke open and stained the bandage red. In the west, the sun was a low ball of dying fire.

The holy well was a low square of stone guarded by the rowan tree. Others who'd come to worship or rest had tied tokens, ribbons and charms, to the branches. Hoyt tethered his horse, then knelt to take the small ladle and sip the cool water. He poured drops on the ground for the god, murmured his thanks. He laid a copper penny on the stone, smearing it with blood from his wound.

His legs felt more full of water than bone, but as twilight crept in, he forced himself to focus. And began to cast his circle.

It was simple magic, one of the first that comes. But his power came now in fitful spurts, and made the task a misery. His own sweat chilled his skin as he struggled with the words, with the thoughts and with the power that seemed a slippery eel wriggling in his hands.

He heard something stalking in the woods, moving in the deepest shadows. And those shadows thickened as the last rays of sunlight eked through the cover of trees.

They were coming for him, waiting for that last flicker to die and leave him in the dark. He would die here, alone, leave his family unprotected. And all for the whim of the gods.

"Be damned if I will." He drew himself up. One chance more, he knew. One. And so he ripped the bandage from his hand, used his own blood to seal the circle.

"Within this ring the light remains. It burns through the night at *my* will. This magic is clean, and none but clean shall bide here. Fire kindle, fire rise, rise and burn with power bright."

Flames shimmered in the center of his circle, weak, but there. As it rose, the sun died. And what had been in the shadows leaped out. It came as a wolf, black pelt and bloody eyes. When it flung itself into the air, Hoyt pulled his dagger. But the beast struck the force of the circle, and was repelled.

It howled, snapped, snarled. Its fangs gleamed white as it paced back and forth as if looking for a weakness in the shield.

Another joined it, skulking out of the trees, then another, another yet, until Hoyt counted six. They lunged together, fell back together. Paced together like soldiers.

Each time they charged, his horse screamed and reared. He stepped toward his mount, his eyes on the wolves as he laid his hands upon it. This at least, he could do. He soothed, lulling his faithful mare into a trance. Then he drew his sword, plunged it into the ground by the fire.

He took what food he had left, water from the well, mixed more herbs—though the gods knew his self-medicating was having no good effect. He lowered to the ground by the fire, sword on one side, dagger on the other and his staff across his legs.

He huddled in his cloak shivering, and after dousing an oatcake with honey, forced it down. The wolves sat on their haunches, threw back their heads, and as one, howled at the rising moon.

"Hungry, are you?" Hoyt muttered through chattering teeth. "There's nothing here for you. Oh, what I wouldn't give for a bed, some decent tea." He sat, the fire dancing in his eyes until they began to close. As his chin drooped to his chest, he'd never felt so alone. Or so unsure of his path.

He thought it was Morrigan who came to him, for she was beautiful and her hair as bold as the fire. It fell straight as rain, its tips grazing her shoulders. She wore black, a strange garb, and immodest enough to leave her arms bare and allow the swell of her breasts to rise from the bodice. Around her neck she wore a pentagram with a moonstone in its center.

"This won't do," she said in a voice that was both foreign and impatient. Kneeling beside him, she laid her hand on his brow, her touch as cool and soothing as spring rain. She smelled of the forest, earthy and secret.

For one mad moment, he longed to simply lay his head upon her breast and sleep with that scent filling his senses.

"You're burning up. Well, let's see what you have here, and we'll make do."

She wavered in his vision a moment, then recrystallized. Her eyes were as green as the goddess's, but her touch was human. "Who are you? How did you get within the circle?"

"Elderflower, yarrow. No cayenne? Well, I said we'd make do."

He watched as she busied herself, as women would, dipping water from the well, heating it with his fire. "Wolves," she murmured, shivered once. And in that shudder, he felt her fear. "Sometimes I dream of the black wolves, or ravens. Sometimes it's the woman. She's the worst. But this is the first time I've dreamed of you." She paused, and looked at him for a long time with eyes of deep and secret green. "And still, I know your face."

"This is my dream."

She gave a short laugh, then sprinkled herbs in the heated water. "Have it your way. Let's see if we can help you live through it."

She passed her hand over the cup. "Power of healing, herbs and water, brewed this night by Hecate's daughter. Cool his fever, ease his pain so that strength and sight remain. Stir magic in this simple tea. As I will, so mote it be."

"Gods save me." He managed to prop himself on an elbow. "You're a witch."

She smiled as she stepped to him with the cup. And sitting beside him, braced him with an arm around his back. "Of course. Aren't you?"

"I'm not." He had just enough energy for insult. "I'm

a bloody sorcerer. Get that poison away from me. Even the smell is foul."

"That may be, but it should cure what ails you." She simply cradled his head on her shoulder. Even as he tried to push free, she was pinching his nose closed and pouring the brew down his throat. "Men are such babies when they're sick. And look at your hand! Bloody and filthy. I've got something for that."

"Get away from me," he said weakly, though the smell of her, the feel of her was both seductive and comforting. "Let me die in peace."

"You're not going to die." But she gave the wolves a wary glance. "How strong is your circle?"

"Strong enough."

"Hope you're right."

Exhaustion—and the valerian she'd mixed in the tea—had his head drooping again. She shifted, so she could lay his head in her lap. And there she stroked his hair, kept her eyes on the fire. "You're not alone anymore," she said quietly. "And I guess, neither am I."

"The sun . . . How long till dawn?"

"I wish I knew. You should sleep now."

"Who are you?"

But if she answered, he didn't hear.

She was gone when he woke, and so was the fever. Dawn was a misty shimmer letting thin beams eke through the summer leaves.

Of the wolves there was only one, and it lay gored and bloody outside the circle. Its throat had been ripped open, Hoyt saw, and its belly. Even as he gained his feet to step closer, the sun beamed white through those leaves, struck the carcass.

It erupted into flame that left nothing behind but a scatter of ashes on blackened earth.

"To hell with you, and all like you."

Turning away, Hoyt busied himself, feeding his horse, brewing more tea. He was nearly done when he noticed his palm was healed. Only the faintest scar remained. He flexed his fingers, held his hand up to the light.

Curious, he lifted his tunic. Bruises still rained over his side, but they were fading. And when he tested, he found he could move without pain.

If what had come to him in the night had been a vision rather than a product of a fever dream, he supposed he should be grateful.

Still, he'd never had a vision so vivid. Nor one who'd left so much of itself behind. He swore he could smell her still, and hear the flow and cadence of her voice.

She'd said she'd known his face. How strange that some-where in the center of him, he felt he'd known hers.

He washed, and while his appetite had come back strong, he had to make do with berries and a heel of tough bread.

He closed the circle, salted the blackened earth outside it. Once he was in the saddle, he set off at a gallop.

With luck, he could be home by midday.

There were no signs, no harbingers, no beautiful witches on the rest of his journey. There were only the fields, rolling green, back to the shadow of mountains, and the secret depths of forest. He knew his way now, would have known it if a hundred years had passed. So he sent his mount on a leap over a low stone wall and raced across the last field toward home.

He could see the cook fire. He imagined his mother sit-ting in the parlor, tatting lace perhaps, or working on one of her tapestries. Waiting, hoping for news of her sons. He wished he brought her better.

His father might be with his man of business or out riding the land, and his married sisters in their own cottages, with young Nola in the stables playing with the pups from the new litter.

The house was tucked in the forest, because his grandmother—she who had passed power to him, and to a lesser extent, Cian—had wanted it so. It stood near a stream, a rise of stone with windows of real glass. And its gardens were his mother's great pride.

Her roses bloomed riotously.

One of the servants hurried out to take his horse. Hoyt merely shook his head at the question in the man's eyes. He walked to the door where the black banner of mourning still hung.

Inside, another servant was waiting to take his cloak. Here in the hall, his mother's, and her mother's tapestries hung, and one of his father's wolfhounds raced to greet him.

He could smell beeswax, and roses cut fresh from the garden. The turf fire simmering in the grate. He left them behind, walked up the stairs to his mother's sitting room.

She was waiting, as he'd known she would be. Sitting in her chair, her hands in her lap, clasped so tightly the knuckles were white. Her face carried all the weight of her grief, and went heavier yet when she saw what was in his eyes.

"Mother—"

"You're alive. You're well." She got to her feet, held out her arms to him. "I've lost my youngest son, but here is my firstborn, home again. You'll want food and drink after your journey."

"I have much to tell you."

"And so you will."

"All of you, if you please, madam. I cannot stay long. I'm sorry." He kissed her brow. "I'm sorry to leave you."

There was food and there was drink, and the whole of his family—save Cian—around the table. But it was not a meal like so many he remembered, with laughter and shouted arguments, with joy or petty disagreements. Hoyt studied their faces, the beauties, the strengths and the sorrows as he told them what had passed.

"If there is to be a battle, I will come with you. Fight with you."

Hoyt looked at his brother-in-law Fearghus. His shoulders were broad, his fists ready.

"Where I go, you can't follow. You're not charged with this fight. It's for you and Eoin to stay here, to protect with my father, the family, the land. I would go with a heavier heart if I didn't know you and Eoin stand in my stead. You must wear these."

He took out the crosses. "Each of you, and all the children who come after. Day and night, night and day. This," he said and lifted one, "is Morrigan's Cross, forged by the gods in magic fire. The vampyre cannot turn any who wear it into its kind. This must be passed on to those who come after you, in song and story. You will swear an oath, each of you, that you will wear this cross until death."

He rose, draping a cross over each neck, waiting for the sworn oath before moving on.

Then he knelt by his father. His father's hands were old, Hoyt noted with a jolt. He was more farmer than warrior, and in a flash, he knew his father's death would come first, and before the Yule. Just as he knew he would never again look in the eyes of the man who'd given him life.

And his heart bled a little.

"I take my leave of you, sir. I ask your blessing."

"Avenge your brother, and come back to us."

"I will." Hoyt rose. "I must gather what I need."

He went up to the room he kept in the topmost tower, and there began to pack herbs and potions without any real sense what would be needed.

"Where is your cross?"

He looked toward the doorway where Nola stood, her dark hair hanging to her waist. She was but eight, he thought, and held the softest spot in his heart.

"She didn't make me one," he said, briskly. "I have another sort of shield, and there's no need for you to be worrying. I know what I'm about."

"I won't cry when you go."

"Why would you? I've gone before, haven't I, and come back handily enough?"

"You'll come back. To the tower. She'll come with you."

He nestled bottles carefully in his case, then paused to study his sister. "Who will?"

"The woman with red hair. Not the goddess, but a mortal woman, one who wears the sign of the witch. I can't see Cian, and I can't see if you'll win. But I can see you, here with the witch. And you're afraid."

"Should a man go into battle without fear? Isn't fear something that helps keep him alive?"

"I don't know of battles. I wish I were a man, and a warrior." Her mouth, so young, so soft, went grim. "You wouldn't be stopping me from going with you the way you stopped Fearghus."

"How would I dare?" He closed his case, moved to her. "I am afraid. Don't tell the others."

"I won't."

Aye, the softest place in his heart, he thought, and lifting her cross, used his magic to scribe her name on the back in ogham script. "It makes it only yours," he told her.

"Mine, and the ones who'll have my name after me." Her eyes glimmered, but the tears didn't fall. "You'll see me again."

"I will, of course."

"When you do, the circle will be complete. I don't know how, or why."

"What else do you see, Nola?"

She only shook her head. "It's dark. I can't see. I'll light a candle for you, every night, until you return."

"I'll ride home by its light." He bent down to embrace her. "I'll miss you most of all." He kissed her gently, then set her aside. "Be safe."

"I will have daughters," she called after him.

It made him turn, and smile. So slight, he mused, and so fierce. "Will you now?"

"It is my lot," she told him with a resignation that made his lips twitch. "But they will not be weak. They will *not* sit and spin and knead and bake all the damn day."

Now he grinned fully, and knew this was a memory he would take with him happily. "Oh won't they? What then, young mother, will your daughters do?"

"They will be warriors. And the vampyre who fancies herself a queen will tremble before them."

She folded her hands, much as their mother was wont to do, but with none of that meekness. "Go with the gods, brother."

"Stay in the light, sister."

They watched him go—three sisters, the men who loved

them, the children they'd already made. His parents, even the servants and stable boys. He took one last long look at the house his grandfather, and his father before, had built of stone in this glade, by this stream, in this land he loved with the whole of his heart.

Then he raised his hand in farewell, and rode away from them and toward the Dance of the Gods.

It stood on a rise of rough grass that was thick with the sunny yellow of buttercups. Clouds had rolled to layer the sky so that light forced its way through in thin beams. The world was so still, so silent, he felt as though he rode through a painting. The gray of the sky, the green of the grass, the yellow flowers and the ancient circle of stones that had risen in its dance since beyond time.

He felt its power, the hum of it, in the air, along his skin. Hoyt walked his horse around them, paused to read the ogham script carved into the king stone.

"Worlds wait," he translated. "Time flows. Gods watch."

He started to dismount when a shimmer of gold across the field caught his eye. There at the edge of it was a hind. The green of her eyes sparkled like the jeweled collar she wore. She walked toward him regally, and changed to the female form of the goddess.

"You are in good time, Hoyt."

"It was painful to bid my family farewell. Best done quickly then."

He slid off the horse, bowed. "My lady."

"Child. You have been ill."

"A fever, broken now. Did you send the witch to me?"

"There's no need to send what will come on its own. You'll find her again, and the others."

"My brother."

"He is first. The light will go soon. Here is the key to the portal." She opened her hand and offered a small crystal wand. "Keep it with you, keep it safe and whole." When he started to remount, she shook her head, took the reins. "No, you must go on foot. Your horse will get safely back home."

Resigned to the whimsy of gods, he took his case, his bag. He strapped on his sword, hefted his staff.

"How will I find him?"

"Through the portal, into the world yet to come. Into the Dance, lift the key, say the words. Your destiny lies beyond. Humankind is in your hands, from this point forward. Through the portal," she repeated. "Into the world yet to come. Into the Dance, lift the key, say the words. Through the portal . . ."

Her voice followed him in, between the great stones. He locked his fear inside him. If he'd been born for this, so be it. Life was long, he knew. It simply came in short bursts.

He lifted the stone. A single beam of light speared out of those thick clouds to strike its tip. Power shot down his arm like an arrow.

"Worlds wait. Time flows. Gods watch."

"Repeat," Morrigan told him, and joined him so that the words became a chant.

"Worlds wait. Time flows. Gods watch."

The air shook around him, came alive with wind, with light, with sound. The crystal in his uplifted hand shone like the sun and sang like a siren.

He heard his own voice come out in a roar, shouting the words now as if in challenge.

And so he flew. Through light and wind and sound. Beyond stars and moons and planets. Over water that made his sorcerer's belly roil with nausea. Faster, until the light was blinding, the sounds deafening and the wind so fierce he wondered it didn't flay the skin from his bones.

Then the light went dim, the wind died, and the world was silent.

He leaned on his staff, catching his breath, waiting for his eyes to adjust to the change of light. He smelled something— leather, he thought, and roses.

He was in a room of some sort, he realized, but like nothing he'd ever seen. It was fantastically furnished with long, low chairs in deep colors, and cloth for a floor. Paintings adorned some of the walls, and others were lined with books. Dozens of books bound in leather.

He stepped forward, charmed, when a movement to his left stopped him cold.

His brother sat behind some sort of table, where the lamp that lit the room glowed strangely. His hair was shorter than it had been, shorn to the jawline. His eyes were vivid with what seemed to be amusement.

In his hand was some sort of metal tool, which instinct told Hoyt was a weapon.

Cian pointed it at his brother's heart and tipped back in the chair, dropping his feet on the surface of the table. He smiled, broadly, and said, "Well now, look what the cat dragged in."

With some confusion, Hoyt frowned, scanning the room for the cat. "Do you know me?" Hoyt stepped forward, farther into the light. "It's Hoyt. It's your brother. I've come to . . ."

"Kill me? Too late. Already long dead. Why don't you just stay where you are for the moment. I see quite well in low light. You're looking . . . well, fairly ridiculous really. But I'm impressed nonetheless. How long did it take you to perfect time travel?"

"I . . ." Coming through the portal might have addled his brains, he thought. Or it might be simply seeing his dead brother, looking very much alive. "Cian."

"I'm not using that name these days. It's Cain, right at the moment. One syllable. Take off the cloak, Hoyt, and let's have a look at what's under it."

"You're a vampyre."

"I am, yes, certainly. The cloak, Hoyt."

Hoyt unhooked the brooch that held it in place, let it drop.

"Sword and dagger. A lot of weaponry for a sorcerer."

"There's to be a battle."

"Do you think so?" That amusement rippled again, coldly. "I can promise you'll lose. What I have here is called a gun. It's quite a good one, really. It fires out a projectile faster than you can blink. You'll be dead where you stand before you can draw that sword."

"I haven't come to fight you."

"Really? The last time we met—let me refresh my memory. Ah yes, you pushed me off a cliff."

"You pushed me off the bloody cliff first," Hoyt said with

some heat. "Broke my bloody ribs while you were about it. I thought you were gone. Oh merciful gods, Cian, I thought you were gone."

"I'm not, as you can plainly see. Go back where you came from, Hoyt. I've had a thousand years, give or take, to get over my annoyance with you."

"For me you died only a week ago." He lifted his tunic. "You gave me these bruises."

Cian's gaze drifted over them, then back to Hoyt's face. "They'll heal soon enough."

"I've come with a charge from Morrigan."

"Morrigan, is it?" This time the amusement burst out in laughter. "There are no gods here. No God. No faerie queens. Your magic has no place in this time, and neither do you."

"But you do."

"Adjustment is survival. Money is god here, and power its partner. I have both. I've shed the likes of you a long time ago."

"This world will end, they will all end, by Samhain, unless you help me stop her."

"Stop who?"

"The one who made you. The one called Lilith."

Chapter 3

Lilith. The name brought Cian flashes of memories, a hundred lifetimes past. He could still see her, smell her, still feel that sudden, horrified thrill in the instant she'd taken his life.

He could still taste her blood, and what had come into him with it. The dark, dark gift.

His world had changed. And he'd been given the privilege—or the curse—of watching worlds change over countless decades.

Hadn't he known something was coming? Why else had he been sitting alone in the middle of the night, waiting?

What nasty little twist of fate had sent his brother—or the brother of the man he'd once been—across time to speak her name?

"Well, now you have my attention."

"You must come back with me, prepare for the battle."

"Back? To the twelfth century?" Cian let out a short laugh as he leaned back in his chair. "Nothing, I promise you, could tempt me. I like the conveniences of this time. The water runs hot here, Hoyt, and so do the women. I'm not interested in your politics and wars, and certainly not in your gods."

"The battle will be fought, with or without you, Cian."

"Without sounds perfectly fine."

"You've never turned from battle, never hidden from a fight."

"*Hiding* wouldn't be the term I'd use," Cian said easily. "And times change. Believe me."

"If Lilith defeats us, all you know will be lost in this time, for all time. Humankind will cease to be."

Cian angled his head. "I'm not human."

"Is that your answer?" Hoyt strode forward. "You'll sit and do nothing while she destroys? You'll stand by while she does to others what she did to you? While she kills your mother, your sisters? Will you sit there while she turns Nola into what you are?"

"They're dead. Long dead. They're dust." Hadn't he seen their graves? He hadn't been able to stop himself from going back and standing over their stones, and the stones of those who'd come after them.

"Have you forgotten all you were taught? Times change, you say. It's more than change. Could I be here now if time was solid? Their fate is not set, nor is yours. Even now our father is dying, yet I left him. I will never see him alive again."

Slowly Cian got to his feet. "You have no conception of what she is, what she is capable of. She was old, centuries old, when she took me. You think to stop her with swords and lightning bolts? You're more fool than I remember."

"I think to stop her with you. Help me. If not for humanity, then for yourself. Or would you join her? If there's nothing left of my brother in you, we'll end this between us now."

Hoyt drew his sword.

For a long moment, Cian studied the blade, considered the gun in his hand. Then he slipped the weapon back in his pocket. "Put your sword away. Christ, Hoyt, you couldn't take me one-on-one when I was alive."

Challenge, and simple irritation, rushed into Hoyt's eyes. "You didn't fare very well the last time we fought."

"True enough. It took me weeks to recover. Hiding around in caves by day, half starving. I looked for her then, you know. Lilith, who sired me. By night, while I struggled to hunt enough food to survive. She abandoned me. So I've a point to square with her. Put the damn sword away."

When Hoyt hesitated, Cian simply leaped. In the blink of an eye he was up, gliding over Hoyt's head and landing lightly at his back. He disarmed his brother with one careless twist of the wrist.

Hoyt turned slowly. The point of the sword was at his throat. "Well done," he managed.

"We're faster, and we're stronger. We have no conscience to bind us. We are driven to kill, to feed. To survive."

"Then why aren't I dead?"

Cian lifted a shoulder. "We'll put it down to curiosity, and a bit of old time's sake." He tossed the sword across the room. "Well then, let's have a drink."

He walked to a cabinet, opened it. Out of the corner of his eye he saw the sword fly across the room and into Hoyt's hand. "Well done on you," he said mildly and took out a bottle of wine. "You can't kill me with steel, but you could—if you were lucky enough—hack some part of me off that I'd rather keep. We don't regenerate limbs."

"I'll put my weapons aside, and you do the same."

"Fair enough." Cian took the gun out of his pocket, set it on a table. "Though a vampire always has his weapon." He offered a brief glimpse of fangs. "Nothing to be done about that." He poured two glasses while Hoyt laid down his sword and dagger. "Have a seat then, and you can tell me why I should get involved in saving the world. I'm a busy man these days. I have enterprises."

Hoyt took the glass offered, studied it, sniffed at it. "What is this?"

"A very nice Italian red. I've no need to poison you." To prove it, he sipped from his own glass. "I could snap your neck like a twig." Cian sat himself, stretched out his legs. Then he waved a hand at Hoyt. "In today's worlds, what we're having here could be called a meeting, and you're about to make your pitch. So . . . enlighten me."

"We must gather forces, beginning with a handful. There is a scholar and a witch, one of many forms and a warrior. That must be you."

"No. I'm no warrior. I'm a businessman." He continued to sit, at his ease, giving Hoyt a lazy smile. "So the gods, as usual, have given you pitifully little to work with, and an all but impossible task. With your handful, and whoever else is fool enough to join you, you're expected to defeat an army led by a powerful vampire, most likely with troops of her kind, and other manner of demon if she deigns to bother with them. Otherwise, the world is destroyed."

"Worlds," Hoyt corrected. "There are more than one."

"You're right about that anyway." Cian sipped, contemplated. He'd nearly run out of challenges in his current persona. This, at least, was interesting.

"And what do your gods tell you is my part in this?"

"You must come with me, teach me all that you can about her kind, and how to defeat them. What are their weaknesses? What are their powers? What weaponry and magic will work against them? We have until Samhain to master these and gather the first circle."

"That long?" Sarcasm dripped. "What would I gain from all this? I'm a wealthy man, with many interests to protect here and now."

"And would she allow you to keep that wealth, those interests, should she rule?"

Cian pursed his lips. Now there was a thought. "Possibly not. But it's more than possible if I help you I'll risk all that and my own existence. When you're young, as you are—"

"I'm the eldest."

"Not for the last nine hundred years and counting. In any case, when you're young you think you'll live forever, so you take all manner of foolish risks. But when you've lived as long as I, you're more careful. Because existence is imperative. I'm driven to survive, Hoyt. Humans and vampires have that in common."

"You survive sitting alone in the dark in this little house?"

"It's not a house," Cian said absently. "It's an office. A place of business. I have many houses, as it happens. That, too, is survival. There are taxes and records and all manner of things to be gotten around. Like most of my kind I rarely stay in one place for long. We're nomadic from nature and necessity."

He leaned forward now, resting his elbows on his knees. There were so few he could speak to about what he was. That was his choice, that was the life he'd made. "Hoyt, I've seen wars, countless wars, such as you could never imagine. No one wins them. If you do this thing, you'll die. Or become. It would be a feather in Lilith's cap to turn a sorcerer of your power."

"Do you think there is a choice here?"

"Oh yes." He sat back again. "There always is. I've made many in my lifetimes." He closed his eyes now, lazily swirling his wine. "Something's coming. There have been rumblings in the world under this one. In the dark places. If it's what you say, it's bigger than I assumed. I should've paid more attention. I don't socialize with vampires as a rule."

Baffled, as Cian had always been sociable, Hoyt frowned. "Why not?"

"Because as a rule they're liars and killers and bring too much attention to themselves. And those humans who socialize with them are usually mad or doomed. I pay my taxes, file my reports and keep a low profile. And every decade or so, I move, change my name and keep off the radar."

"I don't understand half of what you say."

"Imagine not," Cian replied. "She'll fuck this up for everyone. Bloodbaths always do, and those demons who go about thinking they want to destroy the world are ridiculously shortsighted. We have to live in it, don't we?"

He sat in silence. He could focus and hear each beat of his brother's heart, hear the faint electrical hum of the room's climate controls, the buzz of the lamp on his desk across the room. Or he could block them out, as he most often did with background noises.

He'd learned to do, and not do, a great deal over time.

A choice, he thought again. Well, why not?

"It comes down to blood," Cian said, and his eyes stayed closed. "First and last, it comes to blood. We both need it to live, your kind and mine. It's what we sacrifice, for the gods you worship, for countries, for women. And what we spill for the same reasons. My kind doesn't quibble about reasons."

He opened his eyes now, and showed Hoyt how they could burn red. "We just take it. We hunger for it, crave it. Without it, we cease to be. It's our nature to hunt, kill, feed. Some of us enjoy it more than others, just as humans do. Some of us enjoy causing pain, inciting fear, tormenting and torturing our prey. Just as humans do. We're not all of the same cloth, Hoyt."

"You murder."

"When you hunt the buck in the forest and take its life, is it murder? You're no more than that, less, often less, to us."

"I saw your death."

"The tumble off the cliffs wasn't—"

"No. I saw her kill you. I thought it a dream at first. I watched you come out of the tavern, go with her in her carriage. And couple with her as it drove out of the village. And I saw her eyes change, and how the fangs glinted in the dark before she sank them into your throat. I saw your face. The pain, the shock and . . ."

"Arousal," Cian finished. "Ecstasy. It's a moment of some intensity."

"You tried to fight, but she was an animal on you, and I thought you were dead, but you weren't. Not quite."

"No, to feed you simply take, drain the prey dry if you choose. But to change a human, he must drink from the blood of his maker."

"She sliced her own breast, and pressed your mouth to her, and still you tried to fight until you began to suckle on her like a babe."

"The allure is powerful, as is the drive to survive. It was drink or die."

"When she was done, she threw you out into the road, left you there. It was there I found you." Hoyt drank deeply as his belly quivered. "There I found you, covered with blood and mud. And this is what you do to survive? The buck is given more respect."

"Do you want to lecture me?" Cian began as he rose to get the bottle again. "Or do you want to know?"

"I need to know."

"Some hunt in packs, some alone. At wakening we're most vulnerable—from the first when we wake in the grave, to every evening if we've slept through the day. We are night creatures. The sun is death."

"You burn in it."

"I see you know some things."

"I saw. They hunted me when I journeyed home. In the form of wolves."

"Only vampires of some age and power, or those under the protection of another powerful sire can shape shift. Most have to content themselves with the form in which they died. Still, we don't age, physically. A nice bonus feature."

"You look as you did," Hoyt replied. "Yet not. It's more than the garb you wear, or the hair. You move differently."

"I'm not what I was, and that you should remember. Our senses are heightened, and become more so the longer we survive. Fire, like the sun, will destroy us. Holy water, if it's been faithfully blessed, will burn us, as will the symbol of the cross, if held in faith. We are repelled by the symbol."

Crosses, Hoyt thought. Morrigan had given him crosses. Part of the weight eased from his shoulders.

"Metal is fairly useless," Cian continued, "unless you manage to cut off our heads. That would do the trick. But otherwise . . ."

He rose again, walked over and picked up Hoyt's dagger. He flipped it in the air, caught the hilt neatly, then plunged the blade into his chest.

Blood seeped out on the white of Cian's shirt even as Hoyt lunged to his feet.

"Forgot how much that hurts." Wincing, Cian yanked the blade free. "That's what I get for showing off. Do the same with wood, and we're dust. But it must pierce the heart. Our end is agonizing, or so I'm told."

He took out a handkerchief, wiped the blade clean. Then he pulled off his shirt. The wound was already closing.

"We've died once, and aren't easily dispatched a second time. And we'll fight viciously anyone who tries. Lilith is the oldest I've ever known. She'll fight more brutally than any."

He paused, brooded into his wine. "Your mother. How did you leave her?"

"Heartbroken. You were her favorite." Hoyt moved his shoulders as Cian looked up into his face. "We both know it. She asked me to try, to find a way. In her first grief, she could think of nothing else."

"I believe even your sorcery stops short of raising the dead. Or undead."

"I went to your grave that night, to ask the gods to give her heart some peace. I found you, covered with dirt."

"Clawing out of the grave's a messy business."

"You were devouring a rabbit."

"Probably the best I could find. Can't say I recall. The first hours after the Wakening are disjointed. There's only hunger."

"You ran from me. I saw what you were—there had been rumors of such things before—and you ran. I went to the cliffs the night I saw you again, at our mother's behest. She begged me to find a way to break the spell."

"It's not a spell."

"I thought, hoped, if I destroyed the thing that made you . . . Or failing that, I would kill what you'd become."

"And did neither," Cian reminded him. "Which shows you what you're up against. I was fresh and barely knew what I was or what I was capable of. Believe me, she'll have cannier on her side."

"Will I have yours on mine?"

"You haven't a prayer of winning this."

"You underestimate me. I have a great deal more than one prayer. Whether a year has passed or a millennium, you are my brother. My twin. My blood. You said yourself, it's blood, first and last."

Cian ran a finger down his wine glass. "I'll go with you." Then held that finger up before Hoyt could speak. "Because I'm curious, and a bit bored. I've been in this place for more than ten years now, so it's nearly time to move on in any case. I promise you nothing. Don't depend on me, Hoyt. I'll please myself first."

"You can't hunt humans."

"Orders already?" Cian's lips curved slightly. "Typical. As I said, I please myself first. It happens I haven't fed on human blood for eight hundred years. Well, seven hundred and fifty as there was some backsliding."

"Why?"

"To prove that I could resist. And because it's another way to survive—and well—in the world of humans, with their laws. If they're prey, it's impossible to look at them as anything more than a meal. Makes it awkward to do business. And death tends to leave a trail. Dawn's coming."

Distracted, Hoyt glanced around the windowless room. "How do you know?"

"I feel it. And I'm tired of questions. You'll have to stay with me, for now. You can't be trusted to go walking about the city. We may not be identical, but you look too much like me. And those clothes have to go."

"You expect me to wear—what are those?"

"They're called pants," Cian said dryly and moved across the room to a private elevator. "I keep an apartment here, it's simpler."

"You'll pack what you need, and we'll go."

"I don't travel by day, and I don't take orders. I give them now, and have for some time. I have a number of things to see to before I can leave. You need to step in here."

"What is it?" Hoyt poked at the elevator walls with his staff.

"A mode of transportation. It'll take us up to my apartment."

"How?"

Cian finally dragged a hand through his hair. "Look, I've books up there, and other educational matter. You can spend the next few hours boning up on twenty-first-century culture, fashion and technology."

"What is technology?"

Cian pulled his brother inside, pushed the button for the next floor. "It's another god."

* * *

This world, this time, was full of wonder. Hoyt wished he had time to learn it all, absorb it. There were no torches to light the room but instead something Cian called electricity. Food was kept in a box as tall as a man that kept it cold and fresh, and yet another box was used to warm and cook it. Water spilled out of a wand and into a bowl where it drained away again.

The house where Cian lived was built high up in the city, and such a city! The glimpse Morrigan had given him had been nothing compared to what he could see through the glass wall of Cian's quarters.

Hoyt thought even the gods would be stunned by the size and scope of this New York. He wanted to look out at it again, but Cian had demanded his oath that he would keep the glass walls covered, and he would not venture out of the house.

Apartment, Hoyt corrected. Cian had called it an apartment.

He had books, so many books, and the magic box Cian had called a television. Indeed the visions inside it were many, of people and places, of things, of animals. And though he spent only an hour playing with it, he grew weary of its constant chatter.

So he surrounded himself with books and read, and read until his eyes burned and his head was too full for more words or images.

He fell asleep on what Cian had called a sofa, surrounded by books.

He dreamed of the witch, and saw her in a circle of light. She wore nothing but the pendant, and her skin glowed milk-pale in the candlelight.

Her beauty simply flamed.

She held a ball of crystal aloft in both hands. He could hear the whisper of her voice, but not the words. Still, he knew it was an incantation, could feel the power of it, of her across the dream. And he knew she was seeking him out.

Even in sleep he felt the pull of her, and that same impatience he'd sensed from her within his circle, within his own time.

It seemed for an instant that their eyes met across the mists. And it was desire that pierced through him as much as power. In that instant, her lips curved, opened, as if she would speak to him.

"What the hell is that getup?"

He came awake and found himself staring up into the face of a giant. The creature was tall as a tree, and every bit as thick. He had a face even a mother would weep over, black as a moor and scarred at the cheek, and surrounded by knotted hanks of hair.

He had one black eye and one gray. Both narrowed as he bared strong white teeth.

"You're not Cain."

Before Hoyt could react, he was hauled up by the scruff of the neck where he was shaken like a mouse by a very large, angry cat.

"Put him down, King, before he turns you into a small white man."

Cian strolled out of his bedroom, and continued lazily into the kitchen.

"How come he's got your face?"

"He's got his own," Cian retorted. "We don't look that much alike if you pay attention. He used to be my brother."

"That so? Son of a bitch." King dropped Hoyt unceremoniously back on the sofa. "How the hell did he get here?"

"Sorcery." As he spoke, Cian removed a clear packet of blood from a locked cold box. "Gods and battles, end of the world, blah blah."

King looked down at Hoyt with a grin. "I'll be damned. I always thought half of that crap you told me was, well, crap. He's not much for conversation before he's had his evening fix," he said to Hoyt. "You got a name, brother?"

"I am Hoyt of the Mac Cionaoith. And you will not lay hands on me again."

"That's a mouthful."

"Is he like you?" both Hoyt and King demanded in unison.

Wearily Cian poured the blood in a tall, thick glass, then set it in the microwave. "No, to both. King manages my club, the one downstairs. He's a friend."

Hoyt's lips peeled back in disgust. "Your human servant."

"I ain't nobody's servant."

"You've been reading." Cian took out the glass and drank. "Some vampires of rank have human servants. I prefer employees. Hoyt's come to enlist me in the army he hopes to raise to fight the big evil."

"The IRS?"

In better humor, Cian grinned. Hoyt saw something pass between them, something that had once only passed between himself and his brother.

"If only. No, I told you I've heard rumblings. Apparently for a reason. According to the gossip of the gods, Lilith of the Vampires is amassing her own army and plans to destroy humanity, take over the worlds. War, pestilence, plague."

"You can jest?" Hoyt said in barely suppressed fury.

"Christ Jesus, Hoyt, we're talking about vampire armies and time travel. Bloody right I can joke about it. Going with you is likely to kill me."

"Where are you going?"

Cian shrugged at King. "Back to my past, I suppose, to act in an advisory capacity, at least, for General Sobriety there."

"I don't know if we're to go back, or forward, or to the side." Hoyt shoved books over the table. "But we will go back to Ireland. We will be told where we travel next."

"Got a beer?" King asked.

Cian opened the refrigerator, took out a bottle of Harp and tossed it.

"So when do we leave?" King twisted off the cap, took a long slug.

"You don't. I told you before, when it was time for me to leave, I'll give you controlling interest in the club. Apparently, that time's come."

King simply turned to Hoyt. "You raising an army, General?"

"Hoyt. I am, yes."

"You just got your first recruit."

"Stop." Cian strode around the counter that separated the kitchen. "This isn't for you. You don't know anything about this."

"I know about you," King returned. "I know I like a good fight, and I haven't had one in a while. You're talking major battle, good against evil. I like to pick my side from the get."

"If he's a king, why should he take orders from you?" Hoyt put in, and the black giant laughed so hard and long, he had to sit on the sofa.

"Gotcha."

"Misplaced loyalty will get you killed."

"My choice, brother." King tipped the bottle toward Cian. Once again, something silent and strong passed between them with no more than a look. "And I don't figure my loyalty's misplaced."

"Hoyt, go somewhere else." Cian jerked a thumb toward his bedroom. "Go in there. I want a word in private with this idiot."

He cared, Hoyt thought as he obliged. Cian cared about this man, a human trait. Nothing he'd read had indicated vampyres could have true feelings toward humans.

He frowned as he scanned the bedroom. Where was the coffin? The books had said the vampyre slept in the earth of his grave, in a coffin, by day. What he saw here was an enormous bed, one with ticking as soft as clouds and covered with smooth cloth.

He heard the raised voices outside the door, but set about exploring his brother's personal room. Clothes enough for ten men, he decided when he found the closet. Well, Cian had always been vain.

But no looking glass. The books said the vampyre cast no reflection.

He wandered into the bathroom, and his jaw dropped. The expansive privy Cian had showed him before retiring had been amazing and was nothing to this. The tub was large enough for six, and there was a tall box of pale green glass. The walls were marble, as was the floor.

Fascinated, he stepped into the box, began to play with the silver knobs that jutted out of the marble. And yipped in shock when a shower of cold water spurted out of many flat-headed tubes.

"Around here, we take our clothes off before getting in the shower." Cian came in, shut the water off with one violent twist of the wrist. Then he sniffed the air. "On second thought, clothed or otherwise, you could sure as hell use one. You're fucking rank. Clean up," he ordered. "Put on the clothes I've tossed out on the bed. I'm going to work."

He strode out, leaving Hoyt to fumble through on his own.

He discovered, after some time and chill that the temperature of the water could be adjusted. He scalded himself, froze, but eventually found the happy medium.

His brother must have been telling pure truth when he spoke of his wealth, for here was luxury never imagined. The scent of the soap seemed a bit female, but there was nothing else.

Hoyt wallowed in his first twenty-first-century shower, and wondered if he might find a way to duplicate it, by science or magic, once he returned home.

The cloths hanging nearby were as soft as the bed had been. He felt decadent using one to dry his skin.

He didn't care for the clothes, but his own were soaked. He debated going out and getting the spare tunic out of his case, but it seemed best to follow Cian's advice in wardrobe.

It took him twice as long to dress as it would have. The strange fastenings nearly defeated him. The shoes had no laces, but simply slipped on the foot. He was forced to admit that they were quite comfortable.

But he wished there was a bloody looking glass so he could see himself. He stepped out, then came up short. The black king was still on the sofa, drinking from the glass bottle.

"That's an improvement," King observed. "You'll probably pass if you keep your mouth mostly shut."

"What is this fastening here?"

"It's a zipper. Ah, you're going to want to keep that closed, friend." He pushed to his feet. "Cain's gone on down to the club. It's after sunset. He fired me."

"You're burned? I have salve."

"No. Shit. He terminated my employment. He'll get over it. He goes, I go. He don't have to like it."

"He believes we'll all die."

"He's right—sooner or later. You ever see what a vamp can do to a man?"

"I saw what one did to my brother."

King's odd eyes went grim. "Yeah, yeah, that's right. Well, it's this way. I don't figure to sit around and wait for one to do it to me. He's right, there's been rumbling. There's going to be a fight, and I'm going to be in it."

A giant of a man, Hoyt thought, of fearsome face and great strength. "You are a warrior."

"Bet your ass. I'll kick some vampire ass in this, believe me. But not tonight. Why don't we go on down, see what's jumping. That'll piss him off."

"To his . . ." What had Cian called it. "His club?"

"You got it. He calls it Eternity. I guess he knows something about that."

Chapter 4

She was going to find him. If a man was going to drag her into his dreams, push her into out-of-body experiences and generally haunt her thoughts, she was going to track him down and find out why.

For days now she had felt as if she stood on the edge of some high, shaky cliff. On one side there was something bright and beautiful, and on the other a cold and terrifying void. But the cliff itself, while a little unstable, was the known.

Whatever was brewing inside her, he was part of it, that she knew. Not of this time, not of this place. Guys just didn't ride around on horses wearing cloaks and tunics in twenty-first-century New York as a rule.

But he was real; he was flesh and blood and as real as she was. She'd had that blood on her hands, hadn't she? She'd cooled that flesh and watched him sleep off the fever. His face, she thought, had been so familiar. Like something she remembered, or had caught a glimpse of in dreams.

Handsome, even in pain, she mused as she sketched it. Lean and angular, aristocratic. Long narrow nose, strong, sculpted mouth. Good, slashing cheekbones.

His image came true on paper as she worked, first in broad strokes, then in careful detail. Deep-set eyes, she remembered, vividly blue and intense with an almost dramatic arch of brows over them. And the contrast of that black hair, those black brows and wild blue eyes against his skin just added more drama.

Yes, she thought, she could see him, she could sketch him, but until she found him, she wouldn't know whether she should jump off the edge of that cliff or scramble back from it.

Glenna Ward was a woman who liked to know.

So, she knew his face, the shape and feel of his body, even the sound of his voice. She knew, without question, he had power. And she believed he had answers.

Whatever was coming, and every portent warned her it was major, he was tied to it. She had a part to play, had known almost since her first breath that she had a part to play. She had a feeling that she was about to take on the role of her lifetime. And the wounded hunk with the clouds of magic and trouble all around him was slated to costar.

He'd spoken Gaelic, Irish Gaelic. She knew some of it, used the language occasionally in spells, and could even read some in a very rudimentary fashion.

But oddly enough, she'd not only understood everything he'd said in the dream—experience, vision, whatever— she'd been able to speak it herself, like a native.

So somewhere in the past—the good, long past, she determined. And possibly somewhere in Ireland.

She'd done scrying spells and locator spells, using the bloodied bandage she'd brought back with her from that strange and intense visit to . . . wherever she'd been. His blood and her own talent would lead her to him.

She'd expected it to be a great deal of work and effort. Doubled by whatever work and effort would be involved in transporting herself—or at least her essence—to his time and place.

She was prepared to do just that, or at least try. She sat within her circle, the candles lit, the herbs floating on the water in her bowl. Once more she searched for him, focusing on the sketch of his face and holding the cloth she'd brought back with her.

"I seek the man who bears this face, my quest to find his time, his place. I hold his blood within my hand, and with its power I demand. Search and find and show to me. As I will, so mote it be."

In her mind she saw him, brow furrowed as he buried himself in books. Focusing, she drew back, saw the room. Apartment? Dim light, just slanting over his face, his hands.

"Where are you?" she asked softly. "Show me."

And she saw the building, the street.

The thrill of success mixed with absolute bafflement.

The last thing she'd expected was to learn he was in New York, some sixty blocks away, and in the now.

The fates, Glenna decided, were in an all-fired hurry to get things started. Who was she to question them?

She closed the circle, put away her tools and tucked the sketch in her desk drawer. Then she dressed, puzzling over her choices for a bit. What exactly did a woman wear when she went to meet her destiny? Something flashy, subdued, businesslike? Something exotic?

In the end she settled on a little black dress she felt could handle anything.

She traveled uptown by subway, letting her mind clear. There was a drumming in her heart, an anticipation that had been building in her over the past weeks. This, she thought, was the next step to whatever was waiting.

And whatever it was, whatever was coming, whatever would happen next, she wanted to be open to it.

Then she'd make her decisions.

The train was crowded, so she stood, holding the overhead hook and swaying slightly with the movement of the car. She liked the rhythm of the city, its rapid pace, its eclectic musics. All the tones and hues of it.

She'd grown up in New York, but not in the city. The small town upstate had always seemed too limited to her, too closed-in. She'd wanted more, always. More color, more sound, more people. She'd spent the last four of her twenty-six years in the city.

And all of her life exploring her craft.

Something in her blood was humming now, as if it

knew—some part of her knew—she'd been preparing all of her life for these next hours.

At the next station, people filed on, people filed off. She let the sound of them flow over her as she brought the image of the man she sought back into her head.

Not the face of a martyr, she thought. There'd been too much power on him for that. And too much annoyance in him. She'd found it, she could admit, a very interesting mix.

The power of the circle he'd cast had been strong, and so had been whatever hunted him. They chased her dreams, too, those black wolves that were neither animal nor human, but something horribly of both.

Idly, she fingered the pendant she wore around her neck. Well, she was strong, too. She knew how to protect herself.

"She will feed on you."

The voice was a hiss rippling over the back of her neck, icing her skin. Then what spoke moved, seemed to glide and float in a circle around her, and the cold from it had the breath that trembled from between her lips frosting the air.

The other passengers continued to sit or stand, read or chat. Undisturbed. Unaware of the thing that slithered around their bodies like a snake.

Its eyes were red, its eye teeth long and sharp. Blood stained them, dripped obscenely from its mouth. Inside her chest, Glenna's heart tightened like a fist and began to beat, beat, beat against her ribs.

It had human form, and worse, somehow worse, wore a business suit. Blue pinstripes, she noted dully, crisp white shirt and paisley tie.

"We are forever." It swiped a bloody hand over the cheek of a woman who sat reading a paperback novel. Even while red stained her cheek, the woman turned the page and continued to read.

"We will herd you like cattle, ride you like horses, trap you like rats. Your powers are puny and pathetic, and when we're done with you, we'll dance on your bones."

"Then why are you afraid?"

It peeled back its lips in a snarl, and it leaped.

Glenna choked on a scream, stumbled back.

As the train streaked through a tunnel, the thing vanished.

"Watch it, lady." She got an impatient elbow and mutter from the man she'd fallen into.

"Sorry." She gripped the hook again with a hand gone slick with sweat.

She could still smell the blood as she rode the last blocks uptown.

For the first time in her life, Glenna actively feared the dark, the streets, the people who passed by. She had to struggle to not run when the train stopped. Had to suppress the urge to shove and push her way off and race across the platform to the steps leading up.

She walked quickly, and even with the city noises she heard the rapid clip of her heels on the sidewalk and the fearful wheeze of her own breath.

There was a line snaking out from the entrance of the club called Eternity. Couples and singles crammed together hoping to get the signal to go inside. Rather than wait, she walked up to the man on the door. She flashed a smile, did a quick charm.

He passed her through without checking his list or her ID.

Inside was music, blue light and the throb of excitement. For once the press of humanity, the pulse and beat didn't excite her.

Too many faces, she thought. Too many heartbeats. She wanted only one, and the prospect of finding him among so many suddenly seemed impossible. Every bump and jostle as she worked her way into the club jolted through her. And her own fear shamed her.

She wasn't defenseless; she wasn't weak. But she felt both. The thing on the train had been every nightmare. And that nightmare had been sent to her.

For her.

It had known her fear, she thought now. And it had played with it, taunted her until her knees were water and the screams inside her had slashed her mind like razors.

She'd been too shocked, too frightened to reach for the only weapon she held. Magic.

Now anger began to eke through the terror.

She'd told herself she was a seeker, a woman who took risks, valued knowledge. A woman who possessed defenses and skills most couldn't imagine. Yet here she was quivering at the first real whiff of danger. She stiffened her spine, evened her breathing, then headed straight for the huge circular bar.

Halfway across the silver span of the floor she saw him.

The flood of relief came first, then the pride that she'd succeeded in this initial task so quickly. A trickle of interest worked its way through as she veered in his direction.

The guy cleaned up very well.

His hair was carelessly styled rather than ragged, a shining black and shorter than it had been during their first meeting. Then again, he'd been wounded, troubled and in a hell of a fix. He wore black, and it suited him. Just as the watchful, slightly irritable look in those brilliant eyes suited him.

With a great deal of her confidence restored, she smiled and stepped into his path.

"I've been looking for you."

Cian paused. He was accustomed to women approaching him. Not that he couldn't get some enjoyment from it, particularly when the woman was exceptional as this one was. There was a spark in her eyes, jewel green, and a flirtatious hint of amusement. Her lips were full, sensuous and curved; her voice low and husky.

Her body was a good one, and poured into a little black dress that showed a great deal of milky skin and strong muscle tone. He might have amused himself with her for a few moments, but for the pendant she wore.

Witches, and worse, those who played at witchcraft, could be troublesome.

"I enjoy being looked for by beautiful women when I have time to be found." He would have left it at that, moved on, but she touched his arm.

He felt something. And apparently so did she, for her eyes narrowed, and the smile faded.

"You're not him. You only look like him." Her hand tightened on his arm, and he sensed power seeking. "But that's not completely true either. Damn it." She dropped her hand, shook back her hair. "I should've known it wouldn't be so easy."

This time he took her arm. "Let's get you a table." In a dark, quiet corner, Cian thought. Until he knew who or what she was.

"I need information. I need to find someone."

"You need a drink," Cian said pleasantly, and steered her quickly through the crowd.

"Look, I can get my own drink if I want one." Glenna considered causing a scene, but decided it would probably get her tossed out. She considered a push of power, but knew from experience that depending on magic for every irritation led to trouble.

She glanced around, gauging the situation. The place was stacked with people on every level. The music was a throb, heavy on the bass with the female singer purring out the lyrics in a sensual and feline voice.

Very public, very active, Glenna decided with a lot of chrome and blue lighting slicking class over sex. What could he possibly do to her under the circumstances?

"I'm looking for someone." Conversation, she told herself. Keep it conversational and friendly. "I thought you were him. The light in here isn't the best, but you look enough alike to be brothers. It's very important I find him."

"What's his name? Maybe I can help you."

"I don't know his name." And the fact that she didn't made her feel foolish. "And okay, I know how that sounds. But I was told he was here. I think he's in trouble. If you'd just—" She started to shove at his hand, found it hard as stone.

What could he do to her in these circumstances? she thought again. Almost any damn thing. With the first fresh flicker of panic tickling her throat, she closed her eyes and reached for power.

His hand flinched on her arm, then his grip tightened. "So, you're a real one," he murmured, and turned those eyes—as steely as his grip—on her. "I think we'll take this upstairs."

"I'm not going anywhere with you." Something akin to the fear she'd felt on the subway worked its way into her. "That was low wattage. Believe me, you don't want me to up the amps."

"Believe me." And his voice was silky. "You don't want to piss me off."

He pulled her behind the curve of open, spiral stairs. She planted her feet, prepared to defend herself by any and all means at her disposal. She brought the four-inch spike of her heel down on his instep, slammed a back-fist into his jaw. Rather than wasting her breath on a scream, she began an incantation.

Her breath whooshed out when he lifted her off her feet as if she weighed nothing. Her only satisfaction came from the fact that in thirty seconds, when she finished the spell, he'd be flat on his ass.

That didn't stop her from fighting. She reared back, elbows and feet, and sucked in a breath to add a scream after all.

And the doors on what she saw was a private elevator whisked open.

There he was, flesh and blood. And so like the man currently heaving her over his shoulder she decided she could hate him, too.

"Put me down, you son of a bitch, or I'll turn this place into a moon crater."

When the doors of the transportation box opened, Hoyt was assaulted with noise and smells and lights. They all slammed into his system, stunning his senses. He saw through dazzled eyes, his brother with his arms full of struggling woman.

His woman, he realized with yet another jolt. The witch from his dream was half-naked and using language he'd rarely heard even in the seediest public house.

"Is this how you pay someone back for helping you?" She shoved at the curtain of her hair and aimed those sharp green eyes at him. She shifted them, scanned them up and down King, snarled.

"Come on then," she demanded. "I can take all three of you."

As she was currently over Cian's shoulder like a sack of

potatoes, Hoyt wasn't certain how she intended to see the threat through. But witches were tricky.

"You're real then," he stated softly. "Did you follow me?"

"Don't flatter yourself, asshole."

Cian shifted her, effortlessly. "Yours?" he said to Hoyt.

"I couldn't say."

"Deal with it." Cian dropped Glenna back on her feet, caught the fist aimed at his face just before it connected. "Do your business," he told her. "Quietly. Then take off. Keep a lid on the magic. Both of you. King."

He walked off. After a grin and a shrug, King trailed after him.

Glenna smoothed down her dress, shook back her hair. "What the hell's wrong with you?"

"My ribs still pain me a little, but I'm largely healed. Thank you for your help."

She stared at him, then huffed out a breath. "Here's how this is going to work. We're going to sit down, you're going to buy me a drink. I need one."

"I . . . I have no coin in these pants."

"Typical. I'll buy." She hooked an arm through his to make sure she didn't lose him again, then began to wind through the crowd.

"Did my brother hurt you?"

"What?"

He had to shout. How could anyone have a conversation in such noise? There were too many people in this place. Was it some sort of festival?

There were women writhing in what must have been some sort of ritual dance, and wearing even less than the witch. Others sat at silver tables and watched or ignored, drank from clear tankards and cups.

The music, he thought, came from everywhere at once.

"I asked if my brother hurt you."

"Brother? That fits. Bruised my pride for the most part."

She chose the stairs, moving up where the noise wasn't quite so horrific. Still clinging to his arm, she looked right, left, then moved toward a low seat with a candle flickering on the table. Five people were jammed around it, and all seemed to be talking at once.

She smiled at them, and he felt her power hum. "Hi. You really need to get home now, don't you?"

They got up, still chattering, and left the table littered with those clear drinking vessels, some nearly full.

"Sorry to cut their evening short, but I think this takes precedence. Sit down, will you?" She dropped down, stretched out long, bare legs. "God, what a night." She waved a hand in the air, fingered her pendant with the other as she studied his face. "You look better than you did. Are you healed?"

"Well enough. What place are you from?"

"Right to business." She glanced over at the waitress who came to their table to clear it. "I'll have a Grey Goose martini, straight up, two olives. Dry as dust." She cocked a brow at Hoyt. When he said nothing, she held up two fingers.

She tucked her hair behind one ear as she leaned toward him. There were silver coils dangling from her ear in a Celtic knot pattern.

"I dreamed of you before that night. Twice before I think," she began. "I try to pay attention to my dreams, but I could never hold on to these, until the last one. I think in the first, you were in a graveyard, and you were grieving. My heart broke for you, I remember feeling that. Odd, I remember more clearly now. The next time I dreamed of you, I saw you on a cliff, over the sea. I saw a woman with you who wasn't a woman. Even in the dream I was afraid of her. So were you."

She sat back, shuddering once. "Oh yes, I remember that now. I remember I was terrified, and there was a storm. And you . . . you struck out at her. I pushed—I remember I pushed what I had toward you, to try to help. I knew she was . . . she was wrong. Horribly wrong. There was lightning and screams—" She wished actively for her drink. "I woke up, and for an instant, the fear woke with me. Then it all faded."

When he still said nothing, she drew in a breath. "Okay,

we'll stick with me for a while. I used my scrying mirror, I used my crystal, but I couldn't see clearly. Only in sleep. You brought me to that place in the woods, in the circle. Or something did. Why?"

"It was not my work."

"It wasn't mine." She tapped nails painted red as her lips on the table. "You have a name, handsome?"

"I'm Hoyt Mac Cionaoith."

Her smile turned her face into something that all but stopped his heart. "Not from around here, are you?"

"No."

"Ireland, I can hear that. And in the dream we spoke Gaelic, which I don't—not really. But I think it's more than where. It's when, too, isn't it? Don't worry about shocking me. I'm immune tonight."

He waged an internal debate. She'd been shown to him, and she had come within the circle. Nothing that meant harm to him should have been able to come within his protective ring. While he had been told to seek a witch, she was nothing, *nothing* that he'd expected.

Yet she'd worked to heal him, and had stayed with him while the wolves had stalked his ring. She'd come to him now for answers, and perhaps for help.

"I came through the Dance of the Gods, nearly a thousand years in time."

"Okay." She whistled out a breath. "Maybe not completely immune. That's a lot to take on faith, but with everything that's been going on, I'm willing to take the leap." She lifted the glass the waitress set down, drank immediately. "Especially with this to cushion the fall. Run a tab, will you?" Glenna asked and took a credit card out of her purse.

"Something's coming," she said when they were alone again. "Something bad. Big, fat evil."

"You don't know."

"I can't see it all. But I feel it, and I know I'm connected with you on this. Not thrilled about that at this point." She drank some more. "Not after what I saw on the subway."

"I don't understand you."

"Something very nasty in a designer suit," she explained.

"It said she would feed on me. She—the woman on the cliff, I think. I'm going out on a limb here, a really shaky one. Are we dealing with vampires?"

"What is the subway?"

Glenna pressed her hands to her eyes. "Okay, we'll spend some time later bringing you up to date on current events, modes of mass transportation and so on, but right now, I need to know what I'm facing. What's expected of me."

"I don't know your name."

"Sorry. Glenna. Glenna Ward." She held a hand out to him. After a brief hesitation, he took it. "Nice to meet you. Now, what the hell is going on?"

He began, and she continued to drink. Then she held up a hand, swallowed. "Excuse me. Are you saying your brother— the guy who manhandled me, is a vampire?"

"He doesn't feed on humans."

"Oh good. Great. Points for him. He died nine hundred and seventy-odd years ago, and you've come here and now from there and then to find him."

"I am charged by the gods to gather an army to fight and destroy the army the vampyre Lilith is making."

"Oh God. I'm going to need another drink."

He started to offer her his, but she waved him away and signaled the waitress. "No, go ahead. You're going to need it, too, I imagine."

He took a testing sip, blinked rapidly. "What is this brew?"

"Vodka martini. You should like vodka," she said absently. "Seems to me they make it from potatoes."

She ordered another drink and some bar food to counteract the alcohol. Calmer now, she listened to the whole of it without interrupting.

"And I'm the witch."

There wasn't just beauty here, he realized. There wasn't just power. There was a seeking and a strength. Some he would seek, he remembered the goddess saying. And some would seek him.

So she had.

"I have to believe you are. You, my brother and I will find the others and begin."

"Begin what? Boot camp? Do I look like a soldier to you?"

"You don't, no."

She propped a chin on her fist. "I like being a witch, and I respect the gift. I know there's a reason this runs in my blood. A purpose. I didn't expect it to be this. But it is." She looked at him then, fully. "I know, the first time I dreamed of you that it was the next step in that purpose. I'm terrified. I'm so seriously terrified."

"I left my family to come here, to do this thing. I left them with only the silver crosses and the word of the goddess that they would be protected. You don't know fear."

"All right." She reached out, laid a hand on his in a kind of comfort she sensed was innate in her. "All right," she repeated. "You've got a lot at stake. But I've got a family, too. They're upstate. I need to make sure they're protected. I need to make sure I live to do what I'm meant to do. She knows where I am. She sent that thing to scare me off. I'm guessing she's a lot more prepared than we are."

"Then prepared is what we'll get. I have to see what you're capable of."

"You want me to audition? Listen, Hoyt, your army so far consists of three people. You don't want to insult me."

"We have four with the king."

"What king?"

"The black giant. And I don't like working with witches."

"Really?" She drew out the word as she leaned toward him. "They burned your kind just as hot as mine. We're kissing cousins, Merlin. And you need me."

"It may be that I do. The goddess didn't say I had to like it, did she? I have to know your strengths and your weaknesses."

"Fair enough," she said with a nod. "And I have to know yours. I already know you couldn't heal a lame horse."

"That's false." And this time insult edged his voice. "It happens I was wounded, and unable to—"

"Mend a couple of broken ribs and a gash on your own palm. So, you won't be in charge of injuries if and when we manage to build this army."

"It's welcome you are to the task," he snapped. "And building the army is what we'll do. It's my destiny."

"Let's hope it's my destiny to get home in one piece." She signed the check, picked up her purse.

"Where are you going?"

"Home. I have a lot to do."

"That's not the way. We must stay together now. She knows you, Glenna Ward. She knows all of us. It's safer we are, and stronger together."

"That may be, but I need things from my home. I have a lot to do."

"They're night creatures. You'll wait until sunrise."

"Orders already?" She tried for flip, but the image of what had circled her in the subway came to her, very clearly.

Now he gripped her hand, held her in her seat and felt the clash of their emotions in the heat that vibrated between their palms. "Is this a game to you then?"

"No. I'm scared. A few days ago I was just living my life. My terms. Now I'm being hunted, and I'm supposed to fight some apocalyptic battle. I want to go home. I need my own things. I need to think."

"It's fear that makes you vulnerable and foolish. Your things will be there in the morning just as they are now."

He was right, of course. Added to it, she wasn't sure she had the bravado or the courage to step back outside into the night. "And just where am I supposed to stay until sunrise?"

"My brother has an apartment upstairs."

"Your brother. The vampire." She flopped back against her seat. "Isn't that cozy?"

"He won't harm you. You have my word on it."

"I'd rather have his, if you don't mind. And if he tries . . ." She held her palm up on the table, focused on it. A small ball of flame kindled just above her hand. "If the books and movies have it right, his type doesn't do well with fire. If he tries to hurt me, I'll torch him, and your army's down by one."

Hoyt merely laid his hand over hers, and the flame became a ball of ice. "Don't pit your skills against mine, or threaten to harm my family."

"Nice trick." She dumped the ice in her empty glass. "Let's put it this way. I have a right to protect myself, from anyone or anything who tries to hurt me. Agreed?"

"Agreed. It will not be Cian." Now he rose, offered his hand. "I will pledge this to you, here and now. I will protect you, even from him, if he means you harm."

"Well then." She put her hand in his, got to her feet. She felt it, knew he did by the way his pupils dilated. The magic, yes, but more. "I guess we've got our first deal."

As they went down, turned toward the elevator, Cian cut across their path. "Hold it. Where do you think you're taking her?"

"I'm going with him," Glenna corrected, "not being taken."

"It's not safe for her to go out. Not until daylight. Lilith already sent a scout after her."

"Check the magic at the door," Cian told Glenna. "She can have the spare room tonight. Which means you get the couch, unless she wants to share."

"He can have the couch."

"Why do you insult her?" Temper sizzled in the words. "She's been sent; she's come here at risk."

"I don't know her," Cian said simply. "And from now on, I expect you to check with me before you invite anyone into my home." He punched in the code for the elevator. "Once you're up, you stay up. I'm locking the elevator behind you."

"What if there's a fire?" Glenna said sweetly, and Cian merely smiled.

"Then I guess you'd better open a window, and fly."

Glenna stepped into the elevator when the doors opened, then laid a hand on Hoyt's arm. Before the doors shut, she flashed Cian that smile again. "Better remember who you're dealing with," she told him. "We may do just that."

She sniffed when the doors shut. "I don't think I like your brother."

"I'm not very pleased with him myself at the moment."

"Anyway. Can you fly?"

"No." He glanced down at her. "Can you?"

"Not so far."

Chapter 5

The voices woke her. They were muted and muffled so that at first she feared she was having another vision. However much she might have prized her art, she also valued sleep—especially after a night of martinis and strange revelations.

Glenna groped for a pillow to put over her head.

Her attitude toward Cian had leveled a bit after she'd gotten a look at the guest room. It boasted a sumptuous bed with lovely soft sheets and enough pillows to satisfy even her love of luxury.

It hadn't hurt that the room was spacious, decked out with antiques and painted the soft, warm green of forest shadows. The bath had been a killer, too, she recalled as she snuggled in. An enormous jet tub in gleaming white dominated a room nearly half the size of her entire loft, with that same rich green for the acre of counters. But it was the wide bowl of sink in hammered copper that had made her purr with delight.

She'd nearly given in to the temptation to wallow in the tub, indulge herself with some of the bath salts and oils housed in heavy crystal jars and arranged with fat, glossy candles on the counter. But images of movie heroines attacked while bathing had her putting that idea on hold.

All and all, the vampire's pied-à-terre—she could hardly call such luxury a den—made mincemeat of her little loft in the West Village.

Though she admired the vampire's taste, it didn't stop her from putting a protective charm on the bedroom door in addition to turning the lock.

Now, she rolled over, shucked the pillow to stare at the ceiling in the dim light of the lamp she'd left on low through the night. She was sleeping in a vampire's guest room. She'd displaced a twelfth-century sorcerer to the sofa. A gorgeous and serious-minded type who was on a mission, and expected her to join in his battle against an ancient and powerful vampire queen.

She'd lived with magic all of her life, was gifted with skills and knowledge most people never dreamed existed in reality. And still, this was one for the books.

She liked her life the way it was. And knew, without a doubt, that she would never have it quite that way again. Knew, in fact, she might lose that life altogether.

But what were her choices? She couldn't very well do nothing, couldn't put a pillow over her head and hide for the rest of her life. It *knew* her, and had already sent an emissary.

If she stayed, pretended none of it had ever happened, it could come for her, any time, anywhere. And she'd be alone.

Would she fear the night now? Would she glance over her shoulder every time she was outside after sunset? Would she wonder if a vampire only she could see would slink onto the subway the next time she rode uptown?

No, that was no way to live at all. The only way to live— the only real choice—was to face the problem, and handle the fear. And to do just that along with joining her powers and resources to Hoyt's.

Knowing sleep was no longer possible, she glanced at the clock, rolled her eyes at the early hour. Then resigned, she climbed out of bed.

* * *

In the living room, Cian ended his night with a brandy, and an argument with his brother.

He had, on occasion, returned to his living quarters at dawn with the sensation of loneliness, a kind of hollowness. He took no woman in the daylight, even with the drapes closed. Sex was, in Cian's mind, a position of vulnerability as well as power. He didn't choose to share that vulnerability when the sun was up.

It was rare for him to have company after sunrise and before dusk. And those hours were often long and empty. But he'd discovered on stepping into his own apartment and finding his brother there, he preferred the long and empty to the crowded and demanding.

"You expect her to stay here until you decide your next move. And I'm telling you that isn't possible."

"How would she be safe otherwise?" Hoyt argued.

"I don't believe her safety is on my list of immediate concerns."

How much had his brother changed, Hoyt thought in disgust, that he wouldn't immediately stand for a woman, for an innocent? "We're all at risk now, everything's at risk now. We have no choice but to stay together."

"I have a choice, and it isn't sharing my quarters with a witch, or with you, for that matter," he added, gesturing with the snifter. "I don't allow anyone in here during the day."

"I was here through yesterday."

"An exception." Cian got to his feet. "And one I'm already regretting. You're asking far too much from one who cares far too little."

"I haven't begun to ask yet. I know what must be done. You spoke of survival. And it's yours at risk now, as much as hers. As mine."

"More, as your redhead might take it into her head to stake me while I sleep."

"She isn't my . . ." Frustrated, Hoyt waved that off. "I would never let her harm you. I swear it to you. In this place, at this time, you're my only family. My only blood."

Cian's face went blank as stone. "I have no family. No blood but my own. The sooner you come to that, Hoyt, accept that, the better you'll be for it. What I do, I do for myself, not for you. Not for your cause, but for me. I said I'd fight with you, and so I will. But for my own reasons."

"What are they then? Give me that at least."

"I like this world." Cian eased down on the arm of a chair as he sipped brandy. "I like what I've carved out of it, and I intend to keep it, and on my own terms—not on Lilith's whimsy. That's worth the fight to me. Added to it, a few centuries of existence has its eras of boredom. I seem to be in one. But I have limits. Having your woman tucked up in my quarters goes beyond them."

"She's hardly my woman."

A lazy smile curved Cian's mouth. "If you don't make her so, you're even slower than I remember in that area."

"This isn't sport, Cian. It's a fight to the death."

"I know more of death than you will ever know. More of blood and pain and cruelty. For centuries I've watched mortals, again and again, teeter close to their own extinction, by their own hand. If Lilith were more patient, she could simply wait them out. Take your pleasures where you find them, brother, for life is long and often tedious."

He toasted with his glass. "Another reason I'll fight. It's something to do."

"Why not join with her then?" Hoyt spat out. "With the one who made you what you are."

"She made me a vampire. I made myself what I am. As for why I align with you and not with her? I can trust you. You'll keep your word, for that's the way you're made. She never will. It's not her nature."

"And what of your word?"

"Interesting question."

"I'd like the answer to it." Glenna spoke from the doorway. She wore the black silk robe she'd found hanging in the closet with a number of other pieces of intimate female attire. "You two can squabble all you like, it's what men do, and siblings. But since my life's on the line, I want to know who I can count on."

"I see you made yourself at home," Cian commented.

"Do you want it back?"

When she angled her head, reached for the tie, Cian grinned. Hoyt flushed.

"Don't be encouraging him," Hoyt said. "If you'd excuse us for a moment—"

"No, I won't. I want the answer to your question. And I want to know if your brother gets a little peckish, is he going to look to me as a snack?"

"I don't feed on humans. Particularly witches."

"Because of your deep love of humanity."

"Because it's troublesome. If you feed, you have to kill or word gets around. If you change the prey, you're still risking exposure. Vampires gossip, too."

She thought it over. "Sensible. All right, I prefer sensible honesty to lies."

"I told you he wouldn't harm you."

"I wanted to hear it from him." She turned back to Cian. "If you're concerned about me going after you, I'd give you my word—but why should you trust it?"

"Sensible," Cian returned.

"But your brother's already told me he'd stop me if I tried. He may find that more difficult than he believes, but . . . it would be stupid of me to try to kill you, and alienate him, given the situation we're in. I'm afraid, but I'm not stupid."

"I'd have to take your word for that as well."

Idly, she fingered the sleeve of her robe and sent him a mildly flirtatious smile. "If I'd intended to kill you, I'd have already tried a spell. You'd know if I had. You'd feel it. And if there's no more trust than this between the three of us, we're doomed before we start."

"There you have a point."

"What I want now is a shower, and some breakfast. Then I'm going home."

"She stays." Hoyt stepped between them. When Glenna started to step forward, he merely lifted a hand, and the force of his will knocked her back to the doorway.

"Just one damn minute."

"Be silent. None of us leaves this place alone. None

of us. If we're to band together we start now. Our lives are in each other's hands, and a great deal more than our own lives."

"Don't flick your power at me again."

"Whatever I have to do, I'll do. Understand me." Hoyt shifted his gaze between them. "Both of you. Dress yourself," he ordered Glenna. "Then we'll go get whatever it is you think you need. Be quick about it."

In answer, she stepped back, slammed the door.

Cian let out a short laugh. "You certainly know how to charm the ladies. I'm going to bed."

Hoyt stood alone in the living room and wondered why the gods thought he could save worlds with two such creatures at his side.

She didn't speak, but a man who has sisters knows women often use silence as a weapon. And her silence flew around the room like barbs as she filled some sort of carafe with water from the silver pipe in Cian's kitchen.

Women's fashion might have changed radically in nine hundred years, but he believed their inner workings were very much the same.

And still, much of those remained a mystery to him.

She wore the same dress as the night before, but had yet to don her shoes. He wasn't certain what weakness it spoke to in him that the sight of her bare feet should bring on an unwelcomed tinge of arousal.

She shouldn't have flirted with his brother, he thought with considerable resentment. This was a time of war, not dalliance. And if she intended to stroll about with her legs and arms exposed, she'd just have to . . .

He caught himself. He had no business looking at her legs, did he? No business thinking of her as anything but a tool. It didn't matter that she was lovely. It didn't matter that when she smiled it started something like a low fire in the center of his heart.

It didn't matter—couldn't—that when he looked at her, he wanted to touch.

He busied himself with books, returned her silence with his own and lectured himself on proper behavior.

Then the air began to simmer with some seductive aroma. He shot her a glance, wondering if she was trying some of her women's magic. But her back was to him as she rose on the toes of those lovely bare feet to take a cup from a cupboard.

It was the carafe, he realized, filled now with black liquid, and steaming with an alluring scent.

He lost the war of silence. In Hoyt's experience, men always did.

"What are you brewing?"

She simply poured the black liquid from carafe to cup, then turned, watching him with chilly green eyes over the rim as she sipped.

To satisfy himself, he got up, walked into the kitchen and took a second cup down. He poured the liquid as she had, sniffed—detected no poisons—then sipped.

It was electric. Like a quick jolt of power, both strong and rich. Potent, like the drink—the martini—from the night before. But different.

"It's very good," he said then took a deeper drink.

In response, she skirted around him, crossed the room and went back through the doorway of the guest room.

Hoyt lifted his gaze to the gods. Would he be plagued by bad tempers and sulks from both this woman and his brother? "How?" he asked. "How am I to do what must be done if already we fight among ourselves?"

"While you're at it, why don't you ask your goddess to tell you what she thinks about you slapping at me that way." Glenna came back in, wearing the shoes, and carrying the satchel he'd seen her with the evening before.

"It's a defense against what seems to be your argumentative nature."

"I like to argue. And I don't expect you to flick at me whenever you don't like what I have to say. Do it again, and I'll hit back. I have a policy against using magic as a weapon. But I'll break it in your case."

She had the right of it, which was only more annoying. "What is this brew?"

She heaved a breath. "It's coffee. You've had coffee before, I imagine. The Egyptians had coffee. I think."

"Not the like of this," he replied.

And because she smiled, he assumed the worst of it was over. "I'm ready to go, as soon as you apologize."

He should have known better. Such was the way of females. "I'm sorry I was forced to use my will to stop you from arguing the morning away."

"So, you can be a smart-ass. This once, I'll accept that. Let's get moving." She walked to the elevator, pushed its button.

"Is it the fashion for women of this time to be aggressive and sharp-tongued, or is it only you?"

She glanced back at him over her shoulder. "I'm the only one you have to worry about right now." She stepped into the elevator, held the door. "Coming?"

She'd worked out a basic strategy. First, she was going to have to spring for a cab. Whatever the conversation, however strangely Hoyt might behave, a New York City cabbie would have seen and heard it all before.

Added to that, her courage wasn't quite back up to the level to let her ride the subway again.

As she'd anticipated, the minute they were out of the building, Hoyt stopped. And stared. He looked everywhere, up, down, right, left. He studied the traffic, the pedestrians, the buildings.

No one would pay any attention to him, and if they did, they'd mark him as a tourist.

When he opened his mouth to speak, she tapped a finger on her lips. "You're going to have a million questions. So why don't you just line them up and file them? We'll get to them all eventually. For now, I'm going to hail us a cab. Once we're inside, try not to say anything too outrageous."

Questions might have been scrambling in his mind like ants, but he cloaked himself in dignity. "I'm not a fool. I know very well I'm out of place here."

No, he wasn't a fool, Glenna thought as she stepped to the

curb, held up a hand. And he was no coward either. She'd expected him to gawk, but with having the rush and noise and crowds of the city thrust on him, she'd also expected to see some fear, and there was none. Just curiosity, a dose of fascination and a bit of disapproval.

"I don't like the way the air smells."

She nudged him back when he joined her at the curb. "You get used to it." When a cab cruised up to the curb, she whispered to Hoyt as she opened the door. "Get in the way I do, and just sit back and enjoy the ride."

Inside, she reached over him to pull the door shut and gave the cabbie her address. When the cabbie shot back out into traffic, Hoyt's eyes widened.

"I don't know that much about it," she said under the Indian music pumping from the cabbie's radio. "It's a cab, a kind of car. It runs on a combustible engine, fueled by gasoline, and oil."

She did her best to explain traffic lights, crosswalks, skyscrapers, department stores and whatever else came to mind. She realized it was like seeing the city for the first time herself, and began to enjoy it.

He listened. She could all but see him absorbing and tucking all the information, the sights, the sounds, the smells, away in some internal data bank.

"There are so many." He said it quietly, and the troubled tone had her looking over at him. "So many people," he repeated, staring out the side window. "And unaware of what's coming. How will we save so many?"

It struck her then, a sharp, weighted spear in the belly. So many people, yes. And this was just part of one city in just one state. "We can't. Not all. You never can." She reached for his hand, gripped it tight. "So you don't think of the many, or you'll go crazy. We just take it one at a time."

She took out the fare when the cab pulled over—which made her think of finances, and how she'd handle *that* little problem over the next few months. She reached for Hoyt's hand again when they were on the sidewalk.

"This is my building. If we see anyone inside, just smile

and look charming. They'll just think I'm bringing home a lover."

Shock rippled over his face. "Do you?"

"Now and again." She unlocked the door, then squeezed with him into the tiny anteroom to call for the elevator. With an even tighter squeeze, they started up.

"Do all buildings have these . . ."

"Elevators. No, but a lot of them do." When they reached her apartment, she pulled open the iron gate, stepped inside.

It was a small space, but the light was excellent. Her walls were covered with her paintings and her photographs, and were painted the green of minced onions to reflect the light. Rugs she'd woven herself dotted the floor with bold tones and patterns.

It was tidy, which suited her nature. Her convertible bed was made up as a sofa for the day, plumped with pillows. The kitchen alcove sparkled from a recent scrubbing.

"You live alone. With no one to help you."

"I can't afford help, and I like living alone. Staff and servants take money, and I don't have enough of it."

"Have you no men in your family, no stipend or allowance?"

"No allowance since I was ten," she said dryly. "I work. Women work just as men do. Ideally, we don't depend on a man to take care of us, financially or otherwise."

She tossed her purse aside. "I make my living such as it is selling paintings and photographs. Painting, for the most part for greeting cards like notes, letters, messages people send each other."

"Ah, you're an artist."

"That's right," she agreed, amused that her choice of employment, at least, seemed to meet with his approval. "The greeting cards, those pay the rent. But I sell some of the artwork outright now and then. I like working for myself, too. I make my own schedule, which is lucky for you. I don't have anyone to answer to, so I can take time to do, well, what has to be done."

"My mother is an artist, in her way. Her tapestries are beautiful." He stepped up to a painting of a mermaid, rising up out of a churning sea. There was power in the face, a kind of knowledge that he took as inherently female. "This is your work?"

"Yes."

"It shows skill, and that magic that moves into color and shape."

More than approval, she decided. Admiration now, and she let it warm her. "Thanks. Normally, that kind of thumb-nail review would make my day. It's just that it's a very strange day. I need to change my clothes."

He nodded absently, moved to another painting.

Behind him, Glenna cocked her head, then shrugged. She went to the old armoire she used as a closet, chose what she wanted, then carried it into the bathroom.

She was used to men paying a little more attention, she realized as she stripped out of the dress. To the way she looked, the way she moved. It was lowering to be so easily dismissed, even if he did have more important things on his mind.

She changed into jeans and a white tank. Letting the subtle glamour she'd been vain enough to use that morning fade, she did her makeup, then tied her hair back into a short tail.

When she came back, Hoyt was in her kitchen, fiddling with her herbs.

"Don't touch my stuff." She slapped his hand away.

"I was only . . ." He trailed off, then looked deliberately over her shoulder. "Is this what you wear in public?"

"Yes." She turned, and just as deliberately invaded his space. "Problem?"

"No. You don't wear shoes?"

"Not around the house, necessarily." His eyes were so blue, she thought. So sharp and blue against those thick black lashes. "What do you feel when we're like this? Alone. Close."

"Unsettled."

"That's the nicest thing you've said to me so far. I mean, do you feel something? In here." She laid a fist on her belly, kept her eyes locked on his. "A kind of reaching. I've never felt it before."

He felt it, and a kind of burn in and under his heart as

well. "You haven't broken your fast," he managed, and
stepped carefully back. "You must be hungry."

"Just me then," she murmured. She turned to open a cupboard. "I don't know what I'm going to need, so I'm going
to take whatever feels right. I'm not traveling light. You and
Cian have to deal with that. We should probably leave as
soon as possible."

He'd lifted a hand, was on the point of touching her hair,
something he'd wanted to do since he'd first seen her. Now
he dropped it. "Leave?"

"You don't expect to sit around in New York and wait for
the army to come to you? The portal's in Ireland, and we
have to assume the battle's to take place in Ireland, or some
mystical facet thereof. We need the portal, or at some point
we will. So we need to go to Ireland."

He simply stared at her as she loaded bottles and vials
into a case not dissimilar from his own. "Aye, you're right.
Of course, you're right. We need to start back. A voyage will
take much of the time we have. Oh, Jesus, I'll be sick as six
dogs sailing home."

She looked over. "Sailing? We don't have time for the
Queen Mary, sweetie. We'll fly."

"You said you couldn't."

"I can, if it's in a plane. We'll have to figure out how to
get you a ticket. You don't have ID, you don't have a passport. We can do a charm on the ticket agent, the custom's
agent." She brushed it away. "I'll work it out."

"A plain what?"

She focused on him, then leaned back against the counter
and laughed until her sides ached. "I'll explain later."

"It's not my purpose to amuse you."

"No, it wouldn't be. But it's a nice side pocket. Oh hell, I
don't know what to take, what not to take." She stepped back,
rubbed her hands over her face. "It's my first apocalypse."

"Herbs, flowers and roots grow in Ireland, and quite
well."

"I like my own." Which was foolish, and childish. But
still . . . "I'll just take what I consider absolutely essential in
this area, then start on books, clothes and so on. I have to

make some calls, too. I've got some appointments that I need to cancel."

With some reluctance, she closed her already loaded case and left it on the counter. She crossed to a large wooden chest in the far corner of the room, and unlocked it with a charm.

Curiosity piqued, Hoyt moved over to study the contents over her shoulder. "What do you keep here?"

"Spell books, recipes, some of my more powerful crystals. Some were handed down to me."

"Ah, then, you're a hereditary witch."

"That's right. The only one of my generation who practices. My mother gave it up when she married. My father didn't like it. My grandparents taught me."

"How could she give up what's inside her?"

"A question I've asked her many times." She sat back on her heels, touching what she could take, and what she couldn't. "For love. My father wanted a simple life, she wanted my father. I couldn't do it. I don't think I could love enough to give up what I am. I'd need to be loved enough to be accepted for what I am."

"Strong magic."

"Yeah." She took out a velvet sack. "This is my prize." From it she lifted the ball of crystal he'd seen her with in the vision. "It's been in my family a long time. Over two hundred and fifty years. Chump change to a man of your years, but a hell of a run to me."

"Strong magic," he repeated, for when she held it in her hands, he could see it pulse, like a heart beating.

"You're right about that." She looked at him over the orb with eyes that had gone suddenly dark. "And isn't it time we used some? Isn't it time we do what we do, Hoyt? She knows who I am, where I am, what I am. It's likely she knows the same about you, about Cian. Let's make a move." She held the crystal aloft. "Lets find out where she's hiding."

"Here and now?"

"Can't think of a better time or place." She rose, jutted her chin toward the richly patterned rug in the room's center. "Roll that up, will you?"

"It's a dangerous step you're after taking here. We should take a moment to think."

"We can think while you're rolling up the rug. I have everything we need for a locator spell, everything we need for protection. We can blind her to us while we look."

He did as she asked and found the painted pentagram under the rug. He could admit that taking a step, any step, felt right and good. But he'd have preferred, very much, to take it alone.

"We don't know if she can be blinded. She's fed on magic blood, and likely more than once. She's very powerful, and very sly."

"So are we. You're talking about going into battle within three months. When do you intend to start?"

He looked at her, nodded. "Here and now then."

She laid the crystal in the center of the pentagram, and retrieved two athames from her chest. She placed these in the circle, then gathered candles, a silver bowl, crystal wands.

"I won't be needing all these tools."

"Fine for you, but I prefer using them. Let's work together, Merlin."

He lifted an athame to study its carving as she ringed the pentagram with candles. "Will it bother you if I work sky-clad?"

"Aye," he said without looking up.

"All right, in the spirit of compromise and teamwork, I'll keep my clothes on. But they're restricting."

She removed the band from her hair, filled the silver bowl with water from a vial and sprinkled herbs on it. "Generally I invoke the goddesses when casting the circle, and it seems most appropriate for this. Suit you?"

"Well enough."

"You're a real chatterbox, aren't you? Well. Ready?" At his nod she walked to the opposite curve from him. "Goddesses of the East, of the West, of the North of the South," she began, moving around the circle as she spoke. "We ask your blessing. We call to you to witness and to guard this circle, and all within it."

"Powers of Air, and Water, of Fire and of Earth," Hoyt chanted. "Travel with us now as we go between worlds."

"Night and day, day and night, we call you to this sacred rite. We cast this circle, one times three. As we will, so mote it be."

Witches, he thought. Always rhyming. But he felt the air stir, and the water in the bowl rippled as the candles leaped to flame.

"It should be Morrigan we call on," Glenna said. "She was the messenger."

He started to do so, then decided he wanted to see what the witch was made of. "This is your sacred place. Ask for guidance, and cast your spell."

"All right." She laid down the sacred knife, lifted her hands, palms up. "On this day and in this hour, I call upon the sacred power of Morrigan the goddess and pray she grant to us her grace and prowess. In your name, Mother, we seek the sight, ask you to guide us into the light."

She bent, lifted the crystal into her hands. "Within this ball we seek to find the beast who hunts all mankind, while her eyes to us are blind. Make keen our vision, our minds, our hearts so the clouds within this ball will part. Shield us and show us what we seek to see. As we will, so mote it be."

Mists and light swirled within the glass. For an instant he thought he could see worlds inside it. Colors, shapes, movement. He heard it beat, as his heart beat. As Glenna's heart beat.

He knelt as she did. And saw, as she did.

A dark place, mazed with tunnels and washed by red light. He thought he heard the sea, but couldn't be sure if it was within the glass or just the roaring of power in his own head.

There were bodies, bloodied and torn and stacked like cordwood. And cages where people wept or screamed, or simply sat with dull and deadened eyes. Things moved within the tunnels, dark things that barely stirred the air. Some crawled up the walls like bugs.

There was horrible laughter, high, hideous shrieking.

He traveled with Glenna through those tunnels where the

air stank of death and blood. Down, deep down in the earth,
where the stone walls dripped with wet and worse. To a door
scribed with ancient symbols of black magicks.

He felt the breath go cold in his body as they passed
through.

She slept on a bed fit for a queen, four-posted and wide
with sheets that had the sheen of silk and were white as ice.
Droplets of blood stained them.

Her breasts were bare above the sheets, and the beauty of
her face and form were undiminished since last he'd seen her.

Beside her was the body of a boy. So young, Hoyt
thought with a terrible pity. No more than six years, so pale
in death with his cornsilk hair falling over his brow.

Candles were guttering, sending wavering light to flicker
over her flesh, and his.

Hoyt gripped the athame, lifted it over his head.

And her eyes opened, stared into his. She screamed, but
he heard no fear in it. Beside her the boy opened his eyes,
bared fangs and leaped up to scuttle along the ceiling like a
lizard.

"Closer," she crooned. "Come closer, sorcerer, and bring
your witch. I'll make a pet of her once I drain you dry. Do
you think you can *touch* me?"

As she leaped off the bed, Hoyt felt himself flying backward, tearing through air so cold it was shards of ice in his
throat.

Then he was sitting within the circle, staring into
Glenna's eyes. Hers were dark and wide. There was blood
dripping from her nose.

She stanched it with a knuckle while she struggled to get
her breath.

"First part worked," she managed. "The blinded part
didn't take very well, obviously."

"She has power as well. She's not without skill."

"Have you ever felt anything like that?" she asked him.

"No."

"Neither have I." She allowed herself one hard shudder.
"We're going to need a bigger circle."

Chapter 6

Before she packed, Glenna took the time to cleanse the entire loft. Hoyt didn't disagree. She wanted no trace of what they'd touched on, no echoes, no dregs of that darkness in her home.

In the end, she put her tools and books back in the chest. After what she'd seen, what she'd felt, she wasn't going to risk the pick and choose. She was taking the whole lot, along with her travel case, most of her crystals, some basic art supplies, cameras, and two suitcases.

She cast one longing look at the easel standing near the window, and the barely started painting resting on it. If she came back—no *when,* she corrected. When she came back, she would finish it.

She stood beside Hoyt, studying the pile of belongings as he did.

"No comments?" she asked. "No arguments or sarcastic remarks about how I intend to travel?"

"To what end?"

"A wise stand. Now there's the little matter of getting all this out of here, uptown and into your brother's place. At which time, I doubt he'll be as wise as you. But first things first." She toyed with her pendant as she considered. "Do we haul it all by hand, or try a transportation spell? I've never done anything of this scope."

He sent her a bland look. "We'd need three of your cabs and most of what we have left of the day to deal with all of this."

So, he considered the situation as well. "Visualize Cian's apartment," he ordered. "The room where you slept."

"All right."

"Concentrate. Bring it fully into your mind, the details, the shape, the structure."

She nodded, closed her eyes. "I am."

He chose the chest first as he sensed it held the most power. Its magic would aid him in the task. He circled it three times, then reversed, circled again while he said the words, while he opened himself to the power.

Glenna struggled to fix her focus. There was something deeper, richer about his voice, something erotic in the way it spoke the ancient tongue. She felt the heat of what he stirred on her skin, and in her blood. Then a swift and solid punch of air.

When she opened her eyes, the chest was gone.

"I'm impressed." More honestly, she was amazed. She was capable, with considerable preparation and effort, of transporting small, simple objects some distance. But he'd simply and efficiently *poofed* a two-hundred-pound chest.

She could picture him now, in billowing robes on the cliff he'd spoken of in Ireland. Challenging the storm, charging himself with it. And facing what no man should have to face, with faith and with magic.

Her belly tightened with sheer and simple lust.

"Was that Gaelic you were speaking?"

"Irish," he said, so obviously distracted, she didn't speak again.

Once more he circled, focusing now on the cases that contained her photography and art equipment. She nearly yipped a protest, then reminded herself to have faith. Calling on it, she closed her eyes again, brought the guest room back into her mind. Gave him what she could of her own gift.

It took him fifteen minutes to accomplish what she was forced to admit would have taken her hours, if she could have managed it at all.

"Well that was . . . that was something." The magic was still on him, turning his eyes opaque, rippling through the air between them. She felt it like a ribbon wound around both of them, tying them together. Her own arousal was so keen, she had to step back, deliberately break the bond between them.

"No offense, but are you sure they're where we want them?"

He continued to stare at her with those fathomless blue eyes until the heat in her belly grew so strong she wondered it didn't shoot fire from her fingertips.

It was nearly too much, this pressure, this need, the mad beat of it at every pulse. She started to step back again, but he simply lifted a hand and stopped her in her tracks.

She felt the pull, from him, to him, with just enough play for her to resist, to snap that lead and escape. Instead she stood, kept her eyes locked with his as he closed the distance between them with one easy stride.

Then there was nothing easy.

He yanked her to him so that her breath expelled on a quick hitching gasp, and that gasp ended on a moan when their mouths met. The hot, drugging kiss spun through her head, through her body, sizzling in her blood when she clung to him.

Candles she'd left in the room flashed into flame.

At once aggressive and desperate, she dug her hands into his shoulders and plunged headfirst into the storm of sensation. This, this was what she'd craved from the first moment she'd seen him in dreams.

She felt his hands on her hair, her body, her face, and everywhere he touched quivered. No dream now, just need and heat and flesh.

He couldn't stop himself. She was like a feast after the fast, and all he wanted was to gorge. Her mouth was full and soft, and fit so truly to his it was as if the gods had formed it for only that purpose. The power he'd wielded had snapped back on him, inciting an impossible hunger that ached in his belly, in his loins, in his heart and cried out to be sated.

Something burned between them. He'd known it from the first instant, even ill with fever and pain while the wolves stalked beyond his fire. And he feared it nearly as much as he feared what they were fated to face together.

He drew her back, shaken to the bone. What they'd stirred was alive on her face, sultry and tempting. If he accepted and took, what price would they both pay for it?

There was always a price.

"I apologize. I . . . I was caught on the tail of the spell."

"Don't apologize. It's insulting."

Women, was all he could think. "Touching you in that way isn't?"

"If I hadn't wanted you to touch me that way, I'd have stopped you. Oh, don't flatter yourself," she snapped out when she read the expression on his face. "You may be stronger, physically, magically, but I can handle myself. And when I want an apology, I'll ask for one."

"I can't find my balance in this place, or with you." Frustration rippled out from him now, as the magic had. "I'm not liking it, or what I'm feeling for you."

"That's your problem. It was just a kiss."

He caught her arm before she could turn away. "I don't believe, even in this world, that was just a kiss. You've seen what we have to face. Desire is a weakness, one we can't risk. Everything we have must be charged toward what we have to do. I won't risk your life or the fate of the world for a few moments of pleasure."

"I can promise it would be more than a few. But there's no point in arguing with a man who sees desire as a weakness. Let's chalk it up to the moment, and move on."

"I'm not after hurting you," he began with some regret, and she aimed a single, quelling look.

"Apologize again, and you're on your ass." She picked up her keys, her purse. "Put out the candles, would you, and let's go. I want to make sure my things arrived safely, and we've got to arrange for flights to Ireland. And figure out how to smuggle you out of the country."

She grabbed sunglasses from a table, put them on. A great deal of her irritation faded at the baffled expression on his face. "Shades," she explained. "They cut the glare of the sun, and in this case are a sexy fashion statement."

She opened the iron gate, then turned, looked back at her loft, her things. "I have to believe I'll come back here. I have to believe I'll see all this again."

She stepped inside, pushed the button for the ground floor. And left behind much that she loved.

When Cian came out of his room, Glenna was in the kitchen cooking. On their return, Hoyt had taken himself off to the study adjoining the living room, hauling his books with him. Now and again, she felt something ripple out, and assumed he was practicing some spells.

It kept him out of her hair. But it didn't keep him out of her head.

She was careful with men. Enjoying them, certainly, but she didn't share herself recklessly. Which is exactly what she'd done with Hoyt, and she couldn't deny it. It had been reckless, impulsive and apparently a mistake. And though she'd said it had been just a kiss, it had been as intimate an act as she'd ever experienced.

He wanted her, there was no question of that. But he didn't choose to want her. Glenna preferred to be chosen.

Desire wasn't a weakness, not in her mind—but it was a distraction. He was right in that they couldn't afford distractions. That strength of character and good solid sense were two of his appealing traits. But considering her own jumpy system, they were equally irritating ones.

So she cooked, because it kept her busy and settled her down.

When Cian came in looking sleek and sleepy, she was briskly chopping vegetables.

"*Mi casa* is, apparently, *su casa*."

She kept right on chopping. "I brought some perishables— among other things—from home. I don't know if you eat."

He looked dubiously at the raw carrots and leafy greens.

"One of the advantages of my fate is I don't have to eat my vegetables like a good lad." But he'd scented what was on the stove, and moved to it to sniff at the spicy tomato sauce simmering. "On the other hand, this looks appealing."

He leaned back on the counter to watch her work. "So do you."

"Don't waste your questionable charm on me. Not interested."

"I could work on that, just to get under Hoyt's skin. Might be entertaining. He tries not to watch you. He fails."

Her hand hesitated, then she brought down the knife again. "I'm sure he'll succeed eventually. He's a very determined man."

"Always was, if memory serves. Sober and serious, and as trapped by his gift as a rat in a cage."

"Do you see it that way?" She set down the knife, turned to him. "As a trap. It's not, not for him, not for me. It's a duty, yes. But it's a privilege and a joy as well."

"We'll see how joyful you are when you're in Lilith's path."

"Been there. We did a locator spell at my place. She's holed up in a cave with a series of tunnels. Near the sea, I think. Near, I think, that cliffside where Hoyt faced her. She gave us a good solid blast. We won't be so easy to push next time."

"You're mad as Fat Tuesday, the pair of you." He opened his cold box, took out a bag of blood. His face tightened at the small sound Glenna couldn't quite smother. "You'll have to get used to it."

"You're right. I will." She watched him pour the contents in a thick glass, then set it in the microwave to heat. This time it was a snicker she couldn't smother. "Sorry. But it's just so damn odd."

He studied her, obviously saw no rancor, and relaxed. "Want some wine?"

"Sure, thanks. We need to go to Ireland."

"So I'm told."

"No. Now. As soon as it can be arranged. I've got a passport, but we have to figure out how to get Hoyt out of this country and into another. And we'll need a place to set up, to stay and to, well, train and practice."

"Peas in a pod," Cian muttered, pouring her a glass of wine. "It's not a simple matter, you know, to delegate responsibilities for my businesses, particularly since the man I trust to run the club downstairs is bound and determined to join Hoyt's holy army."

"Look, I spent a lot of my time today packing, transferring my rather limited funds so I could pay the rent on my place through October, cancelling appointments and handing off a couple of what would be fairly lucrative jobs to an associate. You'll just have to manage."

He retrieved his own glass. "And what is it you do? These fairly lucrative jobs?"

"Greeting card art, of the mystical variety. I paint. And do some photography."

"You any good?"

"No, I suck. Of course I'm good. The paying photography is mostly weddings. More arty stuff for my own pleasure and the occasional sale. I'm adaptable at keeping the wolf from the door." She lifted her wine. "How about you?"

"Can't survive a millennium otherwise. So, we'll leave tonight."

"Tonight? We can't possibly—"

"Adapt," he said simply and drank.

"We need to check on flights, buy tickets—"

"I have my own plane. I'm a licensed pilot."

"Oh."

"A good one," he assured her. "I've several decades of air time, so you needn't worry on that score."

Vampires who drank blood out of pricey stemware and owned planes. No, what did she have to worry about? "Hoyt doesn't have any identification, no passport, no papers. I can work a charm to get him through Customs, but—"

"No need." He crossed the room, opened a panel on the wall she hadn't detected, and revealed a safe.

Once he'd unlocked it, he took out a lock box, and coming back set it on the counter and flipped the combination.

"He can take his choice," Cian said and pulled out a half a dozen passports.

"Well, wow." She plucked one, opened it, studied the picture. "Handy you look so much alike. The serious lack of mirrors in this place tells me the lore about no reflections hangs true. No problem being photographed?"

"If you're using a reflector camera, you'd have a moment, when the mirror engages when you'd be very puzzled. Then it disengages as you shoot—and there I am."

"Interesting. I brought my cameras. I'd like to try some pictures, when there's time."

"I'll think about it."

She tossed the passport down. "I hope that plane of yours has plenty of cargo space, because I'm loaded."

"We'll manage. I've calls to make, and packing of my own to see to."

"Wait. We don't have a place to stay."

"It won't be a problem," he said as he left the room. "I've something that will suit."

Glenna blew out a breath, looked back at the pot on the stove. "Well, at least we'll get in a good meal first."

It wasn't a simple matter, even with Cian's money and connections laying a path. The luggage and cargo had to be transported the ordinary and laborious way this time. She could see all three of the men she'd hooked her fate with looking for a way to cut down on her load. She cut that route off with a firm: It all goes—and left it at that.

She had no idea what Cian had in the single suitcase or the two large metal chests he packed.

She wasn't sure she wanted to know.

She couldn't imagine what they must have looked like, the two tall, dark men, the enormous black man, and the redhead with enough luggage to resink the *Titanic*.

She enjoyed the privilege of being female, and left it to the men to do the loading, while she explored Cian's sleek and elegantly appointed private jet.

He wasn't afraid of color, or of spending his money, she

had to give him credit for that. The seats were a deep, rich blue in buttery leather, and generous enough to be comfortable for even a man of King's proportions. The carpet was thick enough to sleep on.

It boasted a small, efficient conference room, two sophisticated bathrooms, and what she initially took to be a cozy bedroom. More than that, she realized when she noted it had no windows, no mirrors, and its own half bath. A safe room.

She wandered into the galley, approved it, and appreciated the fact that Cian had already called ahead to have it stocked. They wouldn't starve on the flight to Europe.

Europe. She trailed her finger over one of the fully reclining seats. She'd always planned to go, to spend as much as a month. Painting, taking photographs, exploring. Visiting the ancient sites, shopping.

Now she was going, and getting there well above the first-class level. But she wouldn't be wandering the hills and the sacred grounds at her leisure.

"Well, you wanted adventure in your life," she reminded herself. "Now you've got it." She closed a hand around the pendant she wore and prayed she'd have not only the strength but also the wits to survive it.

She was seated when the men boarded, and making a show out of enjoying a glass of champagne.

"I popped the cork," she said to Cian. "I hope you don't mind. It seemed appropriate."

"Sláinte." He moved directly to the cockpit.

"Want the two-dollar tour?" she asked Hoyt. "Want to look around?" she explained. "I imagine King's flown in this little beauty before and is thoroughly jaded."

"Beats the hell out of commercial," King agreed, and got himself a beer in lieu of champagne. "The boss knows how to handle this bird." He gave Hoyt a slap on the shoulder. "No worries."

Because he looked far from convinced, Glenna rose and poured another glass of champagne. "Here, drink, relax. We're going to be in here all night."

"In a bird made out of metal and cloth. A flying machine." Hoyt nodded, and because it was in his hand, sipped the bubbling wine. "It's a matter of science and mechanics."

He'd spent two full hours reading of the history and technology of aircraft. "Aerodynamics."

"Exactly." King tapped the beer bottle to Hoyt's glass, then Glenna's. "Here's to kicking some ass."

"You look like you're looking forward to it," Glenna commented.

"Damn straight. Who wouldn't? We get to save the frigging world. The boss? He's been restless the last few weeks. He gets restless, I get restless. Ask me, this is just what the doctor ordered."

"And dying doesn't worry you?"

"Everybody dies." He glanced toward the cockpit. "One way or another. 'Sides, a big bastard like me doesn't go down easy."

Cian strolled in. "We're cleared, boys and girls. Have a seat, strap in."

"Got your back, Captain." King followed Cian back into the cockpit.

Glenna sat, offered a smile as she patted the seat beside hers. She was prepared to soothe Hoyt through his first flight. "You'll need your seat belt. Let me show you how it works."

"I know how it works. I read of it." He studied the metal for a moment, then locked the pieces together. "In the event there is turbulence. Pockets of air."

"You're not the least bit nervous."

"I came through a time portal," he reminded her. He began to play with the control panel, amusement crossing his face when the back reclined, came up again. "I think I'll be enjoying this trip. Bloody shame it's got to be done over water."

"Oh, I nearly forgot." She dug into her purse, pulled out a vial. "Drink this. It'll help. Drink it," she repeated when he frowned at the vial. "It's herbs and some powdered crystals. Nothing harmful. It may help the queasiness."

The reluctance was clear on his face, but he downed it. "You have a heavy hand with the cloves."

"You can thank me when you don't have to use the barf bag."

She heard the engines hum, felt the vibration beneath her. "Spirits of the night, give us wings to take this flight. Hold us safe within your hand until we touch upon the land." She slid her eyes to Hoyt. "It never hurts."

He wasn't ill, but she could see that her potion and his will were fighting a hard battle to keep his system steady. She made him tea, brought him a blanket, then reclined his seat, brought up the footrest herself.

"Try to sleep a little."

Too ill to argue, he nodded, closed his eyes. When she was sure he was as comfortable as she could make him, she moved forward to join the others in the cockpit.

There was music playing. Nine Inch Nails, she recognized. In the copilot's seat, King had kicked back and was snoring along with the beat. Glenna looked through the windscreen and felt her heart do a little dance of its own.

There was nothing but the black.

"I've never been in a cockpit before. Awesome view."

"I can kick that one out of here if you want his seat for a bit."

"No. I'm fine. Your brother's trying to sleep. He's not feeling very well."

"He used to turn green crossing the Shannon. I imagine he's sick as a dog by now."

"No, just queasy. I gave him something at takeoff, and he's got an iron will to add to it. Do you want anything?"

He glanced back. "Aren't you the helpful one?"

"I'm too revved up to sleep, too restless to sit. So, coffee, tea, milk?"

"I wouldn't mind the coffee. Thanks for that."

She brewed a short pot, brought him a mug of it. Then stood behind him, staring out into the night sky. "What was he like as a boy?"

"As I told you."

"Did he ever doubt his power? Ever wish he hadn't been given the gift?"

It was a strange sensation, having a woman question him

about another man. Generally if they weren't talking about themselves they were asking about him, trying to nudge aside what some of them saw as a curtain of mystery.

"Not that he ever told me. And he would have," Cian said after a moment. "We were close enough in those days."

"Was there someone—a woman, a girl—for him back there?"

"No. He looked, and he touched, and he had a few. He's a sorcerer not a priest. But he never told me of one special to him. I never saw him look at any of the girls as he looks at you. To your peril, Glenna, I'd be saying. But mortals are fools when it comes to love."

"And I'd say if you can't love when you're facing death, then death's not worth fighting. Lilith had a child with her. Did he tell you that?"

"He didn't, no. You need to understand there's no sentiment there, no softness. A child is just easy prey, and a sweet meal."

Her stomach turned, but she kept her voice even. "Six or eight years old, I'd say," she continued. "In the bed with her, in those caves. She'd made him like her. She'd made that child like her."

"That shocks and angers you, well, that's fine then. Shock and anger can be strong weapons in the right hand. But remember this. If you see that child, or one like him, put your pity away, because he'll kill you without thought or mercy unless you kill him first."

She studied Cian now, that profile that was so like his brother's, yet so completely his own. She wanted to ask if he'd ever turned a child, or fed on one. But she was afraid the answer might be unforgivable, and she needed him.

"Could you do that, destroy a child whatever he'd become?"

"Without thought or mercy." He glanced at her, and she saw he'd known the other question running in her mind. "And you're no good to us or yourself if you can't do the same."

She left him then without a word and went back to stretch out beside Hoyt. Because the conversation with Cian had chilled her, she pulled her own blanket up to her throat, curled toward Hoyt's body heat.

And when she slept, finally slept, she dreamed of children, with sunny hair and bloody fangs.

She woke with a start to find Cian leaning over her. A scream clawed up to her throat until she realized he was shaking Hoyt awake.

She pushed at her hair, skimmed her fingers over her face for a quick glamour. They were speaking in low tones and, she realized, in Irish.

"English, please. I can't follow that much, especially with the accents."

Both turned vibrant blue eyes on her, and Cian straightened as she brought her chair up. "I'm telling him we've about an hour flight time left."

"Who's flying the plane?"

"King's got it for the moment. We'll be landing at dawn."

"Good. Great." She barely stifled a yawn. "I'll throw some coffee and breakfast together so . . . Dawn?"

"Aye, dawn. I need a good cloud cover. Rain would be a bonus. Can you do this? Otherwise King will land it. He's capable, and I'll be spending the rest of the flight and the day in the back of the plane."

"I said I could do it, and I will."

"We can do it," Glenna corrected.

"Well, be quick about it, will you? I've been singed a time or two and it's unpleasant."

"You're welcome," she muttered when he left them. "I'll get a few things from my travel case."

"I don't need them." Hoyt brushed her aside, got up to stand in the aisle. "This time, it'll be my way. He's my brother, after all."

"Your way then. How can I help?"

"Call the vision to your mind. Clouds and rain. Rain and clouds." He retrieved his staff. "See it, feel it, smell it. Thick and steady, with the sun trapped behind the gloom. Dusky light, light without power or harm. See it, feel it, smell it."

He held his staff in both hands, braced his legs apart for balance, then raised it.

"I call the rain, the black clouds that cover the sky. I call the clouds, fat with rain that streams from the heavens. Swirl and close and lay thick."

She felt it spin, spin out from him, spin out to the air. The plane shook, bucked, trembled, but he stood as if he stood on a floor of granite. The tip of the staff glowed blue.

He turned to her, nodded. "That should do it."

"Well. Okay then. I'll make coffee."

They landed in gloom with the rain like a gray curtain. A little overdone, in Glenna's opinion, and it was going to be a miserable drive from the airport to wherever the hell they were going.

But she stepped off the plane and onto Ireland, and there it was. A connection, instant and surprising even to her. She had a quick sense of memory of a farm—green hills, stone fences and a white house with clothes flapping on a line in a brisk wind. There was a garden in the dooryard with dahlias big as dinner plates and calla lilies white as wishes.

It was gone almost as quickly as it had come. She wondered if it was her memory from another time, another life, or simply a call through her blood. Her grandmother's mother had come from Ireland, from a farm in Kerry.

She had brought her linens and her best dishes—and her magic—to America with her.

She waited for Hoyt to deplane. This would always be home for him, she saw it now in the pleasure that ran over his face. Whether it was a busy airport or an empty field, this was his place. And part, very much a part, she understood now, of what he would die to save.

"Welcome home."

"It looks nothing like it did."

"Parts of it will." She took his hand and squeezed. "Nice job with the weather, by the way."

"Well, that at least, is familiar."

King trotted over, wet as a seal. His thick dreads dripped rain. "Cain's arranging for most of the stuff to be delivered by truck. Take what you can carry, or have to have right now. The rest'll be along in a couple hours."

"Where are we going?" Glenna demanded.

"He's got a place here." King shrugged. "So that's where we're going."

They had a van, and even then it was a tight squeeze. And, Glenna discovered, another sort of adventure altogether to sweep along through the pouring rain on wet roads, many of which seemed as narrow as a willow stem.

She saw hedgerows ripe with fuchsia, and those hills of wet emerald rolling up and back into the dull gray sky. She saw houses with flowers blooming in dooryards. Not the one of her quick image, but close enough to make her smile.

Something here had belonged to her once. Now maybe it would again.

"I know this place," Hoyt murmured. "I know this land."

"See." Glenna patted his hand. "I knew some of it would be the same for you."

"No, this place, this land." He pushed up to grab Cian by the shoulder. "Cian."

"Mind the driver," Cian ordered and shook off his brother's hand before turning between the hedgerows and onto a narrow spit of a land that wound back through a dense forest.

"God," Hoyt breathed. "Sweet God."

The house was stone, alone among the trees, and quiet as a tomb. Old and wide, with the jut of a tower and the stone aprons of terraces. In the gloom, it looked deserted and out of its time.

And still there was a garden outside the door, of roses and lilies and the wide plates of dahlia. Foxglove sprang tall and purple among the trees.

"It's still here." Hoyt spoke in a voice thick with emotion. "It survived. It still stands."

Understanding now, Glenna gave his hand another squeeze. "It's your home."

"The one I left only days ago. The one I left nearly a thousand years ago. I've come home."

Chapter 7

It wasn't the same. The furnishings, the colors, the light, even the sound his footsteps made crossing the floor had changed, turning the familiar into the foreign. He recognized a few pieces—some candlestands and a chest. But they were in the wrong places.

Logs had been set in the hearth, but were yet unlit. And there were no dogs curled up on the floor or thumping their tails in greeting.

Hoyt moved through the rooms like a ghost. Perhaps that's what he was. His life had begun in this house, and so much of it had been woven together under its roof or on its grounds. He had played here and worked here, eaten and slept here.

But that was hundreds of years in the past. So perhaps, in a very true sense, his life had ended here as well.

His initial joy in seeing the house dropped away with a weight of sadness for all that he'd lost.

Then he saw, encased in glass on the wall, one of his mother's tapestries. He moved to it, touched his fingers to the glass as she came winging back to him. Her face, her voice, her scent were as real as the air around him.

"It was the last she'd finished before . . ."

"I died," Cian finished. "I remember. I came across it in an auction. That, and a few other things over time. I was able to acquire the house oh, about four hundred years ago now, I suppose. Most of the land as well."

"But you don't live here any longer."

"It's a bit out of the way for me, and not convenient to my work or pleasures. I have a caretaker whom I've sent off until I order him back. And I generally come over once a year or so."

Hoyt dropped his hand, turned. "It's changed."

"Change is inevitable. The kitchen's been modernized. There's plumbing and electricity. Still it's drafty for all that. The bedrooms upstairs are furnished, so take your choices. I'm going up to get some sleep."

He started out, glanced back. "Oh, and you can stop the rain if you've a mind to. King, give me a hand will you, hauling some of this business up?"

"Sure. Very cool digs, if you don't mind a little spooky." King hauled up a chest the way another man might have picked up a briefcase, and headed up the main stairs.

"Are you all right?" Glenna asked Hoyt.

"I don't know what I am." He went to the window, drew back heavy drapes to look out on the rain-drenched forest. "It's here, this place, the stones set by my ancestors. I'm grateful for that."

"But they're not here. The family you left behind. It's hard what you're doing. Harder for you than the rest of us."

"We all share it."

"I left my loft. You left your life." She stepped to him, brushed a kiss over his cheek. She had thought to offer to fix a hot meal, but saw that what he needed most just then was solitude.

"I'm going up, grab a room, a shower and a bed."

He nodded, continued to stare out the window. The rain suited his mood, but it was best to close the spell. Even when he had, it continued to rain, but in a fine, misty drizzle. The fog crawled across the ground, twined around the feet of the rose bushes.

Could they be his mother's still? Unlikely, but they were roses, after all. That would have pleased her. He wondered if in some way having her sons here again, together, would please her as well.

How could he know? How would he ever know?

He flashed fire into the hearth. It seemed more like home with the fire snapping. He didn't choose to go up, not yet. Later, he thought, he'd take his case up to the tower. He'd make it his own again. Instead he dug out his cloak, swirled it on and stepped out into the thin summer rain.

He walked toward the stream first where the drenched foxgloves swayed their heavy bells and the wild orange lilies Nola had particularly loved spread like spears of flame. There should be flowers in the house, he thought. He'd have to gather some before dusk. There had always been flowers in the house.

He circled around, drawing in the scent of damp air, wet leaves, roses. His brother kept the place tended; Hoyt couldn't fault him for that. He saw the stables were still there—not the same, but in the same spot. They were larger than they'd been, with a jut to one side that boasted a wide door.

He found it locked, so opened it with a focused thought. It opened upward to reveal a stone floor and some sort of car. Not like the one in New York, he noted. Not like the cab, or the van they had traveled in from the airport. This was black and lower to the ground. On its hood was a shining silver panther. He ran his hands over it.

It puzzled him that there were so many different types of cars in this world. Different sizes and shapes and colors. If one was efficient and comfortable, why did they need so many other kinds?

There was a long bench in the area as well, and all manner of fascinating-looking tools hanging on the wall or layered in the drawers of a large red chest. He spent some time studying them, and the stack of timber that had been planed smooth and cut into long lengths.

Tools, he thought, wood, machines, but no life. No grooms, no horses, no cats slinking about hunting mice. No litter of wriggling pups for Nola to play with. He closed and locked the door behind him again, moved down the outside length of the stable.

He wandered into the tack room, comforted somewhat by the scents of leather and oil. It was well organized, he saw, just as the stall for the car had been. He ran his hands over a saddle, crouched to examine it, and found it not so different from the one he'd used.

He toyed with reins and bridles, and for a moment missed his mare as he might have missed a lover.

He passed through a door. The stone floor had a slight slope, with two stalls on one side, one on the other. Fewer than there had been, but larger, he noted. The wood was smooth and dark. He could smell hay and grain, and . . .

He moved, quickly now, down the stone floor.

A coal-black stallion stood in the last of three stalls. It gave Hoyt's heart a hard and happy leap to see it. There were still horses after all—and this one, he noted, was magnificent.

It pawed the ground, laid back its ears when Hoyt opened the stall door. But he held up both hands, began to croon softly in Irish.

In response, the horse kicked the rear of the stall and blew out a warning.

"That's all right then, that's fine. Who could blame you for being careful with a stranger? But I'm just here to admire you, to take in your great handsome self, is all I'm about. Here, have a sniff why don't you? See what you think. Ah, it's a sniff I said, not a nip." With a chuckle, Hoyt drew back his hand a fraction as the horse bared his teeth.

He continued to speak softly and stand very still with his hand out while the horse made a show of snorting and pawing. Deciding bribery was the best tack, Hoyt conjured an apple.

When he saw the interest in the horse's eye, he lifted it, took a healthy bite himself. "Delicious. Would you be wanting some?"

Now the horse stepped forward, sniffed, snorted, then nipped the apple from Hoyt's palm. As he chomped it, he graciously allowed himself to be stroked.

"I left a horse behind. A fine horse I'd had for eight years.

I called her Aster, for she had a star shape right here." He stroked two fingers down the stallion's head. "I miss her. I miss it all. For all the wonders of this world, it's hard to be away from what you know."

At length he stepped out of the stall, closed the door behind him. The rain had stopped so he could hear the murmur of the stream, and the plop of rain falling from leaf to ground.

Were there still faeries in the woods? he wondered. Playing and plotting and watching the foibles of man? He was too tired in his mind to search for them. Too tired in his heart to take the lonely walk to where he knew his family must be buried.

He went back to the house, retrieved his case and walked up all the winding steps to the topmost tower.

There was a heavy door barring his way, one that was deeply scribed with symbols and words of magic. Hoyt ran his fingers over the carving, felt the hum and the heat. Whoever had done this had some power.

Well, he wouldn't be shut out of his own workroom. He set to work to break the locking spell, and used his own sense of insult and anger to heat it.

This was *his* home. And never in his life had a door here been locked to him.

"Open locks," he commanded. "It is my right to enter this place. It is my will that breaks this spell."

The door flew open on a blast of wind. Hoyt took himself and his resentment inside, letting the door slam shut behind him.

The room was empty but for dust and spiderwebs. Cold, too, he thought. Cold and stale and unused. Once it had carried the scent of his herbs and candlewax, the burn of his own power.

He would have this back at least, as it had been it would be again. There was work to do, and this was where he intended to do it.

So he cleaned the hearth and lit the fire. He dragged up from below whatever suited him—a chair, tables. There was no electricity here, and that pleased him. He'd make his own light.

He set out candles, touched their wicks to set them to burn. By their light he arranged his tools and supplies.

Settled in his heart, in his mind, for the first time in days, he stretched out on the floor in front of the fire, rolled up his cloak to pillow his head and slept.

And dreamed.

He stood with Morrigan on a high hill. The ground sheered down in steep drops, slicing rolls with shadowy chasms all haunted by the distant blur of dark mountains. The grass was coarse and pocked with rock. Some rose up like spears, others jutted out in gray layers, flat as giant tables. The ground dipped up and down, up again to the mountains where the mists fell into pockets.

He could hear hisses in the mists, the panting breath of something older than time. There was an anger to this place. A wild violence waiting to happen.

But now, nothing stirred on the land as far as his eye could see.

"This is your battleground," she told him. "Your last stand. There will be others before you come here. But this is where you will draw her, and face her with all the worlds in the balance on that day."

"What is this place?"

"This is the Valley of Silence, in the Mountains of Mist, in the World of Geall. Blood will spill here, demon and human. What grows after will be determined by what you, and those with you do. But you must not stand upon this land until the battle."

"How will I come here again?"

"You will be shown."

"We are only four."

"More are coming. Sleep now, for when you wake, you must act."

While he slept the mists parted. He saw there was a maiden standing on that same high ground. She was slim and young with brown hair in a tumble down her back, loose as suited a maiden. She wore a gown of deep mourning, and her eyes showed the ravages of weeping.

But they were dry now, and fixed upon that desolate land,

as his had been. The goddess spoke to her, but the words were not for him.

Her name was Moira, and her land was Geall. Her land and her heart and her duty. That land had been at peace since the gods had made it, and those of her blood had guarded that peace. Now, she knew, peace would be broken, just as her heart was broken.

She had buried her mother that morning.

"They slaughtered her like a spring lamb."

"I know your grief, child."

Her bruised eyes stared hard through the rain. "Do the gods grieve, my lady?"

"I know your anger."

"She harmed no one in her life. What manner of death is that for one who was so good, so kind?" Moira's hands bunched at her sides. "You cannot know my grief or my anger."

"Others will die even a worse death. Will you stand and do nothing?"

"What can I do? How do we defend against such creatures? Will you give me more power?" Moira held out her hands, hands that had never felt so small and empty. "More wisdom and cunning? What I have isn't enough."

"You've been given all you need. Use it, hone it. There are others, and they wait for you. You must leave now, today."

"Leave?" Stunned, Moira turned to face the goddess. "My people have lost their queen. How can I leave them, and how could you ask it of me? The test must be taken; the gods themselves deemed this so. If I'm not to be the one to stand in my mother's stead, take sword and crown, I still must bide here, to help the one who does."

"You help by going, and this the gods deem so. This is your charge, Moira of Geall. To travel from this world so you might save it."

"You would have me leave my home, my people, and on such a day? The flowers have not yet faded on my mother's grave."

"Would your mother wish you to stand and weep for her and watch your people die?"

"No."

"You must go, you and the one you trust most. Travel to the Dance of the Gods. There I will give you a key, and it will take you where you need to go. Find the others, form your army. And when you come here, to this land, on Samhain, you'll fight."

Fight, she thought. She had never been called to fight, had only known peace. "My lady, am I not needed here?"

"You will be. I tell you to go now where you're needed now. If you stay, you're lost. And your land is lost, as the worlds are. This was destined for you since before your birth. It is why you are.

"Go immediately. Make haste. They only wait for sunset."

Her mother's grave was here, Moira thought in despair. Her life was here, and all she knew. "I'm in mourning. A few days more, Mother, I beg you."

"Stay even one day longer, and this is what befalls your people, your land."

Morrigan waved an arm, parting the mists. Beyond them it was black night with only the silver ripple of light from the cold moon. Screams ripped through the air. Then there was smoke, and the shimmering orange glow of fires.

Moira saw the village overlooked by her own home. The shops and cottages were burning, and those screams were the screams of her friends, her neighbors. Men and women ripped to pieces, children being fed on by those horrible things that had taken her mother.

She watched her own uncle fight, slashing with his sword while blood stained his face and hands. But they leaped on him from above, from below, those creatures with fangs and eyes of feral red. They fell on him with howls that froze her bones. And while the blood washed the ground, a woman of great beauty glided over it. She wore red, a silk gown tightly laced at the bodice and bedecked with jewels. Her hair was uncovered and spilled gold as sunlight over her white shoulders.

In her arms was a babe still swaddled.

While the slaughter raged around her, the thing of great beauty bared fangs, and sank them into the babe's throat.

"No!"

"Hold your grief and your anger here, and this will come." The cold anger in Morrigan's voice pierced through Moira's terror. "All you know destroyed, ravaged, devoured."

"What are these demons? What hell loosed them on us?"

"Learn. Take what you have, what you are, and seek your destiny. The battle will come. Arm yourself."

She woke beside her mother's grave, shaking from the horrors she'd seen. Her heart was as heavy as the stones used to make her mother's cairn.

"I couldn't save you. How can I save anyone? How can I stop this thing from coming here?"

To leave all she'd ever known, all she'd ever loved. Easy for gods to speak of destiny, she thought as she forced herself to her feet. She looked over the graves to the quiet green hills, the blue ribbon of the river. The sun was high and bright, sparkling over her world. She heard the song of a lark, and the distant lowing of cattle.

The gods had smiled on this land for hundreds of years. Now there was a price to be paid, of war and death and blood. And her duty to pay it.

"I'll miss you, every day," she said aloud, then looked over to her father's grave. "But now you're together. I'll do what needs to be done, to protect Geall. Because I'm all that's left of you. I swear it here, on this holy ground before those who made me. I'll go to strangers in a strange world, and give my life if my life is asked. It's all I can give you now."

She picked up the flowers she'd brought with her, and laid some on each grave. "Help me do this thing," she pleaded, then walked away.

He was waiting for her on the stone wall. He had his own grief, she knew, but had given her the time she'd needed alone. He was the one she trusted most. The son of her mother's brother—the uncle she'd seen cut down in the vision.

He jumped lightly to his feet when she approached, and simply held open his arms. Going into them, she rested her head on his chest. "Larkin."

"We'll hunt them. We'll find them and kill them. What-ever they are."

"I know what they are, and we will find them, kill them. But not here. Not now." She drew back. "Morrigan came to me, and told me what must be done."

"Morrigan?"

At the suspicion on his face she was able to smile a little. "I'll never understand how someone with your skills doubts the gods." She lifted a hand to his cheek. "But will you trust me?"

He framed her face, kissed her forehead. "You know I will."

As she told him what she'd been told, his face changed again. He sat on the ground, shoving a hand through his mane of tawny hair. She'd envied his hair as long as she'd lived, mourning the fact that she'd been given ordinary brown. His eyes were tawny as well, gilded she'd always thought, while hers were gray as rain.

He'd been gifted with more height, as well as other things she envied.

When she was finished, she drew a long breath. "Will you go with me?"

"I'd hardly let you go alone." His hand closed over hers, firm and steady. "Moira, how can you be sure this vision wasn't simply your heartbreak?"

"I know. I can only tell you that I know what I saw was real. But if it's nothing more than grief, we'll only have wasted the time it takes to go to the Dance. Larkin, I need to try."

"Then we'll try."

"We tell no one."

"Moira—"

"Listen to me." Urgently, she gripped his wrists. "Your father would do his best to stop us. Or to come with us if he believed me. This isn't the way, it isn't my charge. One, the goddess told me. I was to take only one, the one I trusted most. It can only be you. We'll write it down for him. While we're gone, he'll rule Geall, and protect it."

"You'll take the sword—" Larkin began.

"No. The sword isn't to leave here. That was a sacred oath, and I won't be the one to break it. The sword remains until I return. I don't take my place until I lift it, I don't lift it until I've earned my place. There are other swords. Arm yourself, she said, so see that you do. Meet me in an hour. Tell no one."

She squeezed his hands now. "Swear to me on the blood we share. On the loss we share."

How could he deny her when tears were still on her cheeks? "I swear it to you. I'll tell no one." He gave her arms a quick rub in comfort. "We'll be back by supper, I wager, in any case."

She hurried home, across the field and up the hill to the castle where her blood had reigned over the land since it was created. Those she passed bowed their heads to her to show their sympathy, and she saw tears glimmer.

And she knew when they dried, many would look to her for guidance, for answers. Many would wonder how she would rule.

So did she.

She crossed the great hall. There was no laughter here now, no music. Gathering the burdensome skirts of her gown, she climbed the steps to her chamber.

There were women nearby, sewing, tending to children, speaking in low voices so it sounded like doves cooing.

Moira went quietly by, and slipped into her room. She exchanged her gown for riding clothes, laced on her boots. It felt wrong to put off her mourning garb so quickly, so easily, but she would travel more swiftly in the tunic and tewes. She bound her hair back in a braid and began to pack.

She would need little but what was on her back, she decided. She would think of this as a hunting trip—there, at least, she had some skill. And so she got out her quiver and her bow, a short sword and lay them on the bed while she sat to write a message to her uncle.

How did you tell a man who'd stood in as father for so many years that you were taking his son into a battle you didn't understand, to fight what was impossible to comprehend, in the company of men you didn't know?

The will of the gods, she thought, her mouth tight as she wrote. She wasn't certain if she followed that or simply her own rage. But go she would.

I must do this thing, she continued in a careful hand. *I pray you will forgive me for it, and know that I go only for the sake of Geall. I ask that if I don't return by Samhain, you lift the sword and rule in my place. Know that I go for you, for Geall, and that I swear by my mother's blood, I will fight to the death to defend and protect what I love.*

Now I leave what I love in your hands.

She folded the letter, heated the wax and sealed it.

She put on the sword, shouldered her quiver and bow. One of the women bustled out as she left her chambers.

"My lady!"

"I wish to ride out alone." Her voice was so sharp, her manner so curt that there was nothing but a gasp behind her as she strode away.

Her belly shook, but she didn't pause. When she reached the stables, she waved the boy away and saddled her mount herself. She looked down at him, his soft, young face bursting with freckles.

"When the sun sets, you're to stay inside. This night and every night until I tell you. Do you heed me?"

"Aye, my lady."

She wheeled her horse, kicked her heels lightly at its flanks, riding off at a gallop.

She would not look back, Moria thought. She would not look back at home, but forward.

Larkin was waiting for her, sitting loose in the saddle while his horse cropped grass.

"I'm sorry, it took longer."

"Women always take longer."

"I'm asking so much of you. What if we never get back?"

He clicked to his horse, walking it beside hers. "Since I don't believe we're going anywhere, I'm not worried." He sent her an easy smile. "I'm just indulging you."

"I'd feel nothing but relief if this is nothing more than that." But once again she urged her horse to a gallop. Whatever was waiting, she wanted to meet it quickly.

He matched her pace as they rode, as they had so often, over the hills that sparkled in the sunlight. Buttercups dotted the fields with yellow, giving swarms of butterflies a reason to dance in the air. She watched a hawk circle overhead, and some of the heaviness lifted from her.

Her mother had loved to watch the hawk. She'd said it was Moira's father, there to look down on them while he flew free. Now she prayed her mother flew free as well.

The hawk circled over the ring of stones, and raised its cry.

Nerves made her queasy so she swallowed hard.

"Well, we made it this far." Larkin shook back his hair. "What do you suggest?"

"Are you cold? Do you feel the cold?"

"No. It's warm. The sun's strong today."

"Something's watching." She shivered even as she dismounted. "Something cold."

"There's nothing here but us." But when he jumped down from his horse, Larkin laid a hand on the hilt of his sword.

"It sees." There were voices in her head, whispers and murmurs. As if in a trance, she took her bag from the saddle. "Take what you need. Come with me."

"You're acting considerably strange, Moira." With a sigh, Larkin took his own bag, tossing it over his shoulder as he caught up with her.

"She can't enter here. Never. No matter what her power, she can never enter this circle, never touch these stones. If she tries she'll burn. She knows, she hates."

"Moira . . . your eyes."

She turned them on him. They were nearly black, and they were depthless. And when she opened her hand, there was a wand of crystal in it. "You are bound, as I am bound, to do this thing. You are my blood." She took her short sword, cut her palm, then reached for his.

"Well, bollocks." But he held out his hand, let her slice across the palm.

She sheathed the knife, gripped his bloody hand with hers. "Blood is life, and blood is death," she said. "And here it opens the way."

With his hand in hers, she stepped into the circle.

"Worlds wait," she began, chanting the words that swirled in her head. "Time flows. Gods watch. Speak the words with me."

Her hand throbbed in his as they repeated the words.

The wind swirled, whipping the long grass, snapping their cloaks. Instinctively, Larkin put his free arm around her, folding her into him as he tried to use his body as a shield. Light burst, blinding them.

She gripped his hand, and felt the world spin.

Then the dark. Damp grass, misty air.

They still stood within the circle, on that same rise. But not the same, she realized. The forest beyond wasn't quite the same.

"The horses are gone."

She shook her head. "No. We are."

He looked up. He could see the moon swimming behind the clouds. The dying wind was cold enough to reach his bones. "It's night. It was barely midday and now it's night. Where the bloody hell are we?"

"Where we're meant to be, that's all I know. We need to find the others."

He was baffled, and unnerved. And could admit that he hadn't thought beyond the moment. That would stop now, for now he had only one charge. To protect his cousin.

"What we're going to do is look for shelter and wait for sunrise." He tossed her his pack, then started to stride out of the circle. As he walked, he changed.

The shape of his body, the sinew, the bone. In place of skin a pelt, tawny as his hair, in place of hair a mane. Now a stallion stood where the man had been.

"Well, I suppose that would be quicker." Ignoring the knots in her belly, Moira mounted. "We'll ride the way that would be toward home. I think that makes the most sense—if any of this does. Best not gallop, in case that way is different from what we know."

He set off in a trot, while she scanned the trees and the moonstruck hills. So much the same, she thought, but with subtle differences.

There was a great oak where none had been before, and the murmur of a spring in the wrong direction. Nor was the road the same. She nudged Larkin off it, in the direction where home would be if this were her world.

They moved into the trees, picking their way now carefully, following instinct and a rough path.

He stopped, lifted his head as if scenting the air. His body shifted under her as he turned. She felt muscles bunch.

"What is it? What do you—"

He flew, risking low branches, hidden rocks as he broke into a strong gallop. Knowing only he'd sensed danger, she lowered her body, clung to his mane. But it came like lightning, flying out of the trees as if it had wings. She had time to shout, time to reach for her sword before Larkin reared up, striking the thing with both hooves.

It screamed, tumbled off into the dark.

She would have urged him back into a gallop, but he was already shaking her off, already turning back into a man. They stood back-to-back now, swords drawn.

"The circle," she whispered. "If we can get back to the circle."

He shook his head. "They've cut us off," he replied. "We're surrounded."

They came slowly now, slinking out of the shadows. Five, no six, Moira saw as her blood chilled. Their fangs gleamed in the shivering moonlight.

"Stay close," Larkin told her. "Don't let them draw you away from me."

One of the things laughed, a sound that was horribly human. "You've come a long way to die," it said.

And leaped.

Chapter 8

Too restless to sleep, Glenna wandered the house. It was big enough, she supposed, to accommodate an army—certainly large enough to keep four relative strangers comfortable and afford some privacy. There were high ceilings—gorgeous with ornate plaster work—and steps that spiraled or curved to more rooms. Some of those rooms were small as cells, others spacious and airy.

Chandeliers were iron, the style intricate and artful and leaning toward the Gothic. They suited the house more than anything contemporary, or even the elegance of crystal.

Intrigued by the look, she went back for a camera. While she wandered, she paused when the mood struck, framed in a portion of ceiling, or a light. She spent thirty minutes alone on the dragons carved into the black marble of the fireplace in the main parlor.

Wizards, vampires, warriors. Marble dragons and ancient houses secluded in deep woods. Plenty of fodder for her art, she thought. She could very well make up the hit to her income when she got back to New York.

Might as well think positive.

Cian must have spent a great deal of time and money refurbishing, modernizing, decorating, she decided. But then, he had plenty of both. Rich colors, rich fabrics, gleaming antiques gave the house a sense of luxury and style. And yes, she thought, the place just sat here, year after year, empty and echoing.

A pity, really. A waste of beauty and history. She deplored waste.

Still, it was lucky he had it. Its location, its size, and she supposed, its history made it the perfect base.

She found the library and nodded in approval. It boasted three staggered tiers of books, towering to the domed ceiling where another dragon—stained glass this time—breathed fire and light.

There were candlestands taller than a man, and lamps with jeweled shades. She didn't doubt the lake-sized Oriental rugs were the genuine articles and possibly hundreds of years old.

Not only a good base, she mused, but an extremely comfortable one. With its generous library table, deep chairs and enormous fireplace, she deemed this the perfect war room.

She indulged herself by lighting the fire and the lamps to dispel the gloom of the gray day. From her own supply, she gathered crystals, books, candles, arranging them throughout the room.

Though she wished for flowers, it was a start. But more was needed. Life didn't run on style, on luck, or on magic alone.

"What're you up to, Red?"

She turned, saw King filling the doorway. "I guess we could call it nesting."

"Hell of a nest."

"I was thinking the same. And I'm glad you're here. You're just the man I need."

"You and every other woman. What've you got in mind?"

"Practicalities. You've been here before, right?"

"Yeah, a couple times."

"Where are the weapons?" When his eyebrows shot up, she spread her arms. "Those pesky items required for fighting wars—or so I've heard, since this would be my first war. I know I'd feel better if I had a couple of howitzers handy."

"Don't think the boss runs to those."

"What does he run to?"

He considered. "What you got going in here?"

She glanced toward the crystals. "Just some things I've set around for protection, courage, creativity and so on. This struck me as a good place to strategize. A war room. What?" she said when his lips curved in a wide grin.

"Guess you're on to something." He walked over to a wall of books, ran his big fingers along the carved trim.

"You're not going to tell me there's a . . . secret panel," she finished with a delighted laugh when the wall swiveled out.

"Place is full of 'em." King pushed the wall completely around before she could peek through the gap. "I don't know as he'd want you poking around in the passages. But you said weapons." He gestured. "You got weapons."

Swords, axes, maces, daggers, scythes. Every manner of blade hung gleaming on the exposed wall. There were crossbows, long bows, even what she thought was a trident.

"That's just a little bit scary," she declared, but stepped forward to take down a small dagger.

"Little advice," King began. "You use something like that, whatever's coming for you is going to have to get real close before it does you any good."

"Good point." She replaced the dagger, took down a sword. "Wow. Heavy." She replaced it, took down what she thought would be termed a foil. "Better."

"You got any idea how to use that?"

"Hack, hack, hack, jab, jab?" She gave it a testing swing, found herself surprised she liked the feel of it. "Okay, no. Not a clue. Someone will have to teach me."

"Do you think you could slice through flesh with that?" Cian spoke as he came in the room. "Strike bone, spill blood?"

"I don't know." She lowered the sword. "I'm afraid I'm going to have to find out. I saw what she was, what she did, what she has with her. I'm not going into this with only potions and spells. And I'm sure as hell not going to stand there and go *eek* if she tries to bite me."

"You can wound them with that, slow them down. But you won't kill, you won't stop them unless you use it to cut off the head."

With a grimace she studied the slender blade, then resigned, put it back, took down the heavier sword.

"Swinging that around takes a great deal of strength."

"Then I'll get strong, strong enough."

"Muscle's not the only kind of strength you'll need."

She kept her gaze level. "I'll get strong enough. You know how to use this. You and Hoyt, and you," she said to King. "If you think I'm going to sit back, stirring a cauldron when it comes time to fight, think again. I wasn't brought here so I could have men protect me. I wasn't given this gift to be a coward."

"Me," King said with that wide grin in place again, "I like a woman with grit."

Gripping the hilt with both hands, she sliced the air with the blade. "So. When's my first lesson?"

Hoyt descended the stairs. He tried not to mourn what was changed, what was gone. He would get back, back to his true home, back to his family, and his life.

He would see the torches flaming on the walls again, smell his mother's roses in the garden. And he would walk the cliffs beyond his own cottage in Chiarrai again, and know the world was free of the vermin that sought to destroy it.

He'd needed rest, that was all. Rest and solitude in a place he knew and understood. Now he would work, and he would plan. He was done with this sensation of being swept away into what he couldn't understand.

Darkness had fallen, and those lights—those strange, harsh lights that came from electricity rather than fire— illuminated the house.

It irritated him that he found no one about, and could scent no supper cooking from the direction of the kitchen. It was time to be busy, and time the rest understood it was necessary to take the next steps.

A sound made him pause, then hiss out a breath. He followed the sound of clashing steel at a run. Then he swung toward where a doorway had been and cursed when he found sheer wall. He sprinted around it, and burst into the library where he saw his brother slashing a sword toward Glenna.

He didn't think; didn't hesitate. He punched his power toward Cian, and sent his sword spinning away to clatter on the floor. With her forward motion unblocked, Glenna sliced Cian's shoulder.

"Well, shit." Cian flicked a hand at the sword even as Glenna pulled it back in horror.

"Oh God! Oh my God. Is it bad? How bad?" She dropped her sword to rush forward.

"Back!" With another sweep of power, Hoyt had Glenna tumbling back and landing on her ass. "You want blood?" Hoyt plucked up Glenna's discarded sword. "Come then, get mine."

King grabbed a sword from the wall, slapped the blade against Hoyt's. "Back off, magic boy. Now."

"Don't interfere," Cian said to King. "Step away." Slowly, Cian picked up his own sword, met Hoyt's eyes. "You tempt me."

"Stop it! Stop it this minute. What the hell's wrong with you?" Regardless of the blades, Glenna pushed between the brothers. "I've stabbed him, for God's sake. Let me see."

"He attacked you."

"He did not. He was giving me a lesson."

"It's nothing." With his gaze still burning into Hoyt's, Cian nudged Glenna aside. "Shirt's ruined, and it's the second I've trashed on your account. If I'd wanted her blood, I wouldn't take it with a sword, waste it. But for yours, I could make an exception."

Glenna's breath wanted to heave, the words wanted to babble. But if she knew anything about men, she knew it would take only a flick of a finger to have these two spilling each other's blood.

Instead she spoke sharply—annoyed female to foolish boys. "It was a mistake, an accident on all sides. I appreciate you coming to the rescue," she said to Hoyt. "But I didn't, and don't need the white horse. And you—" She jabbed a finger at Cian. "You know very well what it must have looked like to him, so take it down a little. And you," She rounded on King. "You can just stop standing over there adding to it."

"Hey! All I did was—"

"Add more trouble," she interrupted. "Now go, get some bandages."

"I don't need them." Cian walked back to replace his sword. "I heal quickly, which is something you need to bear in mind." He held out a hand for King's sword. The glance Cian gave him might have been affectionate, Glenna thought. Or proud. "Unlike our irritated witch, I appreciate the gesture."

"No big." King handed Cian the sword, then sent Glenna a kind of sheepish shrug.

Unarmed now, Cian turned back to his brother. "You couldn't beat me with a sword when I was human. You damn well couldn't take me now."

Glenna put a hand on Hoyt's arm, felt the muscles quiver. "Put it down," she said quietly. "This needs to stop." She ran her hand down his arm to his wrist, then took the sword.

"The blade needs cleaning," Cian commented.

"I'll take care of it." King stepped away from the wall. "I'll toss something together for dinner while I'm at it. Got my appetite worked up."

Even after he walked out, Glenna thought there was so much testosterone in the room she couldn't have hacked through it with one of Cian's battle-axes.

"Can we move on?" she said briskly. "I thought we could use the library for our war room. And considering the weapons in here, and the books on magic, warfare, vampires and demons, it seems appropriate. I've got some ideas—"

"I bet you do," Cian mumbled.

"The first . . ." She moved to the table, picked up her crystal ball.

"Did you learn nothing the first time?" Hoyt demanded.

"I don't want to look for her. We know where she is. Or was." She wanted to change the mood. If there had to be tension, she thought, at least they could use it constructively.

"Others are coming, that's what we keep being told. There will be others. I think it's time we find some of them."

He'd planned to do exactly that, but could hardly say so now without looking foolish. "Put that down. It's too soon to use it after the last time."

"I've cleansed and recharged it."

"Regardless." He turned to the fire. "We'll do this my way."

"A familiar refrain." Cian stepped over to a cabinet, took out a heavy decanter. "Have at it then, the pair of you. I'm having a brandy. Elsewhere."

"Please stay." Glenna offered a smile, and there was both apology and cajolery in it. "If we find someone, you should be here to see. We need to decide what to do. All of us need to decide. In fact, I should go get King, so the four of us can do this."

Hoyt ignored them, but found it wasn't quite as simple to ignore the little prick that might have been jealousy. Teaching her swordplay and her fretting over the slightest scratch.

He spread his hands and began to focus on the fire, using his annoyance to mix the heat.

"A nice thought." Cian nodded toward Hoyt. "But it seems he's already started."

"Well, for— All right then, all right. But we should cast a circle."

"I don't need one for this. Witches are forever casting circles, spinning rhymes. That's why true sorcery eludes them."

When Glenna's mouth dropped open, Cian grinned at her, added a wink. "Always been full of himself. Brandy?"

"No." Glenna set down her ball, folded her arms. "Thank you."

The fire snapped, rose higher and began to eat greedily at the logs.

He used his own tongue, the language of his birth and blood to draw the fire into a dance. Some part of him knew he was showing off, drawing out the moment and the drama.

With a billow of smoke, a hiss of flame, the images began to form in the flames. Shadows and movement, shapes and silhouettes. Now he forgot all but the magic and the purpose, all but the need and the power.

He felt Glenna move closer—in body and in mind. In magic.

In the flames, the shapes and silhouettes became.

A woman on horseback, her hair in a long braid down her back, a quiver of arrows over her shoulder. The horse was gold and sleek, and moved at a powerful, even reckless gallop through the dark forest. There was fear on the woman's face, and a steely determination along with it as she rode low, one hand clutched in the flying mane.

The man that wasn't a man leaped out of the forest and was struck away. More took shape, sliding out of the dark, moving to surround.

The horse quivered, and in a sudden shimmer of light was a man, tall and lean and young. He and the woman stood back-to-back, blades drawn. And the vampires came for them.

"It's the road leading to the Dance." Cian sprang toward the weapons, grabbed a sword and a two-headed ax. "Go in with King," he ordered Glenna as he raced for the window. "Stay here. Let no one in. No one and nothing."

"But—"

He threw up the window and seemed . . . seemed to *fly* out of it.

"Hoyt—"

But he was already grabbing a sword, a dagger. "Do as he says."

He was out the window himself, nearly as quickly as his brother. Glenna didn't hesitate. She followed.

He made for the stables, throwing his power ahead of him to open the doors. When the stallion charged out, Hoyt held up his hands to stop him. It was no time for niceties.

"Go back," he shouted at Glenna.

"I'm going with you. Don't waste time arguing. I'm in this, too." When she grabbed a handful of mane and sprang onto the horse's back, she tossed back her head. "I'll follow on foot."

He cursed her, but held down his hand for her to grip. The horse reared as King charged the stables. "What the hell's going on?"

"Trouble," Glenna shouted back. "On the road to the Dance." When the horse reared again, she wrapped her arms tight around Hoyt. "Go!"

In the clearing, Moira fought, but no longer for her life. There were too many, and they were too strong. She believed she would die here. She fought for time, each precious moment of breath.

There was no room or time for her bow, but she had her short sword. She could hurt them, *did* hurt them. If her blade pierced flesh, they shrieked, and some fell back. But they rose again and came again.

She couldn't count them, no longer knew how many Larkin battled. But she knew if she fell, they would have him. So she fought to stand, fought just to hold on.

Two came at her, and with her breath sobbing out she hacked at one. His blood gushed out in a horrible scream as those red eyes rolled back to white. To her horror one of his fellows fell on him and began to drink. But still another got past her guard and sent her flying. It pounced on her like a mad dog with greedy fangs and red eyes.

She heard Larkin shout her name, heard the terror in it as she struggled. Those fangs grazed her throat, and the burn was beyond belief.

Something came out of the night, some dark warrior with sword and ax. What was on her was hurled away. Her dazed eyes watched him cleave the ax down, behead the thing. It screamed and flashed, and turned to dust.

"Take their head," the warrior shouted to Larkin, then turned burning blue eyes on her. "Use your arrows. Wood through the heart."

Then his sword began to sing and slice.

She gained her feet, yanked an arrow out of her quiver. Tried to steady her blood-slicked hand to notch it on the bow. Rider coming, she thought dimly when she heard the thunder of hoofbeats.

Another came for her, a girl younger than herself. Moira shifted, but there was no time to shoot. The girl leaped, and the arrow impaled her. There was nothing left but dust.

The horseman jumped down, sword already swinging.

They would not die, Moira thought as sweat dripped into her eyes. They would not die tonight. She notched an arrow, let it fly.

The three men had formed a triangle, and were beating the things back. One slithered through, crouched to charge the horse where a woman sat watching the battle. Moira scrambled forward, trying to find a clear shot, but could only call out a warning.

The second warrior spun around, sword raised as he prepared to attack. But the woman reared back the horse, so its hooves flashed out to strike the thing down.

When the sword sliced through its neck, there was nothing left but blood and dust.

In the silence, Moira sank to her knees, fighting for breath and against a terrible sickness. Larkin dropped down beside her, running his hands over her body, her face. "You're hurt. You're bleeding."

"Not bad. Not bad." Her first battle, she thought. And she was alive. "You?"

"Nicks, scratches. Can you get up? I'll carry you."

"I can get up, yes, and no, you won't carry me." Still kneeling, she looked up at the man who'd come out of the dark. "You saved my life. Thank you. I think we've come to find you, but I'm grateful you found us instead. I'm Moira, and we've come through the Dance from Geall."

He simply looked at her for what seemed like the longest moment. "We need to get back, and inside. It isn't safe here."

"Larkin is my name." He held out a hand. "You fight like a demon."

"True enough." Cian clasped hands briefly. "Let's get them back," he said to Hoyt, and glanced toward Glenna. "The two of you helped yourself to my horse. Good thinking as it turned out. She can ride up with Glenna."

"I can walk," Moira began, only to find herself lifted off her feet and onto the horse.

"We need to move," Cian said briskly. "Hoyt, take point, and you stay beside the women. I'm behind you."

Hoyt laid a hand on the stallion's neck as he passed, and glanced up at Glenna. "You've a steady seat."

"I've been riding since I was four. Don't think about trying to leave me behind again." Then she turned on the horse to look over her shoulder at Moira. "I'm Glenna. Nice to meet you."

"It's the pure truth I can't think of anyone in my life it's been nicer to meet." As the horse moved forward, Moira risked a look back. She couldn't see the warrior. He seemed to have melted into the dark.

"What is his name? The one who came on foot?"

"That would be Cian. Hoyt's up ahead. They're brothers, and there's a great deal to explain on all sides. But one thing's for damn sure, we just survived our first battle. And we kicked some vampire ass."

Moira bided her time. Under normal circumstances she would have considered herself a guest, and behaved accordingly. But she knew that was far from the case. She and Larkin were soldiers now, in what was a very small army.

It may have been foolish, but she was relieved not to be the only woman.

Inside the manor house, she sat in a wondrous kitchen. A huge man with skin dark as coal worked at a stove, though she didn't think he was a servant.

He was called King, but she understood this wasn't his rank. He was a man, like the others. A soldier like her.

"We'll patch you up," Glenna told her. "If you want to clean up first, I can show you upstairs."

"Not until we're all here."

Glenna cocked her head. "All right then. I don't know about the rest of you, but I want a drink."

"I'd kill for one," Larkin said with a quick smile. "Actually, it seems I have. I didn't believe you, not really." He laid a hand on Moira's. "I'm sorry."

"It's all right, it's no matter. We're alive, and where we're meant to be. That's what matters." She looked up as the door opened. But it was Hoyt who came in, not the one called Cian. Still she got to her feet.

"We haven't thanked you properly for coming to help us. There were so many. We were losing until you came."

"We've been waiting for you."

"I know. Morrigan showed you to me. And you," she said to Glenna. "Is this Ireland?"

"It is, yes."

"But—"

Moira merely laid a hand on Larkin's shoulder. "My cousin believes Ireland is a fairy tale, even now. We come from Geall, that which was made by the gods from a handful of Ireland, to grow in peace and to be ruled by the descendent of the great Finn."

"You're the scholar."

"Well, she loves her books, that's for certain. Now this is fine," Larkin said after a sip of wine.

"And the one of many shapes," Hoyt added.

"That'd be me, all right."

When the door opened again, Moira felt relief rush through her like a tide.

Cian flicked a glance at her, then at Glenna. "She needs tending to."

"Wouldn't budge until the gang was all here. Why don't you finish your wine, Larkin? Moira, come on upstairs with me."

"I have so many questions."

"We all do. Let's talk over dinner." Glenna took Moira's hand, drew her out.

Cian poured himself a drink, dropped down at the table. There was blood soaked through his shirt. "Do you usually bring your woman into strange places?"

Larkin took another gulp of wine. "She wouldn't be my woman, but my cousin, and fact of it is, she brought me. Had a vision or a dream or something mystical or other—which isn't that unusual for her. Fanciful sort, she is. But she was bound and determined to do this thing, and I couldn't have stopped her. Those things out there, some came to Geall. They killed her mother."

He took another deep drink. "We buried her this morning, if time's the same here. Ripped her to pieces is what they did. Moira saw it."

"How did she survive to tell it?"

"She doesn't know. At least—well, she won't really speak of it. Not as yet."

Upstairs, Moira washed in the shower as Glenna had showed her. The sheer pleasure of it helped ease her aches and hurts, and she considered the heat of the water nothing short of miraculous.

When the blood and sweat had been washed away, she put on the robe Glenna left her, then came out to find her new friend waiting in the bedchamber.

"No wonder we speak of Ireland like a fairy tale. It seems like one."

"You look better. Some color in your cheeks. Let's have a look at that wound on your neck."

"It burns, considerable." Moira touched her fingers to it. "It's hardly more than a scratch."

"It's still a vampire bite." Examining it closely, Glenna pursed her lips. "Not a puncture though, or just barely, so that's good. I've got something that should help."

"How did you know where to find us?"

"We saw you in the fire." Glenna poked into her case for the right balm.

"You're the witch."

"Mmm-hmm. Here we are."

"And the one called Hoyt is the sorcerer."

"Yes. He's not from this world either—or not from this time. It looks like they're getting us from all over hell and back. How does that feel?"

"Cool." Moira let out a sigh as the balm eased the burn. She raised her eyes to Glenna's. "Lovely, thanks. And Cian, what manner of man is he?"

Glenna hesitated. Full disclosure, she decided. Honesty and trust had to be bywords of their little battalion. "He's a vampire."

Going pale again, Moira pushed to her feet. "Why would you say that? He fought them, he saved my life. He's even now down in the kitchen, inside the house. Why would you call him a monster, a demon?"

"I didn't, because I don't consider him either. He's a vampire, and has been one for over nine hundred years. The one who made him is called Lilith, and she's the one we need to worry about. He's Hoyt's brother, Moira, and he's pledged to fight just like the rest of us."

"If what you say . . . He isn't human."

"Your cousin changes into a horse. I'd say that makes him something more than human, too."

"It's not the same."

"Maybe not. I don't have the answers. I do know Cian didn't ask for what happened to him all those years ago. I know he's helped us get here, and he was the first one out of the house to fight for you when we saw you in the fire. I know how you're feeling."

In her mind Moira saw what had been done to her mother, heard the screams, smelled the blood. "You couldn't know."

"Well, I know I didn't trust him initially either. But I do now. Completely. And I know we need him to win this. Here. I brought you some clothes. I'm taller than you, but you can just roll up the pants until we get you something that fits better. We'll go down, have a meal, talk some of this through. And see what goes."

It seemed they would eat in the kitchen, like family or like servants. Moira wondered if she could eat at all, but found her appetite huge. The chicken was fried juicy and crisp with heaps of potatoes and snap beans.

The vampyre ate little.

"We're gathered," Hoyt began, "and must gather more at some point yet to be known. But it was to start with us, and so it has. Tomorrow we'll begin to train, to learn. Cian, you know best how to fight them. You'll be in charge. Glenna and I will work on the magicks."

"I need to train, too."

"Then you'll be busy. We'll need to find our strengths, and our weaknesses. We need to be ready when the final battle takes place."

"In the world of Geall," Moira said, "in the Valley of Silence, in the Mountains of Mist. On the sabbot of Samhain." Avoiding Cian's eyes she looked at Hoyt. "Morrigan showed me."

"Aye." He nodded. "I saw you there."

"When the time comes, we'll go through the Dance again, and march to the battleground. It's five days' walk, so we'll need to leave in good time."

"Are there those in Geall who'll fight with us?"

"Any and all will fight. Any and all would die to save our home, and the worlds." The burden of it weighed down on her. "I have only to ask."

"You have a lot of faith in your fellow man," Cian commented.

She looked at him now, forced herself to meet his eyes. Blue, she thought, and beautiful. Would they go demon-red when he fed?

"So I do. And in my countrymen, and in humankind. And if I did not, I would order it so. For when I return to Geall, I must go to the Royal Stone, and if I'm worthy, if I'm the one as there is no other, I will pull the sword from that sheath. And I will be queen of Geall. I won't see my people slaughtered by what made you what you are. Not like lambs. If they die, they'll die in battle."

"You should know that the little skirmish you came through tonight was nothing. It was nothing. What were there? Eight, ten of them? There'll be thousands." He got to his feet. "She's had nearly two thousand years to make her army. Your farmers will have to do more than beat their plowshares into swords to survive."

"Then they will."

He inclined his head. "Be ready to train hard, and not tomorrow. Starting tonight. You forget, brother, I sleep days."

He left them with that.

Chapter 9

Glenna signalled to Hoyt, and left the others to
King. She glanced back toward the kitchen, down toward the hall. She had no idea where Cian had gone.

"We need to talk. In private."

"We need to work."

"I won't argue with that, but you and I need to go over
some things. Alone."

He frowned at her, but nodded. If she wanted privacy,
there was one place he could be sure of it. He led the way up
the stairs, wound his way up to his tower.

Glenna wandered the room, studied his work areas, his
books and tools. She went to each narrow window, opened
the glass that had been put there since his day, closed it again.

"Nice. Very nice. Are you going to share the wealth?"

"What is your meaning?"

"I need a place to work—more, I'd say you and I need a
place to work together. Don't give me that look." She waved
a hand at him as she walked over to shut the door.

"What look would that be?"

"The 'I'm a solitary sorcerer and don't care for witches'

look. We're stuck with each other, and with the rest. Some-how, God knows, we have to become a unit. Because Cian's right."

She walked back to one of the windows, looked out into the moonstruck dark. "He's right. She'll have thousands. I never looked that far, never thought that big—though, Jesus, what's bigger than an apocalypse? But of course, she'll have thousands. We have a handful."

"It's as it was told to us," he reminded her. "We're the first, the circle."

She turned back, and though her eyes stayed level, he saw the fear in them. And the doubt. "We're strangers, and far from ready to join hands in a circle and chant some unity spell. We're uneasy and suspicious of each other. Even re-sentful when it comes to you and your brother."

"I don't resent my brother."

"Of course you do." She pushed at her hair, and now he saw frustration as well. "You drew a sword on him a couple of hours ago."

"I thought he—"

"Yes, yes, and more gratitude for rushing to my rescue."

Her dismissive tone insulted his chivalry, and put his back up. "You're bloody welcome."

"If you actually save my life at some point, my gratitude will be sincere, I promise you. But defending the damsel was only part of it, and answering that was only part of why he very nearly fought you. You know it, I know it, and so does he."

"That being the case, there's no need for you to babble on about it."

She stepped forward. He saw with some satisfaction his wasn't the only back up now. "You're angry with him for let-ting himself be killed, and worse, changed. He's angry with you for dragging him into this, and forcing him to remember what he was before Lilith got her fangs into him. All of that's a waste of time and energy. So, we either have to get past those emotions, or we have to use them. Because as it stands, as we stand, she's going to slaughter us, Hoyt. I don't want to die."

"If you're afraid—"

"Of course I'm afraid. Are you stupid? After what we've seen and dealt with tonight, we'd be morons not to be afraid." She pressed her hands to her face, struggled to even her breathing again. "I know what has to be done, but I don't know how to do it. And neither do you. None of us do."

She dropped her hands, went to him. "Let's you and I be honest here. We have to depend on each other, have to trust each other, so let's be honest. We're a handful—with power, yes, with skills—but a handful against untold numbers. How do we survive this, much less win?"

"We gather more."

"How?" She lifted her hands. "How? In this time, in this place, Hoyt, people don't believe. Anyone who goes around talking openly about vampires, sorcerers, apocalyptic battles and missions from gods is either considered eccentric—best case—or put in a padded cell."

Needing the contact, she brushed a hand down his arm. "We have to face it. There's no cavalry coming to the rescue here. We *are* the cavalry."

"You give me problems, but no solutions."

"Maybe." She sighed. "Maybe. But you can't find solutions until you outline the problems. We're ridiculously outnumbered. We're going up against creatures—for lack of a better word—that can only be killed in a limited number of ways. They are controlled or led or driven by a vampire of enormous power and, well, thirst. I don't know much about warfare, but I know when the odds aren't in my favor. So we have to even the odds."

She spoke the kind of cold-blooded sense he couldn't deny. The fact that she would say it was, in his mind, another kind of courage. "How?"

"Well, we can't go out and cut off thousands of heads, it's just not practical. So we find the way to cut off the head of the army. Hers."

"If it were so simple, it would already be done."

"If it were impossible, we wouldn't be here." Frustrated, she rapped a fist on his arm. "Work with me, will you?"

"I haven't a choice in that."

Now there was hurt, just the shadow of it in her eyes. "Is it really so distasteful to you? Am I?"

"No." And more than a shadow of shame in his. "I'm sorry. No, not distasteful. Difficult. Distracting. You're distracting, the way you look, the way you smell, the way you are."

"Oh." Her lips curved up slowly. "That's interesting."

"I don't have time for you, in that way."

"What way? Be specific." It wasn't fair, she knew, to tease and to tempt. But it was a relief to simply be human.

"Lives are at stake."

"What's the point of living without feeling? I feel for you. You stir something in me. Yes, it's difficult, and it's distracting. But it tells me I'm here, and that being afraid isn't all there is. I need that, Hoyt. I need to feel more than afraid."

He lifted a hand to brush his fingers over her cheek. "I can't promise to protect you, but only to try."

"I'm not asking you to protect me. I'm not asking you for anything—yet—more than truth."

He kept his hand on her face, bringing his other up to join it in framing her as he lowered his lips. Hers parted for him, offering. So he took, needing as she did, to feel and to know.

To be human.

It was a slow simmering in the blood, a lazy tightening of muscle, a flutter of pulse—hers and his.

So easy, he thought, so easy to sink into the warm and the soft. To be surrounded by her in the dark and let himself forget, for a moment, for an hour, all that lay before them.

Her arms slid around him, linking his waist as she shifted up on her toes to meet his mouth more truly. He tasted her lips and her tongue, and the promise of them. This could be his. And he wanted to believe it more than he'd ever believed anything.

Her lips moved on his, forming his name—once, then twice. A sudden spark flared, simmer to sizzle. The heat of it rippled over his skin, burned into his heart.

Behind them, the fire that had gone to embers flared up like a dozen torches.

He drew her back, but his hands still lingered on her cheeks. He could see the fire dance in her eyes.

"There's truth in that," he whispered. "But I don't know what it is."

"Neither do I. But I feel better for it. Stronger." She looked toward the fire. "We're stronger together. That means something."

She stepped back. "I'm going to bring my things up here, and we'll work together and find out what it means."

"You think lying together is the answer?"

"It may be, or may be one of them. But I'm not ready to lie with you yet. My body is," she admitted. "But my mind isn't. When I give myself to someone, it's a commitment for me. A big one. Both of us have committed quite a bit already. We'll both have to be sure we're ready to give more."

"Then what was this?"

"Contact," she said quietly. "Comfort." She reached a hand for his. "Connection. We're going to make magic together, Hoyt, serious magic. That's as intimate to me as sex. I'm going to get what I need, bring it up."

Women, he thought, were powerful and mystical creatures even without witchcraft. Add that dose of power and a man was at a serious sort of disadvantage.

Wasn't her scent still wrapped around him, and the taste of her still on his lips? Women's weapons, he decided. Just as slipping away was a kind of weapon.

He'd do well to arm himself against that sort of thing.

She intended to work here in his tower, alongside him. There was good, strong sense in that. But how was a man supposed to work when his thoughts kept drifting to a woman's mouth, or her skin, her hair, her voice?

Perhaps he'd be wise to make use of a barrier, at least temporarily. He moved to his worktable and prepared to do just that.

"Your potions and spells will have to wait," Cian said from the doorway. "And so will romance."

"I don't follow your meaning." Hoyt continued to work.

"I passed Glenna on the stairs. I know when a woman's had a man's hands on her. I could smell you on her. Not that I blame you," Cian added lazily as he strolled into and around the room. "That's a very sexy witch you have there.

Desirable," he added at his brother's stony look. "Alluring. Bed her if you like, but later."

"Who I bed, and when, is nothing to you."

"Who, certainly not, but when's another matter. We'll use the great hall for combat training. King and I have already begun to set up. I don't intend to end up with a stake through my heart because you and the redhead are too busy to train."

"It won't be a problem."

"I don't intend to let it be. The newcomers are unknown entities. The man fights well enough with a sword, but he's protective of his cousin. If she can't stand up in battle, we need to find another use for her."

"It's your job to see that she can, and will, stand up in battle."

"I'll work her," Cian promised. "And the rest of you. But we'll need more than swords and stakes, more than muscle."

"We'll have it. Leave that to me. Cian," he said before his brother could leave the room. "Did you ever see them again? Do you know how they fared, what became of them?"

He didn't have to be told his brother spoke of their family. "They lived and they died, as humans will."

"Is that all they are to you?"

"Shadows are what they are."

"You loved them once."

"My heart beat once as well."

"Is that the measure of love? A heartbeat?"

"We can love, even we can love. But to love a human?" Cian shook his head. "Only misery and tragedy could follow. Your parents sired what I was. Lilith made what I am."

"And do you have love for her?"

"For Lilith." His smile was slow, thoughtful. And humorless. "In my fashion. But don't worry. It won't stop me from destroying her. Come down, and we'll see what you're made of."

"Two hours' hand-to-hand, every day," Cian announced when they were gathered. "Two hours' weapons training, every day. Two hours' endurance, and two on martial arts. I'll work you here at night. King will take over in the daylight when you can train outdoors."

"We need time for study and strategy as well," Moira pointed out.

"Then make it. They're stronger than you, and more vicious than you can imagine."

"I know what they are."

Cian merely looked at her. "You think you do."

"Had you ever killed one before tonight?" she demanded.

"I have, more than one."

"In my world those that would kill their own kind are villains and outcasts."

"If I hadn't, you'd be dead."

He moved so quickly no one had a chance to react. He was behind Moira's back, an arm around her waist. And a knife at her throat. "Of course, I wouldn't need the knife."

"You're not to touch her." Larkin laid a hand on the hilt of his own knife. "You're not to put your hands on her."

"Stop me," Cian invited, and tossed his knife aside. "I've just snapped her neck." He laid his hands on either side of Moira's head, then gave her a little nudge that sent her careening into Hoyt. "Avenge her. Attack me."

"I won't attack the man who fought at my back."

"I'm not at your back now, am I? Show some spine, or don't the men of Geall have any?"

"We've plenty." Larkin drew his knife, crouched. Began to circle.

"Don't play at it," Cian taunted. "I'm unarmed. You have the advantage. Use it—quickly."

Larkin lunged—feinted, then slashed. And found himself flat on his back, with his knife skittering over the floor.

"You never have the advantage over a vampire. First lesson."

Larkin shook back his hair and grinned. "You're better than they were."

"Considerably." Amused, Cian held down a hand, helped Larkin to his feet.

"We'll start with some basic maneuvers, see what you're made of. Choose an opponent. You have one minute to take that opponent down—bare-handed. When I call switch, choose another. Move fast, and hard. Now."

He watched his brother hesitate and the witch turn into him, using her body to shift him off balance, then hooking her foot behind his to send him down.

"Self-defense training," Glenna announced. "I live in New York."

While she was grinning, Hoyt swept her feet out from under her. Her ass hit the floorboards, hard. "Ouch. First request, we get pads for the floor."

"Switch!"

They moved, they maneuvered, grappled. And it was more game and competition than training. Even so, Glenna thought, she was going to have her share of bruises. She faced off with Larkin, sensed he would hold back. So she sent him a flirtatious smile, and when the laugh lit his eyes, flipped him over her shoulder.

"Sorry. I like to win."

"Switch."

The bulk of King filled her vision, and she looked up, up, until she met his eyes. "Me, too," he told her.

She went with instinct, a movement of her hands, a rapid chant. When he smiled blankly, she touched his arm. "Why don't you sit down?"

"Sure."

When he obeyed, she glanced over, saw Cian watching her. And flushed a little. "That was probably against the rules—and it's unlikely I'd be able to pull it off in the heat of battle, but I think it should count."

"There are no rules. She's not the strongest," he called out. "She's not the fastest. But she's the most clever of the lot of you. She uses wile and she uses wit as much as muscle and speed. Get stronger," he said to Glenna. "Get faster."

For the first time he smiled. "And get a sword. We'll start on weapons."

By the end of the next hour, Glenna was dripping sweat. Her sword arm ached like a bad tooth from shoulder to wrist. The thrill of the work, of actually doing something tangible had long since faded into a bitter exhaustion.

"I thought I was in good shape," she complained to Moira. "All those hours of pilates, of yoga, of weights—and I might as well be speaking to you in tongues."

"You're doing well." And Moira herself felt weak and clumsy.

"I'm barely standing. I do regular exercise, hard physical training, and this is turning me into a wimp. And you look beat."

"It's been a very long, very hard day."

"That's putting it mildly."

"Ladies? If I could trouble you to join us. Or would you rather have a seat and discuss fashion?"

Glenna set down her water bottle. "It's nearly three in the morning," she said to Cian. "A dangerous time for sarcasm."

"And prime time for your enemy."

"That may be, but not all of us are on that same clock just yet. And Moira and Larkin have traveled a hell of a long way today and dealt with a very nasty welcome. We need to train, you're absolutely right. But if we don't rest we're not going to get strong, and we're sure as hell not going to get fast. Look at her," Glenna demanded. "She can barely stay upright."

"I'm fine," Moira said quickly.

Cian gave her a long look. "Then we can blame fatigue for your sloppy swordsmanship and poor form."

"I do well enough with a sword." When she reached for it, blood in her eye, Larkin stepped up. He slapped a hand on her shoulder, and squeezed.

"Well enough she does, so she proved earlier tonight. But the blade wouldn't be my cousin's weapon of choice."

"Oh?" A wealth of boredom was contained in the single syllable.

"She's a decent hand with a bow."

"She can give us a demonstration tomorrow, but for now—"

"I can do it tonight. Open the doors."

The tone of command had Cian's brow winging up. "You don't rule here, little queen."

"Nor do you." She strode over, picked up bow and quiver. "Will you open the doors, or will I?"

"You're not to go out."

"He's right, Moira," Glenna began.

"I won't have to. Larkin, if you would."

Larkin moved to the doors and threw them open to the wide terrace beyond. Moira notched an arrow as she moved to the threshold. "The oak, I think."

Cian moved to her side as the others crowded in. "Not much of a distance."

"She wouldn't be meaning the near one," Larkin said and gestured. "But that one there, just to the right of the stables."

"Lowest branch."

"I can barely see it," Glenna commented.

"Can you?" Moira demanded of Cian.

"Perfectly."

She lifted the bow, steadied, sighted. And let the arrow fly.

Glenna heard the whiz, then a faint thunk as the arrow hit home. "Wow. Got ourselves a Robin Hood."

"Nicely shot," Cian said in mild tones, then turned to walk away. He sensed the movement even before he heard his brother's sharp command.

When he turned, Moira had another arrow ready, and aimed at him.

He sensed King prepare to rush forward, and held up a hand to stop him. "Be sure to hit the heart," he advised Moira. "Otherwise you'll just annoy me. Let it be," he snapped to Hoyt. "It's her choice."

The bow trembled a moment, then Moira lowered it. Lowered her eyes as well. "I need sleep. I'm sorry, I need sleep."

"Of course you do." Glenna took the bow from her, set it aside. "I'll take you down, get you settled." Glenna aimed a look at Cian every bit as sharp as the arrow as she led Moira from the room.

"I'm sorry," Moira said again. "I'm ashamed."

"Don't be. You're overtired, overworked. Over everything. We all are. And it's barely begun. A few hours' sleep is what we all need."

"Do they? Do they sleep?"

Glenna understood what she meant. The vampires. Cian. "Yes, it seems they do."

"I wish it was morning so I could see the sun. They crawl back into their holes with the sun. I'm too tired to think."

"Then don't. Here, let's get you undressed."

"I lost my pack in the woods, I think. I don't have a nightdress."

"We'll figure that out tomorrow. You can sleep naked. Do you want me to sit with you awhile?"

"No. Thank you, no." Tears welled up and were willed back. "I'm being a child."

"No. Just an exhausted woman. You'll be better in the morning. Good night."

Glenna debated going back up, then simply turned toward her own room. She didn't give a damn if the men thought she was copping out, she wanted sleep.

The dreams chased her, through the tunnels of the vampire's cave where the screams of the tortured were like slashing knives in her mind, into her heart. Everywhere she turned in the labyrinth, each time she raced into the dark opening, like a mouth waiting to devour her, the screams followed.

And worse than the screams, even worse, was the laughter.

The dreams hunted her along the rocky shore of a boiling sea where red lightning hacked black sky, black sea. There the wind tore at her, there the rocks pierced up out of the ground to stab at her hands, her feet until both were bloody.

Into the dense woods that smelled of blood and death, where the shadows were so thick she could feel them brushing over her skin like cold fingers.

She could hear what craved her coming with the papery snap of wings, the slithery slide of snakes, the sly scrape of claw on earth.

She heard the wolf howl, and the sound was hunger.

They were everywhere she was, and she had nothing but her empty hands and pounding heart. Still she ran blindly, the scream trapped in her burning throat.

She burst out of the trees and onto a cliff above a raging sea. Below her, waves lashed at rocks that rose up, sharp as razors. Somehow in her terror she'd run in a circle, and was back above the cave that held something even death feared.

The wind whipped at her, and power sang in it. His power, the hot, clean power of the sorcerer. She reached for it, strained toward it. But it slipped through her shaking fingers and left her nothing but herself.

When she turned, Lilith stood, regal in red, her beauty luminous against the velvet black. At each side was a black wolf, quivering for the kill. Lilith stroked her hands over their backs, hands that glittered with rings.

And when she smiled, Glenna felt a terrible pull inside her own belly. A deep and terrible yearning.

"The devil or the deep blue." With a laugh, Lilith snapped her fingers for the wolves to sit. "The gods never give their servants decent choices, do they? I have better."

"You're death."

"No, no, no. I'm life. That's where they lie. They're death, flesh and bone moldering in the dirt. What do they give you these days? Seventy-five, eighty years? How small, how limiting."

"I'll take what I'm given."

"Then you'd be a fool. I think you're smarter than that, more practical. You know you can't win. You're already tired, already weary, already questioning. I'll offer you a way out, and more. So much more."

"To be like you? To hunt and kill? To drink blood?"

"Like champagne. Oh, the first taste of it. I envy you that. That first heady taste, that moment when everything falls away but the dark."

"I like the sun."

"With that complexion?" Lilith said with a gay laugh. "You'd fry like bacon after an hour on the beach. I'll show you the coolness. The cool, cool dark. It's inside you already, just waiting to be wakened. Can you feel it?"

Because she could, Glenna only shook her head.

"Liar. If you come to me, Glenna, you'll stand by my side. I'll give you life, eternal life. Eternal youth and beauty. Power so beyond what they've given you. You'll rule your own world. I would give you that, a world of your own."

"Why would you?"

"Why not? I'll have so many. And I'd enjoy the company of a woman such as yourself. What are men, really, but tools to us? If you want them, you'll take them. This is a great gift I offer you."

"It's damnation you offer me."

Her laugh was lilting and seductive. "Gods frighten children with talk of hell and damnation. They use it to keep you bound. Ask Cian if he would trade his existence, his eternity, his handsome youth and lithe body for the chains and traps of mortality. Never, I promise you. Come. Come with me, and I'll give you pleasure beyond pleasure."

When she stepped closer, Glenna held up both hands, drew what she could out of her chilled blood and struggled to cast a protective circle.

Lilith simply struck out a hand. The tender blue of her irises began to redden. "Do you think such puny magic will hold me? I've drunk the blood of sorcerers, feasted on witches. They're in me, as you will be. Come willing, and take life. Fight, and take death."

She moved closer, and the wolves rose to stalk.

Glenna felt the pull, mesmerizing, glorious and dark, a drawing up in the belly that was elemental. It seemed the beat of her blood answered that call. Eternity and power, beauty, youth. All for one moment.

She had only to reach for it.

Triumph lit Lilith's eyes, burned them to red. Fangs flashed as she smiled.

Tears slid down Glenna's cheeks as she turned, as she leaped toward the sea and the rocks. As she chose death.

There was a scream ripping through her head when she shot up in bed. But it wasn't her own, she knew it wasn't her own. It was Lilith's, a scream of fury.

With her breath sobbing, Glenna scrambled out of bed, dragging the blanket with her. She ran, trembling from terror and cold, her teeth chattering with them. She fled down the hallway as if the demons were still after her. Instinct took her to the one place, the only place, she felt safe.

Hoyt sprang out of a sound sleep to find his arms full of

naked, weeping woman. He could barely see her in the dim, predawn light, but he knew her scent, her shape.

"What? What's happened?" He started to shove her aside, to reach for the sword beside his bed. But she clung to him like ivy on an oak.

"Don't. Don't go. Hold on. Please, please, hold on."

"You're like ice." He dragged up the blanket, trying to find warmth for her, trying to find his wits. "Have you been outside? Bloody hell. Have you done some spell?"

"No, no, no." She burrowed into him. "She came. She came. Into my head, into my dream. Not a dream. It was real. It had to be real."

"Stop. Stop this." He took a firm grip on her shoulders. "Glenna!"

Her head jerked back, her breath came shuddering out. "Please. I'm so cold."

"Then hush now, hush." His tone and his touch gentled while he brushed tears from her cheeks. He wrapped her more fully in the blanket, then pulled her close. "It was a dream, a nightmare. Nothing more."

"It wasn't. Look at me." She tilted her head up so he could see her eyes. "It wasn't just a dream."

No, he realized. He could see it hadn't been only a dream. "Then tell me."

"She was inside my head. Or . . . she pulled some part of me outside myself. The way it was when you were in the woods, hurt, with wolves outside your circle. Just as real as that. You know that was real."

"Aye, it was real."

"I was running," she began, and told him all of it.

"She tried to lure you. Now think. Why would she do so unless she knew you were strong, unless she knew you could hurt her?"

"I died."

"You didn't, no, you didn't. You're here. Cold." He rubbed her arms, her back. Would he ever be able to warm her again? "But alive, and here. Safe."

"She was beautiful. Alluring. I don't go for women, if you understand, but I was drawn to her. And part of it was sexual. Even in fear, I wanted her. The idea of her touching me, taking me, was compelling."

"It's a kind of trance, nothing more. And you didn't allow it. You didn't listen, you didn't believe."

"But I did listen, Hoyt. And some part of me did believe. Some part of me wanted what she offered. So much wanted. To live forever, with all that power. I thought, inside me, I thought, yes, oh yes, why shouldn't I have it? And turning away from it—I nearly didn't—because turning away from it was the hardest thing I've ever done."

"Yet you did."

"This time."

"Every time."

"They were your cliffs. I felt you there. I felt you there, but I couldn't reach you. I was alone, more alone than I've ever been. Then I was falling, and I was even more alone."

"You're not alone. Here." He pressed his lips to her forehead. "You're not alone, are you?"

"I'm not a coward, but I'm afraid. And the dark . . ." She shuddered, looked around the room. "I'm afraid of the dark."

He cast his mind toward the bedside candle, toward the logs in the hearth, set them all burning. "Dawn's coming. Here, see." He gathered her into his arms, got out of bed with her to carry her to the window. "There now, look east. The sun's rising."

She saw the light of it, a gilding low in the sky. The cold ball inside her began to ease. "Morning," she murmured. "It's nearly morning."

"You won the night, and she lost it. Come, you need more sleep."

"I don't want to be alone."

"You won't be."

He took her back to bed, drew her against him. Because she still trembled, because he could, he passed his hand over her head. And sent her gently into slumber.

Chapter 10

She woke with sunlight sliding over her face, and she woke alone.

He'd snuffed the candles out, but left the fire burning low. Kind of him, she thought as she sat up, drawing the blanket over her shoulders. He'd been very kind and very gentle, and had given her exactly the comfort and security she'd needed.

Still, the wave of embarrassment came first. She'd run to him like a hysterical child fleeing from the monster in the closet. Sobbing, shaking and incoherent. She hadn't been able to handle it, and had looked for someone—for him—to save her. She prided herself on her courage and her wits, and she hadn't been able to stand up to her first showdown with Lilith.

No spine, she thought in disgust, and no real magic. Fear and temptation had smothered them. No, worse, she thought, fear and temptation had frozen them inside her, deep, where she hadn't been able to reach. Now, in the light of day, she could see how foolish she'd been, how stupid, how *easy*. She'd done nothing to protect herself before, during or after. She'd run through the caves, through the woods, on the cliffs because they'd wanted her to run, and she'd let terror block out everything but the desperate need to escape.

It wasn't a mistake she'd make again.

She wasn't going to sit here wallowing either, not over something that was done.

She got up, wrapped herself in the blanket, then peeked out into the corridor. She saw no one, heard nothing, and was grateful. She didn't want to talk to anyone until she'd put herself back together.

She showered, dressed, then took a great deal of care with her makeup. She hung amber drops at her ears for strength. And when she made the bed, she put amethyst and rosemary under her pillow. After choosing a candle from her supplies, she set it beside the bed. When she prepared for sleep that night, she would consecrate the candle with oil to repel Lilith and those like her from her dreams.

She would also make a stake, and get a sword from the weapons supply. She wouldn't be defenseless and open again.

Before she left the room she took a long look at herself in the mirror. She looked alert, she decided, and capable.

She would be strong.

Because she considered it the heart of any home, she went to the kitchen first. Someone had made coffee, and by process of elimination, she figured it had been King. There was evidence someone had eaten. She could smell bacon. But there was no one around, and no dishes in the sink.

It was some small comfort to know whoever had eaten— or at least whoever had cooked—had also tidied up. She didn't like to live in disorder, but neither would she care to be in charge of all things domestic.

She poured herself a cup from the pot, toyed with making some breakfast. But there was enough of the dream left in her that the sensation of being alone in the house was uncomfortable.

Her next choice was the library, which she thought of as the main artery of the heart. And there, with some relief, she found Moira.

Moira sat on the floor in front of the fire, surrounded by

books. Even now she was hunched over one like a student cramming for an exam. She wore a tunic the color of oatmeal with brown pants and her riding boots.

She looked up as Glenna entered, offered a shy smile. "Good morning to you."

"Good morning. Studying?"

"I am." The shyness faded so those gray eyes shined. "This is the most marvelous room, isn't it? We have a great library in the castle at home, but this rivals it."

Glenna crouched, tapped a finger on a book thick as a beam. Carved into its scrolled leather cover was a single word.

VAMPYRE.

"Boning up?" she asked. "Studying the enemy?"

"It's wise to know all you can about whatever you can. Not all the books I've read so far agree on all things, but there are some elements on which they do."

"You could ask Cian. I imagine he could tell you whatever you wanted to know."

"I like to read."

Glenna only nodded. "Where did you get the clothes?"

"Oh. I went out this morning, early, found my pack."

"Alone?"

"I was safe enough, as I kept to the bright path. They can't come out in the sunlight." She looked toward the windows. "There was nothing left of the ones that attacked us last night. Even the ash was gone."

"Where is everyone else?"

"Hoyt went up to his tower to work, and King said he would go into the town for supplies now that there are more of us. I've never seen a man so big. He cooked food for us, and there was juice from a fruit. Orange. It was wonderful. Do you think I could take some of the seeds of the orange when we go back to Geall?"

"I don't see why not. And the others?"

"Larkin, I imagine, is still sleeping. He tends to avoid the mornings as if they were the plague. The vampyre is in his room, I would think." Moira rubbed her finger over the carved word on the book. "Why does he stand with us? I can find nothing in the books to explain it."

"Then I guess you can't find out everything from books. Is there anything else you need for now?"

"No. Thanks."

"I'm going to grab something to eat, then go up to work. I imagine whenever King gets back, we'll start whatever torture session he has in mind."

"Glenna . . . I wanted to thank you for last night. I was so tired, and upset. I feel so out of my place."

"I know." Glenna put her hand over Moira's. "I think in a way, we all do. Maybe that's part of the plan, taking us out of our place, putting us together so we find ourselves, what there is in us—individually and together—to fight this thing."

She rose. "Until it's time to move, we're going to have to make this our place."

She left Moira to the books and returned to the kitchen. There she found what was left of a loaf of brown bread and slathered butter on a slice. Damned if she'd worry about calories at this point. She nibbled on it as she climbed the stairs to the tower.

The door was closed. She nearly knocked before she reminded herself it was her work area, too, and no longer Hoyt's solitary domain. So she balanced the slice of bread on the mug of coffee, unlatched the door.

He wore a shirt the color of faded denim with black jeans and scarred boots, and still managed to look like a sorcerer. It wasn't just the rich and flowing black hair, she thought, or those intense blue eyes. It was the power that fit him more truly than the borrowed clothes.

Irritation crossed his face first when he glanced at her. She wondered if it was habitual, that quick annoyance at being interrupted or disturbed. Then it cleared, and she found herself being carefully studied.

"So, you're up then."

"Apparently."

He went back to work, pouring some port-colored liquid from a kind of beaker into a vial. "King went for provisions."

"So I'm told. I found Moira in the library, reading, from the looks of it, every book in there."

So, it was going to be awkward, she realized as he continued to work in silence. Better to get past that. "I was going to apologize for disturbing you last night, but that's just an indulgence on my part." She waited, one beat, then two before he stopped to look over at her. "So you could tell me not to worry about it, that of course it was all right. I was frightened and upset."

"That would be true enough."

"It would, and since we both know all that, indulgent. So I won't apologize. But I will thank you."

"It's of no matter."

"It is, for me, on several levels. You were there when I needed you, and you calmed me down. Made me feel safe. You showed me the sun." She set the mug down so her hands would be free as she crossed to him.

"I jumped into your bed in the middle of the night. Naked. I was vulnerable, hysterical. I was defenseless."

"I don't think the last is true."

"At that moment it was. It won't be again. You could have had me. We both know that."

There was a long beat of silence that acknowledged the simple truth more truly than any words. "And what manner of man would I be to have taken you at such a time? To have used your fear for my own needs?"

"A different one from what you are. I'm grateful to the one you are." She skirted the worktable, rose to her toes to kiss both of his cheeks. "Very. You gave me comfort, Hoyt, and you gave me sleep. And you left the fire burning. I won't forget it."

"You're better now."

"Yes. I'm better now. I was caught off guard, and I won't be the next time. I wasn't prepared for her, and I will be the next time. I didn't take precautions, even the simplest ones because I was tired." She wandered to the fire he kept burning low. "Sloppy of me."

"Aye. It was."

She cocked her head, smiled at him. "Did you want me?"

He got busy again. "That's not to the point."

"I'll take that as a yes, and promise the next time I jump into your bed, I won't be hysterical."

"The next time you jump into my bed, I won't give you sleep."

She choked out a laugh. "Well, just so we understand each other."

"I don't know that I understand you at all, but that doesn't stop the wanting of you."

"It's mutual, on both counts. But I think I'm beginning to understand you."

"Did you come here to work, or just to distract me?"

"Both, I guess. Since I've accomplished the latter, I'll ask what you're working on there."

"A shield."

Intrigued she moved closer. "More science than sorcery."

"They're not exclusive, but joined."

"Agreed." She sniffed at the beaker. "Some sage," she decided, "and clove. What have you used for binding?"

"Agate dust."

"Good choice. What sort of shield are you after?"

"Against the sun. For Cian."

She flicked her gaze to his, but he didn't meet it. "I see."

"We risk attack if we go out at night. He dies if he exposes himself to sunlight. But if he had a shield, we could work and train more efficiently. If he had a shield, we could hunt them by day."

She said nothing for a moment. Yes, she was beginning to understand him. This was a very good man, one who held himself to high standards. So he could be impatient, irritable, even autocratic.

And he loved his brother very much.

"Do you think he misses the sun?"

Hoyt sighed. "Wouldn't you?"

She touched a hand to his arm. A good man, she thought again. A very good man who would think of his brother. "What can I do to help?"

"Maybe I begin to understand you as well."

"Is that so?"

"You have an open heart." Now he looked at her. "An open

heart and a willing mind. They're difficult to resist."

She took the vial from him, set it down. "Kiss me, would you? We both want that, and it makes it hard to work. Kiss me, Hoyt, so we settle down."

There might have been amusement, just a sprinkle of it in his voice. "Kissing will settle us down?"

"Won't know unless we try." She laid her hands on his shoulders, let her fingers play with his hair. "But I know, right this minute, I can't think of anything else. So do me a favor. Kiss me."

"A favor then."

Her lips were soft, a yielding warmth under his. So he was gentle, holding her, tasting her the way he'd yearned to the night before. He stroked a hand down her hair, down the length of her back so the feel of her mingled in his senses with her flavor and her scent.

What was inside him opened, and eased.

She skimmed her fingers over the strong edge of his cheekbone and gave herself completely to the moment. To the comfort and the pleasure, and the shimmer of heat flowing under both.

When their lips parted, she pressed her cheek to his, held there a moment. "I feel better," she told him. "How about you?"

"I feel." He stepped back, then brought her hand to his lips. "And I suspect that I'll be needing to be settled again. For the good of the work."

She laughed, delighted. "Anything I can do for the cause."

They worked together for more than an hour, but each time they exposed the potion to sunlight, it boiled.

"A different incantation," Glenna suggested.

"No. We need his blood." He looked at her over the beaker. "For the potion itself, and to test it."

Glenna considered. "You ask him."

There was a thud at the door, then King pushed it open. He wore camo pants and an olive green T-shirt. He'd tied his dreadlocks back into a thick, fuzzy tail. And looked, Glenna thought, like an army all by himself.

"Magic hour's over. Fall in outside. Time to get physical."

If King hadn't been a drill sergeant in another life, karma was missing a step. Sweat dripped into Glenna's eyes as she attacked the dummy Larkin had fashioned out of straw and wrapped in cloth. She blocked with her forearm as she'd been taught, then plunged the stake into the straw.

But the dummy kept coming, flying on the pulley system King had rigged, and knocked her flat on her back.

"And you're dead," he announced.

"Oh, bullshit. I staked it."

"Missed the heart, Red." He stood over her, huge and pitiless. "How many chances you figure you're going to get? You can't get the one in front of you, how are you going to get the three coming at your back?"

"All right, okay." She got up, brushed herself off. "Do it again."

"That's the spirit."

She did it again, and again, until she despised the straw dummy as much as she had her tenth-grade history teacher. Disgusted, she swung around, picked up a sword with both hands, and hacked the thing to pieces.

When she was done, there was no sound but her own labored breathing and Larkin's muffled laugh.

"Okay." King rubbed his chin. "Guess he's pretty damn dead. Larkin, you want to put together another one? Let me ask you something, Red."

"Ask away."

"How come you didn't just tear into the dummy with magic?"

"Magic takes focus and concentration. I think I could use some in a fight—I think I could. But most of me is channelled into handling the sword or the stake, particularly since I'm not used to handling either. If I wasn't centered, I could just send my own weapon flying out of my hand, missing the mark. It's something I'll work on."

She glanced around to make sure Hoyt wasn't anywhere within earshot. "Generally, I need tools, chants, certain rituals.

I can do this." She opened her palm, focused, and brought out the ball of fire.

Curious, he poked at it. And snatched back his singed finger, sucked on it. "Hell of a trick."

"Fire is elemental, like air, earth, water. But if I pulled this out during a battle, tossed it at an enemy, it might hit one of us instead, or as well as."

He studied the shimmering ball with his odd eyes. "Like pointing a gun if you don't know how to shoot. Can't be sure who's going to get the bullet. Or if you'd just end up shooting yourself in your own damn foot."

"Something like that." She vanished the fire. "But it's nice to have it in reserve."

"You go ahead, take a break, Red, before you hurt somebody."

"No argument." She sailed into the house, intending to drink a gallon of water and put together some food. She nearly walked straight into Cian.

"Didn't know you were up and around."

He stood back from the sunlight that filtered through the windows, but she saw he had a full view of the outdoor activities.

"What do you think?" she asked him. "How are we doing?"

"If they came for you now, they'd snack on you like chicken at a picnic."

"I know. We're clumsy, and there's no sense of unity. But we'll get better."

"You'll need to."

"Well, you're full of cheer and encouragement this afternoon. We've been at it over two hours, and none of us is used to this kind of thing. Larkin's the closest King's got to a warrior, and he's green yet."

Cian merely glanced at her. "Ripen or die."

Fatigue was one thing, she thought, and she would deal with the sweat and the effort. But now she was flat-out insulted. "It's hard enough to do what we're doing without one of us being a complete asshole."

"Is that your term for realist?"

"Screw it, and you with it." She stalked around the kitchen, tossed some fruit, some bread, some bottled water into a basket. She hauled it out, ignoring Cian as she passed by.

Outside she dumped the basket on the table King had carried out to hold weapons.

"Food!" Larkin pounced like a starving man. "Bless you down to the soles of your feet, Glenna. I was wasting away here."

"Since it's been two hours for certain since you last stuffed your face," Moira put in.

"The master of doom doesn't think we're working hard enough, and equates us to chicken at a picnic for the vampires." Glenna took an apple for herself, bit in. "I say we show him different."

She took another bite, then whipped around toward the newly stuffed dummy. She focused in, visualized, then hurled the apple. It flew toward the dummy, and as it flew it became a stake. And that stake pierced cloth and straw.

"Oh, that was fine," Moira breathed. "That was brilliant."

"Sometimes temper gives the magic a boost."

The stake slid out again, and splatted as an apple to the ground. She sent Hoyt a look. "Something to work out."

"We need something to unify us, to hold us together," she told Hoyt later. She sat in the tower, rubbing balm into bruises while he pored through the pages of a spellbook. "Teams wear uniforms, or have fight songs."

"Songs? Now we should sing? Or maybe just find a bloody harper."

Sarcasm, she decided, was something the brothers shared as well as their looks. "We need something. Look at us, even now. You and I up here, Moira and Larkin off together. King and Cian in the training room, devising new miseries for us all. It's fine and good to have the whole of the team split into smaller teams, working on their own projects. But we haven't become a whole team yet."

"So we drag out the harp and sing? We've serious work to do, Glenna."

"You're not following me." Patience, she reminded herself. He'd worked as hard as she had today, and was just as tired. "It's about symbolism. We have the same foe, yes, but not the same purpose." She walked to the window, and saw how long the shadows had grown, and how low the sun hung in the sky.

"It'll be dark soon." Her fingers groped for her pendant. It struck her then, so simple, so obvious.

"You were looking for a shield for Cian, because he can't go out in the day. But what about us? We can't risk going out after sundown. And even inside, we know she can get to us, get inside us. What about *our* shield, Hoyt? What shields us against the vampire?"

"The light."

"Yes, yes, but what symbol? A cross. We need to make crosses, and we need to put magic into them. Not only shield, but weapon, Hoyt."

He thought of the crosses Morrigan had given him for his family. But even his powers, even combined with Glenna's fell short of the gods.

Still . . .

"Silver," he mumbled. "Silver would be best."

"With red jasper, for night protection. We need some garlic, some sage." She began going through her case of dried herbs and roots. "I'll start on the potion." She grabbed one of her books, began flipping through. "Any idea where we can get our hands on the silver?"

"Aye."

He left her, went down to the first level of the house and into what was now the dining room. The furnishings were new—to him, at least. Tables of dark, heavy wood, chairs with high backs and ornate carving. The drapes that were pulled over the windows were a deep green, like forest shadows, and made of a thick and weighty silk.

There was art, all of them night scenes of forests and glades and cliffs. Even here, he thought, his brother shunned the light. Or did he prefer the dark, even in paintings?

Tall cupboards with doors of rippled glass held crystal and pottery in rich jewel tones. Possessions, he thought, of a man of wealth and position, who had an eternity of time to collect them.

Did any of the things mean anything to Cian? With so much, could any single thing matter?

On the larger server were two tall candlestands of silver, and Hoyt wondered if they did—or if they had, at least.

They had been his mother's.

He lifted one, and had the image of her—clear as lake water—sitting at her wheel and spinning, singing one of the old songs she loved while her foot tapped the time.

She wore a blue gown and veil, and there was ease and youth in her face, a quiet contentment that covered her like soft silk. Her body was heavy with child, he saw that now. No, he corrected, heavy with children. Himself and Cian.

And on the chest beneath her window stood the two candlestands.

"They were a gift from my father on the day of my wedding, and of all the gifts given, I prized them most. One will go to you one day, and one to Cian. And so this gift will be passed down, and the giver remembered whenever the candle is lit."

He comforted himself that he needed no candle to remember her. But the stand weighed heavy in his hands as he took it up to the tower.

Glenna looked up from the cauldron where she mixed her herbs. "Oh, it's perfect. And beautiful. What a shame to melt it down." She left her work to get a closer look. "It's heavy. And old, I think."

"Aye, it's very old."

She understood then, and felt a little pang in her heart. "Your family's?"

His face, his voice, were carefully blank. "It was to come to me, and so it has."

She nearly told him to find something else, something that didn't mean so much to him. But she swallowed the words. She thought she understood why he had chosen as he had. It had to cost. Magic asked a price.

"The sacrifice you're making will strengthen the spell. Wait." She pulled a ring from the middle finger of her right hand. "It was my grandmother's."

"There's no need."

"Personal sacrifice, yours and mine. We're asking a great deal. I need some time to write out the spell. Nothing in my books is quite right, so we'll need to amend."

When Larkin came to the door they were both deep in books. He glanced around the room and kept to his side of the threshold. "I'm sent to fetch you. The sun's set, and we're going into evening training."

"Tell him we'll be there when we're done," Glenna said. "We're in the middle of something."

"I'll tell him, but I'm thinking he won't like it." He pulled the door shut and left them.

"I've nearly got it. I'm going to draw out what I think they should look like, then we'll both visualize. Hoyt?"

"It must be pure," he said to himself. "Conjured with faith as much as magic."

She left him to it and began to sketch. Simple, she thought, and with tradition. She glanced over, saw he was sitting, eyes closed. Gathering power, she assumed, and his thoughts.

Such a serious face, and one, she realized, she'd come to trust completely. It seemed she'd known that face forever, just as she knew the sound of his voice, the cadence of it.

Yet the time they'd had was short, just as the time they would have was no more than a handful of grains in the sand of an hourglass.

If they won—no when, when they won—he'd go back to his time, his life, his world. And she to hers. But nothing would ever be the same. And nothing would ever really fill the void he'd leave behind.

"Hoyt."

His eyes were different when they met hers. Deeper and darker. She pushed the sketch toward him. "Will this do?"

He lifted it, studied. "Yes, but for this."

He took the pencil from her, added lines on the long base of the Celtic cross she'd drawn.

"What is it?"

"It's ogham script. Old writing."

"I know what ogham is. What does it say?"

"It says light."

She smiled, nodded. "Then it's perfect. This is the spell. It feels right to me."

He took that in turn, then looked at her. "Rhymes?"

"It's how I work. Deal with it. And I want a circle. I'll feel better with one."

Because he agreed he rose, to cast it with her. She scribed fresh candles with her bolline, watched him light them.

"We'll make the fire together." He held out his hand for hers.

Power winged up her arm, struck the heart of her. And the fire, pure and white, shimmered an inch above the floor. He hefted the cauldron, set it on the flames.

"Silver old and silver bright." He set the candlestand in the cauldron. "Go to liquid in this light."

"As we stand in the sorcerer's tower," Glenna continued, adding the jasper, the herbs, "we charge this flame to free your power." She dropped in her grandmother's ring.

"Magicks from the sky and sea, from air and earth we call to thee. We your servants beg this blessing, shield us in this time of testing. We answer your charge with head, heart and hand to vanquish the darkness from the land. So we call you three times three to shield those who serve you faithfully.

"Let this cross shine light to night."

As they chanted the last line, three times three, silver smoke rose from the cauldron, and the white flames beneath it grew brighter.

It flooded her, light and smoke and heat, filled her as her voice rose with his. Through it, she saw his eyes, only his eyes locked on hers.

In her heart, in her belly, she felt it heat and grow. Stronger, more potent than anything she'd ever known. It swirled in her as with his free hand, he threw the last of the jasper dust into the cauldron.

"And each cross of silver a shield will be. As we will, so mote it be."

The room exploded with light, and the force of it shook

the walls, the floor. The cauldron tumbled over, spilling liquid silver into the flame.

The force nearly sent Glenna to the ground, but Hoyt's arms came around her. He spun his body around to shield hers from the sudden spurting flames and roaring wind.

Hoyt saw the door fly open. For an instant, Cian was framed in the doorway, drowned in that impossible light. Then he vanished.

"No! No!" Dragging Glenna with him, Hoyt broke the circle. The light shrank in on itself, swallowed itself and was gone with a crash like thunder. Through the ringing in his ears he thought he heard shouting.

Cian lay on the floor bleeding, his shirt half burned away and still smoking.

Hoyt dropped to his knees, his fingers reaching for a pulse before he remembered there would be none in any case. "My God, my God, what have I done?"

"He's badly burned. Get the shirt off of him." Glenna's voice was cool as water, and just as calm. "Gently."

"What happened? What the hell did you do?" King shoved Hoyt aside. "Son of a bitch. Cian. Jesus Christ."

"We were finishing a spell. He opened the door. There was light. It was no one's fault. Larkin," Glenna continued, "help King carry Cian to his room. I'll be right there. I have things that will help."

"He's not dead." Hoyt said it quietly, staring down at his brother. "It's not death."

"It's not death," Glenna repeated. "I can help him. I'm a good healer. It's one of my strengths."

"I'll help you." Moira stepped up, then eased her body toward the wall as King and Larkin lifted Cian. "I have some skill."

"Good. Go with them. I'll get my things. Hoyt. I can help him."

"What did we do?" Hoyt stared helplessly at his hands. Though they still vibrated from the spell, they felt empty and useless. "It was beyond all I've done."

"We'll talk about it later." She gripped his hand, pulled him into the tower room.

The circle was burned into the floor, scorched in a pure white ring. In its center glinted nine silver crosses with a circle of red jasper at the joining.

"Nine. Three times three. We'll think about all this later. I think we should let them stay there for now. I don't know, let them set."

Ignoring her, Hoyt crossed the circle, picked one up. "It's cool."

"Great. Good." Her mind was already on Cian, and what would have to be done to help him. She grabbed her case. "I have to get down, do what I can for him. It wasn't anyone's fault, Hoyt."

"Twice now. Twice I've nearly killed him."

"This is my doing as much as yours. Are you coming with me?"

"No."

She started to speak, then shook her head and rushed out.

I n the lavish bedchamber, the vampyre lay still on the wide bed. His face was that of an angel. A wicked one, Moira thought. She sent the men out for warm water, for bandages, and mostly to get them out from underfoot.

Now she was alone with the vampyre, who lay on the wide bed. Still as death.

She would feel no heartbeat should she lay her hand on his chest. There would be no breath to fog a glass if she were to hold one to his lips. And he would have no reflection.

She'd read these things, and more.

Yet, he'd saved her life, and she owed him for that.

She moved to the side of the bed, and used what little magic she had to try to cool his burned flesh. Queasiness rose up and was fought down. She'd never seen flesh so scorched. How could anyone—anything—survive such wounds?

His eyes flashed open, searing blue. His hand clamped on her wrist. "What are you doing?"

"You're hurt." She hated to hear the tremor in her voice, but her fear of him—alone with him—was so huge. "An

accident. I'm waiting for Glenna. We'll help you. Lie still."
She saw the instant the pain woke in him, and some of her
fear died. "Lie quiet. I can cool it a little."

"Wouldn't you rather I burn in hell?"

"I don't know. But I know I don't want to be the one who
sends you. I wouldn't have shot you last night. I'm ashamed
I let you believe I would. I owe you my life."

"Go away, and we'll call it quits."

"Glenna's coming. Is it cooling a little?"

He simply closed his eyes; and his body trembled. "I
need blood."

"Well, you won't be having mine. I'm not that grateful."

She thought his lips curved, just the slightest bit. "Not
yours, though I'll bet it's tasty." He had to catch the breath
the pain stole. "In the case across the room. The black case
with the silver handle. I need blood to— I just need it."

She left him to open the case, then swallowed revulsion
when she saw the clear packs that held dark red liquid.

"Bring it over, toss it and run, whatever you want, but I
need it now."

She brought it quickly, then watched him struggle to sit
up, to tear the pack open with his burned hands. Saying nothing, she took the pack, opened it herself, spilling some.

"Sorry." She gathered her strength, then used an arm to
brace him, using her free hand to bring the pack to his lips.

He watched her as he drank, and she made herself look
back into his eyes without flinching.

When he'd drained it dry, she laid his head down again
before going into the bath for a cloth. With it she wiped his
mouth, his chin.

"Small but valiant, are you?"

She heard the edge in his tone, and some return of its
strength. "You haven't a choice because of what you are. I
haven't one because of what I am." She stepped back when
Glenna hurried into the room.

Chapter 11

"Do you want something for the pain?" Glenna coated a thin cloth with balm.

"What have you got?"

"This and that." She laid the cloth gently on his chest. "I'm so sorry, Cian. We should have locked the door."

"A locked door wouldn't have stopped me from coming in, not in my own house. You might try a sign next time, something along the lines . . . Bugger it!"

"I know, sorry, I know. It'll be better in a minute. A sign?" she continued, her voice low and soothing as she worked. "Something like: Flammable Magicks. Keep out."

"Wouldn't hurt." He felt the burn not just on the flesh, but down into the bone, as if the fire had burst inside him as well as out. "What the hell were you doing in there?"

"More than either of us were expecting. Moira, coat more cloth, would you. Cian?"

"What?"

She simply looked at him, deeply, her hands hovering just above the worst of the burns. She felt the heat, but not the release. "It won't work unless you let it," she told him. "Unless you trust me and let go."

"A high price for a bit of relief, adding that you're part of what put me here."

"Why would she hurt you?" Moira continued to coat the cloth. "She needs you. We all do, like it or not."

"One minute," Glenna said. "Give me one minute. I want to help you; you need to believe that. Believe me. Look at me, into my eyes. Yes, that's right."

Now it came. Heat and release, heat and release. "There, that's better. A little better. Yes?"

She'd taken it, he realized. Some of the burn, just for an instant, into herself. He wouldn't forget it. "Some. Yes, some. Thanks."

She applied more cloth, turned back to her case. "I'll just clean the cuts and treat the bruises, then give you something to help you rest."

"I'm not looking for rest."

She shifted back, eased down on the bed intending to clean the cuts on his face. Puzzled, she laid her fingers on his cheek, turned his head. "I thought these were worse."

"They were. I heal quickly from most things."

"Good for you. How's the vision?"

He turned those hot blue eyes on her. "I see you well enough, Red."

"Could have a concussion. Can you get concussions? I imagine so," she said before he could answer. "Are you burned anywhere else?" She started to lower the sheet, then flicked him a wicked glance. "Is it true what they say about vampires?"

It made him laugh, then hiss as the pain rippled back. "A myth. We're hung just as we were before the change. You're welcome to look for yourself, but I'm not hurt in that area. It caught me full on the chest."

"We'll preserve your modesty—and my illusions." When she took his hand the amusement faded from his face. "I thought we'd killed you. So did he. Now he's suffering."

"Oh, *he's* suffering, is he? Maybe he'd like to switch places with me."

"You know he would. However you feel or don't about him, he loves you. He can't turn that off, and he hasn't had all the time that you've had to step back from brotherhood."

"We stopped being brothers the night I died."

"No, you didn't. And you're deluding yourself if you believe that." She pushed off the bed. "You're as comfortable as I can make you. I'll come back in an hour and work on you some more."

She gathered her things. Moira slipped out of the room ahead of her, and waited. "What did that to him?"

"I'm not entirely sure."

"You need to be. It's a powerful weapon against his kind. We could use it."

"We weren't controlling it. I don't know that we can."

"If you could," Moira insisted.

Glenna opened the door to her room, carried her case inside. She wasn't ready to go back to the tower. "It controlled us, as far as I can tell. It was huge and powerful. Too powerful for either of us to handle. Even together—and we were linked as closely as I've been with anyone—we couldn't harness it. It was like being inside the sun."

"The sun's a weapon."

"If you don't know how to use a sword, you're just as likely to cut off your own hand as someone else's."

"So you learn."

Glenna lowered to the bed, then held out a hand. "I'm shaky," she said, watching it tremble. "There are places inside my body I didn't know I had shaking like my hand is."

"And I'm badgering you. I'm sorry. You seemed so steady, so calm when you were treating the vampyre."

"He has a name. Cian. Start using it." Moira's head snapped back as if she'd been slapped, and her eyes widened at the whip in Glenna's tone. "I'm sorry about your mother. Sick and sorry, but he didn't kill her. If she'd been murdered by a blond man with blue eyes, would you go around hating all men with blond hair and blue eyes?"

"It's not the same, not nearly the same."

"Close enough, especially in our situation."

Sheer stubbornness hardened Moira's face. "I fed him blood, and gave what little I could to ease him. I helped you treat his burns. It should be enough."

"It's not. Wait," Glenna ordered as Moira spun around to leave. "Just wait. I *am* shaking, and short-tempered with it. Just wait. If I seemed calm before it's because that's the way it works for me. Handle the crisis, then fall apart. This is the falling apart portion of our program. But what I said goes, Moira.

"Just as what you said in there goes. We need him. You're going to have to start thinking of him, and treating him like a person instead of a thing."

"They tore her to pieces." Moira's eyes filled even as the defense of defiance crumbled. "No, he wasn't there, he had no part of it. He lifted his sword for me. I know it, but I can't feel it."

She slapped a hand on her heart. "I can't feel it. They didn't let me grieve. They didn't give me time to mourn my own mother. And now, now that I'm here it's all grief and all rage. All blood and death. I don't want this burden. Away from my people, from everything I know. Why are we here? Why are we charged with this? Why are there no answers?"

"I don't know, which is another nonanswer. I'm sorry, so horribly sorry about your mother, Moira. But you're not the only one with grief and rage. Not the only one asking questions and wishing they were back in the life they knew."

"One day you will go back. I never can." She yanked open the door and fled.

"Perfect. Just perfect." Glenna dropped her head into her hands.

In the tower room, Hoyt laid each cross on a cloth of white linen. They were cool to the touch, and though the metal had dimmed somewhat, its light was bright enough to glare into his eyes.

He picked up Glenna's cauldron. It was scorched black. He doubted it could ever be used again—wondered if it was meant to be. The candles she'd scribed and lit were no more than puddles of wax on the floor now. It would need to be cleaned. The entire room should be cleansed before any other magic was done here.

The circle was etched into the floor now, a thin ring of pure white. And his brother's blood stained the floor and walls outside the door.

Sacrifice, he thought. There was always payment for power. His gift of his mother's candlestand, Glenna's of her grandmother's ring hadn't been enough.

The light had burned so fierce and bright, so violently hot. Yet it hadn't scorched his skin. He held his hand up, examined it. Unmarked. Unsteady yet, he could admit. But unmarked.

The light had filled him, all but consumed him. It had twined him so truly with Glenna it had been almost as if they'd been one person, one power.

That power had been heady and fantastic.

And it had whirled out like the wrath of the gods at his brother. Struck down the other half of him while the sorcerer had ridden the lightning.

Now he was empty, hollowed out. What power that remained in him was like lead, heavy and cold, and the lead was coated thick with guilt.

Nothing to be done now, nothing to do but put order back into the room. He busied himself, calmed himself, with the basic tasks. When King rushed into the room, he stood still, arms at his sides, and took the blow he saw coming full in the face.

He had a moment to think it was like being hit by a battering ram as he was launched back against the wall. Then simply slid bonelessly to the floor.

"Get up. Get up, you son of a bitch."

Hoyt spat out blood. His vision wavered so he saw several black giants standing over him with ham-sized fists bunched. He braced a hand on the wall, dragged himself to his feet.

The battering ram struck again. This time his vision went red, black, shimmered sickly to gray. King's voice went tinny in his ears, but he struggled to follow the command to get back up.

There was a flash of color through the gray, a stream of heat through the iced pain.

Glenna flew into the tower. She didn't bother to shove at King, but rammed her elbow viciously into his midsection, then all but fell on Hoyt to shield him.

"Stop it! Get away from him. Stupid bastard. Oh Hoyt, your face."

"Get away." He could barely mumble the words, and his stomach pitched violently as he pushed at her and tried to rise again.

"Go ahead and throw one. Come on." King spread his arms, then tapped his chin. "I'll give you a free shot. Hell, I'll give you a couple of them, you miserable son of a bitch. It's more than you gave Cian."

"He's gone then. Get away from me." Hoyt shoved at Glenna. "Go ahead," he told King. "Finish it."

Though his fists remained bunched, King lowered them a fraction. The man was barely standing, and blood ran from his nose, his mouth. One eye was already swelling shut. And he just swayed there, waiting to take another hit.

"Is he stupid, or just crazy?"

"He's neither," Glenna snapped. "He thinks he's killed his brother so he'll stand here and let you beat him to death because he blames himself as much as you blame him. And you're both wrong. Cian's not dead. Hoyt, he's going to be fine. He's resting, that's all. He's resting."

"Not gone?"

"You didn't pull it off, and you won't get a second chance."

"Oh, for God's *sake*!" Glenna whirled to King. "Nobody tried to kill anyone."

"Just step away, Red." King jerked a thumb. "I'm not looking to hurt you."

"Why not? If he's responsible, so am I. We were working together. We were doing what we came here to do, *damn* it. Cian came in at the wrong time, it's as simple and as tragic as that. If Hoyt could, and would, hurt Cian like that purposely, do you think you'd be standing there? He'd cut you down with a thought. And I'd help him."

King's bicolored eyes narrowed, his mouth went grim. But his fists stayed at his side. "Why don't you?"

"It's against everything we are. You couldn't possibly understand. But unless you're brick stupid you should understand that whatever affection and loyalty you feel for Cian, Hoyt feels it, too. And he's felt it since the day he was born. Now get out of here. Just go."

King unbunched his fists, rubbed them on his pants. "Maybe I was wrong."

"A lot of good that does."

"I'm going to check on Cian. If I'm not satisfied, I'm going to finish this."

Ignoring him as he strode out, Glenna turned to try to take some of Hoyt's weight. "Here now, you need to sit down."

"Would you get away from me?"

"No, I won't."

In response, Hoyt merely lowered to the floor.

Resigned, Glenna went for more cloth, poured water from a pitcher into a bowl. "It looks like I'm going to spend the evening mopping up blood."

She knelt beside him, dampening cloth, then gently cleaning blood from his face. "I lied. You are stupid, stupid to stand there and let him pound on you. Stupid to feel guilty. And cowardly, too."

His eyes, bloodied and swollen, shifted to hers. "Have a care."

"Cowardly," she repeated, her voice sharp because there were tears welling at the base of her throat. "To stay up here wallowing instead of coming down to help. Instead of coming down to see what shape your brother was in. Which isn't that much worse than you at this point."

"I'm not in the mood to have you jab at me with words, or flutter about me." He waved her hands away.

"Fine. Just fine." She tossed the cloth back in the bowl so water spewed up and lapped over onto the floor. "Tend to yourself then. I'm tired of every single one of you. Brooding, self-pitying, useless. If you ask me, your Morrigan screwed up royally picking this group."

"Brooding, self-pitying, useless. You forgot your part of the whole. Shrew."

She inclined her head. "That's a weak and old-fashioned term. Today, we just go with bitch."

"Your world, your word."

"That's right. While you're up here wallowing, you might take just a minute to consider this. We did something amazing here tonight." She gestured toward the silver crosses on the table. "Something beyond anything I've ever experienced. The fact that we did, that we could, should, in some way, bring this ridiculous group together. But instead we're all whining in our separate corners. So I guess the magic, and the moment, was wasted."

She stormed out just as Larkin jogged up the steps. "Cian's getting up. He says we've wasted enough time and we'll be training an extra hour tonight."

"You can tell him to kiss my ass."

Larkin blinked, then craned his head around the curve of the stairs to watch her stride down. "Sure it's a fine one," he said, but very quietly.

He peeked into the tower room, saw Hoyt sitting on the floor, bleeding.

"Mother of Christ, did she do that?"

Hoyt scowled at him and decided his punishment for the night wasn't quite done. "No. For God's sake, do I look like I could be beaten by a woman?"

"She strikes me as formidable." Though he would have preferred keeping clear of magic areas, he could hardly leave the man sprawled there. So Larkin walked over to Hoyt, crouched. "Well, that's a mess, isn't it? You're coming up a pair of black eyes."

"Bollocks. Give me a hand up, will you?"

Agreeably, Larkin helped him up, gave him a shoulder to lean on. "I don't know what the bleeding hell's going on, but Glenna's steaming, and Moira's locked in her room. Cian looks like the wrath of all the gods, but he's out of bed and saying we're training. King's opened some whiskey and I'm thinking about joining him."

Hoyt touched fingers gingerly to his cheekbone, hissed as

the pain radiated to his face. "Not shattered, there's some fine luck. She might've done a bit more to help instead of pounding a lecture on my head."

"Words are a woman's sharpest weapon. From the looks of you, you could use some of that whiskey."

"I could." Hoyt braced a hand on the table, prayed he'd regain his balance in a moment. "Do what you can, would you, Larkin, to get the lot of them together in the training area. I'll be along."

"Taking my life in my hands, I'm thinking. But all right. I'll try sweetness and charm with the ladies. They'll either fall for it, or kick me in the balls."

They didn't kick him, but they didn't come happily. Moira sat cross-legged on a table, eyes, swollen from weeping, downcast. Glenna stood in a corner, sulking into a glass of wine. King stood in his own corner, rattling ice in a short glass of whiskey.

Cian sat, drumming his fingers on the arm of his chair. His face was white as bone, and the burns the loose white shirt didn't cover, livid.

"Music might be nice," Larkin said into the silence. "The sort you hear at funeral pyres and the like."

"We'll work on form and agility." Cian cast his glance around the room. "I haven't seen a great deal of that in any of you so far."

"Is there a point to you being insulting?" Moira asked wearily. "A point to any of this? Slapping swords and trading punches? You were burned worse than anyone I've ever seen, and here you are, an hour after, up again. If magic such as that can't take you down, keep you down, what will?"

"I take it you'd be happier if I'd gone to ash. I'm happy to disappoint you."

"That's not what she meant." Glenna shoved irritably at her hair.

"And you interpret for her now?"

"I don't need anyone to speak for me," Moira snapped right back. "And I don't need to be told what to do every bleeding hour of every bleeding day. I know what kills them, I've read the books."

"Oh, well then, you've read the books." Cian gestured toward the doors. "Then be my guest. Go right on out and take out a few vamps."

"It'd be better than tumbling about on the floor in here, like a circus," she shot back.

"I'm with Moira on this." Larkin rested a hand on the hilt of his knife. "We should hunt them down, take the offense. We haven't so much as posted a guard or sent out a scout."

"This isn't that kind of war, boy."

Larkin's eyes glittered. "I'm not a boy, and from what I can see it's no kind of war."

"You don't know what you're up against," Glenna put in.

"Don't I? I fought them, killed three with my own hands."

"Weak ones, young ones. She didn't waste her best on you." Cian rose. He moved stiffly and with obvious effort. "Added to that, you had help and were lucky. But if you came across one with some seasoning, with some skill, you'd be meat."

"I can hold my own."

"Hold it with me. Come at me."

"You're hurt. It wouldn't be fair."

"Fair is for women. If you take me down, I'll go out with you." Cian gestured toward the door. "We'll hunt tonight."

Interest brightened Larkin's eyes. "Your word on it?"

"My word. Take me down."

"All right then."

Larkin came in fast, then spun out of reach. He jabbed, feinted, spun again. Cian merely reached out, gripped Larkin around the throat and lifted him off his feet. "You don't want to dance with a vampire," he said and tossed Larkin halfway across the room.

"Bastard." Moira scrambled up, raced to her cousin's side. "You've half strangled him."

"The half's what counts."

"Was that really necessary?" Glenna got to her feet, moved to Larkin to lay her hands on his throat.

"Kid asked for it," King commented, and had her whipping her head around.

"You're nothing but a bully. The pair of you."

"I'm all right, I'm all right." Larkin coughed, cleared his throat. "It was a good move," he said to Cian. "I never saw it coming."

"Until you can, and do, you don't hunt." He eased back, lowered carefully into the chair. "Time to work."

"I'd ask you to wait." Hoyt came into the room.

Cian didn't bother to look at him. "We've waited long enough."

"A bit more. I have things to say. First to you. I was careless, but so were you. I should have barred the door, but you shouldn't have opened it."

"This is my house now. It hasn't been yours for centuries."

"That may be. But courtesy and caution should approach a closed door, particularly when magic is being done. Cian." He waited until his brother's eyes shifted to him. "I would not have had you hurt. That's for you to believe or not. But I would not have had you hurt."

"I don't know if I can say the same." Cian gestured with his chin toward Hoyt's face. "Did your magic do that?"

"It's another result of it."

"Looks painful."

"So it is."

"Well then, that balances the scales somewhat."

"And this is what we've come to, checks and balances." Hoyt turned to face the room, and the others. "Arguments and resentments. You were right," he said to Glenna. "A great deal of what you said was right, though I swear you talk too much."

"Oh, really?"

"We aren't united, and until we are, we're hopeless. We could be training and preparing every hour of every day of the time we have left, and never win. Because—this is what you said—we have a common enemy, but not a common purpose."

"The purpose is to fight them," Larkin interrupted. "To fight them, and kill them. Kill them all."

"Why?"

"Because they're demons."

"So is he." Hoyt laid a hand on the back of Cian's chair.

"But he fights with us. He doesn't threaten Geall."

"Geall. You think of Geall, and you," he said to Moira, "of your mother. King's here with us because he follows Cian, and in my way, so do I. Cian, why are you here?"

"Because I don't follow. You or her."

"Why are you here, Glenna?"

"I'm here because if I didn't fight, if I didn't try, everything we have and are and know, every one of us, could be lost. Because what's inside me demands that I be here. And above all, because good needs soldiers against evil."

Oh aye, this was a woman, he thought. She put shame to all of them. "The answer. The single one there is, and she's the only one who knew it. We're needed. Stronger than valor or vengeance, loyalty or pride. We're needed. Can we stand with each other and do this thing? Not in a thousand years and with a thousand more of us to fight. We're the six, the beginning of it. We can't be strangers any longer."

He stepped away from Cian's chair as he reached in his pocket. "Glenna said make a symbol and a shield, a sign of common purpose. That unity of purpose made the strongest magic I've ever known. Stronger than I could hold," he said with a glance at Cian. "I believe they can help protect us, if we remember a shield needs a sword, and we use both with one purpose."

He drew the crosses out so the silver glinted in the light. He stepped to King, offered one. "Will you wear it?"

King set his drink aside, took the cross and chain. He studied Hoyt's face as he looped it around his neck. "You could use some ice on that eye."

"I could use a great deal. And you?" He held a cross out to Moira.

"I'll work to be worthy of it." She sent Glenna a look of apology. "I've done poorly tonight."

"So have we all," Hoyt told her. "Larkin?"

"Not just of Geall," Larkin said as he took the cross. "Or no longer."

"And you." Hoyt started to hand Glenna a cross, then stepped closer, looked into her eyes as he put it around her neck himself. "I think tonight you put us all to shame."

"I'll try not to make a habit of it. Here." She took the last cross, put the chain over his head. Then gently, very gently touched her lips to his battered cheek.

At last, he turned and walked back to Cian.

"If you're about to ask if I'd wear one of those, you're wasting your breath."

"I know you can't. I know you're not what we are, and still I'm asking you to stand with us, for this purpose." He held out a pendant, in the shape of a pentagram much like Glenna's. "The stone in the center is jasper, like the ones in the crosses. I can't give you a shield, not yet. So I'm offering you a symbol. Will you take it?"

Saying nothing, Cian held out a hand. When Hoyt poured pendant and chain into it, Cian shook it lightly, as if checking the weight. "Metal and stone don't make an army."

"They make weapons."

"True enough." Cian slipped the chain over his head. "Now if the ceremony's finished, could we bloody well get to work?"

Chapter 12

Seeking solitude and occupation, Glenna poured a glass of wine, got out a pad of paper and a pencil and sat down at the kitchen table.

An hour, she thought, of quiet, where she could settle down, make some lists. Then maybe she would sleep.

When she heard someone approaching, her back went up. In a house this size, couldn't everyone find some place else to be?

But King came in, and stood, shifting his weight, digging his hands into his pockets.

"Well?" was all she said.

"Ah, sorry about breaking Hoyt's face."

"It's his face, you should apologize to him."

"We know where we stand. Just wanted to clear it with you." When she said nothing, he scratched the top of his head through his thick hair, and if a man of six six and two hundred and seventy pounds could squirm, King squirmed.

"Listen, I run up, and that light's blasting, and he's lying there bleeding and burning. Guy's my first sorcerer," King continued after another pause. "I've only known him like a week. I've known Cian since . . . a really long time, and I owe him pretty much everything."

"So when you found him hurt, naturally you assumed his brother tried to kill him."

"Yeah. Figured you had a part in it, too, but I couldn't beat the hell out of you."

"I appreciate the chivalry."

The sting in her tone made him wince. "You sure got a way of cutting a man down to size."

"It would take a chain saw to cut you down to size. Oh, stop looking so pitiful and guilty." With a sigh, she scooped back her hair. "We screwed up, you screwed up, and we're all goddamn sorry about it. I suppose you want some wine now. Maybe a cookie."

He had to grin. "I'll take a beer." He opened the refrigerator, got one out. "I'll pass on the cookie. You're a butt-kicker, Red. Quality I admire in a woman—even if it's my butt getting the boot."

"I never used to be. I don't think."

She was also pretty and pale, and had to be dog tired. He'd worked her, all of them, damned hard that afternoon, and Cian had put them through the wringer tonight.

Sure she'd bitched a little, King thought now. But not nearly as much as he'd expected. And when it came down to it, Hoyt was right. She'd been the only one who'd known the answer to what the hell they were doing here.

"That stuff Hoyt was talking about, what you said, it makes a lot of sense. We don't straighten up, we're easy pickings." He popped the cap off the beer, swallowed half the bottle in one long gulp. "So I will if you will."

She looked at the enormous hand he held out, then placed hers in it. "I think Cian's lucky to have someone who'll fight for him. Who'd care enough to."

"He'd do the same for me. We go back."

"That kind of friendship usually takes time to form, to so-lidify. We're not going to have that kind of time."

"Guess we'd better take some shortcuts then. We cool now?"

"I'd say we're cool now."

He polished off the beer, then dumped the empty bottle in a can under the sink. "Heading up. You ought to do the same. Get some sleep."

"I will."

But when he left her alone, she was bruised and tired and restless, so Glenna sat alone in the kitchen with her glass of wine and the lights on full to beat back the dark. She didn't know the time and wondered if it mattered any longer.

They were all becoming vampires—sleeping through most of the day, working through most of the night.

She fingered the cross around her neck as she continued to write her list. And she felt the press of the night against her shoulder blades like cold hands.

She missed the city, she decided. No shame in admitting it. She missed the sounds of it, the colors, the constant thrum of traffic that was a heartbeat. She yearned for its complexity and simplicity. Life was just life there. And if there was death, if there was cruelty and violence, it was all so utterly human.

The image of the vampire on the subway flashed into her mind.

Or she'd once had the comfort of believing it was human.

Still, she wanted to get up in the morning and wander down to the deli for fresh bagels. She wanted to set her easel in the slash of morning light and paint, and have her strongest concern be how she was going to pay her Visa bill.

All of her life the magic had been in her, and she'd thought she'd valued and respected it. But it had been nothing to this, to know that it was in her for this reason, for this purpose.

That it could very well be the death of her.

She picked up her wine, then jolted when she saw Hoyt standing in the doorway.

"Not a good idea to go creeping around in the dark, considering the situation."

"I wasn't sure I should disturb you."

"Might as well. Just having my own private pity party. It'll pass," she said with a shrug. "I'm a little homesick. Small potatoes compared to how you must feel."

"I stand in the room I shared with Cian when we were boys and feel too much, and not enough."

She rose, got a second glass, poured wine. "Have a seat." She sat down again, set the wine on the table. "I have a brother," she told him. "He's a doctor, just starting. He has a whiff of magic, and he uses it to heal. He's a good doctor, a good man. He loves me, I know, but he doesn't understand me very well. It's hard not to be understood."

How could it be, he wondered, that there had never been a woman in his life other than family he could speak to about anything that truly mattered. And now, with Glenna, he knew he could, and would, talk with her of anything. And everything.

"It troubles me, the loss of him, of what we were to each other."

"Of course it does."

"His memories of me—Cian's—are faded and old while mine are fresh and strong." Hoyt lifted his glass. "Yes, it's difficult not to be understood."

"What I am, what's in me, I used to feel smug about it. Like it was a shiny prize I held in my hands, just for me. Oh, I was careful with it, grateful for it, but still smug. I don't think I ever will be again."

"With what we touched tonight, I'm doubting either of us could be smug again."

"Still, my family, my brother, didn't understand—not fully—that smugness or that prize. And they won't understand—not fully—the price I'm paying for it now. They can't."

She reached out, laid a hand over Hoyt's. "He can't. So, while our circumstances may be different, I understand the loss you're talking about. You look terrible," she said more lightly. "I can help ease that bruising a little more."

"You're tired. It can wait."

"You didn't deserve it."

"I let it take control. I let it fly out of me."

"No, it flew away from us. Who can say if it wasn't meant to." She'd bundled her hair up to train, to work, and now pulled out the pins so it fell, messily, just short of her shoulders.

"Look, we learned, didn't we? We're stronger together than either of us could have anticipated. What we're responsible for now is learning how to control it, channel it. And believe me, the rest of them will have more respect now, too."

He smiled a little. "That sounds a bit smug."

"Yeah, I guess it does."

He drank some wine and realized he was comfortable for the first time in hours. Just sitting in the bright kitchen with night trapped outside the glass, with Glenna to talk with.

Her scent was there, just on the edges of his senses. That earthy, female scent. Her eyes, so clear and green, showed some light bruising of fatigue on the delicate skin beneath them.

He nodded toward the paper. "Another spell?"

"No, something more pedestrian. Lists. I need more supplies. Herbs and so forth. And Moira and Larkin need clothes. Then we need to work out some basic household rules. So far it's been up to me and King for the most part. The cooking, that is. A household doesn't run itself, and even when you're preparing for war, you need food and clean towels."

"There are so many machines to do the work." He glanced around the kitchen. "It should be simple enough."

"You'd think."

"There used to be an herb garden. I haven't walked the land, not really." Put it off, he admitted. Put off seeing the changes, and what remained the same. "Cian might have had one planted. Or I could bring it back. The earth remembers."

"Well, that can go on the list for tomorrow. You know the woods around here. You should be able to tell me where to find the other things I need. I can go out in the morning and harvest."

"I knew them," he said half to himself.

"We need more weapons, Hoyt. And eventually more hands to wield them."

"There will be an army in Geall."

"We hope. I know a few like us, and Cian—it's likely he knows some like him. We may want to start enlisting."

"More vampyres? Trusting Cian's been difficult enough.

As for more witches, we're still learning each other, as we learned tonight. We were to start with those we have. We've barely begun. But weapons. We can make them as we made the crosses."

She picked up her wine again, drank, breathed out slowly. "Okay. I'm game."

"We'll take them with us when we go to Geall."

"Speaking of. When and how?"

"How? Through the Dance. When? I can't know. I have to believe we'll be told when it's time. That we'll know when it's time."

"Do you think we'll ever be able to get back? If we live? Do you think we'll be able to get back home?"

He looked over at her. She was sketching, her eyes on her pad, her hand steady. Her cheeks were pale, he noted, from fatigue and stress. Her hair was bright and bold, swinging forward as she dipped her head.

"Which disturbs you most?" he wondered. "Dying or not seeing your home again?"

"I'm not entirely sure. Death is inevitable. None of us get out of that one. And you hope—or I have—that when the time comes you'll have courage and curiosity, and so face it well."

Absently, she tucked her hair behind her ear with her left hand while her right continued to sketch. "But that's always been in the abstract. Until now. It's hard to think about dying, harder to think about it knowing I might not see home again, or my family. They won't understand what happened to me."

She glanced up. "And I'm preaching to the choir."

"I don't know how long they lived. How they died. How long they looked for me."

"It would help to know."

"Aye, it would." He shook it off, angled his head. "What do you draw there?"

She pursed her lips at the sketch. "It seems to be you." She turned it around, nudged it toward him.

"Is this how you see me?" His voice sounded puzzled, and not entirely pleased. "So stern."

"Not stern. Serious. You're a serious man. Hoyt McKenna."
She printed the name on the sketch. "That's how it would be
written and said today. I looked it up." She signed the sketch
with a quick flourish. "And your serious nature is very attractive."

"Serious is for old men and politicians."

"And for warriors, for men of power. Knowing you, being
attracted to you, makes me realize what I knew before you
were boys. Apparently, I like much older men these days."

He sat, looking at her, with the sketch and the wine between them. With worlds between them, he told himself.
And still he'd never felt closer to anyone. "To sit here like
this with you, in the house that's mine, but not, in a world
that's mine, but not, you're the single thing I want."

She rose, moved to him, put her arms around him. He
rested his head just under her breasts, listened to her heart.

"Is it comfort?" she asked.

"Yes. But not only that. I have such a need for you. I don't
know how to hold it inside me."

She lowered her head, closing her eyes as she rested her
cheek on his hair. "Let's be human. For what's left of tonight, let's be human, because I don't want to be alone in the
dark." She framed his face, lifted it to hers. "Take me to
bed."

He took her hands as he got to his feet. "Such things
haven't changed in a millennium, have they?"

She laughed. "Some things never change."

He kept her hand in his as they walked from the kitchen.
"I haven't bedded many women—being a serious man."

"I haven't been bedded by many men—being a sensible
woman." At the door to her room she turned to him with a
quick, wicked smile. "But I think we'll manage."

"Wait." He brought her to him before she could open the
door, and laid his lips on hers. She felt warmth, and an un-
derlying shimmer of power.

Then he opened the door.

He'd lighted the candles, she saw. Every one of them, so
the room was full of gilded light and soft scent. The fire
burned as well, a low red simmer.

It touched a place in her heart even as it rippled anticipation over her skin.

"A very nice start. Thank you." She heard the click of the key in the lock, pressed a hand to her heart. "I'm nervous. All of a sudden. I've never been nervous about being with someone. Not even that first time. That smugness again."

He didn't mind her nerves. In fact, they added an edge to his own arousal. "Your mouth. This fullness here." He traced a fingertip over her bottom lip. "I can taste it in my sleep. You distract me, even when you're not with me."

"That annoys you." She reached up to link her arms around his neck. "I'm so glad."

She eased toward him, watching his gaze drop to her mouth, linger before it came back to hers. Felt his breath mix with her breath, and his heart beat against her heart. They held there, one endless moment, then their lips met. And they sank into each other.

Nerves fluttered in her belly again, a dozen velvet wings that swept against desire. And still that shimmer of power was like a hum in the air.

Then his hands were in her hair, sweeping it back from her face in a gesture of urgency that had her shuddering in anticipation of what was to come. And his mouth left hers to roam her face, to find that throbbing pulse in her throat.

She could drown him. He knew it even as he took more. This outrageous need for her could take him under, somewhere he'd never been. He knew, wherever that was, he would take her with him.

He molded the shape of her with his hands, steeped himself in it. She found his mouth again, avidly. He heard the shudder of her breath as she stepped back. The candlelight washed over her as she reached up, began to unbutton her shirt.

She wore something white and lacy beneath it that seemed to hold her breasts like an offering. There was more white lace when her pants slid down her hips, an alluring triangle that rode low on her belly, high on her legs.

"Women are the canniest creatures," he mused out loud, and reached out to skim a fingertip over the lace. When she trembled, he smiled. "I like these clothes. Are you always wearing these under the others?"

"No. It depends on my mood."

"I like this mood." He took his thumbs, brushed them up over the lace on her breasts.

Her head fell back. "Oh God."

"That pleasures you. What of this?" He did the same with the lace that sat snug below her belly, and watched the arousal slide over her face.

Soft skin, delicate and smooth. But there was muscle under it. Fascinating. "Just let me touch. Your body is beautiful. Just let me touch."

She reached back, gripped the bedpost. "Help yourself."

His fingers skimmed over her, made her skin quiver. Then pressed and made her moan. She could feel her own bones going to liquid, and her muscles to putty as he explored her. She gave herself to it, to the slow, enervating pleasure that was both triumph and surrender.

"Is this the fastener then?"

She opened heavy eyes as he fiddled with the front hook of her bra. But when she started to undo it, he brushed her hands aside.

"I'll figure it out on my own in a minute. Ah yes, there it is." As he unhooked it, her breasts spilled out and into his hands. "Clever. Beautiful." He lowered his head to them, tasted soft, warm flesh.

He wanted to savor; he wanted to rush.

"And the other part? Where is the fastener?" He ran his hands down her.

"They don't—" And over her. Her breath caught, a half cry as her fingers dug into his shoulders.

"Aye, look at me. Just like that." He skimmed his hands over the lace, under it. "Glenna Ward, who is mine tonight."

And she came where she stood, her body exploding and her eyes trapped by his.

Her head went limp on his shoulder as she shuddered, shuddered. "I want you on me, I want you in me." She dragged at the sweatshirt he wore, drawing it up and away. Now she found muscle and flesh with her hands, with her lips. Now the power seeped back into her as she pulled him with her onto the bed.

"Inside me. Inside me."

Her mouth crushed hungrily to his, hips arching and offering. He fought with the rest of his clothes, struggled to devour more of her as the heat pumped off them both.

When he plunged into her, the fire roared, and the candle flames shot up like arrows.

Passion and power whipped through them, spurring them on toward madness. Still she locked herself around him, stared at him even as tears glazed her eyes.

A wind stirred her hair, bright as fire against the bed. He felt her gather beneath him, tighten like a bow. When the light burst through him, he could only breathe her name.

She felt alight, as if whatever they had ignited between them burned still. She wondered she didn't see beams of its gilded light shooting out of her fingertips.

In the hearth, the fire had settled down to a quiet simmer; another afterglow. But the heat that had bloomed from it, and from them, dewed her skin. Even now her heart moved at a gallop.

His head rested there, on her heart, and her hand on his head.

"Have you ever . . ."

His lips brushed her breast, lightly. "No."

She combed her fingers through his hair. "Neither have I. Maybe it was because it was the first time, or because some of what we made earlier was still stored up."

We're stronger together. Her own words echoed in her mind.

"Where do we go from here?"

When he lifted his head, she shook hers. "An expression," she explained. "And it doesn't matter now. Your bruises are gone."

"I know. Thank you."

"I don't know that I did it."

"You did. You touched my face when we joined." He took

her hand, brought it to his lips. "There's magic in your hands, and in your heart. And still your eyes are troubled."

"Just tired."

"Do you want me to leave you?"

"No, I don't." And wasn't that the problem? "I want you to stay."

"Here then." He shifted, bringing her with him, tucking up sheet and blanket. "I have a question."

"Mmm."

"You have a brand, here." He traced his fingers over the small of her back. "A pentagram. Are witches marked so in this time?"

"No. It's a tattoo—my choice. I wanted to wear a symbol of what I am, even when I was skyclad."

"Ah. I mean no disrespect to your purpose, or your symbol, but I found it . . . alluring."

She smiled to herself. "Good. Then it performed its secondary purpose."

"I feel whole again," he said. "I feel myself again."

"So do I."

But tired, he thought. He could hear it in her voice. "We'll sleep awhile."

She tilted her head up so their eyes met. "You said when you took me to bed you wouldn't give me any sleep."

"This once."

She rested her head on his shoulder, but didn't close her eyes, even when he dimmed the candles. "Hoyt. Whatever happens, this was precious."

"For me as well. And for the first time, Glenna, I believe not only that we must win, but that we can. I believe that because you're with me."

Now she closed her eyes for just a moment, on the pang just under her heart. He spoke of war, she thought. And she'd spoken of love.

She woke to rain, and his warmth. Glenna lay, listening to the patter, absorbing the good, natural feel of a man's body beside hers.

She'd had to lecture herself during the night. What she had with Hoyt was a gift, one that should be treasured and appreciated. There was no point in cursing because it wasn't enough.

And what good did it do to question why it had happened? To wonder if whatever was driving them to the battleground had brought them together, had ignited that passion and need, and yes, love, because they were stronger with it?

It was enough to feel; she'd always believed that. And only doubted it now because she felt so much.

It was time to go back to being practical, to enjoy what she had when she had it. And to do the job at hand.

She eased away from him, started to get out of bed. His hand closed around her wrist.

"It's early, and raining. Come, stay in bed."

She looked over her shoulder. "How do you know it's early. There's no clock in here. Got a sundial in your head?"

"Sure a lot of good it would do as it's pouring rain. Your hair's like the sun. Come back to bed."

He didn't look so serious now, she noted, not with his eyes sleepy and his face shadowed by a night's growth of beard. What he looked was edible.

"You need a shave."

He rubbed a hand over his face, felt the stubble. Rubbed his hand over again, and the stubble was gone. "Is that better for you, *a stór*?"

She reached over, flicked a finger down his cheek. "Very smooth. You could use a decent haircut."

He frowned, scooped a hand through his hair. "What would be wrong with my hair?"

"It's gorgeous, but it could use a little shaping. I can take care of that for you."

"I think not."

"Oh, don't trust me?"

"Not with my hair."

She laughed and rolled over to straddle him. "You trust me with other, and more sensitive parts of you."

"A different matter entirely." His hands walked up and

cupped her breasts. "What's the name of the garment you wore over your lovely breasts last night?"

"It's called a bra, and don't change the subject."

"Sure I'm happier discussing your breasts than my hair."

"Aren't you cheerful this morning."

"You put a light in me."

"Sweet talker." She picked up a hank of his hair. "Snip, snip. You'll be a new man."

"You seem to like the man I am well enough."

Her lips curved as she lifted her hips. And lowered them to take him into her. The candles that had guttered out sparked. "Just a trim," she whispered, leaning over him to rub her lips to his. "After."

He learned the considerable pleasure of showering with a woman, then the fascinating pleasure of watching one dress.

She rubbed creams into her skin, and different ones over her face.

The bra, and what she called panties, were blue today. Like a robin's egg. Over these she pulled rough pants and the short, baggy tunic she called a sweatshirt. On it were words that spelled out WALKING IN A WICCAN WONDERLAND.

He thought the outer clothes made what she wore beneath a kind of marvelous secret.

He felt relaxed and very pleased with himself. And balked when she told him to sit on the lid of the toilet. She picked up scissors, snapped them together.

"Why would a man of sense allow a woman to come near him with a tool like that?"

"A big, tough sorcerer like you shouldn't be afraid of a little haircut. Besides, if you don't like it when I'm done, you can change it back."

"Why are women always after fiddling with a man?"

"It's our nature. Indulge me."

He sighed, and sat. And squirmed.

"Be still, and it'll be done before you know it. How do you suppose Cian deals with grooming?"

He rolled his eyes up, over, to try to see what she was doing to him. "I wouldn't know."

"No reflection must make it a chore. And he always looks perfect."

Now Hoyt slid his eyes toward hers. "You like the way he looks, do you?"

"You're almost mirror images, so it's obvious I do. He has that slight cleft in his chin and you don't."

"Where the faeries pinched him. My mother used to say."

"Your face is a little leaner, and your eyebrows have more of an arch. But your eyes, those mouths and cheekbones—the same."

He watched hair fall into his lap, and inside the mighty sorcerer, his belly trembled. "Jesus, woman, are you shearing me bald?"

"Lucky for you I like long hair on a man. At least I do on you." She dropped a kiss on the top of his head. "Yours is like black silk, with just a little wave. You know, in some cultures, when a woman cuts a man's hair it's a vow of marriage."

His head jerked, but she'd anticipated the reaction and moved the scissors. Her laugh, full of fun and teasing, echoed off the bathroom walls. "Joking. Boy, are you easy. Almost done."

She straddled his legs, standing with hers apart, and her breasts close to his face. He began to think a haircut wasn't such a hardship after all.

"I liked the feel of a woman."

"Yes, I seem to recall that about you."

"No, what I'm meaning is I liked the feel of a woman when I had one. I'm a man, have needs like any other. But it never occupied so much of my mind as it does with you."

She set the scissors aside, then combed her fingers through his damp hair. "I like occupying your mind. Here, have a look."

He stood, studied himself in the mirror. His hair was shorter, but not unreasonably. He supposed it fell in a more pleasing shape—though it had seemed fine to him before she'd gone after it.

Still, she hadn't sheared him like a sheep, and it pleased her.

"It's well enough, thank you."

"You're welcome."

He finished dressing, and when they went downstairs they found all but Cian in the kitchen.

Larkin was scooping up scrambled eggs. "Good morning to you. The man here has a magician's hands with eggs."

"And my shift at the stove's over," King announced. "So if you want breakfast, you're on your own."

"That's something I wanted to talk about." Glenna opened the refrigerator. "Shifts. Cooking, laundry, basic house-keeping. It needs to be spread out among all of us."

"I'm happy to help," Moira put in. "If you'll show me what to do and how to do it."

"All right, watch and learn. We'll stick with the bacon and eggs for this morning." She got to work on it with Moira watching her every move.

"I wouldn't mind more, while you're about it."

Moira glanced at Larkin. "He eats like two horses."

"Hmm. We're going to need regular supplies." She spoke to King now. "I'd say that falls to you or me, as these three can't drive. Both Larkin and Moira are going to need clothes that fit. If you draw me a map, I can make the next run."

"There's no sun today."

Glenna nodded at Hoyt. "I have protection, and it may clear up."

"The household needs to run, as you said, so you can draw up your plans. We'll follow them. But as to other matters, you have to follow. I think no one goes out alone, out of doors, into the village. No one goes out unarmed."

"Are we to be under siege then, held in by a shower of rain?" Larkin stabbed the air with his fork. "Isn't it time we showed them we won't let them set the terms?"

"He has a point," Glenna agreed. "Cautious but not cowed."

"And there's a horse in the stable," Moira added. "He needs to be tended."

The fact was Hoyt had intended to do so himself, while

the others were busy elsewhere. He wondered now if what he'd told himself was responsibility and leadership was just another lack of trust.

"Larkin and I will tend to the horse." He sat when Glenna put plates on the table. "Glenna needs herbs and so do I, so we'll deal with that as well. Cautious," he repeated. And began to devise how it could be done while he ate.

He strapped on a sword. The rain was a fine drizzle now, the sort he knew could last for days. He could change that. He and Glenna together could bring out sun bright enough to blast the sky.

But the earth needed rain.

He nodded to Larkin, opened the door.

They moved out together, splitting right and left, back-to-back to gauge the ground.

"Be a miserable watch in this weather if they just sit and wait," Larkin pointed out.

"We'll stay close together in any case."

They crossed the ground, searching for shadows and movement. But there was nothing but the rain, the smell of wet flowers and grass.

When they reached the stables, the work was routine for both of them. Mucking out, fresh straw, grain and grooming. Comforting, Hoyt thought, to be around the horse.

Larkin sang as he worked, a cheery air.

"I've a chestnut mare at home," he told Hoyt. "She's a beauty. It seemed we couldn't bring the horses through the Dance."

"I was told to leave my own mare behind. Is it true about the legend? The sword and the stone, and the one who rules Geall? Like the legend of Arthur?"

"It is, and some say it was fashioned from it." As he spoke, Larkin poured fresh water in the trough. "After the death of the king or queen, the sword is placed back in the stone by a magician. On the day after the burial, the heirs then come, one by one, and try to take it out again. Only one will succeed, and rule all of Geall. The sword is kept in the great hall for all to see, until that ruler dies. And so it is repeated, generation after generation."

He wiped his brow. "Moira has no brothers, no sisters. She must rule."

Intrigued, Hoyt stopped to glance over. "If she fails, would it come to you?"

"Spare me from that," Larkin said with feeling. "I've no wish to rule. Bloody nuisance if you're asking me. Well, he's set, isn't he?" He rubbed the stallion's side. "You're a handsome devil, that's the truth. He needs exercise. One of us should ride him out."

"Not today, I think. But you're right in that. He needs a run. Still, he's Cian's, so it's for him to say."

They moved to the door, and as before, stepped out together. "That way." Hoyt gestured. "There was an herb garden, and may still be. I haven't walked that way as yet."

"Moira and I have. I didn't see one."

"We'll have a look."

It sprang off the roof of the stables, so quickly Hoyt had no chance to draw his sword. And the arrow struck it dead in the heart while it was still in the air.

Ash flew as a second leaped. And a second arrow shot home.

"Would you let us have one for the sport of it!" Larkin shouted to Moira.

She stood in the kitchen doorway, a third arrow already notched. "Then take the one coming from the left."

"For me," Larkin shouted at Hoyt.

It was twice his size, and Hoyt started to protest. But Larkin was already charging. Steel struck steel. It clashed and it rang. Twice he saw the thing step back when Larkin's cross glinted at him. But he had a reach, and a very long sword.

When Hoyt saw Larkin slip on the wet grass, he lunged forward. He swung the sword at the thing's neck—and met air.

Larkin leaped up, flipped the wooden stake up, caught it neatly. "I was just throwing him off balance."

"Nicely done."

"There may be more."

"There may be," Hoyt agreed. "But we'll do what we came to do."

"I've got your back then, if you've mine. God knows Moira's got them both. This hurt it," he added, touching the cross. "Gave it some trouble anyway."

"They may be able to kill us, but they won't be able to turn us while we wear them."

"Then I'd say that's a job well done."

Chapter 13

There was no herb garden with its creeping thyme and fragrant rosemary. The pretty knot garden his mother had tended was now a gently rolling span of cropped green grass. It would be a sunny spot when the sky cleared, he knew. His mother had chosen it, though it hadn't been just outside the kitchen as was more convenient, so her herbs could bask in the light.

As a child he'd learned of them from her, of their uses and their beauty while sitting by her as she weeded and clipped and harvested. She'd taught him their names and their needs. He'd learned to identify them by their scents and the shapes of the leaves, by the flowers that bolted from them if she allowed it.

How many hours had he spent there with her, working the earth, talking or just sitting in silence to enjoy the butterflies, the hum of bees?

It had been their place, he thought, more than any other.

He'd grown to a man and had found his place on the cliff in what was now called Kerry. He'd built his stone cabin, and found the solitude he'd needed for his own harvest, for his magic.

But he'd always come back home. And had always found pleasure and solace with his mother here, in her herb garden.

Now, he stood over where it had been as he might have a grave, mourning and remembering. A flare of anger lit in him that his brother would let this go.

"This what you're looking for then?" Larkin studied the grass, then tracked his eyes through the rain, toward the trees. "Doesn't seem to be anything left of it."

Hoyt heard a sound, pivoted as Larkin did. Glenna walked toward them, a stake in one hand, a knife in the other. Rain beaded her hair like tiny jewels.

"You're to stay in the house. There could be more of them."

"If there are, there are three of us now." She jerked her head toward the house. "Five as Moira and King have us covered."

Hoyt looked over. Moira was in the near window, her arrow notched, her bow pointed downward. In the doorway to the left, King stood with a broadsword.

"That ought to do it." Larkin sent his cousin a cheeky grin. "Mind you don't shoot one of us in the arse."

"Only if I'm aiming for it," she called back.

Beside Hoyt, Glenna studied the ground. "Was it here? The garden?"

"It was. Will be."

Something was wrong, she thought, very wrong, to have put that hard look on his face. "I have a rejuvenation spell. I've had good luck with it, healing plants."

"I won't need it for this." He stabbed his sword in the ground to free his hands.

He could see it, just as it had been, and honed that image clear into his mind as he stretched out his arms, spread his hands. This, he knew, would come from his heart as much as from his art. This was tribute to the one who had given him life.

And because of it, would be painful.

"Seed to leaf, leaf to flower. Soil and sun and rain. Remember."

His eyes changed, and his face looked carved from stone.

Larkin started to speak, but Glenna tapped a finger to her lips to stop him. There should be no voice, no words now, she knew, but Hoyt's. Power was already thickening the air.

She couldn't help with the visualization as Hoyt hadn't described the garden to her. But she could focus on scent. Rosemary, lavender, sage.

He repeated the incantation three times, his eyes darkening further, his voice rising with each repetition. Beneath their feet, the ground shuddered lightly.

The wind began to lift, then swirl, then blow.

"Rise up! Return. Grow and bloom. Gift from the earth, from the gods. For the earth, for the gods. Airmed, oh ancient one, release your bounty. Airmed, of the *Tuatha de Danaan,* feed this earth. As once this was, let it return."

His face was pale as marble, his eyes dark as onyx. And the power flowed out of him onto, into, the trembling ground.

It opened.

Glenna heard Larkin suck in his breath, heard her own heartbeat rise up to drum in her ears. The plants rose up, leaves unfurling, blooms bursting. The thrill spun into her, released itself of a laugh of pure delight.

Silvery sage, glossy needles of rosemary, tumbling carpets of thyme and camomile, bay and rue, delicate spears of lavender, and more spread out of the ground and into the misting rain.

The garden formed a Celtic knot, she saw, with narrow loops and pathways to make harvesting easier.

As the wind died, as the earth stilled, Larkin blew out a long breath. "Well, that's some damn fine farming."

She laid a hand on Larkin's shoulder. "It's lovely, Hoyt. Some of the prettiest magic I've ever seen. Blessed be."

He pulled his sword out of the ground. The heart that had opened to make the magic was sore as a bruise. "Take what you need, but be quick. We've been out long enough."

She used her bolline, and worked with efficiency, though she wished she could linger, just enjoy the work.

The scents surrounded her. And what she harvested, she knew, would be only more powerful for the manner of their becoming.

The man who'd touched her in the night, who'd held her in the morning, had more power than any she'd ever know. Any she'd ever imagined.

"This is something I miss in the city," she commented. "I do a lot of windowsill pots, but it's just not the same as real gardening."

Hoyt said nothing, simply watched her—bright hair sparkling with rain, slim white hands brushing through the green. It closed a fist over his heart, just one quick squeeze and release.

When she stood, her arms full, her eyes laughing with the wonder of it, that heart tipped in his breast and fell as if an arrow had pierced it.

Bewitched, he thought. She had bewitched him. A woman's magic always aimed first for the heart.

"I can get quite a bit done with these." She tossed her head to swing back her damp hair. "And have enough left to season a nice soup for dinner."

"Best take them in then. We've movement to the west." Larkin nodded toward the west edge of the woods. "Just watching for now."

Bewitched, Hoyt thought again as he turned. He'd forgotten his watch, spellbound by her.

"I count half a dozen," Larkin continued, his voice cool and steady. "Though there may be more hanging back. Hoping to lure us, I'm thinking, into going after them. So they'll be more, aye, more hanging back to cut us down as we come."

"We've done what we need for the morning," Hoyt began, then thought better of it. "But no point letting them think they've pushed us back inside. Moira," he said, lifting his voice enough to carry to her, "can you take one out at this distance?"

"Which one would you like?"

Amused, he lifted a shoulder. "Your choice. Let's give them a bit of something to think about."

He'd barely uttered the words when the arrow flew, and a second so quickly after he thought he imagined it. There were two screams, one melding into the next. And where there had been six there were four—and those four rushed back into the cover of the woods.

"Two would give them more than a bit to think about." With a grim smile, Moira readied another arrow. "I can wing a few back into the woods, drive them back more if you like."

"Don't waste your wood."

Cian stepped to the window behind her. He looked rumpled and mildly irritated. Moira automatically stepped aside. "Wouldn't be wasted if they struck home."

"They'll move on for now. If they were here for more than a nuisance, they'd have charged while they had the numbers."

He walked past her to the side door, and out.

"Past your bedtime, isn't it?" Glenna said.

"I'd like to know who could sleep through all this. Felt like a bleeding earthquake." He studied the garden. "Your work, I assume," he said to Hoyt.

"No." The bitterness from the wound inside him eked out. "My mother's."

"Well, next time you've a bit of landscaping in mind, let me know so I don't wonder if the house is coming down on my ears. How many did you take out?"

"Five. Moira took four." Larkin sheathed his sword. "The other was mine."

He glanced back toward the window. "The little queen's racking up quite the score."

"We wanted to test the waters," Larkin told him, "and see to your horse."

"I'm grateful for that."

"I'm thinking I could take him out for a run now and again, if you wouldn't mind it."

"I wouldn't, and Vlad could use it."

"Vlad?" Glenna repeated.

"Just my little in joke. If the excitement's over, I'll be going back to bed."

"I need a word with you." Hoyt waited until Cian met his eyes. "Privately."

"And would this private word require standing about in the rain?"

"We'll walk."

"Suit yourself." Then he smiled at Glenna. "You look rosy this morning."

"And damp. There are plenty of dry, private places inside, Hoyt."

"I want the air."

There was a moment of humming silence. "He's a slow one. She's waiting to be kissed, so she'll worry less about you getting your throat ripped out because you want a walk in the rain."

"Go inside." Though he wasn't entirely comfortable with the public display, Hoyt took Glenna's chin in his hand, kissed her lightly on the lips. "I'll be fine enough."

Larkin drew his sword again, offered it to Cian. "Better armed than not."

"Words to live by." Then he leaned down, gave Glenna a quick, cocky kiss himself. "I'll be fine, as well."

They walked in silence, and with none of the camaraderie Hoyt remembered they'd shared. Times, he mused, they'd been able to know the other's mind without a word spoken. Now his brother's thoughts were barred to him, as he imagined his were to Cian.

"You kept the roses, but let the herb garden die. It was one of her greatest pleasures."

"The roses have been replaced, I can't count the times, since I acquired the place. The herbs? Gone before I bought the property."

"It's not property as the place you have in New York. It's home."

"It is to you." Hoyt's anger rolled off Cian's back like the rain. "If you expect more than I can or will give, you'll be in a constant state of disappointment. It's my money that bought the land and the house that sits on it, and mine that goes to maintaining both. I'd think you'd be in a better humor this morning, after romping with the pretty witch last night."

"Careful where you step," Hoyt said softly.

"I've good footing." And he couldn't resist treading on tender ground. "She's a prime piece, and no mistake. But I've had a few centuries more experience with women than you. There's more than lust in those striking green eyes of hers. She sees a future with them. And what, I wonder, will you do about that?"

"It's not your concern."

"Not in the least, no, but it's entertaining to speculate, particularly when I haven't a woman of my own to divert me at the moment. She's no round-heeled village girl happy with a roll in the hay and a trinket. She'll want and expect more of you, as women, particularly clever women, tend to."

Instinctively he glanced up, checking the cloud cover. Irish weather was tricky, he knew, and the sun could decide to spill out along with the rain. "Do you think if you survive these three months, satisfy your gods, to ask them for the right to take her back with you?"

"Why does it matter to you?"

"Not everyone asks a question because the answer matters. Can't you see her, tucked into your cottage on the cliffs in Kerry? No electricity, no running water, no Saks around the corner. Cooking your dinner in a pot on the fire. Likely shorten her life expectancy by half given the lack of health care and nutrition, but well then, anything for love."

"What do you know of it?" Hoyt snapped. "You're not capable of love."

"Oh, you'd be wrong about that. My kind can love, deeply, even desperately. Certainly unwisely, which it appears we have in common. So you won't take her back, for that would be the selfish thing. You're much too holy, too pure for that. And enjoy the role of martyr too much as well. So you'll leave her here to pine for you. I might amuse myself by offering her some comfort, and seeing as we share a resemblance, I wager she'll take it. And me."

The blow knocked him back, but not down. He tasted blood, the gorgeous burn of it, then swiped a hand over his bleeding mouth. It had taken longer than he'd assumed it would to bait his brother.

"Well now, that's been a long time coming, for both of us." He tossed his sword aside as Hoyt had. "Let's have a go then."

Cian's fist moved so fast it was only a blur—a blur that had stars exploding in front of Hoyt's eyes. And his nose fountaining blood. Then they charged each other like rams.

Cian took one in the kidneys, and a second strike had his ears ringing. He'd forgotten Hoyt could fight like the devil when provoked. He ducked a jab and sent Hoyt down with a kick to the midsection. And found himself on his ass as his brother slashed out his legs and took his feet out from under him.

He could have been up in a fingersnap, ended it, but his blood was hot. And heated, preferred a grapple.

They rolled over the ground, punching, cursing while the rain soaked them through to the skin. Elbows and fists rammed into flesh, cracked against bone.

Then Cian reared back with a hiss and flash of fangs. Hoyt saw the burn sear into his brother's hand, in the shape of his cross.

"Fuck me," Cian muttered and sucked on burned flesh and welling blood. "I guess you need a weapon to best me."

"Aye, fuck you. I don't need anything but my own fists." Hoyt reached up, had nearly yanked off the chain. Then dropped his hand when he realized the utter stupidity of it.

"This is fine, isn't it?" He spat out the words, and some blood with it. "This is just fine. Brawling like a couple of street rats, and leaving ourselves open to anything that comes. If anything had been nearby, we'd be dead."

"Already am—and speak for yourself."

"This isn't what I want, trading blows with you." Though the fight was still on his face as he swiped blood from his mouth. "It serves nothing."

"Felt good though."

Hoyt's swollen lips twitched, and the leading edge of his temper dulled. "It did, that's the pure truth. Holy martyr, my ass."

"Knew that would get under your skin."

"Sure you always knew how to get there. If we can't be brothers, Cian, what are we?"

Cian sat as he was, absently rubbing at the grass and bloodstains on his shirt. "If you win, you'll be gone in a few months. Or I'll see you die. Do you know how many I've seen die?"

"If time's short, it should be more important."

"You know nothing of time." He got to his feet. "You want to walk? Come on then, and learn something of time."

He walked on through the drenching wet so that Hoyt was forced to fall in beside him.

"Is it all still in your hands? The land?"

"Most of it. Some was sold off a few centuries ago—and some was taken by the English during one of the wars, and given to some crony of Cromwell."

"Who is Cromwell?"

"Was. A right bastard, who spent considerable time and effort burning and raping Ireland for the British royals. Politics and wars—gods, humans and demons can't seem to get by without them. I convinced one of the man's sons, after he'd inherited, to sell it back to me. At quite a good price."

"Convinced him? You killed him."

"And what if I did?" Cian said wearily. "It was long ago."

"Is that how you came by your wealth? Killing?"

"I've had nine hundred years and more to fill the coffers, and have done so in a variety of ways. I like money, and I've always had a head for finance."

"Aye, you have."

"There were lean years in the beginning. Decades of them, but I came around. I traveled. It's a large and fascinating world, and I like having chunks of it. Which is why I don't care for the notion of Lilith pulling her own sort of Cromwell."

"Protecting your investment," Hoyt said.

"I am. I will. I earned what I have. I'm fluent in fifteen languages—a handy business asset."

"Fifteen?" It felt easier now, the walking, the talking. "You used to butcher even Latin."

"Nothing but time to learn, and more yet to enjoy the fruits. I enjoy them quite a bit."

"I don't understand you. She took your life, your humanity."

"And gave me eternity. While I may not be particularly grateful to her as it wasn't done for my benefit, I don't see the point in spending that eternity sulking about it. My existence is long, and this is what you and your kind have."

He gestured toward a graveyard. "A handful of years, then nothing but dirt and dust."

There was a stone ruin overcome by vines sharp with thorns and black with berries. The end wall remained and rose in a peak. Figures had been carved into it like a frame, and had been buffed nearly smooth again by time and weather.

Flowers, even small shrubs forced their way through the cracks with feathery purple heads drooping now, heavy from the rain.

"A chapel? Mother spoke of building one."

"And one was built," Cian confirmed. "This is what's left of it. And them, and the ones who came after. Stones and moss and weeds."

Hoyt only shook his head. Stones had been plunged into the ground or set upon it to mark the dead. Now he moved among them, over uneven ground where that ground had heaved, time and again, and the tall grass was slick with wet.

Like the carving on the ruin, the words etched into some of the stones were worn nearly smooth, and the stones bloomed with moss and lichen. Others he could read; names he didn't know. Michael Thomas McKenna, beloved husband of Alice. Departed this earth the sixth of May, eighteen hundred and twenty-five. And Alice, who'd joined him some six years after. Their children, one who'd left the world only days after coming into it, and three others.

They'd lived and died this Thomas, this Alice, centuries after he'd been born. And nearly two centuries before he stood here, reading their names.

Time was fluid, he thought, and those who passed through it so fragile.

Crosses rose up, and rounded stones tilted. Here and there weedy gardens grew over the graves as if they were tended by careless ghosts. And he felt them, those ghosts, with every step he took.

A rose bush, heavy with rich red blooms grew lushly behind a stone no taller than his knees. Its petals were sheened like velvet. It was a quick strike to the heart, with the dull echoing pain behind it.

He knew he stood at his mother's grave.

"How did she die?"

"Her heart stopped. It's the usual way."

At his sides, Hoyt's fists bunched. "Can you be so cold, even here, even now?"

"Some said grief stopped it. Perhaps it did. He went first." Cian gestured to a second stone. "A fever took him around the equinox, the autumn after . . . I left. She followed three years after."

"Our sisters?"

"There, all there." He gestured at the grouping of stones. "And the generations that followed them—who remained in Clare, in any case. There was a famine, and it rotted the land. Scores died like flies, or fled to America, to Australia, to England, anywhere but here. There was suffering, pain, plague, pillage. Death."

"Nola?"

For a moment Cian said nothing, then he continued in a tone of deliberate carelessness. "She lived into her sixties— a good, long life for that era for a woman, a human. She had five children. Or it might've been six."

"Was she happy?"

"How could I say?" Cian said impatiently. "I never spoke to her again. I wasn't welcome in the house I now own. Why would I be?"

"She said I would come back."

"Well, you have, haven't you?"

Hoyt's blood was cool now, and eking toward cold. "There's no grave for me here. If I go back, will there be? Will it change what's here?"

"The paradox. Who's to say? In any case, you vanished, or so it's told. Depending on the version. You're a bit of a legend in these parts. Hoyt of Clare—though Kerry likes to claim you as well. Your song and story doesn't reach as high as a god, or even that of Merlin, but you've a notch in some guidebooks. The stone circle just to the north, the one you used? It's attributed to you now, and called Hoyt's Dance."

Hoyt didn't know whether to be embarrassed or flattered. "It's the Dance of the Gods, and it was here long before me."

"So goes truth, particularly when fantasy's shinier. The caves beneath the cliffs where you tossed me into the sea? It's said you lie there, deep beneath the rock, guarded by faeries, under the land where you would stand to call the lightning and the wind."

"Foolishness."

"An amusing claim to fame."

For a time they said nothing, just stood, two men of striking physical similarity, in a rainy world of the dead.

"If I'd gone with you that night, as you asked me, ridden out with you, to stop as you said at the pub in the village. A drink and a tumble . . ." Hoyt's throat went hot as he remembered it. "But I had work on my mind and didn't want company. Not even yours. I had only to go, and none of this would be."

Cian slicked back his dripping hair. "You take a lot on yourself, don't you? But then, you always did. If you'd gone, it's likely she'd have had us both—so it's true enough, none of this would be."

What he saw on Hoyt's face brought the fury rushing back into him. "Do I ask for your guilt? You weren't my keeper then or now. I stand here as I did centuries ago, and barring bad luck—or my own idiocy in letting you drag me into this thing and the serious risk of a stake through the heart, I'll stand here again centuries after. And you, Hoyt, food for the worms. So which of us has destiny smiled on?"

"What is my power if I can't change that one night, that one moment? I'd have gone with you. I'd have died for you."

Cian's head whipped up, and on his face was the same hot temper it had held in battle. "Don't put your death, or your regrets, on me."

But there was no answering anger in Hoyt. "And you would have died for me. For any one of them." He spread his arms to encompass the graves.

"Once."

"You are half of me. Nothing you are, nothing that was done changes that. You know it as I know it. Even more than blood, more than bone. We are, beneath all that, what we ever were."

"I can't *exist* in this world feeling this." Emotion swirled now, into his face, his voice. "I can't grieve for what I am, or for you. Or for them. And damn you, goddamn you for bringing me back to it."

"I love you. It's bound in me."

"What you love is gone."

No, Hoyt thought, he was looking at the heart of what he'd loved. He could see it in the roses his brother had planted over their mother's grave.

"You're standing here with me and the spirits of our family. You're not so changed, Cian, or you would not have done this." He touched the petals of a rose. "You could not have done it."

Cian's eyes were suddenly ageless, filled with the torment of centuries. "I've seen death. Thousands upon thousands. Age and sickness, murder and war. I didn't see theirs. And this was all I could do for them."

When Hoyt moved his hand, the petals of an overblown rose spilled down and scattered on his mother's grave. "It was enough."

Cian looked down at the hand Hoyt held out to him. He sighed once, deeply. "Well, damn to us both then," he said and clasped hands with his brother. "We've been out long enough, no point in tempting fate any longer. And I want my bed."

They started back the way they'd come.

"Do you miss the sun?" Hoyt wondered. "Walking in it, feeling it on your face?"

"They've found it gives you cancer of the skin."

"Huh." Hoyt considered it. "Still, the warmth of it on a summer morning."

"I don't think about it. I like the night."

Perhaps it wasn't the time to ask Cian to allow him to do a little experimental bloodletting.

"What do you do in these businesses of yours? And with your leisure? Do you—"

"I do as I please. I like to work; it's satisfying. And makes play more appealing. And it's not possible to catch up on several centuries during a morning's walk in the rain, even if I were inclined." He rested the sword on his shoulder. "But likely you'll catch your death from it, and spare me the questions in any case."

"I'm made of stronger stuff than that," Hoyt said, cheerfully now, "as I proved when I bashed your face not long ago. You've a fine bruise on your jaw."

"It'll be gone quicker than yours, unless the witch intervenes again. In any case, I was holding back."

"Bollocks to that."

The shadows that always fell on him when he visited that graveyard began to lift. "If I'd come at you full, we'd be digging your grave back there."

"Let's go again, then."

Cian slanted Hoyt a look. Memories, the pleasure of them so long suppressed, crept back on him. "Another time. And when I'm finished pounding you, you won't be up to romping with the redhead."

Hoyt grinned. "I've missed you."

Cian stared ahead as the house peeked through the trees. "The bloody hell of it is I've missed you, too."

Chapter 14

With a crossbow armed and ready by her side, Glenna kept watch from the tower window. She'd considered the fact that she'd had very little practice with that particular weapon, and that her aim could be called into serious question.

But she couldn't just sit up there, unarmed and wringing her hands like some helpless female. If the damn sun would come out, she wouldn't have to worry. More than that, she thought with a little hiss, if the McKenna boys hadn't wandered off—obviously to snarl at each other in private—she wouldn't have these images in her head of them being ripped to pieces by a pack of vampires.

Pack? Herd? Gang?

What did it matter? They still had fangs and a bad attitude.

Where had they *gone*? And why had they been out, exposed and vulnerable, so long?

Maybe the pack/herd/gang had already ripped them to shreds and dragged their mutilated bodies off to . . . And oh, God, she wished she could turn off the video in her head for five damn minutes.

Most women just worried about their man getting mugged or run over by a bus. But oh no, *she* had to get herself tangled up with a guy at war with blood-sucking fiends.

Why couldn't she have fallen for a nice accountant or stockbroker?

She had thought of using her skill and the crystal to look for them. But it seemed . . . intrusive, she decided. And rude.

But if they weren't back in ten minutes, she was going to say screw manners and find them.

She hadn't thought through, not completely, the emotional turmoil Hoyt was experiencing, what he missed, and what he risked. More than the rest of them, she decided. She was thousands of miles away from her family, but not hundreds of years. He was in the home where he'd grown up, but it was no longer his home. And every day, every hour, was another reminder of that.

Bringing back his mother's herb garden had hurt him. She should have thought of that, too. Kept her mouth shut about what she'd needed and wanted. Just made a damn list and gone out to find or buy supplies.

She glanced back at some of the herbs she'd already bundled and hung to dry. Small things, everyday things could cause the most pain.

Now he was out there somewhere, in the rain, with his brother. The vampire. She didn't believe Cian would attack Hoyt—or didn't want to believe it. But if Cian were angry enough, pushed hard enough, could he control what must be natural urges?

She didn't know the answer.

Added to that, no one could be sure more of Lilith's forces were not out and about, just waiting for another chance.

It was probably silly to worry. They were two men of considerable power, men who knew the land. Neither of them were solely dependent on swords and daggers. Hoyt was armed, and he wore one of the crosses they'd conjured, so he was hardly defenseless.

And it proved a point, didn't it, the two of them being out, moving freely? It proved they wouldn't be held under siege.

No one else was worried, particularly. Moira was back in

the library, studying. Larkin and King were in the training area doing a weapon inventory. She was, undoubtedly, worked up about nothing.

Where the *hell* were they?

As she continued to scan, she spotted movement. Just shadows in the gloom. She grabbed the crossbow, ordered her fingers to stop shaking as she positioned it and herself in the narrow window.

"Just breathe," she told herself. "Just breathe. In and out, in and out."

That breath came out on a whoosh of relief when she saw Hoyt, Cian beside him. Trooping along, she noted, dripping wet, as if they had all the time in the world, and not a care in it.

Her brows drew together as they came closer. Was that blood on Hoyt's shirt, and a fresh bruise spreading under his right eye?

She leaned out, bumped the stone sill. And the arrow shot out of the bow with a deadly twang. She actually squealed. She'd hate herself for it later, but the purely female sound of shock and distress ripped out of her as the arrow sliced air and rain.

And landed, just a few inches short of the toe of Hoyt's boot.

Their swords were out, a blur of steel, as they pivoted back-to-back. Under other circumstances she would have admired the move, the sheer grace and rhythm of it, like a dance step. But at the moment, she was caught between mortification and horror.

"Sorry! Sorry!" She leaned out farther, waved her arm frantically as she shouted. "It was me. It got away from me. I was just . . ." Oh hell with it. "I'm coming down."

She left the weapon where it was, vowing to take a full hour of practice with it before she shot at anything but a target again. Before she set off in a run, she heard the unmistakable sound of male laughter. A quick glance showed her it was Cian, all but doubled over with it. Hoyt simply stood, staring up at the window.

As she swung down the stairs, Larkin came out of the training room. "Trouble?"

"No, no. Nothing. Everything's fine. It's nothing at all."
She could actually feel the blood rise up to heat her cheeks
as she dashed for the main floor.

They were coming in the front door, shaking themselves
like wet dogs as she sprinted down the last steps.

"I'm sorry. I'm so sorry."

"Remind me not to piss you off, Red," Cian said easily.
"You might aim for my heart and shoot me in the balls."

"I was just keeping watch for you, and I must've pulled
the trigger by mistake. Which I wouldn't have done if the
two of you hadn't been gone so damn long and had me so
worried."

"That's what I love about women." Cian slapped his
brother's shoulder. "They damn near kill you, but in the end
it's your own fault. Good luck with that. I'm going to bed."

"I need to check your burns."

"Nag, nag, nag."

"And what happened? Were you attacked? Your mouth's
bleeding—yours, too," she said to Hoyt. "And your eye's
damn near swollen shut."

"No, we weren't attacked." There was a world of exasper-
ation in his voice. "Until you nearly shot me in the foot."

"Your faces are all banged up, and your clothes are
filthy—ripped. If you weren't . . ." It came to her, when she
saw the expressions on their faces. She had a brother of her
own, after all. "You punched each other? *Each other?*"

"He hit me first."

She gave Cian a look that would have withered stone.
"Well, that's just fine, isn't it? Didn't we go through all this
yesterday? Didn't we talk about infighting, how destructive
and useless it is?"

"I guess we're going to bed without our supper."

"Don't get smart with me." She jabbed a finger into Cian's
chest. "I'm here worried half sick, and the two of you are out
there wrestling around like a couple of idiot puppies."

"You nearly put an arrow in my foot," Hoyt reminded her.
"I think we're quits on foolish behavior for one day."

She only hissed out a breath. "Into the kitchen, both of
you. I'll do something about those cuts and bruises. Again."

"I'm having my bed," Cian began.

"Both of you. Now. You don't want to mess with me at the moment."

As she sailed off, Cian rubbed a finger gently on his split lip. "It's been a long while, but I don't recall you having a particular fondness for bossy women."

"I didn't, previously. But I understand them well enough to know we might as well be after letting her have her way on this. And the fact is, my eye's paining me."

When they came in, Glenna was setting what she needed out on the table. She had the kettle on the boil, and her sleeves rolled up.

"Do you want blood?" she said to Cian, with enough frost in the words to have him clearing his throat.

It amazed him that he actually felt chagrined. It was a sensation he hadn't felt in . . . too long to remember. Obviously living so closely with humans was a bad influence.

"The tea you're making will do, thanks."

"Take off your shirt."

There was a smart comment on the tip of his tongue, she could all but see it. He proved himself a wise man by swallowing it.

He stripped it off, sat.

"I'd forgotten about the burns." Hoyt examined them now. There was no longer any blistering, and they'd gone down to a dull, ugly red. "If I'd remembered," he said as he sat across from Cian, "I'd have put more blows into your chest."

"Typical," Glenna said under her breath, and was ignored.

"You don't fight altogether the way you used to. You use your feet more, and elbows." And Hoyt could still feel the aching result of them. "Then there's that leaping off the ground."

"Martial arts. I have black belts in several of them. Master status," Cian explained. "You need to put more time into training."

Hoyt rubbed his sore ribs. "And so I will."

Weren't they chummy all of a sudden? Glenna thought. What was it about men that made them decide to be pals after they'd smashed their fists into each other's faces?

She poured hot water into the pot, and while it steeped came to the table with her salve.

"I would've said three weeks to heal with what I can do, considering the extent of the burns." She sat, slicked salve on her fingers. "I'm amending that to three days."

"We can be hurt, and seriously. But unless it's a killing blow, we heal—and quickly."

"Lucky for you, especially as you've got a mass of nice bruising to go with the burns. But you don't regenerate," she continued as she applied the salve. "If, say, we were to cut off one of their arms, it wouldn't grow back."

"There's a gruesome and interesting thought. No. I've never heard of anything like that happening."

"Then if we can't get to the heart or the head, we can go for a limb."

She went to the sink to wash the salve from her hands, and make cold packs for the bruising. "Here." She handed one to Hoyt. "Hold that on your eye."

He sniffed at it, then complied. "You shouldn't have worried."

Cian winced. "Bad tact. Wiser to say: 'Ah, my love, we're sorry we worried you. We were selfish and inconsiderate, should likely be flogged for it. We hope you'll forgive us.' Thicken the brogue a bit as well. Women are fools for brogues."

"Then kiss her feet, I suppose."

"Actually, you aim for the ass. Ass kissing is a tradition that never goes out of style. You'll need patience with him, Glenna. Hoyt's still working on the learning curve."

She brought the tea to the table, then surprised them both when she laid a hand on Cian's cheek. "And you're going to teach him how to deal with the modern woman?"

"Well, he's a bit pitiful, is all."

Her lips curved as she lowered her head, brushed them over Cian's. "You're forgiven. Drink your tea."

"Just that easy?" Hoyt complained. "He gets a pat on the cheek and a kiss with it? You didn't nearly put an arrow into him."

"Women are a constant mystery." Cian spoke quietly.

"And one of the wonders of the world. I'll take this up with me." He got to his feet. "I'm wanting some dry clothes."

"Drink all of it." Glenna spoke without turning as she took up another bottle. "It'll help."

"I will then. Let me know if he doesn't learn fast enough to suit you. I wouldn't quibble with being second choice."

"That's just his way," Hoyt told her when Cian left the room. "A kind of teasing."

"I know. So you made friends again while you were bloodying each other."

"It's true enough I hit him first. I spoke to him of our mother, and the garden, and he was cold. Even though I could see what was under that cold, I . . . well, I lashed out, and . . . After, he took me to where our family's buried. And there you have it."

She turned now, and all the pity in her heart swirled into her eyes. "It must've been hard for both of you to be there."

"It makes it real to me, that as I sit here now, they're gone. It didn't seem real before. Not solid and real."

She moved to him, dabbed her tincture on his facial bruises. "And for him, to have lived all this time with no family at all. Another cruelty of what was done to him. To all of them. We don't think of that do we, when we talk about war, and how to destroy them? They were people once, just like Cian."

"They mean to kill us, Glenna. Every one of us that has a heartbeat."

"I know. I know. Something drained them of humanity. But they were human once, Hoyt, with families, lovers, hopes. We don't think of that. Maybe we can't."

She brushed the hair back from his face. A nice accountant, she thought again. A stockbroker. How ridiculous, how ordinary. She had, right here, the amazing.

"I think fate put Cian here, this way, so we understand there's a weight to what we're doing. So that we know, at the end of the day, we've done what we had to do. But not without cost."

She stepped back. "That'll have to do. Try to keep your face from walking into any more fists."

She started to turn, but he took her hand, rising as he drew her back to him. His lips took hers with utter tenderness.

"I think fate put you here, Glenna, to help me understand it's not just death and blood and violence. There's such beauty, such kindness in the world. And I have it." He wrapped his arms around her. "I have it here."

She indulged herself, letting her head rest on his shoulder. She wanted to ask what they'd have when it was over, but she knew it was important, even essential, to take each day as it came.

"We should work." She drew back. "I've got some ideas about creating a safe zone around the house. A protected area where we can move around more freely. And I think Larkin's right about sending out scouts. If we can get to the caves during the day, we might be able to find something out. Even set traps."

"Your mind's been busy."

"I need to keep it that way. I'm not as afraid if I'm thinking, if I'm doing."

"Then we work."

"Moira might be able to help once we have a start," Glenna added as they left the kitchen. "She's reading everything she can get her hands on, so she'd be our prime data source—information," she explained. "And she has some power. It's raw and untrained, but it's there."

While Glenna and Hoyt closed themselves in the tower and the house was quiet, Moira pored over a volume on demon lore in the library. It was fascinating, she thought. So many different theories and legends. She considered it her task to pick them apart for truth.

Cian would know it, or some of it, she concluded. Centuries of existence was plenty of time to learn. And anyone who filled such a room with books sought and respected knowledge. But she wasn't ready to ask him—wasn't sure she would ever be.

If he wasn't like the creatures she read of, those that sought human blood night after night—and thirsted not just for that blood, but the kill—what was he? Now he prepared to make war against what he was, and she didn't understand it.

She needed to learn more, about what they fought, about Cian, about all the others. How could you understand, and then trust, what you didn't know?

She made notes, copious notes, on the paper she'd found in one of the drawers of the big desk. She loved the paper, and the writing instrument. The pen, she corrected, that held the ink inside its tube. She wondered if she could smuggle some of the paper and pens back to Geall.

She closed her eyes. She missed home, and the missing was like a constant ache in her belly. She'd written down her wish, sealed the paper, and would leave it among her things for Larkin to find if it came to pass.

If she died on this side, she wanted her body taken back to Geall for burial.

She continued to write with thoughts circling in her head. There was one she kept coming back to, nibbling at. She would have to find a way to ask Glenna if it could be done—if the others would agree to it, if it could.

Was there a way to seal off the portal, to close the door to Geall?

With a sigh, she looked toward the window. Was it raining in Geall now, too, or was the sun shining on her mother's grave?

She heard footsteps approach, and danced her fingers over the hilt of her dagger. She let them fall away when King came in. For reasons she couldn't name, she felt easier with him than the others.

"Got something against chairs, Shorty?"

Her lips twitched. She liked the way words rumbled out of him, like rocks down a stony hill. "No, but I like sitting on the floor. Is it time for more training?"

"Taking a break." He sat in a wide chair, a huge mug of coffee in his hand. "Larkin could go all damn day. Up there now, practicing some katas."

"I like the katas. It's like dancing."

"Just make sure you're doing the leading if you're dancing with a vampire."

Idly, she turned the page of a book. "Hoyt and Cian fought."

King took a drink. "Oh yeah? Who won?"

"I think neither. I saw them coming back, and from their faces and limps, it seemed to be a draw."

"How do you know they were fighting with each other? Maybe they were attacked."

"No." She traced her fingers over words. "I hear things."

"You got big ears, Shorty."

"So my mother always said. They made peace between them—Hoyt and his brother."

"That eliminates a complication—if it lasts." Given their personalities, King figured a full truce between the brothers had the life expectancy of a fruit fly. "What do you expect to find out in all these books?"

"Everything. Sooner or later. Do you know how the first vampyre came to be? There are different versions in the books."

"Never thought about it."

"I did—do. One is like a love story. Long ago, when the world was young, demons were dying out. Before, long before that, there were more. Scores of them, walking the world. But man grew stronger and smarter, and the time of the demons was passing."

Because he was a man who enjoyed stories, he settled back. "Kind of an evolution."

"A change, yes. Many demons went beneath the world, to hide or to sleep. There was more magic then, because people didn't turn from it. Man and the faeries forged an alliance to wage war on the demons, to drive them under for once and all. There was one who was poisoned, and slowly dying. He loved a mortal woman, and this was forbidden even in the demon world."

"So man doesn't have a lock on bigotry. Keep going," he said when she paused.

"So the dying demon took the mortal woman from her home. He was obsessed with her, and his last wish was to mate with her before his end."

"Not so different from men in that area then."

"I think, perhaps, all living creatures crave love and pleasure. And this physical act that represents life."

"And guys want to get off."

She lost her rhythm. "Get off what?"

He nearly spewed coffee, choked instead. He waved a hand at her as his laugh rumbled out. "Don't mind me. Finish the story."

"Ah . . . Well, he took her deep into the forest and had his way with her, and she, like a woman under a spell, wanted his touch. To try to save his life, she offered her blood to him. So she was bitten, and drank his blood in turn, as this was another kind of mating. She died with him, but she did not cease to exist. She became the thing we call vampyre."

"A demon for love."

"Aye, I suppose. In vengeance against men, she hunted them, fed from them, changed them, to make more of her kind. And still she grieved for her demon lover, and killed herself with sunlight."

"Doesn't quite hit *Romeo and Juliet,* does it?"

"A play. I saw the book of it here, on the shelf. I haven't yet read it." It would take years to read all the books in such a room she thought as she toyed with the end of her braid.

"But I read another tale of the vampyre. It tells of a demon, mad and ill from a spell even more evil than it, thirsting wildly for human blood. He fed, and the more he fed, the more mad he became. He died after mixing his blood with a mortal, and the mortal became vampyre. The first of its kind."

"I guess you like the first version better."

"No, I like truth better, and I think the second is the truth. What mortal woman would love a demon?"

"Led a sheltered life back in your world, haven't you? Where I come from people fall for monsters—or what others consider monsters—all the time. Ain't no logic with love, Shorty. It just is."

She tossed her braid behind her back in a kind of shrug. "Well, if I love, I won't be stupid about it."

"Hope I'm around long enough to see you eat those words."

She closed the book, drew up her legs. "Do you love someone?"

"A woman? Been close a few times, and that's how I know I didn't make it all the way to the bull's-eye."

"How do you know?"

"When you hit the center, Shorty, you're down for the count. But it's fun shooting for it. Gonna take a special woman to get past this." He tapped a finger to his face.

"I like your face. It's so big and dark."

He laughed so hard he nearly spilled his coffee. "You got that one right."

"And you're strong. You speak well and you cook. You have loyalty to your friends."

That big dark face softened. "Want to apply for the position of love of my life?"

She smiled back at him, at ease. "I'm thinking I'm not your bull's-eye. If I'm to be queen, I must marry one day. Have children. I hope it won't be only duty, but that I find what my mother found in my father. What they found in each other. I'd want him to be strong, and loyal."

"And handsome."

She moved her shoulders, because she did hope that as well. "Do women here only look for beauty?"

"Couldn't say, but it don't hurt. Guy looks like Cian, for instance, he's got to beat them off with sticks."

"Then why is he lonely?"

He studied her over the rim of his mug. "Good question."

"How did you come to meet him?"

"He saved my life."

Moira wrapped her arms around her legs and settled in. There was little she liked more than a story. "How?"

"I was in the wrong place at the wrong time. Bad neighborhood in East L.A." He drank again, lifted a shoulder in a half shrug. "See, my old man took off before I was born, and my old lady had what we'll call a little problem with illegal substances. OD'd. Overdosed. Took too much of some bad shit."

"She died." Everything in her mourned for him. "I'm sorry."

"Bad choices, bad luck. You gotta figure some people come into the world set on tossing their life into the shitter. She was one of them. So I'm on the street, doing what I can to get by, and keep out of the system. I'm heading to this place I know. It's dark, steaming hot. I just wanted a place to sleep for the night."

"You had no home."

"I had the street. A couple of guys were hanging out on the stoop, probably waiting to make a score. I got my bad attitude on. Need to get by them to get where I want to go. Car rolls up, blasts at them. Drive-by," he said. "Like an ambush. I'm caught in it. Bullet grazes my head. More coming, and I know I'm going to be dead. Somebody grabs me, pulls me back. Things got blurry, but it felt like I was flying. Then I was someplace else."

"Where?"

"Fancy hotel room. I'd never seen anything like it outside of movies." He crossed his big, booted feet as he remembered. "Big-ass bed, big enough for ten people, and I'm lying on it. Head hurts like a mother, which is why I don't figure I'm dead and this is heaven. He comes out of the bathroom. Got his shirt off, and a fresh bandage on his shoulder. Got himself shot dragging me out of the cross fire."

"What did you do?"

"Nothing much, guess I was in shock. He sits down, studies me like I'm a frigging book. 'You're lucky,' he said, 'and stupid.' He's got that accent. I'm figuring he must be some rock star or something. The way he looks, the fancy voice, the fancy room. Truth is, I thought he was a perv, and he was going to want me to . . . Let's just say I was scared shitless. I was eight."

"You were a child?" Her eyes widened. "You were just a child?"

"I was eight," he repeated. "Grow up like I did, you aren't a kid long. He asks me what the hell I was doing out there, and I give him some sass. Trying to get some of my own back. He asks if I'm hungry, and I shoot back something like I ain't going to . . . perform any sexual favors for a goddamn meal. Orders a steak dinner, a bottle of wine, some soda pop.

And he tells me he isn't interested in buggering young boys. If I've got someplace I'd rather be, I should go there. Otherwise I can wait for the steak."

"You waited for the steak."

"Fucking A." He gave her a wink. "That was the start of it. He gave me food, and a choice. I could go back to where I'd been—no skin off his—or I could work for him. I took the job. Didn't know the job meant school. He gave me clothes, an education, self-respect."

"Did he tell you what he was?"

"Not then. Not long after though. I figured he was whacked, but I didn't much care. By the time I realized he was telling the truth, literal truth, I would've done anything for him. The man I was setting to be died on the street that night. He didn't turn me," King said quietly. "But he changed me."

"Why? Did you ever ask him why?"

"Yeah. That'd be for him to tell."

She nodded. The story itself was enough to think about.

"Break's about over," he announced. "We can get an hour's workout in. Toughen up that skinny ass of yours."

She grinned. "Or we could work with the bow. Improve that poor aim of yours."

"Come on, smart-ass." He frowned, glanced toward the doorway. "You hear something?"

"Like a knocking?" She shrugged, and because she tarried to straighten the books, was several paces behind him out of the room.

G lenna trotted down the steps. What little progress they were making she could leave to Hoyt for the time being. Someone had to see about the evening meal—and since she'd put her name on the list, she was elected. She could toss together a marinade for some chicken, then go back up for another hour.

A good meal would set the tone for a team meeting.

She'd just drop by the library, yank Moira away from the books for a cooking lesson while she was at it. Maybe it was sexist to put the only other woman next on the KP list, but she had to start somewhere.

The knock on the door made her jolt, then pass a nervous hand through her hair.

She nearly called up the stairs for Larkin or King, then shook her head. Talk about sexist. How was she going to fare in serious battle if she couldn't even open the door herself on a rainy afternoon?

It could be a neighbor, dropping by to pay a courtesy call. Or Cian's caretaker, stopping by to make sure they had everything they needed.

And a vampire couldn't enter the house, couldn't step over the threshold, unless she asked it in.

A highly unlikely event.

Still, she looked out the window first. She saw a young woman of about twenty—a pretty blonde in jeans and a bright red sweater. Her hair was pulled back into a tail that swung out of the back of a red cap. She was holding a map—seemed to be puzzling over it as she chewed on a thumbnail.

Someone's lost, Glenna thought, and the sooner she got her on her way and away from the house, the better for everyone.

The knock sounded again as she turned from the window.

She opened the door, careful to keep to her side of the threshold.

"Hello? Need some help?"

"Hello. Thank you, yes." There was relief, and a heavy dose of French in the woman's voice. "I am, ah, lost. *Excusez-moi,* my English, is not so good."

"That's okay. My French is fairly nonexistent. What can I do for you?"

"Ennis? *S'il vous plaît?* May you tell me how the road it goes to Ennis?"

"I'm not sure. I'm not from around here myself. I can look at the map." Glenna watched the woman's eyes as she held out a hand for it—her fingertips on her side of the door. "I'm Glenna. *Je suis* Glenna."

"Ah, *oui. Je m'apelle* Lora. I am in holiday, a student."

"That's nice."

"The rain." Lora held out a hand so rain drops splattered it. "I am lost in it, I think."

"Could happen to anyone. Let's have a look at your map, Lora. Are you by yourself?"

"Pardon?"

"Alone? Are you alone?"

"Oui. Mes amies—my friends—I have friends in Ennis, but I turn bad. Wrong?"

Oh no, Glenna thought. I really don't think so. "I'm surprised you could see the house from the main road. We're so far back."

"Sorry?"

Glenna smiled brilliantly. "I bet you'd like to come in, have a nice cup of tea while we figure out your route." She saw the light come into the blonde's baby blue eyes. "But you can't, can you? Just can't step through the door."

"Je ne comprendrez pas."

"Bet you do, but in case my Spidey sense is off today, you need to go back to the main road, turn left. Left," she repeated and started to gesture.

King's shout behind her had her spinning around. Her hair swung, the tips of it going beyond the doorway. There was an explosion of pain as her hair was viciously yanked, as her body flew out of the house and hit the ground with a bone-wracking thud.

There were two more, and they came out of nowhere. Instinct had Glenna reaching for her cross with one hand, kicking out blindly with her feet. Movement was a blur, and she tasted blood in her mouth. She saw King slicing at one with a knife, holding it off while he shouted at her to get up, to get into the house.

She stumbled to her feet in time to see them surround him, closing in. She heard herself screaming, and thought—hoped—she heard answering shouts from the house. But they would be too late. The vampires were on King like dogs.

"French bitch," Glenna spat out, and charged the blonde. Her fist cracked bone, and there was satisfaction in that, and the sudden spurt of blood. Then she was once more hurdling back, and this time when she hit, her vision went gray.

She felt herself being dragged, struggled. It was Moira's voice buzzing in her ear.

"I have you. I have you. You're back inside. Lie still."

"No. King. They've got King."

Moira was already dashing out, dagger drawn. As Glenna pushed herself up, Larkin vaulted over her and through the door.

Glenna gained her knees, then swayed to her feet. Sickness burned its acrid taste at the base of her throat as she once more stumbled to the door.

So fast, she thought dully, how could anything move that fast? As Moira and Larkin gave chase, they bundled the still struggling King into a black van. They were gone before she got out of the house.

Larkin's body shimmered, shuddered, and became a cougar. The cat flashed after the van and out of sight.

Glenna went to her knees on the wet grass, and retched.

"Get inside." Hoyt grabbed her arm with his free hand. In his other was a sword. "Inside the house. Glenna, Moira, get inside."

"It's too late," Glenna cried, while tears of horror spilled out of her eyes. "They have King." She looked up, saw Cian standing behind Hoyt. "They took him. They took King."

Chapter 15

"In the house," Hoyt repeated. As he started to drag Glenna inside, Cian shoved past him and flew toward the stables.

"Go with him." Glenna struggled past the tears and pain. "Oh, God, go with him. Hurry."

Leaving her, shaking and bleeding, was the hardest thing he'd ever done.

The door where the black machine sat was open. His brother tossed weapons carelessly inside.

"Will this catch them?" Hoyt demanded.

Cian barely spared him a glance with eyes rimmed red. "Stay with the women. I don't need you."

"Need or not, you have me. How the bloody hell do I get inside this thing?" He fought with the door, and when it opened, folded himself inside it.

Cian said nothing, only got behind the wheel. The machine let out a vicious roar, seemed to quiver like a stallion poised to run. And then they were flying. Stones and sod spewed into the air like missiles. Hoyt caught a glimpse of Glenna in the doorway, holding the arm he feared might be broken.

He prayed to all the gods he'd see her again.

She watched him go, and wondered if she'd sent her lover to his death. "Get all the weapons you can carry," she told Moira.

"You're hurt. Let me see to you."

"Get the weapons, Moira." She turned, her face fierce and bloodied. "Or do you intend for us to stay here like children while the men do the fighting?"

Moira nodded. "Do you want blade or bow?"

"Both."

Glenna went quickly to the kitchen, gathered bottles. Her arm was screaming, so she quickly did what she could to block the pain. This was Ireland, she thought grimly, and that should mean plenty of churches. In the churches would be holy water. She carried the bottles, along with a butcher knife and a bundle of garden stakes to the van.

"Glenna." With a longbow and crossbow slung over her shoulders, two swords in her hand, Moira crossed to the van. She put the weapons inside, then held up one of the silver crosses by its chain.

"This was up in the training room. I think it must be King's. He has no protection."

Glenna slammed the cargo door. "He has us."

Hedgerows and hills were no more than a blur through the gray curtain of rain. Hoyt saw other machines—cars, he reminded himself—traveling the wet road, and the edges of a village.

He saw cattle in fields, and sheep, and the ramble of stone fences. He saw nothing of Larkin, or the car that held King.

"Can you track them in this?" he asked Cian.

"No." He spun the wheel, sent up a flood of water. "They'll take him to Lilith. They'll keep him alive." He had to believe it. "And take him to Lilith."

"The caves?" Hoyt thought how long it had taken him to travel from his cliffs to Clare. But that had been on horseback, and he'd been wounded and feverish. Still the journey would take time. Too much time.

"Alive? Cian, why will they take him alive?"

"He'd be a prize to her. That's what he is, a prize. He's alive. She'd want the kill for herself. We can't be that far behind them. Can't be. And the Jag's faster than the bloody van they have him in."

"He won't be bitten. The cross will stop that."

"It won't stop a sword or an arrow. A fucking bullet. Guns and bows aren't the weapons of choice," he said almost to himself. "Too remote. We like close kills, and some tradition with it. We like to look in the eyes. She'll want to torture him first. Wouldn't want it to be quick." His hands tightened on the wheel enough to bruise the leather. "Should buy us some time."

"Night's coming."

What Hoyt didn't say, and they both knew, was there would be more of them at night.

Cian swung around a sedan at a speed that had the Jag fishtailing on the slick road, then the tires bit in and he shot forward again. A flash of headlights in his eyes blinded him, but didn't slow him down. He had a moment to think: bloody tourists, as the oncoming car edged him over. Branches of hedgerows scraped and rattled over the side and windows of the Jag. Loose gravel spat out like stone bullets.

"We should've caught up with them by now. If they took another route, or she's got another hole . . ." Too many options, Cian thought, and pushed for more speed. "Can you do anything? A locator spell?"

"I haven't any . . ." He slapped a hand to the dash as Cian shot around another curve. "Wait." He gripped the cross he wore, pushed power into it. And bearing down, brought its light into his mind.

"Shield and symbol. Guide me. Give me sight."

He saw the cougar, running through the rain, the cross lashing like a silver whip around its throat.

"Larkin, he's close. Fallen behind us. Keeping to the fields. He's tiring." He searched, feeling with the light as if it were fingers. "Glenna—and Moira with her. They didn't stay in the house, they're moving. She's in pain."

"They can't help me. Where's King?"

"I can't find him. He's in the dark."

"Dead?"

"I don't know. I can't reach him."

Cian slammed on the brakes, wrenched the wheel. The Jag went into a sickening spin, revolving closer and closer to the black van that sat across the narrow road. There was a scream of tires and a dull thud as metal slapped metal.

Cian was out before the motion stopped, sword in hand. When he wrenched open the door of the van he found nothing. And no one.

"There's a woman here," Hoyt called out. "She's hurt."

Cursing, Cian rounded the van, yanked open the cargo doors. There was blood, he saw—human blood by its scent. But not enough for death.

"Cian, she's been bitten, but she's alive."

Cian glanced over his shoulder. He saw the woman lying on the road, blood seeping from the punctures in her neck. "Didn't drain her. Not enough time. Revive her. Bring her around," Cian ordered. "You can do it. Do it fast. They've taken her car, switched cars. Find out what she was driving."

"She needs help."

"Goddamn it, she'll live or she won't. Bring her around."

Hoyt laid his fingertips on the wounds, felt the burn. "Madam. Hear me. Wake and hear me."

She stirred, then her eyes flew open, the pupils big as moons. "Rory! Rory. Help me."

Roughly, Cian shoved Hoyt aside. He had some power of his own. "Look at me. Into me." He bent close until her eyes were fixed on him. "What happened here?"

"A woman, the van. Needed help, we thought. Rory stopped. He got out. He got out and they . . . Oh God, sweet God. Rory."

"They took your car. What kind of car was it?"

"Blue. BMW. Rory. They took him. They took him. No room for you. They said no room and threw me down. They laughed."

Cian straightened. "Help me get this van off the road. They were smart enough to take the keys."

"We can't leave her like this."

"Then stay with her, but help me move this bloody van."

Fury had Hoyt spinning around, and the van jumped three feet across the road.

"Nice work."

"She could die out here. She did nothing."

"She won't be the first or the last. It's war, isn't it?" Cian shot back. "She's what they call collateral damage. Good strategy this," he mumbled, and took stock. "Slow us down and switch to a faster car. I won't be catching them now before they reach the caves. If that's where they're going."

He turned toward his brother, considered. "I may need you now after all."

"I won't leave an injured woman on the side of the road like a sick dog."

Cian stepped back to his car, flipped open the center compartment and took out a mobile phone. He spoke into it briefly. "It's a communication device," he told Hoyt as he tossed the phone back into storage. "I've called for help—medical and the garda. All you'll do now by staying is get yourself hauled in, and asked questions you can't answer."

He popped the hood, took out a blanket and some flares. "Put that over her," he instructed. "I'll set these up. He's bait now," Cian added as he set the flares to light. "Bait as much as a prize. She knows we're coming. She wants us to."

"Then we won't disappoint her."

With no hope of cutting off the raiding party before they reached the caves, Cian drove more cautiously. "She was smarter. More aggressive, and more willing to lose troops. So she has the advantage."

"We'll be outnumbered, greatly."

"We always would have been. At this point, she may be willing to negotiate. To take a trade."

"One of us for King."

"You're all the same to her. A human's a human, so you have no particular value in this. You perhaps, because she respects and covets power. But she'd want me more."

"You're willing to trade your life for his?"

"She wouldn't kill me. At least not right away. She'd want to use her considerable talents first. She'd enjoy that."

"Torture."

"And persuasion. If she could bring me over to her side, it would be a coup."

"A man who trades his life for a friend doesn't turn and betray him. Why would she think otherwise?"

"Because we're fickle creatures. And she made me. That gives her quite a bit of pull."

"No, not you. I'd believe you'd trade yourself for King, but I don't think she'd believe it. You'll have to offer me," Hoyt said after a moment.

"Oh, will I?"

"I've been nothing to you for hundreds of years. He's more to you than me. She'd see that. A human for a sorcerer. A good exchange for her."

"And why should she think you'd give yourself for a man you've known for, what a week?"

"Because you'd have a knife to my throat."

Cian tapped his fingers on the steering wheel. "It could work."

The rain had passed into dreary moonlight by the time they reached the cliffs. They rose high above the road, jutted out to cast jagged shadows over the toiling sea.

There was only the sound of the water lashing rock, and the hum of the air that was like the breath of gods.

There was no sign of another car, of human or of creature.

Along the seaside of the road was a rail. Below it was rocks, water and the maze of caves.

"We lure her up." Cian nodded toward the edge. "If we go down to her, we're trapped, with the sea at our backs. We go up, make her come to us."

They started the climb, over slippery rocks and soggy grass. At the headland stood a lighthouse, its beam lancing out into the dark.

They both sensed the attack before the movement. The thing sprang out from behind the rocks, fangs bared. Cian merely pivoted, led with his shoulder and sent it tumbling down to the road. For the second, he used the stake he'd hitched in his belt.

Then he straightened, turned to the third, who appeared more cautious than his fellows.

"Tell your mistress Cian McKenna wants to speak with her."

Vicious teeth gleamed in the moonlight. "We'll drink your blood tonight."

"Or you'll die hungry, and by Lilith's hands because you failed to deliver a message."

The thing melted away, and down.

"There may be more waiting above," Hoyt commented.

"Unlikely. She'd be expecting us to charge the caves, not head to high ground for a hostage negotiation. She'll be intrigued, and she'll come."

So they climbed, then walked the slope to higher ground, and the point where Hoyt had once faced Lilith, and the thing she'd made of his brother.

"She'll appreciate the irony of the spot."

"It feels as it did." Hoyt tucked his cross out of sight under his shirt. "The air. The night. This was my place once, where I could stand and call power with a thought."

"You'd best hope you still can." Cian drew his knife. "Get on your knees." He flicked the point at Hoyt's throat, watched the dribble of blood from the thin slice. "Now."

"So, it comes to choices."

"It always comes to choices. You would have killed me here, if you could."

"I would have saved you here, if I could."

"Well, you did neither, did you?" He slid the knife from Hoyt's sheath, made a V with the blades to hold at his brother's throat. "Kneel."

With the cold edge of the blades on his flesh, Hoyt got to his knees.

"Well, what a handsome sight."

Lilith stepped into the moonlight. She wore emerald green robes with her hair long and loose to spill over her shoulders like sunbeams.

"Lilith. It's been a very long time."

"Too long." The silk rustled as she moved. "Did you come all this way to bring me a gift?"

"A trade," Cian corrected. "Call your dogs off," he said quietly. "Or I kill him, then them. And you have nothing."

"So forceful." She gestured with her hand toward the vampires creeping in at the sides. "You've seasoned. You were hardly more than a pretty puppy when I gave you the gift. Now look at you, a sleek wolf. I like it."

"And still your dog," Hoyt spat out.

"Ah, the mighty sorcerer brought low. I like that, too. You marked me." She opened her robes to show Hoyt the pentagram branded over her heart. "It gave me pain for more than a decade. And the scar never fades. I owe you for that. Tell me, Cian, how did you manage to bring him here?"

"He thinks I'm his brother. It makes it easy."

"She took your life. She's lies and death."

Over Hoyt's head, Cian smiled. "That's what I love about her. I'll give you this one for the human you took. He's useful to me, and loyal. I want him back."

"But he's so much bigger than this one. So much more to feast on."

"He has no power. He's an ordinary mortal. I give you a sorcerer."

"Yet you covet the human."

"As I said, he's of use to me. Do you know how much time and trouble it takes to train a human servant? I want him back. No one steals from me. Not you, not anyone."

"We'll discuss it. Bring him down. I've done quite a bit with the caves. We can be comfortable, have a little something to eat. I've a very Rubenesque exchange student on tap—Swiss. We can share. Oh, but wait." She let out a musical laugh. "I've heard you dine on pigs' blood these days."

"You can't trust everything you hear." Deliberately Cian lifted the knife he'd used to cut Hoyt, flicked his tongue over the bloodied blade.

That first taste of human after so long a fast reddened his eyes, churned his hunger. "But I haven't lived so long to be stupid. This is a one-time offer, Lilith. Bring the human to me, and take the sorcerer."

"How can I trust you, my darling boy? You kill our kind."

"I kill what I like when I like. As you do."

"You aligned yourself with them. With humans. Plotted against me."

"As long as it amused me. It's become boring, and costly. Give me the human, take this one. And, as a bonus, I'll invite you into my home. You can have a banquet on the others."

Hoyt's head jerked, and the blade bit. He cursed, in Gaelic now, with low and steady violence.

"Smell the power in that blood." Lilith crooned it. "Gorgeous."

"Another step, and I cut the jugular, waste it all."

"Would you?" She smiled, beautifully. "I wonder. Is that what you want?" She gestured.

At the edge of the cliff where the lighthouse stood, Cian could see King slumped between two vampires.

"He's alive," she said lightly. "Of course, you only have my word for it, as I have yours that you'd hand that one to me, like a pretty present all wrapped in shiny paper. Let's play a game."

She held her skirts out, twirled. "Kill him, and I give you the human. Kill your brother, but not with the knives. Kill him as you're meant to kill. Take his blood, drink him, and the human is yours."

"Bring me the human first."

She pouted, brushed fussily at her skirts. "Oh, very well." She lifted one arm high, then the other. Cian eased the knives from Hoyt's throat as they began to drag King forward.

They dropped him, and with a vicious kick sent him over the edge.

"Oops!" Lilith eyes's danced with merriment as she pressed a hand to her lips. "Butterfingers. I guess you'll have to pay me back now and kill that one."

With a wild roar, Cian charged forward. And she rose up, spreading her robe like wings. "Take them!" she shouted. "Bring them to me." And was gone.

Cian switched grips on the knives as Hoyt sprang up, yanking free the stakes shoved into the back of his belt.

Arrows flew, slicing through air and hearts. Before Cian could strike the first blow, a half dozen vampires were dust, blown out to sea by the wind.

"More are coming!" Moira shouted from the cover of trees. "We need to go. We need to go now. This way. Hurry!"

Retreat was bitter, a vile taste burning the back of the throat. But the choice was to swallow death. So they turned from battle.

When they reached the car, Hoyt reached for his brother's hand. "Cian—"

"Don't." He slammed in, watched the others leap into the van. "Just don't."

The long drive home was full of silence, of grief and of fury.

Glenna didn't weep. It went too deep for tears. She drove in a kind of trance, her body throbbing with pain and shock, her mind numb with it. And knowing it was cowardice, huddled there.

"It wasn't your fault."

She heard Moira's voice, but couldn't respond to it. She felt Larkin touch her shoulder, she supposed in comfort. But was too numb to react. And when Moira climbed in the back with Larkin to give her solitude, she knew only vague relief.

She turned into the woods, carefully maneuvered the narrow lane. In front of the house where the lights burned, she shut off the engine, the lights. Reached for the door.

It flew open, and she was wrenched out, held inches above the ground. Even then, she felt nothing, not even fear as she saw the thirst in Cian's eyes.

"Tell me why I shouldn't break your neck and be done with it."

"I can't."

Hoyt reached them first, and was flicked away with a careless backward swipe.

"Don't. He's not to blame. Don't," she said now to Hoyt before he could charge again. "Please don't." And to Larkin.

"Do you think that moves me?"

She looked into Cian's eyes again. "No. Why should it? He was yours. I killed him."

"It wasn't her doing." Moira shoved Cian's arm, but didn't budge him an inch. "She isn't to blame for this."

"Let her speak for herself."

"She can't. Can't you see how badly she's hurt? She wouldn't let me tend her before we followed you. We need to get inside. If we're attacked now, we all die."

"If you harm her," Hoyt said quietly, "I'll kill you myself."

"Is that all there is?" Glenna's words were a weary whisper. "Just death? Is that all there'll ever be again?"

"Give her to me." Hoyt cupped his arms, drew her out of Cian's grasp. He murmured to her in Gaelic as he carried her into the house.

"You'll come, and you'll listen." Moira closed a hand around Cian's arm. "He deserves that."

"Don't tell me what he deserves." He wrenched free of her with a force that knocked her back two steps. "You know nothing of it."

"I know more than you think." She left him to follow Hoyt into the house.

"I couldn't catch them." Larkin stared at the ground. "I wasn't fast enough, and I couldn't catch them." He yanked open the cargo doors, unloaded weapons. "I can't turn into one of these." He slammed the doors again. "It has to be alive, what I become. Even the cougar couldn't catch them."

Cian said nothing, and went inside.

They had Glenna on the sofa in the main parlor. Her eyes were closed, her face pale, her skin clammy. Against the pallor, the bruising along her jaw and cheek was livid. Blood had dried at the corner of her mouth.

Hoyt gently tested her arm. Not broken, he thought with relief. Badly wrenched, but not broken. Trying not to jar her, he removed her shirt to discover more bruising over her shoulder, her torso, running down to her hip.

"I know what to get," Moira said and dashed off.

"Not broken." Hoyt's hands hovered over her ribs. "It's good there's nothing broken."

"She's fortunate her head's still on her shoulders." Cian

went directly to a cabinet, took out whiskey. He drank straight from the bottle.

"Some of the injuries are inside her. She's badly injured."

"No less than she deserves for going out of the house."

"She didn't." Moira hurried back in, carrying Glenna's case. "Not the way you're meaning."

"You don't expect me to believe King went out, and she leaped to his defense?"

"He came out for me." Glenna opened eyes glassy from the pain. "And they took him."

"Quiet," Hoyt ordered. "Moira, I need you here."

"We'll use this." She selected a bottle. "Pour it on the bruising." After handing him the bottle, she knelt, rested her hands lightly on Glenna's torso.

"What power I can claim I call now to ease your pain. Warmth to heal and harm none, to take away the damage done." She looked entreatingly at Glenna. "Help me. I'm not very good."

Glenna laid her hand over Moira's, closed her eyes. When Hoyt laid his on top for a triad, Glenna sucked in a breath, let it out on a moan. But when Moira would have yanked her hand away, Glenna gripped it tight.

"Sometimes healing hurts," she managed. "Sometimes it has to. Say the chant again. Three times."

As Moira obeyed, sweat sprang onto Glenna's skin, but the bruising faded a little, going the sickly tones of healing.

"Yes, that's better. Thanks."

"We'll have some of that whiskey here," Moira snapped.

"No. I'd better not." Trying for steady breaths, Glenna pushed up. "Help me sit. I need to see how bad it is now."

"Let's see about this." Hoyt skimmed his fingers over her face. And she grabbed his hand. The tears came now, couldn't be stopped.

"I'm so sorry."

"You can't blame yourself, Glenna."

"Who else?" Cian countered, and Moira shoved up to her feet.

"He wasn't wearing the cross." She dug in her pocket, held it up. "He took it off upstairs and left it behind."

"He was showing me some moves. Wrestling," Larkin explained. "And it got in his way, he said. He must have forgotten about it."

"He never meant to go outside, did he? And wouldn't have but for her."

"He was mistaken." Moira laid the cross on the table. "Glenna, he needs to know the truth. The truth is less painful."

"He thought, he must have thought I was going to let her in, or step out. I wasn't. But I was being cocky, so what's the difference? Smug. He's dead because of it."

Cian took another drink. "Tell me why he's dead."

"She knocked on the door. I shouldn't have answered, but I saw it was a woman. A young woman with a map. I wasn't going out, or asking her in, I swear that to you. She said she was lost. She spoke with an accent, French. Charming, really, but I knew . . . I felt. And I couldn't resist toying with her. God, oh God," she said as more tears spilled. "How stupid. How vain."

She took a deep breath. "She said her name was Lora."

"Lora." Cian lowered the bottle. "Young, attractive, French accent?"

"Yes. You know her."

"I do." He drank again. "I do, yes."

"I could see what she was. I don't know how, but I knew. I should have just shut the door on her. But on the chance I was wrong, I thought I should give her directions and get her moving. I'd just started to when King shouted, and he came running down the hall. I turned around. I was startled, I was careless. She got some of my hair. She pulled me outside by it."

"It was so fast," Moira continued. "I was behind King. I barely saw her move—the vampyre. He went out after them, and there were more. Four, five more. It was like lightning strikes."

Moira poured herself a shot of whiskey, downed it to smooth the raw edge of her nerves. "They were on him, all of them, and he shouted for Glenna to get inside. But she got up instead, she got up and ran to help him. It knocked her back, the female of them, like she was a stone in a sling. She tried to help him, even though she was hurt. Maybe she was careless, but so was he."

Moira picked up the cross again. "And it's a terrible price he paid for it. A terrible price he paid for defending a friend."

With Hoyt's help, Glenna got to her feet. "I'm sorry isn't enough. I know what he meant to you."

"You couldn't possibly."

"I think I do, and I know what he meant to the rest of us. I know he's dead because of me. I'll live with that all of my life."

"So will I. And it's my bad luck that I'll live a great deal longer than you."

He took the whiskey bottle when he walked out.

Chapter 16

In the moment between wake and sleep, there was candlelight, and the bliss of nothing. Easy warmth and sheets scented with lavender, and floating on the comfort of nothing.

But the moment passed, and Glenna remembered.

King was dead, hurled into the sea by monsters with the same carelessness of a boy tossing a pebble into a lake.

She'd gone upstairs alone, by her own request, to seek the solitude and oblivion of sleep.

Watching the candle flicker, she wondered if she would ever be able to sleep in the dark again. If she would ever be able to see night coming and not think their time was coming with it. To walk in the moonlight without fear? Would she ever know that simplicity again? Or would even a rainy day forever send chills down her spine?

She turned her head on the pillow. And she saw him silhouetted by the silver light that slid through the window that overlooked his herb garden. Keeping watch in the night, she thought, over her. Over them all. Whatever burdens they all bore, his were heavier. And still he'd come to stand between her and the dark.

"Hoyt."

She sat up as he turned, and she held out her hands to him.

"I didn't want to wake you." He crossed to her, took her hands while studying her face in the dim light. "Are you in pain?"

"No. No, it's gone under, at least for now. I have you and Moira to thank for that."

"You helped yourself as much as we did. And sleep will help as well."

"Don't go. Please. Cian?"

"I don't know." He sent a troubled look toward the door. "Closed in his rooms with the whiskey." Looking at her, he brushed back her hair, turning her face to take a closer study at the bruising. "We're all using what we can tonight, so the pain goes under."

"She would never have let him go. She would never have released King. No matter what we'd done."

"No." He eased down to sit on the side of the bed. "Cian must have known that somewhere inside him, but he had to try. We had to try."

By pretending to be a bargaining chip, she thought, remembering Hoyt's explanation of what they'd seen on the cliffs.

"Now we all know there can be no bargaining in this," he continued. "Are you strong enough to hear what I have to say?"

"Yes."

"We've lost one of us. One of the six we were told we needed to fight this battle, to win this war. I don't know what it means."

"Our warrior. Maybe it means we all have to become warriors. Better ones. I killed tonight, Hoyt—more from luck than skill—but I destroyed what had once been human. I can and will do it again. But with more skill. Every day with more skill. She took one of us, and she thinks it'll make us weak and frightened. But she's wrong. We'll show her she's wrong."

"I'm to lead this battle. You have great skill in magicks. You'll work in the tower on weapons, shields, spells. A protective circle to—"

"Whoa, wait." She held up a hand. "Am I getting this? I'm consigned to the tower—what, like Rapunzel?"

"I don't know this person."

"Just another helpless female waiting to be rescued. I'll work on the magicks, and I'll work harder and longer. Just like I'll train harder and longer. But what I won't do is sit up in the tower day and night with my cauldron and crystals, writing spells while the rest of you fight."

"You had your first battle today, and it nearly killed you."

"And gave me a lot more respect for what we're up against. I was called to this, just like the rest of us. I won't hide from it."

"Using your strengths isn't hiding. I was given the charge of this army—"

"Well, let me slap some bars on you and call you Colonel."

"Why are you so angry?"

"I don't want you to protect me. I want you to value me."

"Value you?" He shoved to his feet so the red shimmer from the fire washed over his face. "I value you almost more than I can bear. I've lost too much already. I've watched my brother, the one who shared the womb with me, taken. I've stood over the graves of my family. I won't see you cut down by these things—you, the single light for me in all of this. I won't risk your life again. I won't stand over your grave."

"But I can risk your life? I can stand over your grave?"

"I'm a man."

He said it so simply, the way an adult might tell a child the sky is blue, that she couldn't speak for ten full seconds. Then she plopped back against the pillows. "The only reason I'm not working on turning you into a braying jackass this very moment is I'm giving you some slack due to the fact you come from an unenlightened age."

"Un . . . unenlightened?"

"Let me clue you in to mine, Merlin. Women are equals. We work, we go into combat, we vote, and above all, we make our own decisions regarding our own lives, our own bodies, our own minds. Men don't rule here."

"I've never known a world where men rule," he muttered. "In physical strength, Glenna, you're not equal."

"We make up for it with other advantages."

"However keen your minds, your wiles, your bodies are more fragile. They're made to bear children."

"You just gave me a contradiction in terms. If men were responsible for childbearing, the world would've ended a long time ago, with no help from a bunch of glory-seeking vampires. And let me point out one little fact. The one causing this whole mess is a female."

"Somehow that should be my point."

"Well, it's just not. So forget it. And the one who brought us together is also female, so you're way outnumbered. And I have more ammo, but this ridiculous conversation is giving me a headache."

"You should rest. We'll talk more of this tomorrow."

"I'm not going to rest, and we're not going to talk about this tomorrow."

His single light? he thought. Sometimes she was a beam searing straight into his eyes. "You are a contrary and exasperating woman."

"Yes." Now she smiled, and once more held out her hands. "Sit down here, would you? You're worried about me, and for me. I understand that, appreciate that."

"If you would do this thing for me." He lifted her hands to his lips. "It would ease my mind. Make me a better leader."

"Oh, that's good." She drew her hands away to poke him gently in the chest. "Very good. Women aren't the only ones with wiles."

"Not wile, but truth."

"Ask me for something else, and I'll try to give it to you. But I can't give you this, Hoyt. I worry for you, too, and about you. For all of us. And I question what we can do, what we're capable of. And I wonder why in all the world— the worlds—we're the ones who have to do this thing. But none of that changes anything. We are the ones. And we've lost a very good man already."

"If I lose you . . . Glenna, there's a void in me at the very thought of it."

Sometimes, she knew, the woman had to be stronger. "There are so many worlds, and so many ways. I don't think we could ever lose each other now. What I have now is more than I've ever had before. I think it makes us better than we were. Maybe that's part of why we're here. To find each other."

She leaned into him, sighed when his arms encircled her. "Stay with me. Come lie with me. Love me."

"You need to heal."

"Yes." She drew him down with her, touched her lips to his. "I do."

He hoped he had the tenderness in him that she needed. He wanted to give her that, the magic of it.

"Slowly then." He brushed kisses over her cheek. "Quietly."

He used just his lips, skimming kisses over her mouth, her face, her throat. Warm and soothing. He brushed away the thin gown she wore to trace those easy kisses over her breasts, over her bruises. In comfort and with care.

Soft as birds' wings, lips and fingertips to ease her mind and her body, and to stir them.

And when their eyes met, he knew more than he'd ever known. Held more than he'd ever owned.

He lifted her up onto a pillow of air and silver light, making magic their bed. Around the room, the candles came to life with a sound like a sigh. And the light they shed was like melted gold.

"It's beautiful." She took his hands as they floated, closed her eyes on the sumptuous joy of it. "This is beautiful."

"I would give you all I have, and still it wouldn't be enough."

"You're wrong. It's everything."

More than pleasure, more than passion. Did he know what he made of her when he touched her like this? Nothing they faced, no terror or pain, no death or damnation could overcome this. The light inside her was like a beacon, and it would never be dark again.

Here was life at its sweetest and most generous. The taste of him was a balm to her soul even as his touch roused desires. Steeped in him, she lifted her arms, turned up her palms. Rose petals, white as snow, streamed down like rain.

She smiled when he slipped into her, when they moved together, silky and slow. Light and air, scent and sensation surrounded the rise and fall of bodies and hearts.

Once more their fingers meshed, once more their lips met. And as they drifted together, love healed them both.

In the kitchen, Moira puzzled over a can of soup. No one had eaten, and she was determined to make some sort of meal should Glenna awake. She'd managed the tea, but she'd been shown how to conquer that.

She'd only watched King open one of the cylinders with the little machine that made the nasty noise. She'd tried and failed three times to make it work, and was seriously considering getting her sword and hacking the cylinder open.

She had a little kitchen magic—precious little, she admitted. Glancing around to be sure she was alone, she pulled what she had together, and visualized the can open.

It shimmied a bit on the counter, but remained stubbornly whole.

"All right, one more time then."

She bent down, studied the opener that was attached to the underside of the cupboard. With the proper tools she could take it apart, find out how it worked. She loved taking things apart. But if she had the proper tools, she could just open the bloody cylinder in the first place.

She straightened, shook her hair back, rolled her shoulders. Muttering to herself, she tried once again to do the deed. This time, when the machine whirled, the can revolved. She clasped her hands together in delight, then bent close again to watch it work.

It was so clever, she thought. So much here was clever. She wondered if she'd ever be allowed to drive the van. King had said he'd teach her how it was done.

Her lips trembled at the thought of it, of him, and she pressed them hard together. She prayed his death had been quick, and his suffering brief. In the morning, she would put up a stone for him in the graveyard she and Larkin had seen when they'd been walking.

And when she returned to Geall, she would erect another, and ask the harper to write a song for him.

She emptied the contents into a pot and set it on the burner, turning it on as Glenna had showed her.

They needed to eat. Grief and hunger would make them weak, and weakness would make them easier prey. Bread, she decided. They would have some bread. It would be a simple meal, but filling.

She turned toward the pantry, then stumbled back when she saw Cian in the doorway. He leaned against the wall, the nearly empty whiskey bottle dangling from his fingers.

"Midnight snack?" His teeth showed white with his smile. "I've a fondness for them myself."

"No one's eaten. I thought we should."

"Always thinking, aren't you, little queen? Mind's always going."

He was drunk, she could see that. Too much whiskey had dulled his eyes and thickened his voice. But she could also see the pain. "You should sit before you fall over."

"Thanks for the kind invitation, in my own bloody house. But I just came down for another bottle." He shook the one he held. "Someone appears to have made off with this one."

"Drink yourself sick if you want to be stupid about it. But you might as well eat something. I know you eat, I've seen you. I've gone to the trouble to make it."

He glanced at the counter, smirked. "You opened a tin."

"It's sorry I am I didn't have time to kill the fatted calf. So you'll make do."

She turned around to busy herself, then went very still when she felt him behind her. His fingers skimmed the side of her throat, light as a moth's wings.

"I'd have thought you tasty once upon a time."

Drunk, angry, grieving, she thought. All of those made him dangerous. If she showed him her fear, he'd only be more so. "You're in my way."

"Not yet."

"I don't have time for drunkards. Maybe you don't want food, but Glenna needs it, for healing strength."

"I'd say she's feeling strong enough." Bitterness edged his tone as he glanced up. "Didn't you see the lights brighten a bit ago?"

"I did. I don't know what that has to do with Glenna."

"It means she and my brother are having a go at each other. Sex," he said when she looked blank. "A bit of naked, sweaty sex to top off the evening. Ah, she blushes." He laughed, moved closer. "All that pretty blood just under the skin. Delicious."

"Stop."

"I used to like when they trembled, the way you are. It makes the blood hotter, and it adds to the thrill. I'd nearly forgotten."

"You smell of the whiskey. This is hot enough now. Sit down, and I'll make a bowl for you."

"I don't want the fucking soup. Wouldn't mind that hot, sweaty sex, but likely I'm too drunk to manage it. Well then, I'll just get that fresh bottle, and finish the job."

"Cian. Cian, people turn to each other for comfort when death's come. It isn't disrespect, but need."

"You don't want to lecture me on sex. I know more of it than you could ever imagine. Of its pleasures and its pain and its purposes."

"People turn to drink as well, but it's not as healthy. I know what he was to you."

"You don't."

"He talked to me, more than the others, I think, because I like to listen. He told me how you found him, all those years ago, what you did for him."

"I amused myself."

"Stop it." The tone of command, bred into her bones, snapped into her voice. "Now it's disrespect you're showing for a man who was a friend to me. And he was a son to you. A friend and a brother. All of that. I want to put a stone up for him tomorrow. It could wait until sunset, until you could go out and—"

"What do I care for stones?" he said, and left her.

* * *

Glenna was so grateful for the sun she could have wept. There were clouds, but they were thin and the beams burst through them to toss light and shadows on the ground.

She hurt still, heart and body. But she would deal with it. For now, she took one of her cameras and she stepped outside to let the sun bathe her face. Charmed by the music of it, she walked to the stream. Then just laid down on its bank and basked.

Birds sang, pouring joy into air that was fragrant with flowers. She could see foxglove dancing lightly in the breeze. For a moment she felt the earth beneath her sigh and whisper with the pleasure of a new day.

Grief would come and go, she knew. But today there was light, and work. And there was still magic in the world.

When a shadow fell over her, she turned her head, smiled at Moira.

"How are you this morning?"

"Better," Glenna told her. "I'm better. Sore and stiff, maybe a little wobbly yet, but better."

She turned a bit more to study Moira's tunic and rough pants. "We need to get you some clothes."

"These do well enough."

"Maybe we'll go into town, see what we can find."

"I have nothing to trade. I can't pay."

"That's what Visa's for. It'll be my treat." She lay flat, closed her eyes again. "I didn't think anyone else was up."

"Larkin's taken the horse for a run. It should do both of them good. I don't think he slept at all."

"I doubt any of us did, really. It doesn't seem real does it, not in the light of day with the sun showering down and the birds singing?"

"It seems more real to me," Moira said as she sat. "It shows what we have to lose. I have a stone," she continued, brushing her hand through the grass. "I thought when Larkin comes back we could go to where the graves are, make one for King."

Glenna kept her eyes closed, but reached out a hand for Moira's. "You have a good heart," she told her. "Yes, we'll make a grave for King."

* * *

Her injuries prevented her from training, but it didn't stop Glenna from working. She spent the next two days preparing food, shopping for supplies, researching magic.

She took photographs.

More than busy work, she told herself. It was practical, and organizational. And the photos were—would be—a kind of documentation, a kind of tribute.

Most of all it helped keep her from feeling useless while the others worked up a sweat with swords and hand-to-hand.

She learned the roads, committing various routes to memory. Her driving skills were rusty, so she honed them, maneuvering the van on snaking roads, skimming the hedgerows on turns, zooming through roundabouts as her confidence built.

She pored through spell books, searching for offense and defense. For solutions. She couldn't bring King back, but she would do everything in her power to safeguard those who were left.

Then she got the bright idea that every member of the team should be able to handle the van. She started with Hoyt.

She sat beside him as he drove the van at a creeping pace up and down the lane.

"There are better uses for my time."

"That may be." And at this rate, she thought, they'd be a millennium before he got over five miles an hour. "But every one of us should be able to take the wheel if necessary."

"Why?"

"Because."

"Do you plan to take this machine into battle?"

"Not with you at the wheel. Practicalities, Hoyt. I'm the only one who can drive during the day. If something happens to me—"

"Don't. Don't tempt the gods." His hand closed over hers.

"We have to factor it. We're here, and where we are is remote. We need transportation. And, well, driving gives all of us a kind of independence, as well as another skill. We should be prepared for anything."

"We could get more horses."

The wistfulness in his voice had her giving him a bolstering pat on the shoulder. "You're doing fine. Maybe you could try going just a little bit faster."

He shot forward, spitting gravel from the tires. Glenna sucked in a breath and shouted: "Brake! Brake! Brake!"

More gravel flew when the van came to an abrupt halt.

"Here's a new word for your vocabulary," she said pleasantly. "Whiplash."

"You said to go faster. This is go." He gestured toward the gas pedal.

"Yeah. Well. Okay." She drew in a fresh breath. "There's the snail, and there's the rabbit. Let's try to find the animal in between. A dog, say. A nice, healthy golden retriever."

"Dogs chase rabbits," he pointed out, and made her laugh. "That's good. You've been sad. I've missed your smile."

"I'll give you a big, toothy one if we come through this lesson in one piece. We're going to take a big leap, go out on the road." She reached up and closed her hand briefly over the crystal she'd hung from the rearview. "Let's hope this works."

He did better than she'd expected, which meant no one was maimed or otherwise injured. Her heart got a serious workout from leaping into her throat, then dropping hard into her belly, but they stayed on the road—for the most part.

She liked watching him calculate the turns, his brows knit, his eyes intense, his long fingers gripping the wheel as though it were a lifeline in a storm-tossed sea.

Hedgerows closed them in, green tunnels dotted with bloodred drops of fuchsia, then the world would open up into rolling fields, and the dots were white sheep or lazy spotted cows.

The city girl in her was enchanted. Another time, she thought, another world, and she could have found a great deal to love about this place. The play of light and shadows on the green, the patchwork of fields, the sudden sparkle of water, the rise and tumble of rocks that formed ancient ruins.

It was good, she decided, to look beyond the house in the forest, to look and love the world they were fighting to save.

When he slowed, she glanced over. "You have to keep up your speed. It can be as dangerous to go too slow as too fast. Which applies, now that I think about it, to pretty much anything."

"I want to stop."

"You need to pull over to the shoulder—the side of the road. Put the signal on, like I showed you, and ease over." She checked the road herself. The shoulder was narrow, but there was no traffic. "Put it in park. That's all the way up. Good. So— What?" she said when he pushed his door open.

She pulled off her seat belt, grabbed the keys—and her camera as an afterthought—then hurried after him. But he was already halfway across a field, moving quickly toward what was left of an old stone tower.

"If you wanted to stretch your legs or empty your bladder, you just had to say so," she began, huffing a bit as she caught up to him.

The wind danced through her hair, blowing it back from her face. As she touched his arm, she felt the muscles there gone rigid. "What is it?"

"I know this place. People lived here. There were children. The oldest of my sisters married their second son. His name is Fearghus. They farmed this land. They . . . they walked this land. Lived."

He moved inside to what she saw now must have been a small keep. The roof was gone, as was one of the walls. The floor was grass and starry white flowers, the dung of sheep.

And the wind blew through, like ghosts chanting.

"They had a daughter, a pretty thing. Our families hoped we would . . ."

He laid his hand against a wall, left it there. "Just stone now," he said quietly. "Gone to ruin."

"But still here. Hoyt. Still here, a part of it. And you,

remembering them. What we're doing, what we have to do, won't it mean they had the very best chance to live a long, full life? To farm the land and walk it. To live."

"They came to my brother's wake." He dropped his hand. "I don't know how to feel."

"I can't imagine how hard this is for you. Every day of it. Hoyt." She laid her hands on his arms, waiting for his eyes to meet hers. "Part of it stands, what was yours. It stands in what's mine. I think that matters. I think we need to find the hope in that. The strength in it. Do you want some time here? I can go back, wait for you in the van."

"No. Every time I falter, or think I can't bear what's been asked of me, you're there." He bent, plucked one of the little white flowers. "These grew in my time." He twirled it once, then tucked it into her hair. "So, we'll carry hope."

"Yes, we will. Here." She lifted her camera. "It's a place that cries for pictures. And the light's gorgeous."

She moved off to choose her angles. She'd make him a present of one, she decided. Something of her to take with him. And she'd make a copy of the same shot for her loft.

Imagine him studying the photo while she studied hers. Each of them remembering standing there on a summer afternoon with wildflowers waving in a carpet of grass.

But the idea of it hurt more than it warmed.

So she turned the camera on him. "Just look at me," she told him. "You don't have to smile. In fact—" She clicked the shutter. "Nice, very nice."

Inspired, she lowered the camera. "I'm going to set it up on timer, take one of us together. She looked around for something to set the camera on, wished she'd thought to bring a tripod.

"Well, I'll have to mix a little something in." She framed him in. Man and stone and field. "Air be still and heed my will. Solid now beneath my hand, steady as rock upon the land. Hold here what I ask of thee. As I will, so mote it be."

She set the camera on the platter of air, engaged the timer. Then dashed to Hoyt. "Just look at the camera." She slipped an arm around his waist, pleased when he mirrored the gesture. "And if you can manage a little smile . . . one, two . . ."

She watched the light blink. "There we are. For posterity."

He walked with her when she retrieved the camera. "How do you know how it will look when you take it out of the box?"

"I don't, not a hundred percent. I guess you could say it's another kind of hope."

She looked back at the ruin. "Do you need more time?"

"No." Time, he thought, there would never be enough of it. "We should go back. There's other work to do."

"Did you love her?" Glenna asked as they started back across the field.

"Who?"

"The girl? The daughter of the family who lived here."

"I didn't, no. A great disappointment that was to my mother, but not—I think—to the girl. I didn't look for a woman in that way, for marriage and family. It seemed . . . It seemed to me that my gift, my work, required solitude. Wives require time and attention."

"They do. Theoretically, they also give it."

"I wanted to be alone. All of my life it seemed I never had enough of it, the solitude and the quiet. And now, now I'm afraid I may always have too much."

"That would be up to you." She stopped to look back at the ruins a last time. "What will you tell them when you go back?" Even saying it tore little pieces from her heart.

"I don't know." He took her hand so they stood together, looking at what was, imagining what had been. "I don't know. What will you tell your people when this is done?"

"I think I probably won't tell them anything. Let them think as I told them when I called before I left that I took an impulsive trip to Europe. Why should they have to live with the fear of what we know?" she said when he turned to her. "We know what goes bump in the night is real, we know that now, and it's a burden. So I'll tell them I love them, and leave it at that."

"Isn't that another kind of alone?"

"It's one I can handle."

This time she got behind the wheel. When he got in beside her, he took one last look at the ruin.

And, he thought, without Glenna, the alone might swallow him whole.

Chapter 17

It plagued him, the idea of going back to his world. Of dying in this one. Of never seeing his home again. Of living in it the rest of his life without the woman who'd given new meaning to it.

If there was a war to be fought with sword and lance, there was another raging inside him, battering the heart he'd never known could yearn for so much.

He watched her from the tower window as she took pictures of Larkin and Moira sparring, or posed them in less combative stances.

Her injuries had healed enough that she no longer moved stiffly, or tired as quickly. But he would always remember how she'd looked on the ground, bleeding.

Her manner of dress no longer seemed strange to him, but proper and so right for who she was. The way she moved in the dark pants and white shirt, her fiery hair pinned messily atop her head seemed the essence of grace to him.

In her face, he'd found beauty and life. In her mind, intelligence and curiosity. And in her heart both compassion and valor.

In her, he realized, he'd found everything he could want, without ever knowing he'd been lacking.

He had no right to her, of course. They had no right to each other beyond the time of the task. If they lived, if the worlds survived, he would go back to his while she remained in hers.

Even love couldn't span a thousand years.

Love. His heart ached at the word so that he pressed his hand to it. This was love then. The gnawing, the burning. The light and the dark.

Not just warm flesh and murmurs in the candlelight, but pain and awareness in the light of day. In the depths of the night. To feel so much for one person, it eclipsed all else.

And it was terrifying.

He was no coward, Hoyt reminded himself. He was a sorcerer by birth, a warrior by circumstance. He had held lightning in the palm of his hand and called the wind to launch it. He'd killed demons, and twice had faced their queen.

Surely, he could face love. Love couldn't maim him or kill him, or strip him of power. What level of cowardice was it then, for a man to shrink back from it?

He strode out of the room, down the stairs, moving with the rush of impulse. He heard music as he passed his brother's door—something low and brooding. He knew it as the music of grief.

And knew, too, if his brother was stirring, so might others of Cian's kind be stirring. Sunset was close.

He moved quickly through the house, into the kitchen where something simmered on the stove, and out the back.

Larkin was amusing himself, shimmering into a gold wolf while Glenna called out her delight and moved around him with the little machine that took the pictures. The camera, he reminded himself.

He shaped back into a man, and hefting his sword assumed a haughty pose.

"You look better as the wolf," Moira told him.

He raised his sword in mock attack and chased after her. Their shouts and laughter were so opposed to his brother's music, Hoyt could only stand in wonder.

There was still laughter in the world. Still time, and need, for play and fun. There was still light even as the darkness crept closer.

"Glenna."

She turned, the humor still dancing in her eyes. "Oh, perfect! Stand right there. Just there, with the house behind you."

"I want to—"

"Ssh. I'm going to lose the light soon. Yes, yes, just like that. All aloof and annoyed. It's wonderful! I wish there was time to go back in and get your cloak. You were made to wear one."

She changed angles, crouched down, shot up at him. "No, don't look at me. Look off, over my head, think deep thoughts. Look into the trees."

"Wherever it is I look, I still see nothing but you."

She lowered her camera for a moment, with pleasure blooming in her cheeks. "You're just trying to distract me. Give me that Hoyt look, just for a minute. Off into the trees, the serious sorcerer."

"I want to speak with you."

"Two minutes." She changed angles, kept shooting, then straightened. "I want a prop," she muttered, and studied the weapons on the table.

"Glenna. Would you go back with me?"

"Two minutes," she repeated, debating between long sword and dagger. "I need to go in and check the soup anyway."

"I don't mean back into the bloody kitchen. Will you go with me?"

She glanced over, automatically lifting her camera, framing his face and capturing the intensity of it. A good meal, she thought, another solid night's sleep, and she'd be ready for full training by the next morning.

"Where?"

"Home. To my home."

"What?" She lowered the camera, felt her heart do a quick, hard jump. "What?"

"When this is done." He kept his eyes on hers as he

closed the distance between them. "Will you come with me? Will you be with me? Belong to me?"

"Back with you? To the twelfth century?"

"Yes."

Slowly, carefully, she set the camera down. "Why do you want me?"

"Because all I see is you, all I want is you. I think if I have to live five minutes in a world without you in it, it would be eternity. I can't face eternity without seeing your face." He brushed his fingers over her cheek. "Without hearing your voice, without touching you. I think if I was sent here to fight this war, I was sent here to find you as well. Not just to fight with me. To open me. Glenna."

He gathered her hands in his, brought them to his lips. "In all this fear and grief and loss, I see you."

She kept her eyes on his as he spoke, searching. When the words were done, she touched a hand to his heart. "There's so much in there," she said quietly. "So much, and I'm so lucky to be part of it. I'll go with you. I'll go with you anywhere."

The joy of it spread inside him, warmed as he touched his fingertips to her cheek again. "You would give up your world, all you know? Why?"

"Because I've thought of living five minutes without you, and even that was eternity. I love you." She saw his eyes change. "Those are the strongest words in any magic. I love you. With that incantation, I already belong to you."

"Once I speak it, it's alive. Nothing can ever kill it." Now he framed her face. "Would you have me if I stayed here with you?"

"But you said—"

"Would you have me, Glenna?"

"Yes, of course, yes."

"Then we'll see which world is ours when this is done. Wherever, whenever it is, I will love you in it. You." He touched his lips to hers. "And only you."

"Hoyt." Her arms came hard around him. "If we have this, we can do anything."

"I haven't said it yet."

She laughed, rained kisses over his cheeks. "Close enough."

"Wait." He drew her back, just an inch. Those vivid blue eyes locked with hers. "I love you."

A single beam of light shot out of the sky, washed over them, centered them in a circle of white.

"So it's done," he murmured. "Through this life and all the ones to come, I'm yours. And you're mine. All that I am, Glenna."

"All that I'll be. I pledge that to you." She held close again, pressed her cheek to his. "Whatever happens, this is ours."

She tipped back her head so their lips could meet. "I knew it would be you," she said softly, "from the moment I walked into your dream."

They held each other in the circle of light, held close while it bathed them. When it faded, and twilight oozed over the day, they gathered the rest of the weapons, and took them into the house together.

Cian watched them from his bedroom window. Love had flashed and shimmered around them in a light that had all but burned his skin, seared his eyes.

And it had pressed against a heart that hadn't beat in nearly a thousand years.

So his brother had fallen, he thought, for the single blow against which there was no shield. Now they would live their short and painful lives within that light.

Perhaps it would be worth it.

Then he stepped back into the shadows of his room, and the cool dark.

When he came down, it was full dark, and she was in the kitchen alone. Singing at the sink, Cian noted, in an absent and happy voice. The sort, he decided, that a fanciful person would say had little pink hearts spilling out from between her lips with the tune.

She was loading the dishwasher—a homey chore. And the kitchen smelled of herbs and flowers. Her hair was bundled up, and now and then her hips moved with the rhythm of the song.

Would he have had a woman like that if he'd lived? he wondered. One who'd sing in the kitchen, or stand in the light, looking at him with her face alive with love?

He'd had women, of course. Scores of them. And some had loved him—to their loss, he supposed. But if their faces had been alive with that love, those faces were a blur to him now.

And love was a choice he had eliminated from his life.

Or had told himself he had. But the fact was he had loved King, as a father does a son, or a brother a brother. The little queen had been right about that, and damn her for it.

He had given his love and his trust to a human, and as humans were wont to do, it had died on him.

Saving this one, he thought now as Glenna set dishes in the rack. Another thing humans had a habit of doing was sacrificing themselves for other humans.

It was, or had been, a trait that had intrigued him often enough. Easier to understand, in his circumstances, their habit on the other side of the coin—of killing each other.

Then she turned, and jolted. The dish she held slipped out of her hands and shattered on the tiles.

"God. I'm sorry. You startled me."

She moved quickly—and jerkily, he noted, for a woman of easy grace. She took the broom and dustpan from the closet, and began to sweep the shards.

He hadn't spoken to her, nor to any of the others, since the night of King's death. He'd left them to train themselves, or do as they pleased.

"I didn't hear you come in. The others finished dinner. They—they went up to do some training. I had Hoyt out for an hour or so today. Um, driving lesson. I thought . . ." She dumped the shards, turned again. "Oh God, say *something*."

"Even if you live, you're from two different worlds. How will you resolve it?"

"Did Hoyt speak to you?"

"He didn't have to. I have eyes."

"I don't know how we'll resolve it." She put the broom away. "We'll find a way. Does it matter to you?"

"Not in the least. It's of interest to me." He got a bottle of wine from the counter rack, studied the label. "I've lived among you for a considerable amount of time. Without interest, I'd have died of boredom long ago."

She steadied herself. "Loving each other makes us stronger. I believe that. We need to be stronger. So far, we haven't done very well."

He opened the wine, got down a glass. "No, you haven't done very well, particularly."

"Cian," she said as he turned to go. "I know you blame me for King. You have every right to—to blame me and to hate me for it. But if we don't find a way to work together, to mesh, he won't just be the only one of us to die. He'll just be the first."

"I beat him to that by a few hundred years." He tipped the glass toward her in a kind of salute, then walked out with the bottle.

"Well, that was useless," Glenna muttered, and turned back to finish the dishes.

He would hate her, she thought, and likely hate Hoyt as well because Hoyt loved her. Their team was fractured even before it had a genuine chance to become a unit.

If they had time, nothing but time, she would let it lie, wait until Cian's resentment cooled, began to fade. But they didn't have that luxury of wasting any more of the precious little time they'd been given. She'd have to find a way to work around it, or him.

She dried her hands, flung the cloth down.

There was a thump outside the back door, as if something heavy had fallen. Instinctively she stepped back, reached for the sword braced against the counter, and one of the stakes lying on it.

"They can't get in," she whispered, and even the whisper shook. "If they want to spy on me while I'm cleaning up the kitchen, so what?"

But she wished she and Hoyt had had better luck devising a spell to create a protected area around the house.

Still, she couldn't let it frighten her, wouldn't let it. She certainly wasn't going to open the door again to have a chat with something that wanted to rip her throat out.

But there came a kind of scratching, low on the door. And a moan. And the hand gripping the sword went damp with sweat.

"Help me. Please."

The voice was weak, barely audible through the wood. But she thought . . .

"Let me in. Glenna? Glenna? In the name of God, let me in before they come."

"King?" The sword clattered on the floor as she leaped toward the door. Still, she held the stake in a firm grip.

Fool me once, she thought, and kept well out of reach as she opened the door.

He lay on the stones just outside, his clothes bloody and torn. More blood had dried on the side of his face, and his breathing was a thin wheeze.

Alive, was all she could think.

She started to crouch down, pull him inside, but Cian was beside her. He shoved her aside, lowered down himself. Laid a hand on King's battered cheek.

"We need to get him in. Hurry, Cian! I've got things that can help."

"They're close. Tracking me." He groped blindly for Cian's hand. "I didn't think I'd make it."

"You have. Come inside now." He gripped King under the arms, dragged him into the kitchen. "How did you get away?"

"Don't know." King sprawled on the floor, eyes closed. "Missed the rocks. Thought I'd drown, but . . . I got out, got out of the water. Hurt pretty bad. Passed out, don't know how long. Walked, walked all day. Hid at night. They come at night."

"Let me see what I can do for him," Glenna began.

"Close the door," Cian told her.

"Did everybody make it? Did everybody . . . thirsty."

"Aye, I know." Cian gripped his hand, looked into his eyes. "I know."

"We'll start with this." Glenna mixed something briskly in a cup. "Cian, if you'd go get the others. I could use Hoyt and Moira. We'll want to get King into bed, make him comfortable."

She bent to him as she spoke, and the cross around her neck dangled down, swung toward King's face.

He hissed like a snake, bared fangs and skuddled back.

Then to Glenna's horror, he got to his feet. And grinned.

"You never told me how it felt," he said to Cian.

"Words fall short. It needs to be experienced."

"No." Glenna could only shake her head. "Oh God, no."

"You could've taken me here a long time ago, but I'm glad you didn't. I'm glad it was now, when I'm in my prime."

King circled around as he spoke, blocking the door out of the kitchen. "They hurt me first. Lilith—she knows amazing ways to give pain. You know you don't stand a chance against her."

"I'm sorry," Glenna whispered. "I'm sorry."

"Don't be. She said I could have you. Eat you or change you. My choice."

"You don't want to hurt me, King."

"Oh yes, he does," Cian said easily. "He wants the pain in you nearly as much as he wants your blood in his throat. It's how he's made. Had she already given you the gift before they threw you off the cliff?"

"No. I was hurt though, hurt bad. Could hardly stand. They had a rope around me when they tossed me off. If I lived, she'd give me the gift. I lived. She'll take you back," he said to Cian.

"Yes, I know she will."

Glenna looked from one to the other. Trapped, she realized, between them. He'd known—she saw that now. Cian had known what King was before he'd let him in the house.

"Don't do this. How can you do this? To your brother."

"I can't have him," King told Cian. "Neither can you. She wants Hoyt herself. She wants to drink him, the sorcerer. With his blood, she'll ascend even higher. Every world there is will be ours."

The sword was too far away, and she no longer had the stake. She had nothing.

"We're to take Hoyt and the other female to her, alive. This one, and the boy? They're ours if we want them."

"I haven't drunk human blood for a very long time." Cian reached over, trailed a fingertip down the nape of Glenna's neck. "This one, I'd think, would be heady."

King licked his lips. "We can share her."

"Yes, why not?" He tightened his grip on Glenna, and when she fought, when she sucked in her breath, he laughed. "Oh aye, scream for help. Bring the others on down to save you. It'll save us the trip up."

"Rot in hell. I'm sorry for what happened to you," she said to King as he moved toward her. "Sorry for any part I played in it. But I won't make it easy for you."

She used Cian as a brace, swung up her legs and kicked out. She knocked King back a few steps, but he only laughed and moved toward her again.

"They let them run in the caves. So we can chase them. I like when they run. When they scream."

"I won't scream." She rammed back with her elbows, kicked out again.

She heard the rush of footsteps, and thought only, No! So screamed after all as she kicked and struggled.

"The cross. I can't get past the fucking cross. Knock her out!" King demanded. "Get it off her. I'm hungry!"

"I'll fix it." He tossed Glenna aside as the others rushed into the room.

And looking into King's eyes, drove the stake he'd had at his back into his friend's heart.

"It's all I could do for you," he told him, and tossed the stake aside.

"King. Not King." Moira dropped to her knees beside the dust. Then she laid her hands on it, spoke in a voice choked with tears. "Let what he was, the soul of him and the heart, be welcomed in a world again. The demon that took him is dead. Let him have light to find his way back."

"You won't raise a man from a pile of ash."

She looked up at Cian. "No, but maybe free his soul so it can be reborn. You didn't kill your friend, Cian."

"No. Lilith did."

"I thought . . ." Glenna still shook as Hoyt helped her to her feet.

"I know what you thought. Why shouldn't you?"

"Because I should have trusted you. I've said we aren't a unit, but I didn't understand I'm as much to blame for that as any. I didn't trust you. I thought you'd kill me, but you chose to save me."

"You're wrong. I chose to save him."

"Cian." She stepped toward him. "I caused this. I can't—"

"You didn't, no. You didn't kill him, you didn't change him. Lilith did. And sent him here to die once more. He was new, and not yet used to his skin. Injured as well. He couldn't have taken all of us, and she knew it."

"She knew what you would do." Hoyt moved to his brother's side, laid a hand on his shoulder. "And what it would cost you."

"In her way, she couldn't lose. So she'd think. I don't kill him, he takes at least one of you—maybe the lot if I turn. If I go the other way, destroy him, it costs me . . . oh quite a bit, quite a lot indeed."

"The death of a friend," Larkin began, "is a hard death. We all feel it."

"I believe you do." He looked down to where Moira still knelt on the floor. "But it comes to me first because he was mine first. She did this to him not because of you," he said to Glenna. "But because of me. I could've blamed you, and did, if she'd just killed him. Clean. But for this, it's not yours. It's hers and it's mine."

He walked over to pick up the stake he used, studied the killing point. "And when it comes time, when we face her, she's mine. If any of you step up to do the killing blow, I'll stop you. So you see, she miscalculated. I owe her for this, and I'll give her death for it."

Now, he picked up the sword. "We train tonight."

She trained, going one-on-one with Larkin, sword to sword. Cian had paired Moira with Hoyt, and stood back, or moved around them as steel clashed. He called out insults, which Glenna assumed was his style of motivation.

Her arm ached, and her still tender ribs throbbed. While sweat dribbled down her back, into her eyes, she continued to push. The pain, the effort, helped block out the image of King in the kitchen, moving toward her with fangs ready.

"Keep your arm up," Cian shouted at her. "If you can't hold a shagging sword properly you won't last five minutes. And stop dancing with her, for Christ's sake, Larkin. This isn't a bloody nightclub."

"She isn't fully healed," Larkin snapped back. "And what the hell's a nightclub?"

"I need to stop." Moira lowered her sword, wiped her sweaty brow with the back of her free hand. "Rest for a moment."

"You don't." Cian spun toward her. "Do you think you're doing her a favor, asking to rest? Do you think they'll be agreeable to a bloody time out just because your pal here needs to catch her breath?"

"I'm fine. There's no need to snap at her." Glenna struggled to catch her breath, to will some strength back into her legs. "I'm fine. Stop holding back," she told Larkin. "I don't need to be coddled."

"She needs to be looked at." Hoyt gestured Larkin back. "It's too soon for her to train like this."

"That isn't for you to say," Cian pointed out.

"I am saying it. She's exhausted, and she's in pain. And that's enough."

"I said I'm fine, and can speak for myself. Which, though he enjoys being a bastard, is what your brother pointed out. I don't need or want you to speak for me."

"Then you'll have to grow accustomed to it, because so I will when you need it."

"I know what I need and when I need it."

"Maybe the two of you will just talk the enemy to death," Cian said dryly.

Out of patience, Glenna thrust at Cian with her sword. "Come on. Come on then, you and me. You won't hold back."

"No." He tapped his blade to hers. "I won't."

"I said enough." Hoyt slashed his sword between them, and his fury sent a ripple of fire down the steel.

"Which one of us would you like to take on?" Now Cian's tone was like silk. And his eyes darkened with a dangerous pleasure when Hoyt pivoted toward him.

"Should be interesting," Larkin said, but his cousin stepped in.

"Wait," she said. "Just wait. We're upset, all of us. Tired out, and overheated like horses at too long a gallop on top of it. It serves no purpose to hurt each other. If we won't rest, then at least, let's have the doors open. Have some air."

"You want the doors open?" Everything about him suddenly genial, Cian cocked his head. "A bit of air's what you're wanting? Sure we'll have ourselves some fresh air."

He strode to the terrace doors, threw them open. Then in a move fast as a fingersnap, reached out into the dark. "Come in, won't you?" he said and yanked a pair of vampires through the doorway.

"Plenty to eat here." He wandered to the table as both of them leaped up, drew swords. With the tip of his own he speared an apple from the bowl. Then leaned back against the wall, plucking it off to have a bite.

"Let's see what you can do with them," he suggested. "It's two against one, after all. You may just have a shot at surviving."

Hoyt pivoted, instinctively putting Glenna behind him. Larkin was already moving in, flashing his sword. His opponent blocked the slash easily, punched out with its free hand and sent Larkin flying halfway across the room.

It turned, rushed Moira. The first strike hit her sword, and the force knocked her down, sent her skidding over the floor. She groped desperately for her stake as it flew—seemed to fly—through the air toward her.

Glenna buried her terror, dug out her fury. She shot her power out—the first learned, the last lost—and brought the fire. The vampire burst into flames midair.

"Nicely done, Red," Cian commented, and watched his brother battle for his life.

"Help him. Help me."

"Why don't you?"

"They're too close to risk the fire."

"Try this." He tossed her a stake, took another bite of apple.

She didn't think, couldn't think, as she ran forward. As she plunged the stake into the back of the vampire who'd beaten Hoyt to his knees.

And missed the heart.

It howled, but there seemed to be more pleasure than pain in it. It turned, lifted its sword high. Both Moira and Larkin charged, but Glenna saw her death. They were too far away, and she had nothing left.

Then Hoyt sliced his sword through its neck. Blood splattered her face before there was dust.

"Fairly pitiful, but effective enough all in all." Cian wiped his hands. "Now pair off. Playtime's over."

"You knew they were out there." Moira's hand, still holding the stake, trembled. "You knew."

"Well, of course, I knew they were out there. If you'd use your brains, or at least some of your senses, you'd have known it as well."

"You'd have let them kill us."

"More to the point, you nearly let them kill you. You." He gestured at Moira. "Stood there, letting the fear soak you, scent you. You." And now Larkin. "You charged in without using your head, and nearly lost it for the trouble. As for you," he said to Hoyt. "Protecting the womenfolk may be chivalrous, but you'll both die—with your honor intact, of course. While Red, at least, used her head initially—and the power your bloody gods gave her—she then fell apart, and stood meekly waiting to be dead."

He stepped forward. "So, we'll work on your weaknesses. Which are legion."

"I've had enough." Glenna's voice was hardly more than a whisper. "Enough of blood and death, enough for one night. Enough." She dropped the stake and walked out.

"Leave her be." Cian waved a hand when Hoyt turned to follow. "For Christ's sake, an ounce of brain would tell you she wants only her own company—and a strong, dramatic exit like that deserves to stand. Let her have it."

"He's right." Moira spoke quickly. "As much as it pains

me to say it. She needs the quiet." She walked over to pick up the sword that had been knocked out of her hand. "Weaknesses." She nodded her head, faced Cian. "Very well then. Show me."

Chapter 18

Hoyt expected to find her in bed when he came in. He'd hoped she'd be sleeping, so that he could put her under more deeply and work on her injuries.

But she was standing by the window in the dark.

"Don't turn on the light," she said with her back to him. "Cian was right, there are more outside still. If you pay attention, you can sense them. They move like shadows, but there's movement—more a sense of movement. They'll go soon, I think. To whatever hole they burrow in during the day."

"You should rest."

"I know you say that because you're concerned, and I'm calm enough now not to take your head off for it. I know I behaved poorly upstairs. I don't really care."

"You're tired, as I am. I want to wash, and I want to sleep."

"You have your own room. And that was uncalled for," she continued before he could speak. Now she turned. Her face seemed very pale in the dark, pale against the dark robe she wore. "I'm not as calm as I thought. You had no right, no right, to stand in front of me up there."

"Every right. Love gives me the right. And even without that, if a man doesn't shield a woman from harm—"

"Stop right there." She held up a hand, palm out, as if to block his words. "This isn't about men and women. It's about humans. The seconds you took to think of me, to worry for me could have cost you your life. We can't spare it, neither of us. Any of us. If you don't trust that I can defend myself—that all of us can, we're nowhere."

That her words made sense didn't matter a whit as far as he was concerned. He could still see the way that monster had leaped on her. "And where would you be if I hadn't destroyed that thing?"

"Different. A different matter." She moved closer now so that he could scent her, the lotions she used on her skin. So utterly female.

"This is foolishness, and a waste of time."

"It's not foolish to me, so listen up. Fighting with and protecting fellow soldiers is one thing, a vital thing. We all have to be able to count on each other. But to brush me back from battle is another. You have to understand and accept the difference."

"How can I, when it's you, Glenna? If I lost you—"

"Hoyt." She gripped his arms, a kind of impatient comfort. "Any or all of us might die in this. I'm fighting to understand and accept that. But if you die, I won't live with the responsibility of knowing it was for me. I won't do it."

She sat on the side of the bed. "I killed tonight. I know how it feels to end something. To use my power to do that, something I never thought I'd do, need to do." She held out her hands to study them. "I did it to save another human being, and still it weighs on me. I know that if I'd done it with stake or sword I'd accept it more easily. But I used magic to destroy."

She lifted her face to his, and the sorrow was deep in her eyes. "This gift was always so bright, and now there's a darkness in it. I have to understand and accept that, too. And you have to let me."

"I accept your power, Glenna, and what you can and will do with it. I think all of us would be better served by it if you worked solely on the magicks."

"And left the bloody work to you? Off the front line, out of harm's way, stirring my cauldron?"

"Twice this night I nearly lost you. So you'll do as I say."

It took a moment to find her voice. "Well, in a pig's eye. Twice this night I faced death, and I survived."

"We'll discuss this further tomorrow."

"Oh no, oh no, we won't." She flicked out a hand, slammed the door to the bathroom inches before he reached it.

He whirled back, a man obviously at the end of his tether. "Don't slap your power out at me."

"Don't slap your manhood out at me. And that didn't come out the way I meant it." Because there was laughter tickling the back of her throat right along with the temper, she took a breath. "I won't snap to, Hoyt, when you order it, any more than I expect you will for me. You were frightened for me, and oh boy, do I understand that, because I was frightened for me. And for you, for all of us. But we have to get past it."

"How?" he demanded. "How is that done? This love is new for me, this need and this terror that goes with it. When we were called for this, I thought it would be the hardest thing I'd ever done. But I was wrong. Loving you is harder, loving you and knowing I could lose you."

All of her life, she thought, she'd waited to be loved like this. What human didn't? "I never knew I could feel so completely for anyone. This is new for me, too, hard and scary and new. And I wish I could say you won't lose me. I wish I could. But I know the stronger I am, the better chance I have of staying alive. The stronger each one of us is, the better chance we have of surviving this. Of winning."

She stood again. "I looked at King tonight, a man I'd come to like quite a lot. I looked at what they'd made of him. What they made of him wanted my blood, my death, would have rejoiced in it. Seeing that, knowing that, hurt beyond the believing of it. He was a friend. He became a friend so quickly."

Her voice trembled, so that she had to turn away, move back to the window and the dark. "There was a part of me, even as I tried to save myself, that saw what he had been—the man who'd cooked with me, sat with me, laughed with me. I couldn't use my powers against him, couldn't pull it out of me to do that. If Cian hadn't . . ." She turned back now, straight and slim.

"I won't be weak again. I won't hesitate a second time. You have to trust me for that."

"You called out for me to run. Would you say that was putting yourself in front of me in battle?"

She opened her mouth, closed it again. Cleared her throat. "Seemed like the thing to do at the time. All right, all right. Point made and taken. We'll both work on it. And I've some ideas on weaponry that might be helpful. But before we put this, and ourselves to bed, I want to cover one more thing."

"I don't find myself at all surprised."

"Fighting with your brother over me isn't something I appreciate or consider flattering."

"It wasn't only about you."

"I know that. But I was the catalyst. And I'm going to have a word with Moira about it, too. Of course, her idea of distracting Cian from us changed the entire scope of things."

"It was madness for him to bring those things into the house. His own temper and arrogance could have cost us lives."

"No." She spoke quietly now, and with absolute certainty. "He was right to do it."

Stunned, he gaped at her. "How can you say so? How can you defend him?"

"He made a very big and illuminating point, one we won't be able to forget. We won't always know when they'll come, and we have to be ready to kill or be killed every minute, every day. We weren't, not really. Even after King, we weren't. If there'd been more of them, the odds more even, it might've been a very different story."

"He stood by, did nothing."

"Yes, he did. Another point. He's the strongest of us, and the smartest in these circumstances. It's up to us to work toward closing that gap. I have some ideas, at least for the two of us."

She came to him, rising on her toes to brush her lips over his cheek. "Go ahead, wash up. I want to sleep on it. I want to sleep with you."

She dreamed of the goddess, of walking through a world of gardens, where birds were bright as the flowers, and the flowers like jewels.

From a high black cliff, water the color of liquid sapphire tumbled down to strike a pool clear as glass where gold and ruby fish darted.

The air was warm and heavy with fragrance.

Beyond the gardens was a silver sickle of beach where the turquoise water lapped its edges gently as a lover. There were children building sparkling castles of sand, or splashing in the foamy surf. Their laughter carried on the air like the birdsong.

Rising from the beach were steps of shimmering white with diamonds of ruby red along their edges. High above them were houses, painted in dreamy pastels, skirted with yet more flowers, with trees that dripped blossoms.

She could hear music drifting down from the tall hill, the harps and flutes singing of joy.

"Where are we?"

"There are many worlds," Morrigan told her as they walked. "This is just another. I thought you should see that you fight for more than yours, or his, or the world of your friends."

"It's beautiful. It feels . . . happy."

"Some are, some are not. Some demand a hard life, full of pain and effort. But it is still life. This world is old," the goddess said, her robes flowing as she opened her arms. "It earned this beauty, this peace, through that pain and that effort."

"You could stop what's coming. Stop her."

Her bright hair dancing in the wind, she turned to Glenna. "I have done what I can to stop it. I have chosen you."

"It's not enough. Already we've lost one of us. He was a good man."

"Many are."

"Is this how fate and destiny work? The higher powers? So coldly?"

"The higher powers bring laughter to those children, they bring the flowers and the sun. Love and pleasures. And yes, death and pain. It must be so."

"Why?"

Morrigan turned, smiled. "Or it would all mean so little. You are a gifted child. But the gift has weight."

"I used that gift to destroy. All of my life I've believed, been taught, I *knew* what I had, what I was, could never harm. But I used it to harm."

Morrigan touched Glenna's hair. "This is the weight, and it must be carried. You were charged to strike at evil with it."

"I won't be the same again," Glenna stated, looking out to sea.

"No, not the same. And you're not ready. None of you. You're not yet whole."

"We lost King."

"He isn't lost. He's only moved to a different world."

"We're not gods, and we grieve for the death of a friend. The cruelty of it."

"There will be more death, more grieving."

Glenna closed her eyes. It was harder, even harder, to speak of death when she looked at such beauty. "We're just full of good news today. I want to go back."

"Yes, you should be there. She'll bring blood, and another kind of power."

"Who will?" Fear had Glenna jerking back. "Lilith? Is she coming?"

"Look there." Morrigan pointed to the west. "When the lightning strikes."

The sky went black, and the lightning arrowed out of the sky to strike the heart of the sea.

When she whimpered, turned, Hoyt's arms came around her.

"It's dark."

"Nearly dawn." He touched his lips to her hair.

"A storm's coming. She's coming with it."

"Did you dream?"

"Morrigan took me." She pressed closer. He was warm. He was real. "Some place beautiful. Perfect and beautiful. Then the dark came, and the lightning struck the water. I heard them growling in the dark."

"You're here now. Safe."

"None of us are." Her mouth lifted, met his desperately. "Hoyt."

She rose above him, slim and fragrant. White skin against pearled shadows. She took his hands, pressed them to her breasts. Felt his fingers cup her.

Real and warm.

As her heartbeat quickened, the candles around the room began to flicker. In the hearth, the fire woke to simmer.

"There's a power in us." She lowered to him, her lips racing over his face, down his throat. "See it. Feel it. What we make together."

Life, was all she could think. Here was life, hot and human. Here was a power that could strike back the icy fingers of death.

She rose up again, taking him into her, strong and deep. Then bowing back as the thrill washed through her like wine.

He wrapped around her, coming to her so his mouth could take her breast, so he could taste the pounding of her heart. Life, he thought as well. Here was life.

"All that I am." Already breathless, he feasted on her. "This is more. From the first moment, for the rest of time."

She took his face, watched herself in his eyes. "In any world. In all of them."

It poured through her, so fast, so hot, she cried out.

Dawn broke quietly while their passion raged.

"It's the fire," Glenna told him.

They were in the tower, sitting over coffee and scones. She had the door firmly locked, and had added a charm to make certain no one and nothing entered until she was finished.

"It's exciting." His eyes were still sleepy, his body relaxed.

Sex, Glenna thought, could work wonders. She was feeling pretty damn good herself.

"Wake-up sex agrees with you, but I'm not talking about that kind of fire. Or not exclusively. Fire's a weapon, a big one, against what we're fighting."

"You killed one with it last night." He poured more coffee. He was, he realized, developing quite a taste for it. "Effective, and quick, but also—"

"A little unpredictable, yes. If the aim's off, or one of our own is too close—or steps or is shoved in the line, it would be extremely tragic. But . . ." She tapped her fingers against her cup. "We learn to control it, to channel it. That's what we do, after all. Practice, practice. And more, we can use it to enhance the other weapons. The way you did last night, with the fire on the sword."

"I'm sorry?"

"The fire on your sword when you clashed with Cian." She lifted her eyebrows at his blank expression. "You didn't call it, it just came. Passion—in that case anger. Passion, when we're making love. A flame shot down your sword last night, just for an instant. A flaming sword."

She pushed up from the table to pace around the room. "We haven't been able to do anything about creating a protected zone around the house."

"We may yet find the way."

"Tricky, since we have a vampire on the premises. We can't set down a spell to repel vampires without repelling Cian. But yes, in time—if we have the time—we may find a way around that. In the meantime, the fire's not only effective, it's beautifully symbolic. And you bet your gorgeous ass, it'll put the fear of the gods into the enemy."

"Fire takes focus and concentration. A little difficult when you're fighting for your life."

"We'll work on it until it isn't so difficult. You wanted me to work more on magic, and in this case I'm willing. It's time to make ourselves a serious arsenal."

She came back, sat on the table. "When it's time to take this war to Geall, we're going loaded."

She spent the day at it, with him and without him. She buried herself in her own books, and the ones she dragged up from Cian's library.

When the sun set, she lit candles for work light and ignored Cian's banging on the door. She closed her ears to his curses, and his shouts that it was bloody well time for training.

She *was* training.

And she'd come out when she was damn good and ready.

The woman was young, and fresh. And very, very alone.

Lora watched from the shadows, gleefully pleased with her luck. To think she'd been annoyed when Lilith had sent her out with a trio of foot soldiers on a simple scouting mission. She'd wanted to hit one of the outlying pubs, have some fun, have a feast. How long did Lilith expect them to keep to the caves, lying low, picking off the occasional tourist?

The most fun she'd had in *weeks* had been smacking that witch around, and stealing the black man right from under the noses of that tedious, holy brigade.

She wished they could have based somewhere, *anywhere* but in this dreary place. Somewhere like Paris or Prague. Somewhere so full of people she could pluck them like plums. Somewhere full of sound and heartbeats, and the smell of flesh.

She would swear there were more cows and sheep than people in this stupid country.

It was boring.

But now, there was this interesting possibility.

So pretty. So unfortunate.

This one would be a good candidate for the change as well as a quick snack. It would be fun to have a new companion, a woman particularly. One she could train, and play with.

A new toy, she decided, to stave off this endless ennui, at least until the real fun began.

Where, she wondered, had the pretty thing been going after dark in her little car? Such bad luck to have a puncture on this quiet country road.

Nice coat, too, Lora thought as she watched the woman haul out the jack and spare. They were close enough to the same size that she could have the coat as well as what was in it.

All that lovely warm blood.

"Bring her to me." She gestured at the three who stood with her.

"Lilith said we weren't to feed until—"

She whirled, fangs glinting, eyes burning red. And the vampire who'd once been a man of two hundred and twenty pounds of muscle when alive, backed off hurriedly.

"You question me?"

"No." She was here, after all—and he could smell her hunger. Lilith was not.

"Bring her to me," Lora repeated, tapping him on the chest, then wagging that finger playfully in front of his face. "And no tasting. I want her alive. It's time I had a new playmate." Her lips moved over her fangs in a pretty pout. "And try not to damage the coat. I like it."

They moved out of the shadows and onto the road, three males who'd been ordinary in life.

They scented human. And female.

Their hunger, always waiting, woke—and only the fear of Lora's reprisal prevented them from charging like wolves.

She glanced over as they approached. She smiled, quick and friendly as she straightened from her crouch at the side of the car, and raked a hand through short, dark hair that left her throat and neck exposed in the gloomy light.

"I was hoping someone would come along."

"Must be your lucky night." The one Lora had chastised grinned.

"I'll say. Dark, deserted road like this, middle of nowhere. Whew. It's a little scary."

"It can get scarier."

They spread out in a triangle to close her in with the car at her back. She took a step back, eyes going wide, and they growled low in the throat.

"Oh God. Are you going to hurt me? I don't have much money, but—"

"Money's not what we're after, but we'll take that, too."

She still held the tire iron, and when she lifted it, the one closest to her laughed. "Stay back. Just keep away from me."

"Metal's not a big problem for us."

He charged toward her, hands lifted toward her throat. And exploded into dust.

"No, but the pointy end of this is." She wagged the stake she'd held behind her back.

She lunged, kicking one aside with a flashing foot to the belly, blocking a blow with her forearm then leading with the stake. She let the last one come to her, let the momentum of his rage and hunger rush him forward. She swung the tire iron full at his face. She was on him in an instant when he landed on the road.

"Metal's a little problem after all," she said. "But we'll finish up with this."

She staked him, rose. Dusted off her coat. "Damn vampires."

She started back to her car, then stopped, her head lifting like a dog scenting the air.

She spread her legs, shifted her grip on the tire iron, on the stake. "Don't you want to come out and play?" she called out. "I can smell you out there. These three didn't give me much action, and I'm revved."

The scent began to fade. In moments, the air was clear again. She watched, and waited, then with a shrug hooked the stake into the sheath on her belt. When she finished changing the tire, she glanced up at the sky.

Clouds had rolled over the moon, and in the west thunder grumbled. "Storm's coming," she murmured.

I n the training room, Hoyt landed hard on his back. He felt every bone in his body rattle. Larkin pounced, then brought the blunted stake down to tap Hoyt's heart.

"I've killed you six times already tonight. You're off your game." He cursed lightly when he felt the blade at his throat.

Moira eased it back, then leaned over him to give him an upside down smile. "He'd be dust, that's certain, but you'd be bleeding all over what's left."

"Well, if you're going to come at a man from behind—"

"They will," Cian reminded him, giving Moira one of his rare nods of approval. "And more than one. You make your kill, you move on. Quick, fast and in a bloody hurry."

He vised his hands on Moira's head, feigned giving it a twist. "Now the three of you are dead because you spend too much time talking. You need to handle multiple opponents, whether it's sword, stake or bare hands."

Hoyt stood, shook himself off. "Why don't you demonstrate for us?"

Cian lifted his brows at the irritable challenge. "All right then. All of you, on me. I'll try not to hurt you more than is necessary."

"Bragging. That would be talking, wouldn't it?" Larkin crouched into a fighting stance.

"It would be, in this case, stating the obvious." He picked up the blunted stake, tossed it to Moira. "What you want to do here is anticipate each other's moves, as well as mine. Then . . . So you decided to join the party."

"I've been working on something. Making progress." Glenna touched the hilt of the dagger she'd strapped to her waist. "I needed to step away from it awhile. What's the drill here?"

"We're going to kick Cian's arse," Larkin told her.

"Oh. I'll play. Weapons?"

"Your choice." Cian nodded toward the dagger. "You seem to have yours."

"No, not for this." She moved over, selected another blunted stake. "Rules?"

In answer, Cian shot over, flipped Larkin and sent him tumbling to a pad. "Win. That's the only rule."

When Hoyt moved on him, Cian took the blow, let the momentum of it carry him into the air. He kicked off the wall, revolved, and used his body to knock Hoyt into Moira. And took them both down.

"Anticipate," he repeated, and kicked back almost idly to send Larkin into the air.

Glenna grabbed a cross, held it out as she stepped forward.

"Ah, smart." His eyes went red, just at the rims. Outside the doors, thunder began to grumble. "Shield and weapon, put the enemy in retreat. Except . . ." He lashed out, forearm to forearm and knocked the cross away. But when he spun to dispatch the stake, Glenna dived, going under him.

"Now this one's clever." Cian nodded approval, and for a moment, his face was illuminated by a ripple of lightning against the glass. "She uses her head, her instincts—at least when the stakes—haha—are low."

They circled him now, which he considered a small improvement in their strategy. Not quite a team, not yet an oiled machine, but an improvement.

As they closed in, he could see the need to pounce in Larkin's eyes.

Cian chose what he considered the weakest link, pivoted, and using one hand simply lifted Moira off her feet. When he tossed her, Larkin instinctively shifted to catch her. All Cian needed to do was sweep out a leg, take Larkin off his feet, and both of them went down in a tangle of limbs.

He spun to block his brother, gripped Hoyt's shirt. The solid head butt had Hoyt stumbling back, giving Cian the instant he needed to wrench the stake from Glenna.

He had her back against him, his arm hooked tight around her neck.

"What now?" he asked the rest of them. "I've got your girl here. Do you back off, leave her to me? Do you come in, risk me snapping her in half? It's a problem."

"Or do they let me take care of myself?" Glenna gripped the chain around her neck, swung the cross back toward Cian's face.

He released her, vaulted clear to the ceiling. He clung there a moment, a dangerous fly, then dropped lightly to his feet.

"Not bad. And still, the four of you have yet to put me down. And if I were to—" There was a burst of lightning as his hand shot out, snatched the flying stake an inch from his own heart. The end was honed to a killing point.

"We'd call that cheating," he said mildly.

"Back away from him."

They turned to see the woman step through the terrace doors as another flash of lightning ripped the sky behind her. She was slim in a black leather coat that hit her at the knees. Her dark hair was cut short, showcasing a high forehead and enormous eyes of vivid blue.

She dumped the large sack she carried on the floor, and with another stake in one hand, a two-edged knife in the other, she moved farther into the light.

"Who the hell are you?" Larkin demanded.

"Murphy. Blair Murphy. And I'll be saving your lives to-night. How the hell'd you let one of them in the house?"

"It happens I own it," Cian told her. "This is my place."

"Nice. Your heirs should be celebrating really soon. I said keep back from him," she snapped as both Larkin and Hoyt moved in front of Cian.

"I'd be his heir, as this is my brother."

"He's one of us," Larkin said.

"No. He's really not."

"But he is." Moira held up her hands to show they were empty, and moved slowly toward the intruder. "We can't let you hurt him."

"Looked to me like you were doing a piss-poor job of try-ing to hurt him when I came in."

"We were training. He's chosen to help us."

"A vampire helping humans?" Those big eyes narrowed in interest, and what might have been humor. "Well, there's always something new." Slowly Blair lowered the stake.

Cian pushed his shields aside. "What are you doing here? How did you come here?"

"How? Aer Lingus. What? Killing as many of your kind as I can manage. Present company, temporarily, excluded."

"How do you know about his kind?" Larkin asked her.

"Long story." She paused to scan the room, eyebrows lifting

thoughtfully at the stockpile of weapons. "Nice stash. There's something about a battle-ax that warms my heart."

"Morrigan. Morrigan said she'd come with the lightning." Glenna touched a hand to Hoyt's arm, then walked to Blair. "Morrigan sent you."

"She said there'd be five. She didn't mention any undead in the crew." After a moment, she sheathed the knife, tucked the stake into her belt. "But that's a god for you. Just gotta be cryptic. Look, it's been a long trip." She picked up her bag, slung the strap over her shoulder. "Got anything to eat around here?"

Chapter 19

"We have a lot of questions."

Blair nodded at Glenna as she sampled stew. "Bet you do, and right back at you. This is good." She took another spoonful. "Thanks, and compliments to the chef and all that."

"You're welcome. I'm going to start, if that's okay." Glenna scanned the faces of the rest of the group. "Where did you come from?"

"Lately? Chicago."

"The Chicago in the here and now?"

A smile tugged at Blair's wide mouth. She reached for the hunk of bread Glenna had set out, ripped it in two with nails painted a deep candy pink. "That's the one. In the heartland, Planet Earth. You?"

"New York. This is Moira, and her cousin Larkin. They're from Geall."

"Get out." Blair studied them as she ate. "I always figured that for a myth."

"You don't seem particularly surprised it's not."

"Nothing much surprises me, less now after the visit from the goddess. Heavy stuff."

"This is Hoyt. He's a sorcerer from Ireland. Twelfth-century Ireland."

Blair watched as Glenna reached behind her for Hoyt's hand, the way their fingers smoothly intertwined. "You two paired up?"

"You could say that."

Now she lifted her wine, took a small sip. "That's taking going for older men to a new level, but who could blame you?"

"Your host is his brother, Cian, who was made a vampire."

"Twelfth century?" Blair leaned back, took a good, long look at him, with all the interest but none of the amusement she'd shown when studying Hoyt. "You've got nearly a thousand years? I've never met a vamp who lasted that long. The oldest I ever came across was a couple decades shy of five hundred."

"Clean living," Cian said.

"Yeah, that'll be the day."

"He doesn't drink humans." Since it was there, Larkin got another bowl, spooned up stew for himself. "He fights with us. We're an army."

"An army? Talk about delusions of grandeur. What are you?" she asked Glenna.

"Witch."

"So, we've got a witch, a sorcerer, a couple of refugees from Geall and a vampire. Some army."

"A powerful witch." Hoyt spoke for the first time. "A scholar of remarkable skill and courage, a shape-shifter, and a centuries-old vampyre who was made by the reining queen."

"Lilith?" Now Blair set down her spoon. "She made you?"

Cian leaned back against the counter, crossed his ankles. "I was young and foolish."

"And had really bad luck."

"What are you?" Larkin demanded.

"Me? Demon hunter." She picked up her spoon to resume

eating. "I've spent most of my life tracking and dusting his kind."

Glenna angled her head. "What, like Buffy?"

With a laugh, Blair swallowed stew. "No. First, I'm not the only, just the best."

"There are more of you." At that point, Larkin decided he could use some wine as well.

"It's a family thing, has been for centuries. Not all of us, but every generation one or two more of us. My father's one, and my aunt. His uncle was—and like that. I have two cousins on the job now. We fight the fight."

"And Morrigan sent you here," Glenna put in. "Only you."

"I'd have to say yes, since I'm the only one here. Okay, so the last couple of weeks, things have been weird. More un-dead activity than usual, like they're getting some brass ones. And I'm having these dreams. Portentous dreams go with the package, but I'm having them every time I close my eyes. And sometimes when I'm wide awake. Disturbing."

"Lilith?" Glenna asked.

"She made some appearances—cameos we'll say. Up till then, I figured she was another myth. Anyway, in the dream, I thought I was over here—Ireland. It looked like here any-way. I've been to Ireland before, another family tradition. But I'm on this rise. Barren place, rough ground, deep chasms, wicked rocks."

"The Valley of Silence," Moira interrupted.

"That's what she called it. Morrigan. She said I was needed." Blair hesitated, looked around. "I probably don't have to fill in all the details since you're all here. Big battle, possible apocalypse. Vampire queen forming an army to eliminate humankind. There would be five waiting for me, gathered together. We'd have until Samhain to prepare. Not a lot of time considering, you know—goddess, eternity. But that's how it's laid out."

"So you came," Glenna said. "Just like that?"

"Didn't you?" Blair shrugged. "I was born for this. I've dreamed of that place before, as long as I can remember. Me standing on that rise, watching it rage below. The moon, the fog, the screams. I always knew I'd end up there."

Always assumed she would die there.

"I just expected a little more backup."

"In three weeks we've killed more than a dozen," Larkin said with some annoyance.

"Good for you. I don't keep a tally of kills since I had my first thirteen years ago. But I took out three tonight on the road, on the way here."

"Three?" He held up his spoon. "Alone?"

"There was another. It stayed back. Chasing it down didn't seem like a good way to stay alive, which is the first rule in the family handbook. There might have been more of them, but I only scented the one. You've got more stationed around the perimeter of this place. I had to slip through them to get inside."

She pushed her empty bowl away. "That was really good. Thanks again."

"You're welcome again." Glenna took the bowl to the sink. "Hoyt, can I have a word with you? Excuse us, just for a minute."

She drew him out of the kitchen, toward the front of the house. "Hoyt, she's—"

"The warrior," he finished. "Yes, she's the last of the six."

"It was never King." She pressed her fingers to her mouth as she turned away. "He was never one of the six, and what happened to him—"

"Happened." Hoyt took her shoulders, turned her to face him. "Can't be changed. She's the warrior, and completes the circle."

"We have to trust her. I don't know how we begin to do that. She damned near killed your brother before she bothered to say hello."

"And we have only her word she's who she says she is."

"Well, she's not a vampire. She walked right into the house. Added to that, Cian would know."

"Vampyres can have human servants."

"So how do we know? Do we take what she says she is on faith? If she is what she says, she's the last of us."

"We have to be sure."

"It's not like we can check her ID."

He shook his head, not bothering to ask her meaning. "She has to be tested. Upstairs, I think, in the tower. We'll make the circle, and we'll be sure."

When they were gathered upstairs, Blair looked around. "Close quarters. I like things roomier. You're going to want to keep your distance," she warned Cian. "I might stake you, just knee-jerk."

"You can try."

She tapped her fingers on the stake in her belt. There was a ring, a ridged band of silver, on her right thumb. "So, what's all this about?"

"We had no sign you were coming," Glenna began. "Not you specifically."

"So, you're thinking Trojan Horse?"

"It's a possibility we can't dismiss without proof."

"No," Blair agreed, "you'd be stupid just to take my word. And I feel better, actually, knowing you're not stupid. What do you want? My demon hunter's license?"

"You actually have—"

"No." She planted her feet, very like a warrior bracing for battle. "But if you're toying with doing some kind of witchcraft that involves my blood or other bodily fluid, you're out of luck. Line drawn on that."

"Nothing like that. Well, witchcraft, but nothing that requires blood. We're linked, the five of us. By fate, by necessity. And some, yes, by blood. We are the circle. We are the chosen. If you're the last link of that circle, we'll know."

"Otherwise?"

"We can't harm you." Hoyt laid a hand on Glenna's shoulder. "It's against all we are to use power against a human being."

Blair glanced toward the broadsword leaning against the tower wall. "Anything in the rule book about sharp, pointy objects?"

"We won't harm you. If you're Lilith's servant, we'll make you our prisoner."

She smiled, one corner of her mouth rising, then the other. "Good luck with that. All right, let's do it. Like I said, if you'd swallowed everything without a *hmmm,* I'd be more worried about what I'd walked into here. You guys around this white circle, me in it?"

"You know witchcraft?" Glenna asked her.

"I know something about it." She stepped into the circle.

"One of us at each point," Glenna instructed, "to form a pentagram. Hoyt will do the search."

"Search?"

"Of your mind," he assured Blair.

"There are some private things in there, too." Uncomfortable, she moved her shoulders, frowned at Hoyt. "Am I supposed to think of you as my witch doctor?"

"I'm not a witch. It will go more quickly, and without discomfort if you open to this." He lifted his hands, and lit the candles. "Glenna?"

"This is the circle of light and knowledge, formed by like minds, like hearts. Within this circle of light and knowledge no harm will we impart. We seek to link so we may know, within this ring only truth bestow. With mind to mind in destiny, as we will, so mote it be."

The air rippled, and still the candle flames rose straight as arrows. Hoyt held out his hands toward Blair.

"No harm, no pain. Only thoughts within thoughts. Your mind to my mind, your mind to our minds."

Her eyes looked deeply into his, had something flickering in his head. Then they went black, and he saw.

They all saw.

A young girl fighting a monster nearly twice her size. There was blood on her face, and her shirt was torn. They could hear each drawing of her labored breath. A man stood off to the side, and watched the battle.

She was struck to the ground with a vicious backhanded blow, and sprang up. Struck down again. When the thing leaped, she rolled. And stabbed it through the back, into the heart, with a stake.

Slow, the man said. *Sloppy, even for a first kill. You'll need to do better.*

She didn't speak, but the mind inside her mind thought, *I'll do better. I'll do better than anyone.*

Now she was older, and fought beside the man. Ferociously, savagely. The odds were five to two, but it was done quickly. And when it was done, the man shook his head. *More control, less passion. Passion will kill you.*

She was naked, in bed with a young man, moving with him in the low light of the lamp. She smiled as she arched to him, nipped his lip. A diamond winked madly on her finger. Her mind was full of passion, of love, of joy.

And of despair and misery as she sat on the floor in the dark, alone, weeping out the shards of a broken heart. Her finger was bare.

She stood on the rise above the battleground, with the goddess a white shadow beside her.

You were the first to be called, and the last, Morrigan told her. *They're waiting for you. The worlds are in your hands. Take theirs, and fight.*

She thought, *I've been coming toward this all my life. Will it be the end of it?*

Hoyt lowered his hands, brought her slowly back, as he closed the circle. Her eyes cleared, blinked.

"So? Did I pass the audition?"

Glenna smiled at her, then walked to the table, lifted one of the crosses. "This is yours now."

Blair took it, let it dangle. "It's nice. Beautiful craftsmanship, and I appreciate the gesture. But I have my own." She tugged the chain from under her shirt. "Family thing again. Like an heirloom."

"It's lovely, but if you'd—"

"Wait." Hoyt snatched at the cross, stared at it as it lay in his palm. "Where did you get this? Where did it come from?"

"I told you, family. We have seven of them. They've been passed down. You're going to want to let go of that."

When he looked up into her eyes again she narrowed hers. "What's the problem?"

"There were seven, the goddess gave me, on the night she charged me to come here. I asked for protection for my family, the family she ordered me to leave behind. And these were what she gave me."

"That was what, nine hundred years back? It doesn't mean—"

"It's Nola's." He looked over her head to Cian. "I can feel it. This is Nola's cross."

"Nola?"

"Our sister. The youngest." His voice thickened as Cian moved closer to see for himself. "And here, on the back, I inscribed it with her name. She said I'd see her again. And by the gods, I am. She's in this woman. Blood to blood. Our blood."

"There's no question?" Cian said quietly.

"I put this around her neck myself. Look at her, Cian."

"Aye. Well." He looked away again, then moved to the window.

"Forged in the fire of the gods, given by the hand of a sorcerer." Blair breathed deep. "Family legend. My middle name is Nola. Blair Nola Bridgit Murphy."

"Hoyt." Glenna touched his arm. "She's your family."

"I guess you'd be my uncle, a thousand times removed or however it works." She glanced over toward Cian. "And isn't it a kick in the ass? I'm related to a vampire."

In the morning, under a weak and fitful sunlight, Glenna stood with Hoyt in the family graveyard. The storm had soaked the grass, and rain still dripped from the petals of the roses that climbed over his mother's grave.

"I don't know how to comfort you."

He took her hand. "You're here. I never thought I would need anyone to be with me, not the way I need you. It's all so fast, all of this. Loss and gain, discovery, questions. Life and death."

"Tell me about your sister. About Nola."

"She was bright and fair, and gifted. She had sight. She loved animals—had, I think, a special affinity for them. Before I left, there were puppies born to my father's wolfhound. Nola would spend hours in the stables playing with them. And while the world turned, she grew to a woman, had children."

He turned, rested his brow against Glenna's. "I see her in this woman, this warrior who's with us now. And inside of me is another war."

"Will you bring her here? Blair?"

"It would be right."

"You do what's right." She tipped up her head so her lips brushed his. "It's why I love you."

"If we were to marry—"

She took one quick, jerky step back. "Marry?"

"Sure that hasn't changed over the centuries. A man and a woman love, they take vows, make promises. Marriage or handfasting, a tie to bind them to each other."

"I know what marriage is."

"And it disturbs you?"

"Not disturbs, and don't smile at me that way, as if I'm being endearingly stupid. Give me just a minute here." She looked over the stones, toward the sparkling hills beyond. "Yes, people still marry, if they like. Some live together without the ritual."

"You and I, Glenna Ward, we're creatures of ritual."

She looked back at him, felt her stomach jitter. "Yes, we are."

"If we were to marry, would you live here with me?"

It was a second jolt. "Here? In this place, in *this* world?"

"In this place, in this world."

"But . . . don't you want to go back? Need to?"

"I don't think I can go back. Magically, aye, I think it's possible," he said before she could speak. "I don't think I can go back, to what was. To what was home. Not knowing when they'll die. Knowing that Cian is here—that other half of me. I don't think I could go back knowing you would go with me, and pine for what you left here."

"I said I would go."

"Without hesitation," he agreed. "Yet you hesitate at the rite of marriage."

"You caught me off guard. And you didn't actually ask

me," she said with some annoyance. "You more posed a hypothesis."

"If we were to marry," he said a third time, and the humor in his voice had her fighting her own, "would you live with me here?"

"In Ireland?"

"Aye, here. And in this place. It would be a kind of melding of our worlds, our needs. I would ask Cian to let us live in the house, to tend it. It needs people, family, the children we'd make together."

"Leaps and bounds," she murmured. Then took a moment to settle herself, to search herself. Her time, his place, she thought. Yes, it was a loving compromise, could be—would be—a melding of spirits.

"I've always been a confident sort, even as a child. Know what you want, work to get it, then value it once you have it. I've tried not to take anything in my life for granted, or not too much. My family, my gift, my lifestyle."

Reaching out, she brushed her fingers over one of his mother's roses. Simple beauty. Miraculous life.

"But I've learned that I took the world for granted, that it would always be—and that it would roll along, pretty much without my help. I learned otherwise, and that's given me something else to work for, to value."

"Is that a way of saying this isn't the time to speak of marriage and children?"

"No. It's a way of saying I understand the little things— and the big ones—the normal things, life, become only more important when it's all on the line. So . . . Hoyt the Sorcerer."

She touched her lips to his cheek, then the other. "If we were to marry, I would live here with you, and tend this house with you, and make children with you. And I'd work very hard to value all of it."

Watching her, he held up a hand, palm to her. When hers met it, their fingers linked, firm and strong. Light spilled out of their clasped hands.

"Will you marry me, Glenna?"

"Yes."

He cupped the back of her neck, drawing her to him. The kiss spun out, full of promise and possibilities. Full of hope. When her arms came around him, she knew she'd found the strongest part of her destiny.

"We have more to fight for now." He turned his face into her hair. "More to be now."

"Then we will be. Come with me. I'll show you what I'm working on."

She took him with her closer to the house where there were targets set up for archery training. The sound of hoof-beats had her looking over, just in time to see Larkin ride the stallion into the trees.

"I wish he wouldn't ride in the woods. There are so many shadows."

"I doubt they could catch him, if they were lying in wait. But if you asked him," Hoyt said, running a hand down Glenna's hair, "he'd keep to the fields."

Her brows lifted in puzzlement. "If I asked?"

"If he knew you worried, he'd give that to you. He's grateful for what you do for him. You feed him," Hoyt said when she frowned.

"Oh. Well, he certainly likes to eat." Glenna looked to-ward the house. Moira, she imagined, was having her morn-ing session with the books, and Cian would be sleeping. As for Blair, it would take a little time before Glenna learned the newcomer's routine.

"I think we'll have lasagna for dinner. Don't worry." She patted his hand. "You'll like it—and it occurs to me that I'm already tending the house, and the family in it. I never thought of myself as particularly domestic. The things you learn. And now."

She drew her dagger, moving she realized, with complete ease from cookery to weaponry.

The things you learn.

"I worked on this yesterday."

"On the dagger," Hoyt prompted.

"On charming the dagger. I thought I should start small, eventually work up to a sword. We talked about doing some-thing about weapons, but with one thing and the other, we haven't really gotten down to it. Then I thought of this."

He took it from her, skimmed a finger up the edge. "Charmed in what way?"

"Think fire." His gaze moved back to hers. "No, literally," she said as she stepped back a pace. "Think fire. Visualize it, skimming over the blade."

He turned the dagger in his hand, then shifted to a fighting grip. He imagined fire, pictured it coating the steel. But the blade remained cool.

"Are there words to be said?" he asked her.

"No, you just have to want it, to see it. Try it again."

He focused, and got nothing.

"All right, maybe it only works for me—for now. I can refine it." She took it back from him, drew out the image, and pointed the dagger toward the target.

There wasn't so much as a spurt.

"Damn it, it worked yesterday." She took a closer look to make certain she hadn't grabbed the wrong weapon that morning. "This is the right one, I inscribed a pentagram on the hilt. See?"

"Yes, I see it. Perhaps the charm is limited. It wore off."

"I don't see how. I should have to break the charm, and I didn't. I put a lot of time and energy into this, so—"

"What's going on?" Blair strolled out, one hand tucked in the front pocket of her jeans, the other holding a steaming cup of coffee. There was a knife in a sheath at her hip, and the glimmer of moonstones dangling from her ears. "Knife-throwing practice?"

"No. Good morning."

She lifted an eyebrow at the irritation in Glenna's voice. "For some of us anyway. Nice dagger."

"It's not working."

"Let's see." Blair snatched it from Glenna, tested the weight. And sipping coffee, threw it toward the target. It stabbed the bull's-eye. "Works for me."

"Great, so it's got a pointy end, and you've got excellent aim." Glenna stomped toward the target, wrenched out the dagger. "What happened to the magic?"

"Search me. It's a knife, a nice one. It stabs, it hacks, it slices. Does the job. You start counting on magic, you can get sloppy. Then somebody puts that pointy end into you."

"You have magic in your blood," Hoyt pointed out to her. "You should have respect for it."

"Didn't say otherwise. I'm just more comfortable with sharp implements than voodoo."

"Voodoo is a different matter entirely," Glenna snapped. "Just because you can throw a knife doesn't mean you don't need what Hoyt and I can give you."

"No offense—seriously. But I count on myself first. And if you can't fight with that, you should leave the combat to the ones who can."

"You think I can't hit that stupid target?"

Blair sipped more coffee. "I don't know. Can you?"

Riding on insult, Glenna turned, and with curses running through her head flung the knife.

It hit the outer circle. And burst into flame.

"Excellent." Blair lowered her coffee. "I mean your aim's for shit, but the fire show is very cool." She gestured with the mug. "Probably going to need a new target though."

"I was pissed off," Glenna mumbled. "Anger." She turned her excited face to Hoyt's. "Adrenaline. We weren't angry before. I was happy. She pissed me off."

"Always happy to help."

"It's a fine charm, a good weapon." He laid a hand on Glenna's shoulder as the target burned. "How long will the flame last?"

"Oh! Wait." She stepped away, centered herself. Calmed, she put out the fire in her mind. The flame flickered out to smoke.

"It needs work. Obviously, but . . ." She went back to the target, gingerly tested the dagger's hilt. It was warm, but not too hot to touch. "It could give us a real edge."

"Damn straight," Blair agreed. "Sorry about the voodoo crack."

"Accepted." Glenna sheathed the dagger. "I'm going to ask you for a favor, Blair."

"Ask away."

"Hoyt and I need to get to work on this now, but later today . . . Could you teach me to throw a knife like you do?"

"Maybe not like me." Blair grinned. "But I can teach you to throw it better than you do, less like you're shooing pigeons."

"There's more," Hoyt said. "Cian takes charge of the training after sunset."

"A vampire training humans to kill vampires." Blair shook her head. "There's some sort of strange logic in there. Okay, so?"

"We train in the day as well—a few hours. Outside if the sun holds."

"From what I saw last night, you can use all you can get. And don't take insult," Blair added. "I work on it a couple hours a day myself."

"The one in charge of our daylight training . . . we lost him. Lilith."

"Rough. I'm sorry, it's always rough."

"I think you'd be the best to lead that training now."

"Give you guys orders, make you sweat?" Sheer pleasure shone on her face. "Sounds like fun. Just remember you asked when you start to hate me. Where are the others anyway? Daylight shouldn't be wasted."

"I imagine Moira's in the library," Glenna told her. "Larkin took the horse out a little while ago. Cian—"

"I got that part. Okay, I'm going to do a little scouting around, get the lay a little better. We'll get the party started when I get back."

"The trees are thick." Glenna nodded toward the curve of the forest. "You shouldn't go too far in, even during the day."

"Don't worry."

Chapter 20

Blair liked the woods. She liked the smell of them, the look of the big-trunked trees, the play of light and shadow that, for her, made a kind of visual music. The forest floor was carpeted with leaves that had fallen over countless years, and the fairy green of moss. The stream that ran glinting through it only added to that fairy-tale quality. It was slender and curvy, making more music with the water singing over rock.

She'd been to Clare before, had wandered field and forest and hill, and wondered how she'd missed this place if it truly was her beginnings. She supposed she hadn't been meant to find it before, to walk here. To know.

It was now, with these people, in this place.

The witch and the wizard, she mused. They were so full of love, all shiny and new, they all but glistened with it.

Advantage or disadvantage—she'd have to wait and see.

But she knew one thing. She wanted Glenna to make her a fire dagger.

The witch was okay. Great hair, too, and an urban sense of style that showed through even with simple pants and shirts. Lot of smarts going on in there, if Blair was any judge. And she was. She'd gone out of her way to be welcoming, it seemed, the night before. Fixing food, fluffing up the room she'd assigned to Blair.

It was a lot more than she was used to. And it was nice.

The wizard seemed to be on the intense side. Did a lot of watching, didn't have a lot to say. She could respect that. Just as she could, and did, respect the power he wore like skin.

As for the vampire, she was in a holding pattern there. He would be a formidable ally, or foe—and to date, she'd never considered a vamp any kind of ally. Still, she'd seen something in his face when his brother had spoken of Nola. It had been pain.

The other woman was quiet as a mouse. Watchful, oh yeah, and a little on the soft side yet. She hadn't made up her mind about Blair any more than Blair had about her.

And the guy? Larkin. Some serious eye-candy. He had a good, athletic build that should make him an asset in a fight. Boiling with energy, too, she thought. The shape-shifting deal could come in handy, if he was any good at it. She'd have to ask for a demo.

It was a lot—they were a lot—to whip into shape in a very short time. She'd have to be up to it if any of them were going to make it out of this alive.

But for now, it was nice to take a morning stroll through the trees, listening to the water sing, watching the light dance.

She skirted around a rock, cocked her head at what was curled sleeping under its shadow.

"This is your morning wake-up call," she said, and pulled the trigger on the crossbow she carried.

The vampire barely had time to open its eyes.

She retrieved the arrow, set it again.

She took out three more, disturbing another who sprinted off down the path, dodging beams of thin sunlight. Without a clear shot, and unwilling to waste an arrow, she took off after him.

The horse leaped onto the path, a gleaming black beast,

with the gilded god on its back. Larkin sliced down with his sword, and beheaded the fleeing vampire.

"Nice job," she called out.

Through streams of sunlight, Larkin trotted the horse toward her. "What are you doing out here?"

"Killing vampires. You?"

"The horse needed a run. You shouldn't be out here alone, so far from the house."

"You are."

"They couldn't catch this one." He patted Vlad on the neck. "He's the wind. So then, how many have you seen?"

"The four I killed, and yours makes five. There are probably more."

"Four others, you say? Aren't you the busy one. Do you want to hunt them now?"

He looked up to it, but she couldn't be sure. Working with an unknown partner was a good way to die, even if that partner showed a wicked skill with a sword. "That should do it for now. One of them, at least, will run back to Mommy and report we're taking them out of their nests during the day. Should tick her off."

"Tick?"

"Annoy her."

"Ah. Aye, there's that."

"Anyway, we need to do some training so I can see what you're made of."

"You can see?"

"I'm your new sergeant." She could see he wasn't thrilled with that news—and who could blame him? But she held up a hand. "How about a lift, cowboy?"

He reached down, and with a clasp of hands to forearms, she vaulted up behind him.

"How fast will this guy move?" she asked.

"You'd best hold on, and tight."

A tap of his heels sent the horse flying.

Glenna rubbed her thumb and finger together over the cauldron to add another pinch of sulfur to the mix.

"A little at a time," she said absently to Hoyt. "We don't want to overdo it and end up—"

She jerked back as the liquid flashed.

"Mind your hair," Hoyt warned.

She grabbed some pins, bundled it hastily on top of her head. "How's it coming there?"

Inside the metal trough, the dagger continued to burn. "The fire's still unstable. We have to tame it or we'll burn ourselves as well as vampyres."

"It's going to work." She took a sword, slid it into the liquid. Stepping back, she held her hands in the smoke and began her chant.

He stopped what he was doing to watch her, to study the beauty that came into her with the magic. What had his life been before she'd come into it? With no one with whom he could fully share what he was, not even Cian? With no one to look into his eyes in a way that made his heart shine?

Fire licked at the edges of the cauldron, shimmied up the sword, and still she stood, in the smoke and the flame. Her voice like music, her power like dance.

When the flames died, she removed the sword with tongs, set it aside to cure and cool.

"Each has to be done separately. I know it's going to take time, days, but in the end . . . what?" she said when she caught him staring at her. "Have I got magic soot all over my face?"

"No. You're beautiful. When will you marry me?"

She blinked in surprise. "I thought after, when it's over."

"No, I don't want to wait. Every day is a day less, and every day is precious. I want us to be married here, in this house. Before long, we'll travel to Geall, and then . . . It should be here, Glenna, in the home we'll make."

"Of course it should. I know your family can't be here, except for Cian and Blair. Neither can mine. But when it's over, Hoyt. When everyone's safe again, I'd like another ritual here, I'd like my family here then."

"A handfasting now, a wedding ceremony after. Would that suit?"

"Perfect. I'd—now? As in *now*? I can't be ready now. I have to . . . do things first. I need a dress."

"I thought you preferred your rituals skyclad."

"Very funny. A few days. Say the coming full moon."

"The end of the first month." He nodded. "It seems right. I want to—what is all that shouting?"

They walked to the window to see Blair going toe-to-toe with Larkin. Moira stood, hands fisted on her hips.

"Speaking of rituals," Glenna commented. "Looks like the head-butting portion of the daily training's started without us. We'd better get down there."

"She's slow and she's sloppy, and slow and sloppy get you dead."

"She's neither," Larkin shot back at Blair. "But her strengths lie in her bow and in her mind."

"Great, she can think a vamp to death. Let me know how that works out. As for the bow, yeah, eye like an eagle, but you can't always kill at a distance."

"I can speak for myself well enough, Larkin. And you—" Moira jabbed a finger at Blair. "I don't care to be spoken to as if I were addle-brained."

"I've got no problem with your brain, but I've got a big one with your sword arm. You fight like a girl."

"So I am."

"Not during training, not during battle. Then you're a soldier, and the enemy doesn't give a rat's ass about your plumbing."

"King had her working on her strengths."

"King's dead."

There was a moment of utter silence that couldn't have been sliced through with Cian's battle-ax. Then Blair sighed. That, she could admit, had been unnecessarily harsh.

"Look, what happened to your pal is terrible. I sure as hell don't want it to happen to me. If you don't want it to happen to you, you'll work on your weaknesses—and you've got plenty. You can play with your strengths on your own time."

She planted her feet as Hoyt and Glenna came to join them. "Did you put me in charge of this?" Blair demanded.

"I did," Hoyt affirmed.

"And we've nothing to say about it?" Fury tightened Larkin's face. "Nothing at all?"

"You don't, no. She's the best for it."

"Because she's your blood."

Blair rounded on Larkin. "Because I can put you on your ass in five seconds flat."

"Sure of that, are you?" He shimmered and changed, and the wolf he became crouched and snarled.

"Excellent," Blair said under her breath, with temper smothered by pure admiration.

"Oh, Larkin, leave off, would you?" Obviously out of patience, Moira slapped a hand at him. "He's only angry because you were rude to me. And you've no cause to be so insulting. It happens I agree with you about working on the weaknesses." And Cian had said the same, Moira recalled. "I'm willing to practice, but I won't be after standing and being berated while I'm about it."

"More flies with honey than vinegar?" Blair said. "I always wondered why the hell anyone would want to catch flies. Look, you and I can paint our toenails and talk about boys when we're off the clock. While I'm training you, I'm the bitch because I want you alive. Does it hurt when you do that?" Blair asked Larkin when he changed back. "Shifting bones and organs and so on?"

"Some actually." He couldn't recall anyone ever asking him. His temper cooled as quickly as it had flared. "But it's fun, so I don't mind so much."

He slung his arm around Moira's shoulder, gave her arm a little rub as he spoke to Hoyt and Glenna. "Your girl here took out four of them in the forest. I took a fifth myself."

"This morning? Five?" Glenna stared at Blair. "How close to the house?"

"Close enough." Blair glanced toward the woods. "Lookouts, I figure, and not very good ones. Caught them napping. Lilith's going to get word of it. She's going to be unhappy."

* * *

It wasn't a matter of killing the messenger; not in Lilith's long-standing opinion. It was a matter of killing it as painfully as possible.

The young vampire who'd foolishly gone back to the nest after Blair's morning foray was now on a slow roast, belly-down, over a simmering fire. The smell wasn't particularly pleasant, but Lilith understood command required certain sacrifices.

She circled him now, careful to keep the hem of her red gown away from the lick of flames. "Why don't we go over this again?" Her voice was melodious, somewhat like a devoted teacher speaking to a favored student. "The human—female—destroyed everyone I'd posted, save you."

"The man." Pain turned the words to guttural rasps. "The horse."

"Yes, yes. I keep forgetting the man and the horse." She stopped to study the rings she wore. "The one who came along after she'd already cut down—what was it now—four of you?"

She crouched down, a spider of stunning beauty, to stare into his red, wheeling eyes. "And she was able to do this because? Wait, wait, I remember. Because you were *sleeping*?"

"They were. The others. I was at post, Majesty. I swear it."

"At post, and yet, this single female human lives. Lives because—do I have this detail correct? Because you ran?"

"Came back . . . to report." Its sweat dripped into the fire, and sizzled. "The others, they ran away. They ran. I came to you."

"So you did." She tapped him playfully on the nose with each word, then rose. "I suppose I should reward your loyalty."

"Mercy. Majesty, mercy."

She turned around with a silky rustle of skirts to smile at the boy who sat cross-legged on the floor of the cave, systematically ripping the heads off a pile of *Star Wars* action figures.

"Davey, if you break all your toys, what will you have to play with?"

His lips moved to pout as he beheaded Anikin Skywalker. "They're boring."

"Yes, I know." She ran a loving hand over his sunny hair. "And you've been cooped up too long, haven't you?"

"Can we go outside now?" He bounced, and his eyes went round and wide at the prospect of a promised treat. "Can we go outside and play? *Please!*"

"Not quite yet. Now don't sulk." She tipped his chin up to peck a kiss on his lips. "What if your face froze like that? Here now, my sweet boy, what if I gave you a brand-new toy?"

Round cheeks bright with temper, he snapped Han Solo in two. "I'm tired of toys."

"But this will be a new one. Something you've never had before." She turned her head, and with her finger still on his chin, turned his until they both looked at the vampire over the fire pit.

And on the spit, seeing their eyes, it began to struggle and thrash. And weep.

"For me?" Davey said brightly.

"All for you, my own dumpling. But you must promise Mama not to get too close to the fire. I don't want you burned, my precious one." She kissed his little fingers before she rose.

"Majesty, I beg you! Majesty, I came back to you."

"I dislike failure. Be a good boy, Davey. Oh, and don't spoil your dinner." She gestured to Lora, who stood quietly by the door.

The screams began before it was closed behind them. And locked.

"The Hunter," Lora began. "It had to be. None of the other women have the skill to—"

A single look from Lilith silenced her. "I haven't given you leave to speak. My fondness for you is all there is between you and the pit. And my affections only go so far."

Lora bowed her head in deference and followed Lilith into the adjoining chamber. "You lost three of my good men. What can you say to that?"

"I have no excuse."

With a nod, Lilith roamed the chamber, idly picking a ruby necklace from the top of a chest. The single thing she

missed of life was mirrors. She longed, even after two mil-
lennia, to see herself reflected. To be wooed by her own
beauty. She had hired—and fed on—countless sorcerers,
witches and magicians over the centuries to make it so.

It was her greatest failure.

"You're wise not to offer one. I'm a patient woman, Lora.
I've waited more than a thousand years for what's coming.
But I won't be insulted. I dislike having these *people* pick
and pluck us off like flies."

She threw herself into a chair, tapped her long red nails
on its arms. "Speak, then. Tell me about this new one. This
Hunter."

"As the seers prophesied, my lady. The warrior of old
blood. One of the hunters who has plagued our kind for centuries."

"And you know this because?"

"She was too fast to be a mere human. Too strong. She
knew what they were before they moved on her that night,
and she was ready. She completes their number. The first
stage is set."

"My scholars said the black man was their warrior."

"They were wrong."

"Then what good are they?" Lilith heaved the necklace
she still toyed with across the room. "How can I rule when
I'm surrounded by incompetence? I want what's due me. I
want blood and death and beautiful chaos. Is it too much to
ask that those who serve me be accurate on the details?"

For nearly four hundred years Lora had been by Lilith's
side. Friend, lover, servant. No one, she was sure, knew the
queen better. She poured a glass of wine, carried it to the
chair.

"Lilith." She said it gently, offering both it and a kiss.
"We've lost nothing important."

"Face."

"No, not even that. They only believe what they've done in
these past weeks matters. It's good they do, because it makes
them overconfident. And we killed Cian's boy, didn't we?"

"We did." Lilith pouted another moment, then sipped.
"There was satisfaction in that."

"And sending him to them only demonstrated your brilliance, and your strength. Let them take dozens of the meaningless foot soldiers. We cut their heart."

"You're a comfort to me, Lora." Drinking her wine, Lilith stroked Lora's hand. "And you're right, of course, you're right. I'm disappointed, I admit. I so wanted to break their number, to foil the prophecy."

"But it's better this way, isn't it? And it'll be the sweeter when you take them all."

"Better, yes, better. And yet . . . I think we need to make a statement. It would improve my mood, and morale as well. I have an idea. I'll think it through a bit." She watched the wine swirl in her glass. "One day, one day soon, this will be the sorcerer's blood. I'll drink it from a silver cup, and nibble on sugar plums between sips. All that he is will be in me, and all that I am will make even the gods tremble.

"Leave me now. I need to plan."

As Lora rose to go to the door, Lilith tapped on her glass. "Oh, and this irritating business has made me hungry. Bring me someone to eat, will you?"

"Right away."

"Make sure it's fresh." Alone she closed her eyes and began to plot. While she plotted, the screams and squeals from the next chamber battered the cave walls.

Her lips curved. Who could be blue, she thought, with a child's laughter ringing in the air?

$\mathcal{M}$oira sat cross-legged on Glenna's bed and watched Glenna work on the magic little machine she called a laptop. Moira was desperate to get her hands on it. There were worlds of knowledge inside, and so far she'd only been allowed a few peeks.

She'd been promised a lesson, but just at the moment, Glenna seemed so absorbed—and they only had an hour free.

So she cleared her throat.

"What do you think of this one?" Glenna asked and tapped the image of a woman wearing a long white dress.

Angling her head for a better view, Moira studied the screen. "She's very lovely. I was wondering—"

"No, not the model, the dress." Glenna scooted around on the chair. "I need a dress."

"Oh, did something happen to yours?"

"No." With a little laugh Glenna twisted the pendant around her neck. "I need a very special dress. A wedding dress. Moira, Hoyt and I are going to be married. Handfasted. We decided on handfasting, with a wedding ceremony later. After."

"You're betrothed to Hoyt? I didn't know."

"It just happened. I know it might seem rushed, and the timing of it—"

"Oh, but this is wonderful!" Moira sprang up, and in a burst of enthusiasm, threw her arms around Glenna. "I'm so happy for you. For all of us."

"Thanks. For all of us?"

"Weddings, they're bright, aren't they? Bright and happy and human. Oh, I wish we were home so I could have a feast made. You can't make your own wedding feast, and I'm still not very good at the cooking."

"We won't worry about that, not yet. Weddings *are* bright—and happy and human. And I'm human enough to want the perfect dress."

"Well, of course. Why would you want less?"

Glenna let out a long, happy sigh. "Thank God. I've been feeling a little shallow. I should've known all I needed was another girl. Help me, will you? I have a few picked out, and I need to narrow it down."

"I'd love to." Gently, curiously, she tapped the side of the screen. "But . . . how do you get the dress out of the box?"

"We'll get to that, too. I'm going to have to take a few shortcuts. But later, I'll show you how to shop online the conventional way. I want something—I think—along these lines."

While they were huddled, Blair gave the doorjamb a knuckle rap. "Sorry. You got a minute, Glenna? I wanted to talk to you about requisitions and supplies. Figured you were the go-to. Hey. Nice toy."

"One of my favorites. Cian and I are the only ones linked up, so if you need to use—"

"Brought my own, but thanks. Shopping? Neiman's," she said as she moved close enough to see the screen. "Pretty fancy duds for wartime."

"Hoyt and I are getting married."

"No kidding? That's great." She gave Glenna a friendly punch on the shoulder. "Congratulations. So when's the big day?"

"Tomorrow night." When Blair only blinked, Glenna hurried on. "I know how it must seem, but—"

"I think it's terrific. I think it's excellent. Life can't stop. We can't let it. We can't let them make it stop; that's the whole point. Plus, it's great, seriously great, that the two of you found what you've got when everything's so extreme. It's one of the things we're fighting for, right?"

"Yes. Yes, it is."

"Wedding dress?"

"A potential. Blair, thank you."

Blair put a hand on Glenna's shoulder in a gesture that might have been woman-to-woman or soldier-to-soldier. Glenna supposed it was now one and the same.

"I've been fighting for thirteen years. I know better than anyone you need some real, you need things that matter, and that warm you up inside, or you lose the mission. I'll let you get back to it."

"Want to help us shop?"

"Really?" Blair did a little shuffle dance. "Are vampires blood-sucking fiends? I'm so in. One thing, not to put the damper, but how are you going to get the dress here by tomorrow?"

"I've got my ways. And I'd better get started. Would you mind closing the door? I don't want Hoyt coming in while I'm trying them on."

"Trying . . . Sure." Blair obliged while Glenna set several crystals on and around the laptop. She lit candles, then stood back, held her arms out to the side.

"Mother Goddess, I ask your grace to bring this garment to this place. Through the air, from there to here, in the light unto my sight a symbol of my destiny. As I will so mote it be."

With a shimmer and flash, Glenna's jeans and T-shirt were replaced by the white gown.

"Wow. A whole new level of shoplifting."

"I'm not stealing it." Glenna's scowled at Blair. "I'd never use my powers that way. I'm trying it on, and when I find the one, I've got another spell to work the sale. It's just to save time, which I don't have."

"Don't get bent. I was just kidding." Sort of. "Will that work for weapons if we need more?"

"I suppose it would."

"Good to know. Anyway, great dress."

"It's lovely," Moira agreed. "Just lovely."

Glenna turned, studied her reflection in the antique cheval glass. "Thank God Cian didn't strip all the mirrors out of this place. It's beautiful, isn't it? I love the lines. But . . ."

"It's not the one," Blair finished, and settled down on the bed with Moira to watch the show.

"Why do you say that?"

"It doesn't light you up. That light, in the gut, in the heart, that just spreads out right to your fingertips. You put on your wedding dress, take one look at yourself in it and you know. The others are just practice."

So it had gotten that far, Glenna thought, remembering the vision of Blair and the engagement ring on her finger. And the image of her weeping in the dark, her hand bare.

She started to comment, then said nothing. A tender area like that required more than camaraderie. It needed true friendship, and they weren't there yet.

"You're right, it's not the one. I've got four more picked out. So we'll try number two."

She hit it on the third, and felt that light glowing. Heard it in Moira's long, wistful sigh.

"And we have a winner." Blair circled her finger. "Do the turn. Oh, yeah, that one's yours."

It was romantic, and simple, Glenna thought. Just as she'd hoped. There was a little float in the long skirt, and the soft sweetheart neckline was framed by two thin straps that left her shoulders bare then ran down her shoulder blades to spotlight her back.

"It's so exactly right." She glanced at the price again, winced. "Well, maxing out my credit card doesn't seem that big a deal considering the possible apocalypse."

"Seize the day," Blair agreed. "You doing a veil, a headpiece?"

"Traditional Celtic handfastings call for a veil, but in this case . . . Just flowers, I think."

"Even better. Soft, earthy, romantic and sexy all rolled into one. Do the deal."

"Moira?" Glenna looked over, saw Moira's eyes were damp and dreamy. "I can see it has your vote, too."

"I think you'll be the most beautiful of brides."

"Well, this was serious fun." Blair got to her feet. "And I agree with the brain trust here—you look outstanding. But you need to wrap it up." She tapped her watch. "The two of you are due in training. You need some major hand-to-hand practice. Why don't you come with me now?" she said to Moira. "We can get started."

"I'll only be a few minutes," Glenna told them, then turned back to study herself in the glass.

From wedding dresses to combat, she thought. Her life had become a very strange ride.

Because he heard the music playing inside, Hoyt knocked on Cian's door a little before sundown. There'd been a time, he remembered, he wouldn't have thought of knocking, when asking permission to enter his brother's chambers wouldn't have been necessary.

A time, he thought, he wouldn't have needed to ask his brother if he could live with his wife in his own home.

Locks clicked and snicked. Cian wore only loose pants and a sleepy expression when he opened the door. "A bit early for me, for visiting."

"I need a private word with you."

"Which, of course, can't wait on my convenience. Come in then."

Hoyt stepped into a room that was pitch black. "Must we speak in the dark?"

"I can see well enough." But Cian switched on a low light beside a wide bed. The covers on the bed gleamed jewel-like in that light, and the sheets carried the sheen of silk. Cian moved to a cold box, took out a packet of blood. "I haven't had breakfast." He tossed the packet into the microwave sitting on top of the box. "What do you want?"

"When this is done, what do you intend to do?"

"As I choose, as always."

"To live here?"

"I think not," Cian said with a half laugh, and took a crystal glass from a shelf.

"Tomorrow night . . . Glenna and I are to be handfasted."

There was a slight hesitation in his rhythm, then Cian set the glass down. "Isn't that interesting? I suppose congratulations are in order. And you intend to take her back, introduce her to the family. Ma, Da, this is my bride. A little witch I picked up a few centuries from now."

"Cian."

"Sorry. The absurdity of it amuses me." He took the package out, broke it open and poured the warmed contents into the glass. "Well, anyway. *Sláinte.*"

"I can't go back."

After the first sip, the first long stare over the rim, Cian lowered the glass. "More and more interesting."

"It's no longer my place, knowing what I know. Waiting for the day to come when I know they'll die. If you could go back, would you?"

Cian frowned into his glass, then sat. "No. For thousands of reasons. But that would be one of them. But that aside, you brought this war to me. Now you take time from it to handfast?"

"Human needs don't stop. They're only keener, it seems, when the end of days threaten."

"It happens that's true. I've seen it countless times. It also happens war brides don't always make reliable wives."

"That's for me and for Glenna."

"It certainly is." He raised his glass, drank some more. "Well then, good luck to you."

"We want to live here, in this house."

"In my house?"

"In the house that was ours. Setting aside my rights, and our kinship, you're a businessman. You pay a caretaker when you're not in residence. You'd no longer have that expense. Glenna and I would tend this place and the land, at no cost to you."

"And how do you propose to make a living? There isn't much demand for sorcerers these days. Wait, I take it back." Cian laughed, finished off the blood. "You could make a goddamn fortune on television, on the Internet. Get yourself an nine-hundred number, a web site, and off you go. Not your style though."

"I'll find my way."

Cian set the glass aside, looked off into the shadows. "Maybe I hope you do, providing you live, of course. I've no problem with you staying in the house."

"Thanks for that."

Cian shrugged. "It's a complicated life you've chosen for yourself."

"And I intend to live it. I'll let you get dressed."

A complicated life, Cian thought again when he was alone. And it stunned and annoyed him that he could envy it.

Chapter 21

Glenna figured most brides were a little stressed and very busy on their weddings days. But most brides didn't have to fit in sword practice and spells between their facials and pedicures.

At least the pace cut down on the time for the nerves she'd had no idea she'd have. She couldn't squeeze in much of an anxiety attack when she was worried about flower arrangements, romantic lighting and the proper form for beheading a vampire.

"Try this." Blair started to toss the weapon, then obviously changed her mind when Glenna's mouth dropped open. She walked it over. "Battle-ax. More heft than a sword, which would work better for you, I think. You got pretty decent upper body strength, but you'd cut through easier with this than a sword. You need to get used to its weight and its balance. Here."

She walked back, picked up her own sword. "Block me with it."

"I'm not used to it. I could miss, hurt you."

"Believe me, you won't hurt me. Block!" She thrust out,

and more from instinct than obedience, Glenna clanged the ax to the sword.

"Now see, I'd just stab you cheerfully in the back while you're fumbling to turn."

"It's top heavy," Glenna complained.

"It's not. Spread out your grip more for now. Okay, stay forward after the first strike. Come down on the sword, back up at me. Slow. One," she said and thrust. "Two. Again, keep it coming. You want to counter my moves, sure, but what you want is to throw me off balance, to make me counter yours, force me to follow your moves. Think of it as a dance routine where you not only want to lead, but you also really want to kill your partner."

Blair held up a hand, stepped back. "Let me show you. Hey, Larkin. Come be the practice dummy." She tossed him her sword, hilt up, then took the battle-ax. "Take it slow," she told him. "This is a demo."

She nodded. "Attack."

As he moved on her, she called out the steps. "Strike, strike, turn. Thrust up, across, strike. He's good, see?" she said, still calling out to Glenna. "So he's pushing at me while I push at him. So you ad lib as necessary. Turn, kick, strike, strike, pivot. Slice!"

She flipped the dagger strapped to her wrist and swiped it an inch from Larkin's belly. "When his guts are spilling out, you—"

And dodged back from the swipe of what looked like a very large bear claw.

"Wow." She rested the head of her ax on the floor, leaned on the handle. Only his arm had changed shape. "You can do that? Just pieces of you?"

"If I like."

"I bet the girls back home can't get enough of you."

It took him a moment—she'd already turned to go back to Glenna—then he burst into delighted laughter. "Sure that's the truth. But not due to what you're meaning. I prefer my own shape for that kind of sport."

"Bet. Square off with Larkin. I'm going to work with Shorty for a while."

"Don't call me that," Moira snapped.

"Lighten up. I didn't mean anything by it."

Moira opened her mouth, then shook her head. "I'm sorry. That was rude."

"King called her that," Glenna said quietly.

"Oh. Got it. Moira. Resistance training. We're going to pump you up."

"I'm sorry I spoke to you that way."

"Look. We're going to irritate each other a lot before this is done. I don't bruise easily—literally or figuratively. You're going to have to toughen up yourself. Five-pound free weights. You're going to be cut by the time I'm done with you."

Moira narrowed her eyes. "I may be sorry I lashed at you, but I'm not going to let you cut me."

"No, it's an expression. It means . . ." And every other term Blair could think of would be just as confusing. Instead she curled her arm, flexed her biceps.

"Ah." A smile glimmered in Moira's eyes. "Sure I'd like that. All right then, you can cut me."

They worked a full morning. When Blair paused to gulp water from a bottle she nodded at Glenna. "You're coming right along. Ballet lessons?"

"Eight years. Never thought I'd pirouette with a battle-ax, but life's full of surprises."

"Can you do a triple?"

"Not so far."

"Look." Still holding the bottle, Blair whipped her body around three times then shot her leg out to the side, up at a forty-five-degree angle. "That kind of momentum puts a good solid punch in a kick. You need solid to knock one of these things back. Practice. You've got it in you. So." She took another swig. "Where's the groom?"

"Hoyt? In the tower. There are things that need to be done. As important as what we're doing here, Blair," she added when she sensed disapproval.

"Maybe. Okay, maybe. If you come up with more stuff like the fire dagger."

"We've fire charmed a number of the weapons." She

walked to another section of the room, took down a sword to bring it back. "Those that are charmed we've marked. See?"

On the blade near the hilt was a flame, etched into steel.

"Nice. Really. Can I try it?"

"Better take it outside."

"Good point. Okay, we should break for an hour anyway. Grab something to eat. Cross- and longbows, boys and girls, after lunch."

"I'll come with you," Glenna told her. "In case."

Blair used the terrace doors, jogged down to ground level. She glanced at the straw dummy Larkin had hung from a post. You had to give it to the guy, she mused. He had a sense of humor. He'd drawn fangs on the stuffed face and a bright red heart on the chest.

It would be fun to test the fire sword out on it—and a waste of good material. No point burning up Vampire Dummy.

So she began in a fighting stance, her arm arched behind her head, the sword pointing out.

"It's important to control it," Glenna began. "To pull the fire when you need it. If you're just slapping the burning sword around, you could burn yourself, or one of us."

"Don't worry."

Glenna started to speak again, then shrugged. There was nothing and no one to hurt but the air.

Then she watched as Blair began to move, slowly, fluid as water, the sword like an extension of her arm. Yes, a kind of ballet, she thought, a lethal one. But nonetheless compelling. The blade shimmered when the sun struck its edge, but remained cool. Just as Glenna began to assume Blair needed coaching on how to use it, the woman thrust out, and the blade erupted.

"And you're toast. God, I *love* this thing. Will you make me one, out of one of my personal weapons?"

"Absolutely." Glenna lifted her brows as Blair swished the sword through the air and the fire died. "You learn fast."

"Yeah, I do." She frowned, scanning the sky. "Clouds boiling up in the west. Guess we're in for more rain."

"Good thing I planned an indoor wedding."

"Good thing. Let's go eat."

Hoyt didn't come down until late afternoon, and by that time Glenna had given herself permission to take time for herself. She didn't want to do a quick glamour to look her best. She wanted to pamper herself, just a bit.

And she needed flowers to make the circlet for her hair, to make a bouquet. She'd made the facial cream herself, from herbs, so dabbed it on generously as she studied the sky from the bedroom window.

The clouds were moving in now. If she was going to get flowers, she had to get them before the sun was lost and the rain came. But when she opened the door to dash out, Moira and Larkin stood on the other side. He made some sound as his eyes widened, reminding her of the soft green goo on her face.

"It's a female thing, just deal with it. I'm running behind. I haven't got the flowers for my hair yet."

"We . . . Well." Moira brought her hand from behind her back and offered the circlet of white rosebuds with red ribbon braided through it. "I hope it's all right, that it's what you wanted. I know something red's traditional for a handfasting. Larkin and I wanted to give you something, and we don't have anything really, so we did this. But if you'd rather—"

"Oh, it's perfect. It's perfectly beautiful. Oh, *thank* you!" She grabbed Moira in a crushing hug, then turned a beaming smile up to Larkin.

"I've thought it wouldn't be a hardship to have you kiss me," he began, "but just at the moment . . ."

"Don't worry. I'll catch you later."

"There's this as well." He handed her a nosegay of multicolored roses twined with more red ribbon. "To carry, Moira says."

"Oh God, this is the sweetest thing." Tears dribbled through the cream. "I thought this would be hard without family here. But I have family here, after all. Thank you. Thank you both."

She bathed, scented her hair, creamed her skin. White candles burned as she performed the female ritual of preparing herself for a man. For her wedding, and her wedding night.

She was in her robe, brushing her fingers over the skirt of the dress that hung outside the wardrobe when someone knocked.

"Yes, come in. Unless you're Hoyt."

"Not Hoyt." Blair came in carrying a bottle of champagne nestled in an ice bucket. Behind her, Moira brought in three flutes.

"Compliments of our host," Blair told her. "I gotta say, he's got some class for a vampire. This is prime bubbly we got here."

"Cian sent champagne?"

"Yep. And I'm going to get down to popping this cork before we suit you up."

"I have a wedding party. Oh, you should have dresses. I should've thought of it."

"We're fine. Tonight's all about you."

"I've never had champagne. Blair says I'll like it."

"Guaranteed." Blair gave Moira a quick wink then popped the cork. "Oh, I got something for you. It's not much, seeing as I don't have your style with on-line shopping, but anyway." She dug into her pocket. "I didn't have a box either."

She put the pin in Glenna's hand. "It's a claddaugh. Traditional Irish symbol. Friendship, love, loyalty. I'd've gone for the toaster or salad bowl, but time was limited. And I didn't know where you'd registered."

Another circle, Glenna thought. Another symbol. "It's beautiful. Thank you." She turned, pinned it to the ribbon trailing from her bouquet. "Now I'll carry both of your gifts with me."

"I love sentiment. Especially with champagne." Blair poured three glasses, passed them around. "To the bride."

"And her happiness," Moira added.

"And to the continuity represented by what we do tonight. To the promise of the future it represents. I'm going to get all the teary stuff out before I do my makeup."

"Good plan," Blair agreed.

"I know what I found with Hoyt is right, is mine. I know what we're promising each other tonight is right, is ours. But having you here with me, that's right, too. And it's special. I want you to know it's very special to me, having you share this."

They touched glasses, drank, and Moira closed her eyes. "Blair was right. I do like it."

"Told ya. Okay, Moira, let's you and me make ourselves a bride."

Outside the rain splashed down and fog billowed. But in the house was candlelight and the scent of flowers.

Glenna stepped back from the mirror. "Well?"

"You look like a dream," Moira stated. "Like a goddess in a dream."

"My knees are shaking. I bet goddesses don't get shaky knees."

"Take a couple of deep breaths. We'll go down, make sure everything's set up. Including the lucky guy. You're going to blow his socks off."

"Why would she—"

"You know, sweetie," Blair said to Moira as they started for the door. "You're too literal. Start studying contemporary slang while you're buried in books." She pulled open the door, stopped short when she saw Cian. "This is girl territory."

"I'd like a moment with my . . . future sister-in-law."

"It's all right, Blair. Cian. Please come in."

He stepped inside, sent Blair a mild look over his shoulder, then shut the door in her face. Then he turned and took a long look at Glenna. "Well now, you're a vision, aren't you? Truly. My brother's fortune leaps and bounds."

"You probably think this is foolish."

"You'd be wrong. While it may be something I think of as particularly human, it's not one of the things I think of as foolish. Though there are many of those."

"I love your brother."

"Yes, a blind man could see that."

"Thank you for the champagne. For thinking of it."

"My pleasure. Hoyt's ready for you."

"Oh boy." She pressed a hand to her jumpy belly. "I hope so."

Cian smiled at that, stepped closer. "I have something for you. A wedding gift. I thought to put it in your hand as I assume, at least for now, you'd be in charge of the paperwork."

"Paperwork?"

He handed her a thin leather portfolio. After opening it, she sent him a puzzled look. "I don't understand."

"It should be clear enough. It's the deed to this house, the land. It's yours."

"Oh, but we can't. When he asked if we could stay, he only meant—"

"Glenna, I only make grand gestures once every few decades, if the whim happens to strike me. Take it when it's offered. It's more to him than it could ever be to me."

Her throat had filled so she had to wait to speak. "I know what it means to me. It will mean a great deal more to him. I wish you'd give it to him yourself."

"Take it," was all he said, then turned to the door.

"Cian." She set the folder aside, picked up her bouquet. "Would you walk me down? Would you take me to Hoyt?"

He hesitated, then opened the door. Then held out a hand to her.

She heard music as they started down.

"Your handmaidens have been busy. I expected it of the little queen—a lot of sentiment there. But the hunter surprised me."

"Am I shaking? I feel like I'm shaking."

"No." He tucked her hand into his arm. "You're steady as a rock."

And when she stepped into the room filled with candles and flowers, when she saw Hoyt standing in front of the low, gold flames of the fire, she felt steady.

They crossed the room to each other. "I've waited for you," Hoyt whispered.

"And I for you."

She took his hand, scanned the room. It was, as was traditional, madly decked with flowers. The circle had been formed, and the candles lighted, but for the ones they would light during the ritual. The willow wand lay on the table that served as altar.

"I made this for you." He showed her a thick ring of silver, deeply etched.

"One mind," she said, and drew the one she'd made him from her thumb.

They joined hands, walked to the altar. Touched fingers to the candles to light them. After slipping their rings onto the willow wand, they turned to face the others.

"We ask you to be our witnesses at this sacred rite," Hoyt began.

"To be our family as we become one."

"May this place be consecrated for the gods. We are gathered here in a ritual of love."

"Beings of the Air be with us here, and with your clever fingers tie closely the bonds between us." Glenna looked into his eyes as she spoke the words.

"Beings of the Fire be with us here . . ."

And they continued through Water, through Earth, the blessed goddess and laughing god. Her face was luminous as they spoke, as they lit incense, then a red candle. They sipped wine, scattered salt.

She and Hoyt held the wand with the rings gleaming on it between them.

The light grew warmer, brighter as they spoke to each other, the rings under their hands sparkling wildly.

"It is my wish to become one with this man." She slipped the ring from the wand and onto his finger.

"It is my wish to become one with this woman." He mirrored her gesture.

They took the cord from the altar, draped it over their joined hands.

"And so the binding is made," they said together. "Then, as the goddess and the god and the old ones—"

A scream from outside shattered the moment like a rock through glass.

Blair leaped to a window, yanked back the drape. Even her nerves jolted at the vampire's face only inches away behind the glass. But it wasn't that which turned her blood cold; it was what she saw beyond it.

She looked over her shoulders at the others, and said: "Oh, shit."

There were at least fifty, probably more, still in the forest or hidden nearby. Three cages sat on the grass, their occupants bloodied and shackled—and screaming now as they were dragged out.

Glenna shoved her way by to see, then groped behind her for Hoyt's hand. "The blonde one. That's the one who came to the door. When King—"

"Lora," Cian said. "One of Lilith's favorites. I had an . . . incident with her once." He laughed when Lora hoisted a white flag. "And if you believe that, I've all manner of bridges you can buy."

"They have people out there," Moira added. "Injured people."

"Weapons," Blair began.

"Best wait—and see how best to use them." Cian stepped away, and walked to the front door. Wind and rain sliced in when he opened it. "Lora," he called out, almost conversationally. "Why you're good and soaked, aren't you now? I'd ask you and your friends in, but I still have my sanity and my standards."

"Cian, it's been too long. Did you like my present, by the way? I didn't have time to wrap him."

"Taking credit for Lilith's work? That's just sad. And you should tell her she'll pay dearly for it."

"Tell her yourself. You and your humans have ten minutes to surrender."

"Oh? All of ten?"

"In ten minutes, we'll kill the first of these." She grabbed one of the prisoners by the hair. "Pretty, isn't she? Only sixteen. Old enough to know better than to go walking along dark roads."

"Please." The girl wept, and the blood on her neck showed

that something had already tasted her. "Please, God."

"They're always calling for God." With a laugh, Lora threw the girl facedown on the sodden grass. "He never comes. Ten minutes."

"Close the door," Blair said quietly from behind him. "Close it. Okay, give me a minute. One minute to think."

"They'll kill them regardless," Cian pointed out. "Bait is all they are."

"That's not the issue," Glenna snapped. "We have to do something."

"We fight." Larkin drew one of the swords they'd stocked in an umbrella stand near the door.

"Hold your water," Blair ordered.

"We don't surrender, not to the likes of them."

"We fight," Hoyt agreed. "But not on their terms. Glenna, the shackles."

"Yes, I can work that. I'm sure I can."

"We need more weapons from upstairs," Hoyt began.

"I said hold it." Blair grabbed his arm. "You've been in a couple of skirmishes with vampires. That doesn't prepare you. We're not just charging out there and getting cut down like meat. You can work the shackles?"

Glenna drew a breath. "Yes."

"Good. Moira, you're upstairs, bows. Cian, they've probably got guards around the house. Pick a door, start taking them out, quiet as you can manage. Hoyt's with you."

"Wait."

"I know how to do this," she told Glenna. "Are you ready to use that ax?"

"I guess we'll find out."

"Get it. You're up with Moira. They'll have archers too, and they see a hell of lot better in the dark than we do. Larkin, you and me, we're going to create a diversion. Moira, you don't start picking them off until you get the signal."

"What signal?"

"You'll know it. One more thing. Those three out there, they're already gone. All we can do is make a statement. You have to accept that chances are slim to none when it comes to saving any of them."

"We have to try," Moira insisted.

"Yeah, well, that's what we're here for. Let's go."

"Is that one of your trick swords?" Cian asked Hoyt as they approached the east door.

"It is."

"Then keep it well away from me." He touched his finger to his lips, eased open the door. For a moment, there was no sound, no movement but the rain. Then Cian was out, a blur of dark in the dark.

Even as he stepped out to follow, he saw Cian snap two necks and behead a third. "On your left," Cian said quietly.

Hoyt pivoted and met what came at him with steel, and with fire.

Upstairs, Glenna knelt within the circle she'd cast and chanted. The silver around her throat, on her finger glowed brighter with every heartbeat. Moira crouched to the side of the open doorway, a quiver at her back, a bow in her hand.

Moira glanced back at her. "The shackles."

"No, that was for something else. I'll start that now."

"What was it . . . Oh." Moira looked back into the dark, but now thanks to Glenna, with the vision of a cat. "Oh aye, that's a right good one. They've archers back in the trees. I only see six. I can take six."

"Don't go outside. Don't go out until I'm done here." Glenna fought to clear her mind, calm her heart, and call the magic.

Out of the dark, like vengeance, came a gold horse. And the rider on its back wielded death.

With Larkin at a gallop, Blair swung the torch, striking three that burst into flames and took two more into the blaze with them. Then she heaved it, spinning destruction through the air, and flashed a fiery sword.

"It's now, Glenna!" Moira let the first arrow fly. "It's now!"

"Yes, I've got it. I've got it." She grabbed the ax, and a dagger, at a run.

Moira's arrows were winging as they both sprinted into the rain. And the things that were waiting rushed them.

Glenna didn't think, only acted, only felt. She let her

body move into that dance of life and death, striking, blocking, thrusting. Fire rippled over the blades as she swung.

There were screams, such horrible screams. Human,
vampire, how could she tell? She smelled blood, tasted it;
knew some of it was her own. Her heart beat, a war drum in
her chest so she barely registered the arrow that whizzed by
her head as she plunged fire into what leaped at her.

"They've hit Larkin. They've hit him."

At Moira's shout, Glenna saw the arrow in the foreleg of
the horse. But it ran still like a demon with Blair raging destruction from its back.

Then she saw Hoyt fighting fang and sword to get to one
of the prisoners.

"I have to go help. Moira, there are too many down there."

"Go. I've got this. I'll lower the odds, I promise you."

She charged down, screaming to draw some away from
Hoyt and Cian.

She thought it would be a blur, just madness rushing over
her, and through her. But it was clear in every detail. The faces,
the sounds, the scents, the feel of warm blood and cold rain
running over her. The red eyes, the terrible hunger in them.
And the horrible flash and screaming when fire took them.

She saw Cian break off the end of an arrow that had
found his thigh, and plunge it into the heart of an enemy. She
saw the ring she'd put on Hoyt's finger burn like another fire
as he took two with one blow.

"Get them inside," he shouted to her. "Try to get them inside."

She rolled over the wet grass toward the girl Lora had tor-
mented. She half expected to find her dead. Instead she
found her showing fangs in a grin.

"Oh God."

"Didn't you hear her? He doesn't come."

She pounced, knocking Glenna onto her back, then threw
back her head with the joy of the kill. Blair's sword cut it off.

"You'd be surprised," Glenna returned.

"Inside," Blair shouted. "Back in. That's enough of a goddamn statement." She reached down to help Glenna mount
behind her.

They left the field flaming, and covered with dust.

"How many did we kill?" Larkin demanded as he collapsed on the floor. Blood ran down his leg to puddle on the wood.

"At least thirty—damn good ratio. You've got some speed, Golden Boy." Blair looked straight into his eyes. "Winged you a little."

"It's not altogether too bad. It just—" He didn't scream when she yanked the arrow out. He didn't have the breath to scream. When he got it back, all he could manage was a stream of shaky curses.

"You next," she said to Cian, nodding at the broken arrow protruding from his thigh.

He simply reached down, yanked it out himself. "Thanks all the same."

"I'll get supplies. Your leg's bleeding," Glenna told Blair.

"We're all banged up some. But we're not dead. Well." She sent Cian a cocky grin. "Most of us."

"That never gets tired, does it?" Cian speculated and went for the brandy.

"They weren't human. In the cages." Moira held her shoulder where the tip of an arrow had grazed it.

"No. I couldn't tell from in here. Too many of them to separate the scents. It was smart." Blair nodded, a grim acknowledgment. "A good way to engage us and not waste any of their food supply. Bitch has a brain."

"We didn't get Lora." With his breath still heaving out of his lungs, Hoyt eased down. He had a gash on his side, another on his arm. "I saw her when we were fighting our way back into the house. We didn't get her."

"She's going to be mine. My very special friend." Blair pursed her lips when Cian offered her a brandy. "Thanks."

Standing in the center of them on shaky knees, Glenna took stock. "Blair, get Larkin's tunic off. I need to see the wound. Moira, how bad is your wound?"

"More a scratch, really."

"Then get some blankets from upstairs, some towels. Hoyt." Glenna moved to him, knelt, then just took his hands and buried her face in them. However much she wanted to fall apart, it wasn't time. Not time yet. "I felt you with me. I felt you with me every moment."

"I know. You were with me. *A ghrá.*" He lifted her head, pressed his lips to hers.

"I wasn't scared, not while it was happening. I couldn't think to be scared. Then I reached that girl, that young girl, and saw what she was. I couldn't even move."

"It's done. For tonight it's done. And we proved a match for them." He kissed her again, long, deep. "You were magnificent."

She laid a hand over the wound on his side. "I'd say we all were. And we proved more than being able to hold our own. We're a unit now."

"The circle is cast."

She let out a long sigh. "Well, it wasn't the handfasting celebration I was looking for." She struggled to smile. "But at least we . . . No, no, damn it, we didn't. We didn't finish. Just hold everything." She shoved at her dripping hair. "I will not let those monsters ruin this for us." She gripped his hand as Moira rushed down with arms loaded with towels and blankets. "Are you all listening? You're still witnesses."

"We got it," Blair said as she cleansed Larkin's wound.

"Your head's bleeding." Cian passed Moira a damp cloth. "Go right ahead," he told Glenna.

"But Glenna, your dress."

She only smiled at Moira. "It doesn't matter. Only this matters." She clasped hands with Hoyt, locked her eyes with his. "As the goddess and the god and the old ones . . ."

Hoyt's voice joined hers. "Are witness to this rite. We now proclaim we're husband and wife."

He reached down, took her face in his hands. "I will love you beyond the end of days."

Now, she thought, now, the circle was truly cast, strong and bright.

And the light glowed warmer, a wash of gold when their lips met, when their lips clung in hope and promise, and in love.

* * *

"So," the old man said, "with the handfasting complete, they tended to their wounds and began the healing. They drank a toast to the love, the true magic, that had come out of dark and out of death.

"Inside the house while the rain fell, the brave rested and prepared for the next battle."

He sat back, picking up the fresh tea a servant had set beside him. "That is all of the story for today."

The protests were immediate, and passionate. But the old man only chuckled and shook his head.

"There'll be more tomorrow, I promise you, for the story's not finished. Only this beginning. But for now, the sun is out, and so should you be. Haven't you learned from the beginning of the tale that light is to be treasured? Go. When I finish my tea, I'll come out to watch you."

Alone, he drank his tea, watched his fire. And thought of the tale he would tell on the morrow.

Glossary of Irish Words, Characters and Places

a chroi (ah-REE), Gaelic term of endearment meaning "my heart," "my heart's beloved," "my darling"

a ghrá (ah-GHRA), Gaelic term of endearment meaning "my love," "dear"

a stór (ah-STOR), Gaelic term of endearment meaning "my darling"

Aideen (Ae-DEEN), Moira's young cousin

Alice McKenna, descendant of Cian and Hoyt Mac Cionaoith

An Clar (Ahn-CLAR), modern-day County Clare

Ballycloon (ba-LU-klun)

Blair Nola Bridgit Murphy, one of the circle of six, the "warrior"; a demon hunter, a descendant of Nola Mac Cionaoith (Cian and Hoyt's younger sister)

Bridget's Well, cemetery in County Clare, named after St. Bridget

Burren, the, a karst limestone region in County Clare, which features caves and underground streams *cara* (karu), Gaelic for "friend, relative"

Ceara, one of the village women

Cian (KEY-an) *Mac Cionaoith/McKenna*, Hoyt's twin brother, a vampire, Lord of Oiche, one of the circle of six, "the one who is lost"

Cirio, Lilith's human lover

ciunas (CYOON-as), Gaelic for "silence"; the battle takes place in the Valley of Ciunas—the Valley of Silence

claddaugh, the Celtic symbol of love, friendship, loyalty

Cliffs of Mohr (also Moher), the name given to the ruin of forts in the South of Ireland, on a cliff near Hag's Head "Moher O'Ruan"

Conn, Larkin's childhood puppy

Dance of the Gods, the Dance, the place in which the circle of six passes through from the real world to the fantasy world of Geall

Davey, Lilith, the Vampire Queen's "son," a child vampire

Deirdre (DAIR-dhra) *Riddock*, Larkin's mother

Dervil (DAR-vel), one of the village women

Eire (AIR-reh), Gaelic for "Ireland"

Eogan (O-en), Ceara's husband

Eoin (OAN), Hoyt's brother-in-law

Eternity, the name of Cian's nightclub, located in New York City

Faerie Falls, imaginary place in Geall

fàilte à Geall (FALL-che ah GY-al), Gaelic for "Welcome to Geall"

Fearghus (FARE-gus), Hoyt's brother-in-law

Gaillimh (GALL-yuv), modern-day Galway, the capital of the West of Ireland

Geall (GY-al), in Gaelic means "promise"; the land from which Moira and Larkin come; the city which Moira will someday rule

Glenna Ward, one of the circle of six, the "witch"; lives in modern-day New York City

Hoyt Mac Cionaoith/McKenna (mac KHEE-nee), one of the circle of six, the "sorcerer"

Isleen (Is-LEEN), a servant at Castle Geall

Jarl (Yarl), Lilith's sire, the vampire who turned her into a vampire

Jeremy Hilton, Blair Murphy's ex-fiancé

King, the name of Cian's best friend, whom Cian befriended when King was a child; the manager of Eternity

Larkin Riddock, one of the circle of six, the "shifter of shapes," a cousin of Moira, Queen of Geall

Lilith, the Vampire Queen, aka Queen of the Demons; leader of the war against humankind; Cian's sire, the vampire who turned Cian from human to vampire

Lora, a vampire; Lilith's lover

Lucius, Lora's male vampire lover

Malvin, villager, soldier in Geallian army

Manhattan, city in New York; where both Cian McKenna and Glenna Ward live

mathair (maahir), Gaelic word for "mother"

Michael Thomas McKenna, descendant of Cian and Hoyt Mac Cionaoith

Mick Murphy, Blair Murphy's younger brother

Midir (mee-DEER), vampire wizard to Lilith, Queen of the Vampires

miurnin (also sp. miurneach [mornukh]), Gaelic for "sweetheart," term of endearment

Moira (MWA-ra), one of the circle of six, the "scholar"; a princess, future queen of Geall

Morrigan (Mo-ree-ghan), Goddess of the Battle

Niall (Nile), a warrior in the Geallian army

Nola Mac Cionaoith, Hoyt and Cian's youngest sister

ogham (ä-gem) (also spelled ogam), fifth/sixth century Irish alphabet

oiche (EE-heh), Gaelic for "night"

Oran (O-ren), Riddock's youngest son, Larkin's younger brother

Phelan (FA-len), Larkin's brother-in-law

Prince Riddock, Larkin's father, acting king of Geall, Moira's maternal uncle

Region of Chiarrai (kee-U-ree), modern-day Kerry, situated in the extreme southwest of Ireland, sometimes referred to as "the Kingdom"

Samhain (SAM-en), summer's end (Celtic festival); the battle takes place on the Feast of Samhain, the feast celebrating the end of summer

Sean (Shawn) *Murphy*, Blair Murphy's father, a vampire hunter

Shop Street, cultural center of Galway

Sinann (shih-NAWN), Larkin's sister

sláinte (slawn-che), Gaelic term for "cheers!"

slán agat (shlahn u-gut), Gaelic for "good-bye," which is said to the person staying

slán leat (shlahn ly-aht), Gaelic for "good-bye," which is said to the person leaving

Tuatha de Danaan (TOO-aha dai DON-nan), Welsh gods

Tynan (Ti-nin), guard at Castle Geall

Vlad, Cian's stallion

Turn the page for a look at

Dance of the Gods

the second book in the
Circle Trilogy.

Now available from Jove.

Chapter 1

Clare
The first day of September

Through the house, still as a grave, Larkin limped. The air was sweet, fragrant with the flowers gathered lavishly for the handfasting rite of the night before.

The blood had been mopped up; the weapons cleaned. They'd toasted Hoyt and Glenna with the frothy wine, had eaten cake. But behind the smiles the horror of the night's battle lurked. A poor guest.

Today, he supposed, was for rest and more preparation. It was a struggle for him not to be impatient with the training, with the planning. At least last night they'd fought, he thought as he pressed a hand to his thigh that ached from an arrow strike. A score of demons had fallen, and there was glory in that.

In the kitchen, he opened the refrigerator and took out a bottle of Coke. He'd developed a taste for it, and had come to prefer it over his morning tea.

He turned the bottle in his hand, marveling at the cleverness of the vessel—so smooth, so clear and hard. But what was inside it—this was something he'd miss when they returned to Geall.

He could admit he hadn't believed his cousin, Moira, when she'd spoken of gods and demons, of a war for worlds. He'd only gone with her that day, that sad day of her mother's burial, to look after her. She wasn't only blood, but friend, and would be queen of Geall.

But every word she'd spoken to him, only steps away from her mother's grave, had been pure truth. They'd gone to the Dance, they'd stood in the heart of that circle. And everything had changed.

Not just the where and when they were, he mused as he opened the bottle and took that first bracing sip. But everything. One moment, they'd stood under the afternoon sun in Geall, then there'd been light and wind, and a roar of sound.

Then it had been night, and it had been Ireland—a place Larkin had always believed a fairy tale.

He hadn't believed in fairy tales, or monsters, and despite his own gift had looked askance at magic.

But magic there was, he admitted now. Just as there was an Ireland, and there were monsters. Those demons had attacked them—springing out of the dark of the woods, their eyes red, their fangs sharp. The form of a man, he thought, but not a man.

Vampyre.

They existed to feed off man. And now they banded together under their queen to destroy all.

He was here to stop them, at all and any costs. He was here at the charge of the gods to save the worlds of man.

He scratched idly at his healing thigh and decided he could hardly be expected to save mankind on an empty stomach.

He cut a slab of cake to go with his morning Coke and licked icing from his finger. So far, through wile and guile he'd avoided Glenna's cooking lessons. He liked to eat, that was true enough, but the actual making of food was a different matter.

He was a tall, lanky man with a thick waving mane of tawny hair. His eyes, nearly the same color, were wide like his cousin's, and nearly as keen. He had a long and mobile mouth that was quick to smile, quick hands and an easy nature.

Those who knew him would have said he was generous with his time and his coin, and a good man to have at your back at the pub, or in a brawl.

He'd been blessed with strong, even features, a strong back, a willing hand. And the power to change his shape into any living thing.

He took a healthy bite of cake where he stood, but there was too much quiet in the house to suit him. He wanted, needed, activity, sound, motion. Since he couldn't sleep, he decided he'd take Cian's stallion out for a morning run.

Cian could hardly do it himself, being a vampyre.

He stepped out of the back door of the big stone house. There was a chill in the air, but he had the sweater and jeans Glenna had purchased in the village. He wore his own boots—and the silver cross Glenna and Hoyt had forged with magic.

He saw where the earth was scorched, where it was trampled. He saw his own hoofprints left in the sodden earth when he'd galloped through the battle in the form of a horse.

And he saw the woman who'd ridden him, slashing destruction with a flaming sword.

She moved through the mists, slow and graceful, in what he would have taken for a dance if he hadn't known the movements, the complete control in them, were another preparation for battle.

Long arms and long legs swept through the air so smoothly they barely disturbed the mists. He could see her muscles tremble when she held a pose, endlessly held it, for her arms were bared in a snug white garment no woman of Geall would have worn outside the bedchamber.

She lifted a leg behind her into the air, bent at the knee, reaching an arm back to grasp her bare foot. The shirt rose up her torso to reveal more flesh.

It would be a sorry man, Larkin decided, who didn't enjoy the view.

Her hair was short, raven black, and her eyes were bluer than the lakes of Fonn. She wouldn't have been deemed a beauty in his world, as she lacked the roundness, the plump sweet curves, but he found the strength of her form appealing, the angles of her face, the sharp arch of brows interesting and unique.

She brought her leg down, swept it out to the side, then dropped into a long crouch with her arms parallel to the ground.

"You always eat that much sugar in the morning?"

Her voice jolted him. He'd been still and silent, and thought her unaware of him. He should've known better. He took a bite of the cake he'd forgotten he held. "It's good."

"Bet." Blair lowered her arms, straightened. "Earlier rising for you than usual, isn't it?"

"I couldn't sleep."

"Know what you mean. Damn good fight."

"Good?" He looked over the burned ground and thought of the screams, the blood, the death. "It wasn't a night at the pub."

"Entertaining though." She looked as he did, but with a hard light in her eyes. "We kicked some vampire ass, and what could be a better way to spend the evening?"

"I can think of a few."

"Hell of a rush, though." She rolled any lingering tension from her shoulders as she glanced at the house. "And it didn't suck to go from a handfasting to a fight and back again—as winners. Especially when you consider the alternative."

"There's that, I suppose."

"I hope Glenna and Hoyt are getting a little honeymoon time in, because for the most part, it was a pretty crappy reception."

With the long, almost liquid gait he'd come to admire, she walked over to the table they used during daylight training to hold weapons and supplies. She picked up the bottle of water she'd left there and drank deep.

"You have a mark of royalty."

"Say what?"

He moved closer, touched a fingertip lightly to her shoulder blade. There was the mark of a cross like the one around his neck, but in bold and bloody red.

"It's just a tattoo."

"In Geall only the ruler would bear a mark on the body. When the new king or queen becomes, when they lift the sword from the stone, the mark appears. Here." He tapped a hand on his right biceps. "Not the symbol of the cross, but the claddaugh, put there, it's said, by the finger of the gods."

"Cool. Excellent," she explained when he frowned at her.

"I myself have never seen this."

She cocked her head. "And seeing's believing?"

He shrugged. "My aunt, Moira's mother, had such a mark. But she rose to queen before I was born, so I didn't see the mark become."

"I never heard that part of the legend." Because it was there, she swooped a fingertip through the icing of his cake, sucked it off. "I guess everything doesn't trickle down."

"How did you come by yours?"

Funny guy, Blair thought. Curious nature. Gorgeous eyes. Danger, Will Robinson, she thought. That sort of combo just begged for complications. She just wasn't built for complications—and had learned it the hard way. "I paid for it. A lot of people have tattoos. It's like a personal state-ment, you could say. Glenna's got one." She took another drink, watching him as she reached around to tap herself on the small of the back. "Here. A pentagram. I saw it when we were helping her get dressed for the handfasting."

"So they're for women."

"Not only. Why, you want one?"

"I think not." He rubbed absently at his thigh.

Blair remembered yanking the arrow out of him herself, and that he'd barely uttered a sound. The guy had balls to go with the gorgeous eyes and curious nature. He was no slouch in a fight, and no whiner after the battle. "Leg giving you trouble?"

"A little stiff, a little sore. Glenna's a good healer. Yours?"

She bent her leg back, heel to butt, gave it a testing pull. "It's okay. I heal fast—part of the family package. Not as fast as a vamp," she added. "But demon hunters heal faster than your average human."

She picked up the jacket she'd tossed on the table, put it on against the morning cool. "I want coffee."

"I don't like it. I like the Coke." Then he smiled, easy, charming. "Will you be making yourself the breakfast?"

"In a little while. I've got some things I want to do first."

"Maybe you wouldn't mind making enough for two."

"Maybe." Clever guy, too, she thought. You had to respect his finagling. "You got something going now?"

It took him a moment, but he tried to spend a little time each day with the miraculous machine called the television. He was proud to think he was learning new idioms. "I'm after taking the horse for a ride, then feeding and grooming him."

"Plenty of light today, but you shouldn't head into the woods unarmed."

"I'll be riding the fields. Ah, Glenna, she asked if I'd not ride alone in the forest. I don't like to worry her. Were you wanting a ride yourself?"

"I think I had enough of one last night, thanks to you." Amused, she gave him a light punch in the chest. "You've got some speed in you, cowboy."

"Well, you've a light and steady seat." He looked back out at the trampled ground. "You're right. It was a good fight."

"Damn right. But the next one won't be so easy."

His eyebrows winged up. "And that one was easy?"

"Compared to what's coming, bet your ass."

"Well then, the gods help us all. And if you've a mind to cook eggs and bacon with it, that'd be fine. Might as well eat our fill while we still have stomachs."

Cheery thought, Blair decided as she went inside. The hell of it was, he'd meant it that way. She'd never known anyone so offhand about life and death. Not resigned—she'd been raised to be resigned to it—just a kind of confidence that he'd live as he chose to live, until he stopped living.

She admired the viewpoint.

She'd been raised to know the monster under the bed was real, and was just waiting until you relaxed before it ripped your throat out.

She'd been trained to put that moment off as long as she could stand and fight, to slash and to burn, and take out as many as humanly possible. Because under the strength, the wit and the endless training was the knowledge that some day, some way, she wouldn't be fast enough, smart enough, lucky enough.

And the monster would win.

Still there'd always been a balance to it—demon and hunter, with each the other's prey. Now the stakes had been raised, sky-fricking-high, she thought as she made coffee. Now it wasn't just the duty and tradition that had been passed down through her blood for damn near a millennium.

Now it was a fight to save humankind.

She was here, with this strange little band—two of which, vampire and sorcerer, turned out to be her ancestors—to fight the mother of all battles.

Two months, she thought, until Halloween. Till Samhain, and the final showdown the goddess had prophesied. They'd have to be ready, she decided as she poured the first cup. Because the alternative just wasn't an option.

She carried her coffee upstairs, into her room.

As quarters went, it had it all over her apartment in Chicago where she'd based herself over the last year and a half. The bed boasted a tall headboard with carved dragons on either side. A woman could feel like a spellbound princess in that bed—if she was of a fanciful state of mind.

Despite the fact the place was owned by a vampire, there was a wide mirror, framed in thick mahogany. The wardrobe would have held three times the amount of clothes she'd brought with her, so she used it for secondary weapons, and tucked her traveling wardrobe in the chest of drawers.

The walls were painted a dusky plum, and the art on them woodland scenes of twilight or predawn, so that the room seemed to be in perpetual shadow if the curtains were drawn. But that was all right. She had lived a great deal of her life in the shadows.

But she opened the curtains now so morning spilled in and then sat at the gorgeous little desk to check her e-mail on her laptop.

She couldn't prevent the little flicker of hope, or stop it from dying out as she saw there was still no return message from her father.

Nothing new, she reminded herself and tipped back in the chair. He was traveling, somewhere in South America to the best of her knowledge. And she only knew that much because her brother had told her.

It had been six months since she'd had any contact with him, and there was nothing new about that, either. His duty to her had been, in his opinion, fulfilled years ago. And maybe he was right. He'd taught her, he'd trained her, though she'd never been good enough to merit his approval.

She simply didn't have the right equipment. She wasn't his son. The disappointment he'd felt when it had been his daughter instead of his son who'd inherited the gift was something he'd never bothered to hide.

Softening blows of any sort just wasn't Sean Murphy's style. He'd pretty much dusted her off his hands on her eighteenth birthday.

Now she'd embarrassed herself by sending him a second message when he'd never answered the first. She'd sent that first e-mail before she'd left for Ireland, to tell him something was up, something was twitching, and she wanted his advice.

So much for that, she thought now, and so much for trying again, after her arrival, to tell him what was twitching was major.

He had his own life, his own course, and had never pretended otherwise. It was her own problem, her own lack, that she still coveted his approval. She'd given up on earning his love a long time ago.

She turned off the computer, pulled on a sweatshirt and shoes. She decided to go up to the training room and work off frustration, work up an appetite lifting weights.

The house, she'd been told, had been the one Hoyt and his brother, Cian, had been born in. In the dawn of the twelfth century. It had been modernized, of course, and some additions had been made, but she could see from the original structure the Mac Cionaoiths had been a family of considerable means.

Of course Cian had had nearly a millennium to make his own fortune, to acquire the house again. Though from the bits and pieces she'd picked up, he didn't live in it.

She didn't make a habit out of conversing with vampires—just killing them. But she was making an exception with Cian. For reasons that weren't entirely clear to her, he was fighting with them, even bankrolling their little war party to some extent.

Added to that, she'd seen the way he'd fought the night before, with a ruthless ferocity. His allegiance could be the element that tipped the scales in their favor.

She wound her way up the stone stairs toward what had once been the great hall, then a ballroom in later years. And was now their training room.

She stopped short when she saw Larkin's cousin Moira doing chest extensions with five-pound free weights.

The Geallian wore her brown hair back in a thick braid that reached her waist. Sweat dribbled down her temples, and more darkened the back of the white T-shirt she wore. Her eyes, fog gray, were staring straight ahead, focused, Blair assumed, on whatever got her through the reps.

She was, by Blair's gauge about five-three, maybe a hundred and ten pounds, after you'd dragged her out of a lake. But she was game. Having game held a lot of weight on Blair's scale. What Blair had initially judged as mousiness was, in actuality, a watchfulness. The woman soaked up everything.

"Thought you were still in bed," Blair said as she stepped inside.

Moira lowered the weights, then used her forearm to swipe her brow. "I've been up for a bit. You're wanting to use the room?"

"Yeah. Plenty of room in here for both of us." Blair walked over, selected ten-pound weights. "Not hunkered down with the books this morning."

"I . . ." On a sigh, Moira stretched out her arms as she'd been taught. She might have wished her arms were as sleek and carved with muscle as Blair's, but no one would call them soft any longer. "I've been starting the day here, before I use the library. Usually before anyone's up and about."

"Okay." Curious, Blair studied Moira as she worked her triceps. "And you're keeping this a secret because?"

"Not a secret. Not exactly a secret." Moira picked up a bottle of water, twisted off the cap. Twisted it back on. "I'm the weakest of us. I don't need you or Cian to tell me that—though one or the other of you make a point to let me know it with some regularity."

Something gave a little twist inside Blair's belly. "And that sucks. I'm going to tell you I'm sorry about that, because I know how it feels to get slammed down when you're doing your best."

"My best isn't altogether that good, is it? No, I'm not looking for sorry," she said before Blair could speak. "It's hard to be told you're lacking, but that's what I am—for now. So I come up here in the mornings, early, and lift these bloody things the way you showed me. I won't be the weak one, the one the rest of you have to worry about."

"You don't have much muscle yet, but you've got some speed. And you're a frigging genius with a bow. If you weren't so good with it, things wouldn't have turned out the way they did last night."

"Work on my weaknesses, and on my strengths, on my own time. That's what you said to me—and it made me angry. Until I saw the wisdom of it. I'm not angry. You're good at training. King was . . . He was more easy on me, I think, because he was a man. A big man at that," Moira added with sorrow in her eyes now. "Who had affection for me, I think, because I was the smallest of us."

Blair hadn't met King, Cian's friend who'd been captured, then killed by Lilith. Then turned, and sent back as a vampire.

"I won't be easy on you," Blair promised.

By the time she'd finished a session with the weights and grabbed a quick shower, Blair had worked up that appetite. She decided to go for one of her favorites, and dug up the makings for French toast.

She tossed some Irish bacon into a skillet for protein, selected Green Day on her MP3 player. Music to cook by.

She poured her second cup of coffee before breaking eggs in a bowl.

She was beating the batter when Larkin strolled in the door. He stopped, stared at her player. "And what is it?"

"It's a—" How to explain? "A way to whistle while you work."

"No, it's not the machine I'm meaning. There are so many of those, I can't keep them all in my brain. But what's the sound?"

"Oh. Um, popular music? Rock—of the hard variety."

He was grinning now, head cocked as he listened. "Rock. I like it."

"Who wouldn't? Not going for eggs, this morning. Doing up French toast."

"Toast?" Disappointment fell over his face, erasing the easy pleasure of the music. "Just cooked bread?"

"Not just. Besides, you get what you get when I'm manning the stove. Or you forage on your own."

"It's kind of you to cook, of course."

His tone was so long-suffering, she had to swallow a laugh. "Relax, and trust me on this, I've seen you chow down, cowboy. You're going to like it as much as Rock, especially after you drown it in butter and syrup. I'll have it going in a minute. Why don't you flip that bacon over?"

"I'm needing to wash first. Been mucking out the stall and such, and I'm not fit yet to touch anything."

She lifted a brow as he strolled right out. She'd seen him slip out of all manner of kitchen duties already. And she had to admit, he was slick about it.

Resigned, she turned the bacon herself, then heated a second skillet. She was about to dunk the first piece of bread when she heard voices. The newlyweds were up, she realized, and added to the batter to accommodate them.

Effortless style. It was something Glenna had in spades, Blair thought. She wandered in wearing a sage green sweater and black jeans with her bold red hair swinging straight and loose. The urban take on country casual, Blair supposed. When you added the pretty flush of a woman who'd obviously had her morning snuggles, you had quite a package.

She didn't look like a woman who would rush a squad of

vampires while she bellowed war cries and swung a battle-ax, but she'd done just that.

"Mmm, French toast? You must have read my mind." As she moved to the coffeepot, Glenna gave Blair's arm an absent stroke. "Give you a hand?"

"No, I got this. You've been taking the lion's share of KP, and I'm better at breakfast than dinner. Didn't I hear Hoyt?"

"Right behind me. He's talking to Larkin about the horse. I think Hoyt's a little put out he didn't get to Vlad before Larkin did. Coffee's good. How'd you sleep?"

"Like I'd been knocked unconscious, for a couple hours." Blair dipped bread, then laid it to sizzle. "Then, I don't know, too restless. Wired up." She slanted Glenna a look. "And nowhere to put the excess energy, like the bride."

"I have to admit, I'm feeling pretty loose and relaxed this morning. Except." Wincing a little, Glenna massaged her right biceps. "My arms feel like I spent half the night swinging a sledgehammer."

"Battle-ax has weight. You did good work with it."

"*Work* isn't the word that comes to mind. But I'm not going to think about it—at least not until I've gorged myself." Turning, Glenna opened a cupboard for plates. "Do you know how often I had a breakfast like this—fried bread, fried meat—before all this started?"

"Nope."

"Never. Absolutely never," she added with a half laugh. "I watched my weight as if the, well, as if the fate of the world depended on it."

"You're training hard." Blair flipped the bread. "You need the fuel, the carbs. If you put on a few pounds, I can guarantee it's going to be pure muscle."

"Blair." Glenna glanced toward the doorway to ensure Hoyt hadn't started in yet. "You've got more experience with this than any of us. Just between you and me, for now, anyway, how did we do last night?"

"We lived," Blair said flatly. She continued to cook, sliding fried bread onto a plate, dunking more. "That's bottom line."

"But—"

"Glenna, I'll tell you straight." Blair turned, leaning back on the counter for a moment while bread sizzled and scented the air. "I've never been in anything like that before."

"But you've been doing this—hunting them—for years."

"That's right. And I've never seen so many of them in one place at one time, never seen them organized that way."

Glenna let out a quiet breath. "That can't be good news."

"Good or bad, it's fact. It's not—never been in my experience—the nature of the beast to live, work, fight in large groups. I contacted my aunt, and she says the same. They're killers, and they might travel, hunt, even live together in packs. Small packs, and there might be an alpha, male or female. But not like this."

"Not like an army," Glenna murmured.

"No. And what we saw last night was a squad—a small slice of an army. The thing is, they're willing to die for her, for Lilith. And that's powerful stuff."

"Okay. Okay," Glenna said as she set the table. "That's what I get for saying I wanted it straight."

"Hey, buck up. We lived, remember? That's a victory."

"Good morning to you," Hoyt said to Blair as he came in. Then his gaze went straight to Glenna.

They shared coloring, Blair thought, she and her however-many-times great-uncle. She, the sorcerer and his twin brother the vampire shared coloring, and ancestry, and now this mission, she supposed.

Fate was certainly a twisty bastard.

"You two sure have the glow on," she said when Glenna lifted her face to meet Hoyt's lips. "Practically need my shades."

"They shield the eyes from the sun, and are a sexy fashion statement," Hoyt returned and made her laugh.

"Have a seat." She turned off the music, then brought the heaping platter to the table. "I made enough for an army, seeing as that's what we are."

"It looks a fine feast. Thank you."

"Just doing my share, unlike some of us who're a little more slippery." She met Larkin's perfectly timed appearance with a shake of her head. "Right on time."

His expression was both innocent and affable. "Is it ready then? It took me a bit longer to get back as I stopped to tell Moira there was food being cooked. And a welcome sight it is."

"You look, you eat." Blair slapped four slices of French toast on a plate for him. "And you and your cousin do the dishes."

Combining elements of the supernatural with gripping suspense and seduction, number-one *New York Times* bestselling author Nora Roberts presents the second novel in her Circle Trilogy. . . .

He saw where the earth was scorched, where it was trampled. He saw his own hoofprints left in the sodden earth when he'd galloped through the battle in the form of a horse. And he saw the woman who'd ridden him, slashing destruction with a flaming sword. . . .

Blair Murphy has always worked alone. Destined to be a demon hunter in a world that doesn't believe in such things, she lives for the kill. But now, she finds herself the warrior in a circle of six, chosen by the goddess Morrigan to defeat the vampire Lilith and her minions.

Learning to trust the others has been hard, for Blair has never allowed herself such a luxury. But she finds herself drawn to Larkin, a man of many shapes. As a horse, he is proud and graceful; as a dragon, beautifully fierce; and as a man . . . well, Blair has seen her share of hunks, but none quite so ruggedly handsome and playfully charming as this nobleman from the past.

In two months' time, the circle of six will face Lilith and her army in Geall. To complete preparations and round up forces to fight, the circle travels through time to Larkin's world, where Blair must choose between battling her overwhelming attraction to him—or risking everything for a love that can never be. . . .

Don't miss the other books in the Circle Trilogy

Morrigan's Cross
Valley of Silence

Turn the page for a complete list of titles by
Nora Roberts and J. D. Robb from Berkley. . . .

Nora Roberts

HOT ICE
SACRED SINS
BRAZEN VIRTUE
SWEET REVENGE
PUBLIC SECRETS
GENUINE LIES
CARNAL INNOCENCE
HONEST ILLUSIONS
DIVINE EVIL
PRIVATE SCANDALS
HIDDEN RICHES
TRUE BETRAYALS
MONTANA SKY
SANCTUARY
HOMEPORT
THE REEF
RIVER'S END
CAROLINA MOON
THE VILLA
MIDNIGHT BAYOU
THREE FATES
BIRTHRIGHT
NORTHERN LIGHTS
BLUE SMOKE
ANGELS FALL
HIGH NOON
TRIBUTE
BLACK HILLS
THE SEARCH
CHASING FIRE
THE WITNESS
WHISKEY BEACH
THE COLLECTOR
TONIGHT AND ALWAYS
THE LIAR
THE OBSESSION

Series

Ebooks by Nora Roberts

Cordina's Royal Family
AFFAIRE ROYALE
COMMAND PERFORMANCE
THE PLAYBOY PRINCE
CORDINA'S CROWN JEWEL

The Donovan Legacy
CAPTIVATED
ENTRANCED
CHARMED
ENCHANTED

The O'Hurleys
THE LAST HONEST WOMAN
DANCE TO THE PIPER
SKIN DEEP
WITHOUT A TRACE

Night Tales
NIGHT SHIFT
NIGHT SHADOW
NIGHTSHADE
NIGHT SMOKE
NIGHT SHIELD

The MacGregors
PLAYING THE ODDS
TEMPTING FATE
ALL THE POSSIBILITIES
ONE MAN'S ART
FOR NOW, FOREVER
REBELLION/IN FROM THE COLD
THE MACGREGOR BRIDES
THE WINNING HAND
THE MACGREGOR GROOMS
THE PERFECT NEIGHBOR

The Calhouns
COURTING CATHERINE
A MAN FOR AMANDA
FOR THE LOVE OF LILAH
SUZANNA'S SURRENDER
MEGAN'S MATE

Irish Legacy
IRISH THOROUGHBRED
IRISH ROSE
IRISH REBEL

LOVING JACK
BEST LAID PLANS
LAWLESS

BLITHE IMAGES
SONG OF THE WEST
SEARCH FOR LOVE
ISLAND OF FLOWERS
THE HEART'S VICTORY
FROM THIS DAY
HER MOTHER'S KEEPER
ONCE MORE WITH FEELING
REFLECTIONS
DANCE OF DREAMS
UNTAMED
THIS MAGIC MOMENT
ENDINGS AND BEGINNINGS
STORM WARNING
SULLIVAN'S WOMAN
FIRST IMPRESSIONS
A MATTER OF CHOICE

LESS OF A STRANGER
THE LAW IS A LADY
RULES OF THE GAME
OPPOSITES ATTRACT
THE RIGHT PATH
PARTNERS
BOUNDARY LINES
DUAL IMAGE
TEMPTATION
LOCAL HERO
THE NAME OF THE GAME
GABRIEL'S ANGEL
THE WELCOMING
TIME WAS
TIMES CHANGE
SUMMER LOVE
HOLIDAY WISHES

Nora Roberts & J. D. Robb

REMEMBER WHEN

J. D. Robb

Anthologies

FROM THE HEART
A LITTLE MAGIC
A LITTLE FATE

MOON SHADOWS
(with Jill Gregory, Ruth Ryan Langan, and Marianne Willman)

The Once Upon Series
(with Jill Gregory, Ruth Ryan Langan, and Marianne Willman)

ONCE UPON A CASTLE   ONCE UPON A ROSE
ONCE UPON A STAR   ONCE UPON A KISS
ONCE UPON A DREAM   ONCE UPON A MIDNIGHT

SILENT NIGHT
(with Susan Plunkett, Dee Holmes, and Claire Cross)

OUT OF THIS WORLD
(with Laurell K. Hamilton, Susan Krinard, and Maggie Shayne)

BUMP IN THE NIGHT
(with Mary Blayney, Ruth Ryan Langan, and Mary Kay McComas)

DEAD OF NIGHT
(with Mary Blayney, Ruth Ryan Langan, and Mary Kay McComas)

THREE IN DEATH

SUITE 606
(with Mary Blayney, Ruth Ryan Langan, and Mary Kay McComas)

IN DEATH

THE LOST
(with Patricia Gaffney, Mary Blayney, and Ruth Ryan Langan)

THE OTHER SIDE
(with Mary Blayney, Patricia Gaffney, Ruth Ryan Langan, and Mary Kay McComas)

TIME OF DEATH

THE UNQUIET
(with Mary Blayney, Patricia Gaffney, Ruth Ryan Langan, and Mary Kay McComas)

MIRROR, MIRROR
(with Mary Blayney, Elaine Fox, Mary Kay McComas, and R. C. Ryan)

DOWN THE RABBIT HOLE
(with Mary Blayney, Elaine Fox, Mary Kay McComas, and R. C. Ryan)

Also available . . .

THE OFFICIAL NORA ROBERTS COMPANION
(edited by Denise Little and Laura Hayden)

Dance
of the Gods

NORA ROBERTS

JOVE
New York

A JOVE BOOK
Published by Berkley
An imprint of Penguin Random House LLC
penguinrandomhouse.com

Copyright © 2006 by Nora Roberts
Excerpt from *Valley of Silence* copyright © 2006 by Nora Roberts
Penguin Random House supports copyright. Copyright fuels creativity, encourages
diverse voices, promotes free speech, and creates a vibrant culture. Thank you for buying
an authorized edition of this book and for complying with copyright laws by not
reproducing, scanning, or distributing any part of it in any form without permission.
You are supporting writers and allowing Penguin Random House to continue to
publish books for every reader.

A JOVE BOOK, BERKLEY, and the BERKLEY & B colophon
are registered trademarks of Penguin Random House LLC.

ISBN: 9780515141665

First Edition: October 2006

Printed in the United States of America
14   16   18   20   21   19   17   15   13

Cover image by Triff / Shutterstock
Cover design by Rita Frangie
Text design by Kristin del Rosario

To Logan.
You are the future.

What we learn to do, we learn by doing.
—ARISTOTLE

We few, we happy few, we band of brothers.
—SHAKESPEARE

Prologue

When the sun dipped low in the sky, dripping the last of its fire, the children huddled together to hear the next part of the tale. For the old man, their eager faces and wide eyes brought the light into the room. The story he'd begun on a rainy afternoon would continue now, as twilight settled over the land.

The fire crackled in the grate, the only sound as he sipped his wine, as he searched his mind for the right words.

"You know now a beginning, of Hoyt the Sorcerer and the witch from beyond his time. You know how the vampire came to be, and how the scholar and the shifter of shapes from the world of Geall came through the Dance of the Gods, into the land of Ireland. You know how a friend and brother was lost, and how the warrior came to join them."

"They gathered together," one of the wide-eyed children said, "to fight, to save all the worlds."

"This is truth, and this happened. These six, this circle

of courage and hope were charged by the gods, through the messenger Morrigan, to fight the army of vampires led by their ambitious queen, Lilith."

"They defeated the vampires in battle," one of the young ones said, and the old man knew he saw himself as one of the brave, lifting sword and stake to destroy evil.

"This, too, is truth, and this happened. On the night the sorcerer and the witch were handfasted, the night they pledged the love they'd found in this terrible time, the circle of six beat back the demons. Their valor could not be questioned. But this was only one battle, in the first month of the three they'd been given to save worlds."

"How many worlds are there?"

"They can't be counted," he told them. "Any more than the stars in the sky can be counted. And all of these worlds were threatened. For if these six were defeated, those worlds would be changed, just as a man can be changed into demon."

"But what happened next?"

He smiled now with the firelight casting shadows on a face scored by the years. "Well now, I'll tell you. Dawn came after the night of the battle, as dawn will. A soft and misty dawn this was, a quiet after the storm. The rain had washed away the blood, human and demon, but the ground was scorched where fire swords had flamed. And still the mourning doves cooed, and the stream sang. In that morning light, leaves and blossoms, wet from rain, glimmered.

"It was for this," he told them, "these simple and ordinary things they fought. For man needs the comfort of the simple as much as he needs glory."

He sipped his wine, then set it aside. "So they had gathered to preserve these things. And so, now gathered, did they begin their journey."

Chapter 1

Clare
The first day of September

Through the house, still as a grave, Larkin limped.
The air was sweet, fragrant with the flowers gathered
lavishly for the handfasting rite of the night before.

The blood had been mopped up; the weapons cleaned.
They'd toasted Hoyt and Glenna with the frothy wine, had
eaten cake. But behind the smiles, the horror of the night's
battle lurked. A poor guest.

Today, he supposed, was for rest and more preparation.
It was a struggle for him not to be impatient with the training, with the planning. At least last night they'd fought, he
thought as he pressed a hand to his thigh that ached from
an arrow strike. A score of demons had fallen, and there
was glory in that.

In the kitchen, he opened the refrigerator and took out a
bottle of Coke. He'd developed a taste for it, and had come
to prefer it over his morning tea.

He turned the bottle in his hand, marveling at the cleverness of the vessel—so smooth, so clear and hard. But

what was inside it—this was something he'd miss when they returned to Geall.

He could admit he hadn't believed his cousin, Moira, when she'd spoken of gods and demons, of a war for worlds. He'd only gone with her that day, that sad day of her mother's burial, to look after her. She wasn't only blood, but friend, and would be queen of Geall.

But every word she'd spoken to him, only steps away from her mother's grave, had been pure truth. They'd gone to the Dance, they'd stood in the heart of that circle. And everything had changed.

Not just the where and when they were, he mused as he opened the bottle and took that first bracing sip. But everything. One moment, they'd stood under the afternoon sun in Geall, then there'd been light and wind, and a roar of sound.

Then it had been night, and it had been Ireland—a place Larkin had always believed a fairy tale.

He hadn't believed in fairy tales, or monsters, and despite his own gift had looked askance at magic.

But magic there was, he admitted now. Just as there was an Ireland, and there were monsters. Those demons had attacked them—springing out of the dark of the woods, their eyes red, their fangs sharp. The form of a man, he thought, but not a man.

Vampyre.

They existed to feed off man. And now they banded together under their queen to destroy all.

He was here to stop them, at all and any costs. He was here at the charge of the gods to save the worlds of man.

He scratched idly at his healing thigh and decided he could hardly be expected to save mankind on an empty stomach.

He cut a slab of cake to go with his morning Coke and licked icing from his finger. So far, through wile and guile he'd avoided Glenna's cooking lessons. He liked to eat, that was true enough, but the actual making of food was a different matter.

He was a tall, lanky man with a thick waving mane of tawny hair. His eyes, nearly the same color, were long like his cousin's, and nearly as keen. He had a long and mobile mouth that was quick to smile, quick hands and an easy nature.

Those who knew him would have said he was generous with his time and his coin, and a good man to have at your back at the pub, or in a brawl.

He'd been blessed with strong, even features, a strong back, a willing hand. And the power to change his shape into any living thing.

He took a healthy bite of cake where he stood, but there was too much quiet in the house to suit him. He wanted, needed, activity, sound, motion. Since he couldn't sleep, he decided he'd take Cian's stallion out for a morning run.

Cian could hardly do it himself, being a vampire.

He stepped out of the back door of the big stone house. There was a chill in the air, but he had the sweater and jeans Glenna had purchased in the village. He wore his own boots—and the silver cross Glenna and Hoyt had forged with magic.

He saw where the earth was scorched, where it was trampled. He saw his own hoofprints left in the sodden earth when he'd galloped through the battle in the form of a horse.

And he saw the woman who'd ridden him, slashing destruction with a flaming sword.

She moved through the mists, slow and graceful, in what he would have taken for a dance if he hadn't known the movements, the complete control in them, were another preparation for battle.

Long arms and long legs swept through the air so smoothly they barely disturbed the mists. He could see her muscles tremble when she held a pose, endlessly held it, for her arms were bared in a snug white garment no woman of Geall would have worn outside the bedchamber.

She lifted a leg behind her into the air, bent at the knee,

reaching an arm back to grasp her bare foot. The shirt rose up her torso to reveal more flesh.

It would be a sorry man, Larkin decided, who didn't enjoy the view.

Her hair was short, raven black, and her eyes were bluer than the lakes of Fonn. She wouldn't have been deemed a beauty in his world, as she lacked the roundness, the plump sweet curves, but he found the strength of her form appealing, the angles of her face, the sharp arch of brows interesting and unique.

She brought her leg down, swept it out to the side, then dropped into a long crouch with her arms parallel to the ground.

"You always eat that much sugar in the morning?"

Her voice jolted him. He'd been still and silent, and thought her unaware of him. He should've known better. He took a bite of the cake he'd forgotten he held. "It's good."

"Bet." Blair lowered her arms, straightened. "Earlier rising for you than usual, isn't it?"

"I couldn't sleep."

"Know what you mean. Damn good fight."

"Good?" He looked over the burned ground and thought of the screams, the blood, the death. "It wasn't a night at the pub."

"Entertaining though." She looked as he did, but with a hard light in her eyes. "We kicked some vampire ass, and what could be a better way to spend the evening?"

"I can think of a few."

"Hell of a rush, though." She rolled any lingering tension from her shoulders as she glanced at the house. "And it didn't suck to go from a handfasting to a fight and back again—as winners. Especially when you consider the alternative."

"There's that, I suppose."

"I hope Glenna and Hoyt are getting a little honeymoon time in, because for the most part, it was a pretty crappy reception."

With the long, almost liquid gait he'd come to admire, she walked over to the table they used during daylight training to hold weapons and supplies. She picked up the bottle of water she'd left there and drank deep.

"You have a mark of royalty."

"Say what?"

He moved closer, touched a fingertip lightly to her shoulder blade. There was the mark of a cross like the one around his neck, but in bold and bloody red.

"It's just a tattoo."

"In Geall only the ruler would bear a mark on the body. When the new king or queen becomes, when they lift the sword from the stone, the mark appears. Here." He tapped a hand on his right biceps. "Not the symbol of the cross, but the claddaugh, put there, it's said, by the finger of the gods."

"Cool. Excellent," she explained when he frowned at her.

"I myself have never seen this."

She cocked her head. "And seeing's believing?"

He shrugged. "My aunt, Moira's mother, had such a mark. But she rose to queen before I was born, so I didn't see the mark become."

"I never heard that part of the legend." Because it was there, she swooped a fingertip through the icing of his cake, sucked it off. "I guess everything doesn't trickle down."

"How did you come by yours?"

Funny guy, Blair thought. Curious nature. Gorgeous eyes. Danger, Will Robinson, she thought. That sort of combo just begged for complications. She just wasn't built for complications—and had learned it the hard way. "I paid for it. A lot of people have tattoos. It's like a personal statement, you could say. Glenna's got one." She took another drink, watching him as she reached around to tap herself on the small of the back. "Here. A pentagram. I saw it when we were helping her get dressed for the handfasting."

"So they're for women."

"Not only. Why, you want one?"

"I think not." He rubbed absently at his thigh.

Blair remembered yanking the arrow out of him herself, and that he'd barely uttered a sound. The guy had balls to go with the gorgeous eyes and curious nature. He was no slouch in a fight, and no whiner after the battle. "Leg giving you trouble?"

"A little stiff, a little sore. Glenna's a good healer. Yours?"

She bent her leg back, heel to butt, gave it a testing pull. "It's okay. I heal fast—part of the family package. Not as fast as a vamp," she added. "But demon hunters heal faster than your average human."

She picked up the jacket she'd tossed on the table, put it on against the morning cool. "I want coffee."

"I don't like it. I like the Coke." Then he smiled, easy, charming. "Will you be making yourself the breakfast?"

"In a little while. I've got some things I want to do first."

"Maybe you wouldn't mind making enough for two."

"Maybe." Clever guy, too, she thought. You had to respect his finagling. "You got something going now?"

It took him a moment, but he tried to spend a little time each day with the miraculous machine called the television. He was proud to think he was learning new idioms. "I'm after taking the horse for a ride, then feeding and grooming him."

"Plenty of light today, but you shouldn't head into the woods unarmed."

"I'll be riding the fields. Ah, Glenna, she asked if I'd not ride alone in the forest. I don't like to worry her. Were you wanting a ride yourself?"

"I think I had enough of one last night, thanks to you." Amused, she gave him a light punch in the chest. "You've got some speed in you, cowboy."

"Well, you've a light and steady seat." He looked back out at the trampled ground. "You're right. It was a good fight."

"Damn right. But the next one won't be so easy."

His eyebrows winged up. "And that one was easy?"

"Compared to what's coming, bet your ass."

"Well then, the gods help us all. And if you've a mind to cook eggs and bacon with it, that'd be fine. Might as well eat our fill while we still have stomachs."

Cheery thought, Blair decided as she went inside. The hell of it was, he'd meant it that way. She'd never known anyone so offhand about life and death. Not resigned—she'd been raised to be resigned to it—just a kind of confidence that he'd live as he chose to live, until he stopped living.

She admired the viewpoint.

She'd been raised to know the monster under the bed was real, and was just waiting until you relaxed before it ripped your throat out.

She'd been trained to put that moment off as long as she could stand and fight, to slash and to burn, and take out as many as humanly possible. Because under the strength, the wit and the endless training was the knowledge that some day, some way, she wouldn't be fast enough, smart enough, lucky enough.

And the monster would win.

Still there'd always been a balance to it—demon and hunter, with each the other's prey. Now the stakes had been raised, sky-fricking-high, she thought as she made coffee. Now it wasn't just the duty and tradition that had been passed down through her blood for damn near a millennium.

Now it was a fight to save humankind.

She was here, with this strange little band—two of which, vampire and sorcerer, turned out to be her ancestors—to fight the mother of all battles.

Two months, she thought, until Halloween. Till Samhain, and the final showdown the goddess had prophesied. They'd have to be ready, she decided as she poured the first cup. Because the alternative just wasn't an option.

She carried her coffee upstairs, into her room.

As quarters went, it had it all over her apartment in

Chicago where she'd based herself over the last year and a half. The bed boasted a tall headboard with carved dragons on either side. A woman could feel like a spellbound princess in that bed—if she was of a fanciful state of mind.

Despite the fact the place was owned by a vampire, there was a wide mirror, framed in thick mahogany. The wardrobe would have held three times the amount of clothes she'd brought with her, so she used it for secondary weapons, and tucked her traveling wardrobe in the chest of drawers.

The walls were painted a dusky plum, and the art on them woodland scenes of twilight or predawn, so that the room seemed to be in perpetual shadow if the curtains were drawn. But that was all right. She had lived a great deal of her life in the shadows.

But she opened the curtains now so morning spilled in and then sat at the gorgeous little desk to check her e-mail on her laptop.

She couldn't prevent the little flicker of hope, or stop it from dying out as she saw there was still no return message from her father.

Nothing new, she reminded herself and tipped back in the chair. He was traveling, somewhere in South America to the best of her knowledge. And she only knew that much because her brother had told her.

It had been six months since she'd had any contact with him, and there was nothing new about that, either. His duty to her had been, in his opinion, fulfilled years ago. And maybe he was right. He'd taught her, he'd trained her, though she'd never been good enough to merit his approval.

She simply didn't have the right equipment. She wasn't his son. The disappointment he'd felt when it had been his daughter instead of his son who'd inherited the gift was something he'd never bothered to hide.

Softening blows of any sort just wasn't Sean Murphy's style. He'd pretty much dusted her off his hands on her eighteenth birthday.

Now she'd embarrassed herself by sending him a second

message when he'd never answered the first. She'd sent that first e-mail before she'd left for Ireland, to tell him something was up, something was twitching, and she wanted his advice.

So much for that, she thought now, and so much for trying again, after her arrival, to tell him what was twitching was major.

He had his own life, his own course, and had never pretended otherwise. It was her own problem, her own lack, that she still coveted his approval. She'd given up on earning his love a long time ago.

She turned off the computer, pulled on a sweatshirt and shoes. She decided to go up to the training room and work off frustration, work up an appetite lifting weights.

The house, she'd been told, had been the one Hoyt and his brother, Cian, had been born in. In the dawn of the twelfth century. It had been modernized, of course, and some additions had been made, but she could see from the original structure the Mac Cionaoiths had been a family of considerable means.

Of course Cian had had nearly a millennium to make his own fortune, to acquire the house again. Though from the bits and pieces she'd picked up, he didn't live in it.

She didn't make a habit out of conversing with vampires—just killing them. But she was making an exception with Cian. For reasons that weren't entirely clear to her, he was fighting with them, even bankrolling their little war party to some extent.

Added to that, she'd seen the way he'd fought the night before, with a ruthless ferocity. His allegiance could be the element that tipped the scales in their favor.

She wound her way up the stone stairs toward what had once been the great hall, then a ballroom in later years. And was now their training room.

She stopped short when she saw Larkin's cousin Moira doing chest extensions with five-pound free weights.

The Geallian wore her brown hair back in a thick braid

that reached her waist. Sweat dribbled down her temples, and more darkened the back of the white T-shirt she wore. Her eyes, fog gray, were staring straight ahead, focused, Blair assumed, on whatever got her through the reps.

She was, by Blair's gauge, about five-three, maybe a hundred and ten pounds, after you'd dragged her out of a lake. But she was game. Having game held a lot of weight on Blair's scale. What Blair had initially judged as mousiness was, in actuality, a watchfulness. The woman soaked up everything.

"Thought you were still in bed," Blair said as she stepped inside.

Moira lowered the weights, then used her forearm to swipe her brow. "I've been up for a bit. You're wanting to use the room?"

"Yeah. Plenty of room in here for both of us." Blair walked over, selected ten-pound weights. "Not hunkered down with the books this morning."

"I . . ." On a sigh, Moira stretched out her arms as she'd been taught. She might have wished her arms were as sleek and carved with muscle as Blair's, but no one would call them soft any longer. "I've been starting the day here, before I use the library. Usually before anyone's up and about."

"Okay." Curious, Blair studied Moira as she worked her triceps. "And you're keeping this a secret because?"

"Not a secret. Not exactly a secret." Moira picked up a bottle of water, twisted off the cap. Twisted it back on. "I'm the weakest of us. I don't need you or Cian to tell me that—though one or the other of you make a point to let me know it with some regularity."

Something gave a little twist inside Blair's belly. "And that sucks. I'm going to tell you I'm sorry about that, because I know how it feels to get slammed down when you're doing your best."

"My best isn't altogether that good, is it? No, I'm not looking for sorry," she said before Blair could speak. "It's hard to be told you're lacking, but that's what I am—for now. So I come up here in the mornings, early, and lift these bloody things the way you showed me. I won't be the weak one, the one the rest of you have to worry about."

"You don't have much muscle yet, but you've got some speed. And you're a frigging genius with a bow. If you weren't so good with it, things wouldn't have turned out the way they did last night."

"Work on my weaknesses, and on my strengths, on my own time. That's what you said to me—and it made me angry. Until I saw the wisdom of it. I'm not angry. You're good at training. King was . . . He was more easy on me, I think, because he was a man. A big man at that," Moira added with sorrow in her eyes now. "Who had affection for me, I think, because I was the smallest of us."

Blair hadn't met King, Cian's friend who'd been captured, then killed by Lilith. Then turned, and sent back as a vampire.

"I won't be easy on you," Blair promised.

By the time she'd finished a session with the weights and grabbed a quick shower, Blair had worked up that appetite. She decided to go for one of her favorites, and dug up the makings for French toast.

She tossed some Irish bacon into a skillet for protein, selected Green Day on her MP3 player. Music to cook by.

She poured her second cup of coffee before breaking eggs in a bowl.

She was beating the batter when Larkin strolled in the door. He stopped, stared at her player. "And what is it?"

"It's a—" How to explain? "A way to whistle while you work."

"No, it's not the machine I'm meaning. There are so many of those, I can't keep them all in my brain. But what's the sound?"

"Oh. Um, popular music? Rock—of the hard variety."

He was grinning now, head cocked as he listened. "Rock. I like it."

"Who wouldn't? Not going for eggs, this morning. Doing up French toast."

"Toast?" Disappointment fell over his face, erasing the easy pleasure of the music. "Just cooked bread?"

"Not just. Besides, you get what you get when I'm manning the stove. Or you forage on your own."

"It's kind of you to cook, of course."

His tone was so long-suffering, she had to swallow a laugh. "Relax, and trust me on this. I've seen you chow down, cowboy. You're going to like it as much as Rock, especially after you drown it in butter and syrup. I'll have it going in a minute. Why don't you flip that bacon over?"

"I'm needing to wash first. Been mucking out the stall and such, and I'm not fit yet to touch anything."

She lifted a brow as he strolled right out. She'd seen him slip out of all manner of kitchen duties already. And she had to admit, he was slick about it.

Resigned, she turned the bacon herself, then heated a second skillet. She was about to dunk the first piece of bread when she heard voices. The newlyweds were up, she realized, and added to the batter to accommodate them.

Effortless style. It was something Glenna had in spades, Blair thought. She wandered in wearing a sage green sweater and black jeans with her bold red hair swinging straight and loose. The urban take on country casual, Blair supposed. When you added the pretty flush of a woman who'd obviously had her morning snuggles, you had quite a package.

She didn't look like a woman who would rush a squad of vampires while she bellowed war cries and swung a battle-ax, but she'd done just that.

"Mmm, French toast? You must have read my mind." As she moved to the coffeepot, Glenna gave Blair's arm an absent stroke. "Give you a hand?"

"No, I got this. You've been taking the lion's share of KP, and I'm better at breakfast than dinner. Didn't I hear Hoyt?"

"Right behind me. He's talking to Larkin about the horse. I think Hoyt's a little put out he didn't get to Vlad before Larkin did. Coffee's good. How'd you sleep?"

"Like I'd been knocked unconscious, for a couple hours." Blair dipped bread, then laid it to sizzle. "Then, I don't know, too restless. Wired up." She slanted Glenna a look. "And nowhere to put the excess energy, like the bride."

"I have to admit, I'm feeling pretty loose and relaxed this morning. Except." Wincing a little, Glenna massaged her right biceps. "My arms feel like I spent half the night swinging a sledgehammer."

"Battle-ax has weight. You did good work with it."

"*Work* isn't the word that comes to mind. But I'm not going to think about it—at least not until I've gorged myself." Turning, Glenna opened a cupboard for plates. "Do you know how often I had a breakfast like this—fried bread, fried meat—before all this started?"

"Nope."

"Never. Absolutely never," she added with a half laugh. "I watched my weight as if the, well, as if the fate of the world depended on it."

"You're training hard." Blair flipped the bread. "You need the fuel, the carbs. If you put on a few pounds, I can guarantee it's going to be pure muscle."

"Blair." Glenna glanced toward the doorway to ensure Hoyt hadn't started in yet. "You've got more experience with this than any of us. Just between you and me, for now, anyway, how did we do last night?"

"We lived," Blair said flatly. She continued to cook, sliding fried bread onto a plate, dunking more. "That's bottom line."

"But—"

"Glenna, I'll tell you straight." Blair turned, leaning back on the counter for a moment while bread sizzled and scented the air. "I've never been in anything like that before."

"But you've been doing this—hunting them—for years."

"That's right. And I've never seen so many of them in one place at one time, never seen them organized that way."

Glenna let out a quiet breath. "That can't be good news."

"Good or bad, it's fact. It's not—never been in my experience—the nature of the beast to live, work, fight in large groups. I contacted my aunt, and she says the same. They're killers, and they might travel, hunt, even live together in packs. Small packs, and there might be an alpha, male or female. But not like this."

"Not like an army," Glenna murmured.

"No. And what we saw last night was a squad—a small slice of an army. The thing is, they're willing to die for her, for Lilith. And that's powerful stuff."

"Okay. Okay," Glenna said as she set the table. "That's what I get for saying I wanted it straight."

"Hey, buck up. We lived, remember? That's a victory."

"Good morning to you," Hoyt said to Blair as he came in. Then his gaze went straight to Glenna.

They shared coloring, Blair thought, she and her however-many-times great-uncle. She, the sorcerer and his twin brother, the vampire, shared coloring, and ancestry, and now this mission, she supposed.

Fate was certainly a twisty bastard.

"You two sure have the glow on," she said when Glenna lifted her face to meet Hoyt's lips. "Practically need my shades."

"They shield the eyes from the sun, and are a sexy fashion statement," Hoyt returned and made her laugh.

"Have a seat." She turned off the music, then brought the heaping platter to the table. "I made enough for an army, seeing as that's what we are."

"It looks a fine feast. Thank you."

"Just doing my share, unlike some of us who're a little more slippery." She met Larkin's perfectly timed appearance with a shake of her head. "Right on time."

His expression was both innocent and affable. "Is it

ready then? It took me a bit longer to get back as I stopped to tell Moira there was food being cooked. And a welcome sight it is."

"You look, you eat." Blair slapped four slices of French toast on a plate for him. "And you and your cousin do the dishes."

Chapter 2

$\mathcal{M}$aybe it was the post-battle itches, but Blair couldn't settle. After another session with Glenna, everyone's injuries were well on the mend, so they could train. They *should* train, she told herself. Maybe the sweat and effort would work off the restlessness.

But she had another idea.

"I think we should go out."

"Out?" Glenna checked her chart of household duties and noted—God help them—Hoyt was next up on laundry detail. "Are we low on something?"

"I don't know." Blair scanned the charts posted prominently on the refrigerator. "You seem to have the supply and duty lists under control—Quartermaster Ward."

"Mmm, Quartermaster." Glenna sent Blair a twinkling look. "I like it. Can I get a badge?"

"I'll see what I can do. But when I say we should go out, I'm thinking more a little scouting expedition than a supply run. We should go check out Lilith's base of operations."

"Now there's a fine idea." Larkin turned from the sink, where soap dripped from his hands, and he was not at all happy. "Give her a bit of a surprise for a change."

"Attack Lilith?" Moira stopped loading the dishwasher. "Today?"

"I didn't say attack. Throttle back," Blair advised Larkin. "We're outnumbered by a long shot, and I don't think the locals would understand a bloodbath in broad daylight. But the daylight's the key here."

"Go south to Chiarrai," Hoyt said quietly. "To the cliffs and caves, while we have the sun."

"There you go. They can't come out. Nothing they can do about us poking around, taking a look. And it'd be a nice follow-up to routing them last night."

"Psychological warfare." Glenna nodded. "Yes, I see."

"That," Blair agreed, "and maybe we gather some intel. We see what we see, we map out various routes going and coming. And we make a point of letting her know we're there. Or were there."

"If we could lure some of them out. Or go in just far enough to give them some trouble. Fire," Larkin said. "There should be a way to set a fire in the caves."

"Not altogether a bad idea." Blair thought it over. "Bitch could use a good spanking. We'll go prepared for that, and armed. But we go quiet and careful. We don't want some tourist or local calling the cops—then having to explain why we've got a van loaded with weapons."

"Leave the fire to me and to Glenna." Hoyt pushed to his feet.

"Why?"

In answer, Glenna held out her hand. A ball of flame shimmered in her cupped palm.

"Pretty," Blair decided.

"And Cian?" Moira continued to deal with the dishes. "He wouldn't be able to leave the house."

"Then he stays back," Blair said flatly. "Larkin, if you're done there, let's go load up some weapons."

"We have some things in the tower that might be useful." Glenna brushed her fingers over Hoyt's arm. "Hoyt?"

"We can't just leave him without letting him know what we're about."

"You want to wake up a vampire this time of day?" Blair shrugged. "Okay. You go first."

Cian didn't care to be disturbed during his rest time. He figured a closed and locked bedroom door would be a clear signal to anyone that he wanted his privacy. But such things never seemed to stop his brother. So he sat now, awake in the dim light, and listened to the plan for the day.

"So, if I have this right, you woke me to tell me you're going out, down to Kerry to poke at the caves?"

"We didn't want you to wake, find us all gone."

"My fondest dream." Cian waved that lazily away. "Apparently, the good, bloody fight last night isn't enough for the hunter."

"It's good strategy, going there."

"Didn't work out so very well, did it, the last time we went there?"

Hoyt said nothing for a moment, thinking of King, and the loss of him.

"Nor, for you or me, the time before that," Cian added. "You ended up barely able to walk away, and I took a fucking header off a cliff. Not one of my happiest memories."

"Those times were different altogether, and you know it. It's daylight now, and this time she won't know we're coming. And being it's daylight, you'll have to stay behind."

"If you think I'll sulk about that, you'd be wrong. I've plenty to keep me busy. Calls and e-mails, which I've largely neglected these past weeks. I still have businesses that need my attention, which might as well be tended to since you've pulled me out of bed in the middle of the damn day. Let me add it'll be a pure pleasure to have five noisy humans out of the house a few hours, that I can promise you."

He rose, walked to his desk and wrote something on a notepad. "Since you'll be out and about, I'll need you to go here. There's a butcher in Ennis. He'll sell you blood. Pigs' blood," Cian said with a bland smile as he handed his brother the address. "I'll ring him up, so he knows someone's coming. Payment's not a problem as I have an account."

His brother's writing hand had changed over all this time, Hoyt noted. So much had changed. "Doesn't he wonder why . . ."

"If he does, he's wise enough not to ask. And he's no doubt pleased to pocket the extra euros. That's the coin here now."

"Aye, Glenna explained it to me. We'll be back before sunset."

"Better hope you are," Cian warned when Hoyt left him.

Outside, Blair tossed a dozen stakes in a plastic bucket. Swords, axes, scythes were already on board. All of the fiery variety. It was going to be interesting explaining things if they got stopped, but she didn't scout out a vampire nest without going fully loaded.

"Who wants the wheel?" she asked Glenna.

"I know the way."

Blair checked the need to take control, climbed in the back, took the seat behind Glenna as the others joined her. "So, Hoyt, have you ever been in the caves? I don't figure that kind of thing changes much in a few hundred years."

"Many times. But they're different now."

"We've been in them," Glenna explained. "Magically. Hoyt and I did a spell before we left New York. It was intense."

"Fill me in."

Blair listened, one part of her brain marking the route, landmarks, traffic patterns.

In any part, she saw what Glenna described. A labyrinth of tunnels, chambers blocked with thick doors, bodies stacked like so much garbage. People in cages like penned cattle. And the sounds of it—Blair could hear that in the back of her mind—the weeping, the screaming, the praying.

"Luxury vamp condo," she murmured. "How many ways in?"

"I couldn't say. In my time the cliffs were riddled with caves. Some small, barely big enough for a child to crawl through, others big enough for a man to stand. There were more tunnels, wider, taller than I remember."

"So, she excavated. She's had plenty of time to make it all homey."

"If we could block them off," Larkin began, and Moira turned to him in horror.

"There are people inside. People held in cages like animals. Bodies tossed aside without even the decency of burial."

He covered her hand with his and said nothing.

"We can't get them out. That's what he's not saying to you." But it had to be said, Blair thought. "Even if a couple of us wanted to try a suicide run, that's just what it would be. We'd die, they'd die. A rescue isn't an option. I'm sorry."

"A spell," Moira insisted. "Something to blind or bind, just until we free those who've been captured."

"We tried to blind her." Glenna flicked a glance in the rearview to meet Moira's eyes. "We failed. Maybe a transportation spell." She looked at Hoyt now. "Would it be possible for us to transport humans?"

"I've never done it. The risks . . ."

"They'll die in there. Many have already." Moira scooted up in her seat to grip Hoyt's shoulder. "What greater risk is there than death?"

"We could harm them. To use magicks that may harm—"

"You could save them. What choice do you think they would take? What choice would you?"

"She's got a point." If they could do it, Blair thought, if they could save even one, it would be worth it. And it would be a good hard kick in Lilith's ass. "Is there a chance?"

"You need to see what you move from one place to another," Hoyt explained. "And it's more successful if you're close to the object. This would be through rock, and we'd be all but blinded."

"Not necessarily," Glenna countered. "Let's think about this, let's talk it through."

While they talked—argued, discussed—Blair let it all stew around in the back of her mind. Pretty day, she thought absently. The sun shining on all that green. The lovely, long roll of land with cows grazing lazily. Tourists would be out, taking advantage of the weather after yesterday's storm. Shopping in the towns, or driving out to gawk at the Cliffs of Mohr, getting their snapshots and videos of the dolmen in The Burren.

She'd done the same thing herself, once upon a time.

"So, does Geall look anything like this?"

"Quite a bit really," Larkin told her. "It's very like home, except, well, the roads, the cars, most of the buildings. But the land itself, aye, it is. It's very like home."

"What do you do back there?"

"About what, exactly?"

"Well, a guy's got to make a living, right?"

"Oh. We work the land, of course. And we've horses, for breeding, selling. Fine horses. I've left my father short-handed. He may not be too pleased with me right at the moment."

"Odds are he'll understand if you end up saving the world." She should have known he worked with his hands, Blair realized. They were strong and hard, and he had the look, she supposed, of a man who spent the bulk of his time outdoors. All those sun-streaks in his hair, the light golden haze on his skin.

Whoa, settle down, hormones. He was just another member of the team she'd been pulled into. It was smart to learn all you could about who was fighting beside you. And stupid to let yourself get little tingles of lust over them.

"So you're a farmer."

"At the bottom of it."

"How does a farmer know how to use a sword the way you do?"

"Ah." He swiveled around to face her more directly. For a moment, just a short moment, he lost his trend. Her eyes were so deep and blue. "Sure we have tournaments. Games? I like to play in them. I like to win."

She could see that as well, though it was probably more Hollywood than Geallian. "Yeah, me, too. I like to win."

"So then, do you play games?"

There was a teasing, playfully sexy undercurrent in the question. She'd have had to have been brain-dead to miss it. Brain-dead for a month, she decided, not to feel the little buzz.

"Not so much, but I win when I do."

He draped an arm over the back of her seat in a casual move. "In some games, both sides are the winner."

"Maybe. Mostly when I fight, I'm not playing around."

"Play balances out the fighting, don't you think? And our tournaments, well, they'll have served as a kind of preparation for what's to come. There are many men in Geall, and some women besides, who have a good hand with a sword or a lance. If the war goes there, as we're told it will, we'll have an army to meet these things."

"We'll need it."

"What do you do? Glenna says that women must work for a living here. Or that most do. Are you paid in coin to hunt demons?"

"No." He wasn't touching her, and she couldn't say he was putting moves on her. But she felt as if he were. "It's not the way it works. There's some family money. I mean we're not rolling in it or anything, but there's a cushion. We own pubs. Chicago, New York, Boston. Like that."

"Pubs, is it? I like a good pub."

"Who doesn't? Anyway, I do some waitressing. And some personal training."

His brows knit. "Training? For battle?"

"Not really. It's more for health and vanity. Ah, helping people get in shape, lose weight, tone up. I don't need a lot of money, so it works out okay. Gives me some room, too, to take off when I need to."

She glanced over. Moira was staring out the side window like a woman in a dream. In the front, Hoyt and Glenna continued to talk magic. Blair leaned closer to Larkin, lowered her voice.

"Look, maybe our magical lovebirds can pull this transportation bit off, maybe not. If they can't, you're going to have to handle your cousin."

"I don't handle Moira."

"Sure you do. If we've got a shot at executing a little cave-in, or firing up those caves, we have to take it."

Their faces were close now, their voices down to whispers. "And the people inside? We burn them alive, or bury them the same way? She won't accept it. Neither can I."

"Do you know what torment they're in now?"

"It's not of our doing."

"Caged and tortured." She kept her eyes on his, and her voice was low and empty. "Forced to watch when one of them's dragged out of the cage, and fed on. Terrified, or well beyond that while they wonder if they'll be next. Maybe hoping they will just so it ends."

There was no playfulness now, in his face, in his tone. "I know what they do."

"You think you know. Maybe they don't drain them, not the first time. Maybe not the second. They just toss them back in the cage. It burns, the bite. If you live through it, it burns. Flesh, blood, bone, a reminder of the impossible pain when those fangs sank into you."

"How do you know?"

She turned her wrist over, so he could see the faint scar. "I was eighteen, pissed off about something and careless.

In a cemetery up in Boston, waiting for one to rise. I went to school with the guy. Went to his funeral, and heard enough to know he'd been bitten. I had to find out if he'd been turned, so I went, and I waited."

"He did this?" Larkin traced a finger over the scar.

"He had help. No way a fresh one would've managed it. But the one who sired him came back. Older, smarter, stronger. I made some mistakes, and he didn't."

"Why were you alone?"

"Hunting alone is what I do," she reminded him. "But in this case, I was out to prove something to someone. Doesn't matter, except that it made me careless. He didn't bite me, the older one. He held me down while the other one crawled over toward me."

"Wait. Can you tell me, is that the way of it with a sire? To provide . . ."

"Food?"

"Aye, that would be the word for it, wouldn't it?"

It was a good question, she decided, good that he wanted to understand the psychology and pathology of the enemy. "Sometimes. Not always. Depends, I'd say, on why the sire chose to change instead of just drink. They can form attachments, or want a hunting partner. Even just want a younger one around to do the grunt work. You know, sort of work for them."

"I see that. So the sire held you down so the younger could feed first." And how terrifying, he thought, would that have been? To be restrained, probably injured. To be eighteen and alone, while something with a face you'd once known came for you.

"I could smell the grave on him, he was that fresh. He was too hungry to go for the throat, so he got me here. That was the mistake, for both of them. The pain woke me up. It's unspeakable."

She said nothing for a moment. It threw her off her stride, the way he laid his fingers on that scar now, as if to ease an old wound. She couldn't remember the last time anyone had touched her to comfort.

"Anyway. I got a hand on my cross, and I jabbed it right into that bastard's eye, the one holding me down. Christ, did he scream. The other one's so busy trying to eat, he doesn't worry about anything else. He was an easy kill. They were both easy after that."

"You were just a girl."

"No. I was a demon hunter, and I was stupid." She looked Larkin in the eye now, so he would see that comfort, sympathy couldn't stand in front of sense and strategy. "If he'd gone for the throat, I'd be dead. Yeah, probably, I'd be dead and we wouldn't be having this conversation. I know what I felt when I saw that thing coming for me. In the good black suit his mother had picked out for him to be buried in. I know what those people inside those caves feel, at least I know a part of it. If they can't be saved, death's kinder than what's waiting for them."

He closed his hand over her wrist, completely covering the scar, surprising her with the gentleness of the touch. "Did you love the boy?"

"Yeah. Well, the way you do when you're that age." She'd almost forgotten that, nearly forgotten how sad she'd been, even through the pain. "All I could do for him was take him out, and take out the one who'd killed him."

"It cost you more than this." Larkin lifted her hand, brushed his lips over the scar. "More than the pain and the burn."

She'd nearly forgotten, too, she realized, what it was like to have someone understand. "Maybe it did, but it taught me something important. You can't save everyone."

"That's a sad lesson. Don't you think, even when you know you can't, you should try anyway?"

"That's amateur talk. This isn't a game or a contest. Somebody beats you in this, you die."

"Well, Cian's not here to dispute the matter, but would you want to live forever?"

She let out a short laugh. "Hell, no."

There were others along that lonely stretch of cliff and sea. But not as many as Blair had expected. The views were amazing, but she supposed there were others, equally dramatic, and more easily accessible.

They parked, and took what weapons and tools they could most easily conceal. Someone might spot her sword in its back sheath under the long leather coat, Blair decided. But they'd have to be looking. And then, what were they going to do about it?

She studied the lay of the land, the road, the other cars parked along it. A middle-aged couple had climbed to some of the tabletop rocks at the base of the cliff, where it now met the road. Looking out to sea—and completely oblivious to the nightmare that lived below.

"Okay, so it's over the seawall and down. Gonna get wet," she concluded, looking down at the narrow strip of shale, then the teeth of the rocks where the water swirled and plumed. She glanced back at the others. "Can you handle this?"

As an answer, Larkin rolled over the wall. She started to shout at him to wait, to wait one damn minute, but he was already heading down the jagged drop that faced the sea.

He didn't change into a lizard, she observed, but he could sure as hell climb like one. She had to give him A's for balls and agility.

"Okay, Moira. Take it slow. If you slip, your cousin should break your fall." As Moira went over, Blair looked at Glenna.

"Never did any rock climbing," Glenna muttered. "Never could figure out the damn point until now. So, I guess there's always a first time."

"You'll be fine." But Blair watched Moira's progress,

and was relieved she was proving nearly as agile as her cousin. "The drop's not that bad from here. It won't kill you."

She didn't add that bones would be broken. She didn't have to. Hoyt and Glenna went over together, and Blair followed.

There were some reasonably good handholds, she discovered—as long as you weren't worried about your manicure. She concentrated on getting the job done, ignored the cold spray as she worked her way down.

Hands gripped her waist, lifted her down the last couple of feet. "Thanks," she told Larkin, "but I've got it."

"A bit awkward with the sword." He glanced up to the road, grinned. "Fun though."

"Let's keep the party moving. They probably have guards. Maybe some human servants—though it has to be tough keeping humans on tap if there's as many vampires in there as you said."

"I didn't see anyone alive outside of cages," Glenna told her, "not when we looked before."

"This time it's live and in person, so if they've got any, that's who they'll send out. Hoyt you'd better take point, since you know the area."

"It's different, you see it's different than it was." Some of what he was feeling leaked into his voice, the emotion and the sorrow. "Nature and man have done it. That road above us, and the wall, the tower with the light."

Looking up, over, he saw his cliffs, the ledge that had saved his life when he'd fought with what Cian had become. Once, he thought, he'd stood up there and called the lightning as easily as a man calls his hound.

It had changed, he couldn't deny it. But still, in the heart of it, it was his place. He made his way through the rocks, over them, through the spray. "There should be a cave here. And there's nothing but . . ."

He laid his hands on the earth and rock. "This is not real. This is false."

"Maybe you're a little turned around," Blair began.

"Wait." Glenna made her way over to him, put her hands next to his. "A barrier."

"Conjured," Hoyt agreed, "to look and feel like the land, but it isn't the land. This isn't earth and rock. It's illusion."

"Can you break it down?" Larkin thumped a fist against the rock, testing.

"Hold on." Frowning, Blair slicked back her damp hair. "She's got enough mojo for this, or has someone in there with enough, we don't know what else she has. This is smart." Blair tested the wall herself. "Really smart. Nobody gets in unless she wants them in. Nobody gets out unless she wants them out."

"So we just walk away?" Larkin demanded.

"I didn't say that."

"There are more openings, pockets in the wall. Were," Hoyt corrected. "This is a powerful spell."

"And nobody's curious—people who come here, live here—about what happened to them." Blair nodded. "That's powerful, too. She wants her privacy. We're going to have to disappoint her."

Hands on hips, she turned around, searching. "Hey, Hoyt, can you and Glenna carve a message into that big rock over there?"

"It can be done."

"What's the message?" Glenna asked her.

"Gotta think of one, since Up Yours, Bitch seems a little too ordinary."

"Tremble," Moira murmured, and Blair gave her a nod of approval.

"Excellent. Short, to the point, and just a little cocky. Take care of that, will you? Then we'll get started on the rest."

"What is the rest?" Larkin wanted to know. He gave the wall a frustrated kick. "A stronger message would be to break this spell."

"Yeah, it would, but right now I'm thinking she doesn't

know we're out here. That could be an advantage." She heard something like a small blast of gunpowder, and turned to see the word *Tremble* deeply carved into the rock. Below it was another carving, of what she assumed was Lilith. With a stake through her heart.

"Hey, nice job. I really like the artwork."

"A little flourish." Glenna dusted off her hands. "I paint, and I couldn't resist the dig."

"What do you need to try the transportation spell?"

Glenna blew out a breath. "Time, space, focus, and a hell of a lot of luck."

"Not from here." Hoyt shook his head. "The cliffs are mine. The caves are hers. However much time has passed, the cliffs are still mine. We'll work the spell from above." He turned to Glenna. "We have to see first. We can't transport what we can't see. It's likely she'll sense us, and do whatever she can to stop us."

"Maybe not right away. We won't be looking for her this time, but for people. She may not realize what we're doing, and give us the time we need. Hoyt's right, it's better done on the cliffs," Glenna told Blair. "If we can get anyone out, we wouldn't want to bring them out here in any case."

"Good point." Maybe they wouldn't get any solid intel out of this trip, Blair mused, but they might not walk away empty-handed. "So, what do we do with them if it works?"

"Get them to safety." Glenna lifted her hands. "One step at a time."

"I can try to help you. I haven't much magic," Moira added, "but I could try to help."

"Every little bit helps," Glenna said.

"Okay, the three of you go up. Larkin and I will stay here, in case . . . well, in case. Anything that comes out this way to give us trouble has to be human. We'll handle it."

"It could take a while," Glenna warned her.

Blair studied the sky. "Plenty of daylight left."

She waited until they'd started up before she spoke to Larkin. "We can't go in. If this magic deal opens up the caves, we can't go in. I mean it." She punched his arm. "I can see what you're thinking."

"Oh, can you now?"

"Rush in, grab a maiden in distress or two, run out the hero."

"You're wrong about the hero end of it. That wouldn't be what I'm looking for. But now a pretty maiden in distress is hard for a man to resist."

"Resist it. You don't know the caves, you don't know where she's holding the prisoners, and you don't know their numbers or how they're equipped. Listen, I'm not saying a part of me wouldn't like to go charging in there if it opens up, do some damage, maybe save some lives. But we'd never make it out alive, and neither would anyone else."

"We have the swords Hoyt and Glenna charmed. The fire swords."

She struggled with frustration. It was so damn irritating to have to explain basic strategy. "And we'd take some vamps with us, no question. Then they'd have us and the swords."

"I know the sense of what you're saying, but it's hard to stand by and do nothing."

"If the magic team pulls this off, it won't be nothing. You're too good in a fight for us to lose you trying something that can't work."

"Oh, a compliment. Not many of those spill out of your lips." He grinned at her while drops of sea spray glinted in his hair. "I won't go in. I give you my word on it." He held out a hand for hers. When she took it, he gave it an easy squeeze. "But there wouldn't be anything stopping us from slapping some fire in the hole should this bloody rock open. It would be what you call making a statement, wouldn't it?"

"Guess it would. Just don't get cocky, Larkin."

"Sure I was born that way, I'm afraid. What's a man to do, after all?"

He turned to face the wall, and leaned back on one of

the wet rocks as the spume sprayed. And looked relaxed enough, Blair noted, that he might have been sitting in the parlor by the fire.

"Well, likely we've got some time on our hands just now. So, tell me, how did you first know you'd be a demon hunter?"

"You want the story of my life? Now?"

He moved his shoulders. "Might as well pass the time. And I'll admit to some curiosity about it. Before I left Geall, I wouldn't have believed any of this, not at the heart of it. And now, well . . ." He stared thoughtfully at the wall of rock and sod. "What's a man to do?" he repeated.

He had a point she decided. She moved over to join him, angling her body so that she could scan one sweep of the cliff face while he took the other. "I was four."

"Young. Young to have any understanding of matters that dark. That they're real, I'm saying, and not just the shadows a child imagines are monsters."

"Things are a little different in my family. I thought it would be my brother. I was jealous. I guess that's natural enough, the sibling rivalry." She slid her hands into the pockets of her coat, idly toying with the plastic bottle of holy water she'd shoved in there before they'd left. "He'd have been six—six and a half. My father'd been working with him. Simple tumbling, basic martial arts and weaponry. Lots of tension in the house back then. My parents' marriage was falling apart."

"How?"

"It happens." Maybe in his world the sky was rosy pink and love was forever. "People get dissatisfied, feelings change. Added to it my mother was sick of the life, the things that took my father away. She wanted normal, and it was her mistake she'd married someone who'd never give it to her. So she was busy picking fights with my father, and he was busy ignoring her and working with my brother."

Which would mean, Larkin thought, that no one was paying attention to her. Poor little lamb.

"So I was always after my father to train me, too, or trying to do some of the stuff my brother was doing."

"My younger brother trailed after me like a shadow when we were children. This is the same in all worlds, I suppose."

"Bug you? Bother you?" she amended.

"Oh, drove me mad some of the time. Others, I didn't mind so much. If he was close by, it was easier to devil him. And others yet, well, it wasn't so bad as company."

"So pretty much the same as with me and my brother. Then this one day they were down in the training area— a space most people would have a family room." But you had to have a family to rate a family room. "We had equipment—weights, a pommel horse, uneven bars, rings. One whole wall was mirrored."

She could still see it, perfectly, and the way they'd reflected her father and her brother, so close together, while she'd been off to the side. And alone.

"I watched them in the mirrors; they didn't know I was there. My father was giving Mick—my brother—a rash of grief because Mick just couldn't get this move. Back flip," she murmured, "dive, shoulder roll, throw the stake into the target. Mick just couldn't get it, and my father was dead set he would. Finally, Mick got pissy himself, and he threw the stake across the room."

It had almost brushed her fingers, she remembered. As if it had been meant for her hand.

"It rolled right to me. I knew I could do it. I just wanted to show my father I could do it. I just wanted him to look at me. So I did. I called his name: 'Watch me, Daddy,' and I did it, the way I'd watched him do it over and over trying to get Mick to understand the rhythm."

She closed her eyes a moment because she could still see herself, still feel it in her. As if the world had stopped, and only she was in motion for those few seconds.

"Hit the heart. Mostly luck, but I hit the heart. I was so happy. Look what I did! Mick's eyes just about fell out of his head, then . . . there was this little smile in them—just a little. I didn't know what it meant then, I thought he'd just gotten a kick out what I did, because we mostly got along pretty well. My father didn't say anything, not for a few seconds—seemed like an hour—and I thought he was going to yell at me."

"For doing something well?"

"Getting in the way. And, not yell, really. He never raised his voice; that's all about control. I figured he was going to tell me to go back up with my mother. You know, dismiss me. But he didn't. He told Mick to go upstairs, and it was just him and me. Just me and my father, and he was finally looking at me."

"He must have been very proud, very pleased."

"Hell no." Her laugh was short and without any humor. "He was disappointed. That's what I saw when he finally looked at me. He was disappointed that it was me and not Mick. Now he was stuck with me."

"Surely he . . ." Larkin trailed off when she turned her head, met his eyes. "I'm sorry. Sorry his lack of vision hurt you."

"Can't change what you are." Another lesson she'd learned hard. "So he trained me, and Mick got to play baseball. That was the smile. Relief, joy. Mick, he'd never wanted what my father wanted for him. He's got more of my mother in him. When she left, filed for divorce, I mean, she took Mick, and I stayed with my father. I got what I wanted, more or less."

She stiffened when Larkin put an arm around her shoulders, but when she would have shifted away he tightened his grip in the comfort of a one-armed hug. "I don't know your father or your brother, but I do know I'd rather be here with you than either of them. You fight like an avenging angel. And you smell good."

He surprised a laugh out of her, a genuine laugh, and with it, she relaxed against the wet rock, with his arm around her shoulders.

Chapter 3

On the cliffs, the circle was cast. Now and again, there was the sound of a car passing on the road below. But no one walked here, or snapped their pictures, or stood on his headland.

Perhaps, Hoyt thought, the gods did what they could.

"It's so clear today." Moira looked skyward. "Barely a cloud."

"So clear, you can see across the water all the way to *Gaillimh.*"

"Galway." Glenna stood, gathering strength and courage. "I've always wanted to go there, to see the bay. To wander along Shop Street."

"And so we will." Hoyt took her hand now. "After Samhain. Now we look, and we find. You're sure of the location where we'll send any if we can transport?"

Glenna nodded. "I'd better be." She took Moira's hand in turn. "Focus," she told her. "And say the words."

She felt it from Hoyt, that first low rumble of power, the

reaching out. Glenna pushed toward it, pulling Moira with her.

"On this day and in this hour, I call upon the sacred power of Morrigan the goddess and pray she grant to us her grace and prowess. In your name, Mother, we seek the sight, ask you to guide us into the light."

"Lady," Hoyt spoke. "Show us those held beneath this ground, against their will. Help us find what is lost."

"Blind the beasts that seek to kill." Moira struggled to focus as the air began to swirl around her. "That no innocents will pay the cost."

"Goddess and Mother," they said together, "our power unite, to bring into day what is trapped in the night. Now we seek, and now we see. As we will, so mote it be."

Darkness and shadows and dank air, fetid with the foulness of death and decay. Now a shimmer of light, glimmers of shapes in the shadows. There was the sound of weeping, so harsh, so human, and the moans and gibbering of those who had no tears left to shed.

They floated through the maze of tunnels, felt the cold as if their bodies walked there. And even the mind shuddered at what they saw.

Cages, stacked three deep, four high, jammed into a cave washed in a sickly green light. But their minds saw through the gloom of it, to the blood pooled on the floor, to the faces of the terrified and the mad. Even as they watched, a vampire unlocked one of the cages, dragged the woman inside it out. The sound she made was a kind of keening, and her eyes seemed already dead.

"Lora's bored," it said as it pulled her across the filthy floor by the hair. "She wants something to play with."

In one of the cages, a man began to beat the bars and scream. "You bastards! You bastards!"

The tear that spilled down Glenna's cheek was cold.

"Hoyt."

"We'll try. Him, the one who's shouting. He's strong, and it may help. See him. See nothing else."

Because she needed the words as well as the sight, Glenna began to chant. Moira's voice joined her.

And the ground trembled.

Larkin was singing. Something about a black-haired maid from Dara. Blair didn't mind listening; he had a clear, easy voice. The sort, she thought, of a man used to raising it in a pub, or while he walked the fields. And it was calming to have the tune, the steady roar of the sea, and the warm beam of the sun.

Added to it, the simple companionship was a change for her. Usually when she waited, she waited alone.

"You wouldn't have the little thing? The little thing with the music in it with you?"

"No. Sorry. Next time I get a chance, I'm buying myself a pair of those Oakley Thumps, got the MP3 player built in. Sunglasses." She mimed the shape of them over her face—and it occurred to her Larkin would look damn hot wearing a pair himself. "With the little thing with the music inside them."

"You can wear the music?" His whole face lit up. "What a world of miracles this is."

"I don't know about miracles, but it's jammed with technology. Wish I'd thought to bring the player along." Music would be easier than all this conversation. She was used to waiting alone, damn it. Not hanging around with a companion, exchanging small talk and life stories.

It was making her itchy.

"Well, that's all right. Be nice if I had my pipe."

"Pipe." She turned her head. Couldn't quite fit the idea of a pipe with that gilded Irish god face. "You smoke a pipe?"

"Smoke? No, no." He laughed, shifted his weight as he lifted his hands in front of his mouth, wiggled his fingers. "Play. The pipe. Now and again."

"Oh, okay." His eyes were the color of good, dark honey.

Might look hot in a pair of Oakleys, she mused, but it would be a shame to put lenses over those eyes. "That works."

"Do you play anything? Musically?"

"Me? No. Never had time to learn. Unless you count beating out a tattoo on vampires." She mimed again—it seemed they did a lot of charades between them—punching her fists in the air.

"Well now, your sword sings, that's for certain." He gave her a friendly little shoulder bump. "Don't know as I've heard the like of it. And this would be a fine place for a battle, I'm thinking." He tapped fingers rhythmically on the hilt of his sword. "The sea, the rocks, the bright sun. Aye, a fine spot."

"Sure, if you like not having an escape route, or losing your footing on slick rocks. Drowning."

He gave her a pitying look and a sigh. "You're not considering the atmosphere, the dramatic tone of it all. Can vampires drown?" he wondered.

"Not so much. They . . . Did you feel that?" She pushed off the rock as the ground under her vibrated.

"I did. Maybe the spell's breaking down." He drew his sword, scanned the cliff wall. "Maybe the caves behind it will appear now."

"If they do, you're not going in. You gave your word."

"I keep my word." Irritation flickered over his face. This was the soldier now, she noted, and not the pipe-playing farmer. "But if one of them sticks its head out, just a bit . . . Do you see anything? I'm not seeing anything different than it was."

"No, nothing. Maybe it's the magic trio on the cliffs. Seems like they've had enough time to do something." She kept her hand on the stake in her belt as she worked her way as far toward the crashing surf as she dared. "Can't see from here. Can you, like, be a bird? Like a hawk or something? Take a look up there?"

"I can, of course. I don't like to leave you alone down here."

Irritation rippled down her spine. Here she was explaining herself again. "I'm in the sun, vamps can't come out. Besides, I've worked alone for a long time. Let's get a status report on magic time. I don't like not knowing where we stand."

He could do it quickly, he thought. He could be up and back in a matter of minutes. And from the sky, he could see her, and anything that came at her, as well as the group on the cliffs.

So he passed Blair his sword and thought of the hawk. Of its shape, of its vision, and of its heart. The light shimmered into him, over him. In that change, as arms became wings, as lips formed a beak, as talons sprang and curled, there was a sudden and breathless pain.

Then freedom.

He soared up, a gold hawk that took the air, and circled once over Blair with a cry like triumph.

"Wow." She stared up, watching his flight, the sheer power and majesty of it. She'd seen him change before, had ridden on his back when he'd taken the shape of a horse into battle. And still, she was dumbstruck.

"That is so sexy."

While the ground continued to shake, she gripped Larkin's sword, drew her own. And with the sea roaring at her back, faced the blank wall of the cliff.

Overhead, the hawk swept through the air over the cliffs. He could see keenly enough to pick out individual blades of grass, the petals of the rugged wildflowers that forced their way through fissures in rock to seek the sun. He saw the long ribbon of the road, the wide plate of the sea, and all the way to where the land met it again.

The hawk yearned to fly, and to hunt. The man inside it pitted his will against that yearning even as he skimmed the sky.

He could see them below, his cousin, the witch and the sorcerer, hands linked as they stood on the quaking ground. There was light, wild and white, in them, around them, a spinning circle that rose up in a tower to shake the air even as the ground.

The wind caught at him, plucked at his wings like greedy fingers. In it he could hear their voices, blended together as one, and could feel their power, a hot stream that washed the whirling air.

Then that wind slapped at him, and sent him into a rolling, spinning dive.

Blair heard the hawk cry, saw it spiral. Her heart rolled up into her throat, lodged there as Larkin tumbled through the air. It stayed there, a hot, hard ball even as the hawk sheered up, wings spread. Then dived to land gracefully at her feet.

For a moment, she saw the melding of them, hawk and man. Then Larkin stood facing her, his breathing labored, his face pale.

"What the hell was that? What the hell happened? I thought you were going to splat. Your nose is bleeding."

Her voice was tinny to his ears so he shook his head as if to clear it. "Not surprising." He swiped at the blood. "Something's happening up there, something very big from the feel of it. The light damn near blinded me, and the wind's a bloody wicked one. I couldn't tell, not for certain, if they're in trouble. But I think we'd best go up and make certain."

"Okay." She started to hand him his sword, and the ground heaved. Off-balance, she pitched forward. He managed to catch her, but the momentum threw him back against the rock, and nearly sent both of them into the water.

"Sorry, sorry." But it was brace against him or fall. "You hurt?"

"Knocked the bleeding breath out of me again is all."

The next spume of surf soaked them both. "Screw this. We'd better get out of here."

"I'm for that. Steady now."

They linked their arms around each other's waists,

struggling to stay upright. Rock and sod began to spill down the cliff face, making the idea of climbing up it again unappealing if not impossible.

"I can get us up to the others," he told her. "You'll just have to hold on, and I'll—"

He broke off as the wall itself began to waver, to change. To open.

"Well now," he murmured, "what have we here?"

"Spell broke down, or was broken down. Could be trouble."

"I'm hoping."

"Right there with you."

Even as he spoke, they rushed out. Big and burly, and armed with swords.

"How can they—"

"Not vamps." Blair pushed away from Larkin, planted her feet. She figured the quaking ground was as much a problem for the enemy as it was for her and Larkin. "Fight now, explain later."

She swung her sword up, blocked the first blow. The force rippled down her arm even as the ground buckled under her feet. She used it, going down, blocking again as she snatched one of the stakes out of her belt.

She jammed it through his leg. He stumbled, howled, and she came up with her sword.

One down, she thought, and refused the pity. She pivoted, nearly went down as the ground came up, and clashed steel with the one who sprang behind her.

Out of the corner of her eye, she saw Larkin taking on two at once. "Bear claw!" she shouted.

"There's an idea." His arm thickened, lengthened. With the keen black claws that curled out, he swiped even as his sword swung in his other hand.

They were holding their own, Blair thought, but no more than that. There was no room to maneuver, not when a wrong step could have them tumbling into the sea.

Bashed on the rocks, swept away. Worse than the sword.

Still, they couldn't climb, not now. There was no choice but to stand and fight.

She fell, rolled, and the sword plunged into the rocky ground an inch from her face. She kicked up, pumping hard, and sent her opponent into the sea.

Too many of them, too many, she thought as she gained her feet and staggered. But it could be worse. It could . . .

The light changed, dimmed. With the false twilight came the first splatters of rain.

"Christ, Jesus Christ. She's bringing the dark."

With it, vampires began to slink out of the cave. The sea, and a hard, drowning death suddenly seemed the better alternative.

Calculating quickly, she sent fire rippling down her blade. They could block them with fire, hold some back, destroy others. But too many would get through.

"We can't win this, Larkin. Make like a hawk, get to the others. Get them out of here. I'll hold them off as long as I can."

"Don't be foolish. Get on." He threw her his sword. "Hold on."

He changed, but it wasn't a hawk that stood beside her. The dragon's gold wings spread, and as it reared back, its tail sliced down the first that came out of the caves.

She didn't think, just leaped on its back, locking her legs around its serpentine body. She sliced out to the left, hacking at one that charged. Then she was rising up, streaming through the gloom and the mist.

And she couldn't help it, couldn't stop it. She let out a wild cry of sheer delight, throwing back her head as she stabbed the swords into the sky. And set them both to flame.

The wind rushed by her, and the ground rushed away. She sheathed one sword so that she could run a hand over the dragon. The scales, glimmering gold, felt like polished jewels, sun-warmed and smooth. Looking down, she saw earth and sea, and swirling pockets of mists that blanketed the jaws of the rocks.

Then she saw, on the high cliff, three figures sprawled on the tough, wet grass.

"Get down there. Get down there fast!" She knew he could hear and understand her, in any form, but she might have saved her breath.

The rush of speed slapped her back as he arrowed toward the ground. She was jumping off even as he landed, and began to change back.

The fear was bright silver in her belly, but she saw Hoyt push himself up to sit, saw him reach for Glenna. His nose was bleeding, as hers was. When Larkin reached Moira, turned her over, Blair saw blood on her lips.

"We've got to move, we've got to go. They could follow us, and if they want to, they can move fast." She pulled Glenna to her feet. "Let's move faster."

"I'm woozy. Sorry, I . . ."

"Lean on me. Larkin—"

But he'd already chosen his own way. She shoved at her wet hair as she pushed Glenna toward the horse he'd become. "Get up. You and Moira. Hoyt and I are right behind you. Can you walk?" she asked Hoyt.

"I can." If his legs were shaky, he still moved, and quickly as Larkin galloped off. "So much time passed. It's dusk."

"No, she made it. Lilith did it. She's got more power than I figured."

"No. No, not her." Hoyt was forced to brace a hand on Blair's shoulder for balance. "She has someone, something with the power to do this."

"We'll figure it out." She half carried, half dragged him to the van where Larkin was already helping the other women inside "Glenna, keys. I've got the wheel."

Glenna fumbled them out of her pocket. "Just need a minute, a few minutes to recover. That was . . . it was rugged. Moira?"

"I'm all right. Just a bit dizzy is all. And a bit sick in the stomach. I've never . . . I've never touched anything like that."

Blair drove, fast enough to cover some distance, and kept an eye on the rearview for a tail. "Earthquakes, false dusk, a little lightning. Hell of a ride." She slowed as the sun began to break through again. "Looks like she gave up on us. For now. Nobody's hurt? Just shook up?"

"Not hurt, no." Hoyt gathered Glenna against him, brushed the tears from her face with his lips. "Don't. *A ghra*, don't weep."

"There were so many. So many of them. Screaming."

Blair took two careful breaths. "Don't do this to yourselves. You tried, you gave it your best. It was always a long shot you'd be able to get anyone out of there."

"But we did." Glenna turned her face into Hoyt's shoulder. "Five. We got five out, then we couldn't hold it any longer."

Stunned, Blair pulled off to the shoulder, turned around. "You got five out? Where are they?"

"Hospital. I thought . . ."

"Glenna, she thought if we could get them out, we could transport them to a place where they would be safe, and be cared for." Moira looked down at her empty hands.

"Smart. Really smart. It gets them medical attention fast, and keeps us from having to answer awkward questions. Congratulations."

Glenna lifted her head, and her eyes were ravaged. "There were so many of them. So many more."

"And five people are alive, and safe."

"I know, you're right, I know." She straightened, rubbed her face dry with her hands. "I'm just shaken up."

"We did what we came to do. More than."

"What were they?" Larkin asked her. "What were they you and I fought back there? Not vampires, you said."

"Half-vamps. Still human. They've been bitten, probably multiple times, but not drained. And not allowed to mix blood; not changed."

"Then why would they fight us?"

"They're controlled. The best term, I guess, is *thrall*.

They're under a thrall, and do as they're ordered. I counted seven, all big guys. We took out four. She probably doesn't have any more, or not many. It's got to be tough to keep them under control."

"There was a fight?" Glenna asked.

Blair pulled back onto the road. "The caves opened. She sent out the first wave, the half-vamps. Then she did her little weather trick."

"You thought I would leave you there," Larkin broke in. "You thought I would leave you to them."

"First priority is to stay alive."

"That may be, but I don't desert a friend, or a fellow soldier. What manner of man do you think I am?"

"That's a question."

"The answer isn't a coward," he said tightly.

"It's not, and a long way from it." Would she have left him? No, she admitted. Couldn't have, and would have been insulted to be told to go. "It was all I could think of to keep the rest of us alive, to keep her from winning. How was I supposed to know you had a dragon on your repertoire?"

In the back seat, Glenna choked. "A *dragon*?"

"Sorry you missed it. It was wild. But, Jesus, Larkin, a dragon? Someone must have seen it. Of course, everyone else will think they're nuts, but still."

"Why?"

"Why? Because, you know, dragon, and how they don't exist."

Fascinated now, he swiveled in his seat. "You don't have dragons here?"

Blair shifted her gaze toward him. "No," she said slowly.

"Sure that's a pity. Moira, did you hear that? They've no dragons here in Ireland."

Moira opened her tired eyes. "I think she's meaning they don't have them anywhere in this world."

"Well, that can't be. Can it?"

"No dragons," Blair confirmed. "No unicorns or winged horses, no centaurs."

"Ah well." He reached over to pat her arm. "You have cars, and they're interesting. I'm starved," he said after a moment. "Are you starved? That many changes, it just empties me out. Could we stop somewhere, do you think, buy some of those crisps in the bag?"

It wasn't exactly a victory feast, munching on salt-and-vinegar chips and chugging soda from a bottle, but it got them home.

When they arrived, Blair stuck the keys in her pocket. "You three go inside. Larkin and I can take care of the weapons. You're still pretty pale."

Hoyt lifted the bag holding the blood he'd bought at the butcher's. "I'll take this up to Cian."

Blair waited until they were inside. "We're going to have to talk to them," she told Larkin. "Set up some parameters, some boundaries."

"Aye, we are." He leaned on the van as he looked toward the house. It was good, he thought, and somewhat curious, how they understood each other at times with no words. "Are we agreed? They can't use that kind of magic, at least not often, not unless there's no choice."

"Nosebleeds, queasiness, headaches." She pulled weapons out of the cargo area. You had a team, she thought, you had to worry about its members. No choice. "I could just look at Moira and see the headache. It can't be good for them, that kind of physical toll."

"I thought, at first, when I saw them on the ground, I thought . . ."

"Yeah." She let out a long, unsteady breath. "So did I."

"I've come to feel a great deal for Hoyt and Glenna, Cian, too, come to that. It's stronger, deeper even than friendship. Maybe it's even more than kinship. Moira . . . She's always been mine, you know. I don't know how I could live if anything happened to her. If I didn't stop it."

Setting the weapons aside, Blair boosted herself up on

the rear of the van. "It can't be like that. That if the worst happened to her, to any of us, that you didn't stop it. It's up to each of us to do what we have to do to survive, and to do all we can to watch each other's backs. But—"

"You don't understand." His eyes were fierce when they met hers. "She's part of me."

"No, I don't understand, because I've never had anyone like that in my life. But I think I understand her well enough to know she'd be hurt, maybe even pissed off if she thought you felt responsible for her."

"Not responsible. That makes it an obligation, and it's not. It's love. You know what that is, don't you?"

"Yeah, I know what that is." Annoyed, she started to jump down, but he moved, turning his body until it blocked hers. "Do you think I felt nothing for you, nothing, when we stood with our backs to the sea and those demons coming out of the dark? Did you think I felt nothing, so would go, would save myself, because you said to?"

"I didn't know you were going to pull a dragon out of your hat, so—"

She broke off, went rigid when he reached out, gripped her chin in his hand. "Did you think I felt nothing," he said again, and his eyes were deep and gold and thoughtful. "Feel nothing now?"

And hell, she thought. She'd boxed herself in.

"I'm not asking about your feelings," she began.

"I'm telling you whether you ask or not." He moved in a little closer, his legs planted on either side of hers, his eyes on her face. Curiously. "I can't say I know what I feel as I don't think I've felt it before. But there's something when I look at you, now. When I see you in battle. Or when I watched you, just this morning watched you, moving like magic in the mist."

As she'd felt something, she admitted, when she'd ridden on his back into battle. When she'd watched him light up over music. "This is a really bad idea."

"I haven't said I had an idea as yet. But I've feelings, so

many of them I can't seem to pick one out from the others and have a good look at it. And so . . ."

Her head jerked back as his bowed to hers. Her hand slapped on to his wrist.

"Oh, be still a moment," he said with a half laugh. "And let me have a try at this. You can't be afraid of something as easy as a kiss."

Not afraid, but certainly wary. Certainly curious. She sat as she was, the fingers of one hand curled loosely on the back edge of the van, the others around his wrist.

His lips were soft on hers, just a whisper of contact. A brush, a rub, a light and teasing nip. She had a moment to think he was very good at this particular game before the mists floated over her mind.

Strong, he thought. He'd known there'd be strength, and it was a lovely jolt to the system. But there was sweetness as well; he hadn't been sure of that. So that kissing her was like having wine running through his blood.

And there was need, what seemed to be a deep, simmering well of need in him. He hoped in her.

The kiss deepened so he heard the sound of her pleasure purr in her throat. So he felt that wonderful body of hers press, press and yield to his.

When he would have laid her back, back beside the swords, the axes, she put a hand to his chest and held him away.

"No."

"I hear it plain enough, but no isn't what I felt."

"Maybe not, but it's what I'm saying."

He traced a finger from her shoulder to her wrist while his eyes searched her face. "Why?"

"I'm not sure why. I'm not sure, so it's no."

She turned, began to gather weapons.

"I'm wanting to ask a question." He smiled when she glanced over her shoulder. "Do you wear your hair so short so I'll be enchanted by the nape of your neck. The way it slopes there, it make me just want to . . . lick at it."

"No." Just listen to the way he uses that voice, she thought. The women of Geall must scamper after him like puppies. "I wear it short because it doesn't give the enemy much to grab and pull if he wants to fight like a girl." She turned back. "And it looks good on me."

"It does, that it does. Like a faerie queen. I always thought, if they existed, they'd have strength and courage in their faces."

He leaned toward her again, and she laid the blade of a sword against his chest.

He looked down at it, up at her. This time his smile was full of fun. "That's a good bit more than no. I was just going to kiss you again. I wouldn't ask for anything else. Just one more kiss."

"You're awful damn cute," she said after a minute. "And I'd be lying if I said I wasn't tempted. But because you're awful damn cute and tempting, we're going to leave it at one."

"All right then, if that's the way it has to be." He reached past her, picked up an ax, the bucket of stakes. "But I'm just going to be thinking about another one. And so are you."

"Maybe." She started toward the house, arms loaded with weapons. "A little frustration will give me a nice edge."

He shook his head as he looked after her. She was, he thought, the most fascinating of women.

Chapter 4

Blair went straight up to put the weapons in the training area, then went down the back stairs to the kitchen. Larkin could clean the swords, she decided. Work off some of that sexual energy.

She found Glenna there, and the kettle on.

"I'm making some tea, a blend that should take the edge off the day."

"I've heard alcohol does that." And considering it, Blair opened the refrigerator for a beer.

"That's for later—for me. My system's a little twisted up yet. Hoyt went up to see Cian, fill him in."

"Good. We need to talk, Glenna."

"Could I take you through the steps and stages of the spells later, if you need them? It's all a little too hard and bright just now."

"No, I don't need them—that's your territory." Blair boosted herself onto the table, watched Glenna keep her hands busy. "I mean that. When it comes to this area, I'm a civilian. There are some magically inclined, and fairly skilled people, in my family. But nowhere near what you guys have."

"I have more than I did before. Maybe I'm more open to it now." Taking a few pins out of her pocket, Glenna efficiently bundled her hair up. "Maybe it's the connection with Hoyt, the connection we all have to each other. But whatever it is, I'm finding power inside me I never imagined."

"Looks good on you, too. You need to know, to accept, to understand, what the three of you did today was amazing, and it was powerful, and it saved lives. And regardless of that, you have to know, accept and understand it isn't something you can do again. At least not anytime soon."

"We could get more, I think," Glenna said without turning around. "Maybe only one or two at a time. We were greedy, we wanted to get all we could, and we burned it all too long."

"Glenna, it's your territory, like I said. But I'm the one who was looking at the three of you after the serious whammy went down. The fact is, both Larkin and I thought, for a minute there, you were dead. What you were was all but emptied out."

"Yes, that's exactly right. Exactly the right term for it."

"You may not come back from it the next time."

"Isn't that why we're here?" Glenna's hands were steady now as she measured the tea leaves. "To risk it all? Isn't it true that any one of us might not come back each time we walk out the door, each time we pick up a weapon? How many times have you picked up a weapon and the gift you have and risked it all?"

"I couldn't count the times. This is different. You know it. Larkin and I . . . we need you. We need the rest of you strong and healthy."

"You nearly died today, didn't you?"

"Thanks to dragon-boy—"

"Blair." Glenna turned, took the steps over and closed her hand tight over Blair's.

Connections, Glenna had said, and Blair felt it now. You

didn't evade the truth, Blair decided, with someone you were so closely connected to.

"Okay, yeah, it was bad—bad enough I wasn't sure we'd get out of it. But it could've been worse. We all did our jobs, and now I'm having a beer and you're making tea. Good for us."

"You're better at this than I am," Glenna murmured.

"No, I'm not. Just more used to it. Being used to it, I can have a beer because I know we not only beat her today, Glenna. We insulted her, and that feels tingly right down to my toes. And you know what I'd like?"

"I think I do. I think you'd like to go back there and do it all again."

"Bet your ass I would. Nothing better, that's the pure truth. But it would be stupid, self-indulgent, and it would probably get us all killed. Take the victory, Glenna, 'cause you sure as hell earned it. And accept you may not be able to do it just that way again."

"I know it." Glenna walked back to the stove when the water began to boil. "I know you're right. It's hard to accept you're right. In the past few weeks, I've held magicks stronger than anything I ever dreamed existed. It thrills— and it costs. I know we'll need more time, more preparation if we try to do what we did today again."

She poured the water into the pot. "I thought we'd lost Moira," she said quietly. "I felt her falling away, slipping. She's not as strong magically as I am, certainly not as strong as Hoyt." As the tea steeped, she turned back to face Blair. "We let her go. We let her go, only an instant before it exploded. I don't know what would have happened to her if we'd held her in with us."

"Would you have gotten so many out without her?"

"No, no we needed her."

"Take the victory. It was a good day. One question though. How did you know where to send them? Not the magic stuff, just the logistics."

"Oh, I had a map." Glenna smiled a little. "I'd already

calculated the quickest routes to hospitals, in case any of us needed one. So it was just a matter of, well, of following the map."

"A map." After a laugh, Blair took a deep drink. "You're something, Glenna. You are something else. Vampire bitch had you on her team, I think we'd be sunk. Hell of a day," she said with a sigh. "I rode on a freaking dragon."

"It was cute, wasn't it, how surprised he was we didn't have any." Chuckling now, easier now, Glenna got down cups and saucers. "What did he look like? I paint them sometimes."

"Like you'd expect, I guess. He was gold. Long, wicked tail—took a couple of them out with it. And the body's more sinuous than snakelike. Yeah, long and sinuous, the body, the tail, the head. Gold eyes. God, he was beautiful. And the wings, wide, peaked, translucent. Scales big as my hand, that went from pale gold to dark, and all the shades between. And fast? Holy God, he's fast. It's like riding the sun. I was just . . ."

She trailed off when she saw Glenna leaning back against the counter, smiling.

"What?"

"I was just wondering if you have that look in your eye over the dragon or over the man."

"We're talking dragon. But the man's not half bad."

"Gorgeous, fairly adorable, and with the heart of a champion."

Blair raised her eyebrows. "Hey, didn't you recently get married—to somebody else?"

"It didn't strike me blind. Just FYI? Larkin gets that look in his eye, now and again, when he turns in your direction."

"Maybe he does, and maybe I'll think about taking him up on it one of these days. But right now . . ." She slid off the table. "I'm going to go upstairs and take a really long, really hot shower."

"Blair? Sometimes the heart of a champion is tender."

"I'm not looking to bruise hearts."

"I was thinking of yours, too," Glenna replied when she was alone.

Blair heard voices from the library as she passed, and veered just close enough to identify them. Satisfied that Larkin was speaking with Moira, she rerouted for the steps to head upstairs. She wanted nothing more than to wash away the sea salt, the blood and the death.

She paused at the top of the steps when she saw Cian in the shadows of the hallway. She knew her fingers had reached down to skim over the stake in her belt, and didn't bother to pretend she hadn't. It was knee-jerk. Hunter, vampire. They'd both have to accept it, and move on.

"A little early for you to be up and around, isn't it?"

"My brother has no respect for my sleep cycle."

There was something preternaturally sexual, she thought, about a vampire staring out from the cloaked light. Or there was with this one. "Hoyt had a rough one."

"So I could see for myself. He looked ill. But then . . ." The smile was slow and deliberate. "He's human."

"Do you work on that kind of thing? The silky voice, the dangerous smile?"

"Born with it. Died with it, too. Are we going to come to terms, you and me?"

"I think we have." She saw his gaze slide down to her hand, and the stake under it. "Can't help it." But she lifted the hand away, hooked her thumb in her belt. "It's ingrained."

"Do you enjoy your work?"

"I guess I do, on some level. I'm good at it, and you have to like doing what you're good at. It's what I do. It's what I am."

"Yes, we are what we are." He stepped closer. "You look as she must have when she was your age. Younger, I suppose, she'd have been younger, our Nola, when she looked as you did. Women wore down faster then."

"A lot of times vampires look to family for their first kills."

"Home's the place you go where they have to take you in. Do you think any of the others in this house would be alive if I wanted them otherwise?"

"No." So it was time for honesty. "I think you'd have played along with them for a few days, maybe a week. Get some jollies out of it. And wait until they trusted you, let their guards down. Then you'd have slaughtered them."

"You think like a vampire," he acknowledged. "It's part of your skill. So, why haven't I slaughtered the lot of them?"

She kept her eyes on his, struck suddenly by the fact it was nearly like looking into her own. Same color, same shape. "We are what we are. I guess that's not what you are, or not anymore."

"I killed my share in my day. But excepting that I once tried to kill my brother, I never touched my family. I can't say why except I didn't want their lives. You're family, whether either of us is comfortable with that. You come from my sister. You have her eyes. And once I loved her, quite a lot."

She felt something—not pity, it wasn't something he asked for. But she felt a kind of understanding. Following the feeling, she drew the stake out of her belt, keeping the point toward her, and handed it to him. A look of bemusement passed over his face as he studied it.

"I'm not going to have to start calling you Uncle Cian, am I?"

He managed to grin and looked pained at the same time. "Please don't."

They parted ways, with Cian going downstairs, then into the kitchen. He found Glenna fussing with tea trays. She looked a little hollowed out, he thought, and shadowed around the eyes.

"Have you ever considered having someone else play mother?"

She jerked at his voice, clattering the cup she was holding onto the tray. "Guess I'm jumpy." She reset the cup carefully in its saucer. "What did you say?"

"I wonder why one of the others can't deal with food now and then."

"They do. Well, Larkin's slippery, but the others do. Anyway, it keeps me busy."

"From what I'm told you've been busy with things non-domestic."

"Hoyt spoke to you."

"He seems to enjoy waking me in the middle of the day. Which is why I want coffee," he added as he moved to the counter to make it. When he saw her frowning at the stake he set beside the pot, he shrugged. "A sort of peace offering, you could say, from Blair."

"Oh, well, that's good, isn't it?"

He shifted, caught her chin in his hand. "Go lie down, Red, before you fall down."

"That's what the tea's about. It's a restorative. We need it. Batteries dead low here." She managed a smile, but it faded quickly. "She brought a storm, Cian. She has someone with her who has enough power to call a storm, to block the sun, so we need to recharge those batteries. Hoyt and I have to work, and we need to work with Moira. We need to pull out what she has, help her hone it."

She turned back, began to arrange cookies on pretty little plates, anything to keep her hands moving. "We were separated today, the three of us on the high cliffs, Blair and Larkin below. They could've been killed, and we couldn't have helped them, couldn't have stopped it. We didn't see it coming because we were so focused on the transportation spell. And when it came, when the power whipped around and slapped us down, we were already tapped out."

Suffering for it now, he thought. Humans always would suffer for what they'd done, and for what they hadn't. "Now you have a better idea of your limits."

"We're not allowed to have limits."

"Oh, bugger that, Glenna." He snatched up a cookie. "Of course you have limits. You've expanded them, and likely you'll push the box a bit wider before you're done.

She has limits as well, and that's what you're forgetting. Lilith has weaknesses, and is neither invulnerable nor omnipotent. Which you proved today by slipping five of her trophies out from under her."

He bit into the cookie as he got down a mug.

"I know I should think of the five we saved. Blair said to take the victory."

"And she'd be right."

"I know. I *know*. But oh God, I wish I didn't see the ones we left behind. I wish their faces, their screams weren't in my head. We can't save them all, and I said as much to Hoyt when we were in New York. It was easy to say it then."

She shook her head. "And you're right, I need some rest. I have to take this tray up, see that the others get some of it inside them. You could do me a favor."

"I probably could."

"You could take this one into the library. Moira's in there."

"She'll likely think it's poisoned if I take it into her."

"Oh stop."

"All right, all right. But don't blame me if she pours it down some drain." He hefted the tray, muttering to himself as he left the kitchen. "I'm a vampire, for God's sake. Creature of the damn night, drinker of blood. And here I am playing butler to some erstwhile Geallian queen. Mortifying is what it is."

And *he'd* wanted to pass some time in the library, with a book and the fire.

He stepped in, leading with his irritation, and a scathing comment rolling up to the tip of his tongue.

Which would have been wasted, he decided, as she was curled up on one of the sofas, sleeping.

Now what the hell was he supposed to do? Leave her be, wake her and pour the damn tea into her?

Undecided, he stood where he was, studying her.

Pretty enough, he thought, with a potential for true beauty if she put any effort into it. At least when she slept it didn't seem as though her eyes would swallow her face, and whoever she aimed those long, large gray beacons toward with it.

There was a time he'd have found it entertaining to corrupt and defile her kind of innocence. To peel it away slowly, layer by layer, until there was nothing left of it.

These days he preferred the simplicity of the more experienced, women who were in it for no more than he was. A few hours of heat in the dark.

Creatures like this took a great deal of effort. He couldn't remember the last time he'd been stirred enough to play with one.

In the end he decided to leave the tray on the table. If she woke, she'd drink it. If she didn't, well, sleep itself would go a long way to restoring her.

Either way, he'd have done the chore.

He moved to the table, laid the tray down with barely a click of china on wood. But she stirred, nonetheless. A low moan, a little tremor. He backed away, his eyes on her face—and was careless enough to step into a thin slant of sunlight.

The quick, searing pain in his shoulder had him cursing under his breath even as he moved quickly out of the beam. Annoyed with Glenna, with himself, with the sleeping queen, he turned to go.

She began to twitch in her sleep, small sounds of fear gurgling in her throat. Her body rolled up into a tight ball as she shuddered. And in sleep, she began to speak breathlessly.

"No, no, no." Again and again, until she fell into unintelligible Gaelic.

She thrashed, rolling to her back, going stiff as she bowed up, exposing the line of her throat.

He moved quickly, stepping between the couch and the table, and leaning down, gave her a hard shake.

"Wake up," he ordered. "Snap out of it now, I haven't the patience for this."

She moved fast—and he faster—slapping the stake she stabbed out with from her hand. It clattered on the floor ten feet away.

"Don't do that." He gripped her wrist, felt her pulse striking like an anvil against his fingers. "Next time you do, I'll snap this like a twig, I promise you."

"I—I—I—"

"Very succinct. Are you understanding me?"

Her eyes, huge and glassy with fear darted around the room. "She was here, she was here. No, no, not here." Moira came up to her knees, gripping his arm with her free hand. "Where is she? Where? I can still smell her. Too sweet, too heavy."

"Stop." He released her wrist to take hold of her shoulders. Another shake had her teeth chattering. "You were asleep, you were dreaming."

"No. I was . . . Was I? I don't know. It's not dark. It's not dark yet, but it was . . ." She put her hands on his chest, but instead of pushing him away as he expected, she simply dropped her head there. "I'm sorry. I'm sorry. I need a moment."

He caught himself reaching back to stroke her hair—that long thick braid the color of dark oak. He dropped his hand to the side.

"You fell asleep here on the couch," he said in a flat, almost businesslike voice. "You had a dream. Now you're awake."

"I thought Lilith . . ." She reared back. "I nearly staked you."

"No. Not even close."

"I didn't mean—I wouldn't have meant." She closed her eyes in an obvious effort to find some composure. When she opened them, her eyes were clearer, and very direct. "I'm very sorry, but why are you here?"

He stepped to the side, gestured. Now it was simple shock that moved over her face. "You . . . You made me tea and biscuits?"

"Glenna," he corrected, surprisingly embarrassed at the very thought. "I'm just the delivery boy."

"Um. It's very kind of you all the same. I didn't mean to sleep. I thought I would read after Larkin went upstairs. But I . . ."

"Have your tea then. You'll likely be the better for it." When she only nodded, made no move, he cast his eyes to the ceiling. Then he poured out a cup of tea. "Lemon or cream, Your Highness?"

She tipped her head to look at him. "You're annoyed with me, and who could blame you for it? You brought me tea, and I tried to kill you."

"Then don't waste my time or the bloody tea. Here." He pushed the cup into her hands. "Drink it down. Glenna's orders."

Still watching him, she took a sip. "It's very nice." Then her lips trembled, her eyes filled.

His belly tightened. "I'll leave you with it then, and with your tears."

"I wasn't strong enough." The tears didn't fall, just glimmered in her eyes like rain over fog. "I couldn't help them hold the spell, I couldn't do it. So it broke away, it shattered, and it was like shards of glass ripping through us. We couldn't get any of the others, any of the others from the cages."

He wondered if he should tell her that Lilith would only replace the ones they took. Likely twice the number in her fury.

"Now you waste your own time, blaming yourself, and feeling sorry for yourself with it. If you could've done more, you would have."

"In the dream, she said she wouldn't bother to drink me. Being the smallest, the weakest, I wouldn't be worth the trouble."

He sat on the table facing her, helped himself to one of her biscuits. "She's lying."

"How do you know?"

"Creature of the night, remember? The smallest is very often the sweetest. A kind of appetizer, if you will. If I were still in the habit of it, I'd bite you in a heartbeat."

She lowered the tea cup to frown at him. "Is that, in some strange way, a kind of flattery?"

"Take it as you like."

"Well. Thank you . . . I suppose."

"Finish off your tea." He got to his feet. "Ask Glenna for something to block the dreams. She's bound to have it."

"Cian," she said as he started toward the doorway. "I am grateful. For everything."

He only nodded and continued out. A thousand years, he thought, and he still didn't really understand humans— and women in particular.

Blair drank Glenna's tea, and decided she'd stretch out for an hour with her headphones. Ideally, the music would rest her mind, give it time to clear and recharge. But it all circled around with Patty Griffin's soulful voice.

The sea, the cliffs, the battle. That moment, when the sky darkened, of absolute certainty that she'd come to the end. And that tiny cold seed of relief inside her that it would, finally, be over.

She didn't have a death wish, she thought. She *didn't*. But there was that small, secret place in her that was tired, so horribly tired of being alone, of having what she was and what she had to do dictate she would stay alone.

Alone with blood and death and endless violence.

It had cost her the love of a man she'd wanted so much, and the future she'd believed they would have together. Was that when it had started? she wondered. Was that when that little seed had planted itself inside her? The night Jeremy had walked away from her?

Pitiful, she thought and pulled off the headphones. Pathetic. Was she going to let her psyche be twisted up by a man—and one who hadn't been man enough to deal with her? Would she come to accept death just because he hadn't accepted her for who and what she was?

That was just bullshit. She turned to her side, hugging her pillow as she studied the fading light through the window.

She only thought of Jeremy because Larkin had gotten her juices going again. She didn't want to go soft again for a man, to feel herself being taken over and swept off by all that emotion.

Sex was okay, sex was fine, as long as it didn't mean anything more than relief and release. She couldn't go through the pain again, and that awful feeling of abandonment that left the heart a quivering, bleeding mass inside the chest.

No one stayed, she thought as she closed her eyes. Nothing was forever.

She drifted off, the music from the headphones she'd neglected to turn off tinny and distant.

It filled her head, the music that was her own excited blood pumping. It was nearly dawn, the night's work over. But she was so full of energy, so fired up, she knew she could go for hours yet.

She looked down at herself as she walked the last block toward home. She'd ruined another shirt. The job, she thought, was hell on the wardrobe. It was torn and bloody, and her left shoulder was a mass of bruises and throbbing pain.

But she was so juiced!

The suburban street was quiet and pretty—everyone tucked up in bed and safe. And as the sun came up, the dogwoods and tulip trees were so showy and pink. She could smell hyacinths and took a deep breath of soft, sweet spring.

It was the morning of her eighteenth birthday.

So she was going to clean up, rest up, then spend a lot of time making herself irresistible for a very hot birthday date.

As she unlocked the front door of the house where she

lived with her father, she slung her bag off her good shoulder, dumped it. She needed to clean her weapons, but first she wanted about a gallon of water.

Then she spotted the suitcases sitting near the door, and the leading edge of thrill dropped away.

He came down the steps, already wearing his coat. He was so handsome, she thought. Tall and dark, that chiseled face and bold eyes. Just the slightest glint of silver in his hair. A world of love and misery opened inside her.

"So you're back." He glanced at her shirt. "If you're going to let them bloody you, take a change of clothes. You'll draw attention to yourself walking around like that."

"No one saw me. Where are you going?"

"Romania. To research, primarily."

"Romania? Couldn't I go? I'd really like to see—"

"No. I've left a checkbook. There should be enough to run the house for several months."

"Months? But . . . when are you coming back?"

"I'm not." He picked up a small carry-on bag, slung it over his shoulder. "I've done all I can for you. You're eighteen, you're of age."

"But—you can't—Please, don't just go. What did I do?"

"Nothing. I've put the house in your name. Stay, or sell it. Go where you like. It's your life."

"Why? How can you just walk out on me this way? You're my father."

"I've trained you to the best of my ability, and yours. There's nothing else I can do for you."

"You could stay with me. You could love me, just a little."

He opened the door, picked up the suitcases. It wasn't regret she saw on his face, but an absence. He was, she understood, already gone.

"I have an early flight. If I need anything else, I'll send for it."

"Do I mean anything to you?"

He looked at her then, full in the face. "You're my legacy," he said, and walked out the door.

She wept, of course, stood there alone with spring wafting in on the pretty breeze.

She cancelled her date, spent her birthday alone in the house. A few days later, she sat, alone again, in the cemetery, preparing to destroy what the boy she'd cared for had become.

For the rest of her life she would wonder if she'd kept that date, would he have lived?

Now she stood in the bedroom of her Boston apartment, facing the man in whom she'd poured all her love, and her hopes. "Jeremy, please, let's sit down. We need to talk about this."

"Talk?" There was still dull shock in his eyes as he shoved clothing into a duffle. "I can't talk about this. I don't want to *know* about this. Nobody should know about this."

"I did it wrong." She reached out, had him shrug her away in a gesture so sharp and dismissive she felt it cut her to the bone. "I shouldn't have taken you out, shown you. But you wouldn't believe me when I tried to tell you."

"That you kill vampires? What was I thinking, not believing you?"

"I had to show you. We couldn't get married if you didn't know everything. It wasn't fair to you."

"Fair?" He whirled toward her, and she saw it clearly on his face. Not just the fear, not just the rage. Disgust. "This is fair? You lying and deceiving me all this time?"

"I didn't lie. I omitted, and I'm sorry. God, I'm so sorry, but it wasn't something I could tell you when we first . . . and then I didn't know how to tell you what I was, what I do."

"What you are is a freak."

She jerked her head back as if he'd slapped her. "I'm not a freak. I know you're upset, but—"

"Upset? I don't know who you are, what you are. Christ, what I've been sleeping with all these months. But I know this. I want you to stay away from me, away from my family, my friends."

"You need time. I get that, but—"

"I've given you all the time you're going to get. It makes me sick to look at you."

"That's enough."

"It's past enough. Do you think I could be with you, that I could touch you again after this?"

"What's wrong with you?" she demanded. "What I did saved lives. It would have killed people, Jeremy. It would have hunted and killed innocent people. I stopped it."

"It doesn't exist." He dragged the duffle off the bed they'd shared for nearly six months. "When I walk out of here, it doesn't exist, and neither do you."

"I thought you loved me."

"Looks like we were both wrong."

"So you walk out," she said quietly, "and I cease to be."

"That's right."

Not the first time, she thought, no, not the first. The only other man she'd loved had done the same. Slowly, she drew the diamond from her finger. "You'd better have this back."

"I don't want it. I don't want anything that's touched you." He strode to the door, glanced back once. "How do you live with yourself?"

"I'm all I've got," she said to the empty room. Then she set the ring on the dresser, lowered to the floor and wept.

Men are vile creatures, really. Using women up, casting them aside. Leaving them alone and broken. Better to leave them first, isn't it? Better yet to pay them back, and leave them bleeding.

Sick and tired of being the one left behind, aren't you? And all the fighting, all the death. I can help you with that. I'd so like to help you.

Why don't we talk about it, you and me? Just us girls. Let's have a few drinks and trash men, why don't we?

Aren't you going to ask me in?

Blair stood at the window, and the face behind the dark glass smiled at her. Her hands went to the window, started to lift it.

Hurry now. Open up. Ask me in, Blair. That's all you have to do.

She opened her mouth, the words already in her mind.

Then something flew at her from behind, sent her sprawling across the room.

Chapter 5

◆

There was a scream of rage from what floated outside the window. The glass seemed to vibrate from it, almost to bow in from the pressure.

Then it was gone, a blur of motion. Blair felt the room spin.

"Oh no, you don't. There'll be none of that." Larkin took a firm grip on Blair's shoulders, pulled her up to her knees. "What the bloody hell were you doing?"

His face shimmied in and out of focus. "I'm going out. Sorry."

The next thing she knew she was coming to on her own bed, with Larkin tapping her cheeks. "Ah, there you are. Stay with us this time, will you, *muirnin*? I'm going to fetch Glenna."

"No, wait. Give me a minute. I just feel a little sick." She swallowed hard, pressed a hand to her shaky stomach. "Like I've had entirely too many margaritas. I must've been dreaming. I thought I . . . Was I dreaming?"

"You were standing at the window, about to open it. She

was outside, somehow standing out there. The French one."

"Lora. I was going to ask her in." She turned horrified eyes to Larkin. "Oh my God, I was going to ask her in. How can that be?"

"You looked . . . wrong. I'd have said you were asleep, but your eyes were open."

"Sleepwalking. A trance. They got into my head, and they did something. The others!"

He pressed her back down when she started to jump off the bed. "Downstairs, the lot of them. In the kitchen where Glenna's put a meal together, God bless her. She asked if I'd fetch you. I knocked, but you didn't answer." He looked toward the window now, and his face went grim. "I nearly went away again, thinking you were sleeping and could probably use that as much as food. But I thought I heard . . . I heard her talking to you."

"If I'd let her in . . . I've never heard of them being able to do mind control if you haven't been bitten. Something new. We'd better get down, tell the others."

He brushed lightly at her hair. "You're shaky yet. I could carry you."

"Bet you could." It made her smile. "Maybe next time." She sat up, leaned toward him, touched her lips to his. "Thanks for the save."

"You're very welcome." He took her hand to help her off the bed, then wrapped his arms around her when she swayed.

"Whoa. Head rush. They worked something on me, Larkin. They used memories and emotions. Private stuff. That seriously pisses me off."

"You'd be more so if she'd managed the invitation."

"Good point. Okay, let's go down and . . ." She wobbled again, cursed.

"My way then after all." He scooped her off her feet.

"Just need another minute. Need to find my balance."

"You feel balanced enough to me." He looked down, smiled slowly. "You've a lovely shape to you. I like that the

clothes you wear don't hide it away. And just now you've got
a pretty scent to go with it. A bit like green apples."

"Are you distracting me from the fact I nearly invited a
vampire in for dinner?"

"Is it working for you?"

"A little."

"Let's try for a little more then." He stopped, lowered
his head and covered her mouth with his.

A quick jolt. Not so playful as it had been before, and
she realized there was a great deal of anger and fear in him
for her. She didn't know the last time anyone had been
afraid for her. She responded to it before she could stop
herself, turning into him, tangling her fingers in his hair.
Filling up with him that aching loneliness that had followed her out of the dream.

"Fairly effective," she murmured when he lifted his
head again.

"Well, sure it put some of the color back in your cheeks,
so that's fine for now."

"You'd better put me down. If you carry me in there,
it'll scare them. They'll be scared enough when we tell
them what happened."

He shifted her so her feet touched the ground, but kept
his arms around her. "Steady enough?"

"Yeah, better, really."

Still he kept a hand on her arm as they walked the rest
of the way to the kitchen.

"If this can be done, why is it they haven't done it
before?" Hoyt sat at the head of the table in the dining
room, the fire crackling at his back. He looked down the
length of it to Cian.

"I've never heard of it being done before." With a shrug,
Cian sampled the fish Glenna had prepared. "With a personal connection between the vampire and the human, yes,
an invitation can be seduced or cajoled. But that's most often

due to the human's instinctive denial of what it sees. This is a different matter, and from what both you and Larkin said, you were sleeping."

"First time for everything." With no appetite, Blair ate because she needed fuel. "We've got magical types on our team. So, obviously, does she. Some sort of spell."

"I fell asleep in the library, and . . ." Moira sipped water to wet her throat. "There was something. Not what happened to you, Blair, not exactly. But it was as if she was there with me. Lilith. More, that I was with her and it wasn't in the library, at all. We weren't in the library. She was with me in my bedchamber, at home. In Geall."

"What happened?" Blair asked her. "Do you remember?"

"I . . ." Moira's gaze stayed on her plate as her color came up. "I'd been asleep, you see, and it seemed she was just there, as real as you are. She climbed into the bed with me. She . . . touched me. My body. I felt her hands on me."

"That's not unusual." Blair toyed with her fish. "The dream, the clarity of it, maybe, but the content. Vampires are sexual creatures, and very often bisexual. It sounds like she was testing things out with you, playing at it."

"I had an experience right after we came here," Glenna said. "Afterwards, I took precautions, protected myself in sleep. It was stupid, *stupid* of me not to think to protect everyone else."

"Well, that's going on your permanent record." Blair wagged her fork in Glenna's direction. "Glenna doesn't think of everything."

"I appreciate the save by levity, but I should have thought of this."

"We'll figure it out now, because there's no way they're going to put the whammy on one of us and waltz in this house."

"They have someone of power. Not a vampire." Moira glanced toward Cian for confirmation, and got a slight nod. "I've read that there are some vampires who can cause a trance, but they must be there, physically there, with their victim. Or have bitten them before. This bite causes a connection, a bond, between them so that person, the human may be put under the vampire's control."

"Clear of bites here," Blair pointed out.

"Aye. And you were sleeping, as I was—as Glenna was before. You couldn't be caught in their eyes while you slept."

"It takes a lot of juice for a vamp to whammy a human. A lot of energy," Blair explained. "And practice."

"True enough," Cian confirmed.

"So they've turned a witch or sorcerer," Hoyt said.

"No." Moira bit her lip. "I think not. If what I've read is the truth. The vampire can gain power by drinking blood of power, but it becomes diluted. And if this person of power is turned, he would lose most, if not all, of his magic. It's the price for the immortality. The demon he becomes loses the gift, or retains only the dregs of it."

"So it's more likely she has witches or whatever on her payroll, so to speak." Blair considered it as she ate. "Someone who'd already turned to the dark side, we'll say. Or someone she has in thrall. A half-vamp. A potent one."

"I don't know if that has to be." Unlike the others, Larkin had already cleared his plate and was going for more. "I've been listening to all of this."

"How can your ears work when your mouth is so busy?" Blair wondered.

He only smiled as he scooped up more fish, more rice. "It's good food," he said to Glenna. "If I don't eat it, how would you know I appreciated it?"

"I'd like to know where you put all that appreciation. But you were saying," Blair added, gesturing.

"These things happened in sleep, so it would seem to me the spell doesn't work on the conscious mind. Wouldn't it take more power to . . ." He fell back on Blair's term. "To whammy someone when they were awake and aware?"

"It would." Hoyt nodded. "Of course, it would."

"And not just sleeping, not this day. Moira was all but ill with exhaustion from what she was part of today. Blair was worn through as well. I don't know what it was like when it happened to you Glenna, but—"

"I was beat—worn out, upset. It was one of the reasons I didn't think to take any precautions before I fell into bed."

"There you have it then, I'm thinking. Not just sleep, but sleep when the body is weak and the mind at its most vulnerable. So it seems to me that whatever, whoever, she might be using isn't as strong as what we have right here at this table."

"You have been listening." Blair considered him. "Dragon-boy here makes a good point. She hit us when our defenses were down, and she came damn close to getting lucky. What do we do about it?"

"Hoyt and I will work on protection. I've been using the most basic shield to this point." Glenna looked at Hoyt. "We'll pump it up."

"Be good if we could do something for the house, too," Blair pointed out. "Some sort of general woo-woo so they can't get inside, even with an invite."

"You can't block an invitation." Cian sat back with his wine. "You can withdraw it, with the right spell, but it can't be blocked."

"Okay, maybe not. Maybe something that extends the perimeters, creates a safe area around the house itself."

"We've tried." Hoyt laid his hand over Glenna's. "We haven't been able to find the way."

"Something to work on. It would be another layer. The more layers they have to get through the better. Think vamp-free zone."

"Perhaps I should move into a nice B and B," Cian suggested, and had Blair frowning at him until she understood.

"Oh. Oh, right. Sorry. Forgot. Can't have a vamp-free zone with a vamp in residence."

"We haven't been able to find a way to exclude him from it," Glenna explained. "We have a few ideas. More like concepts than actual ideas," she admitted. "And Hoyt's been working for some time on conjuring a kind of shield for you, Cian, so that you could go outside during the day. In the sun."

"Others have tried and failed on that. It can't be done."

"People used to believe the world was flat," Blair pointed out.

"True enough." Cian shrugged. "But I'd think if it could be done it would have been in the thousands of years since our existence. And experimenting with it at this point isn't the best use of time."

"It's my time," Hoyt said quietly.

"We could have used you today." Glenna spoke after a long beat of silence. "In Kerry, at the cliffs. It's worth the time. We think we'd have more success if we had some of your blood."

"Oh?" Cian said dryly. "Is that all?"

"Think about it. Still, our first priority will be protection. Hoyt and I will put that together." She gave his hand a squeeze. "Why don't we get started?"

"Meanwhile, nobody sleeps until we have protection. I've got some extra crosses, some holy water, in my gear." Blair got to her feet. "Cian, unless you're planning to go out, I'd like to set up basic precautions at doors and windows."

"Have at it. But those kind of trinkets won't supercede an invitation."

"Layers," Blair said again.

"I'll help you." Larkin pushed his plate aside. "There's a lot of doors and windows."

"All right, so it looks like we split into teams. Hoyt and Glenna, magic time. Larkin and I will do what we can to block entrances. That leaves Cian and Moira on KP."

It wasn't that she didn't trust Hoyt and Glenna— she did as much as she'd ever trusted anyone. It wasn't that she wasn't open to magic. She had to be.

But even with the charm under her pillow, the candle lit, and the second charm hanging with the cross at her window, Blair slept fitfully that night.

And the night after.

The training helped, the sheer physical exertion of it, and the purpose. She pushed, and pushed hard. No one, including herself, ended any day without bruises and sore muscles. But no one, including herself, ended any day without being just a little stronger, just a little faster.

She watched Moira blossom—or thought of it that way. What Moira didn't have in strength she made up for in speed and flexibility. And sheer determination.

There was no one who could compete with her when she had a bow in her hands.

Glenna polished the skills she already had—the canniness, the solid instincts. And she was coming along with a blade and an ax.

Hoyt brought an intensity to everything. Whether he fought with a blade, with a bow or with his own hands, he had an almost unwavering focus. She thought of him as the most reliable of soldiers.

And Cian as the most elegant, and vicious. He had the superior strength of his kind, and the animal's cunning, but he added style to it all. He would kill, Blair thought, with violent grace.

She thought of Larkin as the utility player. In hand-to-hand, he was a scrapper, and simply didn't give up. He lacked Hoyt's intensity and Cian's elegance with a sword, but he fought tirelessly until he downed his opponents, or they simply dropped from exhaustion. He had a good eye with the bow—not Moira's, but who did?

And you never knew when he'd pull out one of his little tricks, so you'd end up battling with a man who had the head of a wolf, or the claws of a bear, the tail of dragon.

It was handy, and effective.

And damn sexy.

There were times he made her impatient. He was a bit

too impulsive, and often showy. Errol Flynning it, she thought. And showoffs often ended up in the ground.

But when it came down to it, if she had to pick the people she'd want fighting beside her in the battle to save the world, she wouldn't have chosen differently.

But even soldiers in the war to end wars needed to eat, to do laundry, and take out the trash.

Blair took the supply run because she wanted, desperately, to get out of the house. Two days of rain had limited outdoor activities, and made her edgy. If one person, just one, said that the rain is what made Ireland green, she'd split their head open with an ax.

Added to it, since the night of her close encounter with Lora, there'd been no sign of the enemy. The lull ruffled that edge and added twitchy.

Something was brewing. Bound to be brewing.

She had preferred to go alone, to have a couple of hours to herself, with her own thoughts, her own company. But she hadn't been able to argue it was an unnecessary risk.

But she'd drawn the line at giving Larkin a driving lesson on their way into Ennis.

"I don't know why I couldn't do it," he complained. "I've watched Glenna drive the thing. And she's taught Hoyt."

"Hoyt drives like an old blind man from Florida."

"I don't know what that means, except it's an insult of some kind. I could do better than he does, with this, or the beauty Cian keeps in the stable."

"Garage. You keep cars in a garage, and Cian's made it clear he'll bite and drain anyone who touches his Jag."

"You could teach me on this one." He reached over to trail his finger down the side of her neck. "I'd be a fine student."

"Charm won't work." She flipped on the radio. "There, listen to the music and enjoy the ride."

He cocked his head. "That sounds a bit like home."

"Irish station, traditional music."

"It's wonderful, isn't it, that you can have music at the

snap of a finger. Or move so fast from one place to another in a machine."

"Not in Chicago traffic. You do a lot of sitting and cursing instead of moving."

"Tell me about your Chicago."

"It's not my Chicago. Just where I've been based the last couple of years."

"It was the Boston before that."

"Yeah." But Boston was Jeremy, and she'd had to get away from it. "Chicago. It's, ah, it's a city. Major city in the Midwest of the U.S. On a lake—big-ass lake."

"Do you fish in it, this lake?"

"Fish? Me? No. I guess people maybe do. Ah . . . they sail on it. Water sports and stuff. It's wicked cold in the winter, wind like you wouldn't believe. Lake effect, a lot of snow, bone-chilling cold. But, I don't know, it's got a lot happening. Restaurants, great shopping, museums, clubs. Vampires."

"A big city? Bigger than Ennis?"

"A lot bigger." She tried to think what he'd make of the El, and just couldn't.

"How is it that if it's such a large city with so many people, they haven't banded together to fight against the vampires?"

"They don't believe in them, or if some do, they pretend they don't. If somebody gets attacked, or gets dead, they put it down to gangs, or sick bastards. Mostly the vamps keep a low profile—or they did until recently. Prey on the homeless or runaways, transients. People other people don't miss."

"There were legends in Geall of creatures that haunted the night, preyed on humans long ago. I never believed them, until the queen—my aunt—was killed by them. And even then . . ."

"It's hard to believe what you've been taught is fantasy, or the impossible. So you put up the shield. It's natural."

"But not you." He studied her profile. It was strong, yes,

but with such a pretty curve of cheek, and that dark, dark hair such a lovely contrast to the white of her skin. "You've always known. Do you ever wish it otherwise? That you were one of the people with the shields. Who never knew?"

"No point in wishing for what you can't have."

"What's the point of wishing for what you can and do?" he countered.

He had a point, Blair decided. He usually did if you listened long enough.

She found a spot in a car park, dug out the money for the ticket. Larkin just stood, hands in the pockets of the jeans Glenna had bought him on some earlier trip, looking at everything.

It was a relief not to be asked a dozen questions. She knew he'd been to town before, but imagined every visit was a little like a walk through Disney World for him.

"Just stick close, okay? I don't want to have to go hunting for you."

"I wouldn't leave you." He took her hand, tightening his grip a little when she started to shake him off. "You should hold on to me," he said with absolute innocence in his eyes. "I could get lost."

"That's bullshit."

"Not in the least." He linked fingers with hers and set out at a stroll. "Why with all these people, and the street, and the sounds and sights, I could lose my way any moment. At home, the village isn't nearly as big as this, and there aren't so many in it. On market day now, it can be crowded and colorful. But I know what I'm about there."

"You know what you're about everywhere," she said under her breath.

He had good ears, and his lips twitched at the comment. "On market day, people come into the village from all over the land. There's wonderful food—"

"Which would be your first priority."

"A man has to eat. But there's cloths and crafts and music. Lovely stones from the mountains, and shells from the sea. And you bargain, you see, that's the fun of it. When we're at home again, I'll buy you a gift on market day."

He stopped to study the souvenirs and jewelry in a shop window. "I have nothing here to trade, and Hoyt tells me we can't use the coin I brought with me. You like baubles." He flicked a finger at one of the drops in her ears. "So I'll buy you a bauble on market day."

"I think we might be too busy to shop for baubles. Come on." She gave his hand a tug. "We're here for supplies, not shiny things."

"There's no need to hurry. We can have a bit of fun while we're about it. From what I see, you don't have enough fun."

"If we're still alive in November, I'll do cartwheels in the street. I'll do naked cartwheels."

He shot her that quick grin. "That's a new and important reason for me to fight. I haven't thought of the cartwheels, but I have thought about you naked a time or two. Oh, look there. Cakes!"

Sex and food, she thought. If he'd tossed in a beer and a sporting event, he'd be the ultimate guy. "No." She rolled her eyes, halfheartedly dug in her heels as he pulled her across the street. "We're not here for cakes either. I've got a list. A really long list."

"We can see to it soon enough. Ah, would you look at that one? See the long one, with the chocolate."

"Eclair."

"Eclair," he repeated, making the word sound like a particularly pleasurable sex act. "You should have one of those, and so should I." He turned those long, tawny eyes on her. "Be a darling, won't you, Blair? I'll pay you back."

"You ought to be fat as a pig," she muttered, but she went inside the bakery to buy two eclairs.

And came out with a dozen cupcakes as well.

She had no idea how he'd talked her into them, or the detour into half a dozen shops to browse. She was usually—hell, she was *always*—stronger than that.

Then she noticed the way the female clerks, other browsers, women on the street looked at him. Tough to be stronger than that, she decided.

He managed to nudge her into whittling away more than an hour doing nothing before she dragged him with her to finish the supply list.

"Okay, that's it. Foot firmly down. We haul this stuff straight back to the car and head for home. No more window shopping, no more flirting with shop girls."

"Sure it was shameful the way you poured your charm over that dear woman."

Blair gave him a bland look. "You're a real card." She gestured with her chin. "That way. No detours."

"You know, the way this village is built—I'm meaning the way the roads are, it's very like my own. And how the shops are huddled up together. And here, this is very like home, too."

Before she could stop him, he'd opened the door of a pub. "Ah, there's a familiar smell. And there's music. So we'll stop for a moment."

"Larkin, we need to get back."

"So we will. But we should have a beer first. I like beer."

Since her arms were loaded, she didn't put up much resistance when he nudged her inside. "It's nice," he said, "after all the walking to sit and have a tankard. It's not a tankard," he remembered.

"A pint. They usually say a pint here." It was the walking, she decided that made her give in. The man was exhausting. And exhilarating.

She dumped purchases on and around one of the chairs at a low table, sat. "One beer." She held up a finger. "And that's it. I don't want any more trouble from you."

"Have I been trouble to you?" He took her hand, lifted it to kiss her fingers. "Sure I don't mean to be."

Her eyes narrowed. "Wait a minute, wait a minute. Have you been playing me? Is this whole thing been your idea of a date?"

His brows drew together. "I don't know the date. I can't keep track of the days."

"No, I meant . . . never mind. Pint of Guinness," she told the waitress who came over. "Glass of Harp."

"And how's it all going then?" he asked the waitress, and had her beaming him a smile.

"Very fine, and thank you. And for you?"

"A lovely day it's been. Do you live in the village?"

"In Ennis, I do, yes. Are you visiting?"

"We are. My lady is from Chicago."

"Oh, I have cousins there. Well then, welcome to Ireland. I hope you're enjoying your stay. I'll get your beer right away."

Idly, Blair tapped a finger on the table as she studied him. "You don't even have to turn it on, do you? It's just there, all the time."

"I don't understand what you're meaning."

"No, you probably don't. Do the girls back home lap up your cream that way? Blush and flutter?"

He put his hand over hers. "No need at all to be jealous, darling. I've no thought for any woman but you."

"Save it." She had to laugh. "I wouldn't fall for that one even if it wasn't possibly the end of the world."

"There's no one here, or back home, who's caught my eye as you've caught it. I wonder if any will now that I've seen you. You're not like the women I know."

"I'm not like women anyone knows."

The easy smile faded. "You think that's a flaw in you, a fault, or . . . a barrier," he decided. "Something that makes you less appealing than other women. That's false. When I say you're not like other women, I mean you're more interesting, more exciting. More alluring. Stop."

The sudden and unexpected irritation in his voice put her back up. "Stop what?"

"You put that face on. The one that says *bullshit.* I like charming the ladies, for it doesn't do a bit of harm." He waited, and this time Blair could see he had to put some effort into smiling at the waitress when she served them. "Thanks for that." Then he lifted the pint glass, took a long, slow sip.

"You're pissed," she murmured, recognizing the glint in his eye. "What have you got to be pissed about?"

"I don't like the way you demean yourself."

"Demean my—are you whacked?"

"Just be quiet. I said I like charming the ladies, and I do. I enjoy a flirt here and there, and a tumble when I can get one. But I don't hurt women, not with my hands, not with my words. I don't lie. So when I tell you how I see you, it's the simple truth of it. I think you're magnificent."

He drank again, nodding when she only stared at him. "Well, that put the cork back in you right enough. Magnificent," he repeated. "In face and form, in your heart and your mind. Magnificent because of what you do every day, and have done for years, since you were all but a babe. I've never known another like you, and never will. I'm telling you that if a man looks at you and doesn't see what a wonder you are, it's his vision that's at fault, and not a bit of you."

Chapter 6

They fell back into routine, training, strategizing. From the rumbles and flashes coming from the tower, Blair knew there was magic in the work as well.

But what they were doing, under it all, she thought, was waiting.

"We have to make a move." She plowed rapid punches into the heavy bag they'd hung at one end of the once-grand ballroom. "We're caught in a loop, and it's time to do something. Shake things up."

"I'm for that." Larkin watched her, wondering how many levels of frustration she worked through by beating up a big hanging sack. "A daylight attack on the caves is what I was thinking."

"Been there." She pummelled—left, left, right. "Done that."

"No, we went there, but we didn't do the attacking now, did we?"

Annoyed because he was right—worse because he wasn't mentioning the fact she'd been the one to be so nearly used after the mission to Kerry—she shot him a glance. "We go in, we're dead. Or most of us."

"That may be, but we're likely to die in any case before the end of this thing."

Hard truth, she thought. She had to respect it. "Yeah, odds are."

"So there could be a way to give them something to think about without actually going inside and hastening that eventuality. Though I'd like a chance at that—deviling them on their own ground for a change." He picked up a stake, hurled it at the practice dummy.

She understood the sentiment, and felt the same. But knew better. "Whenever possible, you don't fight on their terms, or their turf. The caves are suicide."

"Could be for them, if we lit them up."

She pulled the next punch, turned to him. "Lit them up?"

"Fire. But it would have to be the two of us. The others, Moira in particular, would never agree to it."

Intrigued, she began to unwrap her hands. "I meant to ask you before. The dragon suit. You breathe fire?"

He goggled at her. "Breathe fire?"

"Yeah. Dragons breathe fire, right?"

"No. Why would they want to do that? How could they?"

"That begs the question how can a man turn into one, but okay, another fantasy crushed. So how do you intend to fire up the caves?"

He lifted a sword. "It would only take one of us to get close enough, a few feet in. I'd enjoy that. But . . ." He set the sword down again. "A more practical manner would be flaming arrows."

"Shooting flaming arrows into caves in broad daylight. Well, that shouldn't draw too much attention. I'm not shutting you down," she added before he could speak. "An earthquake and a dragon flight barely made anyone blink. People have blinders. But there's another factor. There are still people in there."

"I know it. Can we save them?"

"Highly unlikely."

"If I were locked in a cage, waiting to be a meal for one of those things, or changed into one, I'd rather burn. You said the same before."

"I don't think you're wrong, but we'd need a full-on attack to make a dent. And you're not wrong either when you say we'd never talk the others into it." She walked over to study his face. "And you're saying it, but you couldn't do it. Not when it came down to it."

He strode over to yank the stake from the dummy. He *wanted* to be able to do it, in his head. But in his heart . . . that was another thing altogether. "Could you?"

"Yeah, I could. Then I'd have to live with it, and I would. I've been fighting this war all my life, Larkin. You don't get through it without casualties. Innocent casualties—collateral damage. If I thought we could end it this way, or put a serious hurt on Lilith, I'd have already done it."

"And you think I can't."

"I know you can't."

"Because I'm weak?"

"No. Because you're not hard."

He pivoted, hurled the stake, hit the heart of the practice dummy. "And you are?"

"I have to be. You haven't seen what I've seen, and for all you know, you still don't know what I know. I have to be hard. What I am makes me hard."

"What you are, a warrior, a hunter, is a gift and a duty. To harden around it, that's a choice. I can do what needs to be done, and if this was the way, this sacrifice of men, I would live with it. It would hurt me, and it would weigh on me, but I would do what needed to be done."

Enough weight, she thought as he left her, you get hard, or you break under it.

And this is why she worked alone, she reminded herself. Why she was alone. So she didn't have to explain herself, or justify herself. Why she'd accepted, after Jeremy, that the only way to do what she'd been born to do, was to stay alone.

She heard a muffled boom from overhead in the tower, glanced up. Sure some people found it—that intimacy, that unity—and made it work. But they had to understand each other first, and accept all the dark places. To not just tolerate them, but embrace them.

And that, when it came to her and her life, just wasn't in the cards. She rewrapped her hands, and went back to pummelling the heavy bag.

"Someone you know?" Cian asked from the doorway.

She barely spared him a glance. She was using her feet now as well as her hands. Side kicks, back kicks, double jumps. She'd worked up enough of a sweat that her breath was short and choppy. "Tenth-grade algebra teacher."

"I'm sure she deserves a good hiding. Ever found a use for that? The algebra business."

"Not a one."

He watched her get a running start, and hit the bag with a flying kick that nearly snapped it off its chain. "Nice form. Oddly, I see Larkin's face on that bag." He smiled a little when she stopped to catch her breath and gulp down water. "I just passed him going down. He looked annoyed—a rarity for him, as he's an affable sort, isn't he?"

"I bring annoyance out in people."

"True enough. He's a likable boy."

"I like him okay."

"Hmm." Cian crossed over to pick up several knives, then began to throw them at the target across the room. "When you've been around humans as long as I have you recognize traits and signals. And, if you're me, you have a curiosity about their choices. So I wonder why the two of you don't just have at each other. Dangerous times, possible end of days, and so on."

Her back went up, she could literally feel the shift in her

spine. "I don't just roll with any guy who's handy—if it's any of your business."

"Your choice, of course." He walked over, tugged out the knives. When he came back, he handed them to her in an easy, almost companionable gesture. "But I think it's a bit more than him being in the vicinity and available."

She gave the knife a testing toss in the air, then hurled it at the target. Hit dead center. "Why this sudden interest in my sex life?"

"Just a study of human reactions. My brother walked out of his world and into this one. The goddess pointed the direction, and he followed."

"He didn't just follow the goddess."

"No," Cian said after a moment. "He came to find me. We're twins, after all, and the attachment runs deep. Added to it, he's by nature dutiful and loyal."

This time she walked over to retrieve the knives. "He's also powerful and courageous."

"He is, yes." Cian took them, threw them. "The odds are I'll watch him die. That's not something I'd choose. Even if he survives this, he'll grow old, his body will shut down, and he'll die."

"Cheery, aren't you? It could be peacefully in his sleep, after a long full life. Maybe after a last bout of really great sex."

Cian smiled a little, but it didn't reach those cool blue eyes. "Whether it's by violence or nature, the result is the same. I've seen more death than you, more than you ever will. But still, you've seen more than most humans have or will. And that separates us, you and me, from the rest."

"We don't have any choice about that."

"Of course we do. I know a bit about loneliness, and what can chase it back, even for the short run."

"So I should jump Larkin because I'm lonely?"

"That would be one answer." Cian retrieved the knives again, and this time replaced them. "The other might be to take a closer look at him, and at what he sees when he looks at you. Meanwhile, the tension and repression gives you a nice edge. Want to go a round or two?"

"Wouldn't say no."

She felt better. Bruised but better. Nothing like a good grapple with a vampire—even one who didn't want to kill you—to clear the head. She'd just go down and grab something to eat before the evening training session.

But first she was going to stop by her room and rub some of Glenna's magic cream into the bruises.

She walked into her room, and onto the rise above the Valley of Silence.

"Oh crap. Crap, crap. I don't need to see this again."

"You do." Morrigan stood beside her, pale blue robes fluttering in the wind. "You need to know it, every rock, every drop, every blade of grass. This is your battleground. This will be the stand of humankind. Not the caves in Kerry."

"So we just wait?"

"There will be more than waiting. You are hunter and hunted now. What you do, what you choose to do, brings you closer to this."

"One battle." Suddenly weary, Blair raked a hand through her hair. "Everything else is just another skirmish leading here. It's all about this. Will it end it?"

Morrigan turned those emerald eyes to Blair's. "It never ends. You know this, in every part of you, you know this single truth. But if she defeats you on this ground, worlds will be tossed into chaos. There will be suffering, death and torment for a time beyond imagining."

"Got that. What's the good news?"

"Everything you need to take this ground is within you. Your circle has the power to win this war."

"But not end it." Blair looked over the ground again, the misery of it. "It's never going to end for me."

"The choice is yours, child, has always been yours."

"I wish I could walk away. Some days I wish that, and others . . . Others I think wow, look what I'm doing, what I can do. And it makes me feel, well, righteous, I guess. Right, anyway. But some days when I go home after a hunt and there's no one there, it all seems too hard, and too empty."

"You should have been cared for, and were not," Morrigan said, gently now. "And still, all that came before, all that comes now has made you. You have more than one battle to win, more than one quest. And always, child, more than one choice."

"Turning away isn't a choice for me. So we'll come here, and we'll win. Because that's what we have to do. I'm not afraid to die. Can't say I look forward to it, but I'm not afraid."

She looked back at the ground, the way the mists filled the pockets in the earth, the way the rocks speared up through it. Now, as always, the look of it shuddered through her. Now, as always, she saw herself lying bloody there. Ended.

She nearly asked if what she saw was truth or imagination, but knew the god wouldn't answer.

"So if I go," Blair decided, "I'm taking a hell of a lot of them with me."

"In one week, you, the circle of six, will go to the Dance of the Gods, and from there to Geall."

Blair turned away from the drop now to look into Morrigan's face. "One week."

"One week from this day. You've done what needed to be done here. You've gathered together, and now, together, you'll make this journey to Geall."

"How?"

"You'll know. In one week. You must trust those with you, and what you hold inside you. If the circle doesn't reach Geall, and come to this place at the appointed time, this world, yours, and all the others are plunged into the dark."

The sun went out. In the black, Blair heard the screams, the howls, the weeping. The air suddenly stank with blood.

"You're not alone," Morrigan told her. "Not even here."

She snapped back, and stared into Larkin's eyes. She felt his fingers digging into her shoulders.

"There you are, there you are now." She was too stunned to evade when he pulled her into his arms, wrapped them around her like bands as he pressed his lips to her hair. "There you are," he repeated. "Was it the vampire?"

"No. Wow. You need to turn me loose."

"In a minute or two. You're shaking."

"I don't think so. I think that's you."

"It may be. I know you scared six lives out of me." He drew her back, barely an inch. "You were just standing there, just standing, staring. You didn't hear me when I spoke to you. Didn't see me when I was right in front of you. And your eyes . . ." He pressed his lips to her forehead now, firmly, the way she imagined parents checked a child for fever. "So dark, so deep."

"It was Morrigan. She took me on a little excursion. I'm okay."

"Do you want to lie down, to rest? Steady yourself a bit. I'll stay with you."

"No, I said I'm fine. I thought you were mad at me."

"I was—am a bit. You're a frustrating creature, Blair, and I've never had to put so much work into wooing a woman."

"Woo?" Something snapped shut in her throat. "I don't like the whole woo thing."

"That's clear enough, but I do. And a man has to please himself as well as the woman who's caught his eye, doesn't he? But in any case, whether or not I'm annoyed and frustrated, I wouldn't leave you alone."

They always do, a little voice whispered in her head. Sooner or later. "I'm okay. Just a little wigged out at getting a message from the land of the gods."

"What is the message?"

"Better get everyone together and deliver it all at once. In the library," she decided. "It's the best setup."

She paced, waiting for Hoyt and Glenna. Apparently, magic couldn't be interrupted even by messages from gods. Struggling against impatience, she toyed with the two crosses around her neck. One, she'd worn nearly all her life. It had come down through her family, through Nola, and all the way back to Hoyt. Morrigan's Cross, one of those given to him at the onset of this battle while he was still in his own time.

The second, he and Glenna had forged with silver and fire and magic. A team emblem, she supposed, as much as a shield, which each of them—but Cian—wore at all times.

The first had saved her life once, she remembered. So magic, she supposed, had priority over impatience.

Still, when Moira offered her tea, she shook her head.

Already she was going over in her mind what had to be done—and she didn't like most of it. Still, it was movement, and that's what they wanted. What they needed.

"There are two outside," Moira said quietly. "We haven't seen any for days, but there are two out there now, just at the edge of the trees."

Blair moved to the window beside her, scanned. "Yeah, I see them. Just barely."

"Should I get my bow?"

"That's a long shot in the dark." Then Blair shrugged. "Sure, why not? Even if you don't hit one, it'll show them we're not sleeping."

Blair glanced around as Moira went out. Cian was sprawled in a chair with a glass of wine and a book. Larkin sat on the couch, sipping at a beer and watching her.

She didn't want the tea Moira had brought in, didn't want to be soothed by it. Nor did she want alcohol to dull the edge.

So she paced a little more, stood at the window again.

She saw the vampire on the left poof. She hadn't even seen the arrow, but she saw the second vamp fade back into the trees.

No, we're not sleeping, she thought.

"Sorry that took so long, but we couldn't leave that in the middle. Tea. Perfect." Glenna went directly to the table when they came in, poured a cup for herself and for Hoyt. "Is something up?"

"Yeah. Moira will be right back. She just went up to take out one of the vamps outside."

"Oh." Glenna let out a little gush of breath as she sat. "So they're back. Well, it was nice while it lasted."

"I could only get one." Moira came in with her bow. "It was too dark to see the second, and I'd have likely wasted an arrow." But she propped the bow and her quiver by the window, in case she had another chance.

"Okay, we're all here. Morrigan paid me a visit—or had me pay her one. However it works."

"You had a vision?" Hoyt demanded.

"I had whatever it is. At the battleground. It was empty. Just wind and fog, her. A lot of cryptic god stuff, the bottom line being she said we're to leave for Geall a week from today."

"We go back?" Moira stepped to Larkin, squeezed a hand on his shoulder. "We go back to Geall."

"That's what the lady said," Blair confirmed. "We've got a week to get ready for it. To figure out what we need, pack it up, finish up what's going on up in the magic tower. We go to the stone circle, the way you got here," she said, nodding at Larkin and Moira. "The way Hoyt came through. I don't know how it works, but—"

"We have keys," Moira told her. "Morrigan gave me a key, and one to Hoyt."

"I'd say travel arrangements are up to you guys. We'll take all the weapons we can carry. Potions, lotions—whatever Hoyt and Glenna figure we can use best. Major glitch that I see is that for Cian to get there, we have to hope for a cloudy day or leave the house after sunset. Since we've got watchers again, they'll know we're on the move. They'll try to stop us, no question."

"And they'll tell Lilith we've gone," Glenna added.

"She'll know where. When we go to Geall, we take her there." Moira's hand tightened on Larkin's shoulder. "I'd bring that plague to my people."

"It can't be helped," Blair began.

"You say that because you've grown used to living with this. I want to go home," Moira said. "I want to go home more than I can say, but to bring something so evil with me. What if the battle didn't take place? If we found her portal, sealed it off somehow. We could change destiny."

Destiny, in Blair's opinion, wasn't something you messed around with. "Then the battle takes place here, where it's not meant to. And I'd have to say our chances of winning drop."

"Moira." Larkin rose, moving around the couch until he faced her. "I don't love Geall less than you, but this is the way. It's what was asked of you, and what you asked of me."

"Larkin."

"The plague you speak of has already infested Geall. It took your mother. Would you ask me to leave my own now, to break this trust. To risk all?"

"No. I'm sorry. I'm not afraid for myself, not any more. But I see the faces of those people in cages, and they take on the faces of those I know, from home. And I'm afraid."

She steadied herself. "It's more than Geall, I know. We'll go, in one week."

"Once we're there we'll raise an army." Hoyt looked at Moira. "You'll ask your people to fight, to unify under this circle."

"They'll fight."

"It's going to involve a lot of training," Blair pointed out. "And it's going to be more complicated than what we've been doing. We're just six. We'd better be able to pull together hundreds, and it's not just putting a stake in their hands. It's teaching them how to kill vampires."

"With one exception." Cian lifted his glass in half salute.

"No one will lay hands on you," Moira told him, and he answered with a lazy smile.

"Little queen, if I thought otherwise, I'd toss some confetti and wish you all bon voyage."

"Okay, here's another thing." Blair passed by the windows again, just to see if any vampires had chanced coming toward the house. "For all we know Lilith may be on the move, too. She may even get there before we do. Anyway, can we rig up the circle—some spell—so we'll know if it's been used to . . . open the door?"

"There should be." Glenna looked at Hoyt. "Yes, I think we can work that."

"You wouldn't have to. She can't use the Dance of the Gods." Larkin reached for his beer again. "Didn't you say, Moira, when we came through that a demon couldn't enter the circle?"

"It's pure," she agreed. "What they are can't enter the ring, much less use it to go between worlds."

"Okay, bigger problem."

Cian acknowledged Blair's comment with another lift of his glass. "Looks like I'll be tossing that confetti after all."

"That's a kick in the arse, isn't it. I'd forgotten." Larkin pursed his lips before drinking again. "So we'll find a way around it. As I understand it, we six must go, so there must be a way to do it. We just need to find it."

"We go together," Hoyt said and set his tea aside, "or we don't go at all."

"Aye." Larkin nodded in agreement. "We leave no one behind. And we're taking the horse this time." He remembered himself, smiled easily at Cian. "If it's all the same to you."

"We work the problem. Any magical solutions spring to mind?" Blair asked Hoyt.

"The goddess must intercede. She must. If we attempt, Glenna and I, to open this ourselves to let Cian through, we could change it all, disrupt the power, close it altogether so no one gets through—or out again."

"Every time you change the nature of something," Glenna explained, "you risk repercussions. Magic has a lot in common with physics, really. The circle is a holy place, sacred ground, and we can't mess with that. But at the same time, Cian's meant to go, and at the goddess's behest. So we'll work on the loophole."

"If there's another way, another portal that Lilith needs to use, maybe Cian's supposed to use that." Blair frowned at him. "It'd be my second choice. I don't like separating, especially on moving day."

"Added to the fact," he reminded her, "that I don't know where in the bloody hell that portal or window might be."

"Yeah, there's that. But maybe we can find out."

"Another search spell?" Glenna reached for Hoyt's hand. "We can try."

"No, I wasn't thinking of spells. Not exactly." Blair angled her head, studied Larkin. "Any living thing, right?"

He set down his beer, smiled slowly. "That's the way of it. What do we have in mind?"

"You're sure you want to do this?" Blair stood in the tower with Larkin. "I know it was my idea, but—"

"And a fine one it is. Ah, now, are you worried for me, *a stor*?"

"Sending you out into a fortified vamp nest, one with magical shields—sending you unarmed. No. What's to worry about?"

"I won't need a weapon, and it wouldn't be easy to carry one the way I'm going."

"Anything seems off, you get out. Don't be a hero."

"I was born to be a hero."

"I'm serious, Larkin, no grandstanding." Her stomach

was already jittering. "This is just for information. Any signs she's getting ready to move, numbers if you can get a clear idea, a look at their arsenal—"

"Sure you've been over this with me already, a time or two. Do I strike you as being addle-brained?"

"We should wait for the morning, then we could drive you as far as the cliffs. We'd be there if you ran into trouble."

"And it's more likely than not they've got the caves blocked off again during the daylight hours, as you said yourself. They'd be less likely to expect anything like this at night. As *I* said so myself. If I'm to be a soldier in this war, Blair, I have to do what I can do."

"Just don't do anything stupid." Giving in to the need, to the worry, she grabbed his hair with both hands, yanked his face to hers.

She kept her fear out of the kiss. It wasn't fear she wanted to send with him. Instead she poured out hope and heat, and held on to him as the punch of the kiss vibrated down to her toes.

"Not so fast," he said when she started to back away. And spun her around so her back was pressed to the tower wall. "Not all of us are done as yet."

This was what he'd looked for, this fire. Like liquid flames that sparked from her to run into his blood. He let it scorch him as he gripped her hips, then ran his hands up her body, down again. So he could take the shape of her with him.

"Cian lured them to the front of the . . ." Moira stopped short, eyes going wide at the sight of her cousin and Blair locked in each other's arms. "I'm sorry."

"It's not a problem. Just getting myself a fine kiss goodbye." He cupped Blair's face in his hands. "I'll be back by morning." Then he turned, opened his arms to Moira.

She rushed into them. "Be careful. I couldn't lose you, I couldn't bear it, Larkin. Remember that, remember we're all waiting for you, and come back safe."

"By first light." He kissed each one of her cheeks. "Keep a candle burning for me."

"We'll be watching." Blair made herself turn and open the window. "In Glenna's crystal, for as long as we can."

"I wouldn't mind having that French toast when I return." He looked straight into her eyes.

They changed first. She hadn't noticed that before, Blair realized. His eyes changed first, pupil and iris, then came the shimmer of light.

The hawk looked at her, as the man had. Then it flew into the night, silent as the air.

"He'll be fine," Blair said under her breath. "He'll be fine."

Moira reached for her hand, and together they watched until the hawk flew out of sight.

Chapter 7

He soared. With his height and the hawk's vision he could see the things that slunk around the house. He counted eight—a small party then, and likely just watchers as Blair had said. Regardless, he took another circle to be sure it was a scouting expedition and not an attack force.

Widening the circle, he spotted the van at the end of the lane, just beyond the turnoff. Of course, he thought, they would need a way to get back and forth from the caves, wouldn't they? But it was nervy, and a bit insulting come to that, for them to leave their machine so close to the house.

He circled again, considering the situation, then dived for the ground.

He remembered what Glenna had said about how the van worked, how a key was needed to spark the—what was it? Ignition. Wasn't it a shame they hadn't left it hanging in there, in the lock of the thing.

But he remembered, too, that she'd explained that the wheels it rolled on were filled with air. If the wheel was punctured, and the air got out, and then the wheel was called a flat. It was a pain in the ass, she'd said.

He thought it would be fruitful, and fun as well, to give the vampires a pain in the ass.

He changed to a unicorn, with a pale gold wash over its white hide. And lowering his head, plunged his keen-tipped horn into the tire. There was a satisfying little pop, then the hiss of escaping air. Wanting to be thorough, he pierced it a second time.

Pleased, Larkin trotted around the van, puncturing each tire until he saw the van sat on four flat wheels. Let's see you try to get this machine to roll now, you bastards, he thought.

Then he rose up again on wings and flew south.

There was enough moonlight to guide him, and a cool wind to aid his speed. He could see the land below, the spread and roll of it. The rise of hills, the patchwork of fields.

Lights glimmered from the villages, and the larger towns.

He thought of the lively pubs, with the music playing, with the scents of beer and pretty women. The voices in conversation and the rise of laughter. One evening, when all this was done, he wanted to sit in a pub with his friends, those five who were so vital to him, and lift a pint with all those voices, all that music around them.

It was a good image to hold on to during a long flight to a nest of monsters.

Below, he saw the long, lovely sweep of river they called Shannon.

It was beautiful land, he thought, as green as home, and with the sea close. He could hear the rumble of it as he angled southwest.

The dragon would be faster, he knew, but it was the hawk he'd agreed to. He wished he could fly here again, in the dragon, with Blair on his back. She could tell him the names of what he saw below, the towns and the ruins, the rivers and lakes. Would she know the name of that water-fall he soared over, the one as high and powerful as his own Faerie Falls back home?

He remembered the feel of her legs locking around him as they rose up into the air. The way she'd laughed. He'd never known another like her, warrior and woman, with such strength and vulnerability. A ready fist and a tender heart.

He liked the way she talked, quick and confident. And the way her lips quirked up on one side, then the other when she smiled.

There was a longing in him for her, which he thought as natural as breath. But there was something tangled with it, something sharp that he didn't recognize. It would be in-teresting to find out what it all meant.

He winged over the waterfall, and a dense forest that framed it. He skimmed over the quiet glimmer of lakes with starshine glinting on the water. And he aimed for the slicing beam of the lighthouse on the cliffs.

He flew down, silent as a shadow.

On the narrow strip of shale, he saw two figures. A woman, he realized, and a young boy. Alarm tightened his heart inside his chest. They would be captured wandering here near the caves in the dark. Imprisoned, then used, then killed. And he had no weapon to defend them.

He landed in the shadow of rock, and nearly changed into a man to do what he could. But the woman turned to laugh at the child, and the cold white moonlight struck her face.

He had seen her only once before, standing on the high cliffs. But he would never forget her face.

Lilith. The self-proclaimed queen of the undead.

"Please, Mama, *please*, I want to hunt."

"Now, Davey, remember what I told you. We don't hunt near our home. We've plenty of food inside, and since you've been so good . . ." She bent down to tap a finger to his nose, a gesture of amused affection. "You can have your pick."

"But it's no fun when they're just *there*."

"I know." She sighed, ruffled his glossy gold hair. "It's more like a chore than a thrill. But it won't be much longer. When we move on to Geall, you can hunt every night."

"When?"

"Soon, my precious lamb."

"I'm tired of being here." Voice petulant, he kicked at the shale.

Larkin could see he had the face of a little imp—round and sweet.

"I wish I had a kitty. Please, can't I have a kitty cat? I wouldn't eat it like last time."

"That's what you said about the puppy," she reminded him with a quick, gay laugh. "But we'll see. But how about this? I'll let one out for you, and it can run through the caves. You can chase it down, hunt it down. Won't that be fun?"

When he grinned, moonlight sent the dusting of freckles on his chubby cheeks into relief. And glinted on his fangs. "Can I have two?"

"So greedy." She kissed him, and not, Larkin saw with a sick revulsion, in the way a mother kisses a son. "That's what I love about you, my own true love. Let's go inside then, and you can pick out the ones you want."

Behind the rock, Larkin changed. A sleek, dark rat darted inside the caves behind the sweep of Lilith's long skirts.

He could smell death, and see the things that moved in the dark. Things that bowed when Lilith glided by.

There was little light—only a scatter of torches clamped to the walls here and there. But as they moved deeper there was a faint green tinge to the light he felt was unnatural. Magic, he knew, just as he knew this magic wasn't clean and white.

She drifted through the maze of it, holding the boy's hand as he trotted at her side. Vampires scuttled up the walls like spiders, or hung from the ceiling like bats.

He could only hope they weren't overly interested in snacking on rat blood.

He followed the swish of Lilith's robes, and kept to the dark corners.

The sounds of unspeakable human suffering began to echo.

"What sort do you want, my darling?" Lilith swung his arm with hers as if they were on an outing to a fair and a promised treat. "Something young and lean, or perhaps something with a little more flesh?"

"I don't know. I want to look in their eyes first. Then I'll know."

"Clever boy. You make me proud."

There were more cages than he'd imagined, and the sheer horror had him struggling to stay in form. He wanted to spring into a man, grab a sword from one of the guards, and start hacking.

He would take down a few of them, and that might be worth dying for. But he would never get any of the people out.

Blair had warned him, but he hadn't fully believed.

The boy had dropped his mother's hand and now strolled, hands behind his back, pacing up and down the length of the cages. A child eyeing treats at the baker's, Larkin thought.

Davey stopped, pursing his lips as he studied a young woman huddled in the corner of a cage. She seemed to be singing, or perhaps she was praying, for the words were unintelligible. But Larkin could see her eyes were already dead.

"This one wouldn't be any fun to hunt." Even when Davey poked at her through the bars, she sat passively. "She's not afraid anymore."

"Sometimes they go mad. Their minds are weak, after all, like their bodies." Lilith gestured to another cage. "What about this one?"

The man in it was rocking a woman who was either

asleep or unconscious. There was blood on her neck, and her face was pale as wax.

"Bitch. You bitch, what have you done to her? I'll kill you."

"Now this one's got some life left in him!" With a broad grin, Lilith tossed back her gilded mane of hair. "What do you think, my sweetie?"

Davey cocked his head, then shook it. "He won't run. He won't want to leave the female."

"Why, Davey, you're so perceptive." She crouched down, kissing his cheeks with obvious pride. "Such a big boy, and so wise."

"I want this one." He pointed at a woman who'd pressed herself to the back of the cage. Her eyes darted everywhere. "She's afraid, and she thinks that maybe, maybe, she can still get out so she'll run, and run and run. And him." Davey gestured up. "He's mad, he wants to *fight*. See the way he shakes the bars."

"I think those are excellent choices." She snapped her fingers at one of the guards, both of whom wore light armor and skullcaps. "Release those two, and pass the word. Except for preventing them from leaving the caves, they're not to be touched. They belong to the prince."

Davey jumped up and down, clapped his hands. "Thank you, Mama! Do you want to play with me? I'll share with you."

"That's so sweet, but I have some work to see to now. And remember to wash up when you're finished eating." She turned to one of the guards again. "Tell Lady Lora I want her to join me, in the wizard's cave."

"That one first." Davey pointed to the woman.

She screamed and struggled as the guard dragged her out of the cage, while another guard beat back at the ones with her who tried to pull her back inside.

Everything inside Larkin strained to do something. Anything.

Davey bent down, sniffing at the shuddering woman to

imprint her scent. "You're mine now, and I get to play with you as long as I want. Isn't that right, Mama?"

"That's right, my darling."

"Let her go," Davey ordered the guard. Then his eyes flashed red as he looked at the woman. "Run. Run, run! Hide-and-seek!" he shouted when she stumbled out.

He leaped onto the wall, clung there as he shot a grin over his shoulder at Lilith. And he slithered out into the dark.

"It's nice to see him having such a good time. Turn the other loose in, oh, fifteen minutes. I'll be with the wizard for the time being."

He could come back, Larkin told himself. Once he'd done what he'd come to do, he could go back, create a diversion, unlock the cages. At least give the prisoners a fighting chance to escape. To survive.

But now, blocking out the moans and screams along with his own needs, he followed Lilith.

The prison was separated from what he supposed were living quarters, storage and work areas, by a long tunnel. She'd built a kind of mansion under the ground, he realized. Chamber flowed after chamber, some of them richly furnished, some sealed off with doors and guarded.

Two, a man and female both in black jeans and sweaters, carried fresh linens down the tunnel. Obviously servants, he decided, and thought they were likely human servants. Both stopped as Lilith approached, bowed deeply.

Lilith glided on as if they weren't there.

He heard the sounds of combat and paused to look down a tunnel. A training area, not that dissimilar from what they used at Cian's. Here the creatures, male and female, practiced with sword or mace, dagger, or bare hands.

Two prisoners, unarmed and shackled, were being used much as he and his circle used practice dummies.

He saw the one called Lora clashing steel with a male of superior size. They wore no protective gear, and the swords, he saw, were honed to a killing edge.

Lora leaped up and over her sparring partner, the movement so fast it was merely a blur. Even as he pivoted, she ran the sword through his chest.

And as he fell, she leaped on him. "You miss that one every time." She leaned down, playfully lapped at the blood. "If you were human, *mon cher*, you'd be dead."

"No one can best you with a sword." His breathing was ragged, but he reached up to stroke a hand down her cheek. "I don't know why I try."

"If Lilith didn't need me, we'd go another round." She trailed a finger down his check, licked the blood from it.

"Perhaps later . . . toward dawn."

"If the queen doesn't want me, I'll come to you." She leaned down again, and the kiss was long, ferocious.

She sheathed the bloody sword and strode out, with Larkin behind her.

She barely paused as the woman who'd been freed to run fell in front of her weeping. Lora merely stepped over her, glanced up to the pair of red eyes glowing in the dark. "Playing tag, Davey?"

"I wanted to play hide-and-seek, but she keeps falling down. Make her get up, Lora! Make her run some more. I haven't finished the game yet."

Lora let out a long-suffering sigh. *"Ca va."* She crouched down, lifted the woman's head by the hair. "If you don't run and keep our darling Davey amused, I'll cut off your fingers, one at a time. Then your toes." She got up, dragging the woman with her. "Now, *allez!* Scamper."

When the woman ran off weeping, Lora looked back up at Davey. "Why don't you give her more of a head start? It's more sporting and the game will last longer."

"It'd be more fun if you played. It's always more fun with you."

"And there's nothing I'd like better, but your mother wants me now. Perhaps later we can have another game." She blew him a kiss and continued on.

Sick to the depths, Larkin followed her.

She entered a chamber. Larkin felt the ripple of magic even as he darted in after her. The door shut with a hollow thud.

"Ah, Lora. We've been waiting for you."

"I was finishing up a bout with Lucius, then I ran into Davey. He's having such a good time."

"He's been pining for a game." Lilith held out a hand. Lora walked over, slipped hers into it. Together, nearly cheek-to-cheek, they looked at the man who stood in the center of the room.

He wore black robes edged in red. His hair was a thick mane of silver around a face that boasted eyes dark as onyx, a long, hooked nose, a thin, unsmiling mouth.

There was a fire behind him that burned without hearth or log or turf. Suspended above it was a cauldron that spilled out pale green smoke, the same color as the light that glowed sickly through the caves. Two long tables held vials and jars. Whatever swam in them looked viscous, and alive.

"Midir." Lilith gestured toward the man with a wide sweep of her arm. "I wanted Lora with us when we had this discussion. She keeps me calm. As you know I've needed time to compose myself after that disaster a few days ago."

She wandered over, picked up a carafe, poured the red liquid from it into a glass. Sniffed. "Fresh?" she asked him.

"Yes, my lady. Tapped and prepared for you."

She sipped, offered the glass to Lora. "I should ask if you're fully recovered from your injuries."

"I am well, my lady."

"I'd apologize for losing my temper, but you disappointed me, Midir. Extremely. Your punishment would have been more severe if Lora hadn't cooled that temper. They snatched those *cows* out from under my nose. They left an insulting message on my very doorstep. It was for you to protect my home from such matters, and you failed, miserably."

"I am prostrate, my lady." He knelt, bowed his head. "I

was not prepared for the attempt, nor for the force of the power they held. It will never happen again."

"It certainly won't if I give you to Lora. Do you know how long she can keep a man alive?" She glanced over at her companion with a soft and knowing smile.

"There was the one in Budapest," Lora recalled. "I kept him six months. I could have gone longer, but I got bored with him. I don't think Midir would bore me for years. But . . ."

Lora ran her hand up and down Lilith's back. "He's of use, *chérie*. He has great power, and he's bound to you, *n'est-ce pas?*"

"He made me promises, a great many promises. Don't speak," she snapped when Midir lifted his head again. "Because of those promises, he's yet to feel my bite. But you're my dog, Midir, and never forget it."

Slowly now, he raised his head. "I serve you, Majesty, and only you. I sought you out, my lady, to give you the portal, so you may walk between worlds, and rule them all."

"And so you can walk between them, wizard, plucking power like daisies with my army at your back. And still this power broke when struck by what the mortals wielded."

"They should never have gotten by him, it's true." Again, Lora soothed. "He allowed them to humiliate you, and that is unforgivable. Still, we are more with him than without him. With him, we'll have all by Samhain."

"See? She keeps me calm." Lilith took the goblet back from Lora as they stood, arms circling each other's waists. "You're alive because of what she said—as I agree with her. And because you at least had the good sense to bring on the dark once we understood we had been breached. Oh, stand up, stand up."

He rose. "My lady, may I speak?"

"I left the tongue in your mouth."

"I have pledged my power and my life to you, and have dedicated that life and power for more than two hundred years to you. I have made this place for you, as you commanded, under the ground, and cloaked it from the human eye. It is I who carved the portal so that you and your army may travel between worlds, so that you, my queen, may go to Geall and ravage, and reign."

She angled her head and a pretty smile curved her mouth. "Yes. But what have you done for me lately?"

"Even my power has limits, my lady, and it takes a great deal to hold the cloak. The magic these others hold is strong, and still, in the end, I felled them."

"True, true. But after they picked my pockets."

"They are formidable, my lady." He folded his hands so they disappeared within the wide sleeves of his robes. "Less would hardly be worthy of you. And your triumph will be only greater when you destroy them."

"Sweet talker."

"He did nearly get me into the house," Lora said. "So close, I could almost taste her. It was a good spell, a strong one to bend the hunter's will. We could try it again."

"We could," Midir agreed. "But it is only two weeks until we reopen the portal. I will need my strength for that, Majesty. And another sacrifice."

"Another?" Lilith rolled her eyes. "How tedious. And a virgin again, I assume."

"If you would, my lady. In the meanwhile, I have a gift which I hope pleases you."

"More diamonds?" She tapped a hand in front of her mouth in a delicate yawn. "I grow weary."

"No, my lady, not diamonds. More precious, I think." He picked a small hand mirror by its bone handle, offered it.

"Do you toy with me? Such a trinket only . . ." She let out a gasp as she twirled it by the handle. "Is this my face!" Stunned, she touched a hand to her own cheek, stared into the glass.

It was as if she looked through a thin mist, but she could see the shape of her face, her eyes, her mouth. The joy of it brought tears to her eyes.

"Oh. Oh, I can see who I am. I'm beautiful. See, my eyes are blue. Such a pretty blue."

"Let me—" Lora squeezed close, her eyes widening as she saw herself in the little glass with Lilith. "Oh! *C'est magnifique! Je suis belle.*"

"Look at us, Lora. Oh, oh, see how wonderful we are!"

"So much better than a photograph or a drawing. See, we move! Look how our cheeks press together."

"I am here," Lilith murmured. "So long ago, before I was given the gift, I saw my face in polished glass, in the clear water of a lake. The shape of it, and how my hair tumbled down to frame that shape."

She touched her hair now, watching her fingers move through it. "The way my lips, my cheeks would move with a smile, the way my eyebrows will lift and fall. And last, the last time I saw this face, it was in the eyes of the one who sired me. Two thousand years have passed since I've looked into my own eyes." A tear trickled down her cheek, and its reflection enchanted her. "I'm here," she said quietly, a voice thick with emotion. "I'm here."

"You're pleased, Your Majesty?" Midir lowered his folded hands to his waist. "I thought it your fondest wish."

"I have never had such a gift. Look! How my mouth moves when I speak. I want a great one, Midir, a big one so I can see the whole of me at once."

"I believe it can be done, but it would take time and power. The portal . . ."

"Of course, of course." Lilith angled the mirror from overhead to try to see more of herself. "I'm as greedy as Davey, demanding more even as I hold a treasure in my hands. Midir, you've pleased me beyond measure. I'll have what you need brought to you."

When he bowed she walked to him, touched his cheek. "Beyond measure," she repeated. "I won't forget that you troubled to touch my heart."

Larkin scurried out after them. Since they spoke of nothing now but the mirror and their own beauty, he veered off to look for their arsenal, to get a clearer idea of their numbers.

He streaked down darkened tunnels, squeezed under doors. In one chamber he found three vampires feasting on a man. When the man moaned, Larkin's shock made him careless. One of them spotted him, and lifted its bloody face in a smile.

"Wouldn't mind a little rat for dessert."

As he pounced, Larkin shot under the doorway again, and across to the next, streaking between the feet of the guard and under.

Into the arsenal.

Weapons for a thousand, he realized. For a thousand and more. Sword and lance, bow and ax, all stored with a military precision that told him this was indeed an army, and not just a pack of animals.

And this they would take to Geall to destroy it.

Well, he'd give them some trouble first.

Turning into a man, he took the single torch from the wall to set the tables, the chests, the cabinets to light.

Distraction and destruction, he thought, tossing the torch aside before turning back into the rat again.

As fast as he could, he went back to the area where the prisoners were kept. He saw the man the boy had chosen was no longer in his cage. So he was too late to save him or the woman. But there were others, more than twenty others, and he would give them a chance at least.

There was only one guard now, leaning up against the wall and despite the moans and pleas, he seemed to be half dozing.

It would take speed and it would take luck, Larkin thought. He was counting on having both. He changed into a man, grabbed the sword at the vampire's side, swung it hard.

As the dust exploded, the screams from the cages were deafening.

"You have to run." He grabbed the keys from the hook

on the wall and began to unlock cages. He shoved the sword into the hands of a man who looked at it blankly.

"You can hurt them with that," Larkin said quickly. "Kill them if you cut off the head. Kill them with fire. There are torches in the tunnels. Use them. Here." He shoved the keys into another pair of hands. "Unlock the rest. Then run. Some of you may get out. I'm going to do what I can to keep the way clear."

Though he knew he risked draining his energy, he changed once more as the chaos whirled around him. Into a wolf that sprang out of the doorway.

He veered left, hoping to buy time and charged the first vampire he saw. He took it by surprise, ripped out its throat. Muzzle dripping, he ran.

He'd hoped the fire he'd set in the arsenal would keep many of them busy. But he heard no alarm as yet.

He saw two carrying bodies to a stack of more dead. Tossed, he thought, like offal. As he ran, he changed, and as he changed he reached for a sword.

He took them both with one blow.

There was shouting now, not the human screaming, but sounds of alarm and fury. Once more he changed into the wolf to use its speed. He could do no more than he had done.

He swung down a tunnel, and he saw the boy.

He was crouched on the ground, feasting on the man who'd been in the cage. The child's shiny hair was streaked with blood, and it dripped from his fingers, from his lips.

The low growl that rumbled out of Larkin's throat had the boy looking up. "Doggie!" Davey grinned, horribly. "None for you until I'm finished. I'm done with that one, so you can have it if you want."

He gestured toward the woman who lay facedown a few feet away.

"She wasn't as much fun as this one, so I finished quick."

Beyond rage, Larkin bunched to spring.

"Davey, there you are!" The one who'd sparred with Lora clipped quickly down the tunnel. "Your mother wants you in your chambers. Some of the humans are loose, and they've managed to set a fire."

"But I haven't finished yet."

"You'll have to finish later. Are these both your kills?" He crouched down to give Davey a congratulatory pat on the back. "Good for you. But if you eat any more, you'll just get sick. I'll send someone down, have these taken to the heap, but for now, you need to come with me."

He glanced over as he spoke, eyeing Larkin. "One of your mother's wolves? I thought she'd sent them all—"

Larkin saw the change on its face, the sudden bracing of its body. He leaped, but missed the throat as the vampire blocked the charge. The force of the blow hurled Larkin against the wall, but he was up quickly, charging again before the thing could clear its sword.

There was screaming, horrible screaming and his own snarls and snaps. The part of him that was wolf lusted for blood as much as the man inside it lusted for vengeance.

He sank his claws into the thing's shoulder, its chest.

Then there was pain, unspeakable pain as the child leaped on his back and used his fangs.

With a howl, Larkin reared back, managed to shake the boy off. But he was up quickly, and the one on the ground was reaching for its sword.

The wolf was done, and Larkin prayed he had enough left in him to get out, and away.

His light sparked, shimmered weakly. There was more pain, and with it now a dragging weakness. But he became the mouse, small and quick, slipping into shadows and hunting the sound of the sea.

The fire in the back of his neck burned to the bone. The caves echoed with screams, running feet. He was nearly trod on as his strength and his speed wavered, but continued to head toward the thin wash of moonlight, the roar of the sea.

There were people running, clawing their way up the cliff wall. Some carried the weak, the wounded. Larkin knew if he attempted a change again, he'd need to be carried himself.

He could do nothing more. With what he had left, he dragged his small body to a rock, wedged himself behind it.

The last thing he saw was the flicker of stars going out as dawn crept closer.

Chapter 8

"He should have been back by now." From the window in the parlor, Blair watched dawn break through the long night. "On his way back anyway. Maybe you should start again." She turned around to Hoyt and Glenna. "Just start again."

"Blair." Glenna crossed over, ran a hand up and down Blair's arm. "I promise you, as soon as he can be seen, we'll see."

"It was a stupid idea. Reckless and stupid. What was I thinking? I sent him in there."

"No." Now Glenna gripped both of her arms. "He went in, and we all agreed. We're all equal in this. None of us bears all the burden."

"He went in there without a weapon, without a shield." She closed her hand over her crosses.

"He could hardly fly or crawl or slither around a nest of vampires with a cross around his neck," Cian pointed out. "A beacon like that? He wouldn't have lasted five minutes."

"So what? He lasts ten going in naked."

"He's not dead." Moira spoke quietly, and continued to sit on the floor, staring at the fire. "I'd know. I think we'd all know. The circle would be broken." She looked over her shoulder at Hoyt. "Isn't that so?"

"I believe it is, yes. It may be as simple as he needed to rest. Maintaining other shapes must take considerable energy and concentration."

"It does. That's why he eats like a plow horse." Scooting to face the room, Moira managed a weak smile. "And he's never, that I know, held a shape above two or three hours."

Another nightmare, Blair thought. To imagine him skulking around the caves as the rat they'd agreed on, then, whoops, he's a human without so much as a Popsicle stick to defend himself.

Alive, she could hold on to that. It made sense that they'd feel it if he'd been killed. But he could be in a cage, hurt, being tortured.

"I'm going to go make some food." Glenna gave Blair's shoulder a comforting pat.

"I'll do it. I should practice more with the cooking," Moira said as she got to her feet. "And I need something to do besides sit and worry."

"I'll give you a hand." Glenna draped an arm over Moira's shoulders. "I'll bring out some coffee in a few minutes."

"I'm going out." Hoyt pushed himself out of the chair. "It may be I can draw something, sense something, outside the confines of the house."

"I'll go with you."

But he shook his head at Blair. "I'd do better alone."

What was she supposed to *do*? She wasn't used to standing and waiting. She was the one who went out, did the job, risked her skin. She wasn't supposed to stand and wring her hands while someone else was on the line.

"Would you mind closing those other drapes? Light's coming in from that side."

Baffled, she looked back. Cian was sprawled lazily in a

chair—and the slant of light coming in the east windows was barely a foot from the tips of his boots.

She imagined most of his kind would have been scampering back in a fast hurry from that spread of light. Not Cian. She doubted they'd get a scamper out of him if they gave him a boot in front of a sunny window.

"Sure." She moved over, drew them, and plunged the room into gloom. She didn't bother with a lamp. Just then the dark was a comfort.

"What will they do to him? Don't lie, don't soften it. If they have him, what will they do to him?"

You know, Cian thought. You know already. "She'll have him tortured. For the entertainment value and for the practical purpose of getting information."

"He won't tell her—"

"Of course he will." Impatience whipped into Cian's voice. It was infuriating that he was attached enough to Larkin to worry about the boy.

"She can do things to a man no human being can withstand—and keep him just this side of alive while she's at it. He'll tell her anything. So would you, so would any of us. And does it matter?"

"Maybe not." She came over, gave in to her weak legs and sat on the table in front of his chair. He was giving her the truth, naked and without sentiment. It was what she needed. "She'll change him, won't she? That's the big coup, siring one of us."

"That would be two of us."

"Right. Right." She dropped her head in her hands because it felt sick. As sick as her gut, as sick as her belly. "Cian. If . . . we'll have to . . ."

"Yes, we will."

"I don't think I can stand it. I don't think I could go on with this. If he's just dead, I can, because otherwise it would be like we wasted his life. But if she sends him back here changed, and we have to . . ." She lifted her head now, rubbed her hands over her damp cheeks. "How did you get through it? After King? Glenna told me you and King were tight, and you had to end him. How did you get through it?"

"I got piss-faced for a couple of days."

"Did it help?"

"Not particularly. I grieved and I drank, then I let the anger in. It's because of what was done to King, more than any other reason, that I'll see this through to the end." He angled his head, studying her. "You've fallen for him."

"What? It's not— I care about him, of course. All of us. We're a unit."

"Humans are so strange, their reactions to what they feel. The expressions of emotions. For you it seems to be embarrassment. Why is that? You're both young, healthy, and caught in a situation filled with passion and jeopardy. Why shouldn't you form an attachment?"

"It's not that simple."

"Not for you, apparently." He glanced over as Hoyt strode back in, and Blair sprang to her feet.

"There's a van on the lane there. The wheels are all ripped. There are some weapons in it."

Blair didn't bother with a jacket, but went out, jogged down the lane. The driver's door was open, she noted, with the key dangling from the ignition, as if someone had tried to start it, then abandoned it in a hurry.

There were a couple of swords and a cooler holding several packets of blood in the cargo area.

"Well, it's theirs," she said to Hoyt. "No question of that. And the chances of all four tires going flat come in at zero." She hunkered down, stuck her finger in the wide hole in the rubber. "Larkin did this, somehow."

"They must have abandoned it, taken to the woods, I'd think, to hide from the sun."

"Yeah." Her smile showed grim purpose. "At last I have something to do. I'll go get armed."

"I'll go with you."

She went into the forest with crossbow and stake, seeking out the shadows, moving like one. At the fork of a path, she and Hoyt separated, each moving deeper into light that was dappled and dim.

She found one cowering, curled on mossy ground in deep shade. A boy, she noted, no more than eighteen when he died. From his clothes—holey jeans and a faded sweatshirt, she imagined he'd probably been a student doing the backpacking thing.

"Sorry about this," she told him.

He hissed at her, crawled over to hide behind the trunk of a tree.

"Oh come on, like I can't still see you? Don't make me come up there."

She didn't hear the one coming behind her, but sensed it. Blair did a half pivot, lowered her right shoulder, so when it leaped at her back, she flipped it over.

This one was about the same age, a girl, and looked a lot more frisky.

"You two a couple? That's cute, and really bad luck."

The female charged, and Blair lowered the crossbow. She didn't just want a kill, she realized, she wanted a fight.

She dodged the kick, taking the brunt of it on the side of the hip, and the second in the small of the back. There was enough force to pitch her forward. She landed on her hands, sprang over, and planted the heel of her boot in the vampire's face.

"Kickboxing classes, huh?" She saw something in the eyes when it came back at her, when they traded blows. It hadn't fed, she realized, remembering the cooler in the van. It was desperate.

And prolonging the kill was only torturing it. This time when it charged, Blair pulled her stake and put it through the heart.

"Bitch. Stupid bitch." The one behind the tree shouted it out, and the heavy dose of New Jersey in the voice nearly amused her.

"Which one of us?"

When he leaped up, she rolled to her toes. But he began

to run away. "Oh, for God's sake." She snatched up the crossbow, and put an arrow in him. "Coward."

She whirled at the sound behind her, then relaxed when she saw Hoyt coming along the path. "Only one," he told her.

"Two here. There may be more, but they'll have gone deeper. We should get back, see if there's any word on Larkin."

"I couldn't sense anything, but neither could I sense his death. He's a clever man, Blair, resourceful, as you can see by what he did with the wheels on the van."

"Yeah. He's nobody's jackass, even if he can change into one."

"I know what it is to care about someone, and to worry for their life." As they walked, Hoyt's eyes tracked through the trees, alert and watchful. "We can defend each other in this, but we can't protect each other. Glenna taught me the difference."

"I never had to worry about anyone before. I don't think I'm very good at it."

"I can tell you that the skill of it comes entirely too easily."

When they stepped out of the woods Moira was running out of the house as if it had burst into flame. The light of absolute joy on her face had all the fear inside Blair dropping away.

"He's coming back!" she shouted. "Larkin, he's coming home."

"There now." Hoyt put an arm around Blair's shoulders as relief shook them. "So you needn't use that worry skill any more today."

It took everything he had to stay the hawk, to stay in the air. Pain and fatigue warred inside him, each threatening to break through and shatter the strength he had left. He'd lost blood, he knew that, but how much he couldn't say. He only knew the bite at the back of his neck was a constant searing fire.

There had been no one—human or vampire—in sight when he'd come to, after dawn, in his own shape. There'd been blood on the shale, not all his own. Not enough, he comforted himself, not enough of it to mean all he'd freed had been slaughtered.

Surely some had made it. Even one . . .

He felt himself falter, felt his wing try to tremble itself into an arm. He bore down, calling the hawk to hold him.

There the river, he thought. There the Shannon. He was well toward home now.

He brought Blair's face into his mind, that two-pointed smile, the strong blue of her eyes, the quick music of her voice. He would make it, he would make these last miles.

He could feel his heart—the hawk's—racing, too fast. Even breathing was a vicious strain, and his vision was no longer sharp. There was something else inside him, something the demon in a child's form had put in him. Inside him, pumping into his own blood, poisoning it.

A weakness, the dark of it, whispered slyly that he should just let go.

Then he heard something else, stronger.

You're almost home, bird-boy. Keep going, you're almost back. We're waiting for you. Going to make you the breakfast of champions—all-you-can-eat buffet. Come on, Larkin, come home.

Blair. He held on to the sound of her voice, and flew.

There were the woods, and the pretty stream, and the stone house and stables. And beyond them, the graveyard where he was damn well determined not to end up now that he was so close.

There! There was Blair, outside the house with her face tipped up to the sky so he could see it. Her eyes. And there was Moira, his sweetheart, and the others save Cian. He gave one heartfelt prayer of thanks to all the gods.

Then his strength simply dissolved. He fell the last ten feet to the ground as a man.

"Oh God, oh God!" Blair sprinted to him, reaching him

a full stride before the others. "Wait, be careful. We have to see if he broke anything."

She began to run her hands over him even as Glenna did the same. Then she felt the raw skin at the back of his neck, and slowly brushed his hair aside.

She stared up into Moira's brimming eyes. "He's been bitten."

"Oh God, sweet God. But he's not changed." Moira lifted one of his limp hands to her lips. "He couldn't be out in the sun if he'd been changed."

"No, not changed. And not broken. Banged up pretty good. His pulse is really thready, Glenna."

"Let's get him inside."

"He needs food." Moira hurried ahead as Hoyt and Blair lifted Larkin. "It would be like one of us going without food for days. Food and liquids. I'll get something."

"The sofa in the parlor," Glenna ordered. "I'll go get what I need."

Once they'd laid him on the sofa, Blair crouched by his head. He was white as death, and bruises were already gathering. "It's okay, you're home now. That's what counts. You're home."

"Cian—Cian said to start with this." Moira rushed in with a large glass of orange juice. "To get the fluids and the sugar into him."

"Yeah, good. Gotta bring him around. Come on, fly-boy."

"Here, let me try this." Glenna knelt at the side of the sofa. She dipped her thumb into a jar of balm, smeared it first on the center of his forehead. "On the chakras," she explained as she worked. "A little chi balancing. Moira, take his other hand, push some of your strength out. You know how. Blair, talk to him again, the way I told you to when he was flying. It'll reach him. Hoyt?"

"Yes." Hoyt laid his hands on either side of Blair's head. "Tell him to come back."

"Come on, Larkin, you've got to wake up. Can't just lie

around all day. Besides, breakfast is ready. Please wake up now. I've been waiting for you." She pressed his hand to her cheek. "Watching for you. His fingers moved! All the way out, Larkin, that's enough damn drama for the day."

His eyelids fluttered. "Why are women always nagging a man?"

"Guess that's just what it takes," she managed.

"Here we are now, here." Moira moved around the couch to lift his head, to hold the glass to it.

He drank like a camel, then managed to smile at her. "There's my sweetheart. Look at this, what a picture. Three beautiful faces. I'd give you all my worldly goods and a lifetime of devotion if you'd get me something to eat."

It was Cian who stepped in, holding a small plate with two pieces of dry toast. "You'll need to start slow." He exchanged a look with Blair. She met it, then squeezed her eyes shut. Nodded.

"Don't bolt it down," she warned.

"Just bread. Can't I have meat? I swear I could eat a whole side of venison. Or that lovely dish you make, Glenna, with the balls of meat and the noodles."

"I'll make it tonight."

"You need to have just enough to take the edge off," Blair began, "to get a little strength back. You eat a full meal, you'll just boot it—vomit," she explained, "when we're taking care of the bite."

"It was the little one, her boy. Little bastard. I was a wolf at the time, so it didn't go as deep as it might have."

"Glenna has balm. She used it on me when I was bitten." Moira stroked Larkin's hair. "It's a terrible burn, I know, but the balm cools it."

"You weren't bitten," Cian said flatly. "A scrape, not a puncture."

"What difference does it make?"

"Quite a bit." Blair straightened. "There's infection, and there's also considerable risk of the one who bit you having some control over you."

"Aye." Larkin frowned, closed his eyes. "I felt something working in me. But—"

"We'll take care of it. It needs to be purified with holy water."

"That's fine. Then if I could have the lovely balm Moira spoke of, and a meal, I'd be good as new—but for the fact every bone of my body feels as if it's been hit with a hammer."

Straight truth, Blair thought. Straight, hard truth. "Do you know the burn you felt when it sank into you? The burn you're feeling now?"

"I do."

"This will be a lot worse. I'm sorry." She walked out, hurried up the steps. And Moira rushed out behind her.

"There must be another way. How can we hurt him again? He's still so weak, and already in pain. I can see the pain in his eyes."

"You think I can't?" She swung into her room. "There is no other way."

"I know it says there isn't in the books. I've read them. But with Glenna and Hoyt—"

Blair pulled a bottle of holy water from her kit, and her face was set when she whirled around. "There *is* no other way. He's infected. That puts him and all of us at risk." She shot out her arm, turned up her wrist to show the scar. "I know what it's like. If there was another way, don't you think I'd try it?"

Moira shuddered out a breath. "What can I do?"

"You can help hold him down."

She took down towels, bandages. She made herself walk to Larkin, look straight into his eyes. "This is going to hurt."

"It's going to hurt," Cian added, "like a motherfucker."

"Oh well." Larkin licked his lips. "That's heartening."

"I might be able to block some of the pain," Glenna began.

"I don't think you can, or should." Blair shook her head.

"It's part of it. It's the way it's done. Here, we need to get him on the floor, facedown. Get those towels under him. Cian, you'd better take his feet. Wouldn't want any to splash on you."

Larkin winced as they shifted him. "What would he need to take my feet for?"

"We're going to hold you down," Blair told Larkin.

"I don't need—"

"Yes, you will."

He met her eyes again, saw what was in them. "You do it then. I trust you to see it through."

With Cian at his feet, Hoyt on one side and both women on the other, Blair opened the bottle. She brushed his hair clear, exposed the raw bite.

"Under these circumstances, it's not considered unmanly to scream. Brace yourself," she warned him, and poured the blessed water on the wound.

He did scream. And his body arched up, bucked. The wound itself seemed to boil, and she let the viscous liquid that bubbled out run as she continued, ruthlessly, to douse it with water.

She flashed back to the night she'd had to go to her aunt, less than a week after her father had left her. And how her aunt's tears had run down her face as she poured the water over the bite on Blair's wrist.

How it had felt as if the flesh, the bones were being seared with a burning knife.

When the wound ran clear and he was gasping for breath, she used towels to wipe it clean, to dry it. "The balm would probably help now."

White as a sheet, Glenna fumbled for the jar. Now her tears fell on him. "I'm sorry, Larkin. I'm so sorry. Can I help him sleep now? Even for an hour?"

Blair swiped the back of her hand over her mouth. "Sure, it's done. He could use a little sleep."

Again, she rushed upstairs. She dashed into her room, slamming the door behind her. Then she dropped down on the floor at the foot of her bed, wrapped her arms around her head and sobbed.

She cringed away when an arm came around her, but it only wrapped tighter. "You were so brave," Moira crooned, like a mother lulling a child. "So strong and so brave. I try to be, and it's so very hard. I want to believe I could have done what you did, for I love him so much."

"I'm sick, I feel sick."

"I know, so do I. Can we hold on to each other for a bit, do you think?"

"I can't feel like this. It doesn't help."

"I think it does. To care, even to hurt. Cian fixed him juice and toasted bread. I couldn't have imagined it. But he cares. It's impossible not to care for Larkin. And if you love him—"

Blair lifted her head, brushed at tears. "I don't want to go there again."

"Well, if you were to love him, you'd have a happy and unusual life. Would you show me how to make the French toast? He'd be pleased to have it when he wakes up."

"Yeah. Yeah, sure. I'll just go splash some water on my face, and be right down." They got up. "Moira? I can't be good for him. I'm not good for anyone."

Moira paused at the door. "That would be up to him, wouldn't it, as much as you?"

He was still pale when he woke, but his eyes were clear. He insisted on eating at the table, within easy reach, he said, of food.

He plowed through French toast, eggs, and bacon with a slow and studied pace. As he ate, he told them what he'd done and seen and heard.

"So many changes, Larkin. You know you shouldn't—"

"Now, don't scold me, Moira. It's all come out all right, hasn't it? Could I have more of the Coke?" He sent a sweet, charming smile with the request.

"It wasn't a rescue mission." Since she was closer, Blair yanked open the refrigerator, grabbed another bottle of Coke. "We specifically talked about that."

"You'd have done the same. Oh, don't shake your head and glower at me." He snagged the bottle. "I had to try, and any of us would have done the same. You didn't see, you didn't hear. It couldn't be walked away from, not without some attempt to help. And the truth of it is, I've been wanting to light a blaze in there for some time."

He looked at Cian now. "Since King."

"He'd have appreciated the gesture."

"It nearly killed you," Blair pointed out.

"War's meant to kill, isn't it? I should have left the boy be—what looked like a boy. But what it was doing . . . I lost the sense of it then, no denying that, and only wanted to end him. That was useless and stupid." He reached around to touch his fingers to the bandage at the back of his neck. "And I won't forget what it cost me."

Then he shrugged, scooped up more eggs. "So . . . She wasn't happy with this wizard, this Midir."

"I know the name," Hoyt put in. "He was infamous—before my time," he added. "Black magicks, raising demons to do his bidding."

Larkin guzzled Coke from the bottle. "He's doing her bidding now."

"It was said he was devoured by his own power. In a way, I suppose he was."

"I think she intended to punish him, or to let the other one—Lora—have a go at him. But when he gave her the mirror, the magic one—she went all soft and dazzled. She and the other one, mesmerized they were by their own faces."

"There's considerable vanity there," Cian told him. "It would be a great thrill to see their reflections after so long."

"It wasn't what I was expecting, their—well, human re-action, or so it seemed. And the, ah, affection between the women seemed genuine."

"He's being delicate," Cian said. "Lilith and Lora are lovers. They both take others, of course, often at the same time, but they're mates, and sincerely devoted to each other. The relationship isn't without its dysfunction, but has held for four hundred years."

"How do you know?" Blair asked him.

"Lora and I had—what should we call it? A fling? This would have been, hmm, in the early 1800s, in Prague, if memory serves. She and Lilith were having one of their spats. Lora and I enjoyed ourselves for a few nights. Then she tried to kill me, and I threw her out the window."

"Tough breakup," Blair murmured.

"Ah, well, she's Lilith's creature, whoever else she might play with from time to time. I knew it before she tried to stake me. As for the boy, I don't know about him. A more recent addition to her cadre, I'd say."

"Family," Larkin corrected. "I know there's something deviant between them, but in some way, she thinks of him as a son, and he of her as his mother."

"That makes them weaknesses." Hoyt nodded. "The boy and the French woman."

"Davey. It's what she called him," Larkin added.

Hoyt nodded. A name was always useful. "If we could capture or destroy either of them, it would be a blow to her."

"She's not leaving for Geall as soon as we are," Blair mused. "Maybe we can set up some traps. We can't know where they'll come out on the other side, not exactly, but we may be able to do something. Anyway, we've got a few days to think about it."

"And we will. Now we're all tired. We all need some sleep." Glenna laid her hands on Larkin's shoulders. "You need to get your strength back, handsome."

"I'm feeling more myself. Thank you. But it's the pure truth I could use a bed." He got to his feet. "There, it seems my legs will hold me now. Would you come up with me, Blair? I'd like to have a word."

"Yeah, all right." She went up the back way with him.

She wanted to keep her hands in her pockets, but he seemed a little unsteady on the stairs. So she took his arm, pulled it around her shoulder. "Here, lean on me."

"I wouldn't mind. I wanted to thank you for taking care of me."

"Don't." It made her stomach clench. "Don't thank me for that."

"You tended to me, and I will thank you. I heard your voice. When I was flying home, and I wasn't sure I could make it, I heard your voice. And I knew I could."

"I thought she had you. I imagined you in a cage, and that was worse than thinking you might be dead. I don't want to be that scared, I don't want to feel that helpless."

"I don't know how to keep that from happening." He was out of breath when they reached his room, grateful for the help to his bed. "Would you lie with me?"

She managed to get him down, then gaped at him. "What?"

"Oh, not that way." With a laugh, he took her hand. "I don't think I've got that in me just yet, but it's a lovely thought for another time. Wouldn't you lie here with me, *a stór*, sleep with me for a while?"

After the pain she'd given him, she'd assumed she'd be the last person he'd want to be with. But here he was, holding out a hand for hers.

"Just sleep." She laid down beside him, turned in so she could see his face. "No fooling around."

"Is having my arm around you fooling around?"

"No."

"And one kiss?"

"One." She touched her lips to his. "Close your eyes."

He did, on a sigh. "It's good to be home again."

"Are you in any pain?"

"Not really. A bit sore is all."

"You're lucky."

He opened his eyes again. "Couldn't you say I was skilled and courageous?"

"Maybe that, too. And I can add smart. Unicorn horn versus Goodyear. I really like that one."

She laid her hand on his heart, closed her eyes. And slept.

Chapter 9

It was the stiffness in his own bones that woke him. Larkin lay there a few minutes wondering if this was how he'd feel every blessed morning when he was an old man. Sort of whifty in the head and heavy in the body. Maybe it was such a gradual thing that the mind adjusted so you forgot what it was to feel young and spry.

He swore he creaked when he rolled over.

Of course she was gone. He probably couldn't have managed to make love with her if she'd stayed—if he'd been able to talk her into it. She was a puzzler, Blair was. So strong, all but steely, and a goddess in battle. But there were all these layers inside, soft ones, bruised ones.

A man just wanted to peel off that hard edge and get to the heart of the matter.

And she was so interesting to look at. The hair like a soft cap, so dark against her white skin. Those deep eyes of magic blue that looked right at you. No coyness at all. Sometimes he just liked to watch her mouth move whatever words were coming out of it, to see all the shapes it could make.

Then there was her form, all lean and tight. Sleek, really. He couldn't say he minded overmuch her trouncing him in hand-to-hand, not when he had that body bumping up against his. Long legs and arms, those strong shoulders that were often bare during training. Those lovely firm breasts.

He'd thought quite a bit about her breasts.

And now he was stirring himself up with no place to go with it.

He got up, wincing. He supposed, all things considered, he was lucky to have gotten off just sore and bruised. He had Glenna to thank for that, and maybe he'd seek her out, see if she could do a bit more now that he was rested.

He took a shower, giving into the luxury of running the water hot as he could stand. He would miss this, that was the sheer truth. He wondered if Moira, who was clever with figuring how things worked, could build one in Geall.

Once he was dressed, he wandered out. The house was quiet enough he wondered if the others were still sleeping, and considered going down to the kitchen. He was hungry again, and no surprise there.

But he doubted he'd find Blair in the kitchen. He thought he knew well enough where she'd be.

He heard her music before he reached the training room. It wasn't the same music as she'd been playing in the kitchen the other day. There was a woman singing now, in a rough, fascinating voice about wanting a little respect when she came home.

Well, it didn't seem too much to be asking, in Larkin's opinion.

And there was Blair, stripped down to the little white shirt and the black pants that sat low on her hips—a personal favorite of his, truth be known.

She was tumbling, he noted. And using most of the big room to do it. Handsprings, kicks and flips. At one point, she rolled to a sword that lay on the floor and began to fight what must have been a multitude of invisible opponents.

He waited until she gave a last thrust, her body posed in a deep warrior position.

"Well, you slaughtered the lot of them."

Only her head moved first, turning until her eyes met his. Then she brought her feet together, lowered the sword. "Nothing but dust."

She walked over to set down the sword, turned the music down, then picked up a bottle of water. Drinking, she took a good long look at him. His face was bruised, scraped along the temple—which for some reason didn't make him less of a looker, she decided.

In any case, his color was good.

"How're you doing?"

"Well enough, though I'd've been better if you'd been beside me when I woke."

"Didn't know how long you'd need to sleep. How's the bite?"

"Barely know it's there." He moved to her, took her hand, turned up her wrist. "We'll both have our scars now."

"Your hair's wet."

"I got in the shower. My bones were aching, and I think I smelled fairly ripe after my night of it."

"You'll have soaked the bandage." She frowned as she nudged him around. "Let me have a look."

"Itches mostly," he said, enjoying having her fingers in his hair, on his skin.

"It's healing fast. Glenna's magic balm. Boy, I wish I'd had some of that after my round. Guess you'll do."

"Will I?" He turned, gripped her waist, then boosted her up so she sat on the table.

"Careful there, Bunky, you're not off the disabled list."

"I don't know what you're talking about. Doesn't matter so much. I was thinking before how I like watching your mouth move." He rubbed his thumb over her bottom lip. "It's got such energy."

"Didn't you wake up all frisky? I think you'd better—"

It was as far as she got before her mouth was very busy.

He didn't just taste this time but feasted. Didn't just sample, but possessed. This was more hunger, more demand than she'd been prepared for, the sort that swamped mind and body and left her floundering with need.

She hadn't put her defenses up, not in time. Now it was too late to do anything but meet the assault.

She'd yielded, just a little, just enough, then the heat flooded back into her. He could feel it, pouring out and up, and through him, a glorious scorching. He ran his hands over her, touching, finally touching, up the lean torso, over firm breasts, along strong shoulders and back again.

He felt her shudder of response, heard the moan of it catch in her throat, and knew she'd belong to him.

But she pressed her hands to his chest. "Wait. Wait. Let's step back a minute."

Her voice was thick and breathy, and made him want to lap her up like cream. "Why?"

"I don't know, but I'll think of a reason in a minute, as soon as my IQ goes back up above the level of a turnip."

"I don't know what your eye queue might be, but the rest of you is perfect."

She managed a laugh but kept her hands firm so his mouth wouldn't take hers again and fry her brain a second time. "I'm not. Not nearly perfect. And it's not that I don't think diving into this would feel really good. *Really* good. More than likely we're going to end up doing just that eventually. But it's complicated, Larkin."

"Things are as simple or as complicated as you make them."

"No. Sometimes things just are. You don't even know me."

"Blair Murphy, demon hunter. That's what you'd think of first—that's what you've been taught to think of first. But it's not nearly the whole of you. Strong, for certain, and full of courage."

She started to interrupt, but he laid a finger on her lips. "But there's more in you than valor and duty. You've soft places in your heart. I saw them when Glenna and Hoyt handfasted. You fussed with the flowers and the candles because you wanted them to have their moment. You knew they loved, and that it's important. There was sweetness in that."

"Larkin—"

"And you've been hurt. The bruises are all inside, all wrapped up where no one should see them. Hurting makes you think you're alone, that you need to be. But you're not. I know you've fought your whole life against something horrible, and you've never turned away from it. And even so, you can smile, and laugh, and get dewy-eyed when two people in love make promises to each other. I don't know your favorite color or what book you last read when you had a moment of leisure, but I know you."

"I don't know what to do about you," she said when she could speak again. "I really don't. That's not the way it's supposed to be for me. I'm always supposed to know."

"And no surprises? I'm happy to change that for you. Well, since I don't think I'm going to be getting the clothes off you right at the moment, why don't we have a walk."

"Ah . . . Hoyt and I did a sweep through the woods this morning. Took out three."

"I didn't say a hunt. A walk. Just a walk. There's plenty of light left in the day."

"Oh. Ah—"

"You'll need a shirt, or a jacket. We'll go down through the kitchen, grab one for you. That way we can get ourselves a box of biscuits."

Just how strange was it, she wondered, to go walking over fields with a man in the late-afternoon sun? With no real purpose but to walk—no mission, no scouting, no hunt. Armed with sword and stake, and sugar cookies.

"Did you know, Hoyt will be staying here with Glenna after this is all done?"

She bit into a cookie, frowned at him. "Here, in Ireland? How do you know?"

"We talk of things, Hoyt and I, when we tend the horse. Here in Ireland, yes. In this place. Cian made them a gift of the house and land."

"Cian gave them the house?" She ate more cookie. "I can't figure him either. I know some vampires—or I've heard—go off the juice. Human juice. There are rumors, legends mostly, of some living among us, passing for human, going off the kill. I never really believed any of it."

"Passing as human doesn't make them so. And yet, Cian's one I'd trust more than most men. I wonder if living so long a life has something to do with it."

"Tell that to Lilith. She's got twice his years."

"Demons would have choices, wouldn't they? Go this way or that. I don't know the answers there. And when this is done, you'll go back to your Chicago?"

"I don't know." There was an itch between her shoulder blades at the thought of it. "Somewhere else, I think. Maybe New York for a while."

"Where Glenna lived. She showed me pictures of it. It's a marvel. Maybe you'll stay in Geall for a while. Like a holiday."

"Holiday in Geall." She shook her head. "Talk about marvels. Maybe. A few days anyway." It wasn't like she had anyone waiting for her to get back.

They walked to the cemetery, and the ruined chapel. Flowers still bloomed here, and the breeze whispered in the high grass.

"These are my people. It's so weird to know that. If it had been traced back this far, no one ever told me."

"Does it make you sad?"

"I don't know. A little I guess. Hoyt brought me here to show me where I came from. That's Nola's grave." She gestured to a stone where the flowers she'd laid days before were faded and dying. "She was the beginning of the family legacy. The start of it. One of her children would have been the first hunter. I don't know which one, and guess I'll never know. But at least one of them."

"Would you change it, if you could?"

"No." She looked over at him when he draped his arm over her shoulder. "Would you give up what you can do?"

"Not for all the gold in the Green Mountains. Especially now. Because it makes a difference now. When you have your holiday in Geall," he said as they walked on, "I'll take you to the Faerie Falls. We'll have a picnic."

"And back to food." She dug out a cookie, stuffed it in his mouth.

"We'll swim in the pool—the water's clear as blue crystal, and warm as well. After I'll make love to you on the soft grass while the water tumbles down beside us."

"And on to sex."

"Food and sex. What could be more pleasant to think about?"

She had to admit, he had a point. And couldn't deny that the simplicity of an afternoon walk had been an unexpected gift, more precious than she would have imagined.

"It's blue," she said. "My favorite color's blue."

He shot her a grin, took her hand so they walked linked over the hill, and down. "Look there. That's a pretty sight."

She saw Glenna and Hoyt in the herb garden, caught in an embrace. The garden thrived around them; the sun showered down. Glenna held a basket of herbs she'd harvested, and her free hand lay on Hoyt's cheek.

"Hear the mockingbird call?" Larkin asked, and she did, the happy little trill of it.

There was a quiet intimacy to the moment, something that couldn't be captured and preserved yet was enduring and universal. A miracle to find this, she thought, this normality, this heart against heart in all the horror.

She realized until she'd come here, she hadn't believed in miracles.

"This is why we'll win," Larkin said quietly.

"What?"

"This is why they can't beat us. We're stronger than they are."

"Not to spoil the moment, but physically they've got it all over the average human."

"Physically. But it's not all about brute strength, is it? It never is. They look to destroy, and we to survive. Survival's always stronger. And we have this." He nodded toward Hoyt and Glenna. "Love and kindness, compassion. Hope. Why else would two people make promises to each other at such a time, and mean to keep them? We won't give all this up, you see. We won't have it taken from us. We'll band together for this, and we'll never stop."

He heard Glenna laugh, and the sound of it reached into him, into that hope as she and Hoyt walked toward the house.

"You're thinking neither will they. Neither will they stop, but that doesn't change it, Blair. In the caves, I saw them in the cages. Some were beaten down, too tired, too frightened to do more than wait to die. But others rattled those cages and they cursed those bastards. And when I let them out, I saw more than fear, even more than hope in some of the faces. I saw bloody vengeance."

When he turned to look at her, Blair saw all of that in his face.

"I saw the stronger helping the weaker," he continued, "because that's what humans do. Terrible times do one of two things to us, they bring out the worst or the best."

"You're counting on the best."

"We've already started on that, haven't we? We're six of us."

She let that play through her mind as they walked on. "The way I was trained," she began, "was to depend on one thing. Yourself. No one else. You're in the battle alone, beginning to end—and it never ends."

"So you're always alone? What would be the point, then?"

"Winning. Coming out of the battle alive, and your enemy dead. Black and white. No grandstanding, no mistakes, no distractions."

"Who could live that way?"

"My father could. Did. Does. After he . . . after I was on my own, I spent some time with my aunt. She had a different philosophy. Sure it's about winning, because if you don't win you're dead. But it's also about living. Family, friends. Going to the movies, sitting on the beach."

"Walking in the sun."

"Yeah. It works for her, for her family."

"You're her family."

"And she always made me feel that way. But it's not the way I was trained. Maybe that's why it's never worked as well for me. I . . . there was someone once, and I loved him. We made some promises to each other, but we couldn't keep them. He couldn't be with me. I couldn't make it work, because what I am didn't just shock and frighten him. It disgusted him."

"Then he wasn't the man for you, or, in my thinking, any kind of a man at all."

"He was just normal, Larkin. A normal, average guy, and I thought I wanted—thought I could have that. Normal, average."

She was made for better, he thought. She was made for more.

"You could say Jeremy—that was his name—taught me I couldn't have that. It's not that I don't have a life outside of what my father calls 'the mission.' I have some civilian friends. I like to shop, eat pizza, watch TV. But it's always in there, the knowing what comes out after sundown. You can't shake it. We're not like other people."

She looked up. "Sun's getting low. Better go in, set up for a training session." She gave him a quiet look. "Playtime's over."

It wasn't a hardship, Larkin thought, to sit and have a beautiful woman tend to you—especially when the woman smelled lovely and had hands like an angel.

"How's this?" Glenna gently kneaded his shoulder, down the arm and back again.

"It's good. It's fine. You can stop anytime in the next hour or two."

She chuckled, but worked her way across his back to his other shoulder. "You took some hard knocks, pal. But you're coming right along. It wouldn't hurt for you to skip training tonight."

"I think it's best I keep up with it. Time's short enough."

"A few days, and we leave." She looked over his head, out the window as she continued to work his back and shoulders. "Strange how quickly this has become home. I still miss New York, but it's not home anymore."

"But you'll go back from time to time."

"Oh yeah, I'll need my fix. You can take the girl out of the city, but . . ." She walked around him, played her fingers over the bruising on the side of his ribs. And made him jolt.

"Sorry. I'm a bit ticklish."

"Suck it in and think of Geall. I'll be quick."

It was torture really, fearing at any minute he might giggle like a girl. "You'll like Geall. At the castle, there are fine gardens, and herbs—oh Jesus, you're killing me. And the river, where it runs behind the castle is nearly wide as a lake. The fish all but jump out into your hands, and . . . Thank God, is that all of it?"

"You'll do. Put your shirt on."

He rolled his shoulders first, circled his head on his neck. "It's better. Thanks for that, Glenna."

"All in a day's work." She walked to the sink to wash balm from her hands. "Larkin, Hoyt and Cian have been talking."

"That's good, seeing as they're brothers." He got up, pulled on his shirt. "But you're not meaning light family conversations."

"No. Logistics, strategies. Hoyt's good with logistics— he doesn't miss details, but Cian's better with strategy, I suppose. Anyway." She turned, drying her hands on a towel. "I asked that they not discuss all this over dinner, so we could just have a meal. A normal . . . well, as normal as you can have with weapons everywhere."

"And a fine meal it was. I saw you and Hoyt earlier, kissing in the herb garden."

"Oh."

"And that was normal. The walk I took with Blair, or Moira cuddled up with a book somewhere. We need all that, so you shouldn't worry I'm offended that I haven't been part of a discussion on logistics and strategy."

"You make it easy. Thanks. The thing is, we're working out not only how to get weapons and the supplies we'll need from here to the Dance, but from here to Geall, and from the Dance in Geall to wherever we're going once we're there."

"The castle would be the place for it."

"The castle." Glenna gave a quiet laugh. "Off to the castle. The transportation might be a bit tricky, and we'd need you and Moira to help with that. Meanwhile, only you and Moira know your way around once we're there. How are you at drawing maps?"

"This would be the whole of Geall." In the library, Larkin drew it out. "This being the shape of it as I've seen on the maps at home. A sort of ragged fan, with these dips being inlets and bays and harbors. And here would be the Dance."

"In the west," Hoyt murmured, "as it is here."

"Aye, and a bit inland. Though if it's a clear day you can see the coast, and out to sea. There's a forest, as there is here, but it spreads just a bit more to the north. The Dance is on a rise, and the Well of the Gods here. And here, ah, about here, would be the castle."

He marked it, drawing a kind of rook and flag. "It's a good hour's ride, if you're going easy, along this road.

There'd be forks here, and again here. To this way, you'd go into the village—Geall City. And this way down to Dragon's Lair, and onto Knockarague. My mother's people came from there, and there are plenty who would come to fight."

"And the battleground?" Hoyt asked him.

"Here, near the center of Geall. These, the mountains, in a kind of half ring running north, curving east, and down to the south. The valley is here. It's wide, and it's rough land, pocked with caves, layered with rock. It's called *Ciunas*. Silence, as a man could wander there, lost, for hours. And no one would hear. In all of Geall, to my knowing, it's the only place nothing lives but the grass and the rocks."

"No point in having an apocalypse in a meadow," Cian commented. "Five days' march, isn't that what Moira said?"

"Hard march, yes."

"Tricky for me, even if I managed to get that far."

"There are places along the way. Shelters, cabins, caves, cottages. We'll see you don't go up like a torch."

"You're a comfort to me, Larkin."

"A man does what he can. There are settlements closer to the valley," he continued, sketching them in. "Men can be called on there as well. But I think there needs to be some fortification done. The enemy would find those locations handy for their own shelter and preparations."

"Boy's got a brain," Cian commented. "She'd attack these." Cian tapped his finger on the map. "Decimate the population, turn those she felt would serve her best, use the rest for food supply. Those would be her first strike."

"Then those will be our first defense." Hoyt nodded.

"You'd be wasting valuable time and effort."

"We can't leave people undefended," Hoyt began.

"Get them out. Leave her without the food source or fresh recruits, at least in that area. I'd say burn the settlement to the ground, but I'd be wasting my time and effort."

"But you'd be right." Blair stepped into the room.

"Leave her with no shelter, no supplies, nothing but ash. It's the cleanest, quickest and most efficient method."

"You're talking of people's homes." Larkin shook his head at her. "Of people's homes and lives and livelihoods."

"Which they won't have when she's done in any case. But they won't do it," she said to Cian. "And if they did, or tried, people would rebel, and we'd be fighting two fronts. So clear out the population, move the old, the weak, those who can't or won't fight to the castle or other fortifications."

"But you agree with him," Larkin insisted. "On the surface of it. Burn it down, the homes, the farms, the shops."

"Yes, I do."

"There are other ways." Hoyt held up a hand. "Glenna and I haven't been able to do a spell to repel the vampires from around this house because of Cian. But we could try one to protect these areas, to keep them out of the homes there. Their wizard may be able to break through that, but it would take time—and have his focus and energies tied up."

"That could work." But she exchanged a look with Cian, understood he was thinking the same as she. So they wouldn't burn the settlements. Lilith would.

"So, this is Geall." She leaned over the map. "And this is the place. Landlocked, slapped up against the mountains. Lots of caves, lots of hiding places, and desolate for all that. A goat would have a hard time beating a retreat out of there."

"We won't be running," Larkin said tightly.

"I was thinking of them. Without other shelter during the day, they'll use the caves. That gives us the high ground, but gives them ambush advantage. It'll be night, another advantage for them. We'll use fire, big advantage us. But before we get there, I've got some ideas about some surprises along the way. Now we don't know where she's going to come out, but we have to figure the odds are it's within this area."

Blair placed a hand on the map. "Battleground, shelter, castle. She's not going to nip behind a rock during the day—not her style, so she's got it worked that she comes in at night and moves with some speed to shelter. Most likely, she'll send an advance to these settlements, get it all taken care of for her arrival. So we need to know the quickest routes from these points to these."

They worked, debated, discussed. She could tell Larkin had backed off from her, stepped away on some basic level. She told herself it couldn't be helped. Told herself she wouldn't be hurt.

What was between them was illusion anyway. Something framed in fantasy, as transient as innocence. The passion was fine, it helped fill voids—temporarily. She knew very well that passion flickered out and died when things got tough. However cold the comfort, she held it to her. Kept it close when she went to her room alone.

Moira bided her time. All through training she could see there was something wrong between Blair and Larkin. They barely spoke, and if they did it was like strangers. When most of the night was gone, she caught him by the arm before he could leave the training room.

"Come on with me, would you? There's something I want to show you."

"What?"

"In my room. It'll take a minute. We'll be home in a few days," she said before he could object. "I wonder if all this will seem like a dream."

"A nightmare."

"Not all of it." Recognizing his poor mood, she bumped him affectionately with her hip. "You know not all of it. Time's moving so fast now. For a while, it seemed we'd been here forever. Now it's flying, and it's like we only arrived."

"I'll feel better when I get there. When I know where I am, what I'm about."

Oh yes, she thought, something was wrong. She opened the door to her room, and didn't speak again until they were both inside, and the door shut.

"What's gone wrong between you and Blair?"

"I don't know what you'd be talking about. What did you want to show me?"

"Not a thing."

"You said—"

"Well, I lied, didn't I? I've seen the two of you together for a while now, and just today out walking, hand-in-hand—and a look in your eye that I'm not mistaking."

"And what of it?"

"Tonight, the air frosted between you every time one of you opened your mouth to the other. You quarreled?"

"No."

She pursed her lips. "Maybe you need to quarrel."

"Don't be foolish, Moira."

"What's foolish about it? She made you happy. She brought something into you I've never seen, and it seemed to me you were bringing the same to her."

He toyed with some of the pretty stones she'd taken from the stream and put on the bureau. "I think you're wrong. I think I was wrong."

"Why is that?"

"She said today I didn't really know her. I didn't believe her, but now . . . Now I wonder if she didn't have the right of it."

"Maybe she does, maybe she doesn't, but it's no question to me she's done or said something to upset you. Are you just going to leave it to lie there? Why don't you kick it to pieces, or at least kick it back at her?"

"I don't—"

"And don't make excuses to me," she snapped, impatient. "Whatever it is can't be bigger than what we're facing. Anything else is petty now. Anything else, I swear, can be fixed. So, go and fix it."

"Why is it up to me to fix things?"

"You might as well because you'll just be sulking and brooding instead of sleeping until you do. And before you get to the sulking and brooding, I'll be badgering you about it until your head's aching."

"All right, all right. You're a true pain in the arse, Moira."

"I know." She touched his cheek. "It's because I love you. Go on now."

"I'm going, aren't I?"

He used his irritation with Moira to carry him out of the room and down to Blair's. He knocked, but didn't wait for an invitation. He opened the door, saw her sitting at the desk at the little computer thing.

He shut the door firm behind him.

"I'll have a word with you."

Chapter 10

She knew that tone—when I want to have a word with you really meant I want to have a *fight* with you. And that was fine, that was great. She was in the perfect mood for a quick, nasty brawl.

But that didn't mean she'd make it easy for him.

She kept her seat. "Obviously, you've missed the fact I'm busy."

"Obviously, you've missed the fact I don't give a bleeding damn."

"My room," she said coolly, "my choice."

"Toss me out then, why don't you?"

She swiveled toward him, stretched out her legs casually in what she knew was an insulting gesture. "Think I couldn't?"

"I think you'd have considerable trouble with it right at the moment."

"From the look of you, you came looking for trouble. Fine." She crossed her feet at the ankles—just a little *more* insulting body language, she thought. Idly, she picked up a bottle of water to gesture with. "Have your word, then get out."

"From the sound of you, *cara*, you've been expecting trouble."

"I know you've got a problem with me. You made that clear enough. So spit it out, Larkin. We haven't got time, and I haven't got the patience for petty grievances."

"Is it petty to talk so callously of destroying people's homes, their life's work, everything they've built and sweated for?"

"It's a legitimate, and proven, strategy in wartime."

"I'd expect to hear that from Cian. He is what he is, and can't help it. But not from you, Blair. And it wasn't just the strategy, but the way it was spoken, and how you talked of those who would defend those homes—rebel as you put it—as a nuisance."

"They would be, creating a liability we couldn't afford."

"But otherwise, you could *afford* to burn them out."

She knew, too well, the look and sound of angry revulsion on a man. All she could do was harden herself against it. "Better to lose brick and wood than flesh and blood."

"A home's more than brick and wood."

"I wouldn't know, I never had one. But that's not the point. In any case, it's moot. It's not being done. So if that's it—"

"What do you mean you never had a home?"

"We'll say I never developed an emotional attachment to the roof over my head. But if I had, I'd rather see it go than me, or anyone I cared about." The muscles in the back of her neck had tightened like wire, shooting a headache straight up into her skull. "And this is a ridiculous discussion because we're not burning down anything."

"No, because we're not the monsters here."

She lost her color at that. He could see it just sink out of her face. "Meaning you're not, Hoyt's not, but Cian and I are another matter. Fine. It's not the first time I've been compared to a vampire."

"That's not what I'm doing."

"You expect it from him, but not from me," she repeated. "Well, expect it. No, strike that, don't expect anything. Now, get out."

"I'm not finished."

"I am." She rose, started for the door. When he stepped in front of her, took her arm, she yanked free. "Move, or I make you move."

"Is that your solution? Threaten, push, shove?"

"Not always."

She hit him. Her fist came up, connected, before the thought of doing it clicked in her brain. It knocked him down, and left her stunned, shocked and shamed. Losing control with another person, physically harming another person, was simply not allowed.

"I'm not going to apologize because you asked for it. But that was crossing the line. The fact that I did means I'm already over the line, and this conversation has got to be over. Here, get up."

She offered a hand.

She didn't see it coming, another mistake, the yank on her hand, the sweep of his leg knocking her feet out from under her. When she hit the floor, he rolled on top of her before she countered.

She had an instant to think he'd been training very well.

"Is that how you win arguments?" he demanded. "A fist to the face?"

"I was done arguing. That was punctuation. You're going to want to get off me, Larkin, and fast. I've got a slippery hold right now."

"Bugger that."

"Bugger *you*." She flipped him off, then sprang to a crouch to block anything he might throw at her. "I won't be played like this. It's all so easy when it's walks in the sunshine, and talking about picnics, but when things get hard, when I have to be hard, then you're revolted. I'm a fucking monster."

"I never called you that, and I'm not revolted. I'm sodding mad is what I am." He dived at her, and they hit the floor again, rolled. Their bodies rammed into a table, tipping it over so the blown glass bowl on it shattered.

"If you'd stop trying to bruise and bloody me for five bloody seconds we could finish this."

"If I wanted you bloody, you'd be pumping from an artery. I don't need you passing judgment on me, or giving me the big chill because I've shocked your sensibilities. I don't need this *bullshit* from you or—"

"What you need is to shut the hell up."

He crushed his mouth to hers in an angry, frustrated kiss even as her elbow found its way into his gut. He had to lift his head to wheeze back in the air she stole.

"Don't tell me to shut up." She grabbed his hair with both hands, yanked his mouth back down to hers.

Just as angry, just as frustrated. Just as needy. The hell with it, she thought. The hell with right and wrong, with sense, with safety. Screw control.

There were times you just took, and let yourself be taken.

Didn't mean anything, she told herself as she dragged at his shirt. It was only flesh, it was only heat. She wanted to weep and rage as much as she wanted to consume.

She shoved him over, straddled him as she pulled her shirt over her head. But he reared up, clamping his arms around her as his mouth found her breast. So she held on, letting her head fall back, letting him plunder.

Now he was riding the dragon, he thought, flying on the power of it. She was like trying to hold flame, so the sheer burn of her made him delirious. He used teeth and tongue, gorging himself as her fingers dug into his shoulders, his back, his sides. Then she was under him again, her hips grinding up while their mouths clashed.

He pulled the loose pants she wore down her hips, and there was nothing beneath them but woman, hot and wet. Hotter and wetter when his hand found her. Her harsh, throaty moan seared across his lips.

When the orgasm ripped through her, she could only think, God, thank God. But the greed whipped back, spun through like a cyclone that had her biting, scratching, tearing. She would give no quarter here, and ask none, but only clamped strong legs around him. Held on to that exquisite shock when he plunged into her.

And drove her like a mad thing, thrust upon urgent thrust, until they were both burned out.

What had she done? She'd just had crazed, kick-your-ass sex without a single thought of self-preservation, of consequences, of . . . anything. No thought, none at all, just brutal, primal need.

He was still inside her, and if felt as though their bodies had melted together in the heat. How would she separate herself again? How could she come out of this whole?

She wasn't supposed to feel like this. She wasn't supposed to want something—someone—so much she forgot herself. Let herself be taken even as she took, and in blind, feral passion.

She hadn't stopped it. She hadn't been able to stop it. And now she would pay.

He murmured something; she couldn't make it out. Then he nuzzled—a kind of nose in the neck like a puppy—before he rolled aside.

The simple sweetness of the gesture after the ferocity all but broke her into pieces.

"Crushing you." He grabbed a couple of ragged breaths. "Well, that was fairly amazing, and not at all the way I'd had it all planned out. Are you all right then?"

Careful, she warned herself. Careful and cool. "No problem."

She sat up, reached for her pants.

"Hang on a minute." He patted her arm. "My head's still spinning here. And I barely took the time to look at you seeing as we were both in a rush."

"Got the job done." She hitched on her pants. "That's what counts."

He pushed himself up, reached her shirt before she did. "Look here at me, would you?"

"I'm not big on postgame analysis, and I've got things to do."

"I don't remember a game. A battle, perhaps. I thought we'd both come out on the winning side of it."

"Yeah, so like I said, no problem." She would start to tremble in a minute, any minute. "I need my shirt."

He studied her face. "Where did you go? You have so many little hiding places."

"I don't hide." She ripped the shirt out of his hand.

"Aye, you do. Someone gets too close, you go sliding off into one of your shadows."

"Okay, why do you want to piss me off?" She dragged on her shirt. "We had sex—really good sex. It's been coming on for a while, and now it's done. We can put the focus back where it belongs."

"I don't think things are so very different here than in Geall that what we just had between us would be just sex."

"Look, cowboy, if you want romance—"

He got to his feet, slowly. It was the look in his eyes that warned her his temper was back. That was fine, in fact, that was good. They'd swipe at each other, and he'd go.

"There wasn't anything romantic about it. I thought there would be the first time we came together, but things took a different turn, and no complaints. Now you're trying to shove me away, knock me back, the way you did before with your fist. Let me say that the fist was more honest than this."

"You got what you were after."

"You know better. You know it wasn't only this."

"What's the point in anything else? What's the god-damn point? It's got nowhere to go."

"Have you been looking into Glenna's crystal? You see tomorrow now, and the day after?"

"I know things like this are doomed before they start. Cian's not the only one who is what he is, Larkin."

"Ah, now we come to it."

"Just—" She lifted her hands, shoved at the air, turned away. "Let it go. If the occasional grope in the dark isn't enough for you, look somewhere else."

So, he'd hurt her along the way, he realized. He was hardly the first, and couldn't quite decide if he was sorry for his part of it as yet. "I don't know what's enough for me when it comes to you." He scooped up his pants, yanked them on. "But I know I care for you. I know you matter."

"Oh please." She grabbed the water from her desk, gulped some down. "You don't even like me."

"Where does that fly from? Why would you say something so foolish and so false?"

"You seem to have forgotten what started this whole thing, what you came in here for in the first place."

"I haven't, but I don't see what that has to do with how I feel about you."

"Well, for God's sake, Larkin, how could you feel anything for someone when you're standing on the other side of a basic line?"

He considered his words now. He was, he knew, being compared to the Jeremy she'd spoken of before. Someone who'd been unable—or unwilling—to love and accept who she was."

"Blair, you're a hardheaded woman, and I've my own streak of stubbornness. My own stands and thoughts and—what did you call it?—sensibilities. And so what?"

"So. You, me." She pointed to him, tapped her own chest, then swiped a finger between them. "Line."

"Oh, bollocks. You think I can't disagree with you, and passionately, come to that, and care for you? Respect you, admire you, even knowing inside my heart you're wrong about the thing we're arguing over? The same, I wager as inside yours you believe I'm wrong. I'm not," he said with the barest hint of a smile, "but that's another matter. If

DANCE OF THE GODS

everyone has to believe the same, if there's never any passionate differences, how do people come together in your world?"

"They don't," she said after a moment. "Not with me."

"Then you're just stupid, aren't you? And narrow in your thinking," he added when she gaped at him. "Hard in the head as well, as I believe I've already mentioned."

She took another careful sip of water. "I'm not stupid."

"Just the rest of it then." He nodded as he took a step toward her. "Blair, it's not always where you end up, is it, that's the most important thing? It's the journey itself, and what you find, what you do along the way. Now I've found you, and that's an important thing."

"Where we're going matters."

"It does. But so does where we are. I have feelings for you, feelings I've never had for anyone. They don't always fit comfortably inside me, but I have a way of shifting things around until I find the fit."

"You maybe. I'm not good at this."

"As I am, you'll just have to follow my lead."

"How did you manage to turn this around on me?"

He only smiled, then kissed her cheek, her brow, her other cheek. "I just managed to get you faced toward me. That's the right direction."

She had to keep her mind focused on the job, the work. If she didn't, Blair found it tended to wander in that direction Larkin had spoken of. Then she'd catch herself daydreaming, smiling for no reason, or remembering what it was like to wake up beside a man who looked at her in a way that made her feel so much like a woman.

There was too much to do to take time indulging in fantasies.

"You have to be practical, Glenna. We all do. Now." Blair tapped Glenna's storage chest with her foot. "What's essential in here?"

"All of it."

"Glenna."

"Blair." Glenna folded her arms. "Are we or are we not going into battle against über evil?"

"Yes, we are. Which means we go in lean, stripped down, mobile."

"No, which means we go in loaded. These are my weapons." Glenna swept out a hand, a bit, Blair thought, like one of those game show models showing off fabulous prizes. "Are you leaving your weapons behind?"

"No, but I can also carry mine on my back, which you can't do with this two-ton chest."

"It doesn't weigh two tons. Seventy-five pounds, tops." Glenna's lips trembled at Blair's long, cool stare. "Okay, maybe eighty."

"The books alone—"

"May make all the difference. Who's to say? I'll worry about the transport."

"This better be a damn big stone circle," Blair muttered. "You know you're taking more than the rest of us combined."

"What can I say? I'm a diva."

Blair rolled her eyes, stalked to the tower window to stare out into the rain.

There was little time here left, she thought. Nearly moving day. And while she could sense—nearly see—a few of Lilith's forces in the trees, there'd be no movement toward the house. No attack.

She'd expected something. After what Larkin had pulled off, the sheer balls of it, she'd expected a reprisal. It seemed impossible Lilith would take such an insult, such a loss, without slapping back.

"Maybe she's too busy gearing up for Geall, too."

"What?"

"Lilith." Blair turned back to Glenna. "Nothing out of her for days now. And Larkin's infiltration had to sting. Jesus, when you think about it, one man—unarmed—not only getting in, but getting prisoners out. It's a kick in the face."

Glenna's eyes glinted. "I wish that was literal as well as figurative."

"Get in line. But anyway, maybe she's too busy preparing to move her front to bother harassing us right now."

"Very likely."

"I'm going to head down to the war room. We need to work out the fine details of the traps we want to set."

"Will it make a difference?"

"What do you mean?"

"I've been thinking about it, all of it. What we've done, what they've done." Glenna rubbed a hand over the top of her chest. "But the time and the place are set. Nothing we do will change that time, that place."

"No, Morrigan made that clear in our last little chat. But what we do, how we handle the time between now and then will set the tone for that time and place. She was saying that, too. Hey, pal, it's okay to be nervous."

"Good." With brisk efficiency, Glenna set vials she'd replenished back in her healing case. "I called my parents today. I told them I'd probably be out of touch for a few weeks. Told them what an incredible time I'm having. I couldn't tell them about any of this, of course. I haven't even told them about Hoyt yet because it's too hard to explain."

She closed the case and turned. "It's not that I'm not afraid to die. I am, of course—maybe more now than I was when this began. I have more to lose now."

"Hoyt, and happy ever."

"Exactly. But I'm prepared to die if that's what it takes. Maybe more now than when this began, for those exact reasons."

"Love sure can twist you up."

"Oh boy," was Glenna's heartfelt agreement. "And I wouldn't change a single moment since I met him. Still, it's so hard, Blair. I have no way of telling my family how or why if I don't make it through this. They'll never know what happened to me. And that weighs on me."

"Then don't die."

Glenna gave a half laugh. "A better idea."

"I'm sorry. I don't mean to make light of it."

"No, it's kind of bolstering, actually. But . . . if anything happens to me, would you take this to my family?" She held out an envelope. "I know it's a lot to ask," she began when Blair hesitated.

"No, but . . . Why me?"

"You and Cian have the best chance of coming through this. I can't ask him to do it. They won't understand, even with this, but at least they won't spend the rest of their lives wondering if I'm alive or dead. I don't want to put them through that."

Blair studied the envelope, the artistic flare of the handwriting forming her parents' names and address. "I tried to contact my father, twice, since this started. E-mail, because I don't actually know where he is. He hasn't answered me."

"Oh, I'm sorry. He must be out of reach for—"

"No, probably not. He just doesn't answer me, that's fairly typical. And I really need to get over it. It isn't that he wouldn't care. Big vamp war—he'd care. And if I died, he'd be sorry. Because he trained me not to, and going down would be a reflection on him."

"That sounds harsh."

"He is." She looked into Glenna's face, clear-eyed. "And he doesn't love me."

"Oh, Blair."

"Time to suck that up, too. Past time. You've got something else here." She tapped the letter. "And it's important."

"It is," Glenna agreed. "But they're not my only family."

"I get that. What we've got, the six of us? It's one of the good things I've picked up along the way."

With a nod, Blair tucked the envelope into the back pocket of her jeans. "I'll give this back to you, November first."

"That'd be good."

"See you downstairs."

"Soon. Oh, and Blair? It's nice, you and Larkin. It's nice to see."

"See what?"

Now Glenna let out a genuine laugh. "What, am I blind? Added to that I have the super X-ray vision of a newlywed. I'm just saying I like the way you are together. It seems like a nice fit."

"It's just— It's not . . . I'm not looking for the big, Hollywood finish, the one where the music crescendos and the light goes all pink and pretty."

"Why not?"

"Just not the way it is. I'll take it a day at a time. People like me look too far down the road, they end up falling into the big hole somebody dug right in front of them."

"If they don't look far enough or hard enough, they don't see what they were really looking for."

"Right now, I'll settle for avoiding the hole."

She headed out. No way to explain, she thought, not to a woman still floating on the wings of new love, that there were some people who just weren't built for it. Some people didn't have that strolling hand-in-hand with the man of their dreams into the sunset in their destiny.

When she strolled into the sunset, she went alone, she went armed and she went looking for death.

Not exactly the stuff of romance and hopeful futures.

She'd tried it once, and it had been a disaster that had blown up in her face. Larkin was no Jeremy, that was for damn certain. Larkin was tougher, and stronger, and sweeter for that matter.

But that didn't change the basics. She had her duty—the mission—and he had his world. Those weren't the elements for a long-term connection.

Her particular branch of the old McKenna family tree would die out with her. She'd made up her mind to that when she'd scraped herself up after Jeremy.

She started to swing toward the stairs, but the music stopped her. Cocking her head, she strained to hear, to recognize. Was that Usher?

Jeez, was Larkin up in the training room fooling around with her MP3? She'd have to kill him.

She jogged up the stairs. It wasn't that she couldn't appreciate the fact he enjoyed her music. But she'd spent a lot of time downloading and setting up that player. He didn't even know how the damn thing worked.

"Listen, cowboy, I don't want you—"

The room was empty, the terrace doors firmly shut. And music poured through the air.

"Okay, weird." She set her hand on the stake she always carried in her belt, and sidestepped slowly toward the weapons. The lights were on full; nothing could hide in shadows. But she closed her hand over the handle of a scythe.

The music shut off; a switch flicked.

Lora stepped through the wall of mirrors.

"Hello, *cherie.*"

"Nice trick."

"One of my favorites." Turning a circle, she seemed to study the room. She wore heeled boots, snug black pants with a fitted jacket that showed a flirty bit of frothy lace between the deep plunge of lapels.

"So, this is where you spar and sweat, and prepare to die."

"This is where we train to kick your ass."

"So tough, so *formidable.*" She floated around the room with the spiked heels of those boots gliding just above the floor.

Not here, Blair told herself. Not really here, just the illusion of her. But to prove it, she hurled a stake. And watched it pass right through Lora's figure to embed itself into the wall.

"That was rude." Lora turned with a little pout. "Hardly a way to welcome a guest."

"You weren't invited."

"No, we were interrupted the last time, before you could invite me in. But still, I brought you a present. Something picked just especially for you. I went all the way to America for it. All the way to Boston."

She did a long, sweeping turn with her eyes bright as suns. "Wouldn't you like to see? Or would you like to guess? Yes, yes, you must guess! Three guesses."

To show complete lack of interest, Blair stood hip-shot, a hand hooked in the pocket of her jeans. "I don't play games with the undead, Fifi."

"You're just no fun, are you? But one day we'll have fun, you and I." She floated closer, running her tongue over fangs before she smiled. "I have so many plans for you. Men have let you down, haven't they? Poor Blair. Withheld their love, and you crying out for it inside."

"The only thing I'm crying out for is an end to this conversation before it makes me sick."

"What you need is a woman. What you need . . ." She trailed a finger in the air, a breath away from Blair's cheek. "Yes, *bien sur*, you need the power and the pleasure I'd give you."

"I don't go for cheap blondes with silly French accents. Plus the outfit? It's so last week."

Lora hissed, her head snapping forward as if to bite.

"I'll make you sorry, and I'll make you grovel. Then I'll make you scream."

Deliberately, Blair widened her eyes. "Golly. Does that mean you don't want to date me anymore?"

With a laugh, Lora spun away. "I like you, I really do. You have, ah . . . flair. That's why I brought you such a special present. I'll just go get it. Wait one minute."

She stepped backward, through the mirrors.

"Fuck this," Blair muttered. She grabbed a crossbow, armed it. With the bow in one hand, the scythe in the other, she began to move cautiously toward the door.

This was Glenna's area, not hers. Time to call in the witch.

But Lora slid through the wall again, and what she pulled with her had Blair's blood freezing.

"No. No, no, no."

"He is handsome." Lora slid a tongue down Jeremy's cheek as he struggled against her hold. "I can see why you feel for him."

"You're not here." Oh God, his face was bleeding. His right eye swollen nearly shut. "It's not real."

"Not here, but real. Say hello, Jeremy."

"Blair? Blair? What's going on? What are you doing here? What's happening?"

"It was so easy." Lora clamped a hand on his throat, choking him as she lifted him an inch off the floor. And laughing when Blair charged them, flew through them and ran hard against the wall. "I just picked him up in a bar. A few drinks, a few suggestions. Men are deceivers ever. That's Shakespeare. 'Why don't we go to your place?' was all I needed to whisper into his ear. And here we are."

She brought him down so his feet touched the ground, but kept her hand around his neck. "I would have fucked him first, but it seemed that would take the shine off the gift."

"Help me." He choked it out, wheezing each breath. "Blair, you have to help me."

"Help me," Lora mimicked and threw him to the ground.

"Why are you wasting your time with him?" Blair felt her stomach twist as Jeremy crawled toward her. "You want me, come for me."

"Oh, I will." Lora leaped, falling on Jeremy. Dragging him to his back, she straddled him. "This weak—yet attractive—human broke your heart. Isn't that so?"

"He dumped me. What do I care what you do to him? You're wasting your time with him when you should be dealing with me."

"No, no, it's never a waste of time. And caring, *chérie*, is what you do." Lora clamped a hand over Jeremy's mouth

as he started to scream, then watching Blair, scraped her
nail down his cheek to draw fresh blood. She licked it from
her fingertip. "Hmm. Fear always gives it such a nice kick.
Beg for him. If you beg, I'll let him live."

"Don't kill him. Please, don't kill him. He means nothing to you. He's not important. Leave him there, just leave
him, you got my attention. I'll meet you, alone, wherever
you want. Just you and me. We'll settle this. The two of us.
We don't need men getting in the way. Don't do this. Ask
for something in return. Just ask."

"Blair." Lora offered her a sweet, sympathetic smile. "I
don't have to ask. I just take. But you begged very well, so
I'll . . . Oh don't be ridiculous. We both know I'm going to
kill him. Watch."

She sank her teeth into him, sliding her body down his
as it convulsed in an awful parody of sex. Blair heard herself screaming and screaming. And screaming.

Chapter 11

When Larkin rushed in all he saw was Blair stabbing a stake over and over into the floor. She was weeping as she did it in wild, screaming sobs, and there was a madness on her face.

He ran to her, but when he grabbed for her, she struck out in a blow that bloodied his lip.

"Get away, get away! She's killing him!"

"There's nothing there." He gripped her wrist, and would have taken another punch if Cian hadn't dragged her back.

She kicked, twisted to attack. Cian slapped her, twice. Hard enough to make the crack of it echo. "Stop. Hysterics are useless."

Enraged, Larkin leaped to his feet. "Take your hands off her. You think you can strike her?" He might have charged, but Hoyt pinned his arm.

"Hold on a bloody minute."

Larkin's answer was to rear back, smash his head into Hoyt's jaw even as Glenna sprinted over to stand between

Larkin and Cian. "Just calm down." Glenna held up her hands. "Just everyone calm down."

But there was shouting, accusations, and Blair's helpless sobbing.

"*Ciunas*!" Moira's voice cut through the mayhem with a cold authority. "Quiet, all of you. Larkin, he did what needed to be done, so stop this nonsense. Let go of her, Cian. Glenna, get her some water. We need to find out what's happened here."

When Cian released her, Blair simply melted to the floor. "She's killed him. I couldn't stop her." She brought up her knees, wrapped her arms around her head as she lowered it. "Oh God, oh my God."

"You have to look at me now." Moira crouched down, firmly took Blair's arms and brought them down again. "You have to look at me, Blair, and tell me what happened here."

"He never believed, not even when I showed him. It was easier to push me away, to throw me away than to believe it. Now he's dead."

"Who is?"

"Jeremy. Jeremy's dead. She brought him here, so I would see her do it."

"There's no one here, Blair. No one here, and no one in the house but the six of us."

"There was." Glenna passed down the water. "I can feel it." She looked at Hoyt for confirmation.

"A smear on the air." He nodded. "A heaviness to it that comes from black magic."

"She came through the wall, and I thought, now we'll fight. You and me, French bitch." Though Blair fought to steady it, her voice continued to hitch. "I threw a stake, but it went right through her. She wasn't really here. She . . ."

"Like on the subway. It happened to me," Glenna explained. "In New York. A vampire on the subway, but no one else could see it. He spoke to me, it moved, but it wasn't really there."

"Boston." Sick to the soul of her, Blair got to her feet. "She went to Boston. I used to live there. It's where I met him—Jeremy. They were in his apartment. She told me where she was. Cian, do you have contacts there?"

"I do."

She gave him an address. "Jeremy Hilton. Someone needs to check. Maybe she was just messing with me. But if . . . They have to make sure she didn't change him."

"I'll take care of it."

She looked down to where she'd hacked and drilled the steak into the floorboards. "Sorry about the floor."

"That'd be Hoyt's and Glenna's problem now." Cian touched her shoulder briefly before he left the room.

"We should go down. You should lie down," Glenna said. "Or sit at least. I can give you something that will help."

"No. I don't want anything." She scrubbed the useless tears away with the heels of her hands. "I knew she'd come back at us, but I never considered, I never thought. Glenna, your family—"

"They're protected. Hoyt and I saw to that. Blair, I'm so sorry we didn't do something for your . . . for your friend."

"I never thought of him. Never considered they would . . . I'm, ah, I'm going to take a few minutes before we get back to work."

"All you need," Glenna told her.

Blair looked at Larkin. "I'm sorry. I'm sorry I hit you."

"It's nothing." Letting her go, letting her go alone, was more painful than any blow.

She didn't weep again. Tears wouldn't help Jeremy, and they certainly wouldn't do her any good.

She contacted her aunt, relayed the details. She could count on family to protect family. In any case, she doubted Lilith, or Lora, any of them would go after people who were prepared, who knew them. And could defend them-selves.

They'd chosen the helpless for a very good reason.

It didn't waste time or effort, was low-risk, and very, very effective.

She was absolutely calm when she armed herself, sliding the sword into the sheath on her back, the stake into the one on her belt. Her mind, her purpose were clear as glass when she went outside.

There wouldn't be many, she thought. It was poor strategy to waste more than a handful at this stage. Which was a pity.

They would expect her to be broken, to be shaking and weeping under the covers. That was a mistake.

She watched the two come toward her, from the right and from the left. "Hello, boys. You looking for a party?"

The sword came out of its sheath with the slick sound of metal on metal. She whirled; a quick, two-handed swing. And decapitated the one coming at her from behind.

"Came to the right place."

When they charged, she was ready. Slicing, piercing, blocking with a sword that sang like vengeance. She took the nick on her forearm. She wanted to feel it, that sting.

They were clumsy, she thought. Young and poorly trained. Fat and soft in the lives they'd led before they'd been turned. Not defenseless, not like Jeremy, but far from seasoned.

She flipped out the stake, eliminated one.

The one that was left dropped its sword, began to run.

"Hey, hey, not done yet." She chased it, took it down with a flying tackle. Then holding the stake to its heart, stared into eyes filled with fear.

"Got a message for Lora. You know her? The French pastry? Good," she said when it nodded. "Tell her she was right about one thing. It will be her and me, and when I end her, it's going to be . . . Oh never mind, I'll tell her myself."

She plunged the stake down. Rising, she tunneled her fingers through her dripping hair. Then picked up the scattered weapons, and started back to the house.

The door swung open before she reached it, and Larkin stormed out. "Have you gone mad?"

"They weren't expecting it." She tossed him one of the swords, moved by him into the house. "Only three anyway. Probably clears the ones she's stationed near the house." She laid the other confiscated swords on the kitchen counter. "And those were lightweights."

"You'd go out alone? Risk your life this way?"

"I went out alone most of my life," she reminded him. "And risking my life is part of the job description."

"It's not a job."

"A job's exactly what it is." She poured herself a large mug of coffee. Hands still steady, she noted. Mission accomplished. "I'm going to go dry off."

"You had no right to take a chance like that."

"Minimal risk," she countered as she walked out. "Excellent results."

When she'd changed her clothes, she joined the others in the library. She could see from their expressions Larkin had informed the rest of the group of her little sortie.

"They were stationed close to the house," she began. "Likely to try to hear or see something they could pass on. That won't be a problem now."

"It would have been a problem if there'd been more of them." Hoyt spoke quietly, but it didn't disguise the steel beneath the words. "It would have been a problem if they'd killed or captured you."

"Didn't happen. We have to be ready to take opportunities. Not only the six of us, but the people we're going to be sending into battle. They have to be trained, how to kill, when to kill. Not just with sword and stake, but with their bare hands, or whatever comes to hand. Because everything's a weapon. And if they're not trained, if they're not ready, they're just going to stand there and die."

"Like Jeremy Hilton."

"Yeah." She nodded at Larkin, absorbed his anger along

with the weight in her heart. "Like Jeremy. Cian, were you able to find anything out?"

"He's dead."

She closed off the part of her that wanted to moan. "Could he have been changed?"

"No. There was too much trauma to the body for that."

"It's still possible he—"

"No." Cian bit off the word to cut her off. "She ripped him to pieces. It's one of her signatures. He's just dead."

She let herself sit. Better to sit, she decided, than to fall over.

"There was nothing you could do, Blair," Moira told her gently. "Nothing you could have done to stop it."

"No, there was nothing. That was her point—look what I can do, right in front of you, and you're helpless. We were engaged, Jeremy and I, a couple years ago. So I had to tell him—in the end I had to show him—what I am, what I do. He walked out, because he wasn't going to believe it, wasn't going to be part of it. Now it's killed him."

"She killed him," Larkin corrected. "Who you are didn't kill him." He waited until she shifted her gaze, met his eyes. "She wants, very much wants, you to blame yourself. Will you give her that victory?"

"She won't win anything from me." Tears stung her eyes again, but she willed them back. "I'm sorry, all around. This messes me up, and I have to live with it awhile on my own before I can put it away."

"We'll put off the meeting." Glenna glanced around at the others for agreement. "You can take some time."

"Appreciate it, but work's better. Thinking's better." If she went upstairs now, were alone now, Blair knew she'd just fall apart again. "So okay. If we're going to set traps on the other side, we'll need to calculate the best locations, and determine how many we'll need on those details."

"We have more immediate concerns," Hoyt interrupted.

"The transportation to Geall itself. If Cian's barred from the Dance, he can't reach the portal."

"There must be an exception." Moira laid a hand on Blair's shoulder, gave it one hard squeeze before moving aside. "Morrigan chose us, all of us."

"Maybe she's finished with me." Cian shrugged. "Gods are fickle creatures."

"You're one of the six," Moira insisted. "Without you in Geall, the circle's broken."

"I could go back to the caves. From the air." Larkin paced in front of the windows. How could he sit at such a time? "Scout. I might be able to find where they're going through."

"We can't separate. Not this close to deadline. We stick together now." Glenna scanned faces, lingering on Blair's. "We stay whole."

"There's another thing, I think I should mention." Moira glanced toward Cian. "When Larkin and I went to the Dance in Geall, it was barely midday. It seemed to happen so quickly, the way we were swept up and away. But when we came out here, it was night. I don't think we can know how long it takes, or if time's the same. Or . . . or if we leave at night as we planned, if it would still be night when we come to Geall."

"Or high bloody noon." Cian cast his eyes up. "Isn't that just perfect?"

"There has to be a way to protect him if there's sunlight."

"Easy for you to say, Red." Cian rose to get a glass of whiskey. "Your delicate skin may burn a bit in strong sunlight, but you don't go to ash, do you?"

"Some sort of block, Hoyt," Glenna began.

"I don't think SPF-forty will do the trick," Cian countered.

"We'll figure it out," she snapped back. "We'll find a way. We haven't come this far to give up, to leave you behind."

Blair let them talk, argue, debate. The voices just buzzed around her. She didn't comment, didn't contribute. When Hoyt finally harangued Cian into giving him a sample of blood, she left them to their magic.

H e didn't try to sleep. A half dozen times he started to go to her room. To offer what? he wondered. Comfort she didn't want, anger she didn't need?

She had suffered a terrible loss, and a hard, hard shock to her heart. She hadn't, perhaps couldn't turn to him. Not even, he thought now, as a fellow warrior.

He couldn't soothe hurts she refused to let him see, or reach wounds she closed in to herself.

She had loved the man, that much was clear. And there was a small part of himself, an ugliness he could despise, that was jealous of the brutalized dead.

So he stood at the window, watching the sun rise on his last day in Ireland.

When someone knocked, he assumed it was Moira. "*Bi istigh.*"

He didn't turn when the door opened, not until Blair spoke. "My Gaelic's pretty crappy, so if that was go to hell, too bad." She hefted the bottle of whiskey she held in one hand. "I raided Cian's supply. Going to get a little drunk, have a wake for an old friend. Want to join me?"

Without waiting for an answer, she walked over to sit on the floor at the foot of the bed, resting her back against it. She opened the bottle, poured a generous two fingers into each of the glasses she'd brought in.

"Here's to just being dead." She lifted the glass, tossed back the contents. "Come on, have a drink, Larkin. You can be pissed at me and still have a drink."

He walked over, lowered to the floor to sit across from her. "I'm sorry you're hurting."

"I'll get over it." She handed him the second glass, poured more whiskey in her own. "*Sláinte.*" She tapped the glasses together, but this time she sipped instead of gulped. "Attachments, my father taught me, were weapons the enemy could use against you."

"That's a hard and cold way to live."

"Oh, he's good at hard and cold. He walked out on me on my eighteenth birthday. Done." She leaned her head back and drank. "You know, he'd hurt me so many times before, cut my heart out, I thought, just by not loving me. But it was nothing, nothing that happened—didn't happen—before came close to what it did to me when he walked away. That's how I got this."

She turned her wrist over, examined the scar. "Going out while I was still reeling, trying to prove I didn't need him. I did need him. Too bad for me."

"He didn't deserve you."

She smiled a little. "He'd completely agree with that, but not the way you mean. I wasn't what he wanted, and even if I had been, he wouldn't have loved me. Took me a long time to come around to that. Maybe he'd have been proud. Maybe he'd have been satisfied. But he never would've loved me."

"And still you loved him."

"Worshiped him." For a moment, Blair closed her eyes as she let that part of her go. That part was over. "I just couldn't rip that out and turn it to dust. So I worked, really hard, until I was better than he'd ever been. But I still had that need inside me. To love somebody, to have them love me back. Then there was Jeremy."

She poured more whiskey for both of them. "I was working at my uncle's pub. My aunt, my cousins and I took shifts. Hunting, or working the bar, waiting tables, just taking the night off. My aunt called it having a life. Work as a family, share the burden, have some normal."

"Sounds like a sensible woman."

"She is. And a good one. So I'm riding the stick—working the bar—when Jeremy comes in with a couple of friends. He's just copped this big account, and they're going to hoist a few. He's a stockbroker." She waved that away. "Hard to explain. Anyway, he's good looking. Great looking, actually. So, he hits on me—"

"He *struck* you?"

"No, no." Finding that wonderfully funny, she snorted out a laugh. "It's parlance, slang. He flirted with me. I flirted back because he gave me the buzz. You know what I mean? That little *zzzz* you get inside?"

"I do." Larkin brushed a hand over hers. "I know that buzz."

"He hung around till closing, and I ended up giving him my number. Well, we don't need every detail. We started seeing each other—going out together. He was fun, sweet. Normal. The kind of guy who sends you flowers the day after your first date."

Her eyes misted over, but she shook her head, downed more whiskey. "I wanted normal. I wanted a chance at it. When things got serious between us, I thought yeah, yeah, this is the way it's supposed to be. The job doesn't mean I can't have somebody, be part of somebody. But I didn't tell him what I did on those nights we weren't together, or what I did some nights after he was asleep. I didn't tell him."

"Did you love him?"

"I did. And I told him that. I told him I loved him, but I didn't tell him what I was." She drew a deep breath. "Honestly? I don't know if that was sheer cowardice or ingrained training, but I didn't tell him. We were together eight months, and he never knew. There had to be signs, there had to be *clues*. Hey, Jeremy, don't you wonder how I got these bruises? Why my clothes are trashed? Where the hell this blood came from? But he never asked, and I never let myself wonder why."

"People, you said, have blinders. Love, I think, can thicken them."

"Bet your ass. He asked me to marry him. Oh God, he pulled out all the stops. The wine, the candles, the music, all the right words. I just rode on it, the big, shiny fantasy of it. Still, I didn't say anything, not for days. Until my aunt sat me down."

She pressed the thumb and finger of one hand to her eyes. "You have to tell him, she said to me. You have to make him believe it. You can't have a life, can never build one with him, not with lies or half-truths or without trust. Dragged my feet another couple of weeks, but it ate at me. I knew she was right. But he loved me, so it would be all right. It would all work out fine. Because he loved me, and he'd see I was doing not just what I had to do, but what was right."

Holding her glass in both hands, she closed her eyes. "I explained it to him as carefully as I knew how, taking him through the family history. He thought I was joking." She opened her eyes now, met Larkin's. "When he realized I wasn't, he got hostile. Figured it was my sick way of breaking the engagement. We went round and round about it. I badgered him into going to the cemetery with me. I knew one was supposed to rise that night, and hey, a picture's worth a thousand. So I showed him what they were, what I was."

She drank again, one long sip. "He couldn't wait to get away from me. Couldn't wait to pack his things and get away. To walk out on me. I was a freak, and he never wanted to see me again."

"He was weak."

"He was just a guy. Now he's a dead guy."

"So it's your fault, is it? Your fault that you cared enough to share what you are with him. To show him not only that there are monsters in the world, but that you're strong enough, courageous enough to fight them? Your fault that he wasn't man enough to see the wonder of you?"

"What wonder? I do what I'm trained to do, follow the family business."

"That's bollocks, and worse, it's self-pity."

"I didn't kill him—you were right about that. But he's dead because of me."

"He's dead because a vicious, soulless demon killed him. He'd dead because he didn't believe in what was in front of his eyes, and didn't hold on to you. And none of that is your doing."

"He left me, like my father left me. I thought that was the worst. But this . . . I don't know what to do with the pain."

He took her glass, set it aside. Reaching out he pulled her into his arms, pressed her head onto his shoulder. "Put a bit of it here for now. Shed your tears, *a stór*. You'll feel better having given them to him."

He held her, stroking her hair and soothing, while she wept for another man.

She woke tucked into his bed, still dressed, and grateful she was alone. The hangover wasn't the clanging bell of a night of foolish indulgence, but the dull gong that came from using whiskey as a cushion.

He'd drawn the drapes so the sun wouldn't wake her, she noted, and checked her watch for the time. The fact that it was already noon made her groan as she threw back the covers to sit on the side of the bed.

Too much to do, she told herself, to coddle a half-assed hangover and a raging case of sorrow. Before she could gather the fortitude to stand, Larkin walked in. He carried a glass that held something murky and brown.

"I'd say good morning, but it likely doesn't feel as such to you."

"It's not too bad," she told him. "I've had worse."

"Regardless, it isn't the day for having a head. Glenna says this will help it."

She looked dubiously at the glass. "Because drinking it will make me throw up everything in my system?"

"She didn't say. But you'll be a brave girl now and take your medicine."

"I guess." She took the glass, sniffed at the contents.

"Doesn't smell as bad as it looks." She took a deep breath, downed all of it. Then shuddered right down to her toes. "Tastes a lot worse. Not just eye of newt, but the whole damn newt."

"Give it a minute or two to settle."

She nodded, then stared down at her hands. "I wasn't at my best last night, to put it extremely mildly."

"No one expects you should be at your best at all times. Certainly not me."

"I want to thank you for the ear, and the shoulder."

"Those seemed to be the parts of me you needed most." He sat beside her. "Were you clear-headed enough to understand what I said to you?"

"Yeah. It's not my fault. In my head I know it's not my fault. There are other parts of me, Larkin, that have to catch up with my head on this."

"They wasted you, these men. I won't." He pushed to his feet again when she stared at him. "Something else for you to catch up with. Come down when you're ready. We've a lot of work."

She kept staring even after he'd gone out and closed the door behind him.

I t helped to have the work. They would carry—the old-fashioned way—as much of the supplies and weapons as possible to the circle. Hoyt and Glenna would continue to work on a shield of some kind for Cian.

With Larkin in the form of a horse, Blair loaded him while Moira loaded Cian's stallion.

"Sure you can ride that thing?" Blair asked her.

"I can ride anything." Moira glanced toward the tower window. "It's the only way to get this done. They need to concentrate on what they're doing. We can't risk trying to carry everything we're taking the full distance after sunset."

"Nope." Blair swung onto Larkin's back. "Keep your eyes open. We may have company in the woods."

They started out, single file. "Can you really smell them?" Moira called out.

"It's more that I sense them. I'll know if one gets close." She scanned the trees, the shadows. Nothing stirred but birds and rabbits.

Sunlight, she thought, and birdsong. It would be a different matter taking this route at night. She and Moira, she decided, on Larkin, with Hoyt and Glenna on the stallion. Cian, she thought, could move nearly as fast as a horse at a gallop if necessary.

It was a twisting and at times a barely trod path. And at times the shadows over it were deep enough to have her fingers twitch toward the crossbow.

She felt the ripple of Larkin's muscles between her thighs, nodded. So he could sense them, too, she thought. Or the horse he was inside could sense them. "They're watching. Keeping their distance, but watching."

"They'll understand what we're about." Moira glanced back. "Or get word to Lilith, and she will."

"Yeah. Pick up the pace a little. Let's get this done."

They came out of the woods, crossed a short fallow field. On the rise of it stood the stone Dance.

"It is big," Blair murmured. Not Stonehenge big, she thought, but impressive. And like Stonehenge, even before she moved into the shadow of the stones, she felt them. Almost heard them.

"Strong stuff." She dismounted.

"In this world, and in mine."

Moira slid off the stallion, then laid her head against Larkin's. "It's our way home."

"Let's hope so." Within the Dance, Blair began to off-load weapons. "You're sure vamps can't come inside the circle?"

"No demon can pass between the stones and step on the sacred ground. It's that way in Geall, and from everything I've read on it, that way in this world as well."

Moira looked as Blair did, toward the woods. But she

thought of Cian and what would become of him if they were forced to leave him behind.

"We'll figure it out."

Moira glanced over. "You're worried, too."

"It's a concern. We've got to get him there, keep him from frying—so make that two really major concerns. Handy this is a safety zone, and we're not going to come back in a few hours and find they've raided our weapons stash, but Cian's the downside."

Without thinking, she rubbed Larkin's flank. When he turned his head, eyed her, she dropped her hand. "Hoyt and Glenna are on it. We all go, that's the deal. So we'll figure it out."

The swish of Larkin's tail slapped her in the butt. "Hey."

"He's a playful sort," Moira commented. "In almost any form."

"Yeah, he's a real jokester. Ought to be careful, one of these days he might stick in one of the four-legged varieties." She came around to his head. "Then where will you be?"

He slurped his tongue from her jaw to her cheekbone. "Eeww."

Moira's laugh bubbled out as she stacked the last of the weapons. "He makes me laugh, even in the worst of times. Ah well," she said when Blair scowled and swiped the slobber from her cheek. "You don't seem to mind his tongue on you when he's a man."

The sound Larkin made was as close to a laugh as a horse could manage. Moira just grinned and swung back onto the stallion. "It's hard to miss when two people are eager to get their hands on each other. I once had a crush on him myself." She reached over, tugged Larkin's mane. "But then I was five. I've gotten well over it now."

"It's the quiet ones you've got to watch out for," Blair muttered. "You." She jerked her head toward Moira as she mounted Larkin. "Quiet type, into the books, little shy around the edges. I wouldn't have figured you'd take the idea of me banging your cousin so casually."

"Banging?" Moira pursed her lips as they rode through the stones. "That would be a term for sexual relations? It fits, doesn't it because . . ." She draped the reins over Vlad's neck so she could slap her hands together. And this time, Blair laughed.

"You're just full of surprises."

"I know what happens between a man and a woman. Theoretically."

"Theoretically. So you've never—" She caught Moira's wincing glance toward Larkin. "Oh, sorry. Big horses have big ears."

"Well, I suppose it's a small thing, considering all the rest. No, I've never. If I'm to be queen, I'll need to marry. But there's time. I'd want to find someone who'd suit, and who understands me. I'd like best to love as my parents loved each other, but at least, I'd want to care for him. And I'd hope he'd be skilled at banging."

This time the sound Larkin made was a kind of mutter.

"Why should you be the only one?" Moira slid her foot from the stirrup to give him a light kick with her boot. "Is he good at it then, our Larkin?"

"He's an animal."

Beneath her, Larkin broke into a fast trot.

Yes, Blair thought, it was good to laugh, even in the worst of times.

Chapter 12

Cian fingered the rough black material with mild distaste. "A cloak."

"But it's a magic cloak." Glenna tried a winning smile. "With hood."

Black cloaks and vampires, he thought with an inward sigh. Such a cliche. "And this . . . thing is supposed to prevent me from going up in flames in direct sunlight."

"It really should work."

He sent her a mildly amused look. "*Should* being the operative word."

"Your blood didn't boil when we exposed it," Hoyt began.

"There's cheery news. It happens I'm made up of more than blood."

"Blood's the key," Hoyt insisted. "Blood's the heart of it. You've said so yourself."

"That was before my flesh and bone were on the line."

"We're sorry there's no time to test it." Glenna pushed a hand through her hair. "It took so long, and until we were reasonably sure, we couldn't ask you to put it on and step outside."

"Considerate of you." He held it up. "Couldn't you have made it a bit more stylish?"

"Fashion wasn't our primary concern." Hoyt didn't quite snap out the words, but it was close. "Protecting your sorry self was."

"I'll be sure to thank you for it if I'm not a pile of inarticulate ash at the end of the day."

"And so you should." Moira condemned him with one quiet look. "They worked through the night, and all through this day with only you in mind. And while you've slept the rest of us have been working as well."

"I had work of my own, Your Highness." He dismissed her simply by turning his back. "Well, it's unlikely to be an issue as your stone circle rejects my sort."

"You have to trust in the gods," Hoyt told him.

"I'm forced to remind you, yet again. Vampire. Vampires and gods aren't drinking buddies."

Glenna stepped up to Cian, laid a hand over his. "Wear it. Please."

"For you, Red." He tipped her face up, kissed her lightly on the lips. Then he stepped back, swirled it on. "Feel like a bloody B movie extra. Or worse, a sodding monk."

He didn't look like a monk, Moira thought. He looked dangerous.

Blair and Larkin came in. "We're as secure as we're going to be," Blair said, then lifted her eyebrows at Cian. "Hey, you look like Zorro."

"I beg your pardon?"

"You know, that scene where he's in the chapel with the girl, and he's pretending to be the priest. Only, jeez, the kind of priest we used to call Father What a Waste. Anyway, sun's down. If we're going to go, we'd better."

Hoyt nodded, looked at Cian. "You'll stay close."

"Close enough."

Blair might have wished they'd taken time to practice

the maneuver, but it was too late for wishes. No more talk, she thought. No more discussion—and no dress rehearsals. It was now or never.

After a quick nod, a quick breath, she and Larkin went through the door first. Even as he changed, she was leaping up, then reaching a hand down to help Moira vault behind her.

They rode away from the stables at a hard run, with the hope of drawing any that waited in ambush. She barely saw Cian streak out. He was at the stable doors in seconds, releasing the stallion.

Then he was gone again, and Hoyt and Glenna were on Vlad's back.

With barely a glimmer of moonlight to guide them, a gallop was risky once they reached the trees. Blair kept Larkin to a trot, trusting him to watch the path as she scanned the woods.

"Nothing yet, nothing. If they're around they're hanging back."

"Can you see Cian?" With her bow ready, Moira tried to look everywhere at once. "Sense him?"

"No, there's nothing." Blair shifted in the saddle to look over Moira's shoulder at Hoyt. "Watch the flank. They may come at us from behind."

They rode in absolute silence, with only the sound of hooves on the path. And that, Blair thought, was a problem. Where were the nightbirds? Where were all the little rustles and peeps of the small animals in a night woods?

Demon hunters, she knew, weren't the only creatures who could sense vampires.

"Be ready," Blair said under her breath.

She heard it then, the clash of steel, a sudden scream. She didn't have to urge Larkin on with words or a nudge of her heels. He was already at a gallop.

She sensed them seconds before they charged out of the trees. Foot soldiers this time, she judged, with some seasoning and wearing light armor. She sliced down with her sword even as Moira's arrows began to fly.

Hooves struck out, and trampled whatever fell beneath them. But the enemy came from everywhere, blocking the circle, and barring the path to the Dance. Blair kicked out, knocking one back as it clawed at her leg. Too many, she thought. Too many to make a stand.

Better, she thought, better to charge, break the line, and get to the stones.

Then the one that leaped down from a branch above her nearly unseated her, knocking her back as she rammed up an elbow to block it. Moira pitched to the ground. With a cry of rage, Blair smashed back with a fist. She'd nearly jumped down when Cian flew across the path.

He swooped Moira up, all but threw her back on Larkin. "Go!" he shouted. "Go now."

She charged the line, the flames from her sword cutting a burning path. She could only hope Cian was out of harm's way as a ball of fire whizzed by her. She felt Larkin vibrate beneath her, and the form of him shift.

Then she was soaring up on the dragon's back, with his claws raking across the line of vampires, slashing out with his tail as Hoyt and Glenna galloped through the gap.

She could see the stones now. Though clouds covered the moon they glowed like polished silver, shining against the dark. She would have sworn even with the rush of wind, the cries of battle, she heard them singing.

As Hoyt and Glenna flew through them and into the circle, Larkin dived.

She leaped from his back, favoring the leg the vampire had scored. "Get ready," she ordered.

"Cian—"

She squeezed Moira's shoulder. "He'll come. Hoyt?"

He drew out his key; Moira did the same. "We don't say the words until Cian's with us." As with the stones themselves, power seemed to pulse from Hoyt as he took

Glenna's hand. "We don't say the words until we're a circle again."

Blair nodded. Whatever the stones held, whatever Hoyt and Glenna had been born with, the full force of the power came from unity. They'd wait for Cian.

She turned to Larkin. "Nice riding, cowboy. How bad is it?"

He pressed a hand to his bleeding side. "Scratches. You?"

"Same. Clawed up a little. Everybody else?"

"We'll do." Glenna was already stanching a gash in Hoyt's arm.

"He's coming," Moira murmured.

"Where?" Hoyt clamped a hand on her arm. "I see nothing."

"There." She pointed. "He's coming."

He was a blur coming out of the trees, a swirl of black up the rise.

"Wasn't that entertaining? They're regrouping, for all the good it will do them." There was blood on his face, and more running down from a slice in his thigh.

"Come." Hoyt held out a hand to him. "It's time."

"I can't." Cian lifted his own hand and pressed it against the air between the stones. "It's like a wall to me. I am what I am."

"You can't stay here," Hoyt insisted. "They'll hunt you down. You'll be alone."

"I'm not such easy prey. Do what you're meant to do. I'll stay to make certain it works."

"If you stay we all stay." Larkin stepped to the gap between two stones. "If you fight, we all fight."

"The sentiment's appreciated," Cian told him. "But this is bigger than one of us, and you have somewhere to be."

"The other portal," Larkin began.

"If I find it, you can buy me a drink in Geall. Go." He met Hoyt's eyes. "What's meant is meant. So you've always believed, and so—in my way—have I. Go. Save worlds."

"I'll find a way." Hoyt reached through the stones to grip Cian's hand. "I'll find a way, I swear it to you."

"Good luck to you." Cian saluted them with his sword. "To you all."

With a heavy heart showing clearly in his eyes, Hoyt stepped back, lifted the crystal. Light beamed in it, and from it.

"Worlds wait. Time flows. Gods watch."

Tears glimmering on her cheeks, Glenna took his hand and repeated the words.

"It's not right." Larkin spoke softly. "It's not right to leave one of us."

"Maybe we can— Oh shit," Blair murmured as the ground began to rumble. The wind swirled up, and light began to pulse.

"*Slan, mo cara.*" With one last look at Cian, Larkin gripped her hand. "It's a hell of a ride," he told her. "Best hold on to me. Moira?"

She held her crystal; she spoke the words. And she stared into Cian's eyes as she felt the world shift. Then she reached out, grabbed his hand. "We are one force, one power. *This* is meant!"

And pulled him into the circle.

It was like being sucked into a tornado, Blair thought. Impossible wind that seemed to pull you away from the earth, spin you in mad circles while the light blasted your eyes.

Would there be munchkins on the other side?

She could see nothing but that wild white light, the spinning whirl of it. Could find no footing, no solid ground, so anchored herself with Larkin's hand.

Then there was dark, and utter stillness. She rubbed her hand over her face, tried to catch her breath. And she saw now there was moonlight, silver streams of it that speared down and struck the standing stones.

"Is this our stop?"

"Oh my *God*!" Glenna's voice was giddy. "What a rush. What a . . . wow. And Cian." Putting both her trembling hands on either side of Cian's face, she kissed him soundly. "How did you do it?" she asked Moira. "How did you bring him inside?"

"I don't know. I just . . . It was meant. You were meant to be here," she said to Cian. "I felt it, and . . ." Moira seemed to realize she was still clutching his hand, and pulled hers away. "And well, here you are."

She pushed at hair that had come loose from its braid. "Well then, *fàilte a Geall.* Larkin." She made a laughing leap into his arms. "We're home."

"And handily enough, it's night." If Cian was shaken, he hid it well—merely glancing around him as he shoved back his hood. "Not that I don't trust your magical powers."

"There's still the matter of getting ourselves, and all this stuff where we're going." Blair gestured widely to encompass the chests, the weapons and cases.

"We can send men for most of it in the morning. I think we carry what we need most," Moira suggested.

"Weapons then. We don't know what we're walking into. Sorry," Blair added. "But you've been gone well over a month. We can't know."

"I can carry three, take the air." Larkin tugged Moira's disordered braid. "I could see if there's anything to worry about. And you can take one on the horse."

"My horse," Cian reminded him before he looked at Moira. "I can take you on my horse."

"Sounds like a plan. Let's get it in motion." Blair slung on her own duffle, then grinned at Hoyt and Glenna. "You guys are going to love this."

Across Geall they flew, with the stallion and its two riders galloping below. As the moonlight dripped like magic, hills and wedges of forest were edged with silver; the river gleamed on its wandering journey through them. Blair saw cottages with thin smoke spiraling from chimneys, the dots that were cattle or sheep lolling in fields. The roads below were narrow and dirt, and empty of travelers but for Cian and Moira.

No cars, she thought, no lights but for the occasional glimmer that might have been a candle or lantern. Just land, she realized, left to roll and spread, and rise to the silhouettes of mountains.

A land, she reminded herself, that until a few weeks ago, she'd believed a fairy tale.

She turned her head, saw the coast with its high, steep cliffs that flowed down to graceful inlets. The sea spread out, velvet black, and cupped a trio of rough little islands on its journey to the horizon.

She heard Glenna give a quick gasp behind her, and looked over again.

The fantasy rose from the high hill, a wide curl of river at its back. Its stones gleamed like jewels in the moonlight, rising up into towers and turrets, stretching out into crenelated walls.

A castle, Blair thought, dumbfounded. And what castle would be complete without a drawbridge, or peaked caps on towers that held silky white flags?

A claddaugh on one, she noted as they waved in the breeze. A dragon on the other.

Glenna leaned forward to speak in her ear. "A hell of a lot to take in, for a couple of twenty-first-century girls."

"I thought nothing was going to surprise me." There was wonder in her voice; Blair could hear it herself. "But wow, a freaking castle."

Larkin circled it so they could keep the horse and riders in view below. Then he glided down to a wide courtyard.

Instantly, Blair found herself surrounded by men in light armor, swords already drawn. She held her hands up in plain sight as she and her companions slid to the ground.

"Your name and your purpose." One of the guards stepped forward.

Larkin shed the dragon. "That's hardly a warm welcome, Tynan."

"Larkin!" The guard sheathed his sword, then grabbed Larkin in a one-armed hug. "Thank the gods! Where the devil have you been all these weeks? We'd all but given up on you. And the princess, where—"

"Open the gates. The princess Moira is waiting to come home."

"You heard Lord Larkin," Tynan snapped. He lacked an inch or two of Larkin's height, but his voice boomed with command. "Raise the gate. You must tell all. Your father will want to be waked."

"There's much to tell. Wake the cook while you're about it. Give welcome to my friends. The warrior Blair, Glenna the witch, Hoyt the sorcerer. We've traveled far today, Tynan. Farther than you can know."

He turned, reaching up to lift Moira down from the horse.

The men bowed, Blair noted, when Moira's feet touched the ground.

"Tynan, your face is a welcome sight." She kissed his cheek. "This is Cian, and this fine fellow is his Vlad. Would you have one of the men take him to the stables, see he's housed and tended?"

"Me or the horse?" Cian murmured, but she pretended not to hear.

"Have my uncle told we've come home, and we wait upon him in the family parlor."

"At once, Highness."

Moira led the way through the courtyard toward a wide archway. The doors were already open for them.

"Nice summer house you've got here," Blair murmured. "*Lord* Larkin."

He shot her a grin. "'Tisn't much, but it's home. In truth, my own family home isn't far from here. My father would be acting as ruler until Moira is crowned."

"If it's meant," Moira said over her shoulder.

"If it's meant," he agreed.

Torches were being lit in the great hall, so Blair assumed word of the return was already spreading. In the floor, fashioned of some sort of tile, the two symbols from the flag here inlaid so that the claddaugh seemed to float over the dragon's head.

They flew again in the glass dome curved into the high ceiling.

She had the impression of heavy furnishings, of colorful tapestries, caught the scent of roses as they started up a curve of stairs.

"The castle has stood more than twelve hundred years," Larkin told her. "Built here, at the order of the gods, on this rise known as Rioga. Royal. All who have ruled Geall since have ruled from here."

Blair glanced back at Glenna. "Makes the White House look like a hovel."

Blair wouldn't have called the room they entered any sort of parlor. It was huge and high-ceilinged, backed by a hearth tall and wide enough for five men to stand in. The fire already roared inside, and over it was a mantel of lapis blue marble.

Overhead, a mural depicted what she assumed were scenes of Geallian history.

There were several long, low seats with jewel-toned fabrics. Chairs with high, ornate backs stood at a long table where servants were already placing tankards and goblets, bowls of apples and pears, plates of cheese and bread.

Paintings and tapestries covered the walls while patterned rugs spread over the floor. Candles flamed in chandeliers, in tall stands, in silver candleabras.

One of the servants, a curvy one with a long spill of gold hair curtseyed in front of Moira. "My lady, we thank the gods for your return. And yours, my lord."

There was a glint in her eye when she looked at Larkin that had Blair's eyebrows raising.

"Isleen. I'm happy to see you." Moira took both her hands. "Your mother is well?"

"She is, my lady. Already weeping with joy."

"Will you tell her I'll see her soon? And we need chambers prepared for our guests." Moira took her aside to explain what she wanted.

Larkin was already heading for the table, and the food. He broke off a hunk of bread, hacked off a wide chunk of cheese, then mashed them together. "Ah, this tastes like home," he said with his mouth full. "Here now, Blair, have some of this."

Before she could object, he was stuffing some in her mouth. "Good," she managed.

"Good? Why it's brilliant as starshine. And what's this?" He lifted a tankard. "Wine, it is? Glenna, you'll have some, won't you?"

"Boy, won't I."

"Little changes," came a voice from the wide doorway. The man who stood there, tall, well built, his dark hair liberally threaded with gray, stared at Larkin. "Surrounded by food and pretty women."

"Da."

They met halfway across the room, and with bear hugs. Blair could see the man's face, the emotion that held it. Then she could see Larkin in the eyes of tawny gold.

The man caught Larkin's face in his big hands, gave his son a hard kiss on the mouth. "I didn't wake your mother. I wanted to be sure before I lifted her hopes."

"I'll go to her as soon as I can. You're well. You look well. A bit tired."

"Sleep hasn't come easy these past weeks. You're injured."

"It's not to worry. I promise."

"No, it's not to worry. You're home." He turned, and he smiled—and again, Blair saw Larkin in him.

"Moira."

"Sir." Then her breath hitched and she was running to him. Her arms clamped around his neck as he lifted her off the ground.

"I'm sorry, I'm sorry I took him from you. I'm sorry I worried you so."

"You're back now, aren't you? Safe and whole. And you bring guests." He set Moira back on her feet. "You're welcome here."

"This is Larkin's father, and the brother of my mother. Prince Riddock. Sir, I would present my friends to you, the best I've ever known."

As Moira introduced them, Larkin stood behind his father's back, signalling the others that they should bow or curtsey. Blair went with the bow, feeling foolish enough.

"There's so much to tell you," Moira began. "If we could sit. Larkin, the doors please? We should be private."

Riddock listened, interrupting occasionally to ask Moira to repeat or expand. Now and then he directed a question to his son, or to one of the others.

Blair could almost see the weight of the words press down on his shoulders, and the grim determination with which he bore it.

"There have been other attacks, at least six, since—" Riddock hesitated briefly. "Since you left us. I did what I could to heed what you wrote to me, Moira, to warn the people to stay in their homes after sunset, to not welcome strangers in the dark. But habits and traditions die hard. As did those who followed them these weeks."

Riddock studied Cian across the long table. "You say we must trust this one, though he is one of them. A demon inside a man."

"Trust is a large word." Idly, Cian peeled an apple. "Tolerate might be smaller, and more easily swallowed."

"He fought with us," Larkin began. "Bled with us."

"He is my brother. If he isn't to be trusted," Hoyt said flatly, "neither am I."

"Nor any of us," Glenna finished.

"You've banded together these weeks. This is to be understood." Riddock took a small sip of his wine as his gaze remained watchful on Cian. "But to believe a demon could and would stand against his own kind, to—tolerate—such a thing, is more than a swallow."

Cian only continued to peel his apple, even as Hoyt started to his feet.

"Uncle." Moira laid a hand over Riddock's. "I would be dead if not for him. But beyond that, he stood with us within the Dance of the Gods, traveled here by their hands. Chosen by them. Will you question their will?"

"Every thinking man questions, but I will abide by the will of the gods. Others may find it more difficult."

"The people of Geall will follow your orders, sir, and your lead."

"Mine?" He turned to her. "The sword waits for you, Moira, as does the crown."

"They will wait awhile longer. I've only just come home, and there's much to be done. Much more important matters than ceremony."

"Ceremony? You speak of the will of the gods one moment, and dismiss it the next?"

"Not dismiss. Only ask that it waits. You have the trust and the confidence of the people. I'm untried. I don't feel ready, not in my heart or in mind." Her eyes were grave as they searched her uncle's face. "Awhile longer, please. I may not be the one to lift the sword, but if I am, I need to know I'm ready to carry it. Geall needs and deserves a ruler of strength and confidence. I won't give it less."

"We'll talk further on it. Now you're weary. You must all be weary, and a mother waits to see her son." Riddock got to his feet. "We'll speak more in the morning, and we'll do all that needs to be done in the coming days. Larkin."

He rose at his father's bidding. "I wish you good night," Larkin said to the others. "And soft dreams on your first night in Geall."

He looked briefly at Blair, then followed his father from the room.

"Your uncle's an imposing man," Blair commented.

"And a good one. With him we'll raise an army that will

send Lilith back to hell. If you're ready, I'll show you to your chambers."

It was a little hard to settle down and sleep, Blair decided, when she was spending the night in a castle. And in a room that was suited to royalty.

Before they'd arrived, she'd been expecting something a little more Dark Ages, she supposed. Tough stone fortress on a windy hill. Smoky torches, mud, animal droppings.

Instead she got something closer to Cinderella's castle.

Instead of a cramped room, something like a barracks with rushes—whatever they were, exactly—on the floor and a lumpy cot, she had a spacious chamber with white-washed walls. The bed was big, soft and draped in a blue velvet canopy. The thick rug had images of peacocks worked into its soft wool.

A check out the windows showed her she looked down on a garden with a pretty spurting fountain. The window seat was padded with more velvet.

There was a small writing desk. Pretty, she thought, not that she'd be making much use of the crystal inkwell or the quill.

The fire was simmering, and its surround was blue-veined white marble.

It was all so fine she could nearly overlook the lack of modern plumbing. The closest the place came to it was the chamber pot tucked behind a painted screen.

She had a feeling she'd be making use of the great out-doors in that area quite a bit.

She stripped down to her underwear and used the basin of water provided to clean the scratches on her leg before dabbing on some of the balm Glenna had given her.

She wondered how the others were doing. She wished it were morning so *she* could be doing.

When the door opened, she picked up the dagger she'd

set beside the basin. Then put it down again when Larkin stepped in.

"Didn't hear you knock."

"I didn't. I thought you might be sleeping." He closed the door quietly behind him, took a quick scan of the room. "Does this suit you then?"

"The room? It's rock star. Feel a little weird, that's all. Like I walked into a book."

"I understand that, as I felt the same not long ago. Your wounds, do they trouble you?"

"They're nothing. Yours?"

"My mother fussed over them. That made her happy, as did weeping all over me. She's anxious to meet you, all of you."

"I guess." Awkward, Blair thought. Why was it all so awkward? "I, ah, it never really computed before. You being royalty."

"Oh well, that's not much to do with me, really. It's more ceremonial than anything. Honorary, you could say." He cocked his head as he moved toward her. "Did you think I wouldn't come to you tonight?"

"I don't know what I thought. It's all pretty confusing."

"Confused, are you?" A smile flirted around his mouth. "I don't mind that. I'll just confuse you a bit more, seduce you."

He traced his finger along the edge of her tank, just teasing the skin.

"You spend a lot of time on seductions? Say, working that on the blonde with the breasts? What was her name? Isleen."

"Flirtation, all in good fun, never seduction. It's not proper or fair to take advantage of one who serves you." He leaned to her, brushed his lips over her shoulder, nudged the strap down. "And while I might have dallied in the past, you weren't here. For it's the God's truth there's not another woman in Geall to compare to you."

He brought his lips to hers, just to nibble. "Blair Murphy," he murmured. "Warrior and beauty."

He played his hands down her back, deepening the kiss just a little. Then just a little more. And when his lips cruised over her face, along her throat, he all but crooned to her in Gaelic.

The sound of it, the feel of him nearly had her eyes rolling back in her head.

"I keep thinking this is a mistake. But it feels so damn good."

"Not a mistake." He caught her chin with his teeth while his thumbs slid up, circled her nipples. "Not at all."

Part of the journey, she told herself as she melted into him. They'd take something good, something strong for themselves along the way.

So she met his lips with hers now, sank herself into him, the warm, solid flesh. There was sweetness in those easy strokes of his hands, and a shivering thrill whenever they found her secrets.

When he lifted her into his arms, she didn't feel like a warrior. She felt conquered.

"I want you." She pressed her face into the curve of his throat as he lay her on the bed. And just breathed him in. "How can I want you so much?"

"It's meant." He lifted her hand, kissed the cup of her palm. "Ssh," he said before she could speak. "Just feel. For tonight, let's both of us just feel."

She could be so soft, he thought, so pliant, so giving. In surrender she made him feel like a king. Those eyes, the drowning blue, watched him as they moved together. They blurred with pleasure as he touched her, tasted her. Those hands, so firm on the hilt of a sword, trembled a little when she drew his shirt aside to find him.

Her lips pressed against his chest, against the heart that was already lost to her.

They took each other slowly, quietly, while the firelight shimmered over their bodies. There were murmurs and sighs instead of words, and a long, lazy climb instead of the frantic race.

When he slipped inside her, he watched her face, watched her as they moved together. As everything in him gathered for that final leap, he watched her still.

And at the end of it, he thought he'd simply fallen into her eyes.

Chapter 13

The guy was a snuggler. He just curved in, body to body, with an arm hooked around her waist—the way she imagined a kid might hold on to a teddy bear.

Blair just wasn't used to having someone hang on to her at night, and couldn't decide if she liked it or not. On one hand, it was sort of sweet and sexy to wake up with him wrapped all over her. Everything was all warm and soft and cozy.

On the other, if she had to move fast, get to a stake or a sword, he was dead weight.

Maybe she should practice breaking loose, rolling out, reaching the closest weapon. And maybe she should relax. It wasn't as if this was a permanent situation.

It was just . . . convenient.

And that was a stupid attitude sunk in bullshit, she admitted. If she couldn't be honest inside her own head, her own heart, then where?

They were more than a convenience to each other, more

than compatriots. More, she was afraid, than lovers. At
least on her side.

Still, in the light of day she had to be realistic. Whatever
it was they were to each other, it couldn't go anywhere.
Not beyond this. Cian had spoken the pure truth in Ireland,
outside of the Dance. The problems they faced were a lot
bigger and more important than one person or their personal needs and wishes. And so their personal needs had to
be, by definition, temporary.

After Samhain it would be over. She had to believe
they'd win, that was essential, but after the victory dance,
the backslapping and champagne toasts there would be
hard facts to face.

Larkin—*Lord* Larkin—was a man of Geall. Once this
was done and she'd completed the mission, Geall would be
for her, in a very real sense, a fairy tale again. Sure, maybe
she could hang around for a few days, have that picnic he'd
talked about. Bask a little. But in the end, she'd have to go.

She had a birthright, she had a duty, she thought as she
touched her fingers to Morrigan's cross. Turning her back
on it wasn't an option.

Love, if that's what she was feeling, wasn't enough to
win the day. Who knew better?

He was more than she'd ever expected to have, even in
the short term, so she couldn't and wouldn't complain
about her luck, or her destiny, or the cold will of gods. He
accepted her, cared for her, desired her. He had courage, a
bone-deep loyalty, and a sense of fun.

She'd never been with a man who possessed all that,
and who still looked at her as if she were special.

She thought maybe—it wasn't impossible—he loved her.

For her, Larkin was a kind of personal miracle. He
would never walk away from her without a backward
glance. He would never shove her aside simply because of
what she was. So when they parted, there could be no regrets.

If things were different they might have been able to make a go of it. At least give it a good, solid try. But things weren't different.

Or, more accurately, things were too different.

So they'd have a few weeks. They'd have the journey. And they'd both take something memorable away from it.

She kissed him, a soft and warm press of lips. Then she poked him.

"Wake up."

His hand slid down her back to rub lazily over her ass.

"Not that way."

"'S the best way. Feel how firm you are, smooth and firm. I dreamed I was making love with you in an orchard in the high days of summer. For you always smell of tart, green apples. Makes me want to take a good bite of you."

"Eat enough green apples, you get a bellyache."

"My belly's iron." His fingers trailed up and down the back of her thigh. "In the dream there was no one but us two, and the trees ladened with fruit under a sky painted the purest of blues."

His voice was all sleepy and slurry, she thought. Sexy. "Like paradise? Adam and Eve? An apple got them in big, bad trouble, if memory serves."

He only smiled. He'd yet to open his eyes. "You look on the dark side of things, but I don't mind that. In the dream, I gave you such pleasure you wept from the joy of it."

She snorted. "Yeah. In your dreams."

"And sobbed my name, again and again. Begging me to take you. 'Use this body,' you pleaded, 'take it with your strong hands, with your skilled mouth. Pierce it with your mighty—'"

"Okay, you're making that up."

He opened one eye, and there was such laughter in it her belly quivered in response. "Well, yes, but I'm enjoying it. And see there, you're smiling. That's what I wanted to see when I opened my eyes. Blair's smile."

Tenderness swamped her. "You're such a goof," she murmured, and rubbed her hand over his cheek.

"The first part of the dream was true. We should look for the orchard one day." He closed his eyes again, started to snuggle in.

"Hold on there. Shut-eye's over. We have to get started."

"In a hurry, are you? Well, all right then."

He rolled onto her. "I didn't mean—" And slipped into her.

The pleasure was so deep, so easy, that her breath caught even as she laughed. "I should've known your mighty would be up and ready."

"And always at your service."

After a later start than she'd planned, she pulled on clothes. "We need to talk about some basics."

"We'll break our fast in the little dining hall."

"I've never known you to have a fast to break. And I wasn't talking about food."

"Oh?" He looked mildly interested as he belted his tunic. "What else then?"

"To get really basic, bathroom facilities. Elimination, hygiene. The chamber pot deal's okay for emergencies, but I'm going to have a problem with it on a regular basis."

"Ah." Brows knit, he scratched his head over it. "There are toilets of sorts in the family wing, and latrines for the castle guards. But they're not what you'd be used to."

"I'll make do. Bathing?"

"The shower." He said it wistfully. "I miss it already. I can have a tub brought up, and water heated. Or there's the river."

"Okay, that's a start." She didn't need plush, Blair thought. She just needed, well, reasonable. "Now we have to talk about training."

"Let's talk about it over food." He took her arm, pulling

her from the room so she wouldn't argue while his stomach was rumbling.

There were spiced apples Larkin seemed particularly fond of, and chunks of potatoes fried in, she assumed, the fat of the thick slices of ham that accompanied them. The tea was black as pitch, and nearly had the same kick as coffee.

"I miss the Coke as well," he commented.

"Going to have to suck that one up."

While the room was smaller than the parlor had been, it was still large enough to fit the big oak table, a couple of enormous servers, and chests she imagined held linens and dishware.

"Does a drawbridge work like a door?" she wondered. "To keep them out," she explained when Larkin gave her a questioning smile. "Do they need an invitation to come into the castle compound? We'd better deal with that, cover our ass. Hoyt and Glenna should be able to come up with something."

"We have a few days."

"If Lilith sticks to the schedule. Either way, we've got our work cut out for us. Organizing, getting civilians transported from the battle area. Hoyt and Glenna might want to try that vamp-free-zone spell, but I have to say, I don't see it working. We're not talking about one house, or even a small settlement."

She shook her head as she ate. "Too much area, too many variables. And, most likely, a waste of their time and energies."

"That may be. Moving people to safety is more important. My father and I spoke of it last night, before I came to you. Even now runners are out so the word spreads."

"Good. We're going to need to put most of our focus on training the troops. You've got guards and—knights, maybe?"

"Aye."

"They have your basic combat skills, but this is a different matter. Then your general population needs to be prepared to defend themselves. We need to get to work on setting those traps. And I'm going to want a firsthand look at the battleground itself."

Her mind clicked off its list while she plowed through breakfast. "We're going to need to set up multiple training areas—military and civilian. Then there's weapons, supplies, transportation. We probably need an area where Hoyt and Glenna can work."

"It will all be seen to."

Something in his tone, the calmness of it, reminded her this was his ground now. He knew it, and its people. She didn't.

"I don't know the pecking order. The chain of command," she said. "Who's in charge of what."

He poured them both more tea. For a moment he thought how nice it was—even if the talk was of war—to sit, just the two of them, over the morning meal.

"Until the sword is drawn from the stone, my father rules as the head of the first family of Geall. He isn't king. He will not be king, but Moira, I think, understands that the men . . . the military as you call it, trust him. They'll follow the ruler, the one whose hand lifts the sword, but . . ."

"This is giving them time. It's letting them follow orders, and absorb the idea of this war, from a man who's been proven to them. I get it. Moira's smart to wait a little longer to take command."

"She is, yes. She's also afraid."

"That she won't be the one to lift the sword?"

He shook his head. "That she will. That she'll be the queen who must order her people to war. To shed their blood, cause their deaths. It haunts her."

"It's Lilith who sheds their blood, causes their death."

"And it will be Moira who tells them to fight. The farmers and the shopkeepers, the tinkers and the cooks. For generations Geall has been ruled in peace. She'll be the first to change that. It weighs on her."

"It should. It should never be easy to send a world to war. Larkin, what if it's not her? What if she's not the one, through destiny, or just because she doesn't have it in her to pull that sword out of stone?"

"She was the queen's only child. There's no other in her line."

"So lines can shift. There's you."

"Bite your tongue." When she didn't smile, he sighed. "There would be me. My brother, my sister. My sister's children. The oldest is but four. My brother, he's hardly more than a boy himself, and it's the land that calls to him. My sister wants nothing more than to tend her babies and her home. They could never do this thing. I can't believe the gods would put this into their hands."

"But yours?"

He met her eyes. "I've never wanted it, to rule. War or peace."

"People would follow you. They know you, and they trust you."

"That may be. And if it comes to it, what choice would I have? But the crown isn't my wish, Blair." Nor was it his destiny, of that he was sure. He reached over, took her hand. "You must know what I wish."

"Wishes, dreams. We don't always get what we ask for. So we have to take what there is."

"And what's in your heart? In mine? I want—"

"I'm sorry." Moira stopped at the doorway. "I'm sorry to disturb you, but my uncle has spoken to the guards, and to the inner circle of knights. You're to come to the great hall."

"Then we'd better get started," Blair said.

She felt under-dressed in jeans and a black sweater. For the first time since Blair had met her, Moira wore a dress. A gown? Whatever the term it was simple and elegant, in a kind of russet tone that fell straight down her body from a high, gathered waist.

Her silver cross hung between her breasts, and a thin circlet of gold sat on her head.

Even Glenna seemed polished up, but then again, her favorite witch had a way of giving a casual shirt and pants an air of style and grace.

The cavernous room was heated by fires on either side and fronted by a wide platform, up two steps where a deep red carpet ran. On it stood a throne. An actual throne, Blair mused, in regal red and gold.

Riddock sat on it now, with Moira standing at his side.

To the other side sat a woman. Her blond hair was bound back in what Blair thought was called a snood. A younger woman, obviously pregnant, sat beside her. Two men stood at their backs.

The first family of Geall, Blair decided. Larkin's family.

And at a glance from his father, he touched Blair's arm, murmured: "It'll be fine." Then he left her to go up the steps and stand between his parents.

"Please." Riddock gestured. "Take your ease." He waited until they'd taken chairs at the base of the platform. "Moira and I have talked at length. At her request, I have spoken to the guards and many of the knights to tell them of the threat, and the coming war. It is Moira's wish that you, and the other who came with you, be given the authority of command. To recruit, to train, to forge our army."

He paused, studied them. "You are not Geallian."

"Sir," Larkin objected. "They are proven."

"This war is brought to our soil, and it will be paid in our blood. I ask why those from outside should lead our people."

"May I speak?" Hoyt got to his feet, waited until Riddock nodded. "Morrigan herself has sent us here, just as she sent two Geallians to Ireland, to us, so that we would gather into the first circle. We who have come here have left our worlds and our families, and have pledged our lives to fight this pestilence that comes to Geall."

"This pestilence murdered our queen, my sister, before ever you came." Riddock gestured toward them. "You are two women, a demon, and a man of magic. And you are strangers to me. I have seasoned men, who are proven to me. Men whose names I know, whose families I know. Men who know Geall and are unquestioned in loyalty. Men who I know will lead our people strong into battle."

"Where they'll be slaughtered like lambs." Though Riddock's stare at the interruption was frigid, Blair pushed to her feet. "Sorry, but that's the way it is. We can dance around it, play protocol, waste time, but the fact is your seasoned warriors don't know squat about fighting vampires."

When Hoyt laid a hand on Blair's arm, she shook it off. Testily. "And I didn't come here to be shuffled aside because I wasn't born here, or because I'm a woman. And I didn't come here to fight for Geall. I came here to fight for it all."

"Well said," Glenna murmured. "And ditto. My husband is accustomed to matters of court and princes. We're not. So you'll have to forgive us mere women. Mere women of power."

She held out a hand, and a ball of fire, then flicked the ball into the hearth on the side of the room. Testily.

"Mere women who have fought and bled, and watched friends die. And the demon you spoke of is my family. He's also fought and bled and watched a friend die."

"Warriors you may be," Riddock acknowledged with what could only be termed a regal nod. "But to lead takes more than magic and courage."

"It takes experience, a cool head. And cold blood."

Riddock glanced back to Blair with a slight lift of eyebrows. "These, aye, and the trust of the people you would lead."

"They have mine," Larkin said. "They have Moira's. Earned every hour of every day these past weeks. Sir, have I not earned yours?"

"You have." He said nothing for a moment, then again gestured to Hoyt, Glenna and Blair. "I would ask that you instruct, and that you take your commands from Lord Larkin and the Princess Moira."

"We can start with that," Blair decided. "Will you fight?" she asked Riddock.

Now the look in his eye had a kinship with a wolf. "To the last breath."

"Then you're going to need instruction, too, or that last breath's going to come sooner than you think."

Larkin cast his eyes heavenward, but laid a hand on his father's shoulder and spoke lightly. "Blair has a warrior's spirit."

"And an unruly tongue. The gaming area then," Riddock decided. "For our first instructions."

"Your father doesn't like me."

"That's not so." Larkin gave Blair a friendly elbow nudge. "He's merely working his way around to understanding you, and all of this."

"Uh-huh." She looked at Glenna as they walked outside. "Do you think we should tell Riddock how our people felt about kings?"

"I think we could let that one alone. But running up against what we did in there makes me realize it's not going to be a snap convincing a bunch of macho Geallian men that women should teach them how to fight a war."

"I've got some thoughts on that. And I think you should work with the women anyway."

"Excuse me?"

"Don't get a wedgie. You have more diplomacy and patience than I do." Probably, Blair thought, anyone did. "And the women will probably relate better to you. They have to be trained, too, Glenna. To defend themselves, their families. To fight. Someone has to do it. And someone has to know which ones should stay home, and which ones should go."

"Oh God."

"We're going to have the same deal with men. The ones who don't measure up have to be put to other use. Treating the injured, protecting the kids, the elderly, supplying food, weapons."

"And what do you suggest I do, Cian do," Hoyt asked, "while the two of you are so busy?"

"His nose is out of joint because we mouthed off to Riddock," Glenna murmured.

"My nose is fine and well, thanks all the same." Hoyt spoke with unwavering dignity. "He needed to be told, though there could have been considerably more tact. If we offended him, it only takes more time and effort to repair the damage."

"He's a reasonable man," Larkin insisted. "He wouldn't let a few breaches of protocol interfere with what needs doing." Frustrated himself, Larkin raked a hand through his hair. "He hasn't been in a position to rule before this. The queen was crowned very young, and he's had only the position as an adviser now and then."

He'd have to be a fast learner, Blair thought.

Men were already gathered in what Blair saw was an area they held their jousts, their tournaments and games. There was a long rope where colored hoops hung. Scoreboard, she decided. And the royal box, the rougher seats for the masses. Paddocks for horses, tents where competitors readied themselves for whatever sport was on the ticket.

"You ever see that movie, *Knight's Tale*?" Blair muttered.

"We will, we will rock you," Glenna responded and made Blair grin.

"Sure helps having you here. Coming up on show time. Pick out one you figure you can take."

"What? Why? What?"

"Both of you," Blair said, adding Hoyt. "Just in case."

Larkin stepped up to the lines of men. "My father has told you what it is we face, and what is coming. We have until Samhain to prepare, and on that day we must be in the Valley of Silence to do battle. We must win. To win you must know how to fight and how to kill these things that are not human. They are not men, and cannot be killed as men can be killed."

Hanging back as Larkin spoke, Blair studied the men. Most of them looked fit and able. She spotted Tynan, the guard both Larkin and Moira had greeted on arrival. He, Blair decided, looked not only fit and able. He looked ready.

"I have fought them," Larkin continued, "as the princess Moira has fought them. As those who came with us from outside this world have fought them. We will teach you what you need to know."

"We know how to fight." A man who stood beside Tynan called out. "What can you teach me I haven't taught you on this very field?"

"This won't be a game." Blair stepped forward. This one was a big bruiser, she noted. Looked cocky with it. Good strong shoulders, tough built, hard attitude.

Perfect.

"You won't get the consolation prize and a pat on the back if you come in second in this. You'll be dead."

His face didn't sneer at her, but his tone did. "Women don't instruct men on the art of combat. They tend the fires, and keep the bed warm."

He got some appreciative male laughter and a look of pity from Larkin.

"Niall," he said, with cheer, "you've stepped full into the bog with that one. These women are warriors."

"I see no warriors here." With his hands on his hips, Niall elbowed toward the front of the line. "But two women dressed as men, and a sorcerer who stands with them. Or behind them."

"I'll go first," Blair murmured to Glenna. "I'll take you on," she told Niall. "Here and now. Your choice of weapons."

He snorted. "Do you expect me to spar with a girl?"

"Choose your weapon," Riddock ordered.

"Sir. At your command." He was snickering as he strode away.

Immediately the wagers began.

"Hey, now!" Larkin gave Blair a quick pat on the shoulder, moved into the men. "I'll have some of that."

Niall strode back with two thick fencing poles. Blair studied the way he held them, the way he moved. Full swagger now.

"This will be quick," he assured Blair.

"Yeah, it will. It's a good choice of weapon," she called out over the voices still calling out odds and wagers. "Wood kills a vampire, if you have the strength and the aim to get it through the heart. You look strong enough." She eyed Niall up and down. "How's your aim?"

He grinned, wide. "I've not yet had a woman complain of it."

"Well, let's see what you got, big guy." She gripped the pole lengthwise, nodded. "Ready?"

"I'll give you the first three hits, out of fairness."

"Fine."

She took him down in two, ramming the end of the pole in his gut, then sweeping down to crack it hard against his legs. Ignoring the laughter and whoops, she stood over him, the pole pressed to his heart.

"Now if you were a vampire, I'd put this right through you till it came out the other side. Then you'd be dust." She stepped back. "I think you should hold your bets, guys. That was just practice." She cocked her head at Niall. "Ready now?"

He got to his feet, and she saw the shock and embarrassment at being knocked down by a woman had lit a fire in him. He came in hard, the force of his pole against hers shooting up her arms. She leaped up and over when he aimed for her legs, then cracked her stick against his chest.

He fought well, she decided, and with a bullish strength—but he lacked creativity.

She used her pole like a vault, planting it in the ground, swinging up over her opponent. When she landed, she spun a kick into the small of his back, caught her pole. And tripped him with it.

This time she held it to his throat as he panted for breath.

"Three out of five?" she suggested.

He let out a roar, knocking at the pole. She let his forward motion carry her back, then pumped up with her feet to flip him over her. And flat onto his back again.

His eyes were still dazed as she pressed the pole to his throat again. The last fall had knocked the wind out of him, and stolen the color from his cheeks.

"I can do this all day, and you'll end up on your ass every time."

She got to her feet, and now planted her pole beside him to lean negligently against it. "You're strong, but so am I. Plus, you're heavy in the feet—and you weren't thinking on them. Just because you're bigger doesn't mean you'll win, and it sure as hell doesn't mean you'll live. I'd say you got close to a hundred pounds on me, but I knocked you flat three times."

"The first didn't count." Niall sat up, rubbed his sore head. "But I'll give you the two."

When he grinned at her, Blair knew she'd won.

"Larkin, come take this pole," Niall called out. "I'll fight you for her, for this one's a woman for certain."

Blair held out a hand. "He'd beat you, too. I helped train him."

"Then you'll teach me. And them?" He jerked his chin toward Hoyt and Glenna. "Can they fight like you?"

"I'm the best, but they're pretty damn good."

She turned to the group of men, waited while money

finished changing hands. Tynan, she noted, was one of the few besides Larkin that collected any.

"Anyone else need a demonstration?"

"Wouldn't mind one from the redhead," someone called out, and had more laughter rolling.

Glenna fluttered her lashes, added a coy smile. Then drew her dagger from its sheath and shot a line of fire from it.

Men scrambled back, en masse.

"My husband's is bigger," she said sweetly.

"Aye." Hoyt swept forward. "Perhaps one of you would like a demonstration from me instead of my lovely wife. Sword? Lance?" He turned up his palms, let the fire dance above them. "Bare hands? For I don't stand behind these women, but I'm proud and honored to stand with them."

"Down boy," Blair murmured. "Fire's a weapon against them. Powerful weapon, as is wood, if used right. Steel will hurt them, slow them down, but it won't kill them unless you cut off the head. They'll just keep coming until they rip out your throat."

She tossed her fencing pole to Niall. "It won't be quick and clean like this little bout," she told them. "It will be bloody, and vicious, and cruel beyond the telling of it. Many of them, maybe most, will be stronger and faster than you. But you'll stop them. Because if you don't, they won't just kill you, the soldiers who meet them in combat. They'll kill your children, your mothers. Those they don't kill they'll change, they'll turn into what they are, or enslave them for food, for sport. So you'll stop them, because there's no choice."

She paused because now there was silence, now every eye there was on her. "We're going to show you how."

Chapter 14

Blair debated between the river and the tub. The river was very likely freezing, and that would be a bitch. But she just couldn't resign herself to having some servant haul up steaming buckets of water, to pour them into what essentially would be a bigger bucket. Then after she'd bathed, they'd have to repeat the whole deal in reverse.

It was just too weird.

Still, after several hours working with a bunch of men, she needed soap and water.

Was that too much to ask?

"You did very well." Moira fell into step beside her. "I know this must be frustrating for you, like starting over. And with men who feel, in some ways, they already know as much—if not more—than you. But you did very well. You've made a fine start."

"Most of those guys are in good to excellent shape, and that's a plus. But the bulk of them still think it's a game, for the most part. Just don't believe. That's a big strike in the minus column."

"Because they haven't seen. They know of my mother, but many still believe—need to believe—it was some sort of wild dog. It might be if I hadn't seen myself what killed her, I could refuse to believe it."

"It's easier to refuse. Refusing is one of the reasons Jeremy's dead now."

"Aye. That's why I think people need to see, need to believe. We need to hunt down the ones that killed the queen, the ones that have killed others since that night. We need to bring at least one of them back here."

"You want to take one alive?"

"I do." Moira remembered how Cian had once pulled a vampire into the training room, then stood back so the rest of them would have to fight it. And understand it. "It will make a point."

"Not impossible to refuse what's in front of your face, but harder." Blair thought it through quickly. "Okay. I'll go out tonight."

"Not alone. Don't, don't," Moira said wearily when Blair started to argue. "You're used to hunting alone, capable of hunting alone. But you don't know the land here. They will by now. I'll go with you."

"You've got a point, and a strong one. But no, you're not the one for this hunt. I'm not saying you're not capable either. But you're not the best when it comes to close-in fighting. It'll have to be Larkin, and I'll need Cian."

In a gesture of annoyance, Moira tugged a blossom from a bush. "Now you have the strong point. I feel I've done nothing but matters of state since I've come home."

"You've got my sympathy. But I think that kind of thing has to be important, too. Statesmen—women—people— they raise armies. You've already taken steps to move people out of what's going to be a war zone. That's saving lives, Moira."

"I know it. I do. But . . ."

"Who's going to stir up the general population, fire them up into putting their lives on the line? We'll train them, Moira. But you've got to get them to us."

"You're right, I know."

"I'll get you a vampire—two if I can manage it. You get me people I can teach to kill one. But right now, I've got to wash up. A vamp could smell me a half a mile away."

"I'll have a bath readied for you, in your chambers."

"I was thinking I'd just use the river."

"Are you mad?" Finally, Moira's face relaxed into a smile. "The river's freezing this time of year."

It was never comfortable for Moira to speak with Cian. Not just because of what he was, as she'd reconciled herself to that. She thought of it, when she thought of him, as a condition; a kind of disease.

At their first meeting he had saved her life, and since had proven himself again and again.

His kind had murdered her mother, and yet he had fought beside her, had risked his life—or more accurately his existence—in doing so.

No, she couldn't hold what he was against him.

Still there was something inside her, something she couldn't quite see clearly, or study, or understand. Whatever it was made her uneasy, even nervy around him.

He knew it, or sensed it, she was sure. For he was so much cooler to her than the others. It was so rare that he would spare her a smile, or an easy word.

After the attack on their way to Geall, he'd swooped her up off the ground. His arms were the arms of a man. Flesh and blood, strong and real.

"Hold on," he'd said. And that was all.

She'd ridden with him to the castle, and his body had been that of a man. Lean and hard. And her heart had been raging for so many reasons, she'd been afraid to touch him.

What had he said to her then, in that sharp, impatient voice of his?

Oh yes: Get a grip on me before you fall on your ass again. I haven't bitten you yet, have I?

It had made her embarrassed and ashamed, and grateful he couldn't see the color flame into her cheeks.

Likely he'd have had something cutting to say about her virginal blushes as well.

Now she had to go to him, to ask him for help. It wasn't something she would pass off to Blair, or Larkin, certainly not to a servant. It was her duty to face him, to speak the words, ask the boon.

She would ask him to leave the castle, the comfort and safety of it, and go out into a strange land to hunt one of his own.

And he would do it, she knew, already she knew he would do it. Not for her—the request of a princess, the favor of a friend. He would do it for the others. For the whole of it.

She went alone. The women who attended her wouldn't approve, of course, and would consider the idea of their princess alone in a man's bedchamber unseemly, even shocking.

Such matters were no longer an issue for Moira. What would her ladies think if they knew she'd once fed him blood when he was wounded?

She imagined they would shriek and hide their faces— those who didn't swoon away. But they would have to look straight on at such things very soon. Or face much worse.

Her shoulders went tight as she stepped to the door of his chamber. But she knocked briskly, then stood to wait.

When he opened the door, the lights from the corridor washed over his face, and plunged the rest into shadow. She saw the faintest flicker of surprise come and go in his eyes as he studied her.

"Well, look at you. I barely recognized you. Your Highness."

It reminded her she was wearing a dress, and the gold mitre of her office. And remembering, she felt foolishly exposed.

"There were matters of state to attend to. I'm expected to attire myself appropriately."

"And fetchingly, too." He leaned lazily on the door. "Is my presence required?"

"Yes. No." *Why* did he forever make her clumsy? "May I come in? I would speak with you."

"By all means."

She had to brush against him to step inside. The room was like midnight, she thought. Not a single candle lit, nor the fire, and the drapes were pulled tight at the windows.

"The sun's gone down."

"Yes, I know."

"Would you mind if we had some light?" She picked up the tinderbox, fumbling a bit. "I can't see so well as you in the dark." The quick flare of light did quite a bit to calm her jumping stomach. "There's a chill," she continued, lighting more candles. "Should I light the fire for you?"

"Suit yourself."

He said nothing while she knelt in front of the hearth, set the turf. But she knew he watched her, and his watching made her hands feel cold and stiff.

"Are you comfortable here?" she began. "The room isn't so large or grand as you're used to."

"And separate enough from the general population so they can be comfortable."

Stunned, she turned, kneeling still while the turf caught flame at her back. She didn't flush. Instead her cheeks went very pale. "Oh, but no, I never meant . . ."

"It's no matter." He picked up a glass he'd obviously poured before she'd come in. And now he drank deliberately of the blood with his eyes on hers. "I imagine your people would be put off by some of my daily habits."

Distress hitched into her voice. "It was never a concern. The room, it faces north. I thought . . . I only thought there would be less direct sun, and you'd be more comfortable. I would never insult a guest—a friend. I wouldn't insult someone who welcomed me into their home when they have come to mine."

She got quickly to her feet. "I can have your things moved, right away. I—"

He held up a hand. "There's no need. And I apologize for assuming." It was rare for him to feel the discomfort of guilt, but he felt it now. "It's a considerate choice. I shouldn't have expected less."

"Why are we . . . I don't understand why we seem to be so often at odds."

"Don't you?" he murmured. "Well, that's likely for the best. So, to what do I owe the honor of your presence?"

"You make fun of me," she said quietly. "You're so hard when you speak to me."

She thought he sighed, just a little. "I'm in a mood. I don't rest well in unfamiliar places."

"I'm sorry. And I'm here to impose again. I've asked Blair to hunt the vampires now in Geall, to bring at least one of them back here. Alive."

"Contradiction in terms."

"I don't know how else to express it," she snapped. "My people will fight because it's asked of them. But I can't ask them to believe—can't make them believe—what seems impossible. So they need to be shown."

It would be a good queen, he thought, who didn't expect to be followed blindly. And see how she stood there now, he noted. So still, so serious, when he knew a war raged inside of her.

"You want me to go with her."

"I do—she does. I do. God, I am forever stumbling with you. She asked that you and Larkin go with her. She doesn't want me. She feels, and so do I, that I'm of more use gathering the forces, helping lay the traps she devised."

"Ruling."

"I don't rule yet."

"Your choice."

"Aye. For now. I'd be grateful if you would go with her and Larkin, if you can find a way to bring back a prisoner."

"I'd rather be doing than not. But there's the matter of knowing where to look."

"I have a map. I've already spoken with my uncle, and know where the attacks—the known attacks—took place. Larkin knows the land of Geall. You can have no better guide. And you know you can have no better companion, in leisure or in battle."

"I've no problem with the boy, or with a hunt."

"Then as soon as you're ready, if you'd come to the outer courtyard. I can have someone show you the way."

"I remember the way."

"Well. I'll go see to your mounts and provisions." She went to the door, but he was there before her—without seeming to have moved at all. She looked up into his face. "Thank you," she said and slipped quickly out.

Those eyes, he thought as he shut the door behind her. Those long gray eyes could kill a man.

It was lucky he was already dead.

But he could do nothing about the scent she'd left behind her, the scent of woodland glades and cool spring water. Not a bloody thing he could do about that.

"We'll be watching." Glenna laid a hand on Blair's leg when Blair mounted her horse. "If you get into trouble we'll know. We'll do what we can to help."

"Don't worry. I've got thirteen years of this under my belt."

Not in Geall, Glenna thought, but she stepped back. "Good hunting."

They rode through the gates, and turned south.

It was a good night for it, Blair thought. Clear and cool. It would be easier to track them by night when they were active than by day when they would have gone to nest somewhere. In any case, she wouldn't have Cian, which she considered an advantage, if they hunted by day.

She rode between the two men at an easy trot. "I didn't want to ask Moira," she began. "But her mother was the first attack reported."

"Aye, the queen was the first death we know of."

"And there were no other attacks that night? No one taken?"

"No." Larkin shook his head. "Again that we know of."

"Target-specific then," Blair mused. "They came for Moira's mother—we assume. We don't know how they got in."

"I've thought of it," Larkin admitted. "Before the queen's death, there would have been no reason to stop someone from coming in. A wagon of supplies, perhaps, or any reasonable bit of business. They would have been passed through."

"Plays." Blair nodded after a moment. "Come in shortly after sundown. Stay in a bolt hole until everyone settles in for the night. Lure the queen outside, kill her." She glanced at Larkin. "We don't have more specifics?"

"Moira won't speak of it, really. I'm not sure she remembers the details of it."

"Maybe it doesn't matter—for our purposes. So they kill the queen, then they stay. Maybe they can't get back through except at specific times. But they don't rampage," she pointed out. "A handful of deaths in all these weeks. That's pretty low profile for the breed."

"There will have been more," Cian commented. "Travelers, whores, those not as quickly missed as others. But they've been careful, and avoided what we're doing now. The hunt. I don't think they're only hiding from us."

"Who then?" Larkin glanced over and saw Blair was studying Cian thoughtfully.

"He means Lilith. You think they're trying to stay off her radar? Why?"

"Because it could be you're only half right in your theory.

Target-specific, yes," Cian agreed. "But I doubt the target was the queen. It's Moira who was chosen as a link in the first circle."

"Moira." There was alarm in Larkin's voice as he swiveled in the saddle to look back at the castle growing smaller with distance. "If they tried to kill her once—"

"They've tried to kill all of us, more than once," Cian pointed out. "Without success. She's as safe as she can be, where she is."

Blair outlined it in her mind. "You're thinking Lilith tried an end-run. Take one of us out before she was, essentially, one of us."

"It's a possibility, a strong one. Why waste the time and what must have been some effort to send a couple of assassins here? If you're going to buy in to the whole destiny business," Cian went on, "it's Moira and not Moira's mother who was the threat."

"They screwed up," Blair mused. "Took out the wrong target. So it may not be a matter of them not being able to get back, but not wanting to."

"Lilith isn't particularly tolerant of mistakes. Having a choice of being tortured and ended by her, or going to ground, snacking on the locals here, which would you do?"

"Door number two," Blair said. "And if you buy in to the whole destiny business, her first mistake was in turning you all those years ago. You're a more formidable enemy as a vampire than you might be as a man. No offense."

"None taken."

"Then you get Hoyt fired up, and start the whole Morrigan's Cross thing."

Thoughtfully, Blair fingered the two crosses she wore around her neck. "You've got Glenna connected to Hoyt— maybe, if you want the romantic—destined to find and love each other. And by doing so, exponentially increasing each other's power. You've got Larkin's connection to Moira, and due to it, his coming with her through the Dance and into Ireland."

"So makes a nice, tidy circle," Cian concluded. "Convoluted, but that's gods for you."

"She was meant to die. The queen." Larkin took a steadying breath. "Meant to die in Moira's place. If Moira comes to this herself, it will hurt her immeasurably."

"With her clever and questing mind, I'd be surprised if she wasn't already dealing with it. And dealing with it is what she'll do," Cian added. "What other choice is there?"

Larkin let it lie in his heart, on his head as they crossed a field.

"The next attack was here. I'm told the man who farms this land thought wolves had been at his sheep. It was his boy who found him next morning. My father came here himself that day, to see the body, and it was as the queen's had been."

Blair shifted in the saddle. "About two miles, due south of the castle. No place to hide around here. Just open fields. But a couple of experienced vamps could cover a couple of miles fairly quickly. They can go in and out of the castle grounds as they've had an invite, but . . ."

"Not a good place to nest," Cian agreed. "Easy pickings, certainly, but too much exposure. No, it would be caves, or deep forest."

"Why not a house or cabin?" Larkin suggested. "If they chose with any care, they could find one out of the way, where it's not as likely someone would come by."

"Possible," Cian told him. "But the trouble with a cottage, a building, is daylight attack. Your enemy has one more weapon against you—and only has to pull a covering from a window to win the day."

"All right then." Larkin gestured across the field. "The next two attacks reported were just east of here. There's forest, but the hunting's good. There are plenty who track deer and rabbit there and might disturb a vampire's daytime rest."

"You know that," Blair told him. "They may not have. They're strangers here. It's a good place to start."

They rode in silence for a time. She could see sheep or cattle lolling in the fields—more easy pickings if a vampire couldn't take down a human. There were flickers of light she assumed were candles or lanterns in cottages. She could smell the smoke—the rich tang of peat rather than seasoned wood.

She smelled grass and animal dung, a deeper, loamy scent from fields planted and waiting for the coming harvest.

She could smell the horses, and Larkin, and knew how to separate Cian's scent from others like him.

But when they came to the edge of a wood, she couldn't be sure.

"Horses have been through here, and not long ago."

She looked at Larkin with eyebrows raised. "Well, listen to Tonto here."

"Tracks." He slid off his horse to study the ground. "Not shoed. Gypsies likely, though I don't see signs from a wagon, and they travel that way. They're leading out, in any case."

"How many?"

"It would be two. Two horses, coming out of the woods here to cross the field."

"Can you follow them in?" she asked him. "See where they came from?"

"I can." He mounted. "If they're on horseback, they could cover considerable distance. It would take the gods' own luck for us to track them down in one night."

"We backtrack the riders here, see what we see. The other attacks were east, right? Straight through these woods, out the other side."

"Aye. Another three miles at most."

"This would be a good hub." She looked at Cian as she spoke. "If they have decent shelter in here, it's a good spot to nest during the day, spread out for food at night."

"Leaves are still thick this time of year," he agreed. "And there'd be small game as well if they needed to make do."

Larkin took the lead, following the trail until the trees thickened to block the light. He dismounted again, tracking now on foot. By signs, Blair assumed she couldn't see.

Then again, she'd done the majority of her hunting in urban forests and suburban trails. But Larkin moved with the confidence of a man who knew what he was doing, pausing only to crouch down now and then, studying the tracks more carefully.

"Wait," she said abruptly. "Just wait. You get that?" she asked Cian.

"Blood. It's not fresh. And death. Older yet."

"Better get back on your horse, Larkin," she told him. "I think we've got some of the gods' luck after all. We can track it from here."

"I can't smell a thing but the woods."

"You will," she murmured, and drew her sword from the sheath on her back as they walked the horses down the path.

The wagon was pulled into the trees, off the path, and sheltered by them. It was a kind of small caravan, Blair thought, covered in the back with its red paint faded and peeling.

And the smell of death seemed to soak it.

"Tinkers," Larkin told them. And she'd been right, he could smell the death now. "Gypsies who travel the roads selling whatever wares they might make. The wagon's harnessed for two horses."

"A good nest," Blair decided. "Mobile if you need it to be. And you could drive around at night, no one would pay any attention."

"You could take it right into the village," Larkin said grimly. "Drive it up to someone's cottage and ask for hospitality. In the normal course of things, you'd get it."

He thought of the children who might run outside to see if there would be toys for sale they could beg their parents to buy or trade for. And the thought sickened him even more than the stench.

He dismounted with the others, moved to the rear of the

wagon where the doors were tightly shut, and bolted from the outside. They drew weapons. Blair slid the bolt free, tested the door.

When it gave, she nodded to her companions, mentally counted to three, then yanked it open.

The fetid air came first, crawling into the throat, pouring into the eyes. She heard the hungry hum of flies and fought against the need to gag.

It leaped out at her, the thing with the face of a pretty young woman whose eyes were red and mad. The stink rolled off her, where it was matted in her dark hair, streaked over her homespun dress.

Blair pivoted aside so it landed in the brush on its hands and knees, snarling like the animal it had become.

It was Larkin who swung his sword and ended it.

"Oh God, sweet Jesus. She couldn't have been fourteen." He wanted to sit, just sit there on the ground while his belly heaved. "They changed her. How many others—"

"Unlikely more," Cian said, cutting him off. "Then they'd have to compete for food, worry about keeping it under control."

"She didn't come through with them," Larkin insisted. "She wasn't one of them before. She was Geallian."

"And young, pretty, female. Food isn't the only need."

Blair saw when the full impact of Cian's words hit Larkin. She saw not just by the shock but the sheer outrage on his face.

"Bastards. Bloody fucking bastards. She was hardly more than a child."

"And this surprises you because?"

He whirled on Cian, and would, Blair was sure, have vented some of that horror and outrage. Perhaps Cian was giving him a target for it. But there wasn't time for indulgences.

She simply stepped between them and shoved Larkin back a full three paces. "Close it down," she ordered him. "Just settle it down."

"How can I? How can you?"

"Because you can't bring her back, or the ones that are in there." She jerked a chin toward the wagon. "So we figure out how to use this to capture the ones who did it."

Burying her own revulsion, she pulled herself up into the wagon. Into a nightmare.

What must have been the girl's parents were shoved together under a kind of bunk on one side of the wagon. The man had probably died quickly, as had the younger boy whose body lay under the bunk on the opposite side.

But the woman, they'd have taken more time there. No point in tearing off her clothes if you didn't intend to play with her first. Her hands were still bound, and what was left of her was covered in bites.

Yes, they'd taken time with her.

She could see no weapons, but one of the bunks was stained with blood fresher than what was staining the other bunk, the floor and the walls. That was where the girl had died, she assumed. And had waked again.

"The woman's only been dead a couple of days," Cian said from behind her. "The man and boy longer. A day or more longer."

"Yeah. Jesus." She had to get out, had to breathe. She climbed out of the back to draw in air she hoped would clear the smear in her throat, in her lungs.

"They'll come back for her." She bent over, bracing her hands on her thighs so the nausea, the dizziness would fade. "Bring her something so she can feed. She was new. Probably only woke tonight."

"We need to bury them," Larkin said. "The others. They deserve to be buried."

"It has to wait. Look, be pissed at me if you have to, but—"

"I'm not. I'm sick in my heart, but I'm not angry with you. Or you," he said to Cian. "I don't know why it should be this way inside me. I saw what was in the caves back in Ireland. I know how they kill, how they breed. But knowing they made a monster of that girl only so they could use her between them, it makes my heart sick."

She didn't have any words, any real ones, to offer. She wrapped her fingers around his arm, squeezed. "Let's make them pay for it. They'll be back before sunrise. Well before if they can find what they're after quickly enough and get it back. They know she'll have risen tonight, and need to feed. That's why they—"

"That's why they left the bodies inside," Larkin said when she cut herself off. "So she'd have something until they could bring her fresh blood. I'm not slow-witted, Blair. They left her own family for her to feed on."

Nodding, she looked back toward the wagon. "So we close up the wagon, and we wait. Will they be able to smell us? The human?"

"Hard to say," Cian told her. "I don't know how old they are, how experienced. Enough so Lilith thought they could handle this assignment. Which they bungled. But it's possible they'll catch the scent of live blood, even through all this. Then there's the horses."

"Okay, I've got that covered. Most likely they'll come back to the wagon from the same direction they left it. We'll take the horses farther into the woods, downwind. Tether them. All but mine. If I'm walking him when they see me, they'll figure he came up lame. And they'll be too happy with their luck of coming across a lone female to think beyond that."

"So, you think you're going to be bait," Larkin began, with a look on his face that warned Blair they were in for a fight about it.

"I'll just take the horses back while you two argue this out." Cian took the reins, melted into the trees.

Calm, Blair ordered herself. Reasonable. She should remember it was nice to have someone who actually cared enough to worry about her.

"If they see a man, they're more likely to attack. A

woman, they're going to want me alive—temporarily. Gives them each a playmate. It's the most logical way."

That was the end of her calm and reasonable. "And, here's what. If your ego has a problem with the fact that if I *were* out here alone I could still handle two of them, you'll just have to deal with it."

"My ego has nothing to do with the matter. It's just as logical for the three of us to lay back and wait, then move on them as one."

"No, because if they scent either you or me, we lose the element of surprise. Moira wants them—or at least one of them alive. That's why we're out here instead of having a nice glass of wine in front of a roaring fire. If we have to go full scale attack we'll probably have to kill them both. Surprise gives us a better chance of capture."

"There are other ways."

"Probably a dozen of them. But while they may not be back for five hours, they could also be back in five minutes. This will work, Larkin, because it's simple and it's basic. Because they wouldn't expect a woman by herself to be any kind of threat. I want to bag these two as much as you do. Let's make sure we do."

Cian slipped back out of the trees. "Have you settled it, then, or will we be debating this much longer?"

"It seems to be settled." Larkin brushed a hand over Blair's hair. "I've just been wasting my breath." Then he tipped back her chin. "If you have to speak to them to hold the illusion until we move in, they'll know you're not from Geall."

"Sure you think I can't manage a bit of an accent." She slathered on the brogue, and gave him a wide-eyed help-less look. "And give every appearance of being a defense-less female?"

"That's not altogether bad." He lowered his lips to hers. "But for myself, I'd never believe the defenseless part of it."

Chapter 15

An hour passed, then another. Then a third. There was little for her to do but eat some of the bread and cheese Moira had provided for them, wash it down with the water in her bag.

At least Larkin and Cian had each other for company, while all she had was her own head. She frowned when that thought passed through. She was used to hunting alone, to waiting alone in dark, quiet places.

Strange, it had only taken a matter of weeks for her to break that lifetime habit.

In any case, the waiting was taking longer than she'd hoped, and Blair hadn't factored in the boredom. It made her think of her first night in Ireland this time around, and the luck—fate—of getting a flat on a dark, lonely road.

There'd been three vampires that time, and the element of surprise had added to her advantage. Mostly, vamps didn't expect to get clocked with a tire iron, especially by a woman who was a hell of a lot stronger than they'd calculated.

They sure as hell hadn't expected her to pull out a stake and dust them.

These two—if they ever got back—wouldn't be expecting it either. Only she had to remember dusting them wasn't the mission. A tough one to swallow for a bred in the blood demon hunter.

Her father wouldn't approve of this little adventure, she mused. In his book you ended them, period. Quickly, efficiently. No flourishes, no conversation.

Of course, he'd have done his best to end Cian by now, she decided. Family connection and will of the gods be damned. He would never have worked with Cian or fought beside him, trained with him.

And one of them, possibly both of them, would be dead now.

Maybe that was why she'd been brought here instead of her father. Why she could admit now, as she waited on the rutted forest path, she hadn't told him about Cian. Not that her father bothered to actually read her e-mails, but still she hadn't brought up an allegiance to the undead in the ones she'd sent him.

There simply were no allegiances in demon hunting, not to her father's mind. It was you and the enemy. Black and white, live and die.

Only another reason she'd never earned his approval, she realized. It wasn't only because she wasn't his son, but because she'd seen the gray, and had questioned.

Because like Larkin she had felt, more than once, a pity and regret for the things she ended. She knew what her father would say. That an instant of pity or regret could mean an instant of hesitation. And an instant's hesitation could kill you.

He'd be right, she thought. But not completely, no, not absolutely, as there were shades of gray there, too. She could feel that pity and still do her job. She *had*.

Wasn't she standing here now, alive? And she damn well intended to stay alive.

She only wondered, for the first time since Jeremy, if it was possible to have a life along with a heartbeat. She'd stopped letting herself wish or want or ask if she could have someone to love her. Now there was Larkin, and she believed he did. Or close enough to love to care for and want.

In time maybe it could be love. The kind she'd never had before, the kind that crossed all the lines and accepted.

It was brutal, she thought, just brutal that there couldn't be enough time. There just wasn't enough of the commodity to span entire worlds.

But when she went back to her own, she would know there was someone who had looked at her, had seen who and what she was, and still had cared.

If she did make it back, if they won this thing and the worlds kept spinning, she would tell him what he'd given her. Tell him that he'd changed something inside her, so much for the better.

But she wouldn't tell him she loved him. Words like that would only hurt them both. She wouldn't tell him what she was finally able to admit to herself.

That she would always love him.

She *felt* the movement rather than saw it, and turned toward it, braced for attack. But it was Cian, the shape and scent of him, off the path and in the shadows.

"Heads up," he murmured. "Two riders starting into the woods. They're dragging a body behind them. Alive yet."

She nodded and thought: Curtain up.

She began to walk the horse slowly, in the direction of the wagon so they'd come up behind her. So it would seem, she thought, that she'd ridden into the woods before her horse had come up lame.

She felt them first, something that was beyond scent. It was more a knowledge, which covered all the senses. But she waited until she heard the hoofbeats.

She'd taken off her coat. She didn't think Geallian women walked around in black leather. Against the chill she wore one of Larkin's tunics, belted snugly enough to show she had breasts. Her crosses were tucked under the cloth, out of sight.

She looked like an unarmed woman, hoping for some help.

She even called out as the sound of the horses grew closer, making sure her voice was blurred with brogue and a little fear.

"Hello, the riders! I'm having a bit of trouble here— ahead on the path."

The hoofbeats stopped. Oh yeah, Blair thought, talk it over for a minute, figure it out. She called out again, increasing the quaver in her voice.

"Are you there? My horse picked up a stone, I'm afraid. I'm on my way to Cillard."

They were coming again, slowly, and she fixed what she hoped was a mixture of relief and concern on her face. "Well, thank the gods," she said when the horses came into view. "I thought I'd end up walking the rest of the way to my sister's, and alone in the dark for all that. Which serves me right, doesn't it, for starting out so much later than I should."

One dismounted. He looked strong, Blair judged, solidly built. When he pushed back the hood of his cloak she saw a tangle of white blond hair and a deep, V-shaped scar above his left eyebrow.

There was no sign of anyone being dragged behind the horses, so she assumed they'd dropped their prey off for the moment.

"You're traveling alone?"

Slavic, she thought. Just the faintest of accents. Russian, Ukrainian maybe.

"I am. It's not so very far, and I meant to leave earlier in the day. But one thing and another, and now this . . ." She gestured to her horse. "I'm Beal, of the o Dubhuir family. Would you be heading toward Cillard by chance?"

The second dismounted to hold the reins of both their horses.

"It's dangerous to be out in the woods, alone in the dark."

"I know them well enough. But you, you don't sound like you come from this part of Geall." She backed up a step as a frightened woman might. "Are you a stranger to the area then?"

"You could say that." And when he smiled, his fangs glimmered.

She gave a little shriek, decided such things couldn't be overplayed. He laughed when he grabbed for her. She brought her knee up hard between his legs, then topped it off with a solid roundhouse. When he went down to his knees, she kicked him full in the face, then planted her feet to meet the second attack.

The second wasn't as toughly built as the first, but he was faster. And he'd drawn his sword. Blair flipped back, landing on her hands to kick out at his sword arm. It gave her time and a little distance. When the first gained its feet, Larkin burst out of the woods.

"Let's see how you do against a man."

Blair took the fast running steps she needed to give the flying kick momentum. She hit the first mid-body as Larkin clashed swords with the other. She grabbed her sword from its sheath on her saddle as all three of the horses shied. Instinct had her whirling, bringing the blade up two-handed to block the down sweep of her enemy's sword.

She'd been right about his strength, she discovered, as the force of the blow rippled straight down to her toes. Because he had her in reach, she went in close. His advantage was she didn't want to kill him—but he didn't know that. She stomped hard on his instep, brought the hilt of her sword up in a vicious blow to his chin.

The hit knocked him back, into her mount. All three horses whinnied in alarm as they scattered.

He just kept coming, hacking and swinging until sweat rolled into her eyes. She heard someone—something—

scream, but couldn't risk a look. Instead, she feinted, drawing his sword to the left, then plowed her foot into his belly. It took him down long enough for her to leap on him, hold her sword across his throat.

"Move and you're dust. Larkin?"

"Aye."

"If you're done playing around with that one, I could use a little help over here."

He stepped over. Then kicked the vampire in the head, in the face—several times.

"Yeah, that ought to do it." Breathless, she sat back on her haunches to look up at Larkin. Blood was spattered over his shirt, his face. "Is much of that yours?"

"Not a great deal of it. It would be his, for the most part." He stepped back, gestured so she could see the vampire he'd skewered into the ground with a sword.

"Ouch." She got to her feet. "We need to round up those horses, get these two in chains and . . ." She trailed off as Cian walked toward them, leading the horses.

He glanced at the vampires bleeding on the path. "Untidy," he decided. "But effective. This one's not in the best of shape." He nodded toward the bleeding man slung over one of the horses. "But he's alive."

"Nice work." She wondered, not for the first time, how hard it was for him to resist the smell of fresh human blood. But it didn't seem like the time to ask. "We'd better get these two contained. This one wakes up, he's trouble." Blair circled her aching shoulder. "That one's like a goddamn bull."

While the men chained the prisoners, she examined the unconscious man. He was bloodied and battered, but unbitten. Going to take him back to the wagon, she thought. Share him with the female. Have a little party.

"We need to bury the dead," Larkin said to her.

"We can't take the time now."

"We're not just leaving them."

"Listen, just listen." She gripped his hands before he

could turn away. "That man's hurt, and hurt bad. He needs help as soon as we can get it for him, or he might not make it. Then we'd be digging another grave. Added to it, we need to get Cian back and inside before sunrise. We're going to be cutting it close as it is."

"I'll stay behind, deal with it myself."

"Larkin, we need you. If we don't make good time, Cian's going to have to go ahead, or go to ground, and that leaves me with two vampires and one wounded human. I could handle it alone if I had to, but I don't. We'll send someone back to bury them. I'll come back with you, and we'll do it ourselves if you'd rather. But we have to leave them for now. We have to go."

He said nothing, only nodded then strode to his horse.

"He's taking the female he ended to heart," Cian murmured.

"Some are harder than others. You have that cloak thing, right? In case."

"I do, but I'll be frank and tell you I'd rather not risk my skin on it."

"Can't blame you. If and when you have to ride ahead, you ride." She looked over where the two vampires were shackled, gagged and tied across one of their horses. "We can handle them."

"You could handle them on your own, we both know that."

"Larkin shouldn't have to deal with what's back there in that wagon by himself." She swung onto her horse. "Let's get this done."

They rode in silence through the dark of the woods, across the fields dappled with pale moonlight. Once, just ahead, a white owl swooped over a gentle rise with only the whisper of wings. Blair thought, for an instant, she saw the glitter of its eyes, green as jewels. Then there was only the murmur of the wind through the high grass and the hushed silence of predawn.

She saw the vampire she fought lift its head. When its

eyes met hers she saw the blood lust, and the fury. But over them both she saw the fear. He struggled against his chains, eyes wheeling toward the east. The one beside him lay weakly, and Blair thought the sounds he made behind his gag were sobs.

"They feel dawn coming," Cian said from beside her. "The burn of it."

"Go. Larkin and I can handle it."

"Oh, there's time yet, a bit of time yet."

"We should only be a couple miles out."

"Less," Larkin told her. "A bit less. The wounded man's coming around some. I wish he wouldn't."

The ride couldn't be doing him any good, Blair thought, but they couldn't afford to keep it slow and smooth any longer. The stars had faded out.

"Let's pick up the pace." She kicked her horse into a gallop, and hoped the man slumped over the horse she led would live another mile.

She saw the lights first, the flicker of them—candle and torch—through the rising mists. And there, the silhouette of the castle, high on the rise with its white flags waving against a sky that was no longer black, but a deep, dense blue.

"Go!"

The vampires bucked and jerked, making sounds far from human as the first streaks of red bled over the horizon behind the castle.

But Cian rode straight in the saddle, hair flying. "I so rarely see it from out of doors."

There was pain, the rip and the burn of it. And there was wonder, and a faint regret as he galloped through the gates and into the shadow of the keep.

Moira was there, her face tight and pale. "Go inside, please. Your horse will be tended. Please," she repeated, the strain cutting through the word as Cian slowly dismounted. "Be quick."

She gestured for the men with her to take the prisoners.

"Got a handy dungeon?" Blair asked her.

"We don't, no."

Riddock watched the men drag the chained prisoners away. "Arrangements have been made, as Moira requested. They'll be held in the cellars, and guarded."

"Leave the chains on them," Larkin ordered.

"Hoyt and Glenna are waiting inside," Moira told him. "We'll add magic to the chains. You're not to worry. You need food and rest, all of you."

"This one's human. And wounded." Blair stepped over, laid her fingers on the pulse in the man's throat. "Alive, but he needs attention."

"Right away. Sir?"

"We'll send for the physician." Riddock signalled to some men. "See to him," he ordered before turning to his son. "Are you hurt?"

"No. I have to go back, there are some we had to leave, back in the forest on the path to Cillard." Larkin's face was pale, and it was set. "They need to be buried."

"We'll send a party out."

"I have a need to see to it myself."

"Then you will. But come inside first. You need to wash, break your fast." He slung an arm around Larkin's shoulders. "It's been a long night for all of us."

Inside, Cian stood speaking with Hoyt and Glenna. He broke off when the others entered and lifted a brow at Moira.

"You have your prisoners. What do you intend to do with them?"

"We'll speak of it, all of it. I've ordered food to the family parlor. If we could meet there, we have much to discuss."

She swept away with two of her women hurrying behind her.

Blair went to her own room where a fire was lit and fresh water waited. She washed away the blood, changing the borrowed tunic for one of her own shirts.

Then she braced her hands on the bureau and studied her face in the mirror.

She'd looked better, she decided. She needed sleep, but wasn't going to get it. Nor for a while yet. She'd have paid a lot for an hour in a bed, but that wasn't in the cards any more than a couple days at a nice spa.

Instead, she was going to take half the day to ride back out, bury three strangers. There wasn't time for it, not when she should have been working with the troops, devising strategies, checking on weapon production. A dozen practical and necessary tasks.

But if she didn't go, Larkin would do it alone. She couldn't let that happen.

He was already in the parlor when she walked in. And he was alone by the window, watching morning strike mist.

"You think I'm wasting valuable time," he said without turning around. "With something unnecessary and useless."

So he read her, she thought. And damn clearly. "It doesn't matter. You need to do it, so we'll do it."

"Families should be safe on the roads of Geall. Young girls should not be raped and tortured and killed. Should not be turned into something that must be destroyed."

"No, they shouldn't."

"You've lived with it longer than I. And perhaps you can face it more . . ."

"Callously."

"No." He turned now. He looked older, she thought, in the hard light, with the violence of the night still on him. "That wasn't the word, and would never be one I'd use for you. Coolly perhaps, practically for certain. So you must. I won't hold you to going with me."

Because he wouldn't, she knew she could do nothing else but go. "I said I would, and I will."

"Yes, you will, so thanks for that. Can you understand that I'm stronger for knowing you'll do this thing with me, that you'd understand my need to do it enough to take the time?"

"I think it takes a strong man to need to do what's human, and humane. That's enough for me."

"There's so much I have to say to you, so many things I want to say. But today isn't the day. I feel . . ." He looked down at his sword hand. "Stained. Do you know what I'm saying?"

"Yeah, I know what you're saying."

"Ah well. Come, we'll drink strong tea and wish it was Coke." He smiled a little as he walked to her. Then he laid his hands lightly on her shoulders, pressed his lips to her brow. "You are so beautiful."

"Your eyes must really be tired."

He eased back. "I see you," he told her, "exactly as you are."

He pulled her chair out for her, something she couldn't remember him doing before. As she sat, Hoyt and Cian came in. Cian flicked a glance toward the windows, then moved away from them to the table Moira had had set away from the light.

"Glenna will be along," Hoyt said. "She wanted to check on the man you brought in. The prisoners are secured." He looked at his brother. "And very unhappy."

"They haven't fed." Cian poured his own tea. "The castle boasts a fine wine cellar, which you didn't mention," he said to Larkin. "A corner of it is nicely dark and damp enough to keep them. But unless your cousin simply intends to starve them to death, they'll need to be fed if they're chained in there above another day."

"I have no intention of starving them." Moira came in. She wore riding gear now, with a feminine flare, in forest green. "And neither will they be fed. They've had enough Geallian blood, animal and human. My uncle and I will ride out shortly, to rally the people and spread the word. As many as can manage will come here by sundown. And when the sun has set, what is in the cellars will be shown to them. Then destroyed."

She looked directly at Cian. "Do you find that hard, cold, with no drop of human emotion or mercy?"

"No. I find it practical and useful. I hardly thought you had us hunt them down to bring them here for counseling and rehabilitation."

"We'll show the people what they are, and how they must be killed. We're sending troops out now to lay the traps you want, Blair. Larkin, I've asked Phelan to take charge of the task."

"My sister's husband," Larkin explained. "Aye, he'd be up for that. You chose well."

"The man you brought back is awake, though the physician wishes to dose him. Glenna agrees. He told us he went outside, hearing what he thought was a fox in his henhouse. They set upon him. He has a wife and three children, and shouted for them to stay in the house. It was all he could do, and we can thank the gods they obeyed. We're sending for them."

"Until Larkin and Blair return, Glenna and I can help with the training. And Cian perhaps," Hoyt added, "if there's somewhere inside."

"Thank you. I'd hoped that would suit you. Ah, we have the village smithy and two others forging weapons. We'll have more, but some who come will have their own arms."

"You've got trees," Blair pointed out. "You're going to want to start making stakes out of some of them. More arrows, lances, spears."

"Yes, of course. Yes. I need to go as my uncle and our party is waiting. I want to thank you for your night's work. We'll be back before sundown."

"She's starting to look like a queen," Blair said when Moira left.

"Worn out is what she looks."

Blair nodded at Larkin. "Being a queen's bound to be hard work. Add a war, and it's got to be brutal. Cian, you okay to fill the others in on our party last night?"

"I've already given them the highlights. I'll fill in the details."

"Then why don't you and I get started," she said to Larkin.

She went to the stables with him where he gathered the tools they'd need.

"I could fly us there quicker than we could ride. Would that suit you?"

"That'd be good."

He led the way around to the courtyard garden she recognized from her window. "The bag's heavy. Hang it round my neck once I've changed."

He passed it to her; became the dragon.

He dipped his head so that she could work the strap over it. Then she looked into his eyes, stroked his jeweled cheek. "You sure are pretty," she murmured.

He lowered so she could mount his back.

They were rising up, above the towers, the turrets, over the waving white flags.

The morning was like a gem of blue and green and umber, spreading around her. She tipped her head back, let the wind rush over her, let it blow away the fatigue of the long night.

She saw horses below on the road now, and carriages, wagons, people walking. The little village she'd yet to explore was a spread of pretty buildings, bright colors, busy stalls. The people who looked up raised caps or hands as they flew over, then went back about the business of the day.

Life, Blair thought, didn't just go on, it insisted on thriving.

She turned her face toward the mountains, with their mists and their secrets. And their valley called silence where in a matter of weeks there would be blood and death.

They would fight, she thought, and some would fall. But they would fight so life could thrive.

They reached the woods and circled before Larkin wove delicately through the trees to the ground.

She slid off him, took the bag.

When he was a man again, he took her hand.

"It's beautiful," she said. "Before we do this, I want to tell you Geall is beautiful."

Together they walked through the trees, then stopped to dig three graves in the soft, mossy ground. The work was physical, and mechanical, and they did it without conversation. Going back into the wagon, removing the bodies was a horror. Neither spoke, but simply did what needed to be done.

She felt the weariness dragging back into her bones, and the sickness that sat deep in the belly as they closed the ground over the bodies.

Larkin carried stones for each of the graves, then a fourth for the young girl he couldn't bury.

When it was done, Blair leaned on the shovel. "Do you want to, I don't know, say some words?"

He spoke in Gaelic, taking her hand as he said the words, then saying them again in English so she could understand.

"They were strangers to us, but to each other they were family. They died a hard death, and now we give them back to the earth and the gods where they will have peace. They will not be forgotten."

He stepped back, drawing her with him. "I'll pull the wagon into the field, away from the trees. We'll burn it."

Everything they'd owned, she thought as they set the wagon to light. Everything they'd had, these people who had no name for her. The idea of it was so sad, as the wagon burned and the smoke rose, that when she climbed onto the dragon's back again, she laid her head on his neck, closed her eyes and dozed as they flew over the ashes.

Chapter 16

She heard thunder, and thought groggily that they'd have to outrace a storm. Straightening, more than a little amazed she'd dozed off on the back of a dragon, she opened her eyes. Shook her head to clear it.

Not thunder, she realized and gaped at the towering fall of water that gushed over twin spires of rock into a wide blue pool.

There were trees here, still leafy and green, and the surprising tropical touch of palms. Lilies floated on the pool, pink and white, as if they'd been painted there. Beneath the surface of blue, she could see the dart of fish, bright and elegant as jewels.

The air smelled of flowers and clear water.

She was so stunned she stayed where she was when he landed. The dragon's head bent down so the strap of the bag slid off. And she was sitting piggyback on Larkin.

"What? We take a wrong turn?"

He turned his head to smile into her dazzled eyes. "I told you I would bring you here. Faerie Falls, it is. There's no picnic this time, but I thought . . . I wanted an hour, alone with you, somewhere there's only beauty."

"I'll take it." She jumped off his back, turned a circle.

There were starry little flowers in the grass, and a tangle of vines, blooming purple, winding right up the rocks, almost like frames for that plunge of water. The pool itself was clear as a mirror, blue as a pansy while the cups of lilies floated over it, and overhead the falls spilled fifty feet down.

"It's incredible, Larkin, a little slice of paradise. And I don't care how cold that water is, I'm having a swim."

She yanked off her boots, started on her shirt. "Aren't you?"

"Sure." He kept grinning at her. "I'll be right behind you."

She stripped, tossing her clothes carelessly on the soft ground. Poised on the bank, she sucked in her breath, braced for the shock. And dived.

When she surfaced, she let out a joyful yell. "Oh my God, it's *warm*! It's warm and it's silky and it's wonderful." She did a surface dive, came up again. "If I were a fish, I'd live here."

"Some say the faeries warm it every morning with their breath." Larkin sat, pulled off his own boots. "Others less fanciful talk of hot springs under the ground."

"Faeries, science, I don't care. It feels so damn good."

He jumped in, and as men were prone to do, hit the water hard so it would splash her as much as possible. She only laughed and splashed him back.

They went under together, tugging each other deeper or pinching bare flesh, playing like seals. She swam under, cutting through with strong strokes until she felt the vibration of water striking water. She sprang off the bottom and into the tumble.

It beat on her shoulders, the back of her neck, the base of her spine. She shouted out with a combination of relief and joy as it pummeled away the aches and fatigue. When he joined her, wrapped his arms around her, they laughed as the water plunged over them. The force pushed them back toward the heart of the pool where she could simply float with him.

"I was thinking earlier how much I'd like a couple days at a good spa. This is better." She sighed and let her head rest on his shoulder. "An hour here is better than anything."

"I wanted you to have something unspoiled. I needed, I think, to remind myself there are such places." Not only graves to be dug, he thought. Not only battles to be fought. "There isn't another woman I know, but Moira, who would have done what you did with me today. For me today."

"There aren't many men I know who would have done what you did today. So we're even."

He brushed his lips over her temple, her cheek, found her mouth. The kiss was soft and warm as the water. His hand that stroked over her as gentle as the air.

It seemed that nothing beyond this place, beyond this precious time existed. Here, for now, they could just be. While they drifted, she saw a white dove soar overhead, and circle. She saw the sparkle of its green eyes.

So the gods do watch, she thought, remembering the white owl. In the good times, and in the bad.

Then she turned her lips to his. What did she care for gods now? This was their time, this was their place. She sank into the kiss, letting the water and his arms carry her.

"I need you." His eyes were on hers as he took her mouth again. "Do you, can you know how much it is I need you? Take me in." He murmured it as he cupped her hips, slid into her.

They watched each other as they joined, fingers stroking faces, lips brushing lips.

It was more than pleasure that moved through her, more even than the joy of life. If it was truth, she thought, this need, this sharing, then she could live on it the rest of her life.

She wrapped herself around him, gave herself to that truth.

And knew the name of that truth was love.

It was probably possible to be more tired, to be more frustrated, but Glenna hoped she never found out. She'd done what Moira had asked and taken a group of women to one end of the gaming fields to try to give them the first basic lesson of self-defense.

They were more interested in gossiping and giggling, or trying to flirt with the men Hoyt worked with across the field than moving their asses.

She'd taken some twenty of the younger ones assuming they'd be more enthusiastic and in better physical shape. And that, she decided, might have been her first mistake.

Time, she thought, to get mean.

"Be quiet!" The sharp edge of her voice silenced the group into a single gasping breath. "You know, I like to ogle beefcake as much as the next girl, but we're not here so you can pick out your date for the harvest ball. We're here so I can teach you how to stay alive. You." She chose one at random, pointed at a pretty brunette who looked sturdy. "Step over here."

There were a few giggles, and the woman smirked as she strutted up to Glenna.

"What's your name?"

"Dervil, lady." Then she squeaked and stumbled back when Glenna's fist swung up and stopped a bare inch from her face.

"Is that what you're going to do when someone tries to hurt you, Dervil? Are you going to squeal like a girl, gulp like a fish?" She grabbed Dervil's arm yanked it up so that it blocked Dervil's face as Glenna shot her fist out again. Their forearms rammed together.

"That hurt!" Dervil's mouth fell open in shock. "You have no right to hurt me."

"Hurting someone isn't about rights, it's about intent. And a forearm block hurts less than a bare-fisted punch in the face. They'll like the look of you, Dervil. Block! No, don't throw your arm up like it's a dishrag. Firm, strong. Again!" She worked Dervil backward with each punch. "You've got some meat on you, and all that blood swimming in your veins. Squealing and flapping won't help you. What will you do when they come for you?"

"Run!" someone called out, and though there was some laughter at this, Glenna stopped and nodded.

"Running could be an option. There might be a time it's the only option, but you'd better be fast. A vampire can move like lightning."

"We don't believe in demons." Dervil thrust up her chin, rubbed her bruised forearm. From the mutinous set of her mouth, the glitter in her eyes, Glenna understood she'd made her first enemy in Geall.

So be it.

"You can bet they believe in you. So run. End of the field and back. Run like the demons of hell are after you. Goddamn it, I said *run*." To get them moving, she spurted a little fire at their feet.

There were some screams, but they ran. Like girls, Glenna thought in despair. Waving arms, mincing feet, flapping skirts. And at least three of them tripped, which she considered an embarrassment for all females, everywhere.

Since she calculated she'd lose half of them if she made them run back, she jogged after them.

"Okay, from here. A couple of you actually have some speed, but for the most part, you're all slow and silly. So we'll run every day, one length of the field. You're going to have to wear, what are they? Tewes or leggings. Pants," she said, patting her own sweats. "Men's attire for training. Skirts are only going to trip you up, be in the way."

"A lady—" one of them began, only to freeze when Glenna lasered a stare at her.

"You're not ladies when I'm training you. You're soldiers." A different tack, she decided. "Who here has children?"

Several raised hands, so she chose one she thought was at least watching her with some interest. "You? Your name?"

"Ceara."

"What would you do, Ceara, if something came after your child?"

"I would fight, of course, I would. I would die fighting to protect my child."

"Show me. I'm after your baby. What do you do?" When Ceara looked blank, Glenna pushed down her own impatience. "I've killed your husband. He's dead at your feet, now the only thing that stands between me and your child is you. Stop me."

Ceara lifted her hands, fingers curled into claws, and made a halfhearted lunge at Glenna. And the breath went out of her as she was flipped over Glenna's shoulder to land on her back.

"How does that stop me?" Glenna demanded. "Your child's screaming for you. Do something!"

Ceara got into a crouch, sprang up. Glenna let herself be tackled, then simply flipped Ceara over, pressed an elbow to her throat.

"That was better, that was positive. But it was too slow, and your eyes, your body told me just what you were going to do."

When Glenna stood, Ceara sat up, rubbed the back of her head. "Show me," she said to Glenna.

By the end of the session, Glenna put her first students in two camps. The Ceara camp consisted of those who showed at least some interest and aptitude. Then there was the Dervil camp, which not only showed neither, but a strong resistance to spending time doing something that wasn't traditionally a woman's task.

When they were gone, she simply sat down on the ground. Moments later, Hoyt dropped down beside her, and she had the pleasure, at least, of resting her head on his shoulder.

"I think I'm a poor teacher," he told her.

"That makes two of us. How are we going to do this, Hoyt? How are we going to pull this together, turn these people into an army?"

"We have no choice but to do it. But gods's truth, Glenna, I'm tired already and we've only begun."

"It was different when we were in Ireland, the six of us. We knew, we understood what we'd be facing. At least you're dealing with men, and some of them are already well trained with a sword or a bow. I've got a gaggle of girls here, Merlin, and most of them couldn't fight off a blind, one-legged dwarf much less a vampire."

"People rise when they have no choice. We did." He turned his head to kiss her hair. "We have to believe we can do this thing, then we'll do it."

"Believing counts," she agreed. "A lot of them don't believe what we're telling them."

He watched two of the guards carrying iron posts, watched as they began to hammer them into the ground. "They soon will." He got to his feet, reached for her hand. "We should see if the others are back."

B lair didn't know that she'd ever been sent for— unless you counted the occasional summons to the vice principal's office in high school. She doubted Moira intended to give her detention, but it was weird, being escorted to the princess.

Moira answered the door herself, and the smile she gave Blair was quiet and serious. "Thank you for coming. That will be all, Dervil, thank you. You should go now, secure your place in the stands."

"My lady—"

"I want you there. I want everyone there. Blair, please

come in." She stepped back to allow Blair inside, then shut the door in Dervil's face.

"You sure come over all royal."

"I know it must seem that way." Moira rubbed a hand up and down Blair's arm before she turned to walk farther into the room. "But I'm the same."

She might have been wearing what Blair considered Moira's training gear—the simple tunic, pants and sturdy boots—but there was something different about her.

The room might have added to it. It was, Blair assumed, a kind of sitting room, and plush for all that. Cushions of richly worked tapestries, velvet drapes, the lovely little marble hearth with its turf fire simmering all spoke of position.

"I asked you here to tell you how the demonstration will be done."

"To tell me," Blair repeated.

"I don't imagine you'll like what I've chosen to do, but the decision is made. There's no other way for me."

"Why don't you tell me what you've chosen to do, then I'll tell you if I like it or not."

She didn't. And she argued. She threatened and she cursed. But Moira remained both implacable and immovable.

"What have the others said about this?" Blair demanded.

"I haven't told them. I've told you." Thinking they could both use it, Moira poured them each a glass of wine. "Put yourself in my position, please. These are the monsters who killed my mother. They murdered the queen of Geall."

"And the idea was—is—to show people they exist. What they are, how they need to be fought and destroyed."

"Aye, that's an essential point." Moira sat a moment, to sip wine, to settle. All through the worries of the night, the duties of the day, she'd been gathering herself for what was to come. "In a few days, I'll go to the stone. Again, before the people of Geall who've gathered there, I'll take hold of the sword. If I lift it, I will be queen. And as queen I'll lead my people into war—the first war in Geall. Can I send them into battle, can I send them to their deaths when I'm unproven?"

"Moira, you don't have to prove anything to me."

"Not to you, but to others. And to myself—do you understand? I won't take up sword and crown until I feel worthy of both."

"From where I'm standing you are. I wouldn't tell you that if I thought otherwise."

"You wouldn't, no. That's why I asked for you, and not one of the others. You'll speak to me plainly, and I can speak plainly to you. It matters that you think I'm ready for the sword and the crown. It matters a great deal. But I have to feel it, don't you see?"

"Yeah. Shit." Because she did see, Blair raked her hands through her hair. "Yeah."

"Blair, I'm afraid of what's been asked of me. Of what I need to do, of what's to come. I'm asking you to help me do this thing tonight, as a friend, a fellow warrior, and as a woman who knows how cold the path of destiny can be."

"And if I refuse, you'll do it anyway."

"Of course." Now a glimmer of a smile. "But I'd feel stronger and surer with your understanding."

"I do understand. I don't have to like it, but I can understand."

Moira set her wine aside, got to her feet to take Blair's hand. "That's enough."

They'd made it into a kind of party, Blair thought. Torches blazed, lining the field of play. Flames rose up toward the sky where the nearly full ball of moon beamed like a spotlight.

People crammed into the stands, jostled for position behind wooden barriers. They'd brought children, she noted, right down to babies—and the mood was festive.

She was armed—sword, stake, crossbow—and heard the murmurs as she passed through on her way to the royal box.

She slipped in next to Glenna.

"So what do you think the insurance would go for on a gig like this? Fire, wood, all this flammable clothing."

Glenna shook her head as she scanned the crowd. "They don't understand it. They're like fans waiting for the concert to begin. For God's sake, Blair, there are vendors selling meat pies."

"Never underestimate the power of free enterprise."

"I tried to get to Moira before we were brought here. We don't even know the plan."

"I do. And you're not going to like it." Before she could elaborate, there was a blare of trumpets. The royal family came into the box. "Just don't blame me," Blair said over the cheers of the crowd.

Riddock stepped forward, raising his hands to quiet the crowd. "People of Geall, you are here to welcome home Her Highness, the princess Moira. To give thanks for her safe return to us, and that of Larkin, lord of MacDara."

There were more cheers as Moira and Larkin stepped up to stand on either side of Riddock. Larkin shot Blair a quick, cocky grin.

He doesn't know, she thought, and felt her stomach twist.

"You are here to welcome the valiant men and women who accompanied them to Geall. The sorcerer Hoyt of the family Mac Cionaoith. His lady Glenna, *cailleach dearg*. The lady Blair, *gaiscioch dorcha*. Cian, of the Mac Cionaoith, and brother to the sorcerer. They are welcome to our land, to our home, to our hearts."

The cheers rolled. Give them a few hundred years, Blair thought, and there'd be little witch and wizard action figures. If the world survived that long.

"People of Geall! We have known a dark time, one of heartbreak and of fear. Our beloved queen was cruelly taken from us. Murdered by what are not men, but beasts. On this night, on this ground, you will see what has taken your queen. They are brought here by order of her Royal Highness, and through the valor of Lord Larkin, the lady Blair and Cian of the Mac Cionaoith."

Riddock stepped back, and by the way his jaw tightened, Blair thought he knew the drill—and wasn't happy about it.

Moira moved forward, waited for the crowd to subside. "People of Geall, I have come home to you, but not to bring you joy. I come to bring you war. I have been charged by the goddess Morrigan herself to fight what would destroy our world, the world of my friends, all the worlds of humankind. I am charged, with these five whom I trust with my life, with my land, with the crown I may one day bear if the gods deem it, to lead you into this battle."

She paused, and Blair could see she was judging the tone of the crowd, the murmurs, pacing herself.

"It is not a battle for land or wealth, not for glory or vengeance, but for life itself. I have not been your ruler, I have not been a warrior, but a student, a dutiful daughter, a proud citizen of Geall. Yet I would ask you to follow me and mine, to give your lives for me, and for all that come after. For on the night of the feast of Samhain we will face an army of these."

The vampires were dragged onto the field. Blair knew what the people saw. They saw men in chains, murderers yes, but not demons.

There were shouts and gasps, there were calls for justice, there were even tears. But there was no true fear.

The guards fixed the chains to the iron posts, and at Moira's nod, left the field.

"These that killed my mother, that murdered your queen have a name. It is vampire. In her world, the lady Blair has hunted them, destroyed them. She is the hunter of this demon. She will show you what they are."

Blair let out a breath, turned briefly to Larkin. "Sorry."

Before he could speak, she vaulted out of the box and crossed the field.

"What is this?" Larkin demanded.

"You will not interfere." Moira gripped his arm. "This is my wish. More, this is my order. You won't interfere. None of you."

As Blair began to speak, Moira left the box.

"Vampires have one purpose. To kill." Blair circled them, letting them draw her scent, the scent that would stir the terrible hunger. "They feed on human blood. They will hunt you, and drink you. If food is their only purpose you'll die quickly. In pain, in horror, but quickly. If they want more, they'll torture you, as they tortured the family Larkin, Cian and I found dead in the forest on the night we hunted these down."

The larger one tried to lunge at her. His eyes were red now, and those closest to the field would see the fangs he exposed.

"Vampires aren't born. They aren't conceived, they don't grow inside a womb. They're made. Made from humans. A bite from a vampire, if not fatal, infects. Some that are infected become half-vampires, slaves to them. Others are drained almost to the point of death, the very edge of life. Then they're fed the blood of their sire, and they die only to rise again. Not as a human, but as a vampire."

She continued to move, circling just out of reach.

"Your child, your mother, your lover can be turned like this. They won't be your child, your mother, your lover anymore. They'll be a demon, like these, with the blood lust that drives them to feed, to kill, to destroy."

She turned, and behind her the vampires strained against their chains, howling in frustration and hunger as she stood just out of range. "This is what's coming for you. Hundreds, maybe thousands of them. This is what you have to fight. Steel won't kill them. It hurts them."

She whirled, sliced the tip of her sword across the chest of the larger one. "They bleed, but they heal, and a wound like this will barely slow one down. These are the weapons that destroy a vampire. Wood."

She drew a stake, and when she feinted toward the smaller one, he cringed back, hunching to defend his chest. "Through the heart. Fire." She grabbed a torch, and when she flourished it in the air, both of them shrieked.

"They're night feeders because the direct light of the sun will end them. But they can lurk in the shadows, walk in the rain. Kill when the clouds block the sun. The symbol of the cross will burn them, and if you're lucky hold them back. Holy water burns them. If a sword is used it must cut through the neck, taking their head."

She, too, could judge the mood of the crowd, Blair thought. Excitement, confusion, those first whiffs of fear. And a great deal more disbelief. They still saw men in chains.

"These are your weapons, these are what you have along with your wits, your courage, against creatures that are stronger, faster and harder to kill than you are. If we don't fight, if we don't win, a little more than a month from now, they'll devour you."

She paused while Moira walked across the field to her. "Be sure," Blair murmured.

"I am." She gripped Blair's hand briefly then turned to the crowd where voices rippled with concern, confusion.

Moira lifted her voice over it. "Morrigan is called the queen of the warrior, yet it is said she has never fought in battle. Still, I bow to her command. This is faith. I cannot, will not ask that you have the faith in me that you would in a god. I am a woman, mortal as you are. But when I ask you to follow me into battle, you will follow a warrior. Proven. Whether or not I wear a crown, I will carry a sword. I will fight beside you."

She drew her sword, lifted it high. "Tonight, on this ground, I will destroy what took your queen and my mother. What I do here I do for her, by her blood. I do for you, for Geall, and all humankind."

She faced Blair. "Do it. If you have any love for me," she said when Blair hesitated. "Warrior to warrior, woman to woman."

"It's your show."

She chose the smaller of the two, though she judged he still had thirty pounds on Moira. "On your knees," she ordered, holding her sword to his throat.

"Easy for you to kill when I'm in chains." He hissed it, but he dropped to his knees.

"Yeah, it would be. And I already regret I'm not getting a piece of you." She held the sword against his throat as she moved behind him. Then taking the key Moira had given her, unlocked the chains.

With pride and fear, she plunged the sword into the ground beside him, and walked away.

"What have you done?" Larkin demanded when Blair took her position in front of the box.

"What she asked me to do. What I'd want her to do for me if the situation were reversed." She looked up at him now. "If you can't trust her, why should they?" She reached up for his hand. "If we can't trust her, how can she trust herself?"

She released his hand, and facing the field, prayed she'd done the right thing.

"Pick up the sword," Moira ordered.

"With a dozen arrows pointed at me?" it demanded.

"None flies unless you try to run. Are you afraid to fight a human on equal ground? Would you have run that night if my mother had held a sword?"

"She was weak, but her blood was rich." His eyes slanted to the left, to his companion, still chained and staked too far away to be of any help. "It was meant to be you."

The knife from that had already been in her heart. The words only twisted it. "Aye, and you killed her for nothing. But now it could be me. Will Lilith have you back if you taste my blood tonight? You want it." Deliberately she cut a shallow slice across her palm. "It's so long since you fed."

She watched his tongue flick out to lick his lips as she held up her hand so the blood would drip down her arm and onto the ground. "Come. Strike me down and feed."

He yanked the sword free, and raising it, charged.

She didn't block the first blow, but pivoted aside, kicked out to send him sprawling.

A good move, Blair decided. Add some humiliation to the fear and the hunger. He came up, rushed Moira with that eerie, preternatural speed some of them possessed. But she was ready for him. Maybe, Blair thought, she'd been ready all of her life.

Sword struck sword, and Blair could see that while he had more speed, more strength, Moira had the better form. Moira drove his sword up, aside, then plunged her own into his chest. She danced back, once more took her stance.

Showing the crowd, Blair knew, that while such a wound might be mortal in a human, it barely broke a vampire's stride.

She ignored the screams, the shouts, even the sounds of panic and running feet and watched the combat on the field.

The vampire cupped a hand on his wound, brought the blood from it to his mouth. From behind her, Blair heard the sound of a body hitting the ground as someone fainted.

He came at her again, but this time he anticipated Moira's move. His sword nicked her arm, and he cracked the back of his hand across her face. She stumbled back, blocking the next blow, but was driven back toward the second vampire.

Blair lifted her crossbow, prepared to break her word.

Instead, Moira dived down, rolled aside. She came up with her legs pistoning in a hard double kick that simply made Blair's heart sing.

"Atta girl, atta girl. Now take him out. Stop fooling around."

But it had gone beyond that, beyond merely showing the people what a vampire was capable of withstanding in battle. Moira brought her sword down to cleave a gash in its shoulder, and still she moved back rather than strike a killing blow.

"How long did she live?" Moira demanded. "How long did she suffer?" She continued to block, to drive even when the hand that gripped the hilt of her sword was slick with her own blood.

"Longer than you will, or the coward who sired you."

He charged through her shock. She barely saw the move, would never know how she defended herself against it. There was pain, the sting as the sword grazed her side. There was her own scream as she swung her sword through the air, and took its head.

She went to her knees as much with the sudden tearing grief than from any wounds. She shook from it, and the roars of the crowd were like a distant ocean.

She gained her feet, turned to Blair. "Unlock the other."

"No. That's enough, Moira. It's enough."

"That's for me to say." She strode over, yanked the key from Blair's belt. "It's for me to do."

All sound dropped away as she started across the field. Moira saw the sudden light, a kind of glee in the vampire's eyes as she approached it. The hunger, and the pleasure of what was to come.

Then she saw the arrow whizz by, and strike its heart.

Moira whirled, the rage of betrayal ripping through her. But it wasn't Blair who held the bow. It was Cian.

He tossed it down. "Enough," was all he said before he walked away.

Chapter 17

oira didn't think, she didn't wait. She didn't take her place back in the royal box to speak to her people again. As she rushed away, she could hear Larkin's voice lifted, strong and clear. He would stand in for her, and that would have to do.

She still carried her bloody sword as she sprinted after Cian.

"How dare you! How dare you interfere!"

He continued, reaching the courtyard now, moving across it. "I don't take orders from you. I'm not one of your subjects, not one of your people."

"You had no right." She spun ahead of him to block him from entering the castle. And seeing his face, saw cold rage.

"I'm not concerned about rights."

"Couldn't you stand it? Watching me fight one of them, torment it, destroy it. You couldn't stand by and see me beat down a second."

"If you like."

He didn't push past her but changed direction to continue across the courtyard and through an archway.

"You will not turn from me." This time when she rounded him, she laid the flat of her sword on his chest. Her rage wasn't cold, but hot, bubbling through her like the wrath of gods. "You're here because I wish it, because I permit it. You aren't master here."

"Didn't take long, did it, for you to drape on the mantle. But understand this, princess, I'm here because I wish it, and your *permission* is less than nothing to the likes of me. Now either use that sword or lower it."

She threw it aside so it clattered on the stones. "It was for *me* to do."

"For you to die in front of a roaring crowd? You're a bit small for the gladiator title."

"I would—"

"Have given a hungry vampire his last meal," Cian snapped. "You couldn't have bested the second of them. Maybe, just maybe, you'd have stood a small chance against him if you were fresh and not wounded. But Blair chose the smaller of them to begin with because it was your best chance at proving your point. And so you did, be satisfied with that."

"You think you know what I can do?"

He simply squeezed a hand to the cut on her side, releasing it when she went dead white and swayed back against the wall. "Yes. And so did he. He'd have known exactly where to come at you." Cian lifted the bottom edge of her tunic, wiped the blood from his hand. "You wouldn't have lasted above two minutes before you were as dead as the mother you're so hell-bound to avenge."

Her eyes went from fog to smoke. "Don't speak of her."

"Then stop using her."

Her lips trembled once before she firmed them. "I would have beaten him because I had to."

"Bollocks. You were done, and too proud, too stupid to admit it."

"We can't know, can we, because you ended it."

"You think you could have stopped him from sinking his teeth into this?" Cian skimmed a finger down the side of her throat, barely lifting an eyebrow when she slapped his hand aside. "Stop me then. You'll need more than a peevish slap to manage it."

He stepped back, picked up the sword she'd tossed down. Smiled grimly when she winced at the pull in her side as he threw it to her. "There, you have a sword, I don't. Stop me."

"I've no intention of—"

"Stop me," he repeated, and moved quickly to give her a light shove back against the wall.

"You won't put your hands on me."

"Stop me." He shoved her again, then simply batted the sword aside.

She slapped him, hard across the face before he gripped her shoulders, pressed her back against the wall. She felt something that might have been fear, that might have been, as his eyes held hers transfixed.

"For God's sake, stop me."

When his mouth crushed down on hers, she felt everything. Too much. It was dark and it was bright, it was hard, and unbearably soft. All that was inside her rushed toward it, reckless and crazed.

Then he was standing aside, a foot away from her, and it seemed all the breath had left her body.

"That's not the way he'd have tasted you."

Cian left her trembling against the wall before he compounded an already enormous mistake.

He scented rather than saw Glenna. "She needs to be seen to," he said and continued away.

Inside, Blair sat in front of the fire in the family parlor, trying to get her bearings. "Just don't start on me," she warned Larkin. "She wheedled my word out of me, and the fact is, I understood why she needed to do it."

"Why didn't you tell me?"

"Because you weren't *there*. Because she left it for the last minute. Ambushed me. Which was damn good strategy, if you want my opinion. I argued with her, and maybe I could have argued harder, but she was right. Mostly right. And, Jesus, she made her point, didn't she? In spades."

He handed her a cup of wine, crouched in front of her. "You think I'm angry with you. I'm not. With her, a bit. With her because she didn't trust me with this. Because it wasn't just her mother those things killed, but my aunt. And I loved her. It wasn't just her people she sought to rally with this business tonight, but mine. And I can promise you, Moira and I will speak of it."

"Okay. Okay." She drank, looked at Hoyt. "Have you got two cents to put into this?"

"If you're meaning do I have an opinion on it, I do. She shouldn't have taken this on herself. She's too valuable to risk, and we're meant to be a circle. No one of us should make such important decisions without the others."

"Well, if you're going to be logical." Blair sighed. "You're not wrong, and if there'd been time, I'd have insisted she bring everyone in on it. We wouldn't have stopped her, but we'd have all been prepared. She went all queen on me." Sighing again, Blair rubbed at the tension at the base of her neck. "Man, she took some hits."

"And Glenna will tend to her," Hoyt answered. "She would have taken more if Cian hadn't acted."

"I wouldn't have let it happen. I'm not going to kick at him for jumping in, grabbing the crossbow out of my hands, but I wouldn't have let her take on number two. She was finished." She drank again. "But I'm not sorry she's tearing the skin off his hide instead of mine."

"His is thick enough." Idly Hoyt poked at the fire. "We'll have our army now."

"We will," Larkin agreed. "None can doubt what we'll come to face. We're not a people of war, but we're not cowards. We'll have an army come Samhain."

"Lilith will be here any day," Blair pointed out. "We've got a lot of work ahead of us. We'd better get some sleep, get an early start on it tomorrow."

But as she started to get up, Dervil came to the doorway. "I beg your pardon, but I'm sent for the lady Blair. My mistress wishes to speak with her."

"Another command performance," Blair muttered.

"I'll wait in your chambers." Larkin laid a hand on her arm. "You'll come, tell me how she is."

"I'll let you know." Blair started out, glanced at Dervil. "I know the way now."

"I'm asked to bring you."

At the door of Moira's chambers, Dervil knocked. It was Glenna who answered, let out a breath of relief when she saw Blair. "Good, thanks for coming."

"My lady." When Glenna lifted a brow, Dervil cleared her throat. "I would apologize for my poor behavior today, and ask at what time you wish to have the women gathered for instruction."

"An hour past dawn."

"Can you teach me to fight?"

"I will teach you," Glenna corrected.

Dervil's smile was hard and tight. "We'll be ready."

"Something I missed?" Blair asked Glenna when Dervil left them.

"Just part of a very long day. Something else you missed." She kept her voice low. "I found Moira arguing with Cian at the edge of the courtyard."

"Not a big surprise."

"It was when he finished the argument with his lips."

"Come again?"

"He kissed her. Hard, steamy, passionate."

"Ho boy."

"She was pretty shaken." Glenna glanced over her shoulder. "And not, in my opinion, due to insult and outrage."

"I repeat: Ho boy."

"I'm telling you because I don't want to be worried about this all by myself."

"Thanks for sharing."

"What are friends for?" Glenna stepped back. "Finish that potion, Moira," she said, lifting her voice now to conversational level. "I mean it."

"I am. I will. You've fussed enough."

Moira sat near the fire. She wore robes now, with her hair loose down her back. The bruising on her face stood out against her pallor. "Blair, thank you for coming. I know you must be tired, but I didn't want you to go to bed before I thanked you."

"How are you holding up?"

"Glenna's fussed and tended and dosed me." She held up the cup, drank the contents down. "I feel well enough."

"It was a good fight. You had some nice moves out there."

"I toyed with him too long." Moira lifted her shoulders, then winced as the wound in her side objected to the movement. "That was foolish and prideful. More foolish, more prideful to tell you to release the second. You were right not to."

"Yeah, I was." Blair came over to sit on the hassock at Moira's feet. "I'm not going to tell you I know anything about being a queen. But I do know that being a leader doesn't mean doing it all yourself. Being a warrior doesn't mean fighting when the fight isn't necessary."

"I let my needs cloud my judgment. I know that. I won't do so again."

"Well, all's well that ends." She patted Moira's knee.

"You're the best friends I've known, save Larkin. And the closest women to me but my mother. I saw by your faces when you stood in the door that Glenna told you what she saw between me and Cian."

Unsure how to answer, Blair rubbed her hands on her thighs. "Okay."

"I think we might have some wine." When Moira started to rise, Glenna laid a hand on her shoulder to stop her.

"I'll get it. I didn't tell Blair to talk behind your back, or gossip."

"I know that as well. It was concern, as a friend, as another woman. There's no need for concern. I was angry. No, enraged," Moira corrected as Glenna came back with the wine. "That he would take it upon himself to end what I wanted to do."

"He only beat me to it by a couple seconds," Blair told her.

"Well. Well. I went after him when it was my duty to stay, to speak to my people. But I went after him, and I deviled him. He'd done what he did to stop me from making a foolish and perhaps fatal mistake. And he told me as much, but I wasn't ready to listen, to accept. He showed me as much, and it's all of a piece, what happened at the end of it. He only showed me that I wasn't strong enough to stop any sort of attack. It meant nothing more than that."

"Okay . . ." Blair searched for words. "If you're satisfied with that."

"It's difficult for a woman to be satisfied when she's kissed in such a way, then coldly rejected." Still Moira lifted a shoulder. "But it was done in anger on both sides. I won't apologize to him, nor do I expect he will to me. We'll simply go on, remembering there are more important things than pride and temper."

"Moira." Glenna stroked a hand over Moira's hair. "Do you have feelings for him?"

As if to search inside herself, Moira closed her eyes. "There are times it seems I'm nothing but feelings. But I know where my duty lies. I've agreed to go to the stone, take hold of the sword. Not tomorrow. There's much to do tomorrow. But by week's end. I've shown my people they have a warrior in me. Soon, if the gods' will it, I'll show them a queen."

When they stepped out, Moira remained in the chair, watching the fire.

"What I gave her will help her sleep, and soon, I hope." Blowing out a breath, Glenna dug her hands into her pockets.

"This could get complicated."

"What *isn't*? I should have seen something like this coming."

"Time to turn in your crystal ball on a newer model?"

"Oh well." They walked together toward their own rooms. "Should we talk to Cian about this?"

"Sure. You go first."

With a half laugh, Glenna shook her head. "Okay, we leave it alone. Stay out of it—at least for now. You know, I'm a firm believer in full disclosure in relationships. But I'm not going to say anything to Hoyt about this."

"If you think I'm going to blab to Larkin, think again. We've all got enough on our minds."

The morning was soggy and cold, but there were a flock of women on the gaming field. Most of them wore pants—what the locals called *braes*—and tunics.

"More than twice the turnout I had yesterday," Glenna told Blair. "That's Moira's doing."

"She sure as hell drove the point home last night. Look, I'll give you an hour, get them started. Then I'm going to want to get my pet dragon up in the air."

Whether it was the gloom of the morning or the dregs of the tension from the night before, Blair was antsy. "I want to check out the battlefield firsthand, make sure those settlements near it are cleared out. And I want to swing by, make sure the traps are up and running."

"Just another day in paradise. Well, I guess we ought to move this indoors." Hands on hips, Glenna turned a circle. "See if there's a space we can work with."

"Why?"

"In case you haven't noticed, it's raining."

"Yeah, I got that with all the water dripping off my hair. Point is, we don't know what conditions will be like on

Samhain. For that matter, we don't know what they'll be like if any of these women have to tangle with a vamp before that. Might as well get used to fighting dirty, so to speak."

"Crap."

"Buck up, soldier." Blair gave her a friendly punch in the arm.

At the end of an hour, Blair was filthy, mildly bruised and in the best of moods. A little down-and-dirty training had gone a long way toward smoothing down the restlessness.

She started across the courtyard with the goal of finding Larkin, then stopped short when she recognized his mother and sister coming her way.

Perfect, she thought. Aces. She was covered with mud and sweat, and about to cross paths with the mom of the guy she was sleeping with. Just her lucky day.

Since there was nowhere to duck out of sight, she toughed it out. "Good morning."

"And to you. I am Deirdre, and this is my daughter, Sinann."

Blair nearly extended a hand before she remembered herself. Since she didn't think she could pull off a curtsey under current conditions, she simply nodded. "It's nice to meet you. I've, ah, been training some of the women."

"We watched." In the way of pregnant women, Sinann folded her hands over the mound of her belly. "You have skill—and energy."

She smiled when she said it, so Blair ordered herself to relax. "They're coming along."

"My son speaks well of you."

"Oh." Blair looked back at Deirdre, cleared her throat. Relax, hell. "That's good to know. Thank you. I was just looking for him. We need to do a little scouting."

"He's in the stables." Deirdre gave Blair a long, quiet look. "Do you think I don't know he shares your bed?" Before Blair could speak, could think to speak, Sinann made a sound that might have been muffled laughter.

"I'm his mother, after all," Deirdre continued in that same mild tone. "I'm aware he's shared beds of other women before you. But he's never spoken to me of them, as he speaks of you. So that changes the matter. I'll beg your pardon. From what he's said, I believed you'd prefer plain speaking."

"I do. I would. Oh boy, I'm sorry. I've just never had a conversation like this, and not with someone like you."

"A mother?"

"For starts. I don't want you to think I just share my bed with anyone who's . . ." Could this be more embarrassing? Blair wondered as Deirdre simply continued to study her with what looked like amused interest. "He's a good man. He's, well, he's an amazing man. You've done your job very well."

"No compliment is dearer to a mother's heart, and I certainly agree with you." The amusement faded now. "This war comes to us, and he'll do battle. I've never faced such a thing, so I have to believe, deep in my heart, that he does what he must, and will live."

"I believe it, if that helps."

"It does. I have other children." Deirdre touched a hand to her daughter's arm. "Another son, the husband of my daughter who is a son to me. I'll have the same faith in them. But my daughter can't fight like the women you teach."

"The child is to be born before the yule," Sinann told Blair. "My third. My children are too young to fight, and this one not yet born. How do I protect them?"

Blair thought of the crosses Hoyt and Glenna had made. She believed the others would agree Larkin's pregnant sister should have one. "There's a lot you can do," Blair assured her. "I'll help you."

Now she turned to Deirdre. "But you shouldn't worry about your daughter, your grandchildren. Your sons, your husband, my friends and I will never let what's coming here get this far."

"You give me peace of mind, and I'm grateful. We may not be able to fight, but we won't be idle. There are many things women who are no longer young, and women who carry life, can do. We'll do them. Now, you have work so we won't keep you longer. Good day to you, and gods protect."

"Thank you."

Blair stood a moment, watching them walk away. Women with spine, she thought. Lilith was going to be so out of her league.

Satisfied, she hunted Larkin down in the stables where he was stripped down to the waist, slicked with sweat, and helping forge weapons.

Her mood only improved. What could be better than watching a half-naked, great-looking guy beat hot steel into a sword?

She could see they'd made a good start from the number of weapons set aside to cure. The anvil rang with hammer strokes, and smoke billowed as a red-hot blade was plunged into a vat of water.

Was it a wonder, she asked herself, that her mind clicked over to sex?

"Can I get one of those engraved?" she called out. "Something like: 'To the woman who pierced my heart.' Corny, yet amusing."

He looked up, grinned. "You look like you've been rolling in the mud."

"Have been. I was about to go clean up."

He handed his hammer off to one of the other men, then picked up a cloth to scrub the sweat from his face as he walked to her. "We'll have every man and woman in Geall armed by Samhain. Cian's remark some time ago about beating the plowshares into swords isn't that far off. Word's gone out."

"Good. It needs to. Can you break away from here?"

He used his finger to rub some of the mud from her cheek. "What did you have in mind?"

"A couple of flybys. Weather's crappy, I know, but we can't wait for sunshine and rainbows. I need to see the battlefield, Larkin. I need a firsthand look."

"All right then." He grabbed the tunic he'd discarded earlier and called out a quick stream of Gaelic to the men working behind them.

"They'll push on well enough without me."

"Have you seen Moira this morning?"

"Aye. We had a discussion, with considerable heat. Then cooled off and made up. She's gone into the village to speak to people, the merchants. To bargain for more horses, wagons, supplies, whatever it is she's scribbled down on her list of things we'll need in the coming weeks."

"It's good thinking. And smart to make sure she's seen after last night. Anyone who wasn't there would have heard by now. The more visible she is, the better."

In the coming weeks, Blair thought as she went inside to clean up, the shopping, list-making, supply-gathering were all something women like Deirdre and Sinann could deal with. Keep them busy, she mused. And keep the royal family visible.

She scraped off the mud, changed into a reasonably fresh shirt, then strapped on her standard weapons.

When she met Larkin in the courtyard, she took the sheaths for his sword, his stakes. "Got something for you." She picked up the harness she'd set on the ground, slid the sheaths into the loops. "Put this together for you so you can carry your weapons when you're zipping around up there."

"Well, isn't this fine!" He grinned like a kid presented with a shiny new red wagon. "This was thoughtful of you, Blair." He leaned over to give her a kiss.

"Do your thing, and we'll try it out."

"I owe you a gift." He kissed her again.

When he'd become the dragon, Blair looped the harness over his body, gave it a quick cinch. "Not bad, if I do say so myself." She vaulted onto him. "Let's fly, cowboy."

She'd never get used to it. Even in the rain it was a thrill to feel the wonder of what was beneath her, and rise up and up. Into mists now, drenched with wet, that curtained the land below. It was like flying inside a cloud, she thought, where the sound was muffled and there was nothing but the flight.

She decided she'd never be satisfied with anything as ordinary as an airplane again.

The rain thinned, and as the sun struggled to carve beams through the clouds, she saw the rainbow. It arched, a bleeding blur of delicate colors that seemed to drip through the rain. With a lazy sweep of wings, Larkin turned so that the arch glimmered like a doorway ahead. And the colors deepened, seemed to shine like wet silk. As shafts of sunlight cut through the clouds, the rain and those soft, arching colors turned the sky to wonder.

There was a trumpeting call, a kind of joyful blare. Then the sky was filled with dragons.

She lost her breath, literally felt it whiz out of her lungs as beautiful winged beasts soared beside her, in front of her, behind. In more colors than the rainbow, she realized, with their emeralds and rubies and sapphires. She felt Larkin's body ripple as he answered their call, and grinned like a fool when he turned his head and fixed a laughing gold eye on her.

She was flying with a flock of dragons. Herd? Pack? Pod? What did it matter? The wind from their wings blew over her face and hair, sent her coat billowing as they soared through the rainbow sky. The other dragons circled, looped, somersaulted in playful dances. Anticipating, she gripped the harness, shouted for Larkin to: "Do it! Do it!"

And screamed with excitement as he dived and rolled. Hanging upside down as he soared belly-up, she could see the mists tear and reveal the sparkling green and deep, deep brown of the land of Geall.

He skimmed the treetops, dipped over the rush of a river, then climbed, climbed, climbed into air that gleamed now with the strengthening sun.

They flew on, past rainbows and jeweled wings, until it was only the two of them and the sky. Overcome, she lowered to him, laid her cheek on his neck. He'd said he'd owed her a gift, she remembered. He had given her one beyond price.

They flew through sunlight now, and occasional and surprising showers of rain. Below she could see small villages or settlements, the rough roads that joined them, the tangle of streams or narrow rivers, tough little knuckles of forest.

But ahead lay the mountains, dark and mist-shrouded and somehow foreboding.

She could see the edge of the valley that lay at their feet, broken land scarred with rock. The first shudder rippled down her spine as she looked down on what she'd too often seen in dreams.

The sun didn't sparkle here. It was as if the light was absorbed, just sucked away into the dark belly of gullies and chasms, rejected by the dull grass that fought with the spears and juts of weather-pocked rock.

The land dipped and rose, tightened in on itself into folds. And the looming mountains cast great shadows across it, shadows that seemed to cause the land itself to move and shift.

It was more than a shudder that ran through her now. It was an unreasonably, atavistic fear. A fear that this hard and forbidding land would be her grave.

As Larkin veered off, she closed her eyes and let the fear have its way for a moment. Because it couldn't be beaten off, she thought, couldn't be battered down by fists or weapons. It had to be recognized, and accepted.

Once it had, she could control it. If she were strong enough, she could use that fear to fight, and to survive.

When he touched down, she slid off. Legs a little shaky, she admitted to herself. But they held her up, and that's what counted. Her fingers might have felt stiff, but they worked, and she used them to uncinch the weapon harness.

Then Larkin stood beside her.

"It's an evil place."

It was almost a relief to her to hear him say it. "Yeah, oh yeah, it is."

"You can almost feel that evil rising up out of the ground. I've been there before, and it always seemed to me to be a place out of Geall. Not quite a part of it. But it never felt as it did today, as though the ground itself wanted to open up and swallow you whole."

"Oh boy. It got to me, I've got to be honest. Turned my blood cold." She rubbed her hands over her face, then glanced around. "Where are we?"

"Just a ways off from it. I didn't want to set down there. It's an easy walk from here, and I wanted a few moments first."

"I'll take them."

He touched her cheek. "A long way from rainbows here."

"The wrong side of them, I'd say. And I want to say something else, before we head back and face that place. That flight—the rainbow, the other dragons, the whole ball of it, it was the most incredible experience of my life."

"Is that the truth of it?" He cocked his head. "I thought the most incredible experience of your life would be making love with me."

"Oh yeah, right. Well, next to that."

"All right then." He tipped up her chin to kiss her. "I'm glad you enjoyed it."

"It was more than enjoyment. It was just flat down amazing. The best gift anyone's ever given me."

"Handy for me, that rainbow. Dragons can't resist one."

"Really? They're so gorgeous. I thought my eyes would pop out of my head."

"Happens you've seen a dragon before," he reminded her.

"And you're the most gorgeous and handsome of them,

blah blah, but honestly, Larkin, they're extreme. All those colors, and the power . . . Hold on—do people ride them, the way I've been riding you?"

"No one rides like you, *a stór*. And they don't, no. They're not horses, after all."

"But if they could. You talked to them."

"It's not what you'd call conversation. It's a kind of communication to be sure. A sort of expression of thought of feeling. And something I can only do when I'm in the dragon, so to speak."

"Aerial warfare would give us a big, fat advantage. I want to think about this."

"They're gentle creatures, Blair."

"So, for the most part, are the women Glenna and I are training to fight. When worlds are on the line, pal, you use everything that comes to hand." She could see the resistance clearly enough on his face. "Let me just play with it in my head awhile. It's this way, right?"

"It is."

They walked the narrow road, framed in hedges and lined with spears of orange lilies. He bent, plucked one, then passed it to her.

Blair stared down at it, delicate petals in a strong and vibrant color. Something wild and lovely.

She talked of war, she thought. And he gave her a flower.

Maybe it was foolish—maybe both of them were—but she slid its stem into one of the buttonholes of her coat. And she breathed in its sweet scent as they walked toward the battleground.

Chapter 18

They'd walked only minutes when Blair heard the sound of horses, and a rattle she assumed was a wagon or cart. When they cleared the curve in the road, she saw she'd been right. There were two wagons, both loaded with people and possessions. There were riders on horseback as well, some no more than children.

Mules were tethered to the back of each wagon and clopped along with a look she could only describe as extreme irritation.

The first wagon pulled up, with the man driving it lifting his cap to Blair, then addressing himself to Larkin.

"It's the wrong way you're traveling," he said. "For by orders of the royal family all in this province are to go into Dunglas, or farther, even into Geall City itself if they can manage it. There are demons coming, it's said, and war with them."

Beside him, the woman clutched the baby she carried closer to her breast. "It won't be safe here," she told them. "All are leaving their homes behind. The princess Moira herself has decreed that every citizen of Geall must be indoors by sunset. You're welcome to a seat in the wagon, and to ride with us as far as my cousin in Dunglas."

"It's kind of you, mistress, and thank you for the offer of hospitality, but we're on business here for the royal family and for Geall. We'll make our way."

"We had to leave our sheep, our crops." The man looked behind him. "But the riders who came from the castle said there was no choice in it."

"They'd be right."

The man turned back to study Blair. "And it's said, too, that warriors and wizards have come from beyond Geall to fight this war and drive the demons out of the world."

"It's truth." But Larkin saw both fear and doubt. "I've gone out of this world, and back into it. I'd be Larkin, lord of Mac Dara."

"My lord." Now the man removed his cap altogether. "It's our honor to speak with you."

"This is the lady Blair, a great warrior from beyond Geall."

The boy who sat on horseback beside the wagon all but bounced in the saddle. "Have you killed demons, then? Have you fought and killed them, Lady?"

"Seamas." The woman, obviously his mother, spoke sharply. "You haven't been given leave to speak, much less to pester with questions."

"It's all right." Blair stroked a hand over his horse. The boy had a wide-open face, she thought, where freckles had exploded like ginger over cream. He couldn't have been more than eight. "I have fought them, and killed them. So has Lord Larkin."

"And so will I!"

She hoped not. She hoped to God he was safely tucked into bed by nightfall, and every night after. "A strong boy like you has another job. To stay inside, every night until the war's over, guarding his mother, his brothers and sisters. Keeping them safe will take courage."

"No demon will touch them!"

"Best make your way now, and safe travels," Larkin said.

"And to you my lord, my lady."

He clicked to the horses, snapped the reins. Blair watched them until both wagons had rumbled by. "That's a lot of faith in your family, to pack up, leave your home. That's another strong weapon, that kind of faith."

"You spoke well to that boy, made him see that staying inside with his mother was a duty. Lilith's whelp was about that age—a bit younger, actually." Larkin reached under his hair, traced the scar on the back of his neck with his fingers. "Sweet-faced, too. He was some mother's son before she turned him into a monster."

"She'll be paying for that, and a lot more. That bite give you any trouble?" she asked as they started to walk again.

"It doesn't. Not something I forget though, that's for certain. As I'm sure you know for yourself." He lifted her hand, turned her wrist over and kissed her scar. "Still pissed, as you say, that the little bugger got a taste of me. Hardly more than a baby, and damn near killed me."

"Kiddie vampires aren't any less lethal than the full grown variety. And actually, in my opinion, more creepy."

The hedgerows dropped away, and the Valley of Silence lay before them.

"And speaking of creepy," she murmured. "It's no less goosebumping from down here. I'm no sissy, but I wouldn't be insulted if you held my hand."

"I wouldn't be insulted if you held mine."

So they stood, clutching hands, on what seemed to Blair to be the end of the world.

The land fell off in a steep, jagged, ankle-breaking incline. It heaved up in nasty hillocks or rippled tables of rock. Acres of it, she thought. Acres of misery and shadows with only the undulating moan of a cold wind through the wild grass.

"Lots of places to hide," she commented. "We can use that as well as they can. Most of the fighting's going to have to be done on foot. Only the best riders could handle a mount on that ground."

She narrowed her eyes. "We'd better go down, take a look at what we're dealing with."

"How do you feel about riding a goat?"

"Unenthusiastic." But she gave his hand a squeeze. "Besides, if we can't negotiate it now, daylight, no pressure, we're not going to do very well at night, in the heat of battle."

Plenty of footholds, she discovered as they started down. And the ground was too mean and stubborn to crumble away under her boots. Maybe she'd have preferred a nice flat field for the mother of all battles, but there were ways to use what they had to their advantage.

"Some of these crevices, shallow caves could be useful. Hiding men and weapons."

"They would." Larkin crouched down, peered into a small opening. "They'd think of that as well, as you said back in Ireland."

"So we get here first, block off some strategic points. Magically maybe—we can talk to Hoyt and Glenna about that. Or with crosses."

He nodded, straightened. "We'd want the high ground there, and perhaps there." He gestured as he studied the lay. "Flood down on them, that's what we'd do. Flood down on the bloody bastards, keeping archers on the high ground."

Blair climbed up on a shelf of rock. "We'll need light, that's essential."

"We can't count on the moon."

"Glenna conjured some sort of light the night we went head-to-head with Lora in that skirmish back at Cian's place. They'll slaughter us like flies if we fight in the dark. That's their turf. We can't lay traps here," she added with a thoughtful frown. "Can't risk our own men stumbling over or falling into one."

Larkin held up a hand for her as she prepared to jump

down. "She'll come here as well, at night, to study, to work out her strategy. She may have been here before, before we were born. Before those who birthed us were born. Spinning out her web and dreaming of that single night to come."

"Yeah, she'll have been here. But . . ."

"What?"

"So have I. I've seen this place in my head as long as I can remember. From up there, from down here. In sunlight and silence, in the dark with the screams of battle. I know this place," she whispered. "I've been afraid of it all my life."

"Yet you come to it. You stand on it."

"Feels like I've been pushed here, closer and closer, every day. I don't want to die here, Larkin."

"Blair—"

"No, I'm not afraid to die. Or not obsessed with the idea of it. But, oh God, I don't want to end here, in this hard, lonely place. Drowning in my own blood."

"Stop." He took her shoulders. "Stop this."

Her eyes were huge now, and deep, deep blue. "You see, I don't know if I've seen it, or just imagined it because of the fear. I don't know if I've watched myself die here. Damn gods, anyway, for their mixed messages and unreasonable demands."

She patted her hands on his chest to ease him back, give herself a little space. "It's okay, I'm okay. Just a little panic attack."

"It's this place, this evil place. Slides under the skin and freezes the blood."

"So, advantage them. But you know what? You know something that tips onto our side? The people who'll come here, who'll take this ground and fight on this place, they'll have something inside them. Whatever it is, it'll already have given evil the finger."

"What finger?"

She hadn't thought it possible, not in this awful silence, not in this nightmare place, but she laughed until her sides ached.

She explained as they walked the broken ground. And it seemed easier then, to cross it, study it, to think clearly. When they climbed back up she felt more steady, more sure.

She brushed off her hands, started to speak. Then simply froze.

The goddess stood in a stream of light. It seemed to pulse from her white robe, and still it was dim compared to her luminous beauty.

I'm awake, Blair thought, so this is new. Wide awake, and there she is.

"Larkin, do you see—"

But he was going down on one knee, bowing his head. "My lady."

"My son, you would kneel before what you have never truly believed?"

"I have come to believe in many things."

"Then believe this," Morrigan said. "You are precious to me. Each of you. All of you. I've watched you travel here, through the light and the dark. And you, daughter of my daughters, will you not kneel?"

"Is that what you need?"

"No." And she smiled. "I only wondered. Rise up, Larkin. You have my gratitude, and my pride."

"Would either of those come with an army of gods?" Blair asked her, and earned a shocked hushing sound from Larkin.

"You are my army, you and what you both carry inside you for tomorrow and tomorrow. Would I ask this thing of you if it were not possible?"

"I don't know," Blair answered. "I don't know if gods only ask the possible."

"And yet you come, you prepare, you battle. So you have my gratitude, my pride, and my admiration. This, the second month, the time of learning is nearly done. So will come the time of knowing. You must know if you are to win this thing."

"What, my lady, must we know?"

"You will know when you know."

"See." Blair spread her hands. "Cryptic. Why does it always have to be cryptic?"

"It frustrates you, I know." There might have been a laugh in Morrigan's eyes as she stepped closer. But there was no doubt of the affection in the brush of her fingers— warm and real—over Blair's cheek. "Mortals may see the path the gods have carved, but it's up to them to choose a direction and follow it. I will tell you that you are my hope, you and the four with you who forged the circle. You are my hope, the hope of mankind. You are my joy, and the future."

She touched Larkin's cheek now. "And you are blessed."

She stepped back, the laughter gone. In its place was a sorrow and a kind of steely strength. "What is coming must come. There will be pain, and blood and loss. There is no life without its price. The shadows will fall, dark upon dark, and demons rise from it. A sword flames through it, and a crown shines. Magic beats like a heart, and what was lost can be regained if that heart is willing. Give these words to all the circle, and remember them. For it is not the will of gods that will win the day, but the will of humankind."

She vanished with the light so Blair stood with Larkin on the edge of the cursed ground.

"Remember it?" Blair lifted her hands, let them fall. "How are we supposed to remember all that? Did you get it?"

"I'll remember it. It's my first conversation with a goddess, so I can promise you I won't be forgetting the details of it."

They flew again, away from the valley to the first of the three points Blair had devised for traps. They set down in a green glade with a pretty river winding through it.

Standing beside the river, she took out the map the six of them had worked on. "Okay, if we go by the fact that our portal stands in nearly the same spot here as it does in Ireland, then we make the big leap of faith that the same would hold true for Lilith's way in, the cliffs are roughly twenty miles west."

"They are, as you see here." He traced his finger on the map, along the coastline. "And caves as well, which she could use for her base."

"Could," Blair agreed. "And she might put some troops there. But it makes more sense to base closer to the battleground. Even if she doesn't, at some point she'll have to move west to east, and if she's taking the most direct route, she'd have to cross this way. And this river." She nodded toward the water. "Smarter to cross it near this point, where it narrows. Moira said she took care of the mojo."

"She had the holy man brought here, as you wanted. The water was blessed."

"Not to question your holy man, but I'd feel better if I checked it out."

She dug in her pocket for a vial of blood. "Courtesy of the vampire you skewered into the ground the other night. Let's try a little chemistry."

Larkin took the water bag to the river to fill it. While he was there he cupped his hand, sampled straight from the river itself. "Fresh and cool in any case. Pity its not deep enough for a swim just here, or I'd talk you out of your clothes again."

"On the clock here, pretty boy." She crouched down beside him and opened the vial. "Just a couple of drops. It's either going to work or it's not."

He tapped a few drops into the vial. And the blood bubbled and steamed with the water mixed with it.

"All right! You've got yourself a happening holy man. Look at that boil." She straightened to do a quick happy dance. "Picture this. Along marches the evil vampire army. Gotta cross the river, if not at this point, at some point. Crap, going to get our feet wet, but we're the evil vampire army, we're not afraid of a little stinking water. Then they start across. Man, I can just *hear* it. 'Yipe, yipe, shit, fuck!' Splashing across, splashing back, just making it worse. Wet feet, hell. Searing, burning feet—worse if some of them panic and knock each other down, slip. Oh joy, oh rapture."

Larkin stayed in his crouch, grinning at her pleasure. "It was damn clever of you."

"It was freaking brilliant. High five!" She grabbed his hand, slapped her palm to his. "It's a thing."

He got up, yanked her to him and kissed her long and deep. "It's a thing I like better."

"Who could argue? Wouldn't it be great, oh, wouldn't it be sweet, if Lilith was leading the way, starts her strut across the stream. The ultimate hot foot. I'm just loving this."

She took a huge breath. "Okay, that's enough fun and frivolity. Let's go check out the others."

A good day, Blair thought as they headed toward the second location. Rainbows, dragons, goddesses. She'd faced one of her personal nightmares by walking in the valley, and she'd come out of it again. Now she was seeing her guerilla warfare tactics take shape.

Lilith's army was going to take a few hard kicks in the ass long before Samhain. Since vamps weren't known for tending their wounded without a strong connection between them, she was likely going to lose a nice chunk of troops on the march toward destiny.

When Larkin started his descent she prepared herself for another pat on the back. Then he changed directions. Puzzled, she looked down and saw the overturned wagon.

There was a man lying beside it, and a woman standing with a toddler in her arms, and another at her skirts.

The youngest let out a squeal that might have been delight, might have been terror as a gold dragon with a woman on its back soared down to the road.

The young mother went pale as a sheet and stumbled back when the dragon shifted shape into a man.

"Oh, blessed mother!"

"Don't be frightened." Larkin spoke gently, added what Blair thought of as his thousand-watt smile. "Just a bit of magic, is all. I'm Larkin, son of Riddock."

"My lord." Her cheeks remained colorless, but she managed a curtsey.

"You've some trouble here. Your man is hurt?"

"It's me leg." The man struggled to sit up, but could only moan. "I fear it's broke."

"Let me have a look." Blair knelt down. His face was gray, she noted, with a good-sized bruise along his jaw-line.

"The axle, it broke. Thank the gods my family wasn't hurt, but I took a bad fall. Then the bloody horse runs off."

"Might have a small fracture here." Blair gave him a bolstering smile. "It's not as bad as your axle, but you're not going to be walking for a while. He's going to need help, Larkin."

Larkin studied the wheel. "There's no fixing that without some new wood. Where are you bound?" he asked the woman.

"My lord, we were going to stop at the wayfarers on the road to Geall City, then travel on from there on the morrow. My husband has relations in Geall City. His brother, Niall, is with the castle guards."

"I know Niall well. If you'd get what you feel you can't do without for the evening, we'll see you to the wayfarer."

The older child, a girl of about four, tugged on Larkin's tunic. "Where did your wings go?"

"I've just tucked them away for now, but I'll show them to you again. Help your mother now." He gestured to Blair.

"Can he ride?" he asked her.

"You'd have to go at a walk. We can put a temporary

splint on that leg, but I don't think it should be jostled around. He's in a lot of pain."

"All right then, it'll have to be flying. It's only a few miles to the inn."

"You take them. Two adults—one of them hurt—a couple of kids. That's about all you can manage."

"I don't like leaving you alone."

"Broad daylight," she reminded him, "and I'm armed. I can head over, check out the next trap. It's what, about a quarter mile that way, right?"

"It is, but you could wait here. I wouldn't be much above a half hour."

"Kick my heels by a broken wagon? I can check it out and be back here by the time you make the round trip. Then we can swing by the last of them, and maybe do a sweep of the area, see if there are any stragglers that need a hand. We'll be back home before sunset, with time to spare."

"All right then, for you'll go anyway the minute I've gone."

"Nice to be so well understood."

It took time, not just to load the family on, but to first convince the woman that it could be done. That it had to be done.

"Now don't worry a bit, Breda." Larkin gave her full-power charm. "I'll be staying as low to the ground as I'm able. We'll have you and your family at the inn quick as a wink, and send off for help for your man here. I'll see that someone comes and fixes your wagon in the morning, and delivers it straight to you. Can't ask better than that."

"No, my lord, no. You're so kind." Still she stood, all but wringing her hands. "I've heard, of course, of your gift. All of Geall knows of it, but to see . . . And the idea of riding a dragon—"

"Won't your daughter have stories to tell? Come now, your husband needs help."

"Aye. Well, of course, of course."

He changed before she could balk, and left it to Blair to deal with the rest. She helped the injured man up, taking his weight as Larkin bellied to the ground. Using rope from the wagon, she tied him on.

"I'm grateful to you," he said to Blair. "I don't know how we'd have managed."

"If you're anything like your brother, you'd have figured something. He's a good man. You get on behind him," Blair instructed his wife. "Keep the kids between you. I'm going to tie you on his back. You'll be secure, I promise you."

"I like his wings." The girl clambered on before her mother could make a peep. "They shine."

When it was done, Larkin picked up the pack of possessions in his jeweled legs. Then turned his head to give Blair a nuzzle on the arm.

And he was rising up. Blair heard the little girl shouting with absolute delight as they skimmed down the road and away.

"Know just how you feel," Blair said with a laugh. With the map in hand, she crossed the road and started across the first field.

It felt good to walk, and to have a little alone time. Not that she wasn't nuts about the guy, Blair thought as she brushed her finger over the flower in her buttonhole. But she was so used to being on her own. This whole business had all but eliminated her solo time.

Since it started, she'd been part of a team—a circle, she corrected. People she respected and believed in, no question, but people who needed to be consulted.

All in all, she was better at teamwork than she'd imagined she would be. Maybe, she decided, it was all a matter of who was making up the team.

And somehow, through that team, she'd ended up being half of a couple. She hadn't believed that was in the cards for her, not again. Certainly not with a man who knew everything there was to know about her, and not only got it, but valued it.

She already knew it was going to rip her to pieces when they went their separate ways. No choice there that she could see, so there wasn't much point in brooding about it, less point in wasting the time they had feeling sorry for herself.

In any case, they both had to live first before they could be miserable and alone.

It was better, all around better, to enjoy, and to cherish the time they had. When that time was done she could look back at it and know she'd loved, and had been loved.

She glanced up at the sky, wondering how the farmer and his family were faring with their first—and if she was any judge of the mother of the brood, their last—dragon flight.

Larkin would take care of them. It was one of the things he was good at. Taking care. When you added the fairy-tale-prince looks, the kick-ass attitude in battle, that quick grin and the excellent stamina in bed, he was just about perfect.

She checked her map again, hopped over a low stone fence to the next field.

Beyond it were a few trees, and the most direct route from the coast to the valley.

They'd move through here, Blair thought, two, maybe three hours before they reached the stream with the blessed water. And at night, go quickly through this open area toward the shelter of woods another few miles inland.

This route was logical, and it was efficient. Add in the scatter of farms, cottages sprinkled through, there was the possibility of fresh food.

Oh yeah, Blair mused, this is the way she'll come. Has to. In stages, maybe, leaving some at the caves, at various safe points along the way. For hunting, for ambushes, quick raids.

"It's what I'd do," Blair murmured, and with a last

check of the map, headed southeast into a small, thin grove of trees.

She saw it almost immediately, and her first thought was some kid or passer-by had stumbled over the trap. And into it.

Her heart bounced straight into her throat. She sprinted toward the wide hole, terrified she'd see bodies impaled on the wooded spikes below.

What she saw was a scatter of weapons, and one very dead horse.

"Moved up the schedule," she said softly, and despite the sunlight, reached behind her to draw her sword.

Moved things up, Blair decided, when the reports came in that they'd gone to the Dance with supplies and weapons. And vanished.

She'd have known where they'd vanished, Blair thought. So Lilith's army was already in Geall, already on the march. And had already passed this point. The trap had worked. From the weapon count, it looked to have taken out at least a dozen—and the very unlucky horse.

She crouched down, wishing she had some of the rope she'd used earlier. They needed to retrieve those weapons—waste not, want not—and get that poor horse out of there.

She was puzzling over how she and Larkin might do that when she realized the light had changed. Looking up, she saw the sky overhead was black with clouds.

As twilight fell in a fingersnap, she got to her feet. "Oh shit."

She backed up, backed away from the hole, and thought it wasn't just a dozen vamps who'd walked into a trap. She'd just walked into one herself.

And they came up, out of the ground.

Chapter 19

She took two out fast, an instinctive and wide sweep of her sword, before they were fully disinterred. But there were alarms shrilling in the back of her mind that said she was in big, bad trouble.

Eight, she counted, after the two she'd dusted. They had her surrounded, cutting off any chance of retreat. And she'd walked right into it, all but whistling a tune. If she managed to live—and the odds were against it—she'd curse herself for it later. Right now since flight wasn't an option, fight was all that was left.

The one thing she had, Blair reminded herself, was a lot of fight in her. She pulled her stake, blocked the first blade with her sword even as she pumped out a back kick. She spun, swinging out with the sword, scoring flesh, buying time. Spotting an opening, she rammed the stake.

One more down.

But these weren't green recruits who'd make many sloppy and fatal mistakes. What she was facing were trained and seasoned soldiers, and it was still seven against one.

She envisioned the fire, sending it rippling down the sword Glenna had charmed. "Yeah, come on. Come *on*!" Hacking out, she sent one falling back, his arm ablaze.

Then went flying as one caught her foot on the next kick and hurled her into the air. She slammed hard into the trunk of a tree, saw stars floating on a gray field edged with sickly red. But the one that charged her met fire and steel, and fell screaming into the trap.

She rolled, and with pain bursting through her, struck out with the flaming sword. Her left arm was numb from the shoulder down, and she'd lost the stake. She hacked, thrust, sliced, took a hard punch to the face that nearly sent her into the trap. She managed to spring over it, fight for footing. And with vicious, screaming blows, beat back the next attack.

One went for her throat, so she cracked the hilt of the sword on the bridge of his nose. She felt the chain that held her crosses snap as he fell back.

No stake, no cross. And five of them left. She wasn't going to make it, no longer hoped she could hold them back until Larkin got to her to even the odds.

So she wouldn't die in the valley, but here and now. But by God, she'd take as many as she could with her first so that when Larkin came for her, he could finish the rest.

Her left arm was nearly useless, but she still had her feet, and kicked up, kicked out as she sliced out fire. They'd weakened her, breaking her form, her rhythm. She blocked an oncoming sword, but the tip of it scored a line down her thigh on the down swing. Her slight stumble left her open enough so that when another kicked, the blow plowed into her belly, stealing her breath as her body flew back.

She went down hard, felt something tear inside her. With what she had left, she thrust up blindly, had the grim satisfaction of seeing one burst into flame.

Then the sword was knocked out of her hand, and she had nothing left.

How many left? she wondered. Three? Maybe three. Larkin could take three. He'd be all right. Head swimming, she struggled back to her feet. She didn't want to die on her back. She fisted her hands, fought to get her balance.

Maybe, maybe she could take one more, just one more, bare-handed, before they killed her.

But they'd stepped back, she saw. Three? Four? Her vision was doubling on her. But she willed it to focus, and saw Lora glide over the ground.

Weren't going to kill me, Blair thought dimly. Just working me over, wearing me down. Saving me for her. Worse than death, she realized as her blood went cold. She wondered if she could find a weapon and a way to end her own life before Lora made her a monster.

If she could manage it, she might be able to throw herself into the trap. Better staked than changed.

"I'm so impressed." Clapping her hands together lightly, Lora smiled. "You defeated seven of our seasoned warriors. I've lost a bet with Lilith. I wagered you'd take out no more than four."

"Happy to help you lose."

"Well, you did have a slight advantage. They were ordered not to kill you. That pleasure will be mine."

"You think?"

"Know. And that coat? I've admired that coat since I first saw you on the side of the road in Ireland. It's going to look marvelous on me."

"So that was you? Sorry, all of you smell the same to me."

"I can say the same about you mortals." Lora beamed out a gay smile. "Speaking of mortals, I have to say your Jeremy was absolutely delicious." Still smiling, she touched her fingertips to her lips, flicked them out as if reliving the moment.

Don't think about Jeremy, Blair ordered herself. Don't give her the satisfaction. So she said nothing, meeting Lora's laugh with stony silence.

"But where are my manners? We've met, of course, but haven't been formally introduced. I'm Lora, and I'll be your sire."

"Blair Murphy, and I'll be the one dusting you. And the coat looks better on me than it would on you."

"You're going to be the most delightful playmate! I can hardly wait. Because I have admiration and respect for you, we'll fight this out. Just you and I." Lora pointed a finger toward the trio of soldiers, wagged it. "Back, back, back now. This is between us girls."

"So, you want to fight?" Think, think, think, Blair ordered herself. Think over the pain. "Swords, knives, hand-to-hand?"

"I do love bare hands." Lora lifted hers, wiggled her fingers. "It's so intimate."

"Works for me." Blair spread her coat open to show she had no weapons. "Can I ask you a question?"

"Bien sur."

"Is that accent real, or do you just put it on?" She unhooked the water bottle from her belt.

"I was born in Paris, in the year fifteen-eighty-five."

Blair let out a snort. "Come on."

"All right," Lora said with a laugh, "fifteen-eighty-three. But what woman doesn't fudge a little about her age?"

"You were younger than me when you died."

"Younger when I was given true life."

"It's all a matter of perspective." Blair lifted the water sack, twisted it open. "Mind? Your boys gave me quite a workout. Feeling a little dehydrated."

"Be my guest."

Blair tipped the bag back, drank. The water felt like a miracle on her dry throat. "If I take you, are your boys going to finish me off?"

"You won't take me."

Blair angled her head, said a quick prayer. "Bet?"

And swung the bag so the blessed water splashed over Lora's face and throat.

The screams were like rusty razors slicing through Blair's brain. There was smoke, the nasty stench of burning flesh. She stumbled away from it as Lora ran shrieking.

A weapon, Blair thought, fighting to see, just to stay on her feet. Everything, anything was a weapon.

She grabbed a low branch of the tree as much for support as a last-ditch effort. Calling on whatever she had left she pulled at it, felt it crack. With something between a sob and a scream, she swung it at the three vampires who charged toward her.

The dragon dived out of the sky, tail lashing. Blair saw one of them fly headfirst into the trap as the man stood, drawing the sword from the harness that spilled around his feet.

The last thing she saw before she fell was the bright flame of it cleaving through the dark.

He fought like a madman, without a thought for his own safety. If they landed blows, he never felt them. His rage and his fear were beyond pain. There had been three, but if there'd been thirty he still would have cut through them like an avenging god.

His dragon had swept one into the stakes, and now he hacked through the shoulder of another. The arm that fell went to dust, and the creature that was left ran screaming across the field. The third rushed to retreat. Larkin swept up a stake on the run, flung it. And sent it to hell.

With his sword hand ready for however many more might spring out of the dark, he crouched to Blair. The words poured out of him, and were all her name. Her face had no color but the blood that streaked it, and the bruises already going black.

When her eyes fluttered open, he saw they were glassy with pain.

"My hero." Her voice was barely more than a thick whisper. "Gotta move, gotta go, could be more. Oh God, oh God, I'm hurt. You gotta help me up."

"Just be still a moment. I need to see how bad it is."

"It's bad. Just . . . is the light coming back or am I heading into that stupid white tunnel people talk about?"

"The sun's coming back. It's all right now."

"Ten, there were ten, and the French whore makes eleven. My head—damn it. Concussion. Vision keeps doubling on me. But—" She couldn't bite back the scream when he moved her shoulder.

"I'm sorry. *A stór, a stór,* I'm sorry."

"Dislocated. Don't think broken, just out of joint. Oh God. You have to fix it. I can't . . . I can't. You have to take care of it, okay? Then . . . Jesus, Jesus. Go get a wagon. I can't ride."

"You'll trust me now, won't you, my darling? Trust me to take care of you now."

"I do. I will. But I need you to—"

He did it quickly, bracing her back against the tree, pressing his body hard to her as he yanked her shoulder back into place.

She didn't scream this time. But he was watching her face, and saw her eyes roll up white before she slumped against him.

Ripping the sleeve of his tunic, he used the material to field dress the gash on her thigh before checking along her torso for broken ribs. When he'd done the best he could for her, Larkin laid her down gently before springing up to gather the weapons. After securing them in the harness, he draped it over himself and hoped it would hold.

Shimmered from man to dragon.

He picked her up, cradling her in his claws as if she were made of glass.

"Something's wrong." Glenna gripped Moira's arm as they stood on the practice field working with a handful of the more promising students. "Something bad, big. Wake Cian. Wake him now."

They both saw the black boil of the sky to the southeast, and the rippling curtain of darkness that fell from it.

"Larkin. Blair."

"Get Cian," Glenna repeated, and began to run.

She didn't have to shout for Hoyt; he was already sprinting toward her. "Lilith," was all she said.

"Midir, her wizard." He took hold of her arm, pulling her toward the castle. "This would be his work."

"She's already here. Larkin and Blair are out there, out there in the dark. We need to do something, quickly. Counteract the spell. There must be a way."

"Riddock should send riders out."

"They'd never get there in time. It's miles off, Hoyt."

"They'll go in any case."

When they rushed inside, Cian was already coming down, Moira hard on his heels.

"He was already coming," Moira said.

"I felt the change. False night. I can get there quicker than you, or any mortal."

"And what good will it do if the sun comes back?" Moira demanded.

"Time I gave that bloody cloak a try."

"We don't separate. We can't risk it. And sending riders, Hoyt." Glenna shook her head. "They won't help now. We need a circle, and a counter spell." Maybe a miracle, she thought. "We need it fast."

"It has to be outside, under the sky." Hoyt looked into his brother's eyes. "Will you risk it? We can try it without you," he said before Cian could speak. "The three of us."

"But the odds are better with me. Let's get it done."

They gathered what they needed. Hoyt and Glenna were already outside making hurried preparations when Cian came down again with the cloak.

Moira stepped forward when he got to the base of the stairs. "I think faith in your brother will strengthen the spell."

"Do you?"

"I think," she said in the same measured tones, "your willingness to risk so much for friends has already given you protection."

"We're about to find out." He swirled the cloak on, pulled the hood up. "Nothing ventured," he added. And for the first time in nearly a thousand years stepped into the sun.

There was heat. He felt it weigh down on him—lead heated almost to burning. It pressed on his chest, shortened his breath, but he crossed the courtyard.

"I haven't turned into a human torch yet," he said, "but I wouldn't object if this didn't take long."

"Fast as we can," Glenna told him. "Bright blessings on you, Cian."

"Let's keep the bright off it, if it's all the same."

"Carnelian for speed." She began placing crystals in a pentagram pattern on the stones. "Sunstone for light. Agates—dendritic for protection, plume for binding."

Now she took up herbs, dropping them into a bowl. "Garlic for protection. Sorry," she said to Cian.

"That's a myth."

"Okay, good. Holly, restoration of balance. Rose and willow. Power and love. Join hands. Keep yours inside the cloak, Cian, we'll come to you."

"Focus," Hoyt ordered, with his eyes on the black sky, the bubble of night to the south and east. "Draw out what you have. Both of you have power inside you. Draw it out and forge the circle."

"Guardians of the Watchtowers," Glenna called out. "We summon you."

"Of the east, of the south, of the west, of the north, we call your fire to cast here this circle."

At Hoyt's words the yellow candles Glenna had chosen to represent the sun sprang to light.

"Morrigan the mighty, join with us now," he continued. "We are your servants, we are your soldiers."

Casting her eyes to the sky, Glenna pulled everything she had inside her, and pushed. "Blessed are you and blessed are we who seek to fight this infamy. Magic against magic, white and pure against the black, here springs our power against this attack. Might and right push back the night. With our power joined we raise our cry, break this dark spell in the eastern sky. Hear our love and loyalty. As we will, so mote it be."

Her hand trembled in Hoyt's as the power spun round the circle. With her eyes still cast up, she saw the battle rage. Flashing lights, gushing black clashing together like swords to raise a thunder that sent the ground to quiver.

"We refute the dark magicks!" Hoyt shouted. "We cast them back, we cast them out. We call the sun to flame through the false night."

Overhead the war between the black and the white raged on.

Blair swam dizzily toward consciousness, and into the pain. She felt the wind rush by her, and thought she saw the blur of land below.

Flying? She was flying? Is this what happened after you were dead? But if she was dead, why the hell did she hurt so much?

She tried to move, but she was tied down, strapped in. Or maybe her body simply refused to work any longer. Then she managed to turn her head, and she was looking up at a golden throat.

She thought: Larkin. Then floated away once more.

He felt her stir, gently tightened his grip in hopes it would reassure her, make her feel more secure. He angled his head to look down at her, but her eyes were already closing again.

She looked so pale. She felt so fragile.

He'd left her alone.

He would live, all of his life, he would live with the image of her bleeding, left with nothing more than a tree branch for defense while monsters circled her like vultures.

If he'd been even seconds later, she would be dead. Because he hadn't been with her. He'd seen to the safety of others, and he'd tarried just a little longer so a young girl could pet his wings.

When the darkness had come, he hadn't been with her.

The fear ate through him that no matter how fast he'd flown to reach her, no matter if he'd stopped the three demons who'd stalked her from feeding, he'd still been too late to save her life.

Even when he saw the castle, the fear gnawed. He saw Moira rush out, and Hoyt, Glenna, his father and others. But still he knew nothing but that fear.

He'd barely touched the ground when he changed, and held Blair in his arms. "She's hurt. She's hurt."

"Bring her in, quickly." Sprinting alongside him, Glenna reached over to check the pulse in Blair's throat. "Up to her room. I'll get what I need. Moira, go with him, do what you can for her. I'll be quick."

"How bad?" Cian swung around to rush up the stairs beside Glenna.

"I don't know. Pulse is weak, thready. Her face . . . she took a beating."

"Bites?"

"I didn't see any." She grabbed her healing kit from her room, dashed out again.

Larkin had laid Blair on the bed, and stood as Moira laid hands on Blair's face, her shoulders, her heart.

"How long has she been unconscious?" Glenna snapped as she swept in.

"I . . . I don't know. She fainted," Larkin managed. "I had to . . . her shoulder, it was out of the joint. I had to . . . she fainted when I snapped it back. I think she came around once on the way back, but I can't be sure. The dark, it came. I wasn't with her, and they set on her, and she was alone."

"You brought her back. Moira, help me get her coat off, her clothes. I have to see where she's hurt."

Cian stepped up himself to take off her boots.

"The men should go," Moira began.

"She isn't the first I've seen naked, and I don't think

she'd be worried about it. How many were there?" Cian asked Larkin.

"She said ten. Ten and the French one as well. There were only three when I got to her."

"She made them pay." Cian gently tugged down her pants.

Glenna bit back a sound of distress as she saw the bruising, the cuts. "Ribs." She made her voice brisk. "Probably kidney. Bruised. Shoulder's bad, too. The gash on her leg is fairly shallow. But God, her knee. Not broken, at least. Nothing broken."

"She . . ." Larkin reached down, took one of Blair's limp hands. "She said her vision was going double. Concussion, she said."

Now Glenna spoke gently. "Why don't you step out? Let Moira and me take care of her."

"No, I won't leave her again. She had pain. A lot of pain. You need to give her something that will take away the pain."

"I will, I promise I'll give her what I can for it. Why don't you build up the fire then? I want it warm for her."

Blair could hear them, the voices. She couldn't quite separate one from the other or pick out words, but the sounds were enough to assure her she was alive.

The pain spoke to her as well and that told her she'd gotten her ass thoroughly kicked.

She caught scents as well now. Peat smoke, Glenna, and something strong and floral. But when she tried to open her eyes, they wouldn't cooperate. That had panic trickling into her chest like nasty little drops of acid.

Coma? She didn't want to be in a coma. People fell into comas and sometimes they never climbed out. She'd rather be dead than trapped inside the dark, hearing, feeling, but not being able to see or speak.

Then she felt something slide over her, like silk. Just a flutter over her skin, under it, then deeper, deeper still to where the pain was clenched in fists.

Then the silk heated, then it burned. Oh God. And the fire of it forced those fists open until the pain spread and broke into a thousand jagged pieces.

Her eyes flew open in blinding light that had her flailing out.

"Son of a *bitch*!" In her mind she screamed it, but it came out as a hoarse croak.

She sucked in breath to curse again, but the worst of it ebbed and became a slow, steady throbbing.

"It hurts, I know, it hurts to heal. Can you look at me? Blair? No, stay up here now, and look at me."

Blair forced her eyes open again. Glenna swam into view, her face close. Her hand cupped the back of Blair's neck, lifted it gently up. "Drink a little of this. Just a little now. I can't give you too much because of the head trauma. But this will help."

Blair swallowed, winced. "Tastes like liquid tree bark."

"Not that far off. Do you know where you are?"

"I'm back."

"What's your name?"

"Blair Murphy. Do you want rank and serial number?"

Glenna's lips curved. "How many fingers?"

"Two and a half. Vision's a little blurry." But she struggled to use it, to see. The room was full of people, she realized—the whole team. "Hey. Dorothy, Scarecrow, the Tin Man." She realized then her hand was gripping Larkin's, probably hard enough to grind bone to bone. She relaxed her fingers, managed a smile. "Thanks for saving my life back there."

"It was no trouble. You'd taken care of most of it yourself."

"I was done." She closed her eyes again. "Tapped out."

"I shouldn't have left you alone."

"Cut that out." Blair would have given him a light punch to go with the words if she'd had the strength. "It's wrong and it's useless."

"Why did you?" Cian asked him. "Why did you separate?"

As Larkin told them about the injured man, Blair closed her eyes again. She could hear Glenna and Moira murmuring to each other. Floating a little, she thought Glenna had a voice like silk—sort of sexy and sleek. Moira's was more like velvet, soft and warm.

And that was a really strange thought, she decided. But at least she was having thoughts.

As they worked on her, the pain bloomed, then backed off, bloomed and died. She began to anticipate the rhythm of it before she made another realization.

"Am I naked?" She would have pushed up to her elbows, at least tried to, if Glenna hadn't eased her back. "I'm naked. Oh man."

"You're covered well enough with a sheet. We had to see your injuries," Glenna told her. "You're pretty well covered with gashes and bruises, too, so I wouldn't worry about modesty right now."

"My face." Blair lifted a hand to feel for herself. "How bad is my face?"

"Modesty and vanity," Glenna said. "Good signs. You wouldn't make the finals of the Miss Demon Hunter contest at the moment, but you look damn good to me."

"You're beautiful." Larkin took her hand, kissed it. "You couldn't be more beautiful."

"That bad, huh? Well, I heal fast. Not as fast as you guys," she said to Cian, "but fast enough."

"Can you tell us what happened when you and Larkin were apart?" Hoyt touched her ankle. "He said there were ten."

"Yeah, ten, and Lora, so that's eleven. Trap worked. Dead horse down there, and weapons. We should get those weapons. They were in the ground."

"The weapons?" Hoyt prompted.

"No, the vamps. Dug into the ground. Trap in a trap. It got dark—bam. Like a solar eclipse, but faster. And they came up out of the ground. I got the first two before they got all the way out. Realized after, later, they weren't trying to kill me—which to be honest, is why I'm not dead. They were just softening me up for her. Cowardly bitch."

"But you killed her."

She shook her head at Larkin, and immediately regretted the movement. "No. Don't think so. Couldn't have taken her in a fight, could barely keep my feet. She knew it. Comes strutting out, talking trash. Thinks she'll make me her lesbian vamp lover. As if. She's hurting now, too, oh yeah. And she doesn't look so good either. Water bag."

"Holy water," Larkin murmured. "Aren't you the clever one?"

"Everything's a weapon. I tossed as much as I could into her face. Hit her, too. Face, down the throat. I heard her screaming when she ran off. But that was it for me, pretty much all I had left. Good thing you came."

"You had a branch."

"A branch of what?"

"A tree branch," he told her, kissing her fingers again. "You were swinging a tree branch."

"Yeah. Huh, good for me. It's sort of blurry here and there."

"That's enough for now." Glenna held the cup back to Blair's lips. "A little more of this."

"Rather have a frozen margarita."

"Who wouldn't?" Glenna passed a hand over Blair's face. "Now sleep."

Chapter 20

She swam in and out, and the pain was waiting each time she surfaced. Weakness would drag her under again, but not before she heard whispers and murmurs. Not before she heard herself answering questions that seemed to be peppered over her every time she came back to the world.

Why wouldn't they just let her sleep?

Then someone would pour more tree bark down her throat, and she'd float away again.

Sometimes when she floated she went back to that field and relived every blow, every block, every movement of what she'd believed were the last moments of her life.

Sometimes she simply floated into nothing.

Larkin sat beside her, watching as Moira and Glenna took turns tending her. Watching as one of them came in to light candles, or add turf to the fire. Or just lay a hand over Blair's brow to check for fever.

Every two hours by the clock, one of them would wake her, ask questions of her. Because of the concussion,

Glenna had said. It was a precaution because she'd suffered such hard blows to her head.

Then he would think what might have happened if one of those blows had knocked her unconscious, what they would have done to her while she was alone.

Every time he thought of it, imagined it, he'd take her hand to feel her pulse beat under the scar on her wrist.

He passed the time talking nonsense to her, and for a time playing the pipe that Moira had brought to him. He thought—he hoped—she rested easier with the music.

"You should go, rest now for an hour or two." Moira stroked a hand down her hair as she spoke. "I'll sit with her."

"I can't."

"No. Nor could I in your place. She's so strong, Larkin, and Glenna so skilled. I wish you wouldn't worry so."

"I didn't know it was inside me. That I could feel so much for one person. That I could know, without question, without a single doubt, that this woman is . . . well, everything there is for me."

"I knew it. Not that it would be her, but that there would be someone. And that when you found her, she'd change everything." Moira bent to press her lips to the top of his head. "I'm a little jealous. Do you mind?"

"No." He turned her head, pressed his face to her side. "I'll love you all my life. I think I could be a thousand miles from you, and still reach out my hand and touch yours."

Tears stung Moira's eyes. "I couldn't have chosen better for you if I'd chosen her myself. Still, she's the luckiest of women."

"She's waking."

"All right, talk to her now. We'll keep her with us a few moments, then I'll give her more medicine."

"There you are." Larkin spoke quietly, standing to take her hand. "*Mo chroi*. Open your eyes."

"What?" They fluttered open. "What is it?"

"Give me your name now."

"Scarlett O'Hara. Can't you remember it for five minutes?" she said testily. "Blair Murphy. I don't have brain damage. I'm just tired and annoyed."

"She's lucid enough," Moira decided, and poured more of Glenna's potion into a cup.

"I don't want any more of that." Hearing the petulance in her own voice, Blair closed her eyes a moment. "Look, I don't mean to be pissy. Or, okay, maybe I do. So what? But that gunk makes me feel foggy and out of it. Which wouldn't be so bad if someone wasn't waking me up every freaking ten minutes to ask me my name."

Not at all displeased with the rant, Moira set the cup aside. "Glenna said I should wake her if Blair refused."

"Oh jeez, don't go get Nurse Rachett."

"I'll be a moment."

Larkin eased down on the side of the bed as Moira slipped out of the room. "Your color's come back, you know. It's a relief to me."

"I bet I'm all kinds of colors right now. Blue, black, purple, that sick-looking yellow. Good thing it's dark in here. Look, you don't have to hang around."

"I'm not going anywhere."

"I appreciate it. But . . . listen, can we talk about something other than me and my severely kicked ass? Tell me something. Tell me . . . when's the first time you knew you could shape-shift?"

"Oh, I'd have been about three. I wanted a puppy, you see. My father had his wolfhounds, but they were too dignified to play with the likes of me, to chase balls around and fetch sticks."

"A puppy." She relaxed with the sound of his voice. "What kind of puppy."

"Oh, any sort would do, but my mother said she wasn't after having another dog in the house, and that she already had me and the baby to deal with. That would be my brother, who would have been barely more than a year old.

And I was unaware at the time she was already carrying my sister as well."

"Small wonder she wasn't up for housebreaking a dog."

"She's been in to see you, my mother. Twice tonight. My sister, my father as well."

"Oh." Blair patted her face, imagined how she looked. "Terrific."

"So, to continue the tale, I begged for the pup relentlessly, and to no avail. She would not be moved. I had a good sulk about it up in the nursery, imagining running off with the gypsies where I could have as many pups as I pleased, and so on. And I kept thinking about the pup, and then there was this . . . moving inside me. And this light was spinning around. I was frightened, and called out for my mother. And barked."

"You turned into a puppy."

Her eyes were clearer now; he could see it, see the fun in them as he told the story. "Oh, what terror—and what a thrill with it. I couldn't have a puppy, so I'd made myself one, and wasn't that an amazing thing."

"I'd make some crack about being able to play with yourself, but it's a cheap shot. Keep going."

"Well now, I went running out, and down the stairs where my mother caught sight of me. And thinking I'd gone and snuck a pup in the house despite her, she set off chasing me. I thought she'd hide me good when she realized what I'd done, and tried to run outside. But she cornered me. She's always been quick. Hauled me up, she did, by the scruff of the neck. I must have whimpered and looked plain pitiful, for she sighed, deep, and scratched my ears."

"Softie."

"Aye, she's a good, warm heart my mother. I heard her speak, plain as day. That boy, she said, what am I to do with that boy. And with you, she said to me—not knowing I *was* that boy. She sat down with me in her lap. When she began to pet me, I turned back."

"And when she regained consciousness?"

"Oh, she's made of sterner stuff than that, my mam. I remember her eyes popped wide—but mine must've been as big. I threw my arms around her neck, so glad to be a boy again. She laughed and laughed. Her granny, it seemed, had the same skill."

"Excellent. So it's a family trait."

"Here and there, it seems. By the end of the week, her granny, who I swear was older than the moon itself, came to stay with us and teach me what I needed to know. And she brought with her a little spotted puppy I named Conn, for the warrior of a thousand battles."

"That's a nice story." Her eyelids began to droop. "What happened to Conn?"

"He lived twelve good years, then went over the Bridge of Rainbows where he could be a puppy again, and play all day in the sun. Sleep now, *a ghrá*. I'll be with you when you wake."

He glanced over as Glenna came quietly in, and even managed a smile. "She's gone off to sleep again. Natural sleep. That would be good, wouldn't it?"

"Yes. No fever," Glenna said after laying her palm on Blair's forehead. "If she refused the medicine, I'd guess the pain's lessened. And her color's good. Moira says you won't leave her."

"How can I?"

"If it were Hoyt, I'd say the same. But why don't you lie down with her, get a little rest yourself?"

"I might jostle her in sleep. I don't want to hurt her."

"You won't hurt her." Glenna moved to the windows, drawing the drapes. "I don't want the sun to wake either of you. If you need me, come for me, or send for me. But I think she'll rest easy enough for a few hours now."

She put a hand on Larkin's shoulder, then leaned down to kiss his cheek. "Lie down beside her for a while, and do the same."

When he did, Blair stirred and turned, just a little, just

enough so that her body curled toward his. As gently as he could, he took her hand. "She'll pay for what she did to you. I swear to you, she'll pay."

Listening to her low, steady breathing, he closed his eyes. And finally slept.

I n another room a fire blazed, and the drapes were drawn tight against the glass. Against the dawn.

Lora's wild wails echoed through the room. She thrashed as Lilith, once again, slathered a pale green balm over the burns and the boils that covered Lora's face, her neck, even her breasts.

"There, there, don't. Don't, my darling, my sweet, sweet girl. Don't fight me. This will help."

"It burns! It burns!"

"I know." Tears gathered in Lilith's throat, in her eyes, as she coated the vicious burns on Lora's neck. "Oh, my poor baby, I know. Here now, there now. Drink a little of this."

"I don't want it!" Lora turned her head away, clamping her eyes and mouth tightly shut.

"But you must." Though it scored her heart to cause Lora more pain, Lilith took a firm grip on the back of Lora's neck to force some of the liquid down. "Just a bit more, just a bit. Good, that's good, my own darling."

"She hurt me. Lilith, she hurt me."

"Hush, hush now. We'll fix it."

"She scarred me." Fresh tears spilled over the balm as Lora once again turned her face away. "I'm ugly and scarred. How can you even look at me after what she did to my face?"

"You're only more beautiful to me now. More precious to me." She laid her lips, gently, gently, on Lora's. Lilith had allowed no one else to tend Lora but herself. No one, she vowed, would touch that burned skin but herself. "You're my sweetest girl. My bravest."

"I had to hide in the dirt!"

"Ssh. It means nothing. You came back to me." Lilith took Lora's hand, turning it palm up to press kisses there. "I have you back."

The door opened, and Davey came in. He carried a crystal goblet on a silver tray, his lips pressed hard in concentration. "I didn't spill any. Not one drop."

"Such a big boy." Lilith took the goblet, ran her other hand down his hair.

Once again, Lora turned her face away. "He shouldn't see me like this."

"No. He should know what they're capable of, these *mortals*. Come, Davey, come sit with our Lora. Gently now, don't jostle her."

He climbed carefully onto the bed. "Does it hurt very bad?"

Lora nodded. "Very bad."

"I wish it didn't. I can bring you a toy."

In spite of the pain, Lora smiled. "Perhaps later."

"I brought you blood. It's still warm. I didn't sneak any," he added, stroking her hand as he'd seen Lilith do. "Mama said you need it all, so you can be strong and well again."

"That's right. Here now." Lilith held the goblet to Lora's lips. "Drink it, but slowly."

The blood calmed her, and the drug Lilith had given her earlier helped fog the worst of the pain. "It helps." She laid back, shut her eyes. "But I feel so weak. I thought, oh, Lilith, I thought at first I'd been blinded. It burned my eyes so. She tricked me. How could I have been so *stupid*?"

"You mustn't blame yourself. No, I won't have it."

"You should be furious with me."

"How could I be, at such a time? We've centuries together, my love, the good and the bad. Can I say you were foolish? Of course, but I might have done the same. What good is the kill without the flourish?" She lowered the bodice of her robes to reveal the pentagram scar between her breast. "Don't I carry this because I toyed too long with a mortal once?"

"Hoyt." Lora spat out the name. "You battled a sorcerer. There was no magic in that bitch who scarred me."

"When Mama kills the sorcerer, I can lap up his blood like a puppy does milk."

Lilith laughed, ruffled Davey's hair. "That's my boy. And don't be sure that demon hunter is without magic." She reached for Davey, setting him on her lap. "I don't believe she could have hurt you so without it."

"She was hurt, at least. Perhaps mortally."

"There, you see, always a bright side." Lilith kissed Davey. "It's Midir who must do better. Didn't night slip through his fingers? Didn't the white magic defeat his?"

Lilith had to take a moment to calm herself over the outrage of her wizard's incompetence. "I'd be rid of him if we had another nearly as powerful. But I promise you this, I swear this to you. They will pay. You'll bathe in her blood come Samhain, my darling girl. We'll all drink, long and deep. And when I rule, you'll be by my side."

Comforted, Lora reached out. "Will you stay awhile longer? Will you stay while I sleep?"

"Of course. We're family, after all."

Blair woke in stages. Her mind stirred first, circling slowly around where she was, what had happened. Her head began to ache in a low, steady drumming, then her eyes throbbed with it. She became aware of other pain—shoulder, ribs, belly, legs. As she lay quiet, taking stock, she realized there wasn't a spot on her that didn't hurt.

But it was manageable rather than the breath stealing pain that had flattened her. The aftertaste of the potion Glenna had poured down her coated her throat. Not horribly unpleasant, she decided. Just sort of smoky and thick, so that she wished for a gallon or two of water to clear it away.

Cautiously, she let her eyes open. Candlelight, firelight. So it was still shy of dawn, she decided. Good. She felt reasonably good, all in all.

In fact, she felt good enough to be hungry, which had to be a positive sign. She worked at sitting up just as she spotted Larkin crossing back toward the bed from the far window.

"Hey, go get some sleep."

He stopped, just stared for a moment. "You're awake."

"Yeah, and before you ask, my name's Blair Murphy, I'm in Geall, and I got my ass whooped by a bunch of vampires. Do you think I could get something to eat?"

"You're hungry." He all but sang the words as he rushed to the bed.

"Yeah. Maybe just a little midnight snack—or whatever time it is."

"You're having pain."

"The grandmother of all headaches," she admitted. "And some other twinges. Mostly, I feel sort of groggy and dopey. Also," she added with a quick wince, "I have an amazing need to pee. So, you know, shoo for a minute."

Instead, he picked her up, carried her to the chamber pot behind the painted screen.

"I can't do this with you in here. I just can't. Go outside the room and count to thirty." She squirmed as her bladder strained. "Make that forty. Come on, give a girl a private moment."

He rolled his eyes, but did as she asked. In exactly forty seconds he was back in the room where she was taking a few hesitant steps. He was at her side, taking her arm in an instant.

"Glenna said you might be dizzy."

"Little bit. Little dizzy, little wobbly, and it hurts pretty much everywhere. But it could be a whole lot worse, in that I could be dead or craving a nice slug of blood at this moment. I want to take a look."

With his help, she limped to the mirror. Her left cheek

was scraped from nose to temple, and she was sporting two black eyes. Glenna had fashioned a kind of butterfly bandage to close the gash on her forehead. She turned, noted that while her shoulder was a mass of bruises, they were already going the sickly yellow-green of healing.

"Yeah, could've been worse." She ran a hand down her own ribs. "Pretty tender yet, but nothing got busted. There's a plus."

"I've never been so frightened in all my life."

"Me, either." She met his eyes in the glass. "I don't know if I thanked you or dreamed I did on one of my trips to La-La Land, but you saved me. I'll never forget watching you whip through those three vamps like they were nothing."

"If I'd been sooner—"

"Isn't this a lot about destiny, this whole business? If you were meant to be there sooner, you would've been. You were there in time, and that's what counts."

"Blair." He lowered his head to her good shoulder. He spoke in a quiet murmur, and in Gaelic.

"What was all that?"

"For later." He straightened. "But for now, I'll get you some food."

"I could use it. Feel like I haven't eaten in days. I'm not getting back in bed. I'll sit."

He helped her to the chair by the fire, then brought over a blanket for her legs. "Do you want the drapes open?"

"Yeah, sure. Listen, after you get someone to throw some food together, you should go, catch some sleep for the rest of the night—oh!"

She blinked, threw up a hand to block the glare of the sun through the glass.

"I slept a bit," he told her with a quick grin.

"Yeah, well, apparently so did I. What time is it?"

"I'd say well past midday."

"Mid—" She blew out a breath. "Guess my advanced healing powers have been getting a hell of a workout."

"I'll go see about some food if you promise to stay where I've put you."

Gingerly, she rubbed her aching knee. "I'm not going anywhere."

Obviously, he didn't take her at her word as Glenna came in moments later.

"You look better."

"Then I must've looked like the wrath of God."

"You did." Glenna set her case on a table, opened it.

And Blair gave it a long, meaningful frown. "I really don't need any more of that magic tree bark."

"We'll switch to something else. Double vision?"

"Down to the regular kind. Head aches like a mother."

"I can help with that." Glenna came over, laid her fingers on Blair's temples. "How's the shoulder?"

"Achy, worse than the ribs, but they're not too bad. Must've cracked my knee pretty good, too. It's a little wobbly."

"Considering it was about twice its normal size when Larkin got you here, a little wobbly's good. You know, this is the first time he's left this room since he brought you back."

"But he said he slept some."

"I convinced him to lie down next to you for a while."

"He blames himself. It's stupid."

"It's stupid, I agree. But that's only part of it. He's watched over you all night because he's desperately in love with you. How's the head now?"

"The what? Oh . . . Better," she realized. "A lot better. Thanks. Oh God, what am I going to do?"

"You'll figure it out. They'll be sending up some tea—one of my infusions. We'll add a little of this and that to it. You'll drink it all. Let's see what I can do about that shoulder."

"If I stayed here in Geall, I'd be turning my back on what I was born for. On what brought me to him in the first place. Glenna, I can't. Whatever I feel, whatever I want, I can't not be what I am."

"Duty and love. They can make their own nasty little wars, can't they? Relax now. Try some yoga breathing. You're a strong woman, Blair. Mind, body, heart. A lot of people don't understand how difficult it can be to be a strong woman. If I were taking bets, I'd say Larkin's a man who does."

Later, when she'd eaten and felt steadier, she convinced Larkin she needed to walk. She sensed he was waiting to scoop her up at the first sign of weakness. She did feel weak, but in heart rather than body. She had to tell him, he deserved to be told, that she couldn't make promises to him. When what they'd been charged to do had been done, she would have to leave him.

She knew what it was to be rejected, and wished with everything inside her things could be different. That she could be.

They walked to the courtyard with the fountain she could see from her window, where the sun was strong and the air cool with the first brush of autumn.

"Only a month left," he said, and sat with her on a bench of deep blue marble.

"We'll be ready."

"Aye, we will. In a few days, Moira will take her sword."

"What if it's not her? What if it's you?"

"It isn't." He lifted his shoulder. "I've searched myself on that, and I'd know if it was. I'd have always known, as in some part of her, Moira knows. And thank God."

"But your family. This place. You're tied to it, by birth. By blood."

"True enough." He took her hand, idly toying with her fingers. "It's the place of my birth, and I'll always miss it."

"You'll . . . what? Miss it? Why? We're going to win. Just because I got slapped around doesn't mean they're going to beat us."

"No, it doesn't, and they won't." He looked up from her

fingers, into her eyes. And his were like gold steel. "Because we'll fight to the last man. To the last drop."

"So why—"

"Let me ask you a question, one none of us have voiced as yet. Have all the vampires from your world come here to follow Lilith?"

"No, of course not."

"Then when this battle's won, the fight goes on. You'll have to hunt, as you've always hunted. Here, if some survive, they'll be an army always to fight them. The people of Geall know what they are, as the people of your world don't."

"Yes." So he did understand. "I wish— I'm sorry. Going back, it's not a choice for me. If it were . . . But it's not."

"No, it can't be a choice for you. But it can be for me. So I'll be going back with you, to fight beside you."

"Excuse me?"

"*A stór*. Did you think I'd let you get away from me?"

"You can't leave here."

"Why? It's Moira who will rule, and my father will advise her as need be. There's my brother and my sister's husband to work the land, and tend the horses."

She thought of his mother, his sister, brother. Of his father, and the look on Riddock's face when he'd embraced Larkin after his return. "You can't leave your family."

"It's hard, yes, to leave loved ones. It should be hard, I think, and should only be done when it needs to be done. It isn't, could never be, the way it was when your father left you, Blair."

"The result's the same."

"It's not, no. Not when the leaving is with love, all around. And it's true enough that a man often moves away from his parents. It's the way of things, a natural order."

"They move to the next town, or across the country. Not to another world."

"Trying to talk me out of it's a waste of breath. My mind's been made up to it for a while now. Moira knows it, though we haven't spoken of it right out. As does my mother."

He looked straight into her eyes. "Do you think I would fight, risk everything, then step aside from the one that matters most in this world, in any world to me? I'd give my life for this if that's what's needed. But if I live, you'll belong to me. And that's the end of it."

"The end of it?"

"I'm thinking, as you have no close family at home, we could be married here. We can do the whole business again in your Chicago if you like."

"Married? I didn't say I would marry you. Anybody."

"Of course you'll marry me, don't be foolish." He gave her a friendly pat on her good knee. "You love me. And I love you," he said before she could speak. "I nearly told you that first night we were together. But a man shouldn't say such words when he's inside a woman, I think. How would she know, for certain, he was speaking with his heart and not, well, not with his . . ."

"Oh boy."

"I thought to tell you at other times, but told myself it should wait. I realize I nearly waited too long. You asked what I said to you, inside after you woke. I'll tell you now. So look at me when I do."

He laid his fingers on her cheeks. "I said you're my breath, and my pulse, my heart, my voice. I said, I'll love you even when all of them stop. I'll love you, and only you, until all the worlds are ended. So you'll marry me, Blair. And I'll go where you go, and fight beside you. We'll live together, and love together, and make a family."

"I have to . . . I have to stand up a minute." She got to her feet, shaky now, and walked to the fountain. Just to breathe, she thought, to let the cool spray of water wash her face.

"No one's ever loved me like this. I don't know, not for certain, that anyone's ever loved me at all until you. No one's ever offered me what you're offering me." She turned back to him. "I'd be a fool to push it away. I'm not a fool. I thought I loved someone once, but that was so pale compared to what I feel for you. I thought I'd have to be strong enough to leave you behind. I didn't know you could be strong enough to come with me. I should have."

She came back to him, offering her hand when he rose. "I'd marry you anywhere. I'd be so proud to marry you."

He kissed her hands, then drew her gently into his arms to meet her lips.

"Get a good grip, will you?" she murmured. "I'm a demon hunter. I'm not fragile."

He laughed, and swung her right off her feet.

"Have a care with her! Have you lost your mind?"

As Moira sprinted toward them, Larkin only grinned, and spun Blair again. "A bit. We're betrothed."

"Oh." Moira stopped, her hands fluttering up to her heart. "Oh, well, that's wonderful. Blessings on you both. I'm so pleased for you."

She stepped up, kissed Blair's cheek, then Larkin's. "We need a celebration. I'll go back, tell the others. Cian had a notion . . . but it can wait."

"What notion?" Blair demanded.

"A way . . . how did he put it? To thumb our noses at Lilith. But—"

"I'm for that." Blair patted Larkin's arm. "Why don't you go in. I'll be right behind you. I just want a second with Moira."

"All right. But don't stay on your feet too long."

"Listen to him, after he's tossing you around in the air. I do wish you happy, Blair."

"I want you to know I'm going to try, every day of my life, to make him happy. I want you to know that."

"You do make him happy." Moira angled her head. "We're friends, aren't we, you and I?"

"You, Glenna, Hoyt, Cian. Best friends I ever had in my life."

"I feel the same, so I'm going to be honest with you. It will hurt when he goes. It will hurt my heart, and when

he's out of sight I'll weep until my heart's dry of tears.
Then I'll be light, and I'll be happy. Because I know he'll
have what he needs, what he wants, what he deserves."

"If there's a way we can come back, to spend some
time, to visit, you, his family, we'll find it."

"That's a nice thought to hold on to. And I will. Come
now. He's right, you should be off your feet."

"I think I feel better than I ever have in my life."

"That's love for you, but still, you'll need your strength
for what Cian has in mind."

It was nose-thumbing, Blair thought. And chest-
beating. And it was perfect.

"Are you sure you're up for this?" Glenna asked her.

"I am so up for this. It's so in-your-face." Blair grinned
at Cian. "Good thinking."

He looked up at the sky, watched the stars wink to life.
"Good clear night for it. It's not what you'd call battle strategy, but—"

"Damn straight it is. Demoralizing the enemy is always
good strategy." Blair turned the swords she held. "So I'm
set?" she asked Glenna.

"You're set."

"Okay, handsome. Make like a dragon."

"In a moment. First, I have something for you, and I want
to give it to you here, in front of our circle. One of the symbols of Geall is the dragon. One of our symbols as well, you
and I. So I want you to wear this, for our betrothal."

He drew out a ring of bright gold shaped like a dragon.

"Glenna drew a picture of it when I told her what I'd
like. And the goldsmith used it to make the ring."

"It's perfect," she murmured when he slipped it on her
finger.

"And to seal it." He framed her face, kissed her warmly.
And shot her a grin when he eased back. "Now let's go
thumb our noses at this bitch."

He flashed into the dragon. Leaping onto his back, Blair lifted both swords high.

"They rose into the sky," the old man said. "Across the moon and stars and the dark behind them. And over the world of Geall, those swords flashed flame for all to see. With them, the demon hunter carved these words into that sky.

"Bright blessings on Geall and all humankind. We," she wrote in fire, "are the future."

The old man lifted the wine that sat beside him. "It was said that the queen of the vampires stood below, cursing, shaking her fists as those words shone bright as the sun."

He sipped the wine, held up a hand when the children spread around him protested that couldn't be the end of the tale.

"Oh, there's more to tell. More indeed. But not tonight. Go on now, for I was told there'd be gingercakes in the kitchen for a treat before bedtime. I've a fondness for gingercake."

When he was alone, and the room quiet again, he sipped his wine. He nodded off with the fire warming his bones, and his mind drifting to the last of the story.

To the time of knowing.

Glossary of Irish Words, Characters and Places

a chroi (ah-REE), Gaelic term of endearment meaning "my heart," "my heart's beloved," "my darling"

a ghrá (ah-GHRA), Gaelic term of endearment meaning "my love," "dear"

a stór (ah-STOR), Gaelic term of endearment meaning "my darling"

Aideen (Ae-DEEN), Moira's young cousin

Alice McKenna, descendant of Cian and Hoyt Mac Cionaoith

An Clar (Ahn-CLAR), modern-day County Clare

Ballycloon (ba-LU-klun)

Beal (Bale), name Blair uses when acting as bait

bi istigh (vee-ISHtee), Gaelic term meaning "come in"

Blair Nola Bridgitt Murphy, one of the circle of six, the "warrior"; a demon hunter, a descendant of Nola Mac Cionaoith (Cian and Hoyt's younger sister)

braes (BRO-sh), underdrawers or trousers, worn by the people of Geall

Breda (BREE-da), mother of family with overturned wagon

Bridget's Well, cemetery in County Clare, named after St. Bridget

Burren, the, a karst limestone region in County Clare, which features caves and underground streams

cailleach dearg (CAH-lic JAR-eg), witch with red hair, epithet for Glenna

cara (karu), Gaelic for "friend, relative"

Ceara, one of the village women

Cian (KEY-an) *Mac Cionaoith/McKenna*, Hoyt's twin brother, a vampire, Lord of Oiche, one of the circle of six, "the one who is lost"

Cillard, place in County Clare

Cirio, Lilith's human lover

ciunas (CYOON-as), Gaelic for "silence"; the battle takes place in the Valley of Ciunas—the Valley of Silence

claddaugh, the Celtic symbol of love, friendship, loyalty

Cliffs of Mohr (also Moher), the name given to the ruin of forts in the South of Ireland, on a cliff near Hag's Head, "Moher O'Ruan"

Conn, Larkin's childhood puppy

Dance of the Gods, the Dance, the place in which the circle of six passes through from the real world to the fantasy world of Geall

Dara (DARE-a), in modern day County Kildare

Davey, Lilith, the Vampire Queen's "son," a child vampire

Deirdre (DAIR-dhra) *Riddock*, Larkin's mother

Dervil (DAR-vel), one of the village women

Dunglas, place in Geall

Eire (AIR-reh), Gaelic for "Ireland"

Eogan (O-en), Ceara's husband

Eoin (OAN), Hoyt's brother-in-law

Eternity, the name of Cian's nightclub, located in New York City

Faerie Falls, imaginary place in Geall

fàilte à Geall (FALL-che ah GY-al), Gaelic for "Welcome to Geall"

Fearghus (FARE-gus), Hoyt's brother-in-law

Gaillimh (GALL-yuv), modern-day Galway, the capital of the west of Ireland

gaiscioch dorcha (GA-shuk DOR-ka), dark warrior or dark hero, epithet for Blair

Geall (GY-al), in Gaelic means "promise"; the city from which Moira and Larkin come; the city which Moira will someday rule

Glenna Ward, one of the circle of six, the "witch"; lives in modern-day New York City

Hoyt Mac Cionaoith/McKenna (mac KHEE-nee), one of the circle of six, the "sorcerer"

Isleen (Is-LEEN), a servant at Castle Geall

Jarl (Yarl), Lilith's sire, the vampire who turned her into a vampire

Jeremy Hilton, Blair Murphy's ex-fiance

King, the name of Cian's best friend, whom Cian befriended when King was a child; the manager of Eternity

Knockarague (KNOCKA-rig), town in Geall; home of Larlin's mother

Larkin Riddock, one of the circle of six, the "shifter of shapes," a cousin of Moira, Queen of Geall

Lilith, the Vampire Queen, aka Queen of the Demons; leader of the war against humankind; Cian's sire, the vampire who turned Cian from human to vampire

Lora, a vampire; Lilith's lover

Lucius, Lora's male vampire lover

Mac Dara, surname; part of one of Larkin's titles

Malvin, villager, soldier in Geallian army

Mam, term for mother

Manhattan, city in New York; where both Cian McKenna and Glenna Ward live

mathair (maahir), Gaelic word for "mother"

Michael Thomas McKenna, descendant of Cian and Hoyt Mac Cionaoith

Mick Murphy, Blair Murphy's younger brother

Midir (mee-DEER), vampire wizard to Lilith, Queen of the Vampires

miurnin (also sp. miurneach [mornukh]), Gaelic for "sweetheart," term of endearment

Mo chroi (mo-kree), Gaelic term meaning "my heart," "my sweetheart," "my darling" (see **a chroi**)

Moira (MWA-ra), one of the circle of six, the "scholar"; a princess, future queen of Geall

Morrigan (Mo-ree-ghan), Goddess of the Battle

Niall (Nile), a warrior in the Geallian army

Nola Mac Cionaoith, Hoyt and Cian's youngest sister

o Dubhuir (o DOVE-er), surname Blair uses when acting as bait

ogham (ä-gem) (also spelled ogam), fifth/sixth century Irish alphabet

oiche (EE-heh), Gaelic for "night"

Oran (O-ren), Riddock's youngest son, Larkin's younger brother

Phelan (FA-len), Larkin's brother-in-law

Prince Riddock, Larkin's father, acting king of Geall, Moira's maternal uncle

Region of Chiarrai (kee-U-ree), modern-day Kerry, situated in the extreme southwest of Ireland, sometimes referred to as "the Kingdom"

Samhain (SAM-en), summer's end (Celtic festival); the battle takes place on the Feast of Samhain, the feast celebrating the end of summer

Sean (Shawn) *Murphy*, Blair Murphy's father, a vampire hunter

Shop Street, cultural center of Galway

Sinann (shih-NAWN), Larkin's sister

sláinte (slawn-che), Gaelic term for "cheers!"

slán agat (shlahn u-gut), Gaelic for "good-bye," which is said to person staying

slán leat (shlahn ly-aht), Gaelic for "good-bye," which is said to the person leaving

Tuatha de Danaan (TOO-aha dai DON-nan), Welsh gods

Tynan (Ti-nin), guard at Castle Geall

Vlad, Cian's stallion

Turn the page for a look at

Valley of Silence

the third book in the
Circle Trilogy.

Available now from Jove.

She didn't sleep. How could a woman sleep on what was, in Moira's mind, essentially the last night of her life? If in the morning it was her destiny to free the sword from its stone scabbard, she would be queen of Geall. As queen she would rule and govern and reign, and those were duties she'd been trained for since birth. But as queen on this coming dawn and the ones to follow, she would lead her people to war. If it wasn't her destiny to raise the sword, she would follow another, willingly, into battle.

Could weeks of training prepare anyone for such an action, such a weight of responsibility? So this night was the last she could be the woman she'd believed she would be, even the queen she'd hoped she might be.

Whatever dawn brought her, she knew nothing would ever be quite the same again.

Before her mother's death, she'd believed this coming dawn was years away. She'd assumed she would have years of her mother's company and comfort and counsel, years of peace and study so that when her time came she'd be not only ready for the crown, but worthy of it.

A part of her had assumed her mother would reign for decades longer, and she herself would marry. In the dim and distant future, one of the children she bore would take the crown in her stead.

All of that had changed on the night of her mother's death. No, Moira corrected, it had changed before, years before when her father had been murdered.

Perhaps it had not changed at all, but was simply unfolding as the pages of the book of fate were written.

Now she could only wish for her mother's wisdom, and look inside herself for the courage to bear both crown and sword.

She stood now on the high reaches of the castle under a thumbnail moon. When it waxed full again, she would be far from here, on the cold ground of a battlefield.

She'd come to the battlement because she could see the torches lighting the playing field. Here the sights and sounds of night training could reach her. Cian, she thought, used hours of his night to teach men and women how to fight something stronger and faster than humans. He would push them, she knew, until they were ready to drop. As he had pushed her, and the others of the circle, night after night during their weeks in Ireland.

Not all of them trusted him, she knew that as well. Some actively feared him, but that might be to the good. She understood he wasn't after making friends here, but warriors.

In truth, he'd had a strong part of making one of her.

She thought she understood why he fought with them— or at least had a glimmer of understanding why he would risk so much for humankind. Part of it was pride of which she knew he had abundance. He would not bow to Lilith. Part, whether he admitted it or not, was loyalty to his brother. And the rest, well, it dealt with courage and his own conflicted emotions.

For he had emotions, she knew. She couldn't imagine

how they struggled and whirled inside him after a thousand years of existence. Her own were so conflicted and torn after only two months of blood and death she hardly recognized herself.

What must it be like for him, after all he'd seen and done, all he'd gained and lost? He knew more than any of them of the world, of its pleasures, its pains, its potentials. No, she couldn't imagine what it was like to know all he knew and still risk his own survival.

That he did risk it, that he was even now lending his time and skill to train troops, earned her respect. While the mystery of him, the hows and whys of him, continued to fascinate.

She couldn't be sure what he thought of her. Even when he'd kissed her—that single hot and desperate moment— she couldn't be sure. And getting to the inside of matters had always been irresistible to her.

She heard footsteps, and turning, saw Larkin coming toward her.

"You should be in your bed," he said.

"I'd only stare at the ceiling. The view's better here." She reached for his hand—her cousin, her friend—and was instantly comforted. "And why aren't you in yours?"

"I saw you. Blair and I went out to help Cian for a bit." Like hers, his gaze scanned the field below. "I saw you standing up here alone."

"I'm poor company, even for myself tonight. I only wish it were done, then there would be what happens next. So I came up here to brood over it." She tipped her head toward his shoulder. "It passes the time."

"We could go down to the family parlor. I'll let you beat me at chess."

"Let me? Oh, will you listen to him." She looked up at him. His eyes were golden brown, long-lidded like her own. The smile in them didn't quite mask his concern. "And I suppose you've *let* me win the hundreds of matches we've had over the years."

"I thought it good for your sense of confidence."

She laughed even as she poked him. "It's confident I am I can beat you at chess nine times out of every ten."

"We'll just put that to the test then."

"We will not." Now she kissed him, brushing his tawny hair away from his face. "You'll go to your bed and to your lady, and not spend these hours distracting me from my sorry mood. Come, we'll go in. It may be the limited view of my ceiling will bore me to sleep after all."

"You've only to tap on the door if you're wanting company."

"I know it."

Just as she knew she would keep her own counsel until the first light of dawn.

But she did not sleep.

In the way of tradition she would be dressed and tended to by her ladies in the last hour before dawn. Though it was urged on her, she refused the red gown. Moira knew well enough it wasn't a color that flattered her, however royal it might be. In its stead she wore the hues of the forest, a deep green over a paler green kirtle.

She agreed to jewels—they had been her mother's after all. So she allowed the heavy stones of citrine to be fastened around her neck. But she would not remove the silver cross.

She would wear her hair down and uncovered, and sat letting the female chatter chirp around her as Dervil brushed it tirelessly.

"Will you not eat just a little, Highness?"

Ceara, one of her women, once again urged a plate of honey cakes on her. "After," Moira told her. "I'll feel more settled after."

Moira got to her feet, her relief profound when Glenna stepped into the room. "How wonderful you look!" Moira held out her hands. She'd chosen the gowns herself for both Glenna and Blair, and saw now she'd chosen well. Then again, she thought, Glenna was so striking there was nothing that wouldn't flatter her.

Still, the choice of deep blue velvet highlighted her creamy skin and the fire of her hair.

"I feel a bit like a princess myself," Glenna told her. "Thank you so much. And you, Moira, look every inch the queen."

"Do I?" She turned to her glass, but saw only herself. But she smiled when she saw Blair come in. She'd chosen russet for Blair, with a kirtle of dull gold. "I've never seen you in a dress."

"Hell of a dress." Blair studied her friends, then herself. "We've got that whole fairy tale thing going." She threaded her fingers through her short, dark hair to settle it into place.

"You don't mind then? Tradition requires the more formal attire."

"I like being a girl. I don't mind dressing like one, even one who's not in my own fashion era." Blair spotted the honey cakes, and helped herself to one. "Nervous?"

"Well beyond it. I'd like a moment with the ladies Glenna and Blair," Moira told her women. When they scurried out, Moira dropped into the chair in front of the fire. "They've been fussing around me for an hour. It's tiring."

"You look beat." Blair sat on the arm of the chair. "You didn't sleep."

"My mind wouldn't rest."

"You didn't take the potion I gave you." Glenna let out a sigh. "You should be rested for this, Moira."

"I needed to think. It's not the usual way of it, but I want both of you, and Hoyt and Larkin to walk with me to the stone."

"Wasn't that the plan?" Blair asked with her mouth full.

"You would be part of the procession, yes. But in the usual way, I would walk ahead, alone. This must be, as it always has been. But behind me, would be only my family.

My uncle, and my aunt, Larkin, my other cousins. After them, according to rank and position would walk others. I want you to walk with my family, as you are my family. I do this for myself, but also for the people of Geall. I want them to see what you are. Cian isn't able to be part of this, as I wish he could."

"It can't be done at night, Moira." Blair touched a hand to Moira's shoulder. "It's too much of a risk."

"I know. But while the circle won't be complete at the place of the stone, he'll be in my thoughts." She rose now to go to the window. "Dawn's coming," she murmured. "And the day follows."

She turned back as the last stars died. "I'm ready for what comes with it."

Her family and her women were already gathered below. She accepted the cloak from Dervil, and fastened the dragon brooch herself.

When she looked up from the task, she saw Cian. She assumed he might have stopped for a moment on his way to retire, until she saw he carried the cloak Glenna and Hoyt had charmed to block the killing rays of the sun.

She stepped away from her uncle's side, and up to Cian. "You would do this?" she said quietly.

"I rarely have the opportunity for a morning walk."

However light his words, she heard what was under them. "I'm grateful you've chosen this morning to take one."

"Dawn's broke," Riddock said. "The people wait."

She only nodded, then drew up her hood as was the custom before stepping out into the early light.

The air was cool and misty with barely a breeze to stir the fingers of vapor. Through the rising curtain of it, Moira crossed the courtyard to the gates alone, while her party fell in behind her. In the muffled quiet, she heard the morning birds singing, and the faint whisper of the damp air.

She thought of her mother, who had once walked this way on a cool, misty morning. And all the others who'd walked before her out of the castle gates, across the brown road, over the green grass so thick with dew it was like wading through a river. She knew others trailed behind her, merchants and craftsmen, harpers and bards. Mothers and daughters, soldiers and sons.

The sky was streaked with pink in the east, and the ground fog sparkled silver.

She smelled the river and the earth, and continued up, over the gentle rise with the dew dampening the hem of her gown.

The place of the stone stood on a faerie hill where a little glade of trees offered shelter. Gorse and moss grew, pale yellow, quiet green, over the rocks near the holy well.

In the spring there would be the cheery orange of lilies, dancing heads of columbine, and later the sweet spires of foxglove, all growing where they would.

But for now, the flowers slept and the leaves of the trees had taken on that first blush of color that portended their death.

The sword stone itself was wide and white, altarlike on an ancient dolmen of flat gray.

Through the leaves and the mists, beams of sun lanced, crossing that white stone and glinting on the silver hilt of the sword buried in it.

Her hands felt cold, so very cold.

All of her life she had known the story. How the gods had forged the sword from lightning, from the sea, and the earth and the wind. How Morrigan had brought it and the altar stone herself to this place. And there she had buried it to the hilt, carved the words on the stone with her fiery finger.

> SHEATHED BY THE HAND OF GODS
> FREED BY THE HAND OF A MORTAL
> AND SO WITH THIS SWORD
> SHALL THAT HAND RULE GEALL

Moira paused at the base of the stones to read the words again. If the gods deemed it, that hand would be hers.

With her cloak sweeping over the dew-drenched grass, she walked through sun and mist to the top of the faerie hill. And took her place behind the stone.

For the first time she looked, and she saw. Hundreds of people, her people, with their eyes on hers spread over the field, down toward that brown ribbon of road. Every one of them, if the sword came to her, would be her responsibility. Her cold hands wanted to shake.

She calmed herself as she scanned the faces and waited for the trio of holy men to take their places behind her.

Some were still coming over that last rise, hurrying lest they miss the moment. She wanted her breath steady when she spoke, so waited a little longer and let herself meet the eyes of those she loved best.

"My lady," one of the holy men murmured.

"Yes. A moment."

Slowly, she unpinned the brooch, passed her cloak behind her. The wide sweep of her sleeves flowed back as she lifted her arms, but she didn't feel the chill against her skin. She felt heat.

"I am a servant of Geall," she called out. "I am a child of the gods. I come here to this place to bow to the will of both. By my blood, by my heart, by my spirit."

She took the last step toward the stone.

There was no sound now. It seemed even the air held its breath. Moira reached out, curled her fingers around the silver hilt.

And oh, she thought as she felt the heat of it, as she heard somewhere in her mind the murmur of its music. Of course, aye, of course. It's mine, and always was.

With a whisper of steel against rock, she drew it free and raised its point to the sky.

She knew they cheered, and some of them wept. She knew that to a man they lowered to one knee. But her eyes were on that point and the flash of light that streaked from the sky to strike it.

She felt it inside her, that light, a burst of heat and color and strength. There was a sudden burn on her arm, and as if the gods etched it, the symbol of the claddaugh formed there to brand her queen of Geall. Rocked by it, thrilled and humbled, she looked down at her people. And her eyes met Cian's.

All else seemed to melt away in that moment, for a moment. There was only him, his face shadowed by the hood of his cloak, and his eyes so brilliant and blue.

How could it be, she wondered, that she should hold her destiny in her hand, and see only him? How, meeting his eyes like this, could it be like looking deeper, deeper yet, into her own destiny?

"I am a servant of Geall," she said, unable to look away from him. "I am a child of the gods. This sword, and all it protects is mine. I am Moira, warrior queen of Geall. Rise, and know I love you."

She stood as she was, the sword still pointing skyward as the hands of the holy man placed the crown on her head.

He was no stranger to magic, the black or the white, but Cian thought he'd never seen anything more powerful. Her face, so pale when she'd removed her cloak, had bloomed when her hand had taken the sword. Her eyes, so heavy, so somber, had gone as brilliant as the blade.

And had simply sliced through him, keen as a sword, when they'd met his.

There she stood, he thought, slender and slight, and as magnificent as any Amazon. Suddenly regal, suddenly fierce, suddenly beautiful.

What moved inside him had no place there.

He stepped back, turned to go. Hoyt laid a hand on his arm.

"You must wait for her, for the queen."

Cian lifted a brow. "You forget, I have no queen. And I've been under this bloody cloak long enough."

He moved quickly. He wanted to get away from the light, from the smell of humanity. Away from the power of those gray eyes. He needed the cool and the dark, and the silence.

He was barely a league away when Larkin trotted up to him. "Moira asked me to see if you wanted a ride back."

"I'm fine, but thanks."

"It was amazing, wasn't it? And she was . . . well, brilliant as the sun. I always knew she'd be the one, but seeing it happen is a different matter. She was queen the moment she touched the sword. You could see it."

"If she wants to stay queen, have anyone to rule, she better make use of that sword."

"So she will. Come now, Cian, this isn't the day for gloom and doom. We're entitled to a few hours of joy and celebration. And feasting." With another grin, Larkin gave Cian an elbow poke. "She might be queen, but I can promise the rest of us will eat like kings this day."

"Well, an army travels on its belly."

"Do they?"

"So it was said by . . . someone or another. Have your feasting and celebration. Tomorrow queens, kings and peasants alike best be preparing for war."

"Feels like we've been doing nothing else. Not complaining, mind," he continued before Cian could speak. "I guess the matter is I'm tired of preparing for it, and want to get to it."

"Haven't had enough fighting the last little while?"

"I've payment to make for what was nearly done to Blair. She's still tender along the ribs, and wears down quicker than she'd admit." His face was hard and grim as he remembered it. "Healing fast, as she does, but I won't forget how they hurt her."

"It's dangerous to go into battle with a personal agenda."

"Ah, bollocks. We've all of us something personal to settle, or what's the point? And you won't tell me that a part of you won't be going into it with what that bitch did to King in your mind and in your heart."

Because Cian couldn't deny it, he left it alone. "Are you . . . escorting me back, Larkin?"

"As it happens. There was some mention of me throwing myself bodily over you to shield you from the sunlight should the magic in that cloak fade out."

"That would be fine. We'd both go up like torches." Cian said it casually, but he had to admit he felt easier when he stepped into the shadow cast by Castle Geall.

"I'm also asked to request you come to the family parlor if you're not too weary. We're to have a private breakfast there. Moira would be grateful if you could spare a few minutes at least."

She would have liked a few minutes herself, alone. But Moira was surrounded. The walk back to the castle was a blur of movement and voices wrapped in mists. She felt the weight of the sword in her hand, the crown on her head even as she was swept along by her family and friends. Cheers echoed over the hills and fields, a celebration of Geall's new queen.

"You'll need to show yourself," Riddock told her. "From the royal terrace. It's expected."

"Aye. But not alone. I know it's the way it's been done," she continued before her uncle could object. "But these are different times. My circle will stand with me." She looked at Glenna now, then Hoyt and Blair. "The people won't just see their queen, but those who have been chosen to lead this war."

"It's for you to say, you to do," Riddick said with a slight bow. "But on such a day, Geall should be free of the shadow of war."

"Until Samhain has passed, Geall remains always in the shadow of war. Every Geallian must know that until that day, I rule with a sword. And that I'm part of six the gods have chosen."

She laid a hand on his as they passed through the gates. "We will have feasting and celebration. I value your advice, as always, and I will show myself, and I will speak.

But on this day, the gods have chosen both queen and warrior in me. And this is what I will be. This is what I'll give to Geall, to my last breath. I won't shame you."

He took her hand from his arm, brought it to his lips. "My sweet girl. You have and always will bring me nothing but pride. And from this day, to my last breath, I am the queen's man."

The servants were gathered, and knelt when the royal party entered the castle. She knew their names, their faces. Some of them had served her mother before Moira herself was born.

But it was no longer the same. She wasn't the daughter of the house now, but its mistress. And theirs.

"Rise," she said, "and know I am grateful for your loyalty and service. Know, too, that you and all of Geall have my loyalty and service as long as I am queen."

Later, she told herself as she started up the stairs, she would speak with each of them individually. It was important to do so. But for now, there were other duties.

In the family parlor the fire roared. Flowers cut fresh from garden and hothouse spilled from vases and bowls. The table was set with the finest silver and crystal, with wine waiting for Moira's inner circle to toast the new queen.

She took a breath, then two, trying to find the words she would say, her first, to those she loved best.

Then Glenna simply wrapped arms around her. "You were magnificent." She kissed both Moira's cheeks. "Luminous."

The tension she'd held tight in her shoulders eased. "I feel the same, but not. Do you know?"

"I can only imagine."

"Nice job." Blair stepped up, gave her a quick hug. "Can I see it?"

Warrior to warrior, Moira thought and offered Blair the sword.

"Excellent," Blair said softly. "Good weight for you. You expect it to be crusted with jewels or whatever. It's good that it's not. It's good and right that it's a fighting sword, not just a symbol."

"It felt as though the hilt was made for my hand. As soon as I touched it, it felt . . . mine."

"It is." Blair handed it back. "It's yours."

For the moment, Moira set the sword on the table to accept Hoyt's embrace. "The power in you is warm and steady," he said close to her ear. "Geall is fortunate in its queen."

"Thank you." Then she let out a laugh as Larkin swept her off her feet and in three dizzying circles.

"Look at you. Majesty."

"You mock my dignity."

"Always. But never you, *a stór*."

When Larkin set her back on her feet, she turned to Cian. "Thank you for coming. It meant a great deal to me."

He neither embraced nor touched her, but only inclined his head. "It was a moment not to be missed."

"A moment more important to me that you would come. All of you," she continued and started to turn when her young cousin tugged on her skirts. "Aideen." She lifted the child, accepted the damp kiss. "And don't you look pretty today."

"Pretty," Aideen repeated, reaching up to touch Moira's jeweled crown. Then she turned her head with a smile both shy and sly for Cian. "Pretty," she said again.

"An astute female," Cian observed. He saw the little girl's gaze drop to the pendant he wore, and in an absent gesture lifted it so that she could touch.

Even as Aideen reached out, her mother all but flew across the room. "Aideen, don't!"

Sinann pulled the girl from Moira, gripped her tight against her belly, burgeoning with her third child.

In the shocked silence, Moira could do no more than breathe her cousin's name.

"I never had a taste for children," Cian said coolly. "You'll excuse me."

"Cian." With one damning look toward Sinann, Moira hurried after him. "Please, a moment."

"I've had enough moments for the morning. I want my bed."

"I would apologize." She took his arm, holding firm until he stopped and turned. His eyes were hard; blue stone. "My cousin Sinann, she's a simple woman. I'll speak with her."

"Don't trouble on my account."

"Sir." Pale as wax, Sinann walked toward them. "I beg your pardon, most sincerely. I have insulted you, and my queen, her honored guests. I ask your forgiveness for a mother's foolishness."

She regretted the insult, Cian thought, but not the act. The child was on the far side of the room now, in her father's arms. "Accepted." He dismissed her with barely a glance. "Now if you'll release my arm. Majesty."

"A favor," Moira began.

"You're racking them up."

"And I'm in your debt," she said evenly. "I need to go out, onto the terrace. The people need to see their queen, and, I feel, those who are her circle. If you'd give me a few minutes more of your time I'd be grateful."

"In the buggering sun."

She managed a smile, and relaxed as she recognized the frustration in his tone meant he'd do as she asked. "A few moments. Then you can go find some solitude with the satisfaction of knowing I'll be envying you for it."

"Then make it quick. I'd enjoy some solitude and satisfaction."

Moira arranged it deliberately, with Larkin on one side of her—a figure Geall loved and respected—and Cian on the other. The stranger some of them feared. Having them flank her would, she hoped, show her people she considered them equals, and that both had her trust.

The crowd cheered and called her name, with the cheers rising to a roar when she lifted the sword. It was also a deliberate gesture for her to pass that sword to Blair to hold for her while she spoke. The people should see that the woman Larkin was betrothed to was worthy to hold it.

"People of Geall!" She shouted it, but the cheering continued. It came in waves that didn't ebb until she stepped closer to the stone rail and raised her hands.

"People of Geall, I come to you as queen, as citizen, as protector. I stand before you as did my mother, as did her sire, and as did all those back to the first days. And I stand as part of a circle chosen by the gods. Not just a circle of Geallian rulers, but a circle of warriors."

Now she spread her arms to encompass the five who stood with her. "With these who stand with me, that circle is formed. These are my most trusted and beloved. As a citizen I ask you give them your loyalty, your trust, your respect as you do me. As your queen, I command it."

She had to pause every few moments until the shouts and cheers abated again. "Today, the sun shines on Geall. But it will not always be so. What is coming seeks the dark, and we will meet it. We will defeat it. Today, we celebrate, we feast, we give thanks. Come the morrow, we continue our preparations for war. Every Geallian who can bear arms will do so. And we will march to *Ciunas*. We will march to the Valley of Silence. We will flood that ground with our strength and our will, and we will drown those who would destroy us in the light."

She held her hand out for the sword, then held it high again. "This sword will not, as it has since the first days, hang cool and quiet during my reign. It will flame and sing in my hand as I fight for you, for Geall, and for all humankind."

The roars of approval rose like a torrent.

Then there were screams as an arrow streaked the air.

Before she could react, Cian shoved her down. Under the shouting and chaos, she heard his low, steady cursing. And felt his blood warm on her hand.

"Oh God, my God, you're shot."

"Missed the heart." He spoke through gritted teeth. She saw the pain on his face as he pushed away from her to sit.

When he reached up to grip the arrow out of his side, Glenna dropped to a crouch, pushed his hand aside. "Let me see."

"Missed the heart," he repeated, and once again gripped the arrow. He yanked it out. "Bugger it. Bloody fucking hell."

"Inside," Glenna began briskly. "Get him inside."

"Wait." Though her hand trembled a little, Moira gripped Cian's shoulder. "Can you stand?"

"Of course I can bloody stand. What do you take me for?"

"Please, let them see you." Her free hand fluttered over his cheek for just an instant, like a brush of wings. "Let them see us. Please."

When she linked her fingers with his she thought she saw something stir in his eyes, and felt its twin shift inside her heart.

Then it was gone, and his voice was rough with impatience. "Give me some damn room then."

She got to her feet again. Below was chaos. The man she assumed was the assassin was being kicked and pummeled by every hand or foot that could reach him.

"Hold!" She shouted it with all her strength. "I command you, hold! Guards, bring that man to the great hall. People of Geall! You see that even on this day, even when the sun shines on us, this darkness seeks to destroy us. And it fails." She gripped Cian's hand, lifted it high with her own. "It fails because there are champions in this world who would risk their lives for another."

She laid a hand on Cian's side, felt his wince. Then held

up her bloody hand. "He bleeds for us. And by this blood he shed for me, for all of you, I rise him to be Sir Cian, Lord of Oiche."

"Oh, for Christ's sake," Cian muttered.

"Be quiet." Moira said it softly, with steel, and her eyes on the crowd.